THE PARIS APARTMENT

ALSO BY **LUCY FOLEY**

Praise for
The Paris Apartment

"Told in rotating points of view, this Tilt-A-Whirl of a novel brims with jangly tension—an undeniably engrossing guessing game."
—*Vogue*

"As you patiently await season two of *Only Murders in the Building*, cozy up with Lucy Foley's latest whodunit." —*Parade*

"Another well-paced, suspenseful locked-room mystery with shifting points of view." —*Library Journal*

"An enticing Parisian locked-room mystery with enough twists and turns to keep even the most seasoned of thriller fans guessing."
—PopSugar

"Super-twisty." —*Cosmopolitan*

"Paris is always a good idea . . . until it isn't. . . . You can expect some plot twists and Agatha Christie-esque whodunit vibes."
—The Skimm

"A modern-day Agatha Christie." —*Entertainment Weekly*

"A fast-paced, twisty bit of escapism that mixes compelling, messy characters, deft narrative red herrings, shifting perspectives, and a few genuine surprises to create a story that'll keep you up reading well into the night." —*Paste*

"Lucy Foley keeps you guessing with multiple first-person narrators and short chapters designed to leave you hanging."
—Associated Press

"*The Paris Apartment* grabbed me from the get-go. . . . A little bit *Emily in Paris* meets *Rear Window* to me. It's *totalement* satisfying in the end." —Vulture

"If you binged *Only Murders in the Building*, then this book sounds like it may be right up your alley." —BuzzFeed

"Foley turns up the creep factor and expertly plays with our precon-
ceptions to make this an involving follow-up to her 2020 bestseller,
The Guest List."   —Air Mail

"*The Paris Apartment* is cleverly and intricately plotted, told from
several different points of view and occasionally moving forward
and backward chronologically. This gives readers just enough clues
to allow them to try to solve the mystery while continually pulling the rug out from under them so they remain off-balance and
surprised. The book takes a classic formula but makes it feel fresh
and modern using contemporary storytelling techniques, ensuring
that readers will come away from it eagerly awaiting Foley's next
fiendishly clever puzzle of a mystery."   —Bookreporter.com

"Another glamorous mystery with a sprawling, secretive cast—
namely, the inhabitants of the titular apartment complex."
                                                      —*BookPage*

"Will keep you guessing until the very end. It may be pure fiction,
but fans of true crime novels will gobble it right up."
                                                 —*Reader's Digest*

"But it's not only the intelligent and riveting storyline or the carefully
conceived and fully developed characters that elevates this book far
above mundane thrillers. Foley's precise prose rings with echoes of
her British background and the elegance of her French setting. . . .
With confidence and cunning, Foley provides pleasures that chill as
they captivate."   —*Fredericksburg Free Lance-Star* (VA)

"An atmospheric thriller wrapped in a mystery, lots of mysteries. . . .
Her writing is spare, her plotting intricate, and she is stingy with
clues along the way—as a good mystery/thriller writer should be.
I recommend *The Paris Apartment* for fans of this genre who especially enjoy being in the dark for most of the book and quite
surprised at the end."   —*Florida Times-Union* (Jacksonville, FL)

"Foley is the master of the slow reveal, and gives a little bit at a time
to lead up to the big reveal. You never quite know what to expect,
which makes the plot even more exciting. This well-written and
entertaining read is perfect for fans of Ruth Ware, Agatha Christie,
and Foley's previous books."   —Mystery & Suspense Magazine

THE PARIS APARTMENT

A NOVEL

LUCY FOLEY

wm

WILLIAM MORROW

An Imprint of HarperCollinsPublishers

P.S.™ is a trademark of HarperCollins Publishers.

THE PARIS APARTMENT. Copyright © 2022 by Lost and Found Books Ltd. Excerpt from THE HUNTING PARTY copyright © 2019 by Lost and Found Books Ltd. All rights reserved. Printed in the United States of America. No part of this book may be used or reproduced in any manner whatsoever without written permission except in the case of brief quotations embodied in critical articles and reviews. For information, address HarperCollins Publishers, 195 Broadway, New York, NY 10007.

HarperCollins books may be purchased for educational, business, or sales promotional use. For information, please email the Special Markets Department at SPsales@harpercollins.com.

Published in 2022 by HarperFiction, an imprint of HarperCollins UK.

A hardcover edition of this book was published in 2022 by William Morrow, an imprint of HarperCollins Publishers.

FIRST WILLIAM MORROW PAPERBACK EDITION PUBLISHED 2023.

Designed by Bonni Leon-Berman

Library of Congress Cataloging-in-Publication Data has been applied for.

ISBN 978-0-06-300306-4

23 24 25 26 27 LBC 8 7 6 5 4

FOR AL, FOR EVERYTHING.

Ben

HIS FINGERS HOVER OVER THE keyboard. Got to get it all down. This: this is the story that's going to make his name. Ben lights another cigarette, a Gitane. Bit of a cliché to smoke them here but he does actually like the taste. And fine, yeah, likes the way he looks smoking them too.

He's sitting in front of the apartment's long windows, which look onto the central courtyard. Everything out there is steeped in darkness, save for the weak greenish glow thrown by a single lamp. It's a beautiful building, but there's something rotten at its heart. Now he's discovered it he can smell the stench of it everywhere.

He should be clearing out of here soon. He's outstayed his welcome in this place. Jess could hardly have chosen a worse time to decide to come and stay. She barely gave him any notice. And she didn't give much detail on the phone but clearly something's up; something wrong with whatever crappy bar job she's working now. His half sister has a knack for turning up when she's not wanted. She's like a homing beacon for trouble: it seems to follow her around. She's never been good at just *playing the game*. Never understood how much easier it makes life if you just give people what they want, tell them what they want to hear. Admittedly, he did tell her to come and stay "whenever you like," but he didn't really mean it. Trust Jess to take him at his word.

When was the last time he saw her? Thinking about her always makes him feel guilty. Should he have been there for her more, looked out for her . . . ? She's fragile, Jess. Or—not fragile exactly, but vulnerable in a way people probably don't see at first. An "armadillo": softness beneath that tough exterior.

Anyway. He should call her, give her some directions. When her phone rings out he leaves a voicenote: "Hey Jess, so it's number twelve, Rue des Amants. Got that? Third floor."

His eye's drawn to a flash of movement in the courtyard beneath the windows. Someone's passing through it quickly. Almost running. He can only make out a shadowy figure, can't see who it is. But something about the speed seems odd. He's hit with a little animal spike of adrenaline.

He remembers he's still recording the voicenote, drags his gaze from the window. "Just ring the buzzer. I'll be up waiting for you—"

He stops speaking. Hesitates, listens.

A noise.

The sound of footsteps out on the landing . . . approaching the apartment door.

The footsteps stop. Someone is there, just outside. He waits for a knock. None comes. Silence. But a weighted silence, like a held breath.

Odd.

And then another sound. He stands still, ears pricked, listening intently. There it is again. It's metal on metal, the scrape of a key. Then the clunk of it entering the mechanism. He watches the lock turn. Someone is unlocking his door from the outside. Someone who has a key, but no business coming in here uninvited.

The handle begins to move downward. The door begins to open, with that familiar drawn-out groan.

He puts his phone down on the kitchen counter, voicenote forgotten. Waits and watches dumbly as the door swings forward. As the figure steps into the room.

"What are you doing here?" he asks. Calm, reasonable. Nothing to hide. Not afraid. Or not yet. "And why—"

Then he sees what his intruder holds.

Now. Now the fear comes.

Jess

FOR CHRIST'S SAKE, BEN. ANSWER your phone. I'm freezing my tits off out here. My Eurostar was two hours late leaving London; I should have arrived at ten-thirty but it's just gone midnight. And it's cold tonight, even colder here in Paris than it was in London. It's only the end of October but my breath smokes in the air and my toes are numb in my boots. Crazy to think there was a heatwave only a few weeks ago. I need a proper coat. But there's always been a lot of things I need that I'm never going to get.

I've probably called Ben ten times now: as my Eurostar pulled in, on the half hour walk here from Gare du Nord. No answer. And he hasn't replied to any of my texts. Thanks for nothing, big bro.

He said he'd be here to let me in. "Just ring the buzzer. I'll be up waiting for you—"

Well, I'm here. Here being a dimly lit, cobblestoned cul-de-sac in what appears to be a seriously posh neighborhood. The apartment building in front of me closes off this end, standing all on its own.

I glance back down the empty street. Beside a parked car, about twenty feet away, I think I see the shadows shift. I step to the side, to try and get a better look. There's . . . I squint, trying to make out the shape. I could swear there's someone there, crouched behind the car.

I jump as a siren blares a few streets away, loud in the silence. Listen as the sound fades away into the night. It's different from the ones at home—"nee-naw, nee-naw," like a child's impression—but it still makes my heart beat a little faster.

I glance back at the shadowy area behind the parked car. Now I can't make out any movement, can't even see the shape I thought I glimpsed before. Maybe it was just a trick of the light, after all.

I look back up at the building. The others on this street are beautiful, but this one knocks spots off them all. It's set back from the road behind a big gate with a high wall on either side, concealing what must be some sort of garden or courtyard. Five or six stories, huge windows, all with wrought-iron balconies. A big sprawl of ivy growing all over the front of it which looks like a creeping dark stain. If I crane my neck I can see what might be a roof garden on the top, the spiky shapes of the trees and shrubs black cut-outs against the night sky.

I double-check the address. Number twelve, rue des Amants. I've definitely got it right. I still can't quite believe this swanky apartment building is where Ben's been living. He said a mate helped sort him out with it, someone he knew from his student days. But then Ben's always managed to fall on his feet. I suppose it only makes sense that he's charmed his way into a place like this. And charm must have done it. I know journalists probably earn more than bartenders, but not by this much.

The metal gate in front of me has a brass lion's head knocker: the fat metal ring held between snarling teeth. Along the top of the gate, I notice, is a bristle of anti-climb spikes. And all along the high wall either side of the gate are embedded shards of glass. These security measures feel kind of at odds with the elegance of the building.

I lift up the knocker, cold and heavy in my hand, let it drop. The clang of it bounces off the cobblestones, so much louder than expected in the silence. In fact, it's so quiet and dark here that it's hard to imagine it's part of the same city I've trundled across this evening from Gare du Nord: all the bright lights and crowds, people spilling in and out of restaurants and bars. I think of the area around that huge cathedral lit up on the hill, the Sacré-Coeur, which I passed beneath only twenty minutes ago: throngs of tourists out taking selfies and dodgy-looking guys in puffer jackets sharking between them, ready to nick a wallet or two. And the streets that I walked through with the neon signs, the blaring music, the all-night food, the crowds spilling out of bars, the queues for clubs. This is a different universe. I look back down the street behind me: not another person in sight. The only real sound comes from a scurry of dead ivy across the cobblestones. I can hear the roar of traffic at a distance, the honking of car horns—but even that seems muffled, like it wouldn't dare intrude on this elegant, hushed world.

I didn't stop to think much, pulling my case across town from the station. I was mainly concentrating on not getting mugged, or letting the broken wheel of my suitcase stick and throw me off balance. But now, for the first time, it sinks in: I'm here, in Paris. A different city, a different country. I've made it. I've left my old life behind.

A LIGHT SNAPS on in one of the windows up above. I glance up and there's a dark figure standing there, head and shoulders in silhouette. Ben? If it were him, though, he'd wave down at me, surely. I know I must be lit up by the nearby streetlamp. But the figure at the window is as still as a statue. I can't make out any features or even whether they're male or female. But they're watching me. They must be. I suppose I must look pretty shabby and out of place with my broken old suitcase trying to bust open despite the bungee cord wrapped around it. A strange feeling, knowing they can see me but I can't see them properly. I drop my eyes.

Aha. To the right of the gate I spot a little panel of buttons for the different apartments with a lens set into it. The big lion's head knocker must just be for show. I step forward and press the one for the third floor, for Ben's place. I wait for his voice to crackle through the intercom.

No answer.

Sophie

SOMEONE IS KNOCKING ON THE front door to the building. Loud enough for Benoit, my silver whippet, to leap to his feet and let out a volley of barks.

"*Arrête ça!*" I shout. "Stop that."

Benoit whimpers, then goes quiet. He looks up at me, confusion in his dark eyes. I can hear the change in my voice as well—too shrill, too loud. And I can hear my own breathing in the silence that follows, rough and shallow.

No one ever uses the door knocker. Certainly, no one familiar with this building. I go to the windows on this side of the apartment, which look down into the courtyard. I can't see onto the street from here, but the front door from the street leads into the courtyard, so if anyone had come in I would see them there. But no one has entered and it must have been a few minutes since the knocking. Clearly it's not someone the concierge thinks should be admitted. Fine. Good. I haven't always liked that woman, but I know I can trust her in this at least.

In Paris you can live in the most luxurious apartment and the scum of the city will still wash up at your door on occasion. The drug addicts, the vagrants. The whores. Pigalle, the red-light district, lies just a little way away, clinging to the coattails of Montmartre. Up here, in this multi-million-euro fortress with its views out over the city's rooftops, all the way to the Tour

Eiffel, I have always felt comparatively safe. I can ignore the grime beneath the gilt. I am good at turning a blind eye. Usually. But tonight is . . . different.

I go to check my reflection in the mirror that hangs in the hallway. I pay close attention to what I see in the glass. Not so bad for fifty. It is partly due to the fact that I have adopted the French way when it comes to maintaining my *forme*. Which essentially means always being hungry. I know that even at this hour I will be looking immaculate. My lipstick is flawless. I never leave the apartment without it. Chanel, "La Somptueuse": my signature color. A bluish, regal color that says: "stand back," not "come hither." My hair is a shining black bob cut every six weeks by David Mallet at Notre Dame des Victoires. The shape perfected, any silver painstakingly concealed. Jacques, my husband, made it quite clear once that he abhors women who allow themselves to go gray. Even if he hasn't always been here to admire it.

I am wearing what I consider my uniform. My armor. Silk Equipment shirt, exquisitely-cut dark slim trousers. A scarf—brightly patterned Hermès silk—around my neck, which is excellent for concealing the ravages of time to the delicate skin there. A recent gift from Jacques, with his love of beautiful things. Like this apartment. Like me, as I was before I had the bad grace to age.

Perfect. As ever. As expected. But I feel dirty. Sullied by what I have had to do this evening. In the glass my eyes glitter. The only sign. Though my face is a little gaunt, too—if you were to look closely. I am even thinner than usual. Recently I have not had to watch my diet, to carefully mark each glass of wine or morsel of croissant. I couldn't tell you what I ate for breakfast this morning; whether I remembered to eat at all. Each day my waistband hangs looser, the bones of my sternum protrude more sharply.

I undo the knot of my scarf. I can tie a scarf as well as any born and bred Parisian. By it you know me for one of them, those chic moneyed women with their small dogs and their excellent breeding.

I look at the text message I sent to Jacques last night. **Bonne nuit, mon amour. Tout va bien ici.** *Good night, my love. Everything is fine here.*

Everything is fine here. HA.

I don't know how it has come to this. But I do know that it started with him coming here. Moving into the third floor. Benjamin Daniels. He destroyed everything.

Jess

I PULL OUT MY PHONE. Last time I checked Ben hadn't replied to any of my messages. One on the Eurostar: **On my way!** And then: **At Gare du Nord! Do you have an Uber account?!!!** Just in case, you know, he suddenly felt generous enough to send a cab to collect me. Seemed worth a shot.

There is a new message on my phone. Only it's not from Ben.

You stupid little bitch. Think you can get away with what you've done?

Shit. I swallow past the sudden dryness in my throat. Then I delete it. Block the number.

As I say, it was all a bit last minute, coming here. Ben didn't sound that thrilled when I called him earlier and told him I was on my way. True, I didn't give him much time to get used to the idea. But then it's always felt like the bond between us is more important to me than it is to my half brother. I suggested we hang out last Christmas, but he said he was busy. "Skiing," he said. Didn't even know he could ski. Sometimes it even feels like I'm an embarrassment to him. I represent the past, and he'd rather be cut loose from all that.

I had to explain I was desperate. "Hopefully it'll only be for a month or two, and I'll pay my way," I said. "Just as soon as I get on my feet. I'll get a job." Yeah. One where they don't ask too many questions. That's how you end up in the places I've worked at—there aren't that many that will take you when your references are such a shitshow.

Up until this afternoon I was gainfully employed at the Copacabana bar in Brighton. The odd massive tip made up for it. A load of wanker bankers, say, down from London celebrating some Dick or Harry or Tobias' upcoming nuptials and too pissed to count the notes out right—or maybe to guys like that it's just so much loose change anyway. But, as of today, I'm unemployed. Again.

I press the buzzer a second time. No answer. All the building's windows are dark again—even the one that lit up before. Christ's sake. He couldn't have turned in for the night and totally forgotten about me . . . could he?

Below all the other buzzers there's a separate one: *Concierge*, it reads in curly script. Like something in a hotel: further proof that this place is seriously upmarket. I press the button, wait. No answer. But I can't help imagining someone looking at the little video image of me, assessing, then deciding not to open up.

I lift up the heavy knocker again and slam it several times against the wood. The sound echoes down the street: someone must hear it. I can just make out a dog barking, from somewhere deep inside the building.

I wait five minutes. No one comes.

Shit.

I can't afford a hotel. I don't have enough for a return journey to London—and even if I did there's no way I'm going back. I consider my options. Go to a bar . . . wait it out?

I hear footsteps behind me, ringing out on the cobblestones. Ben? I spin round, ready for him to apologize, tell me he just popped out to get some ciggies or something. But the figure walking toward me isn't my brother. He's too tall, too broad, a parka hood with a fur rim up over his head. He's moving quickly and there's something purposeful about his walk. I grip the handle of my suitcase a little tighter. Literally everything I own is in here.

He's only a few meters away now, close enough that by the light of the streetlamp I can make out the gleam of his eyes under the hood. He's reaching into his pocket, pulling his hand back out. Something makes me take a step backward. And now I see it. Something sharp and metallic, gleaming in his hand.

Concierge

I WATCH HER ON THE intercom screen, the stranger at the gate. What can she be doing here? She rings the buzzer again. She must be lost. I know, just from looking at her, that she has no business being here. Except she seems certain that this is the place she wants, so determined. Now she looks into the lens. I will not let her in. I cannot.

I am the gatekeeper of this building. Sitting here in my *loge*: a tiny cabin in the corner of the courtyard, which would fit maybe twenty times into the apartments above me. But it is mine, at least. My private space. My home. Most people wouldn't consider it worthy of the name. If I sit on the pull-down bed, I can touch nearly all the corners of the room at once. There is damp spreading from the ground and down from the roof and the windows don't keep out the cold. But there are four walls. There is a place for me to put my photographs with their echoes of a life once lived, the little relics I have collected and which I hold onto when I feel most alone; the flowers I pick from the courtyard garden every other morning so there is something fresh and alive in here. This place, for all its shortcomings, represents security. Without it I have nothing.

I look again at the face on the intercom screen. As the light catches her just so I see a familiarity: the sharp line of the nose and jaw. But more than her appearance it is something about the way she moves, looks around her. A hungry, vulpine quality that reminds me of another. All the more reason not to let her in. I don't like strangers. I don't like change. Change has always been dangerous for me. He proved that: coming here with his questions, his charm. The man who came to live in the third-floor apartment: Benjamin Daniels. After he came here, everything changed.

Jess

HE'S COMING STRAIGHT FOR ME, the guy in the parka. He's lifting his arm. The metal of the blade gleams again. Shit. I'm about to turn and run—get a few yards on him at least—

But wait, no, *no* . . . I can see now that the thing in his hand isn't a blade. It's an iPhone, in a metallic case. I let out the breath I've been holding and lean against my bag, hit by a sudden wave of tiredness. I've been wired all day, no wonder I'm spooking at shadows.

I watch as the guy makes a call. I can make out a tinny little voice at the other end; a woman's voice, I think. Then he begins to talk, over her, louder and louder, until he's shouting into his handset. I have no idea what the words mean exactly but I don't need to know much French to understand this isn't a polite or friendly chat.

After he's got his long, angry speech off his chest he hangs up and shoves the phone back in his pocket. Then he spits out a single word: "*Putain.*"

I know that one. I got a D in my French GCSE but I did look up all the swear words once and I'm good at remembering the stuff that interests me. *Whore*: that's what it means.

Now he turns and starts walking in my direction again. And I see, quite clearly, that he just wants to use the gate to this building. I step aside, feeling a total idiot for having got so keyed up over nothing. But it makes sense; I spent the whole Eurostar journey looking over my shoulder. You know, just in case.

"*Bonsoir*," I say in my best accent, flashing my most winning smile. Maybe this guy will let me in and I can go up to the third floor and hammer on Ben's apartment door. Maybe his buzzer's simply not working or something.

The guy doesn't reply. He just turns to the keypad next to the gate and punches in a series of numbers. Finally he gives me a quick glance over his shoulder. It's not the *most* friendly glance. I catch a waft of booze, stale and sour. Same breath as most of the punters in the Copacabana.

I smile again. "Er . . . *excuse moi?* Please, ah—I need some help, I'm looking for my brother, Ben. Benjamin Daniels—"

I wish I had a bit more of Ben's flair, his charm. "Benjamin Silver-Tongue," Mum called him. He's always had this way of getting anyone to do what he wants. Maybe that's why he ended up a journalist in Paris while I've been working for a bloke affectionately known as The Pervert in a shithole bar in Brighton serving stag dos at the weekends and local lowlifes in the week.

The guy turns back to face me, slowly. "Benjamin Daniels," he says. Not a question: just the name, repeated. I see something: anger, or maybe fear. He knows who I'm talking about. "Benjamin Daniels is not here."

"What do you mean, he's not here?" I ask. "This is the address he gave me. He's up on the third floor. I can't get hold of him."

The man turns his back on me. I watch as he pulls open the gate. Finally he turns round to face me a third time and I think: maybe he is going to help me, after all. Then, in accented English, very slowly and loudly, he says: "Fuck off, *little girl*."

Before I even have time to reply there's a clang of metal and I jump backward. He's slammed the gate shut, right in my face. As the ringing fades from my ears I'm left with just the sound of my breathing, fast and loud.

But he's helped me, even though he doesn't know it. I wait a moment, take a quick look back down the street. Then I lift my hand to the keypad and punch in the same numbers I watched him use only a few seconds ago: 7561. Bingo: the little light flickers green and I hear the mechanism of the gate click open. Dragging my case after me, I slip inside.

Mimi

FOURTH FLOOR

MERDE.

I just heard his name, out there in the night. I lift my head, listening. For some reason I'm on top of the covers, not under them. My hair feels damp, the pillow cold and soggy. I shiver.

Am I hearing things? Did I imagine it? His name . . . following me everywhere?

No: I'm sure it was real. A woman's voice, drifting up through the open window of my bedroom. Somehow I heard it four stories up. Somehow I heard it through the roar of white noise inside my head.

Who is she? Why is she asking about him?

I sit up, pulling my bony knees tight against my chest, and reach for my childhood *doudou*, Monsieur Gus, a scraggy old penguin stuffed animal toy I still keep beside my pillow. I press him against my face, try to comfort myself with the feel of his hard little head, the soft, shifting scrunch of the beans inside his body, the musty smell of him. Just like I did as a little girl when I'd had a bad dream. You're not a little girl any longer, Mimi. He said that. Ben.

The moon is so bright that my whole room is filled with a cold blue light. Nearly a full moon. In the corner I can make out my record player, the case of vinyls next to it. I painted the walls in here such a dark blackish-blue that they don't reflect any light at all but the poster hanging opposite me seems to glow. It's a Cindy Sherman; I went to her show at the Pompidou last year. I got completely obsessed with how raw and freaky and intense her work is: the kind of thing I try to do with my painting. In the poster, one of the Untitled Film Stills, she's wearing a short black wig and she stares out at you like she's possessed, or like she might be about to eat your soul. "*Putain!*" my flatmate Camille laughed, when she saw it. "What happens if you bring some guy back? He's gonna have to look at that angry bitch while you're screwing? That'll put him off his rhythm." As if, I thought at the time. Nineteen years old and still a virgin. Worse. A convent-school-educated virgin.

I stare at Cindy, the black bruise-like shadows around her eyes, the jagged line of her hair which is kind of like my own, since I took a pair of scissors to it. It feels like looking in a mirror.

I turn to the window, look down into the courtyard. The lights are on in the concierge's cabin. Of course: that nosy old bitch never misses a trick. Creeping out from shadowy corners. Always watching, always there. Looking at you like she knows all your secrets.

This building is a U-shape around the courtyard. My bedroom is at one end of the U, so if I peer diagonally downward I can see into his apartment. Nearly every evening for the last two months he sat there at his desk working late into the night, the lights on. For just a moment I let myself look. The shutters are open but the lights are off and the space behind the desk looks more than empty, or like the emptiness itself has a kind of depth and weight. I glance away.

I slide down from my bed and tiptoe out into the main part of the apartment, trying not to trip over all the stuff Camille leaves scattered around like it's an extension of her bedroom: magazines and dropped sweaters, dirty coffee cups, nail varnish pots, lacy bras. From the big windows in here I've got a direct view of the front entrance. As I watch, the gate opens. A shadowy figure slips through the gap. As she comes forward into the light I can make her out: a woman I have never seen before. No, I say silently. No no no no no. Go away. The roar in my head grows louder.

"Did you hear that knocking?"

I spin around. *Putain.* Camille's lounging there on the couch, cigarette glowing in her hand, boots up on the armrest: faux-snakeskin with five-inch heels. When did she get in? How long has she been lurking there in the dark?

"I thought you were out," I say. Normally, if she goes clubbing, she stays till dawn.

"*Oui.*" She shrugs, takes a drag on her cigarette. "I've only been back twenty minutes." Even in the gloom I see how her eyes slide away from mine. Normally she'd be straight into some story about the crazy new club she's been at, or the guy whose bed she's just left, including an overly detailed description of his dick or exactly how skilled he was at using it. I've often felt like I'm living vicariously through Camille. Grateful someone like her would choose to hang out with me. When we met at the Sorbonne she told me she likes collecting people, that I interested her because I have this "intense energy." But when I've felt worse about myself I've suspected this apartment probably has more to do with it.

"Where have you been?" I ask, trying to sound halfway normal.

She shrugs. "Just around."

I feel like there's something going on with her, something she's not telling me. But right now I can't think about Camille. The roaring in my head suddenly feels like it's drowning out all my thoughts.

There's just one thing I know. Everything that has happened here happened because of him: Benjamin Daniels.

Jess

I'M STANDING IN A SMALL, dark courtyard. The apartment building proper wraps around it on three sides. The ivy has gone crazy here, winding up almost to the fourth floor, surrounding all the windows, swallowing drainpipes, a couple of satellite dishes. Ahead a short path winds between flowerbeds planted with dark shrubs and trees. I can smell the sweetish scent of dead leaves, fresh-turned earth. To my right there's a sort of cabin structure, only a bit bigger than a garden shed. The two windows seem to be shuttered. On one side a tiny chink of light shows through a crack.

In the opposite corner I make out a door, which seems to lead into the main part of the building. I head that way along the path. As I do a pale face looms suddenly out of the darkness on my right. I stop short. But it's the statue of a nude woman, life-size, her body wound about with more black ivy, her eyes staring and blank.

The door in the corner of the courtyard has another passcode, but it clicks open with the same set of numbers, thank God. I step through it into a dark, echoing space. A stairwell winds upward into deeper darkness. I find the little orange glow of a light switch on the wall, flick it. The lights hum on, dimly. A ticking sound: some sort of energy-saving timer maybe. I can see now that there's a dark reddish carpet beneath my feet, covering a stone floor then climbing up the polished wooden staircase. Above me the bannister coils around on itself and inside the staircase there's a lift shaft—a tiny, ancient, rickety-looking capsule that might be as old as the apartment itself, so ancient-looking I wonder if it's actually still in use. There's a trace of stale cigarette smoke on the air. Still, all pretty posh, all a long, long way from the place I've been crashing at in Brighton.

There's a door to the left of me: *Cave*, it says. I've never let a closed door stay closed for long: I suppose you could say that's my main problem in life. I give it a push, see a flight of steps leading down. I'm hit by a waft of cold underground air, damp and musty.

I hear a noise then, somewhere above me. The creak of wood. I let the door swing shut and glance up. Something moves along the wall several flights up. I wait to see someone appear around the corner, in the gaps between the bannisters. But the shadow stops, as though waiting for something. And then suddenly everything goes dark: the timer must have run out. I reach over, flick it back on.

The shadow's gone.

I walk over to the lift in its metal cage. It's definitely on the antique side, but I'm too exhausted to even think about lugging my stuff up those stairs. There's barely room for me and the suitcase inside. I close the little door, press the button for the third floor, put a hand against the structure to steady myself. It gives under the pressure of my palm; I hastily pull my hand away. There's a bit of a shudder as the lift sets off; I catch my breath.

Up I go: each floor has one door, marked with a brass number. Is there only one apartment per floor? They must be pretty big. I imagine the sleeping presence of strangers behind those doors. I wonder who lives in them, what Ben's neighbors are like. And I find myself wondering which apartment the dickhead I met at the gate lives in.

The lift judders to a halt on the third floor. I step out onto the landing and drag my suitcase after me. Here it is: Ben's apartment, with its brass number 3.

I give it a couple of loud knocks.

No answer.

I crouch down and look at the keyhole. It's the old-fashioned kind, easiest in the world to pick. Needs must. I take out my hoop earrings and bend them out of shape—the convenience of cheap jewelry—leaving me with two long, thin pieces of metal. I make my rake and my pick. Ben actually taught me this when we were little so he can hardly complain. I got so good at it I can unpick a simple pin tumbler mechanism in less than a minute.

I wiggle the earrings back and forth in the lock until there's a click, then turn the handle. Yes—the door begins to open. I pause. Something about this doesn't feel right. I've had to rely on my instincts quite a lot over the years. And I've also been here before. Hand clasped around the door handle. Not knowing what I'm going to find on the other side—

Deep breath. For a moment it feels like the air contracts around me. I find myself gripping the pendant of my necklace. It's a St. Christopher: Mum gave us both one, to keep us safe—even if that was her job, not something to be outsourced to a little metal saint. I'm not religious and I'm not sure Mum was either. All the same, I can't imagine ever being parted with mine.

With my other hand I push the handle down. I can't stop myself from squeezing my eyes shut tight as I step into the space.

It's pitch-black inside.

"Ben?" I call out.

No answer.

I step farther inside, grope about for a light switch. As the lights come on the apartment reveals itself. My first thought is:

Christ, it's huge. Bigger even than I expected. Grander. High-ceilinged. Dark wooden beams up above, polished floorboards below, huge windows facing down onto the courtyard.

I take another step into the room. As I do something lands across my shoulders: a blunt, heavy blow. Then the sting of something sharp, tearing into my flesh.

Concierge

A FEW MINUTES AFTER THE knocking I watched through the windows of my lodge as the first figure entered the courtyard, his hood pulled up. Then I saw a second figure appear. The newcomer, the girl. Clattering that huge suitcase across the cobbles of the courtyard, making enough noise to wake the dead.

I watched her on the intercom screen until the buzzer stopped ringing.

I am good at watching. I sweep the residents' hallways, I collect their post, I answer the door. But also, I watch. I see everything. And it gives me a strange kind of power, even if I'm the only one who's aware of it. The residents forget about me. It's convenient for them to do so. To imagine that I'm nothing more than an extension of this building, just a moving element of a large machine, like the lift that takes them up to their beautiful apartments. In a way I have become part of this place. It has certainly left its mark on me. I am sure the years of living in this tiny cabin have caused me to shrink, hunching into myself, while the hours spent sweeping and scrubbing the corridors and stairs of the apartment building have winnowed my flesh. Perhaps in another life I would have grown plump in my old age. I have not had that luxury. I am sinew and bone. Stronger than I look.

I suppose I could have gone and stopped her. Should have done. But confrontation is not my style. I have learned that watching is the more powerful weapon. And it had a feeling of inevitability, her being here. I could see her determination. She would somehow have found her way in, no matter what I did to try and prevent her.

Stupid girl. It would have been far, far better if she'd turned and left this place and never returned. But it's too late now. So be it.

Jess

MY HEART IS BEATING DOUBLE-TIME, my muscles tensed.

I look down at the cat as it weaves its way between my legs, purring, a blur of movement. Slinky, black, a white ruff. I put a hand down the back of my top. My fingers come away with a sheen of blood. *Ouch.*

The cat must have jumped onto my back from the counter next to the door, digging its claws in for grip when I fell forward. It looks up at me now through narrowed green eyes and gives a squawk, as though asking me what the hell I think I'm doing here.

A cat! Jesus Christ. I start laughing and then stop, quickly, because of the strange way the sound echoes around the high space.

I didn't know Ben had a cat. Does he even like cats? It suddenly seems crazy that I don't know this. But I suppose there's not all that much I do know about his life here.

"Ben?" I call out. Again the sound of my voice bounces back at me. No answer. I don't think I expected one: it feels too silent, too empty. There's a strange smell, too. Something chemical.

I suddenly really need a drink. I wander into the little kitchen area to my right and start raiding the cupboards. First things first. I come up with half a bottle of red wine. I'd prefer something with more of a kick, but beggars can't be choosers and that might as well be the motto for my whole bloody life. I slosh some into a glass. There's a pack of cigarettes on the side too, a bright blue box: Gitanes. I didn't know Ben still smoked. Typical of him to favor some fancy French brand. I fish one out, light up, inhale, and cough like I did the first time a fellow foster kid gave me a drag: it's strong, spicy, unfiltered. I'm not sure I like it. Still, I push the rest of the pack into the back pocket of my jeans—he owes me—and take my first proper look around the place.

I'm . . . surprised, to say the least. I'm not sure what I imagined, but this isn't it. Ben's a bit creative, a bit cool (not that I'd ever describe him that way to his face), and in contrast this whole apartment is covered in antique-looking old-lady wallpaper, silvery with a floral pattern. When I put out a hand and touch the nearest wall I realize it's not paper after all: it's a very faded silk. I see brighter spots where there were clearly once pictures hanging, small rusty age spots on the fabric. From the high ceiling hangs a chandelier, curls of metal holding the bulbs. A long strand of cobweb swings lazily back and forth—there must be a breeze coming from somewhere. And maybe there were once curtains behind those window shutters: I see an empty curtain rail up above, the brass rings still in place. A desk plumb in front of the windows. A shelf holding a few ivory-colored books, a big navy French dictionary.

In the near corner there's a coat stand with an old khaki jacket on it; I'm sure I've seen Ben wearing it before. Maybe even the last time I saw him, about a year ago, when he came down to Brighton and bought me lunch before disappearing back out of my life again without a backward glance. I reach into the pockets and draw out a set of keys and a brown leather wallet.

Is it a bit strange that Ben's gone but left these behind?

I open the wallet: the back pocket's stuffed with a few euro notes. I take a twenty and then, for good measure, a couple of tens. I'd have asked to borrow some money if he was here anyway. I'll pay it back . . . sometime.

A business card is stuffed into the front of the section that holds credit cards. It reads: **Theo Mendelson. Paris editor,** *Guardian*.

And scribbled on it, in what looks like Ben's handwriting (sometimes he remembers to send me a birthday card): *PITCH STORY TO HIM!*

I look at the keys next. One of them's for a Vespa, which is odd as last time I saw him he was driving an old eighties Mercedes soft top. The other's a large antique-looking thing that looks like it might be for this place. I go to the door and try it: the lock clicks.

The uneasy feeling in the pit of my stomach grows. But he might have another set of keys. These could be spares, the set he's going to lend me. He probably has another key for the Vespa, too: he might even have gone off on it somewhere. As for the wallet, he's probably just carrying cash.

I find the bathroom, next. Nothing much to report here, other than the fact that Ben doesn't appear to own any towels at all, which seems bizarre. I step back out into the main room. The bedroom must be through the closed pair of French double doors. I walk toward them, the cat following, pressing close as a shadow. Just for a moment, I hesitate.

The cat squawks at me again as if to ask: what are you waiting for? I take another long slug of wine. Deep breath. Push open the doors. Another breath. Open my eyes. Empty bed. Empty room. No one here. Breathe out.

OK. I mean, I didn't really think I was going to find anything like that. That's not Ben. Ben's sorted; I'm the fuck-up. But when it's happened to you once—

I drain the dregs from my glass, then go through the cupboards in the bedroom. Not much by way of clues except that most of my brother's clothes seem to come from places called Acne (why would you wear clothes named after a skin condition?) and A.P.C.

Back out in the main room I pour the remainder of the bottle into the glass and neck it back. Drift over to the desk by the large windows, which look down onto the courtyard. There's nothing on the desk beyond a ratty-looking pen. No laptop. Ben seemed surgically attached to it when he took me for lunch that time, getting it out and typing something while we waited for our order. I suppose he must have it with him, wherever he is.

All at once I have the definite feeling that I'm not alone, that I'm being watched. A prickle down the back of my neck. I spin around. No one there except the cat, which is sitting on the kitchen counter. Perhaps that's all it was.

The cat gazes at me for a few moments, then turns its head on one side like it's asking a question. It's the first time I've seen it sit still like this. Then it raises a paw to its mouth and licks. This is when I notice that both the paw and the white ruff at its throat are smeared with blood.

Jess

I'VE GONE COLD. WHAT THE—

I reach out to the cat to try to get a closer look, but it slinks out from under my hand. Maybe it's just caught a mouse or something? One of the families I fostered with had a cat, Suki. Even though she was small she could take down a whole pigeon: she came back once covered in blood like something out of a horror film and my foster parent Karen found the headless body later that morning. I'm sure there's some small dead creature lying around the apartment, just waiting for me to step on it. Or maybe it killed something out there in the courtyard—the windows are open a crack, which must be how it gets in and out of this place, walking along the guttering or something.

Still. It gave me a bit of a jolt. When I saw it for a moment I thought—

No. I'm just tired. I should try and get some sleep.

Ben will turn up in the morning, explain where he's been, I'll tell him he's a dick for leaving me to basically break in and it'll be like old times, the *old* old times, before he went to live with his shiny rich new family and got a whole new way of speaking and perspective on the world and I got bounced around the care system until I was old enough to fend for myself. I'm sure he's fine. Bad stuff doesn't happen to Ben. He's the lucky one.

I shrug off my jacket, throw it onto the sofa. I should probably take a shower—I'm pretty sure I stink. A bit of B.O. but mainly of vinegar: you can't work at the Copacabana and not reek of the stuff, it's what we use to sluice the bar down after every shift.

But I'm too tired to wash. I think Ben might have mentioned something about a camp bed, but I don't see any sign of one. So I take a throw from the sofa and lie down in the bedroom on top of the covers in all my clothes. I give the pillows some thumps to try and rearrange them. As I do something slithers out of the bed onto the floor.

A pair of women's knickers: black silk, lacy, expensive-looking. *Ew.* Christ, Ben. I don't want to think about how those got here. I don't even know if Ben has a girlfriend. I feel a little pang of sadness, in spite of myself. He's all I've got and I don't even know this much about him.

I'm too tired to do much more than kick the knickers away, out of sight. Tomorrow I'll sleep on the sofa.

Jess

A SHOUT RIPS THROUGH THE silence. A man's voice. Then another voice, a woman's.

I sit up in bed listening hard, heart kicking against my ribs.
It takes a second for me to work out that the sounds are coming
from the courtyard, filtering through the windows in the main
room. I check the alarm clock next to Ben's bed. 5 A.M.: morning,
just, but still dark.

The man is shouting again. He sounds slurred, like he's been
drinking.

I creep across the main room to the windows and crouch
down. The cat pushes its face into my thigh, mewing. "Shh," I
tell it—but I quite like the feel of its warm, solid body against
mine.

I peer into the courtyard. Two figures stand down there: one
tall, one much smaller. The guy is dark-haired and she's blonde,
the long fall of her hair silver in the cool light of the courtyard's
one lamp. He's wearing a parka with a fur rim that looks familiar,
and I realize it's the guy I "met" outside the gate last night.

Their voices get louder—they're shouting over one another
now. I'm pretty sure I hear her say the word "police." At this his
voice changes—I don't understand the words but there's a new
hardness, a threat, to his tone. I see him take a couple of steps
toward her.

"*Laisse-moi!*" she shouts, sounding different now, too—scared
rather than angry. He takes another step closer. I realize I'm
pressed so close to the window that my breath has misted up the

glass. I can't just sit here, listening, watching. He raises a hand. He's so much taller than her.

A sudden memory. Mum, sobbing. *I'm sorry, I'm sorry*: over and over, like the words to a prayer.

I lift my hand to the window and slam it against the glass. I want to distract him for a few seconds, give her a chance to move away. I see both of them glance up in confusion, their attention caught by the sound. I duck down, out of sight.

When I look back out again it's just in time to see him pick something up from the ground, something big and bulky and rectangular. With a big petulant shove he throws it toward her—at her. She steps back and it explodes at her feet: I see it's a suitcase, spilling clothes everywhere.

Then he looks straight up at me. There's no time to crouch down. I understand what his look means. *I've seen you. I want you to know that.*

Yeah, I think, looking right back. *And I see you, dickhead. I know your sort. You don't scare me.* Except all the hairs on the back of my neck are standing to attention and the blood's thumping in my ears.

I watch as he walks over to the statue and shoves it viciously off its plinth, so that it topples to the ground with a crash. Then he makes for the door that leads back into the apartment building. I hear the slam echoing up the stairwell.

The woman is left on her knees in the courtyard, scrabbling around for the things that have fallen out of the suitcase. Another memory: Mum, on her knees in the hallway. Begging . . .

Where are the other neighbors? I can't be the only one who heard the commotion. It's not a choice to go down and help: it's something I have to do. I snatch up the keys, run down the couple of flights of stairs and out into the courtyard.

The woman starts as she spots me. She's still on her hands and knees and I see that her eye make-up has run where she's been crying. "Hey," I say softly. "Are you OK?"

In answer she holds up what looks like a silk shirt; it's stained with dirt from the ground. Then, shakily, in heavily accented English: "I came to get my things. I tell him it's over, for good. And this—this is what he does. He's a . . . a son-of-a-bitch. I never should have married him."

Jesus, I think. This is why I know I'm better off single. Mum had exceptionally terrible taste in men. My dad was the worst of all of them though. Supposedly a good guy. A real fucking bastard. Would have been better if he'd disappeared off into the night like Ben's dad did before he was born.

The woman's muttering under her breath as she shovels clothes into the suitcase. Anger seems to have taken over from fear. I go over and crouch down, help her pick up her things. High heels with long foreign names printed inside, a black silk, lacy bra, a little orange sweater made out of the softest fabric I've ever felt. "*Merci*," she says, absent-mindedly. Then she frowns. "Who are you? I've never seen you here before."

"I'm meant to be staying with my brother, Ben."

"*Ben*," she says, drawing out his name. She looks me up and down, taking in my jeans, my old sweater. "He's *your* brother? Before him I thought all Englishmen were sunburnt, no elegance, bad teeth. I did not know they could be so . . . so beautiful, so *charmant*, so *soigné*." Apparently there aren't enough words in English for how wonderful my brother is. She continues shoveling clothes into the suitcase, a violence to her movements, scowling every so often at the door into the apartment building. "Is it so strange I got bored of being with a stupid fucking . . . loser *alcoolique*? That I wanted a little flirtation? And, *d'accord*, maybe

I wanted to make Antoine jealous. Care about something other than himself. Is it such a surprise I started to look elsewhere?"

She tosses her hair over her shoulder in a shining curtain. It's quite impressive, being able to do that while crouched down picking your lacy underwear out of a gravel path.

She looks toward the building and raises her voice, almost as though she wants her husband to hear. "He says I only care about him because of his money. Of *course* I only care about him because of his money. It was the only thing that made it—how do you say—worthwhile? But now . . ." she shrugs, "it's not worth it."

I pass her a silky, electric blue dress, a baby pink bucket hat with JACQUEMUS printed across the front. "Have you seen Ben recently?" I ask.

"*Non*," she says, raising an eyebrow at me like I might be insinuating something. "*Pour quoi*? Why do you ask?"

"He was meant to be here last night, to let me in, but he wasn't—and he hasn't been answering my messages."

Her eyes widen. And then, under her breath, she murmurs something. I make out: "*Antoine . . . non. Ce n'est pas possible . . .*"

"What did you say?"

"Oh—*rien*, nothing." But I catch the glance she shoots toward the apartment building—fearful, suspicious, even—and wonder what it means.

Now she's trying to clip shut her bulging suitcase—brown leather with some sort of logo printed all over it—but I see that her hands are trembling, making her fingers clumsy.

"*Merde.*" Finally it snaps closed.

"Hey," I say. "Do you want to come inside? Call a cab?"

"No way," she says, fiercely. "I'm never going back in there. I have an Uber coming . . ." As if on cue, her phone pings. She checks it and gives what sounds like a sigh of relief. "*Merci. Putain*, he's here. I have to go." Then she turns and looks up at the apartment building. "You know what? Fuck this evil place." Then her expression softens and she blows a kiss toward the windows above us. "But at least one good thing happened to me here."

She pulls up the handle of the little case then turns and begins stalking toward the gate.

I hurry after her. "What do you mean, evil?"

She glances at me and shakes her head, mimes zippering her lips. "I want my money, from the divorce."

Then she's out onto the street and climbing into the cab. As it pulls away, off into the night, I realize I never managed to ask whether what she had with my brother was ever more than a flirtation.

I TURN BACK toward the courtyard and nearly jump out of my skin. Jesus Christ. There's an old woman standing there, looking at me. She seems to glow with a cold white light, like something off *Most Haunted*. But after I've caught my breath, I realize it's because she's standing beneath the outdoor lamp. Where the hell did she appear from?

"*Excuse-moi?*" I say. "*Madame?*" I'm not even sure what I want to ask her. *Who are you*, maybe? *What are you doing here?*

She doesn't answer. She simply shakes her head at me, very slowly. Then she's retreating backward, toward that cabin in the corner of the courtyard. I watch as she disappears inside. As the shutters—which I see now must have been open—are quickly drawn closed.

Nick

SECOND FLOOR

I LEAN FORWARD ONTO THE handlebars of the Peloton bike, standing up in the saddle for the incline. There's sweat running into my eyes, stinging. My lungs feel like they're full of acid, not air, my heart hammering so hard it feels like I might be about to have a heart attack. I pedal harder. I want to push beyond anything I've done before. Tiny stars dance at the edges of my vision. The apartment around me seems to shift and blur. For a moment I think I'm going to pass out. Maybe I do—next thing I know I'm slumped forward over the handlebars and the mechanism is whirring down. I'm hit by a sudden rush of nausea. I force it down, take huge gulps of air.

I got into spinning in San Francisco. And bulletproof coffee, keto, Bikram—pretty much any other fad the rest of the tech world was into, in case it provided any extra edge, any additional source of inspiration. Normally I'd sit here and do a class, or listen to a Ted Talk. This morning wasn't like that. I wanted to lose myself in pure exertion, push through to a place where thought was silenced. I woke just after five A.M., but I knew I wasn't going to sleep, especially during that fight in the courtyard, the latest—and worst—of many. Getting on the bike seemed like the only thing that made sense.

I climb down from the saddle, a little unsteadily. The bike is one of the few items in this room besides my iMac and my books. Nothing up on the walls. No rugs on the floor. Partly because I like the whole minimal aesthetic. Partly because I still feel like I haven't really moved in, because I like the idea that I could up and leave at any moment.

I pull the headphones out of my ears. It sounds like things have quieted down out there in the courtyard. I walk over to the window, the muscles in my calves twitching.

I can't see anything at first. Then my eye snags on a movement and I see there's a girl down there, opening the door to the building. There's something familiar about her, about the way she moves. Difficult to put my finger on, but my mind gropes around as if for a forgotten word.

Now I see the lights come on in the apartment on the third floor. I watch her move into my line of sight. And I know that she has to be something to do with him. With my old mate and—as of very recently—neighbor, Benjamin Daniels. He told me about a younger sister, once. Half sister. Something of a tearaway. Bit of a problem case. From his old life, however much he'd tried to sever himself from all that. What he definitely didn't tell me was that she was coming here. But then it wouldn't be the first time he's kept something from me, would it?

The girl appears briefly at the windows, looking out. Then she turns and moves away—toward the bedroom, I think. I watch her until she's out of sight.

Jess

MY THROAT HURTS AND THERE'S an oily sweat on my forehead. I stare up at the high ceiling above me and try and work out where I am. Now I remember: getting here last night . . . that scene in the courtyard a couple of hours ago. It was still dark out so I got back into bed afterward. I didn't think I'd be able to sleep but I must have drifted off. I don't feel rested though. My whole body aches like I've been fighting someone. I think I *was* fighting someone, in my dream. The kind you're relieved to wake up from. It comes back to me in fragments. I was trying to get into a locked room but my hands were clumsy, all fingers and thumbs. Someone—Ben?—was shouting at me not to open the door, *do not open the door*, but I knew I had to, knew I didn't have any other choice. And then finally the door was opening and all at once I knew he was right—oh why hadn't I listened to him? Because what greeted me on the other side—

I sit up in bed. I check my phone. Eight A.M. No messages. A new day and still no sign of my brother. I call his number: straight to voicemail. I listen to the voicenote he left me again, with that final instruction: "Just ring the buzzer. I'll be up waiting for you—"

And this time I notice something strange. How his voice seems to cut off mid-sentence, like something has distracted him. After this there's a faint murmur of sound in the background—words, maybe—but I can't make anything out.

The uneasy feeling grows.

I walk out into the main living space. The room looks even more like something from a museum in the light of day: you can see the dust motes hanging suspended in the air. And I've just spotted something I didn't see last night. There's a largish, lighter patch on the floorboards just a few feet before the front door. I walk toward it, crouch down. As I do the smell—the strange smell I noticed last night—catches me right at the back of the throat. A singe-the-nostrils chemical tang. Bleach. But that's not all. Something's caught here in the gap between the floorboards, glinting in the cold light. I try to wiggle it out with my fingers, but it's stuck fast. I go and get a couple of forks from the drawer in the kitchen, use them together to pry it loose. Eventually, I work it free. A long gilt chain unspools first, then a pendant: an image of a male saint in a cloak, holding a crook.

Ben's St. Christopher. I reach up and feel the identical texture of the chain around my neck, the heavy weight of the pendant. I've never seen him without it. Just like me, I suspect he never takes it off, because it came from Mum. Because it's one of the few things we have from her. Maybe it's guilt, but I suspect Ben's almost more sentimental about stuff like that than me.

But here it is. And the chain is broken.

Jess

I SIT HERE TRYING NOT to panic. Trying to imagine the rational explanation that I'm sure must be behind all this. Should I call the police? Is that what a normal person would do? Because it's several things now. Ben not being here when he said he would and not answering his phone. The cat's blood-tinged fur. The bleach stain. The broken necklace. But more than any of this it's the way it all . . . feels. It feels wrong. *Always listen to your inner voice*, was Mum's thing. *Never ignore a feeling*. It didn't work out so well for her, of course. But she was right, in a way. It's how I knew I should barricade myself in my bedroom at night when I fostered with the Andersons, even before another kid told me about Mr. Anderson and his preferences. And way before that, before foster care even, it's how I knew I shouldn't go into that locked room—even though I did.

I don't want to call the police, though. *They might want to know things about you*, a little voice says. *They might have questions you don't want to answer.* The police and I have never got on all that well. Let's just say I've had my share of run-ins. And even though he had it coming, what I did to that arsehole is, I suppose, technically still a crime. Right now I don't want to put myself on their radar unless I absolutely have to.

Besides, I don't really have enough to tell them, do I? A cat that might just have killed a mouse? A necklace that might just have been innocently broken? A brother who might have just fucked off, yet again, to leave me to fend for myself?

No, it's not enough.

I put my head in my hands, try to think what to do next. At the same moment my stomach gives a long, loud groan. I realize I can't actually remember the last time I ate anything. Last night I'd sort of imagined I'd get here and Ben would fix me up some scrambled eggs or something, maybe we'd order a takeaway. Part of me feels too queasy and keyed up to eat. But perhaps I'll be able to think more clearly with some food in my belly.

I raid the fridge and cupboards but besides half a pack of butter and a stick of salami they're bare. One cupboard is different from all the rest: it's some sort of cavity with what looks like a pulley system, but I can't work out what it's for at all. In desperation I cut off some of the salami with a very sharp Japanese knife that I find in Ben's utensil pot, but it's hardly a hearty breakfast.

I pocket the set of keys I found in Ben's jacket. I know the code now, I've got the keys: I can get back into this place.

The courtyard looks less spooky in the light of day. I pass the ruins of the statue of the naked woman, the head separated from the rest, face up, eyes staring at the sky. One of the flowerbeds looks like it has recently been re-dug, which explains that smell of freshly turned earth. There's a little fountain running, too. I look over at the tiny cabin in the corner and see a dark gap between the closed slats of the shutters; perfect for spying on anything that's going on out here. I can imagine her watching me through it: the old woman I saw last night, the one who seems to live there.

I take in the strangeness of my surroundings as I close the apartment's gates, the foreignness of it all. The crazily beautiful buildings around me, the cars with their unfamiliar number-plates. The streets also look different in daylight—and much busier when I get away from the hush of the apartment building's cul-de-sac. They smell different, too: moped fumes and cigarette smoke and roasted coffee. It must have rained in the night as the cobbles are gleaming wet, slippery underfoot. Everyone seems to know exactly where they're going: I step into the street out of the way of one woman walking straight at me while talking on her phone and nearly collide with a couple of kids sharing an electric scooter. I've never felt so clueless, so like a fish out of water.

I wander past shop fronts with their grilles pulled down, wrought-iron gates leading onto courtyards and gardens full of dead leaves, pharmacies with blinking neon green crosses—there seems to be one on every street, do the French get sick more?—doubling back on myself and getting lost a couple of times. Finally, I find a bakery, the sign painted emerald green with gold lettering—BOULANGERIE—and a striped awning. Inside the walls and the floor are decorated with patterned tiles and it smells like burnt sugar and melted butter. The place is packed: a long queue doubles back on itself. I wait, getting hungrier and hungrier, staring at the counter which is filled with all sorts of things that look too perfect to be eaten: tiny tarts with glazed raspberries, eclairs with violet icing, little chocolate cakes with a thousand very fine layers and a touch of what looks like actual gold on top. People in front of me are putting in serious orders: three loaves of bread, six croissants, an apple tart. My mouth waters. I feel the rustle of the notes I nicked from Ben's wallet in my pocket.

The woman in front of me has hair so perfect it doesn't look real: a black, shining bob, not a strand out of place. A silk scarf tied around her neck, some kind of camel-colored coat and a black leather handbag over her arm. She looks rich. Not flashy rich. The French equivalent of posh. You don't have hair that perfect unless you spend your days doing basically nothing.

I look down and see a skinny, silver-colored dog on a pale blue leather lead. It looks up at me with suspicious dark eyes.

The woman behind the counter hands her a pastel-colored box tied with a ribbon: "*Voilà, Madame Meunier.*"

"*Merci.*"

She turns and I see that she's wearing red lipstick, so perfectly applied it might be tattooed on. At a guess she's about fifty—but a very well-preserved fifty. She's putting her card back into her wallet. As she does something flutters to the ground—a piece of paper. A banknote?

I bend down to pick it up. Take a closer look. Not a banknote, which is a shame. Someone like her probably wouldn't miss the odd ten euros. It's a handwritten note, scribbled in big block capitals. I read: *double la prochaine fois, salope.*

"*Donne-moi ça!*"

I look up. The woman is glaring at me, her hand outstretched. I think I know what she's asking but she did it so rudely, so like a queen commanding a peasant, that I pretend not to understand.

"Excuse me?"

She switches to English. "Give that to me." And then finally, as an afterthought, "please."

Taking my time about it, I hold out the note. She snatches it from my hand so roughly that I feel one of her long fingernails scrape at my skin. Without a thank you, she marches out through the door.

"*Excusez-moi? Madame?*" the woman behind the counter asks, ready to take my order.

"A croissant, please." Everything else is probably going to be too expensive. My stomach rumbles as I watch her drop it into the little paper bag. "Two, actually."

On the walk back to the apartment through the cold gray morning streets I eat the first one in big ravenous bites and then the second slower, tasting the salt of the butter, enjoying the crunch of the pastry and the softness inside. It's so good that I could cry and not much makes me cry.

Back at the apartment building I let myself in through the gate with the code I learned yesterday. As I cross the courtyard I catch the scent of fresh cigarette smoke. I glance up, following the smell. There's a girl sitting there, up on the fourth-floor balcony, cigarette in her hand. A pale face, choppy dark hair, dressed in head-to-toe black from her turtleneck to the Docs on her feet. I can see from here that she's young, maybe nineteen, twenty. She catches sight of me looking back at her, I can see it in the way her whole body freezes. That's the only way I can describe it.

You. You know something, I think, staring back. And I'm going to get you to tell me.

Mimi

SHE'S SEEN ME. THE WOMAN who arrived last night, who I watched this morning walking around in his apartment. She's staring straight at me. I can't move.

In my head the roar of static grows louder.

Finally she turns away. When I breathe out my chest burns.

I WATCHED HIM arrive from here, too. It was August, nearly three months ago, the middle of the heatwave. Camille and I were sitting on the balcony in the junky old deckchairs she'd bought from a *brocanter* shop, drinking Aperol Spritzes even though I actually kind of hate Aperol Spritz. Camille often persuades me to do things I wouldn't otherwise do.

Benjamin Daniels turned up in an Uber. Gray T-shirt, jeans. Dark hair, longish. He looked famous, somehow. Or maybe not famous but . . . special. You know? I can't explain it. But he had that thing about him that made you want to look at him. *Need* to look at him.

I was wearing dark glasses and I watched him from the corner of my eye, so it didn't seem like I was looking his way. When he opened the boot of the car I saw the stains of sweat under his arms and, where his T-shirt had ridden up, I also saw how the line of his tan stopped beneath the waistband of his jeans, where the paler skin started, an arrow of dark hair descending. The muscles in his arms flexed when he lifted the bags out of the trunk. Not like a jacked-up gym-goer. More elegant. Like a drummer: drummers always have good muscles. Even from here I could imagine how his sweat would smell—not bad, just like salt and skin.

He shouted to the driver: "Thanks, mate!" I recognized the English accent straightaway; there's this old TV show I'm obsessed with, *Skins*, about all these British teenagers screwing and screwing up, falling in love.

"Mmm," said Camille, lifting up her sunglasses.

"*Mais non*," I said. "He's really old, Camille."

She shrugged. "He's only thirty-something."

"*Oui*, and that's old. That's like . . . fifteen years older than us."

"Well, think of all that *experience*." She made a vee with her fingers and stuck her tongue out between them.

I laughed at that. "Beurk—you're disgusting."

She raised her eyebrows. "*Pas du tout*. And you'd know that if your darling papa ever let you near any guys—"

"Shut up."

"Ah, Mimi . . . I'm kidding! But you know one day he's going to have to realize you're not his little girl any longer." She grinned, sucked up Aperol through her straw. For a second I wanted to slap her . . . I nearly did. I don't always have the best impulse control.

"He's just a little . . . protective." It was more than that, really. But I suppose I also never really wanted to do anything to disappoint Papa, tarnish that image of me as his little princess.

I often wished I could be more like Camille, though. So chill about sex. For her it's just another thing she likes doing: like swimming or cycling or sunbathing. I'd never even had sex, let alone with two people at the same time (one of her specialties), or tried girls as well as boys. You know what's funny? Papa actually approved of her moving in here with me, said living with another girl "might stop you from getting into too much trouble."

Camille was in her smallest bikini, just three triangles of pale crocheted material that barely covered anything. Her feet were pressed up against the ironwork of the balcony and her toenails were painted a chipped, Barbie-doll pink. Apart from her month in the South with friends she'd sat out there pretty much every hot day, getting browner and browner, slathering herself in La Roche-Posay. Her whole body looked like it had been dipped in gold, her hair lightened to the color of caramel. I don't go brown; I just burn, so I sat tucked in the shade like a vampire with my Francoise Sagan novel, wearing a big man's shirt.

She leaned forward, still watching the guy getting his cases out of the car. "Oh my God, Mimi! He has a cat. How *cute*. Can you see it? Look, in that carry basket. *Salut minou!*"

She did it on purpose, so he would look up and see us—see her. Which he did.

"Hey," she called, standing up and waving so hard that her *nénés* bounced around in her bikini top like they were trying to escape. "*Bienvenue*—welcome! I'm Camille. And this is Merveille. Cute pussy!"

I was so embarrassed. She knew exactly what she was saying, it's the same slang in French: *chatte*. Also, I hate that my full name is Merveille. No one calls me that. I'm Mimi. My mum gave me that name because it means "wonder" and she said that's what my arrival into her life was: this unexpected but wonderful thing. But it's also completely mortifying.

I sank down behind my book, but not so much that I couldn't still see him over the top of it.

The guy shielded his eyes. "Thanks!" he called. He put up a hand, waved back. As he did I saw again that strip of skin between his T-shirt and jeans. "I'm Ben—friend of Nick's? I'm moving into the third floor."

Camille turned to me. "Well," she said, in an undertone. "I feel like this place has just got a *lot* more exciting." She grinned. "Maybe I should introduce myself to him properly. Offer to look after the pussy if he goes away."

I wouldn't be surprised if she's fucking him in a week's time, I thought to myself. It would hardly be a surprise. The surprising thing was how much I hated the thought of it.

SOMEONE'S KNOCKING ON the door to my apartment.

I creep down the hall, look through the peephole. *Merde*: it's her: the woman from Ben's apartment.

I swallow—or try to. It feels like my tongue is stuck in my throat.

It's hard to think with this roaring in my ears. I know I don't have to open the door. This is my apartment, my space. But the *knock knock knock* is incessant, beating against my skull until I feel like something in me is going to explode.

I grit my teeth and open the door, take a step back. The shock of her face, close up: I see him in her features, straightaway. But she's small and her eyes are darker and there's something, I don't know, hungry about her which maybe was in him too but he hid it better. It's like with her all the angles are sharper. With him it was all smoothness. She's scruffy, too: jeans and an old sweater with frayed cuffs, dark red hair scragged up on top of her head. That's not like him either. Even in a gray T-shirt on a hot day he looked kind of . . . pulled-together, you know? Like everything fit him just right.

"Hi,' she says. She smiles but it's not a real smile. "I'm Jess. What's your name?"

"M—Mimi." My voice comes out as a rasp.

"My brother—Ben—lives on the third floor. But he's . . . well, he's kind of disappeared on me. Do you know him at all?"

For a crazy moment I think about pretending I don't speak English. But that's stupid.

I shake my head. "No. I didn't know him—don't, I mean. My English, sorry, it's not so good."

I can feel her looking past me, like she's trying to see her way into my apartment. I move sideways, try to block her view. So instead she looks at me, like she's trying to see into *me*: and that's worse.

"This is your apartment?" she asks.

"*Oui.*"

"Wow." She widens her eyes. "Nice work if you can get it. And it's just you in here?"

"My flatmate Camille and me."

She's trying to peer into the apartment again, looking over my shoulder. "I was wondering if you'd seen him lately, Ben?"

"No. He's been keeping his shutters closed. I mean—" I realize, too late, that wasn't what she was asking.

She raises her eyebrows. "OK," she says, "but do you remember the last time you saw him generally about the place? It would be so helpful." She smiles. Her smile is not like his at all. But then no one's is.

I realize she's not going to go unless I give her an answer. I clear my throat. "I—I don't know. Not for a while—I suppose maybe a week?"

"*Quoi? Ce n'est pas vrai!*" *That's not true!* I turn to see Camille, in just a camisole and her *culotte*, wandering into the space behind me. "It was yesterday morning, remember Mimi? I saw you with him on the stairs."

Merde. I can feel my face growing hot. "Oh, yes. That's right." I turn back to the woman in the doorway.

"So he *was* here yesterday?" she asks, frowning, looking from me to Camille and back. "You *did* see him?"

"Uh-huh," I say. "Yesterday. I must have forgotten."

"Did he say if he was going anywhere?"

"No. It was only for a second."

I picture his face, as I passed him on the stairs. *Hey Mimi. Something up?* That smile. No one's smile is like his.

"I can't help you," I say. "Sorry." I go to close the door.

"He said he'd ask me to feed his kitty if he ever went away," Camille says and the almost flirtatious way she says "kitty" reminds me of her "Cute pussy!" on the day he arrived. "But he didn't ask this time."

"Really?" The woman seems interested in this. "So it sounds like—" Maybe she's realized I'm slowly closing the door on her because she makes a movement like she's about to step forward into the apartment. And without even thinking I slam the door in her face so hard I feel the wood give under my hands.

My arms are shaking. My whole body's shaking. I know Camille must be staring at me, wondering what's going on. But I don't care what she thinks right now. I lean my head against the door. I can't breathe. And suddenly I feel like I'm choking. It rushes up inside me, the sickness, and before I can stop it I'm vomiting, right onto the beautifully polished floorboards.

Sophie

I'M COMING UP THE STAIRS when I see her. A stranger inside these walls. It sends such a jolt through me that I nearly drop the box from the boulangerie. A girl, snooping around on the penthouse landing. She has no business being here.

I watch her for a while before I speak. "*Bonjour,*" I say coolly. She spins around, caught out. Good. I wanted to shock her.

But now it's my turn to be shocked. "You." It's her from the boulangerie: the scruffy girl who picked up the note I dropped.

Double la prochaine fois, salope. *Double the next time, bitch.*

"Who are you?"

"I'm Jess. Jess Hadley. I'm staying with my brother Ben," she says, quickly. "On the third floor."

"If you are staying on the third floor then what are you doing up here?" It makes sense, I suppose. Sneaking around in here as though she owns the place. Just like him.

"I was looking for Ben." She must realise how absurd this sounds, as though he might be hiding in some shadowy corner up here in the eaves, because she suddenly looks sheepish. "Do you know him? Benjamin Daniels?"

That smile: a fox entering the henhouse. The sound of a glass smashing. A smear of crimson on a stiff white napkin.

"Nicolas's friend. "Yes. Although I've only met him a couple of times."

"Nicolas? Is that 'Nick'? I think Ben might have mentioned him. Which floor's he on?"

I hesitate. Then I say: "The second."

"Do you remember when you last saw him about?" she asks. "Ben, I mean? He was meant to be here last night. I tried asking one of the girls—Mimi?—on the fourth floor, but she wasn't too helpful."

"I don't recall." Perhaps my answer sounds too quick, too certain. "But then he keeps so much to himself. You know. Rather— what's the English expression?—reserved."

"Really? That doesn't sound anything like Ben! I'd expect him to be friends with everyone in this building by now."

"Not with me." That at least is true. I give a little shrug. "Anyway, maybe he went away and forgot to tell you?"

"No," she says. "He wouldn't do that."

COULD I REMEMBER the last time I saw him? Of course I can.

But I am thinking now about the first time. About two months ago. The middle of the heatwave.

I did not like him. I knew it straightaway.

The laughter, that's what I heard first. Vaguely threatening, in the way male laughter can be. The almost competitive nature of it.

I was in the courtyard. I had spent the afternoon planting in the shade. To others gardening is a form of creative abandon. To me it is a way of exerting control upon my surroundings. When I told Jacques I wanted to take care of the courtyard's small garden he did not understand. "There are people we can pay to do it for us," he told me. In my husband's world there are people you can pay for anything.

The end of the day: the light fading, the heat still oppressive. I watched from behind the rosemary bushes as the two of them entered the courtyard. Nick first. Then a stranger, wheeling a moped. Around the same age as his friend, but he seemed somehow older. Tall and rangy. Dark hair. He carried himself well. A very particular confidence in the way he inhabited the space around him.

I watched as Nick's friend plucked a sprig of rosemary from one of the bushes, tearing hard to wrench it free. How he crushed it to his nose, inhaled. There was something presumptuous about the gesture. It felt like an act of vandalism.

Then Benoit was running over to them. The newcomer scooped him up and held him.

I stood. "He doesn't like to be held by anyone but me."

Benoit, the traitor, turned his head to lick the stranger's hand.

"*Bonjour* Sophie," Nicolas said. "This is Ben. He's going to be living here, in the apartment on the third floor." Proud. Showing off this friend like a new toy.

"Pleased to meet you, Madame." He smiled then, a lazy smile that was somehow just as presumptuous as the way he'd ripped into that bush. *You will like me*, it said. *Everyone does.*

"Please," I said. "Call me Sophie." The Madame had made me feel about a hundred years old, even though it was only proper.

"Sophie."

Now I wished I hadn't said it. It was too informal, too intimate. "I'll take him, please." I held out my hands for the dog. Benoit smelled faintly of petrol, of male sweat. I held him at a little distance from my body. "The concierge won't like that," I added, nodding at the moped, then toward the cabin. "She hates them."

I had wanted to assert myself, but I sounded like a matron scolding a small boy.

"Noted," he said. "Cheers for the tip. I'll have to butter her up, get her on side."

I stared at him. Why on earth would he want to do that?

"Good luck there," Nick said. "She doesn't like anyone."

"Ah," he says. "But I like a challenge. I'll win her over."

"Well watch out," Nick said. "I'm not sure you want to encourage her. She has a knack for appearing round corners when you least expect it."

I didn't like the idea of it at all. That woman with her watchful eyes, her omnipresence. What might she be able to tell him if he did "win her over"?

When Jacques got home I told him I had met the new inhabitant of the third–floor apartment. He frowned, pointed to my cheekbone. "You have dirt, there." I rubbed at my cheek—somehow I must have missed it when I had checked my appearance . . . I thought I had been so careful. "So what do you make of our new neighbor?"

"I don't like him."

Jacques raised his eyebrows. "I thought he sounded like an interesting young man. What don't you like?"

"He's too . . . charming." That charm. He wielded it like a weapon.

Jacques frowned; he didn't understand. My husband: a clever man, but also arrogant. Used to having things his way, having power. I have never acquired that sort of arrogance. I have never been certain enough of my position to be complacent. "Well," he said. "We'll have to invite him to drinks, look him over."

I didn't like the sound of that: inviting him into our home.

The first note arrived two weeks later.

I know who you are, Madame Sophie Meunier. I know what you really are. If you don't want anyone else to know I suggest you leave €2000 beneath the loose step in front of the gate.

The "Madame": a nasty little piece of faux formality. The mocking, knowing tone. No postmark; it had been hand-delivered.

My blackmailer knew this building well enough to know about the loose step outside the gate.

I didn't tell Jacques. I knew he would refuse to pay, for one thing. Those who have the most money are often the most close-fisted about handing it over. I was too afraid not to pay. I took out my jewelry box. I considered the yellow sapphire brooch Jacques had given me for our second wedding anniversary, the jade and diamond hair clips he gave me last Christmas. I selected an emerald bracelet as the safest, because he never asked me to wear it. I took it to a pawnbroker, a place out in the *banlieues*, the neighborhoods outside the *peripherique* ring road that encircles the city. A world away from the Paris of postcards, of tourist dreams. I had to go somewhere no one could possibly recognize me. The pawnbroker knew I was out of my depth. I think he could sense my fear. Little did he know it was less to do with the neighborhood than my horror at finding myself in this situation. The debasement of it.

I returned with more than enough cash to cover it—less than I should have got, though. Ten €200 notes. The money felt dirty: the sweat of other hands, the accumulated filth. I slid the wedge of notes into a thick envelope where they looked even dirtier against the fine cream card and sealed them up. As though it would somehow make the fact of the money less horrific, less demeaning. I left it, as directed, beneath the loose step in front of the apartment building's gate.

For the time being, I had covered my debts.

"PERHAPS YOU'LL WANT to return to the third floor now," I tell the strange, scruffy girl. His sister. Hard to believe it. Hard, actually, to imagine him having had a childhood, a family at all. He seemed so . . . discrete. As though he had stepped into the world fully formed.

"I didn't catch your name," she says.

I didn't give it. "Sophie Meunier," I say. "My husband Jacques and I live in the penthouse apartment, on this floor."

"If you're in the penthouse apartment, what's up there?" She points to the wooden ladder.

"The entrance to the old *chambres de bonne*—the old maids' quarters—in the eaves of the building." I nod my head in the other direction, toward the descending staircase. "But I'm sure you'll want to get back to the third floor now."

She takes the hint. She has to walk right by me to go back down. I don't move an inch as she passes. It is only when my jaw begins to ache that I realize how hard I have been gritting my teeth.

Jess

I CLOSE THE APARTMENT DOOR behind me. I think of the way Sophie Meunier looked at me just now: like I was something she'd found on the sole of her shoe. She might be French, but I'd know her type anywhere. The shining black bob, the silk scarf, the swanky handbag. The way she stressed "penthouse." She's a snob. It's not exactly a new feeling, being looked at like I'm scum. But I thought I sensed something else. Some extra hostility, when I mentioned Ben.

I think of her suggestion that he might have gone away. "It's not a great time," he'd said, on the phone. But he wouldn't just up and go without leaving word . . . would he? I'm his family— his *only* family. However put out he was, I don't think he would abandon me.

But then it wouldn't be the first time he's disappeared out of my life with little more than a backward glance. Like when suddenly he had some shiny new parents ready to whisk him away to a magical new life of private schools and holidays abroad and family Labradors and *sorry but the Daniels are only looking to adopt one child. Actually it can be best to separate children from the same family, especially when there has been a shared trauma.* As I said, my brother's always been good at getting people to fall in love with him. Ben, driving away in the back seat of the Daniels' navy blue Volvo, turning back once and then looking forward, onward to his new life.

No. He left me a voicenote giving me directions, for Christ's sake. And even if he did have to leave for some reason, why isn't he answering any of my calls or texts?

I keep coming back to the broken chain of his St. Christopher. The bloodstains on the cat's fur. How none of Ben's neighbors seem prepared to give me the time of day—more than that, seem actively hostile. How it just feels like something here is *wrong*.

I search Ben's social media. At some point he seems to have deleted all his socials except Instagram. How have I only just realized this? No Facebook, no Twitter. His Instagram profile picture is the cat, which right now is sitting on its haunches on the desk, watching me through narrowed eyes. There isn't a single photo left on his grid. I suppose it's just like Ben, master of reinvention, to have got rid of all his old stuff. But there's something about the disappearance of all his content that gives me the creeps. Almost like someone's tried to erase him. I send him a DM, all the same. **Ben, if you see this: answer your phone!**

My mobile buzzes: **You have only 50MB of Roaming Data remaining. To buy more, follow this link . . .**

Shit. I can't even get by on the cheapest plan.

I sit down on the sofa. As I do I realize I've sat on Ben's wallet, I must have tossed it here earlier. I open it and pull out the business card stuck in the front. **Theo Mendelson, Paris editor,** *Guardian*. And scribbled on the card: PITCH STORY TO HIM! Some-one Ben's working for, maybe, someone he might have been in touch with recently? There's a number listed. I call but it rings out so I fire off a quick text:

Hi. It's about my brother Ben Daniels. Trying to find him. Can you help?

I put the phone down. I just heard something odd.

I sit very still, listening hard, trying to work out what the noise is. It sounds like footsteps passing down a flight of stairs. Except the sound isn't coming from in front of me, from the landing and the staircase beyond the apartment's entrance. It's behind my head. I stand up from the sofa and study the wall. And it's now, looking properly, that I see something there. I run my hands over the faded silk wall covering. There's a break, a gap in the fabric, running horizontally above my head and vertically down. I step back and take in the shape of it. It's cleverly hidden, and the sofa's pushed in front of it, so you wouldn't notice it at all unless you were looking pretty closely. But I think it's a door.

Sophie

BACK IN THE APARTMENT I reach into my handbag—black leather Celine, ferociously expensive, extremely discreet, a gift from Jacques—take out my wallet and am almost surprised to find the note hasn't burnt a hole through the leather. I cannot believe I was so clumsy as to drop it earlier. I am never normally clumsy.

Double the next time, bitch.

It arrived yesterday morning. The latest in the series. Well. It has no hold over me now. I rip it into tiny pieces and scatter them into the fireplace. I pull the tasseled cord set into the wall and flames roar into life, instantly incinerating the paper. Then I walk quickly through the apartment, past the floor-to-ceiling windows with their view out over Paris, along the hallway hung with its trio of Gerhard Richter abstracts, my heels tapping briefly over the parquet then silenced on the silk of the antique Persian runner.

In the kitchen I open the pastel box from the boulangerie. Inside is a quiche Lorraine, studded with lardons of bacon, the pastry so crisp it will shatter at the slightest touch. The dairy waft of the cream and egg yolk briefly makes me want to gag. When Jacques is away from home on one of his business trips I usually exist on black coffee and fruit—perhaps the odd piece of dark chocolate broken from a Maison Bonnat bar.

I did not feel like going out. I felt like hiding in here away from the world. But I am a regular customer and it is important to stick to the usual routines.

A couple of minutes later, I open the door to the apartment again and wait a few moments listening, looking down the staircase, making sure no one's there. You cannot do anything in this building without half-expecting the concierge to appear from some dark corner as if formed from the shadows themselves. But for once it isn't her that I'm concerned about. It's this newcomer, this stranger.

When I am certain I am alone, I walk across the landing to the wooden stairs that lead up to the old *chambres de bonne*. I am the only one in the building with a key to these old rooms. Even the concierge's access to the public spaces of this building ends here.

I fasten Benoit to the bottom rung of the wooden steps with his leash. He wears a matching set in blue leather from Hermès: both of us, with our expensive Hermès collars. He'll bark if he sees anyone.

I take the key out of my pocket and climb the stairs. As I put the key into the lock my hand trembles a little; it takes a couple of attempts to turn.

I push the door open. Just before I step inside I check, again, that I am not being watched. I can't afford to be too careful. Especially not with her here now, snooping around.

I spend perhaps ten minutes up here, in the *chambres de bonne*. Afterward I lock the padlock again just as carefully, pocket the little silver key. Benoit is waiting for me at the bottom of the steps, looking up at me with those dark eyes. My secret-keeper. I put a finger to my lips.

Shh.

Jess

I GRAB HOLD OF THE sofa, drag it away from the wall. The cat jumps down from the desk and trots over, maybe hoping I'm going to reveal a mouse or some creepy crawlies. And yes, here it is: a door. No handle but I get a hold of the edge, wedge my fingers into the gap and pull. It swings open.

I let out a gasp. I don't know what I'd expected: a hidden cupboard, maybe. Not this. Darkness greets me on the other side. The air as cold as if I'd just opened a fridge. There's a smell of musty old air, like in a church. As my eyes adjust to the gloom I make out a stone staircase, spiraling up and down, dark and cramped. It couldn't be more different from the grand sweeping affair beyond the apartment's main door. I suppose from the looks of it this was probably some kind of servants' staircase, like the maids' rooms Sophie Meunier told me about upstairs.

I step inside and let the door swing closed behind me. It's suddenly very dark. But I notice a chink of light showing through the door, slightly lower than head-height. I crouch and put my eye to it. I can see into the apartment: the living area, the kitchen. It looks like some kind of homemade spy hole. I suppose it could always have been here, as old as the building itself. Or it could have been made more recently. Someone could have been watching Ben through here. Someone could have been watching *me*.

I can still hear the footsteps heading downward. I turn on my phone's flashlight and follow, trying not to trip over my own feet as the steps twist tightly round on themselves. This staircase must have been made for a time when people were smaller: I'm not exactly large, but it still feels like a tight squeeze.

A second of hesitation. I have no idea where this might lead. I'm not sure this is the best idea. Could I even be heading toward some sort of danger?

Well. It's not like that's ever stopped me before. I carry on downward.

I come to another door. Here, too, I spot another little spy hole. I press my eye to it quickly, look in. No sign of anyone about. I'm feeling a little disorientated but I suppose this must be the second-floor apartment: Ben's friend Nick's place. It looks like it might be pretty much the same layout as Ben's, but it's all whitewashed walls with nothing on them. Beyond the giant computer in the corner, some books, and what looks like a piece of exercise equipment it's practically empty, with about as much character as a dentist's surgery. It seems Nick has barely moved in.

The footsteps below me continue, urging me to follow. I carry on down, the light from my phone bouncing in front of me. I must be on the first floor now. Another apartment and there it is: another spy hole. I look through. This place is a mess: stuff everywhere, empty sharing-size crisp packets and overflowing ashtrays, side tables crowded with bottles, a standing lamp lying on its side. I take an involuntary step back as a figure looms into view. He's not wearing his parka but I recognize him instantly: the guy from the gate, from that fight in the courtyard. Antoine. He appears to be swigging from a bottle of Jack Daniel's. He drains the last dregs then lifts up the bottle. Jesus: I jump as he smashes it against the side table.

He sways on the spot, looking at the jagged stump like he's wondering what to do with it. Then he turns in my direction. For a horrible moment it feels like he's staring directly at me. But I'm peering through a chink only a few millimeters wide . . . there's no way he could possibly see me here. Right?

I'm not going to hang around to find out. I hurry on down. I must be passing the ground floor level, the entrance hall. A further flight of steps: I think I'm underground now. The air feels heavier, colder; I can imagine the earth surrounding me. Finally the staircase leads me to a door, swinging on its hinges—whoever I'm following has just stepped through it. My pulse quickens, I must be getting closer. I push through the door and even though it's still just as dark on the other side I have the impression of having stepped into a wide, echoing space. Silence. No sound of footsteps. Where can they have gone? I must only be moments behind.

It's colder down here. It smells of damp, of mold. My phone throws only a very weak beam into the darkness but I can see the orange glow of a light switch across from me. I press it and the lights come on, the little mechanical timer clicking down: *tick tick tick tick tick*. I've probably only got a couple of minutes before it goes dark again. I'm definitely in the basement: a wide, low-ceilinged space easily double the size of Ben's apartment; several doors leading off it. A rack in the corner that holds a couple of bikes. And leaning against one wall there's a red moped. I walk over to it, take out the set of keys I found in Ben's jacket, fit the Vespa one into the ignition and turn. The lights hum on. It hits me: so Ben can't be away on his bike somewhere. I must have been leaning against it because it tilts under me. It's now that I see that the front wheel is flat, the rubber completely shredded. An accident? But there's something about the total decimation that feels intentional.

I turn back to the basement. Perhaps whoever it was has disappeared behind one of those doors. Are they hiding from me? A shiver of unease as I realize I may now be the one being watched.

I open the first door. A couple of washing machines—one of which is on, all the clothes whizzing around in a colorful jumble.

In the next room I smell the bins before I see them, that sweetish, rotten scent. Something makes a scuffling sound. I shut the door.

The next is some sort of cleaning cupboard: mops and brooms and buckets and a pile of dirty-looking rags in the corner.

The next one has a padlock on the door but the door itself is open. I push inside. It's stuffed full of wine: racks and racks of it, floor to ceiling. There might be well over a thousand bottles in here. Some of them look seriously old: labels stained and peeling, the glass covered in a layer of dust. I pull one out. I don't know much about wine. I mean, I've worked in plenty of bars but they've been the sort of place where people ask for "a large glass of red, love" and you get the bottle thrown in for an extra couple of quid. But this, it just *looks* expensive. Whoever's keeping this stuff down here clearly trusts their neighbors. And probably won't notice if just one little bottle goes missing. Maybe it'll help me think. I'll pick something that looks like it's been down here for ages, something that they'll have forgotten about. I find the dustiest, most cobweb-covered bottles on the bottom racks, search along the rows, pull one out a little way. *1996.* An image of a stately home picked out in gold. Château Blondin-Lavigne, the label reads. That'll do.

The lights go out. The timer must have run down. I look for a light switch. It's so dark in here; I'm immediately disorientated. I step to the left and brush up against something. Shit, I need to be careful: I'm basically surrounded by teetering walls of glass.

There. Finally I spot the little orange glow of another light switch. I press it, the lights hum back on.

I turn to find the door. That's odd, I thought I left it open. It must have swung shut behind me. I turn the handle. But nothing happens when I pull. The door won't budge. What the hell? That can't be right. I try it again: nothing. And then again, putting everything into it, throwing all my weight against it.

Someone's locked me in. It's the only explanation.

Concierge

THE LOGE

AFTERNOON AND ALREADY THE LIGHT seems to be fading, the shadows growing deeper. A rap on the door of my cabin. My first thought is that it's him, Benjamin Daniels. The only one who would deign to call on me here. I think of the first time he knocked on my door, taking me by surprise:

"*Bonjour Madame.* I just wanted to introduce myself. I'm moving in on the third floor. I suppose that makes us neighbors!" I assumed, at first, that he was mocking me, but his polite smile said otherwise. Surely he had to know there was no world in which we were neighbors? Still, it made an impression.

The knock comes again. This time I hear the authority in it. I realize my mistake. Of course it isn't him . . . that would be impossible.

When I open the door, there she stands on the other side: Sophie Meunier. Madame to me. In all her finery: the elegant beige coat, the shining black handbag, the gleaming black helmet of her hair, the silk knot of her scarf. She's part of the tribe of women you see walking the smarter streets of this city, with shopping bags over their arms made from stiff card with gilded writing, full of designer clothes and expensive *objets*. A little pedigree dog at the end of a lead. The wealthy husbands with their *cinq-à-sept* affairs, the grand apartments and white, shuttered holiday homes on the Île de Ré. Born here, bred here, from old French money—or at least so they would like you to believe. Nothing gaudy. Nothing *nouveau*. All elegant simplicity and quality and heritage.

"*Oui Madame?*" I ask.

She takes a step back from the doorway, as though she cannot bear to be too close to my home, as though the poverty of it might somehow infect her.

"The girl," she says simply. She does not use my name, she has never used my name, I am not even sure she knows it. "The one who arrived last night—the one staying in the third-floor apartment."

"*Oui Madame?*"

"I want you to watch her. I want you to tell me when she leaves, when she comes back. I want to know if she has any visitors. It is extremely important. *Comprenez-vous?*" Understand?

"*Oui Madame.*"

"Good." She is not much taller than I am but somehow she manages to look down at me, as though from a great height. Then she turns and walks away as quickly as possible, the little silver dog trotting at her heels.

I watch her go. Then I go to my tiny bureau and open the drawer. Look inside, check the contents.

She may look down upon me but the knowledge I have gives me power. And I think she knows this. I suspect, even though she would never think to admit it, that Madame Meunier is a little afraid of me.

Funny thing: we share more than meets the eye. Both of us have lived in this building for a long time. Both of us, in our own way, have become invisible. Part of the scenery.

But I know just what sort of woman Madame Sophie Meunier really is. And exactly what she is capable of.

Jess

"HELLO?" I SHOUT. "CAN ANYONE hear me?"

I can feel the walls swallowing the sound, feel how useless it is. I shove at the door with all my strength, hoping the weight of my body might break the lock. Nothing: I might as well be ramming myself against a concrete wall. Panicking now, I pummel the wood.

Shit. *Shit.*

"Hey!" I shout, desperately now. "HEY! HELP ME!"

The last two words. A sudden flashback to another room. Shouting at the top of my lungs, shouting until my voice went hoarse, but it never felt loud enough . . . there was no one coming. *Help me help me help me someone help she's not . . .*

My whole body is trembling.

And then suddenly the door is opening and a light flashes on. A man stands there. I take a step back. It's Antoine, the guy I just watched casually smashing a bottle against a side table—

No . . . I can see now that I'm wrong. It was the height, maybe, and the breadth of the shoulders. But this guy is younger and in the weak light I can see that his hair is lighter, a dark golden color.

"*Ça va?*" he asks. Then, in English: "Are you OK? I came down to get my laundry and I heard—"

"You're British!" I blurt. As British as the Queen, in fact: a proper, plummy, posh-boy accent. A little like the one Ben adopted after he went to live with his new parents.

He's looking at me like he's waiting for some kind of explanation. "Someone locked me in here," I say. I feel shivery now that the adrenaline's wearing off. "Someone did this on purpose."

He pushes a hand through his hair, frowns. "I don't think so. The door was jammed when I opened it. The handle definitely seems a bit sticky."

I think of how hard I threw myself against it. Could it really just have been stuck? "Well, thanks," I say weakly.

"No worries." He steps back and looks at me. "What are you doing here? Not in the *cave*, I mean: in the apartment?"

"You know Ben, on the third floor? I'm meant to be staying with him—"

He frowns. "Ben didn't tell me he had anyone coming to stay."

"Well it was kind of last minute," I say. "So . . . you know Ben?"

"Yeah. He's an old friend. And you are?"

"I'm Jess," I say. "Jess Hadley, his sister."

"I'm Nick." A shrug. "I—well, I'm the one who suggested he come and live here."

Nick

I SUGGESTED JESS COME UP to my place, rather than us chatting in the chilly darkness of the *cave*. I'm slightly regretting it now: I've offered her a seat but she's pacing the room, looking at my Peloton bike, my bookcases. The knees of her jeans are worn, the cuffs of her sweater frayed, her fingernails bitten down to fragments like tiny pieces of broken shell. She gives off this jittery, restless energy: nothing like Ben's languor, his easy manner. Her voice is different too; no private school for her, I'm guessing. But then Ben's accent often changed depending on who he was speaking to. It took me a while to realize that.

"Hey," she says, suddenly. "Can I go splash some water on my face? I'm really sweaty."

"Be my guest." What else can I say?

She wanders back in a couple of minutes later. I catch a gust of Annick Goutal Eau de Monsieur; either she wears it too (which seems unlikely) or she helped herself when she was in there.

"Better?" I ask.

"Yeah, much, thanks. Hey, I like your rain shower. That's what you call it, right?"

I continue to watch her as she looks around the room. There's a resemblance there. From certain angles it's almost uncanny. . . . But her coloring's different from Ben's, her hair a dark auburn to his brown, her frame small and wiry. That, and the curious way she's prowling around, sizing the place up, makes me think of a little fox.

"Thanks for helping me out," she says. "For a moment I thought I'd never get out."

"But what on earth were you doing in the *cave*?"

"The what?"

"*Cave*," I explain, "it means 'cellar' in French."

"Oh, right." She chews the skin at the edge of her thumbnail, shrugs. "Having a look around the place, I suppose." I saw that bottle of wine in her hand. How she slipped it back into the rack when she didn't think I was looking. I'm not going to mention it. The owner of that cellar can afford to lose a bottle or two. "It's huge down there," she says.

"It was used by the Gestapo in the war," I tell her. "Their main headquarters was on Avenue Foch, near the Bois de Boulogne. But toward the end of the Occupation they had . . . overspill. They used the *cave* to hold prisoners. Members of the Resistance, that kind of thing."

She makes a face. "I suppose it makes sense. This place has an atmosphere, you know? My mum was very into that sort of thing: energy, auras, vibrations."

Was. I remember Ben telling me about his mum. Drunk in a pub one night. Though even drunk I suspect he never spilled more than he intended to.

"Anyway," she says, "I never really believed in that stuff. But you can feel something here. It gives me the creeps." She catches herself. "Sorry—didn't mean to offend—"

"No. It's fine. I suppose I know what you mean. So: you're Ben's sister." I want to work out exactly what she's doing here.

She nods. "Yup. Same mum, different dads."

I notice she doesn't say anything about Ben being adopted. I remember my shock, finding out. But thinking that it also made sense. The fact that you couldn't pigeonhole him like you could the others in our year at university—the staid rowing types, the studious honors students, the loose party animals. Yes, there was the public school accent, the ease—but it always felt as though there was some other note beneath it all. Hints of something rougher, darker. Maybe that's why people were so intrigued by him.

"I like your Gaggia," Jess says, wandering toward the kitchen. "They had one like that in a café I used to work in." A laugh, without much humor in it. "I might not have gone to a posh school or uni like my brother but I do know how to make a mean microfoam." I sense a streak of bitterness there.

"You want a coffee? I can make you one. I'm afraid I've only got oat milk."

"Have you got any beer?" she asks, hopefully. "I know it's early but I could really do with one."

"Sure, and feel free to sit down," I say, gesturing to the sofa. Watching her prowl around the room, combined with the lack of sleep, is making me feel a little dizzy.

I go to the fridge to get out a couple of bottles: beer for her, kombucha for me—I never drink earlier than seven. Before I can offer to open hers she's taken a lighter out of her pocket, fitted it between the top of her index finger and the bottom of the cap and somehow flipped the lid off. I watch her, amazed and slightly appalled at the same time. Who is this girl?

"I don't think Ben mentioned you coming to stay," I say, as casually as I can. I don't want her to feel like I'm accusing her of anything—but he definitely didn't. Of course we didn't speak much the last couple of weeks. He was so busy.

"Well, it was kind of last minute." She waves a hand vaguely. "When did you last see him?" she asks. "Ben?"

"A couple of days ago—I think."

"So you haven't heard from him today?"

"No. Is something the matter?"

I watch as she tears at her thumbnail with her teeth, so hard it makes me wince. I see a little bead of blood blossom at the quick. "He wasn't here when I arrived last night. And I haven't heard from him since yesterday afternoon. I know this is going to sound weird, but could he have been in some sort of trouble?"

I cough on the sip I've just taken. "Trouble? What kind of trouble?"

"It just . . . feels all wrong." She's fidgeting with the gold necklace around her neck now. I see the metal saint come free; it's the same as his. "He left me this voicenote. It . . . kind of cuts out halfway through. And now he isn't answering his phone. He hasn't read any of my messages. His wallet and his keys are still in the apartment—and I know he hasn't taken his Vespa because I saw it in the basement—"

"But that's just like Ben, isn't it?" I say. "He's probably gone off for a few days, chasing some story with a couple of hundred euros in his back pocket. You can get the train to most of Europe from here. He's always been like that, since we were students. He'd disappear and come back a few days later saying he'd gone to Edinburgh 'cause he fancied it, or he'd wanted to see the Norfolk Broads, or he'd stayed in a hostel and gone hiking in the Brecon Beacons."

The rest of us in our little bubble, hardly remembering—some of us wanting to forget—that there was a world outside it. It wouldn't have occurred to us to leave. But off he'd go, on his own, like he wasn't crossing some sort of invisible barrier. That hunger, that drive in him.

"I don't think so," Jess says, cutting into these memories. "He wouldn't do that . . . not knowing I was coming." But she doesn't sound all that certain. She sounds almost as though she's asking a question. "Anyway, you seem to know him pretty well?"

THE PARIS APARTMENT   79

"We hadn't seen much of each other until recently." That much, at least, is true. "You know how it is. But he got in touch with me when he moved to Paris. And meeting back up . . . it felt like it had been no time at all, really."

I'm drawn back to that reunion nearly three months ago. My surprise—shock—at finding the email from him after so long, after everything. A sports bar in Saint-Germain. A sticky floor and sticky bar, signed French rugby shirts tacked to the wall, moldy-looking chunks of charcuterie with your beer and French club rugby playing on about fifteen different screens. But it felt nostalgic; almost like the kind of place we would have gone to as students nursing pints and pretending to be real men.

We caught up on the missed decade between us: my time in Palo Alto; his journalism. He got out his phone to show me his work.

"It's not exactly . . . hard-hitting stuff," he said, with a shrug. "Not what I said I wanted to do. It's fluff, let's be honest. But it's tough right now. Should have gone the tech route like you."

I coughed, awkwardly. "Mate, I haven't exactly conquered the tech world." That was putting it mildly. But I was almost more disappointed by his lack of success than my own. I'd have expected him to have written his prize-winning novel by now. We'd met on a student paper but fiction always seemed more his thing, not the factual rigors of journalism. And if anyone was going to make it I'd been so sure it would be Ben Daniels. If he couldn't, what hope was there for the rest of us?

"I feel like I'm really hunting around for scraps," he said. "I get to eat in some nice restaurants, a free night out once in a while. But it's not exactly what I thought I'd end up doing. You need a big story to break into that, make your name. A real coup. I'm sick and tired of London, the old boys' club. Thought I'd try my luck here."

Well, we both had our big plans, back when we'd last seen each other. Even if mine didn't involve much more than getting the fuck away from my old man and being as far away from home as possible.

A sudden clatter brings me back into the room. Jess, on the prowl again, has knocked a photograph off the bookshelf: one of the rare few I've got up there.

She picks it up. "Sorry. That's a cool boat, though. In the photo."

"It's my dad's yacht."

"And this is you, with him?"

"Yes." I'm about fifteen in that one. His hand on my shoulder, both of us smiling into the camera. I'd actually managed to impress him that day, taking the helm for a while. It might have been one of the only times I've ever felt his pride in me.

A sudden shout of laughter. "And this one looks like something out of Harry Potter," she says. "These black cloaks. Is this—"

"Cambridge." A group of us after a formal, standing on Jesus Green by the River Cam in the evening light, wearing our gowns and clutching half-drunk bottles of wine. Looking at it I can almost smell that green, green scent of the fresh-cut grass: the essence of an English summer.

"That's where you met Ben?"

"Yup, we worked on *Varsity* together: him in editorial, me on the website. And we both went to Jesus."

She rolls her eyes. "The names they give those places." She squints at it. "He's not in this photo, is he?"

"No. He was taking it." Laughing, getting us all to pose. Just like Ben to be the one behind the camera, not in front of it: telling the story rather than a part of it.

She moves over to the bookcases. Paces up and down, reading the titles. It's hard to imagine she ever stops moving. "So many

THE PARIS APARTMENT 81

of your books are in French. That's what Ben was doing there, wasn't it? French studies or something."

"Well, he was doing Modern Languages at first, yes. He switched to English Literature later."

"Really?" Something clouds her face. "I didn't—I didn't know that about him. He never told me."

I recall the fragments that Ben told me about her while we were traveling. How she had it so much harder than him. No one around to pick up the pieces for her. Bounced around the care system, couldn't be placed.

"So you're the friend that helped him out with this place?" she asks.

"That's me."

"IT SOUNDS INCREDIBLE," he'd said, when I suggested it the day we met up again. "And you're sure about that, the rent? You reckon it would really be that low? I have to tell you I'm pretty strapped for cash at the moment."

"Let me find out," I told him. "But I'm pretty sure, yes. I mean, it's not in the best shape. As long as you don't mind some slightly . . . antique details."

He grinned. "Not at all. You know me. I like a place with character. And I tell you, it's a hell of a lot better than crashing on people's sofas. Can I bring my cat?"

I laughed. "I'm sure you can bring your cat." I told him I'd make my inquiries. "But I think it's probably yours if you want it."

"Well . . . thanks mate. I mean . . . seriously, that sounds absolutely amazing."

"No problem. Happy to help. So that's a yes, you're interested?"

"It's a hell yes." He laughed. "Let me buy you another drink, to celebrate."

We sat there for hours with more beers. And suddenly it was like we were back in Cambridge with no time having passed between us.

He moved in a couple of days later. That quick. I stood there with him in the apartment as he looked around.

"I know it's a little retro," I told him.

"It's certainly . . . got character," he said. "You know what? I think I'll keep it like this. I like it. Gothic."

And I thought how great it was, having my old buddy back. He grinned at me and for some reason I suddenly felt like everything might be OK. Maybe more than OK. Like it might help me find that guy I had been, once upon a time.

"CAN I USE your computer?"

"What?" I'm jolted out of the memory. I see Jess has wandered over to my iMac.

"Those bloody roaming charges are a killer. I just thought I could check Ben's Instagram again, in case something's happened to his phone and he's messaged me back."

"Er—I could give you my Wifi code?" But she's already sitting down, her hand on the mouse. I don't seem to have any choice in the matter.

She moves the mouse and the screen lights up. "Wait—" she leans forward, peering at the screensaver, then turns around to me. "This is you and Ben, isn't it? Jeez, he looks so young. So do you."

I haven't switched on my computer in several days. I force myself to look. "I suppose we were. Not much more than kids." How strange, to think it. I felt so adult at the time. Like all the mysteries of the world had suddenly been unlocked to me. And yet we were still children, really. I glance out of the windows. I don't need to look at the photo; I can see it with my eyes shut. The light golden and slanting: both of us squinting against the sun.

"Where were you, here?"

"A group of us went interrailing, the whole summer after our finals."

"What, on trains?"

"Yes. All across Europe . . . it was amazing." It really was. The best time of my life, even.

I glance at Jess. She's gone quiet; seems lost in her own thoughts. "Are you OK?"

"Yeah, sure." She forces a smile. A little of her energy seems to have evaporated. "So . . . where was this photo taken?"

"Amsterdam, I think."

I don't think: I know. How could I forget?

Looking at that photo, I can feel the late July sun on my face, smell the sulphur stink of the warm canal water. So clear, that time, even though those memories are over a decade old. But then everything on that trip seemed important. Everything said, everything done.

Jess

"I'VE JUST REALIZED," NICK SAYS, looking at his watch. "I've actually got to get going. Sorry, I know you wanted to use the computer."

"Oh," I say, a little thrown. "No worries. Maybe you could lend me your code? I'll see if I can get on the Wifi from up there."

"Sure."

He suddenly looks very eager to be gone; maybe he's late for something. "What is it," I ask, "work?"

I've been wondering what he does for a living. Everything about this guy says money. But whispers it rather than shouts it. As I've been looking around his place I've noticed some very swanky-looking speakers (Bang & Olufsen, I'll look it up later but I can just tell they're expensive), a fancy camera (Leica), a massive screen in the corner (Apple) and that professional-looking coffee machine. But you have to really look to see the wealth. Nick's are the possessions of someone who is loaded but doesn't want to boast about it . . . might even be a little embarrassed by it. But they tell a story. As do the books on his shelves—the titles that I can understand, anyway: *Fast Forward Investing*, *The Technologized Investor*, *Catching a Unicorn*, *The Science of Self-Discipline*. As did the stuff in his bathroom. I spent about three seconds splashing my face with cold water and the rest of the time having a good root through his cabinets. You can learn a lot about someone from their bathroom. I learned this when I was taken to meet prospective foster families. No one's ever going to stop you if you ask to use the toilet. I'd go in there, poke around—sometimes nick a lipstick or a bottle of perfume, sometimes explore the rooms on the way back—find out if they were concealing anything scary or weird.

In Nick's bathroom I found all the usual: mouthwash, toothpaste, aftershaves, paracetamol, posh toiletries with names like "Aesop" and "Byredo" and then—interesting—quite a large supply of oxycodone. Everyone has their poison, I get that. I dabbled with some stuff, back in the day. When it felt like it might be easier to stop caring about anything, to just kind of slip out the back door of life. It wasn't for me, but I get it. And I guess rich boys feel pain, too.

"I'm—well, between jobs at the moment," Nick says.

"What were you doing before?" I ask, reluctantly moving away from the desk. I'm fairly certain his last job didn't involve working in a dive with inflatable palm trees and flamingos dangling from the ceiling.

"I was in San Francisco for a while. Palo Alto. Tech start-ups. An Angel, you know?"

"Er . . . no?"

"An investor."

"Ah." It must be nice to be so casual about looking for work. Clearly "between jobs" doesn't mean that he's scrabbling for cash.

He squeezes past me to get to the doorway; I've been blocking his way and being a nice posh English boy he's probably too polite to ask me to budge. I smell his cologne as he does: smoky and expensive and delicious, the same one I had a spray of in his bathroom.

"Oh," I say. "Sorry. I'm holding you up."

"It's OK." But I get the impression he's not as relaxed as he sounds: something in his posture, perhaps, a tightness about his jaw.

"Well. Thanks for your help."

"Look," he says. "I'm sure it's nothing to worry about. But I'm still keen to help. Anything I can do, any questions I can answer—I'll try to."

"There is one thing," I say. "Do you know if Ben's seeing anyone?"

He frowns. "Seeing anyone?"

"Yeah. Like a girlfriend, or something more casual."

"Why do you ask?"

"Just a hunch." It's not like me to be prudish, but there's something in me that gets the ick at describing the knickers I found in Ben's bed.

"Hmm . . ." He puts a hand up to his hair and runs his fingers through it, which only makes his curls stand out more messily. He's beautiful. Yes, all my focus is on finding Ben but I'm also not blind. I've always had a stupid weakness for a polite posh boy; I'm not saying I'm proud of it. "Not that I know of," he says, finally. "I don't *think* he has a girlfriend. But I suppose I don't know everything about his life here in Paris. I mean, we'd kind of fallen out of touch before he arrived here."

"Yeah." I know how that is.

But that's just like Ben, isn't it? Nick had said, just before. *He's always been like that, since we were students.* And all I could think was: *is* he? *Has* he? And if he was always rushing off at the drop of a hat when he was at Cambridge, how did he not find more time to come and see me? He was always saying he was "so busy with essays" or "I can't miss any of my tutorials. You know how it is." But I didn't, of course. He knew I didn't. One of the only times he came to see me—I was fostering in Milton Keynes at the time—was when I suggested a trip to Cambridge. I had an inkling that the threat of his scuzzy foster-kid sister turning up and damaging his image might work. Thinking about it, I feel a little spike of something that I hope is anger, not hurt. Hurt is the worst.

"Sorry not to be more use," Nick says, "but if you need me, I'm right here. Just one floor down."

Our eyes meet. His are a very dark blue, not the brown I'd taken them for. I try to see past the little tug of attraction. Can I trust this guy? He's Ben's mate. He says he's keen to help. The problem is I'm not good at trusting people. I've been used to fending for myself for too long. But Nick could be useful. He knows Ben—apparently better than I do, in some ways. He clearly speaks French. He seems like a decent guy. I think of weird, jumpy Mimi and frosty Sophie Meunier: it's nice to think someone in this building might be a useful ally.

I watch as he pulls on a smart navy wool coat, wraps a soft-looking gray scarf around his neck.

He goes to the door and opens it for me. "It's nice to meet you, Jess," he says, with a small smile. He looks like a painting of an angel. I don't know where the thought comes from—maybe it's because he used the word himself just now—but I know that it's right; perfect even. A fallen angel. It's the dark gold curls, those purple shadows under his navy eyes. Mum had a thing about angels, too, she was always telling me and Ben we all have one looking out for us. Shame hers didn't seem up to the job. "And, look," Nick says. "I'm sure Ben will turn up."

"Thanks. I think so too." I try to believe it.

"Here, let me give you my number."

"That would be great." I give him my phone: he puts his details in.

As I take it from him our fingers brush, and he quickly drops his hand.

BACK UP IN Ben's apartment I'm relieved to find I can get onto Nick's Wifi using the password he gave me. I head to Ben's Instagram and look for "Nick Miller"—the name he's put in my phone—but I can't see him among Ben's followers. I try a more general search and get Nick Millers from all over the place: the

States, Canada, Australia. I look through them until my eyes sting. But they're too young, too old, too bald, from the wrong country. Google is useless, too: there's some fictional guy called Nick Miller from a TV show which fills all the Google results. I give up. Just as I'm about to put it back in my pocket my phone vibrates with a text. And for a moment I think: *Ben*. It's from Ben! How amazing would that be, after all this—

It's from an unknown number:

Got your message about Ben. Haven't heard from the guy. But he'd promised me a couple of pieces of work and a pitch. I'm working at the Belle Epoque café next to the Jardin du Luxembourg all day. You can meet me here. T.

I'm confused for a moment, then I scroll up to my message above and I realize it's the guy I texted earlier. I take Ben's wallet out of my back pocket to remind me of his full name. Theo Mendelson, Paris editor, *Guardian*.

I'm coming now, I text back.

Just before I slide the card back into the wallet, I notice another one sitting behind it. It catches my eye because it's so simple, so unusual. Made from metal, it's a dark midnight blue with an image like an exploding firework, picked out in gold. No text or numbers or anything. Not a credit card. Not a business card either, surely. Then what? I hesitate, feel the surprising weight of it in my palm, then pocket it.

When I open the door that leads onto the courtyard I realize it's already starting to get dark, the sky the color of an old bruise. When did that happen? I haven't noticed the hours passing. This place has swallowed time, like something from a fairytale.

As I walk through the courtyard I hear a sound close by, a rasping: *scritch, scritch, scritch*. I turn and start as I see a small, stooped figure standing only a couple of meters away to my right. It's the old woman, the one I saw last night. She wears a scarf tied about her gray hair, and some sort of long shapeless cardigan over an apron. Her face is all nose and chin, hollow eye-sockets. She could be anything from seventy to ninety. She's holding a broom, which she's using to sweep dead leaves into a heap. Her eyes are fixed on me.

"*Bonsoir*," I say to her. "Um. Have you seen Ben? From the third floor?" I point up to the windows of the apartment. But she just keeps on sweeping: *scritch, scritch, scriiiitch*, all the while watching me.

Then she steps even closer. Her eyes on me the whole time, barely even blinking. But just once, quickly, she looks up at the apartment building, as though checking for something. Then she opens her mouth and speaks in a low hiss, a sound not un-like the rasping of those dead leaves: "*There is nothing for you here.*"

I stare at her. "What do you mean?"

She shakes her head. And then she turns and walks away, goes back to her sweeping. It all happened so quickly I could almost believe I imagined the whole thing. Almost.

I stare after her stooped, retreating figure. For Christ's sake: it feels like everyone I meet in here is speaking in riddles—except Nick, maybe. I have this sudden, almost violent urge to run up to her and, I don't know, shake her or something . . . force her to tell me what she means. I swallow my frustration.

When I turn to open the gate I'm sure I can feel her gaze across my shoulder blades, definite as the touch of fingertips. And as I step onto the street I can't help but wonder: was that a warning or a threat?

Concierge

THE GATE CLANGS SHUT BEHIND the girl. She thinks that she's staying in a normal apartment building. A place that follows ordinary rules. She has no idea what she has got herself into here.

I think of Madame Meunier's instructions. I know that I have no option but to obey. I have too much at stake here not to cooperate. I will tell her that the girl has just left, as she asked me to do. I will tell her when she comes back, too. Just like the obedient member of staff I am. I do not like Madame Meunier, as I have made clear. But we have been forced into an uneasy kind of alliance by this girl's arrival. She has been sneaking around. Asking questions of those that live here. Just like he did. I can't afford to have her drawing attention to this place. He wanted to do that too.

There are things here that I have to protect, you see. Things that mean I can never leave this job. And up until recently I have felt safe here. Because these are people with secrets. I have been too deep into those secrets. I know too much. They can't get rid of me. And I can never be rid of them.

He was kind, the newcomer. That was all. He noticed me. He greeted me each time he passed in the courtyard, on the staircase. Asked me how I was. Commented on the weather. It doesn't sound like much, does it? But it felt like such a long time since someone had paid any attention to me, let alone shown me kindness. Such a long time since I had even been noticed as a human being. And soon afterward he began asking his questions.

"How long have you worked here?" he inquired, as I washed the stone floor at the base of the staircase.

"A long time, Monsieur." I wrung out my mop against the bucket.

"And how did you come to work here? Here—let me do that." He carried the heavy bucket of water across the hallway for me.

"My daughter came to Paris first. I followed her here."

"What did she come to Paris for?"

"That was all a very long time ago, Monsieur."

"I'm still interested, all the same."

That made me look at him more closely. Suddenly I felt I had told him enough. This stranger. Was he *too* kind, *too* interested? What did he want from me?

I was very careful with my answer. "It isn't a very interesting story. Perhaps some other time, Monsieur. I have to get on with my work. But thank you, for your help."

"Of course: don't let me hold you up."

For so many years my insignificance and invisibility have been a mask I can hide behind. And in the process I have avoided raking up the past. Raking up the shame. As I say, this job may have its small losses of dignity. But it does not involve shame.

But his interest, his questions: for the first time in a very long time I felt seen. And like a fool, I fell for it.

And now this girl has followed him here. She needs to be encouraged to leave before she is able to work out that things are not what they seem.

Perhaps I can *persuade* her to go.

Jess

IT'S STRANGE TO BE BACK among people, traffic, noise, after the hush of the building. Disorientating, too, because I still don't really know where I am, how all the roads around here connect to one another. I check the map on my phone quickly, so as not to burn too much more data. The café where I'm meeting this Theo guy turns out to be all the way across town on the other side of the river so I decide to take the Metro, even though it means I'll have to break another of the notes I nicked from Ben.

It feels like the further I move away from the apartment the easier I can breathe. It's like a part of me has smelled freedom and never wants to go back inside that place, even though I know I have to.

I walk along cobbled streets, past crowded pavement cafés with wicker chairs, people chatting over wine and cigarettes. I pass an old wooden windmill erupting from behind a hedge and wonder what on earth that's doing in the middle of the city, in someone's garden. Hurrying down a long flight of stone steps I have to climb around a guy sleeping in a fort of soggy-looking cardboard boxes; I drop a couple of euros into his paper cup. A little way on I cut through a couple of smart-looking squares that look almost identical, except in the middle of one there are these old guys playing some kind of *boules* and in the other a merry-go-round with a candy-striped top, kids clinging onto model horses and leaping fish.

When I get to the more crowded streets around the Metro stop there's an odd, tense feeling, like something's about to happen. It's like a scent in the air—and I have a good nose for trouble.

Lo and behold, I spot three police vans parked in a side street. I glimpse them sitting inside wearing helmets, stab vests. On instinct, I keep my head down.

I follow the stream of people underground. I get stuck in the turnstile because I forget to take the little paper ticket out; I don't know how to unlatch the doors on the train when it arrives so a guy has to help me before it pulls away without me. All of it makes me feel like a clueless tourist, which I hate: clueless is dangerous, it makes you vulnerable.

As I stand in the crowded, smelly, too-warm crush of bodies on the train I get the feeling I'm being watched. I glance around: a cluster of teenagers hanging from the rails, looking like they've stepped out of a nineties skate park; a young woman in a leather jacket; a few elderly women with tiny dogs and grocery trollies; a group of bizarrely dressed people with ski goggles on their heads and bandannas round their necks, one of them carrying a painted sign. But nothing obviously suspicious and when we get to the next stop a man playing an accordion steps on, blocking half the carriage from view.

Up out of the Metro the quickest way seems to be through a park, the Jardin du Luxembourg. In the park the light is purple, shifting, not quite dark. On the path leaves crunch under my feet where they haven't been swept into huge glowing orange pyramids; the branches of the trees are nearly bare. There's an empty bandstand, a shuttered café, chairs stacked in piles. Again I have that feeling of being watched, followed: certain I can feel someone's gaze on me. But every time I turn back no figure stands out.

Then I see him. *Ben.* He flashes right by me, jogging alongside another guy. What the hell? He must have seen me: why didn't he stop?

"Ben!" I shout, quickening my step, "Ben!" But he doesn't look back. I start to jog. I can just about make him out, disappearing into the dim light. Shit. I'm lots of things but I'm not a runner. "Hey, Ben! For fuck's sake!" He doesn't turn around, though several other runners glance at me as they pass. Finally I'm just behind him, breathing hard. I reach out, touch his shoulder. He turns around.

I take a step backward. It isn't Ben. His face is totally wrong: eyes too close together, weak chin. I see Ben's raised eyebrow, clear as if he really were standing in front of me. *You mistook me for that guy?*

"*Qu'est-ce que tu veux?*" the stranger asks, looking irritated, then: "What do you want?"

I can't answer, partly because I can't breathe and talk at once but mainly because I'm so confused. He makes a little "crazy" gesture to his mate as they jog off.

Of course it wasn't Ben. As I watch him move away, I can see everything's wrong—he runs clumsily, his arms loose and awkward. There's never been anything awkward about Ben. I'm left with the same feeling I had when he ran by me. It was like seeing a ghost.

THE CAFÉ BELLE EPOQUE has a kind of festive look to it, glimmering red and gold, light spilling onto the pavement. The tables outside are crowded with people chatting and laughing and the windows are steamy with condensation from all the bodies crowded around tables inside. Round the corner, where they haven't turned on the heat-lamps, there's one guy on his own hunched over a laptop; somehow I just know this is him.

"Theo?" I feel like I'm on a Tinder date, if I bothered going on those anymore and it wasn't all catfishers and arseholes.

He glances up with a scowl. Dark hair long overdue a cut and the beginnings of a beard. He looks like a pirate who's decided to dress in ordinary clothes: a woolen sweater, frayed at the neck-line, under a big jacket.

"Theo?" I ask again. "We texted, about Benjamin Daniels—I'm Jess?"

He gives a curt nod. I pull out the little metal chair opposite him. It sticks to my hand with cold.

"Mind if I smoke?" I think the question's rhetorical, he's already pulled out a crumpled pack of Marlboro Reds. Everything about him is crumpled.

"Sure, I'll have one thanks." I can't afford a smoking habit but I'm feeling jittery enough to need one—even if he didn't actually offer.

He spends the next thirty seconds struggling to light his cigarette with a crappy lighter, muttering under his breath: *"Fuck's sake"* and *"Come on, you bastard."* I think I detect a slight accent as he does.

"You're from East London?" I ask, thinking that maybe if I ingratiate myself he'll be more willing to help. "Whereabouts?"

He raises a dark eyebrow, doesn't answer. Finally, the lighter works and the cigarettes are lit. He draws on his like an asthmatic on an inhaler, then sits back and looks at me. He's tall, uncomfortable-looking in the little chair: one long leg crossed over the other knee at the ankle. He's kind of attractive, if you like your men rough around the edges. But I'm not sure I do—and I'm shocked at myself for even thinking about it, in the circumstances.

"So," he says, narrowing his eyes through the smoke. "Ben?" Something about the way he says my brother's name suggests there's not that much love lost there. Maybe I've found the one person immune to my brother's charm.

Before I can answer a waiter comes over, looking pissed off at having to take our order, even though it's his job. Theo, who looks equally pissed off at having to talk to him and speaking French with a determined English accent, orders a double espresso and something called a Ricard. "Late night, on a deadline," he tells me, a little defensively.

Mainly to warm up I ask for a *chocolat chaud*. Six euros. Let's assume he's paying. "I'll have the other thing too," I tell the waiter.

"*Un Ricard?*"

I nod. The waiter slouches off. "I don't think we served that at the Copacabana," I say.

"The what?"

"This bar I worked in. Until a couple of days ago, actually."

He raises a dark eyebrow. "Sounds classy."

"It was the absolute worst." But the day The Pervert decided to show his disgusting little dick to me was the day I'd finally had enough. Also the day I decided I'd get the creep back for all the times he'd lingered too long behind me, breath hot and wet on the back of my neck, or "steered" me out of the way, hands on my hips, or the comments he'd made about the way I looked, the clothes I wore—all those things that weren't quite "things" except were, making me feel a little bit less myself. Another girl might have left then and never come back. Another might have called the police. But I'm not that girl.

"Right," Theo says—clearly he has no time for further chit-chat. "Why are you here?"

"Ben: does he work for you?"

"Nah. No one works for anyone these days, not in this line of work. It's dog eat dog out there, every man for himself. But, yeah, sometimes I commission a review from him, a travel piece. He's been wanting to get into investigative stuff. I guess you know that." I shake my head. "He's due to deliver a piece on the riots, in fact."

"The riots?"

"Yeah." He peers at me like he can't believe I don't know. "People are seriously fucked off about a hike in taxes, petrol prices. It's got pretty nasty . . . tear gas, water cannons, the lot. It's all over the news. Surely you've seen something?"

"I've only been here since last night." But then I remember: "I saw police vans near the Pigalle Metro stop." I remember the group with the ski goggles on the train. "And maybe some protestors."

"Yeah, probably. Riots have been breaking out all over town. And Ben's meant to be writing me a piece on them. But he was also going to tell me about a so-called 'scoop' he had for me—this morning, in fact. He was very mysterious about it. But I never heard from him."

A new possibility. Could that be it? Ben dug too deep into something? Pissed off someone nasty? And he's had to . . . what? Do a runner? Disappear? Or—I don't want to think about the other possibilities.

Our drinks come; my hot chocolate thick and dark and glossy in a little jug with a cup. I pour it out and take a sip and close my eyes because it may be six euros but it is also the best fucking hot chocolate I have had in my life.

Theo pours five sachets of brown sugar into his coffee, stirs it in. Then he takes a big glug of his Ricard. I give mine a sip—it tastes of licorice, a reminder of all the sticky shots of Sambuca I've done behind the bar, bought for me by punters or snuck from the bottle on a slow evening. I down it. Theo raises his eyebrows.

I wipe my mouth. "Sorry. I needed that. It's been a really shitty twenty-four hours. You see, Ben's disappeared. I know you haven't heard from him, but you don't have any idea where he might be, do you?'

Theo shrugs. "Sorry." I feel the small hope I'd been holding onto fizzle and die. "How do you mean disappeared?"

"He wasn't in his apartment last night when he said he would be. He's not answering any of my calls or even reading my messages. And there's all this other stuff . . .' I swallow, tell him about the blood on the cat's fur, the bleach stain, the hostile neighbors. As I do I have a moment where I think: how has it come to this? Sitting here with a stranger in a strange city, trying to find my lost brother?

Theo sits there dragging on his cigarette and squinting at me through the smoke and his expression doesn't change at all. The guy has a great poker face.

"The other strange thing," I say, "is he's been living in this big, swanky building. I mean, I can't imagine Ben makes that much from writing?" Judging by the state of Theo's outfit, I suspect not.

"Nope. You certainly don't get into this business for the money."

I remember something else. The strange metal card I took from Ben's wallet. I slide it out of the back pocket of my jeans.

"I found this. Does it mean anything to you?"

He studies the gold firework design, frowning. "Not sure. I've definitely seen that symbol. But I can't place it right now. Can I take it? I'll get back to you." I hand it over, a little reluctantly, because it's one of the few things I have that feels like a clue. Theo takes it from me and there's something about the way he grabs it that I don't like. It suddenly seems too eager, despite the fact he's told me he doesn't know Ben all that well and doesn't seem all that concerned for his welfare. He doesn't exactly give off a Good Samaritan vibe. I'm not sure about this guy. Still, beggars can't be choosers.

"There's one other thing," I say, remembering. "Ben left this voicenote for me last night, just before I got into Gare du Nord."

Theo takes my phone. He plays the recording and Ben's voice sings out. "Hey Jess—"

It's strange hearing it again like this. It sounds different from the last time I listened, somehow not quite like Ben, like he's that much further out of reach.

Theo listens to the whole thing. "It sounds like he says something else, at the end. Have you been able to work out what?"

"No—I can't hear it. It's too muffled."

He puts up a finger. Hang on. Then he reaches into the rucksack by his chair—as crumpled as everything else about him—and pulls out a tangled pair of headphones. "Right. Noise-canceling and they go really loud. Want one?' He holds out a bud to me.

I stick it in my ear.

He dials up the volume to the max and presses play on the voicenote again.

We listen to the familiar part of the recording. Ben's voice: "Hey Jess, so it's number twelve, rue des Amants. Got that? Third floor" and "Just ring the buzzer. I'll be up waiting for you—" His voice seems to cut off mid-sentence, just like every time I've listened to it before. But now I hear it. What sounded like a crackle on the voicemail is actually a creaking of wood. I *recognize* that creak. It's the hinges of the door to the apartment.

And then I hear Ben's voice at a distance, quiet but still much clearer than what had been only a mumble before: "What are you doing here?" A long pause. Then he says: "What the fuck . . . ?"

Next there's a sound: a groan. Even at this volume it's difficult to tell if it's a person making the sound or something else—a floorboard creaking? Then: silence.

I feel even colder than I did before. I find myself taking hold of my necklace, reaching for the pendant, gripping it hard.

Theo plays the recording again. And finally a third time. Here it is. Here's the proof. Someone was there in the apartment with Ben, the night he left this voicenote.

We each remove an earbud. Look at each other.

"Yeah," Theo says. "I'd say that's a little fucking weird."

Mimi

SHE'S NOT IN THE APARTMENT right now. I know because I've been watching from my bedroom window. All the lights are off on the third floor, the room in darkness. But for a moment I actually think I see him; appearing out of the shadows. Then I blink and of course there's no one there.

But it would be like him. He had this habit of showing up unannounced. Just like he did the second time I met him.

I'd stopped by this old vinyl store on my way back from the Sorbonne: Pêle-Mêle. It was so hot. We have this expression in French, *soleil de plomb*, for when the sun feels as heavy as lead. That was what it was like that day—hard to imagine now, when it's so cold out. It was horrible: exhaust fumes and sweaty sunburnt tourists crammed together on the pavements. I always hate the tourists but I hate them most of all in the summer. Bumbling around, hot and angry that they came to the city rather than the beach. But there were no tourists in the store because it looks so gloomy and depressing from the outside, which is exactly why I like it. It was dark and cool, like being underwater, the sounds from outside muted. I could spend hours in there in my own little bubble, hiding from the world, floating between the stacks of vinyl and listening to record after record in the scratched glass booth.

"Hey."

I turned around.

There he was. The guy who'd just moved in on the third floor. I saw him most days, wheeling his Vespa across the courtyard or sometimes moving around in his apartment: he always left the shutters open. But close up, it was different. I could see the stubble on his jaw, the coppery hairs on his arms. I could see he wore a chain around his neck, disappearing beneath the neckline of his T-shirt. I wouldn't have expected that, somehow: he seemed too preppy. Up close I could catch the tang of his sweat, which sounds kind of gross—but it was a clean peppery smell, not the fried onion stink you get on the Metro. He was kind of old, like I'd said to Camille. But he was also kind of beautiful. Actually, he took my breath away.

"It's Merveille, isn't it?"

I nearly dropped the record I was holding. He knew my name. He'd remembered. And somehow, even though I hate my name, on his lips it sounded different, almost special. I nodded, because I didn't feel like I could speak. My mouth tasted of metal; maybe I'd bitten my tongue. I imagined the blood pooling between my teeth. In the silence I could hear the ceiling fan, *whoomp, whoomp, whoomp,* like a heartbeat.

Finally, I managed to speak. "M—most people call me Mimi."

"Mimi. Suits you. I'm Ben." His English accent; the bluntness of it. "We're neighbors: I moved into the apartment on the third floor, a few days ago."

"*Je sais,*" I said. It came out like a whisper. *I know.* It seemed crazy that he thought I might not know.

"It's such a cool building. You must love living there." I shrugged. "All that history. All those amazing features: the *cave,* the elevator—"

"There's a dumbwaiter, too." I blurted it out. It's one of my favorite things in the building. I wasn't sure why, but I suddenly wanted to share it with him.

He leaned forward. "A dumbwaiter?" He looked so excited; I felt a warm glow that I'd been the cause of it. "Really?"

"Yeah. From back when the building was a proper *hôtel particulier*—it belonged to this countess or something and there was a kitchen down in the *cave*. They'd send food and drink up in it and the laundry would come back down."

"That's amazing! I've never actually seen one of those in real life. Where? No, wait—don't tell me. I'm going to try and find it." He grinned. I realized I was smiling back.

He pulled at the collar of his T-shirt. "Christ it's hot today."

I saw the small pendant on the end of the chain come free. "You wear a St. Christopher?" Again, I just kind of blurted it out. I think it was the surprise at seeing it, recognizing the little gold saint.

"Oh." He looked down at the pendant. "Yeah. This was my mum's. She gave it to me when I was small. I never take it off—I kind of forget it's there." I tried to see him as a child and couldn't. Could only see him tall, broad, the tanned skin of his face. He had lines, yes, but now I realized they didn't make him look old. They just made him seem more interesting than any of the guys I knew. Like he'd been places, seen stuff, done stuff. He grinned. "I'm impressed you recognized it. You're a Catholic?"

My cheeks flamed. "My parents sent me to a Catholic school." A Catholic girls' school. *Your papa really hoped you'd turn out a nun*, Camille said. *The closest thing he could find to a chastity belt.* Most kids I know, like Camille, went to big lycées where they wore their own clothes and smoked cigarettes and ate each other's faces in the street at lunch break. Going to a place like the Soeurs Servantes du Sacré Coeur makes you into a total freak. Like something out of the kids' book *Madeline*. What it means is you get stared at in your uniform by a certain kind of creep on the Metro and ignored by all the other guys. Makes you unable to talk to them like a normal human being. Which is probably exactly why Papa chose it for me.

Of course, I didn't stay the whole time at the SSSC. They had some trouble with a teacher there, a young man: my parents thought it best I leave and for the last few years I had a private tutor, which was even worse.

I saw Benjamin Daniels looking at the record I was holding. "Velvet Underground," he said. "Love them." The design on the front of the vinyl sleeve—by Andy Warhol—was a series of pictures showing wet red lips opening to suck soda from a straw. Suddenly it seemed somehow dirty and I felt my cheeks grow warm again.

"I'm getting this," he said, holding up his record. "The Yeah Yeah Yeahs. You like them?"

I shrugged. "*Je ne sais pas.*" I'd never heard of them. I'd never listened to the Velvet Underground record I'd picked up, either. I'd just liked the Warhol design; had planned to copy it in my sketchbook when I got home. I go to the Sorbonne, but what I'd really like to do (if it were left up to me) is art. Sometimes, when I've got a stick of charcoal or a paintbrush in my hand, it feels like the only time I'm complete. The only way I can speak properly.

"Well—I've got to run." He made a face. "Got a deadline to meet." Even that sounded kind of cool: having a deadline. He was a journalist; I'd watched him working late into the night at his laptop. "But you guys are on the fourth floor, right? Back at the apartment? You and your flatmate? What's her name—"

"Camille." No one forgets Camille. She's the hot one, the fun one. But he'd forgotten her name. He'd remembered mine.

* * *

A FEW DAYS later a note was pushed under the apartment door.

I found it!

I couldn't work out what it meant at first. Who had found what? It didn't make any sense. It had to be something for Camille. And then I remembered our conversation in the record store. Could it be? I went to the cupboard that contained the dumbwaiter, pulled out the hidden handle, cranked it to bring the little cart upward. And I saw there was something in it: the Yeah Yeah Yeahs record he'd bought in the store. A note was attached to it. *Hey Mimi. Thought you might like to try this. Let me know what you think. B x*

"Who's that from?" Camille came over, read the note over my shoulder. "He lent it to you? Ben?" I could hear the surprise in her voice. "I saw him yesterday," she said. "He told me he'd love it if I could feed his kitty, if he ever goes away. He's given me his spare key." She flipped a lock of caramel-colored hair behind one ear. I felt a little sting of jealousy. But I reminded myself he hadn't left *her* a note. He hadn't sent *her* a record.

There's this expression in French. *Être bien dans sa peau.* To feel good in your own skin. I don't feel that way often. But holding that record, I did. Like I had something that was just mine.

NOW, I LOOK at the cupboard that has the dumbwaiter hidden inside it. I find myself drifting over to it. I open the cupboard to expose the pulleys, crank the handle, just like I did that day in August. Wait for the little cart to come into view.

What?

I stare. There's something inside it. Just like when he sent me the record. But this isn't a record. It's something wrapped in cloth.

I reach down to pick it up and, as I close my hand around it, I feel a sting. Hold my hand up and see blood beading from my palm. *Merde.* Whatever is inside here has cut me, biting through the fabric. I drop it and the cloth spills its contents onto the ground.

I take a step back. Look at the blade, crusted with something that looks like rust or dirt but isn't, something that's also streaked all over the cloth it was wrapped in.

And I start to scream.

Jess

I CAN'T STOP THINKING ABOUT how Ben sounded at the end of that message. The fear in his voice. "What are *you* doing here?" The emphasis. Whoever was there in the room, it sounded like he knew them. And then the "What the fuck?" My brother, always so in control of any situation. I've never heard him like that. It hardly even sounded like Ben.

There's a sick feeling in the pit of my stomach. It's been there all along, really, growing since last night. But now I can't ignore it any longer. I think something happened to my brother last night, before I arrived. Something bad.

"Are you going to go back to that place?" Theo asks. "After hearing that?"

I'm kind of struck by his concern, especially as he doesn't seem the sensitive sort.

"Yeah," I say, trying to sound more confident than I feel, "I need to be there."

And I do. Besides—I don't say this—I don't have anywhere else to go.

I DECIDE TO walk back instead of taking the Metro—it's a long way but I need to be out in the air, need to try and think clearly. I look at my phone to check my route. It buzzes:

You have used nearly all your Roaming Data! To buy more, follow this link . . .

Shit. I put it back in my pocket.

I pass little chi-chi shops painted red, emerald-green, navy blue, their brightly lit windows displaying printed dresses, candles, sofas, jewelry, chocolates, even some special bloody meringues tinted pale blue and pink. There's something for everyone here, I suppose, if you've got the money to spend. On the bridge I push through crowds of tourists taking selfies in front of the river, kissing, smiling, talking and laughing. It's like they're living in a different universe. And now the beauty of this place feels like so much colorful wrapping hiding something evil inside. I can smell things rotting beneath the sweet sugary scents from the bakeries and chocolate shops: fish on the ice outside a fishmonger's leaving stinking puddles collecting on the pavement, the reek of dog shit trodden into the pavement, the stench of blocked drains. The sick feeling grows. What happened to Ben last night? What can I do?

There have been times in my life when I've been pretty desperate. Not quite sure how I'm going to make the rent that month. Times I've thanked God I have a half brother with deeper pockets than me. Because, yeah, I might have resented him in the past, for having so much more than I ever did. But he has got me out of some pretty tight spots.

He came and collected me from a bad foster situation once in the Golf his parents had bought him, even though it was in the middle of his exams:

"We have to stick together, us orphans. No: worse than orphans. Because our dads don't want us. They're out there but they don't want us."

"You're not like me," I told him. "You've got a family: the Daniels. Look at you. Listen to how you talk. Look at this frigging car. You've got so much of everything."

A shrug. "I've only got one little sister."

Now it's my turn to help him. And even though every part of me recoils from calling the police, I think I have to.

I take out my phone, search the number, dial 112.

I'm on hold for a few moments. I wait, listening to the engaged tone, fiddling with my St. Christopher. Finally someone picks up: "*Comment puis-je vous aider?*" A woman's voice.

"Um, *parlez-vous anglais?*"

"*Non.*"

"Can I speak to someone who does?"

A sigh. "*Une minute.*"

After a long pause another voice—a man's. "Yes?"

I begin to explain. Somehow the whole thing sounds so much flimsier out loud.

"Excuse me. I do not understand. Your brother left you a voice message. From his apartment? And you are worried?"

"He sounded scared."

"But there was no sign of a break-in in his home?"

"No, I think it was someone he knew—"

"Your brother is . . . a child?"

"No, he's in his thirties. But he's disappeared."

"And you are certain he has not, for example, gone away for a few days? Because that seems like the likeliest possibility, *non?*"

I have this growing feeling of hopelessness. I don't feel like we're getting anywhere here. "I'm fairly certain, yeah. It's all pretty fucking weird—sorry—and he's not answering his phone, he's left his wallet, his keys."

A long pause. "OK, Mademoiselle. Give me your name and your address, I will make a formal record and we will come back to you."

"I—" I don't want to be on any formal record of anything. What if they compare notes with the UK, run my name? And the way he says, "formal record," in that bored flat voice, sounds like—yeah, we'll think about doing something in a couple of years after we've done all the stuff that actually matters and maybe a bit of the stuff that doesn't.

"Mademoiselle?" he prompts.

I hang up.

That was a total waste of time. But did I really expect anything else? The British police have never helped me before. Why did I think their French counterparts would be any different?

When I look up from my phone I realize I've lost my bearings. I must have been wandering aimlessly while I was on the call. I go to the map on my phone but it won't load. As I try to get it to work my phone buzzes and a notification pops up:

You have used up all of your Roaming Data. To buy more, follow this link . . .

Shit, shit . . . It's getting darker, too and somehow this only makes me feel more lost.

OK. Pull yourself together Jess. I can do this. I just need to find a busier street, then I can find a Metro station and a map.

But the streets get quieter and quieter until I can hear just one other set of footsteps, a little way behind me.

There's a high wall on my right and I realize, glimpsing a little plaque nailed to it, that I'm skirting a cemetery. Above the wall I can just make out the taller tombs, the wing tips and bent head of a mourning angel. It's almost completely dark now. I stop.

The footsteps behind me stop, too.

I walk faster. The footsteps quicken.

Someone is following me. I knew it. I round the curve of the wall so I'll be out of sight for a few seconds. Then, instead of carrying on I stop and press myself back against the wall on the other side. My heart's beating hard against my ribs. This is

probably really fucking stupid. What I should be doing is running away, finding a busy street, surrounding myself with other
people. But I have to know.

I wait until a figure appears. Tall, a dark coat. My chest is
burning: I realize I've been holding my breath. The figure turns,
slowly—looking around. Looking for me. They're wearing a
hood, and for a moment I can't see their face.

Then they take a sudden step back; I know they've seen me.
The hood falls down. I can see their face now in the light from
the streetlamp. It's a woman: young, beautiful enough to be a
model. Dark brown hair cut in a sharp fringe, a mole on her high
cheekbone, like a piece of punctuation. A hoodie under a leather
jacket. She's staring at me in surprise.

"Hello," I say. I take a cautious step toward her, the shock ebbing away, especially now I can see she's not the threatening figure
I'd imagined. "Why were you following me?" She backs away. It
feels like I have the upper hand now. "What do you want?" I ask,
more insistently.

"I—I'm looking for Ben." A strong accent, not French. Eastern
European, maybe—the thick sound of the "I." "He isn't answering.
He told me—only if it's very important—to come to the apart-
ment. I heard you asking about him last night. In the street."

I think back to when I first arrived at the building, when I
thought for a moment I saw a figure crouched in the shadows
behind a parked car. "Was that you? Behind the car?"

She doesn't say anything, which I suppose is as much of an
answer as I'm going to get. I take another step toward her. She
takes a step back.

"Why?" I ask her. "Why are you looking for Ben? What's
important?"

"Where is Ben?" is all she says. "I must speak with him."

"That's exactly what I'm trying to work out. I think something's happened. He's disappeared."

It happens so quickly. Her face goes white. She looks so scared that I suddenly feel pretty scared myself. Then she swears in another language—it sounds like "*koorvah.*"

"What is it?" I ask her. "Why are you so frightened?"

She's shaking her head. She takes a few more steps backward, almost tripping over her feet. Then she turns and begins walking, quickly, in the other direction.

"Wait," I say. And then, as she gets farther away, I shout it: "Wait!" But she starts running. I hurry after her. Shit, she's fast—those long legs. And I'm skinny but not fit. "Stop—please!" I try calling.

I chase her down onto a busier street—people are turning to look at us. At the last minute she veers off to the left and clatters down the stairs of a Metro station. A couple walking up the steps, arm in arm, break apart in alarm to let her through.

"Please," I call, pounding down the stairs behind her, gasping for breath, feeling like I'm moving in slow motion, "wait!"

But she's through the barrier already. Luckily there's an out-of-order gate that's been left open: I charge through after her. But as I get to a junction, the right fork leading to eastbound trains and the left to westbound, I realize I have no idea which way she's gone. I've got a fifty percent chance, I suppose: I choose right. Panting, I make it down to the platform to find her standing on the opposite side of the tracks. Shit. She's staring back at me, white-faced.

"Please!" I shout, trying to catch my breath, "please, I just want to talk to you—"

People are turning to stare at me, but I don't care.

"Wait there!" I shout. There's a big rush of warm air, the thunder of an approaching train down the tunnel. I sprint up the stairs, up over the bridge that leads to the other platform. I can feel the rumble of the train passing beneath me.

I clatter down the other side. I can't see her. People are piling onto the train. I try to get on but it's full, there are too many bodies packed in there, people are stepping back down onto the platform to wait for the next train. As the doors close I see her face, pale and scared, staring out at me. Now the train's pulling away, *clackety-clacking* its way into the tunnel. I glance at the board displaying the route: there are fifteen stations before the end of the line.

A link to Ben, a lead—finally. But I've got no chance of working out where she's going, where she might get off. Or, most likely, of ever seeing her again.

Jess

THE APARTMENT IS AS BRIGHT as I can make it. I've turned on every single lamp. I've even put a vinyl on Ben's posh record player. I'm trying not to panic and it seemed a good idea to have as much noise and light as possible. It was so quiet when I entered the building just now. Too quiet, somehow. Like there was no one behind the doors I passed. Like the place itself was listening, waiting for something.

It's totally different now, being here. Before, it was just a feeling I couldn't put my finger on. But now I've heard the end of the voicenote. Now I know that the last time I heard from Ben he was afraid, and that there was someone in this apartment with him.

I think about the girl, too. The look on her face when I said I thought something had happened to Ben. She was scared but it also seemed like she'd somehow been expecting it.

Suddenly I'm very aware of how, if you looked across from the right spot in any of the other apartments, you'd be able to see me sitting here, lit up like I'm onstage. I go to the windows and slam all the big wooden shutters closed. Better. There were definitely curtains here once: I notice that the rings on the rail are all broken, as though at some point they've been pulled down.

I can't just sit here and run through everything in my head over and over. There must be something else I'm missing. Something that will provide a clue as to what might have happened.

I tear through the apartment. I crouch down to look under the bed, rip through the shirts in Ben's wardrobe, hunt through the kitchen cabinets. I yank his desk away from the wall. Bingo:

something falls out. Something that had been trapped between the wall and the back of the desk. I pick it up. It's a notebook. One of those posh leather ones. Just the kind Ben would use.

I flick it open. There are a few scribbled notes that look like they're for restaurant reviews, that kind of thing. Then, on a page near the back, I read:

LA PETITE MORT
Sophie M knows.
Mimi: how does she fit in?
The Concierge?

La Petite Mort. Even I can translate that: *the little death.*

Sophie M—it has to be Sophie Meunier, the woman who lives in the penthouse apartment. *Sophie M knows.* What does she know? Mimi, that's the girl on the fourth floor, the one who looked like she was going to hurl her breakfast when I asked about Ben. How *does* Mimi fit in? What *is* the concierge's connection? Why was Ben writing in his notebook about these people, about "little deaths"?

I flip through the rest of the notebook, hoping to discover more, only to find it's blank after this. But this does tell me something. There is something strange going on with the people in this building. Ben was keeping notes about them.

I drink more of Ben's wine, waiting for it to take the edge off my nerves but it doesn't seem to be helping. It only starts to make me feel groggy. I put the wine glass down because I have an urge to stay awake, to keep watch, to keep thinking. I don't want to fall asleep here. Suddenly it doesn't feel safe.

When my eyes start closing of their own accord I realize I don't have a choice. I have to sleep. I need the energy to keep going. I drag myself into the bedroom and fall onto the bed. I know I can't do any more today, not while I'm this knackered. But as I turn out the light I realize that a whole day has now passed without word from my brother and the feeling of dread grows.

MY EYES SNAP open. It feels like no time has passed, but the neon numbers on Ben's alarm clock read: 3:00. Something woke me. I know it, even if I'm not sure what. Could it have been the cat, knocking something over? But no, it's here at the end of the bed, I can feel the weight of its body against my feet and, as my eyes adjust to the dark, I can make it out more clearly in the green glow of the alarm clock. It's sitting up, alert, ears pricked and twitching like radars trying to catch a signal. It's listening to something.

And then I hear it. A creak, the sound of a floorboard giving under someone's foot. Someone's here, in the apartment with me, just the other side of the French doors.

But . . . could it be Ben? I open my mouth to call out. Then I hesitate. Remember the voicenote. There's no light beneath the French doors: my visitor is moving around in the dark. Ben would have switched on the lights by now.

Suddenly I'm wide awake. More than awake: wired. My breathing sounds too loud in the silence. I try to calm it, make it as quiet as possible. I close my eyes and fake sleep, lying as still as I can. Has someone broken in? Wouldn't I have heard the glass shattering, the door splintering?

I wait, listening to every tiny creak of the footsteps making their way around the room. It doesn't feel as though they're in any particular rush. I pull the throw up so I'm almost completely covered by it. And then, through the thundering of my own blood in my ears, I hear the doors to the bedroom begin to open.

My chest is so tight it's hard to breathe. My heart is jumping against my ribs. I'm still pretending to sleep. But at the same time I'm thinking about the lamp next to the bed, the metal base nice and heavy. I could snatch out an arm—

I wait, head pressed against the pillow, trying to decide whether to grab for the lamp now or—

But . . . now I hear the soft pad of footsteps retreating. I hear the French doors closing. And then, a few moments later, further away, the groan of the main door to the apartment opening and shutting.

They've gone.

I LIE STILL for a moment, my breathing coming in rough pants. Then I jump up, push through the French doors and run out into the main room. If I move quickly, I might catch them. But first—I rummage through the kitchen cupboards, come up with a heavy frying pan, just in case, then pull open the apartment's main door. The corridor and stairwell are dark and silent. I close the door, go to the windows instead. Maybe I'll catch someone out there in the courtyard. But it's just a dark pit: the black shapes of trees and bushes, no flicker of movement. Where did they go?

I turn on a light. The place looks completely untouched. No broken glass and the front door looks undamaged. Like they just walked right in.

I could almost believe I dreamt it. But someone was here, I'm certain. I heard them. The cat heard them. Even if, right now, it couldn't look more chilled, sprawled on the sofa, cleaning delicately between its outspread toes.

I glance at Ben's desk, and that's when I realize the notebook is gone. I search the drawers, behind the gap in the desk where I found it before. Shit. I'm an idiot. Why did I leave it out there in full view? Why didn't I hide it somewhere?

It seems so obvious now. After hearing that voicenote I should have taken extra precautions. I should have put something in front of the door. Should have known that someone might come in here, poke around. Because they wouldn't need to break in. If it's the same person Ben was speaking to on that recording, they already have a key.

Ben

EVERYTHING GOES BLACK. JUST FOR a moment. Then it all becomes terrifyingly clear. It is going to happen here, now, in this apartment. Right here, on this innocuous spot of flooring just beyond the door, he is going to die.

He understands what must have happened. Nick. Who else? But one of the others in this place might be involved . . . because of course they are all connected—

"Please," he manages, "I can explain." He has always been able to talk himself out of any situation. *Benjamin Silver-Tongue* she called him. If he can only find the words. But speech seems suddenly very difficult . . .

The next attack comes with astonishing suddenness, astonishing force. His voice is pleading, high as a child's. "No, no—please, please . . . don't—" The words tumbling out of him, he who is always so poised. No time for explanations now. He is begging. Begging for mercy. But there is none in the eyes gazing down upon him.

He sees the blood spatter onto his jeans but he doesn't understand what it is immediately. Then he watches as spots of crimson begin to fall onto the parquet floor. Slowly at first, then faster, faster. It doesn't look real: such a brilliant, intense red and there is so much of it, all at once. How can all of this have come from him? More and more every second. It must be spilling out of him.

Then it happens again, the next attack, and he is falling and on the way down his head bounces against something hard and sharp: the edge of the kitchen counter.

He should have known. Should have been less arrogant, less cavalier. Should at least have had a chain put on the door. And yet he thought he was invincible, thought that he was the one in control. He has been so stupid, so arrogant.

Now he's down on the floor and he cannot imagine ever being able to stand again. He tries to put up his hands, to beg without words, to defend himself, but his hands won't obey him either. His body is no longer within his control. With this comes a new terror: he is utterly helpless.

The shutters . . . the shutters are open. It's dark outside: which means that this whole scene must be illuminated to the outside world. If someone saw—if someone could come to help—

With a vast effort he opens his eyes, turns and begins to crawl toward the windows. It's so hard. Each time he places a hand it slips out from under him: it takes a moment for him to realize that this is because the floor is slick with his own blood. Eventually he reaches the window. He raises himself a little way above the sill, he reaches out a hand and marks a gory handprint against the pane. Is there someone out there? A face turned up toward him, caught by the light spilling from the windows, out there in the gloom? His vision is blurring again. He tries to beat his palm, to mouth the word: *HELP.*

And then the pain hits him. It is huge, more overwhelming than anything he has experienced in his life. He can't bear this, surely: it must be too much. This is where the story ends.

And his last lucid thought is: Jess. Jess will be coming tonight, and no one will be here to meet her. From the moment she arrives, she too will be in danger.

Nick

SECOND FLOOR

MORNING. I ENTER THE BUILDING'S stairwell. I've been running for hours. I have no idea how long, actually, or how far I went. Miles, probably. Normally I'd have the exact stats, would be checking my Garmin obsessively, uploading it all to Strava the second I'd got back. This morning I can't even be bothered to look. Just needed to clear my head. I only stopped because the agony in my calf began to cut through everything else—though for a while I almost enjoyed running through the pain. An old injury: I pushed a Silicon Valley quack to prescribe me oxycodone for it. Which also helped dull the sting when my investments started to go bad.

On the first floor I hesitate outside the apartment. I knock on the door once, twice—three times. Listen for the sound of footsteps inside while I take in the scuffed doorframe, the stink of stale cigarette smoke. I linger perhaps a couple of minutes but there's no answer. He's probably passed out in there in a drunken stupor. Or maybe he's avoiding me . . . I wouldn't be surprised. I have something I want—need—to say to the guy. But I suppose it'll have to wait.

Then I close the door, start climbing the stairs, my eyes stinging. I lift the hem of my sweat-soaked T-shirt to rub at them, then carry on up.

I'm just passing by the third-floor apartment when the door is flung open and there she stands: Jess.

"Er—hi," I say, pushing a hand through my hair.

"Oh," she says, looking confused. "It looked like you were going upstairs?"

"No," I say, "No . . . actually, I was coming to see how you were. I meant to say—sorry for running off yesterday. When we were talking. Did you have any luck tracking Ben down?"

I look at her closely. Her face is pale. No longer the sly little fox she seemed yesterday, now she's a rabbit in the headlamps.

"Jess," I say. "Are you all right?"

She opens her mouth but for a moment no sound comes out. I get the impression she's fighting some sort of internal battle. Finally she blurts, "Someone was in here, very early this morning. Someone else must have a key to this apartment."

"A key?"

"Yeah. They came in and crept around." Less rabbit-in-the-headlamps now. That tough veneer coming back up.

"What, *into* the apartment? Did they take anything?"

She shrugs, hesitates. "No."

"Look, Jess," I say. "It sounds to me like you should speak to the police."

She screws up her face. "I called them yesterday. They weren't any help."

"What did they say?"

"That they'd make a record," she says with an eyeroll. "But then, I don't know why I even bothered. I'm the fucking idiot who comes to Paris alone, barely able to speak the language. Why I thought they'd take me seriously . . ."

"How much French can you speak?" I ask her.

She shrugs. "Hardly anything. I can just about order a beer, but that's it. Pretty bloody useless, right?"

"Look, why don't I come with you to the *Commissariat*? I'm sure they'd be more helpful if I spoke to them in French."

She raises her eyebrows. "That would be—well, that would be amazing. Thank you. I'm . . . look, I'm really grateful." A shrug. "I'm not good at asking for favors."

"You didn't ask—I offered. I told you yesterday I want to help. I mean it."

"Well, thanks." She tugs at the chain of her necklace. "Can we go soon? I need to get out of this place."

Jess

WE'RE OUT ON THE STREET, walking along in silence. My thoughts are churning. That voicenote made me feel like I shouldn't trust anyone in the building—including Ben's old uni mate, friendly as he might be. But on the other hand, Nick's the one who suggested going to the police. Surely he wouldn't do that if he had something to do with Ben's disappearance?

"This way," Nick takes hold of my elbow—my arm tingles slightly at his touch—and steers me into an alleyway, no, more like a kind of stone tunnel between buildings. "A cut-through," he says.

In contrast with the crowded street we left behind there's suddenly no one else in sight and it's much darker. Our footsteps echo. I don't like that I can't see the sky.

It's a relief when we pop out at the other end. But as we turn onto the street I see it ends in a police barricade. There are several guys wearing helmets and stab vests, holding batons, radios crackling.

"Fuck," I say, heart thudding.

"*Merde*," says Nick, at the same time.

He goes over and speaks to them. I stay where I am. They don't seem friendly. I can feel them looking us over.

"It's the riots," Nick says, striding back. "They're expecting a bit of trouble." He looks closely at me. "You OK?"

"Yeah, fine." I remind myself that we're literally on the way to talk to the police. They might be able to help. But it suddenly feels important to get something off my chest. "Hey—Nick?" I start, as we begin walking again.

"Yup?"

"Yesterday, when I spoke to the police, they said they wanted to take my name and address, for their records or whatever. I, er . . . I don't want to give them that information."

Nick frowns at me. "Why's that?"

Because even though he had it coming, I think, what I did to that arsehole is technically still a crime.

"I—it's not worth getting into." But because he's still looking at me oddly and I don't want him to think I'm some sort of hardened criminal, I say: "I had a little trouble at work, just before I came here."

More than a little trouble. Two days ago I walked into the Copacabana, smile on my face, as though my boss hadn't flashed his dick at me the day before. Oh, I can play along when I need to. I needed that bloody job. And then at lunch before opening, while The Pervert was taking a crap (he went in there with a dirty magazine, I knew I had a while), I went and got the little key from his office and opened the till and took everything in it. It wasn't loads; he was too wily for that, refilled it every day. But it was enough to get here, enough to escape on the first Eurostar I could book myself onto. Oh, and for good measure I heaved two kegs in front of the toilet door, one stacked on the other and the top one just under the door handle so he couldn't turn it. Would have taken him a while to get out of that one.

So no, I'm not desperate to be on any official record of anything. It's not like I think Interpol are after me. But I don't like the idea of my name in some sort of system, of the police here comparing notes with the UK. I came here for a new start.

"Nothing major," I say. "It's just . . . sensitive."

"Er, sure," Nick says. "Look, I'll give them my details as a contact. Does that work?"

"Yes," I say, my shoulders slumping with relief . . . "Thank you, that would be great."

"So," he says, as we wait at some traffic lights, "I'm thinking of what I say to the police. I'll tell them you thought there was someone in the apartment last night, of course—"

"I don't *think* there was someone," I interject, "I know."

"Sure," he nods. "And is there anything else you want me to say?"

I pause. "Well . . . I spoke to Ben's editor."

He turns to me. "Oh yes?"

"Yeah. This guy at the *Guardian*. I don't know if it's important but it sounded like Ben had an idea he was excited about, for an article."

"What about?"

"I don't know. Some big investigative piece. But I suppose if he got mixed up in something . . ."

Nick slows down slightly. "But his editor doesn't know what the piece was about?"

"No."

"Ah. That's a shame."

"And look, I found a notebook. But it was missing this morning. It had these notes in it—about people in the building. Sophie Meunier—you know the lady from upstairs? Mimi, from the fourth floor. The concierge. There was this line: *La Petite Mort*. I think it means 'the little death'—"

I see something shift in Nick's expression.

"What is it? What does it mean?"

He coughs. "Well, it's also a euphemism for orgasm."

"Oh." I'm not all that easy to embarrass but I feel my cheeks growing warm. I'm also suddenly really aware of Nick's eyes on me, how near we are to each other in the otherwise empty street. There's a long, awkward silence. "Anyway," I say. "Whoever was creeping around this morning took the notebook. So there must be something in it."

We turn into a side street. I spot a couple of ragged posters pasted to some hoardings. Pause for a moment in front of them. Ghostly faces printed in black and white stare out at me. I don't need to understand the French to know what—who—these are: Missing Persons.

"Look," Nick says, following my gaze. "It's probably going to be tough. Loads of people go missing every year. They have a certain . . . cultural issue here. There's this view that if someone goes missing, it may be for their own reasons. That they have a right to disappear."

"OK. But surely they won't think that's what's happened to Ben. Because there's more . . ." I hesitate, then decide to risk telling Nick about the voicenote.

A long pause, while he digests it. "The other person," he says. "Could you actually hear their voice?"

"No. I don't think they said anything. It was just Ben talking." I think of the *what the fuck?* "He was scared. I've never heard him like that. We should tell the police about that too, right? Play it for them."

"Yes. Definitely."

We walk in silence for a couple more minutes, Nick setting the pace. And then suddenly he stops in front of a building: big and modern and seriously ugly, a total contrast to all the fancy apartment blocks flanking it.

"OK. Here we are."

I look up at the building in front of us. COMMISSARIAT DE POLICE, it says, in large black letters above the entrance.

I swallow, then follow Nick inside. Wait just inside the front door as he speaks in fluent-sounding French to the guy on the desk.

I try to imagine what it must be like to have the confidence Nick has in a place like this, to feel like you have a right to be here. To my left there are three people in grimy clothes being held in cuffs, faces smeared with what looks like soot, yelling and tussling with the policemen holding them. More protestors? I feel like I have much more in common with them than I do with the nice rich boy who's brought me here. I jump back as nine or ten guys in riot gear burst into the reception and shove past me and out into the street, piling into a waiting van.

The guy behind the desk is nodding at Nick. I see him pick up a telephone.

"I asked to speak to someone higher up," Nick says as he comes over. "That way we'll actually be listened to. He's just calling through now."

"Oh, great," I say. Thank God for Nick and his fluent French and his posh boy hustle. I know if I'd walked in here I'd have been fobbed off again—or, worse, bottled it and left before I'd spoken to anyone.

The receptionist stands and beckons us through into the station. I swallow my unease about heading farther into this place. He leads us down a corridor into an office with a plaque that reads COMMISSAIRE BLANCHOT on the door and a man—in his late fifties at a guess—sitting behind a huge desk. He looks up. A bristle of short gray hair, a big square face, small dark eyes. He stands and shakes Nick's hand then turns to me, looks me up and down, and sweeps a hand at the two chairs in front of his desk. *"Asseyez vous."*

Clearly Nick pulled some strings: the office and Blanchot's air of importance tell me he's some sort of bigwig. But there's something about the guy I don't like. I can't put my finger on it. Maybe it's the pitbull face, maybe it's to do with the way he looked at me just now. It doesn't matter, I remind myself. I don't have to like him. All I need is for him to do his job properly, to find my brother. And I'm not so blind that I can't see I might be bringing my own baggage to all of this.

Nick starts speaking to Blanchot in French. I can barely pick up a word they're saying. I catch Ben's name, I think, and a couple of times they glance in my direction.

"Sorry," Nick turns back to me. "I realize we were talking pretty fast. I wanted to get everything in. Could you follow any of it? He doesn't speak much English, I'm afraid."

I shake my head. "It wouldn't have made much difference if you'd gone slowly."

"Don't worry: I'll explain. I've laid out the whole situation to him. And basically we're coming up against what I was telling you about before: the 'right to disappear.' But I'm trying to convince him that this is something more than that. That you—that we—are really worried about Ben."

"You've told him about the notebook?" I ask. "And what happened last night?"

Nick nods. "Yes, I went through all that."

"How about the voicenote?" I hold up my phone. "I have it right here, I could play it."

"That's a great idea." Nick says something to Commissaire Blanchot, then turns to me and nods. "He'd like to listen to it."

I hand over the phone. I don't like the way the guy snatches it from me. *He's just doing his job, Jess,* I tell myself. He plays the voicenote through some kind of loudspeaker and, once again, I hear my brother's voice like I've never heard it before. "*What the fuck?*" And then the sound. That strange groan.

I look over at Nick. He's gone white. He seems to be having the same reaction as I did: it tells me my gut feeling was right.

Blanchot turns it off and nods at Nick. Because I don't speak French, or I'm a woman—or both—it feels like I barely exist to him.

I prod Nick. "He has to do something now, yes?"

Nick swallows, then seems to pull himself together. He asks the guy a question, turns back to me. "Yes. I think that's helped. It gives us a good case."

Out of the corner of my eye I see Blanchot watching the two of us, his expression blank.

And then suddenly it's all over and they're shaking hands again and Nick is saying: "*Merci*, Commissaire Blanchot" and I say "*Merci*" too and Blanchot smiles at me and I try to ignore the uneasiness that I know is probably less to do with this guy than everything he represents. Then we're being shown back out into the corridor and Blanchot's door is closing.

"How do you think it went?" I ask Nick, as we walk out of the front door of the station. "Did he take it seriously?"

He nods. "Yes, eventually. I think the voicenote clinched it." He says, his voice hoarse. He still looks pale and sickened by what he just heard, on the voicenote. "And don't worry—I've given myself as a contact, not you. As soon as I hear anything I'll let you know."

For a moment, back out on the street, Nick stops and stands stock-still. I watch as he covers his eyes with his hand and takes a long, shaky breath. And I think: here is someone else who cares about Ben. Maybe I'm not quite as alone in this as I thought.

Sophie

I'M SETTING UP THE APARTMENT for drinks. The last Sunday of every month, Jacques and I host everyone in our penthouse apartment. We open some of the finest vintages from the store in the cellar. But this evening will be different. We have a great deal to discuss.

I pour the wine into its decanter, arrange the glasses. We could afford staff to do this. But Jacques never wanted strangers in this apartment capable of nosing around through his private affairs. It has suited me well enough. Though I suppose if we did have staff I might have been less alone here, over the years. As I place the decanter on the low table in the sitting area, I can see him there in the armchair opposite me: Benjamin Daniels, exactly as he sat nearly three months ago. One leg crossed over the knee at the ankle. A glass of wine dangling from one hand. So at ease in the space.

I watched him. Saw him sizing the place up, the wealth of it. Or perhaps trying to find a flaw in the furnishings I had chosen as carefully as the clothes I wear: the mid-century Florence Knoll armchair, the Ghom silk rug beneath his feet. To signify class, good taste, the kind of breeding that cannot be bought.

He turned and caught me watching. Grinned. That smile of his: a fox entering the hen coop. I smiled back, coolly. I would not be wrong-footed. I would be the perfect hostess.

He asked Jacques about his collection of antique rifles.

"I'll show you." Jacques lifted one down—a rare honor. "Feel that bayonet? You could run a man straight through with it."

Ben said all the right things. Noticed the condition, the detailing on the brass. My husband: a man not easily charmed. But he was. I could see it.

"What do you do, Ben?" he asked, pouring him a glass. A hot, late summer night: white would have been better. But Jacques wanted to show off the vintage.

"I'm a writer," Ben said.

"He's a journalist," Nick said, at the same time.

I watched Jacques' face closely. "What sort of journalist?" He asked it so lightly.

Ben shrugged. "Mainly restaurant reviews, new exhibitions, that sort of thing."

"Ah," Jacques said. He sat back in his chair. King of all he surveyed. "Well, I'm happy to suggest some restaurants for you to review."

Ben smiled: that easy, charismatic smile. "That would be very helpful. Thank you."

"I like you, Ben," Jacques told him, pointing. "You remind me a little of myself at your age. Fire in the belly. Hunger. I had it too, that drive. It's more than can be said for some young men, these days."

Antoine and his wife Dominique arrived then, from the first-floor apartment. Antoine's shirt was missing a button: it gaped open, the soft flesh pushing through. Dominique, however, had made what could be described as an effort. She wore a dress made of a knit so fine that it clung to every ripe curve of her body. *Mon Dieu*, you could see her nipples. There was something Bardot-like about her: the sullen moue of her mouth, those dark, bovine eyes. I found myself thinking all that ripeness would fade, run to fat (just look at Bardot, poor cow), anathema to so many French men. Fat in this country is seen as a sign of weakness, even of stupidity. The thought gave me a nasty sort of pleasure.

I watched her look at Ben. Look up and down and *all over* him. I suppose she thought she was subtle; to me she resembled a cheap whore, touting for a fare. I saw him gaze back. Two attractive people noticing one another. That *frisson*. She turned back to Antoine. I watched her mouth curve into a smile while she talked to him. But the smile was not for her husband. It was for Ben. A carefully calculated display.

Antoine was drinking too much. He drained his glass and held it out for a refill. His breath, even from a couple of feet away, smelled sour. He was embarrassing himself.

"Does anyone smoke?" Ben asked. "I'm going to go for a cigarette. Terrible habit, I know. I wondered if I might use the roof terrace?"

"It's that way," I told him. "Past the bookcase there and to the left, out of the doorway: you'll see the steps."

"Thanks." He smiled at me, that charming smile.

I waited for the sensor lights to come on, which would be the sign that he had found his way to the roof terrace. They did not. It should have only taken him a minute or so to climb the steps.

As the others talked I got up to investigate. There was no sign of him out on the terrace, or in the other half of the room beyond the bookcase. I had that cold, creeping feeling again. The sense that a fox had entered the henhouse. I walked along the shadowed corridor that leads to the other rooms in the apartment.

I found him in Jacques' study, the lights off. He was looking at something.

"What are you doing in here?" My skin was prickling with outrage. Fear, too.

He turned in the dark space. "Sorry," he said. "I must have got confused with the directions."

"They were quite clear." It was difficult to remain civil, to suppress the urge to simply tell him to get out. "It was left," I said. "Out of the doorway. The opposite direction."

He pulled a face. "My mistake. Perhaps I've had too much of that delicious wine. But tell me, while we're here—this photograph. It fascinates me." I knew instantly which one he was looking at. A large black and white, a nude, hung opposite my husband's desk. The woman's face turned sideways, her profile dissolving into the shadows, her breasts bared, the dark triangle of her pubic hair between white thighs. I had asked Jacques to get rid of it. It was so inappropriate. So seedy.

"It belongs to my husband," I said, curtly. "This is his study."

"So this is where the great man works," he said. "And do you work, yourself?"

"No," I said. He must know that, surely. Women in my position do not work.

"But you must have done something before you met your husband?"

"Yes."

"Sorry," he said, after the pause had grown so long it felt like a physical presence in the air between us. "It's the journalist in me. I'm just . . . curious about people." He shrugged. "It's incurable, I'm afraid. Please, forgive me."

I had thought it that first time I met him: that he wielded his charm like a weapon. But now I was sure of it. Our new neighbor was dangerous. I thought of the notes. My mystery blackmailer. Could it be a coincidence that they had arrived almost at the same time—this man, with his air of knowing—and the demand for money, threatening to reveal my secrets? If so, I would not allow it. I would not let this random stranger dismantle everything I had built.

I managed to find my voice. "I'll show you to the roof terrace," I told him. Followed him until he walked through the right door. He turned around and gave me a grin, a brief nod. I did not smile back.

I went back and joined the others. A few moments later Dominique stood up, announced that she, too, was going for a cigarette. Perhaps she was embarrassed by her husband drinking himself into a stupor on the sofa. Or—I thought of the way she looked at Ben when she arrived—she was simply shameless.

Antoine's arm shot out; his hand gripped her wrist, hard. The wine glass in her hand jerked, a crimson splash landed on the pale knit of her dress. "*Non*," he said. "*Tu ne feras rien de la sorte.*"

You'll do no such thing.

Dominique glanced at me, then. Her eyes wide. Woman to woman. *See how he treats me?* I looked away. You have made your choices, *chérie*, just as I have made mine. I knew what sort of man my husband was when I married him; I'm sure it was the same for you. If not—well, you're even more of a foolish little tart than I thought.

I watched as she wrenched her hand away from her husband's grip and stalked off in the direction of the roof terrace. I imagined the two of them up there, could see the scene play out. The rooftops of Paris laid out before them, the illuminated streets like strings of fairy lights. Her bending forward as she lit her cigarette from his. Her lips brushing his hand.

They came back down a short while later. When he spotted them Antoine rose from the seat where he had been slumped. He lumbered over to Dominique. "We're going."

She shook her head. "No. I don't want to."

He leaned in very close and hissed, loud enough for all of us to hear: "We're going, you little slut." *Petite salope.* And then he turned to Ben. "Stay away from my wife, you English bastard.

Comprends-tu? Understand?" Like a final piece of punctuation he gestured with his full wine glass, and I could not tell if it was because he was drunk or if it was on purpose that it flew from his hand. An explosion of glass. Wine smattered up the wall.

Everything went very still and quiet.

Ben turned to Jacques: "I'm very sorry, Monsieur Meunier, I—"

"Please," Jacques stood. "Do not apologize." He stalked over to Antoine. "No one behaves like that in my apartment. You are not welcome here. Get out." His voice was cold, heavy with menace.

Antoine's mouth opened. I saw his teeth, stained by the wine. For a moment I thought he was about to say something unforgivable. Then he turned and looked at Ben. A long look that said more than any words could.

The silence that followed their exit rang like a tuning fork.

LATER, WHILE JACQUES took a phone call, I went and took a shower in my bathroom. I found myself almost idly directing the shower head between my legs. The image that came to my mind was of the two of them: Dominique and Ben, up in the roof garden. Of all the things that might have occurred between them while the rest of us made small talk downstairs. And as my husband barked instructions—just audible through the wall—I had a silent orgasm, my head pressed against the cool tiles. The little death, it's called. *La petite mort.* And perhaps that was only appropriate. A small part of me had died that evening. Another part had come alive.

Jess

IT'S EVENING AND I'M BACK in the apartment. Gazing out into the courtyard, looking up and down at the illuminated squares of my neighbors' windows, trying to catch a glimpse of one of them moving around.

I've texted Nick a couple of times to ask if he's heard anything from the police but I haven't had anything back yet. I know it's way too soon, but I couldn't help myself. I'm grateful for his help earlier. It's good to feel I have an ally in this. But I still don't trust the police to do anything. And I'm starting to feel itchy again. I can't just sit around waiting to hear.

I shrug on my jacket and step out of the apartment onto the landing, not knowing what I'm going to do but knowing I need to do *something*. As I pause, trying to decide what that is, I realize I can hear raised voices somewhere above me, echoing down the stairwell. I can't resist following the sound upward. I start to climb the stairs, up past Mimi's on the fourth floor, listening for a moment to the silence behind the door. The voices must be coming from the penthouse. I can hear a man speaking over the others, louder than the rest. But I can hear other voices now, too, they all seem to be talking at once. I can't make out any of the words, though. Another flight of stairs and I'm on the top landing, with the door to the penthouse apartment in front of me and to my left that wooden stepladder leading up to the old maids' quarters.

I creep toward the door of the penthouse apartment, wincing at every creak in the floorboards. Hopefully the people inside are too distracted by the sounds of their own voices to pay attention to anything outside. I get right up close to the door, then drop down and put my ear to the keyhole.

The man starts to speak again, louder than before. Crap—it's all in French, of course it is. I think I hear Ben's name and I go tense, craning to hear more. But I can't make out a single—

"*Elle est dangereuse.*"

Wait. Even I can guess what that means: *She is dangerous.* I press my ear closer to the keyhole, listening hard for anything else I might understand.

Suddenly there's the sound of barking, right up close to my ear. I stumble away from the keyhole, half-fall backward, try and scrabble my way to standing. Shit, I need to get out of here. I can't let them see—

"You."

Too late. I turn back. She stands there in the doorway, Sophie Meunier, wearing a cream silk shirt and black trousers, crazily sparkling diamonds at her earlobes—her expression so frosty that they might be tiny icicles she just sprouted there. There's a small gray dog at her feet—a whippet?—looking at me with gleaming black eyes.

"What are you doing here?"

"I heard voices, I . . ." I trail off, realizing that hearing voices behind someone else's apartment door isn't exactly a good excuse to go and eavesdrop. Silver-tongued Ben might be able to, but I can't find a way of talking myself out of this one.

She looks like she's trying to decide what to do with me. Finally, she speaks. "Well. As you are here, perhaps you will come in and join us for a drink?"

"Er—"

She's watching me, waiting for an answer. Every instinct is telling me that going inside this apartment would be a very bad idea.

"Sure," I say. "Thanks." I look down at my outfit—Converse, shabby jacket, jeans with a rip at the knee. "Am I dressed OK?"

Her expression says she thinks there's nothing remotely OK about anything I'm wearing. But she says, "You're fine as you are. Please, come with me."

I follow her into the apartment. I can smell the perfume she's wearing, something rich and floral—although really it just smells like money.

Inside, I stare. The apartment is at least double the size of Ben's, perhaps bigger. A brightly lit, open-plan space bisected by a giant bookcase. Floor-to-ceiling windows look out over the rooftops and buildings of Paris. In the darkness the illuminated windows of all the apartment buildings surrounding us make a kind of tapestry of light.

How much would an apartment like this cost? Lots, that's all I can guess. Millions? Probably. Fancy rugs on the floor, huge works of modern art on the walls: bright splashes and streaks of color, big bold shapes. There's one small painting, nearest to me, a woman holding some kind of pot, a window behind her. I spot the signature in the bottom-right corner: Matisse. OK. Holy shit. I don't know much about art but even I've heard of Matisse. And everywhere, displayed on side tables, are little figurines, delicate glass vases. I bet even the smallest would fetch me more than I earned in a whole year in that shitty bar. It would be so easy to slip one—

I'm suddenly aware of feeling watched. I look up and meet a pair of eyes. Painted, not real. A huge portrait: a man sitting in an armchair. Strong jaw and nose, gray at the temples. Kind of handsome, if a little cruel-looking. It's the mouth, maybe, the curl to it. The funny thing is, he seems familiar. I feel like I've seen his face before but I can't for the life of me think where. Could he be someone a bit famous? A politician, something like that? But I'm not sure why I'd recognize some random politician, let alone a French one: I don't know anything about that stuff. So it must be from somewhere else. But where on earth—

"My husband, Jacques," Sophie says, behind me. "He's away on business at the moment but I'm sure will be . . ." a small hesitation, "eager to meet you."

He looks powerful. Rich. Obviously rich, just frigging look at the place. "What does he do?"

"He's in wine," she says.

So that explains the thousands of bottles of wine in the cellar. The *cave* must also belong to her and her husband.

Next my eye travels to a strange display on the opposite wall. At first I think it's some kind of abstract art installation. But on second glance I see it's a display of old guns. Each with a sharp, knife-like protrusion attached to the end.

Sophie follows my gaze. "From the First World War. Jacques likes to collect antiques."

"One's missing," I say.

"Yes. It's gone for a repair. They require more upkeep than you might think. *Bon*," she says, curtly. "Come through and meet the others."

WE WALK TOWARD the bookcase. It's only now that I become aware of the presence of people behind it. As we skirt round it I see them facing each other on two cream-colored sofas. Mimi, from the fourth floor, and—oh no—Antoine from the first floor. He's staring at me as though he is exactly as pleased to see me as I am him. Surely he's the sort of neighbor you just give a wide berth and leave to their own devices? When I look back he's still staring at me. It feels like something's crawling down my spine.

It's such a random grouping of people, nothing in common

with each other beyond the fact that they live nearby: weird quiet Mimi, who can only be nineteen or twenty; Antoine, a middle-aged mess; Sophie in her silk and diamonds. What could they have been talking about just now? It didn't sound like a polite, neighborly conversation. I can feel their eyes on me, feel like they're all looking at me like I'm an unknown specimen brought into a laboratory. *Elle est dangereuse.* I'm sure I didn't mishear.

"Perhaps you would like a glass of wine?" Sophie asks.

"Oh, yeah. Thanks." She lifts the bottle and as the wine glugs out into a glass I see the gold image of the chateau on the front and realize it's familiar, the match of the bottle I picked up from the cellar downstairs.

I take a long sip of my wine; I need it. I sense three pairs of eyes watching me. They're the ones with the power in this room, the knowledge; I don't like it. I feel outnumbered, trapped. And then I think: fuck it. One of them must know something about what happened to Ben. This is my chance.

"I still haven't heard from Ben," I say. "You know, I'm really starting to think something must have happened to him." I want to shock them out of their watchful silence. So I say, "When I went to the police today—"

It happens so quickly, too quickly for me to see how it unfolded. But there's a sudden commotion and I see that the girl, Mimi, has spilled her glass of wine. The crimson liquid has spattered over the rug, up one leg of the sofa.

No one moves for a second. Maybe, like me, the other two are watching as the dark liquid soaks into the fabric and feeling grateful that it wasn't them.

The girl's face is a livid, beetroot red. "*Merde,*" she says.

"It's all right," Sophie says. "*Pas de problème.*" But her voice is steel.

Mimi

FOURTH FLOOR

PUTAIN. I WANT TO LEAVE right now but that would cause another scene so I can't. I have to just sit here and take it while they all stare at me. While *she* stares at me. The white noise in my head becomes a deafening roar.

Suddenly I can feel the sickness rising inside me. I have to leave the room. It's the only way. I feel like I'm not quite in control of myself. The wine glass . . . I'm not even sure whether it was an accident or whether I did it on purpose.

I jump up from the sofa. I can still feel her watching me. I stumble down the corridor, find the bathroom.

Get a grip, Mimi. *Putain de merde.* Get a fucking grip.

I vomit into the toilet bowl and then look in the mirror. My eyes are pink with burst blood vessels.

For a moment I actually think I see him; appearing behind me. That smile of his, the way it felt like a secret shared just between the two of us.

I COULD WATCH him for hours. Those hot early-autumn nights while he worked at his desk with all the windows open and I lay on my bed with the fan blowing cool air onto the back of my neck and the lights off so he couldn't see me in the shadows. It was like watching him on a stage. Sometimes he walked about shirtless. Once with just a towel wrapped around his waist so I could see the dark shadow of hair on his chest, that line of hair that arrowed from his stomach down beneath the towel: a man, not a boy. He hardly ever remembered to close the shutters. Or maybe he left them open on purpose.

I got out my painting materials. He was my new favorite subject. I'd never painted that well before. I'd never covered the canvas so quickly. Normally I had to stop, check, correct my mistakes. But with him I didn't need to. I imagined that one day, perhaps, I would ask him to sit for me.

Sometimes I could hear his music drifting out across the courtyard. It felt like he wanted me to hear it. Maybe he was even playing it for me.

One night he looked up and caught me watching.

My heart stopped. *Putain.* I'd watched him for so long I forgot that he could see me too. It was so embarrassing.

But then he raised his hand to me. Like he did on that first day, when we saw him arriving in the Uber. Except then he was just saying hi, and it was to Camille too: mainly to Camille, probably, in her tiny bikini. But this time it was different. This time it was just to me.

I raised mine back.

It felt like a private sign to each other.

And then he smiled.

I know I have this tendency to get a little fixated. A little obsessed. But I reckoned he was obsessive too; Ben. He sat there and typed until midnight, sometimes later. Sometimes with a cigarette in his mouth. Sometimes I smoked one too. It felt almost like we were smoking together.

I watched him until my eyes burned.

* * *

NOW, IN THE bathroom I splash cold water on my face, rinse the sourness of the vomit from my mouth. I try to breathe.

Why did I agree to come this evening? I think of Camille, throwing her little wicker basket over her arm, tripping out in the city earlier to hang out with friends, not a care in the world. Not trapped here like me, friendless and alone. How badly I longed to trade places with her.

I can hear him speaking, suddenly. As clearly as if he were standing behind me whispering in my ear, his breath warm against my skin: "You're strong, Mimi. I know you are. So much stronger than everyone thinks you are."

Jess

THERE'S A LONG SILENCE AFTER Mimi disappears. I take a sip of my wine.

"So," I say at last. "How do you all—"

I'm interrupted by the sound of a knock on the door. It seems to echo endlessly in the silence. Sophie Meunier gets up to answer it. Antoine and I are left facing each other. He stares at me, unblinking. I think of him smashing that bottle in his apartment while I watched through the spyhole, how violent it seemed. I think of that scene with his wife in the courtyard.

And then, under his breath, he hisses at me: "What are you doing here, little girl? Haven't you got the message yet?"

I take a sip from my glass. "Enjoying some of this nice wine," I tell him. It doesn't come out as flippant as I'd hoped: my voice wavers. I like to think I'm not scared of much. But this guy scares me.

"Nicolas," I hear Sophie say, using the French pronunciation of the name. And then, in English: "Welcome. Come and join us—would you like a drink?"

Nick! Part of me feels relieved at his being here, that I'm not going to be stuck alone with these people. At the same time I wonder: what is he doing here?

A few moments later he appears around the bookcase behind Sophie Meunier, holding a glass of wine. Apparently living in Paris has given him more style than the average British guy: he's in a crisp white shirt, open at the neck and setting off his tan perfectly, and navy trousers. His curling, dark gold hair is pushed back from his brow. He looks like someone from a perfume ad: beautiful, aloof—I catch myself. What am I doing . . . lusting after this guy?

"Jess," Sophie says, "this is Nicolas."

Nick smiles at me. "Hey." He turns back to Sophie. "Jess and I know each other."

There's a slightly awkward pause. Is this just something rich people who live in apartments like this do, all hang out together? It's not like any neighbors I've ever had. But then again I haven't exactly lived in very *neighborly* places.

Sophie gives a wintry smile. "Perhaps, Nicolas, you could show Jess the view from the roof garden?"

"Sure." Nick turns to me. "Jess, you want to come and have a look?"

I feel like Sophie's trying to get rid of me, but at the same time it's a chance to talk to Nick without the others listening. I follow him back past the bookcase, up another flight of stairs.

He pushes open a door. "After you."

I have to step past him as he holds open the door, close enough that I can smell his expensive cologne, the faint tang of his sweat.

A blast of freezing air hits me first. Then the night sky, the lights below. The city spread out beneath me like an illuminated map, bright ribbons of streets snaking away in all directions, the blurry red glow of taillights . . . for a second it feels like I've stepped out into thin air. I reel back. No: not quite thin air. But there's not much separating me from the streets five floors down beside a flimsy-looking iron rail.

Suddenly uplighters are humming on all around us: they must be on some kind of sensor. Now I can see shrubs and even trees in big stoneware pots, a big rose bush which still has some white blooms attached to it, statues not unlike the one that got smashed to pieces in the courtyard.

Nick steps up onto the terrace behind me. Because I've been rooted to the spot, staring, I haven't given him any space; he has to stand pretty close behind me. I can feel the warmth of his breath on the back of my neck, such a contrast to the freezing air. I have a sudden crazy impulse to lean back against him. What would his reaction be if I did? Would he pull away? But at the same time I have an equally crazy urge to dive forward into the night. It feels like I could swim in it.

When you're this high up, do you ever get the urge to jump?

"Yes," Nick says, and I realize I must have spoken the question out loud.

I turn to him. I can barely make him out, just a dark silhouette stitched against the glow from the lights behind him. He's tall, though. Standing this close I'm aware of the difference between our heights. He takes a tiny step back.

I look beyond him and notice that there's an extra layer of building above us: the windows dark and small and dust-smeared, ivy wound all over them, like something from a fairytale. I wouldn't be surprised to see a ghostly face appearing behind the glass.

"What's up there?"

He follows my gaze. "Oh, it'll be the old *chambres de bonne*—where the former maids' quarters were." That must be where the wooden ladder leads. Then he gestures back out at the city. "Pretty good view from up here, isn't it?"

"It's insane," I say. "How much do you reckon a place like this costs? A couple million? More than that?"

"Er . . . I've got no idea." But he must have some sort of idea; he must know what his own apartment is worth. It probably makes him feel awkward. I suspect he's too classy to talk about this sort of thing.

"Have you heard anything?" I ask him. "From that guy at the police station? Blanchot?"

"Unfortunately not." It's strange, not being able to see his expression. "I know it's frustrating. But it's only been a few hours. Let's give it time."

I feel a swoop of despair. Of course he's right, of course it's too soon. But I can't help panicking that I'm no closer to finding Ben. And no closer to working any of these people out.

"You all seem pretty friendly in there," I say, trying to keep my tone light.

Nick gives a short laugh. "I wouldn't say that."

"But do you all get together often? I've never had drinks with my neighbors."

I can hear his shrug. "No—not that often. Sometimes. Hey, do you want a cigarette?"

"Oh, sure. Thanks."

I hear the click of his lighter and when the flame sparks I see his face lit up from beneath. His eyes are black holes, blank as that statue's in the courtyard. He passes me my cigarette and I feel the quick warm touch of his fingers, then his breath on my face as I lean closer for him to light the tip. A shiver of something in the air between us.

I take a drag. "I don't think Sophie likes me much."

He shrugs. "She doesn't like anyone much."

"And Jacques? Her husband? The one in that massive portrait. What's he like?"

He screws up his face. "A bit of a cunt, to be honest. And she's definitely just with him for his money."

I almost choke on my cigarette smoke. It was so casual; the way he said it. But with a real emphasis on the "cunt." I wonder what he has against the couple. And if he's clearly not a fan, what on earth is he doing coming for drinks in their apartment?

"How about that guy from the downstairs flat? Antoine?" I ask. "I can't believe she'd invite him up here. I'm surprised she even lets him sit on her couch. And when I first arrived he told me to fuck off—talk about hostile."

Nick shrugs. "Well . . . it's no excuse but his wife just left him."

"Yeah?" I say. "If you ask me she had a pretty lucky escape."

"Look," he says, pointing beyond me, "you can see the Sacré-Coeur, over there." Clearly he doesn't want to talk about his neighbors any more. We gaze together at the cathedral: illuminated, seeming to float above the city like a big white ghost. And in the distance . . . yes—there—I can see the Eiffel Tower. For a few seconds it lights up like a giant Roman candle and a thousand moving lights shimmer up and down its height. I'm suddenly aware of how huge and unknowable this city is. Ben's out there somewhere, I think, I hope . . . Again, that feeling of despair.

I give myself a mental shake. There must be something else I can learn, some new angle to this I haven't explored. I turn to Nick. "Ben never mentioned what he was looking into, did he?" I ask. "The thing he was writing? The investigative piece?"

"He didn't say anything to me about it," Nick says. "As far as I knew, he was still working on restaurant reviews, that kind of thing. But then that's typical of him, isn't it?" I think I hear a note of bitterness.

"What do you mean?"

"Well, you have to ask whether anyone really knows the real Benjamin Daniels." You're telling me, I think. Still, I wonder exactly what he means by it. "Anyway, it's what he always wanted to do." He sounds different now, more wistful. "Investigative stuff. That or write a novel. I remember him saying that he wanted to write something that would have made your mum proud. He talked all about it on the trip."

"You mean the one you took after uni?" The way he said "the trip" made it sound important. The Trip. I think of that screen-saver. Some instinct tells me to press him on it. "What was it like? You went all across Europe, right?"

"Yeah." His tone is different again: lighter, excited. "We spent a whole summer doing it. Four of us: a couple of other guys, Ben and me. I mean, we were really roughing it. Grotty trains with no air-con, blocked loos. Days, weeks, of sleeping sitting up in hard plastic seats, eating stale bread, hardly washing our clothes. And then when we did we had to use launderettes."

He sounds thrilled. Babe, I think, if you think that's roughing it you don't know you're born. I think of his minimalist apart-ment: the Bang & Olufsen speakers, the iMac, all that stealth wealth. I kind of want to hate him for it, but I can't. There's something melancholy about the guy. I remember the oxycodone I found in his bathroom.

"Where did you go?" I ask.

"All over," he says. "We'd be in Prague one day, Vienna the next, Budapest a few days later. Or sometimes we'd just spend a whole week lying on the beach and hitting the clubs every night—like we did in Barcelona. And we lost a whole weekend to food poisoning in Istanbul."

I nod, like I know what he's talking about, but I'm not sure I could point to all those places on a map.

"So that's what Ben was up to," I say. "Sounds a long way from a one-bed in Haringey."

"Where's Haringey?"

I give him a look. He even pronounced it wrong. But of course a rich kid like him wouldn't have heard of it. "North London? It's where we come from, Ben and I. Even then he couldn't wait to escape, to travel. Actually, it reminds me of something—"

"What?"

"My mum, she used to leave us on our own quite a lot, while she went out. She did shift work and she'd lock us in from about six, so we couldn't get up to any trouble—it can be a rough part of town—and we'd be so bored. But Ben had this old globe . . . you know, one of those light-up ones? He'd spend hours spinning it round, pointing out the places we might go. Describing them to me—spice markets, turquoise seas, cities on mountaintops . . . God knows how he knew any of that. Actually, he probably made it all up." I pull myself out of the memory. I'm not sure I've spoken to anyone else about all of that. "Anyway. It sounds like you had a ball. The photo on your screensaver, that was Amsterdam, right?"

I look at Nick but he's staring out into the night. My question is left hanging in the chill autumn air.

Concierge

THE LOGE

I'M WATCHING THE ROOF TERRACE from my position in the courtyard. I saw the lights come on a few moments ago. Now I see someone step close to the rail. I catch the sound of voices, the faint strains of music floating down. Rather a contrast with the sounds coming from a few streets away, the whine of police sirens. I heard it just now on the radio: the riots are beginning again in earnest tonight. Not that any of them up there will know or care.

The radio was a gift from him, actually. And only a few weeks ago I watched him up there on the roof terrace, too, smoking a cigarette with the wife of the drunk on the first floor.

As the figure next to the rail turns I realize it's her, the girl staying in his apartment. She has somehow gained access to the penthouse. Invited in? Surely not. If she is anything like her brother I can imagine she may have invited herself.

In a couple of days she has gained access to parts of this building that I have never entered, despite working here for so many years. This is only to be expected. I am not one of them, of course. In all the time I have worked here I can only recall the great Jacques Meunier looking at me twice, speaking to me once. But of course to a man like that I am barely human. I am something less than visible.

But this girl is an outsider, too. Just as much as I am—maybe more so. Also apparently given to climbing, like her brother. Insinuating herself. Does she really know what she has got herself into here? I think not.

I see another figure appear behind her. It's the young man from the second floor. I snatch in a breath. She really is very close to the rail. I only hope she knows what she is doing. Climbing so high, so quickly: it only makes for further to fall.

Nick

SECOND FLOOR

TELLING JESS ABOUT IT HAS brought it back—that thrill. The buzz of shunting between different cities, playing endless rounds of poker with a battered old deck of cards, drinking warm cans of beer. Talking shit, talking about the deep stuff—often a mixture of both. Something real. All my own. Something money couldn't buy. It's why I leapt at the chance to reunite with Ben, in spite of everything. It's not the first time I've longed to go back there, to that innocence.

I catch myself. Talk about rose-tinted glasses. Because it wasn't all innocent, was it?

Not when our mate Guy nearly OD-d in a Berlin nightclub and we found him pouring water into his face, had to save him from basically drowning himself.

Not when we had to pass a bribe to a Hungarian train guard, because our tickets had expired and he was threatening to dump us in the middle of a vast pine forest.

Not when we nearly got our throats slit by a gang in a back alley in Zagreb after they'd stolen all our remaining cash.

Not in Amsterdam.

I watch Jess now as she takes a drag on her cigarette. I remember Ben telling me about her in a Prague beer hall: "My half sister, Jess . . . She was the one who found Mum. She was only a kid. The bedroom door was locked, but I'd taught her how to trip a lock with a piece of wire . . . An eight-year-old should never have to see something like that. It . . . *fuck*—" I remember how his voice broke a little, "it eats me up, that I wasn't there."

I wonder what that would do to you. I study Jess, think of finding her yesterday, about to steal that bottle of wine. Or appearing in this apartment tonight, uninvited. There's something reckless about her—it feels as though she might do anything. Unpredictable. Dangerous. And given this morning's outing she's clearly got issues with the police.

"I've never been anywhere outside the UK," she says, suddenly. "Apart from here, of course. And look how well this is turning out."

I stare at her. "What—this is the first time you've been abroad?"

"Yeah." She shrugs. "Haven't had any reason to go before. Or the cash, for that matter. So . . . what was Amsterdam like?"

I think back to it. The stink of the canals in the heat. We were a group of young guys so of course we went straight to the red-light district. De Wallen, it's called. The neon glow of the windows: orange, fuchsia pink. Girls in lingerie, pressing themselves against the glass, signaling that there was more to see if you were happy to pay. And then a sign: Live Sex Show in Basement.

The others wanted to do it: of course they wanted to. We were basically still horny kids.

Down a tunnel, down some stairs. The light growing dimmer. Into a small room. Smell of stale sweat, stale cigarette smoke. Harder to breathe, like the air was getting thinner, like the walls were pressing closer. A door opening.

"I can't do this," I said, suddenly.

The others looked at me like I'd lost it.

"But this is what you *do* in Amsterdam," Harry said. "It's just for fun. You're not telling me you're scared of a bit of snatch? And anyway, it's legal here. So it's not like we'll get in any trouble, if that's what you're worried about."

"I know," I said. "I know but I just . . . I can't. Look, I'll—I'll hang around . . . and meet all of you afterward."

I could tell they thought I was a pussy, but I didn't care. I couldn't do it. Ben looked at me then. And even though he couldn't know, I felt like somehow he got it. But that was Ben all over. Our de facto leader. The grown-up of our little group: somehow more worldly than the rest of us. The one who could talk his way into any nightclub, any hostel that claimed to be full—and out of situations too: he was the one who passed that bribe. I was so envious of that. You can't learn or buy that sort of charm. But I had wondered if maybe just a little of that confidence, that sureness, might rub off on me.

"I'll come with you, mate," he said. Howls of disappointment from the others: "It'll be weird if it's just the two of us," and "What's wrong with you both? Fuck's sake."

But Ben slung an arm around my shoulders. "Let's leave these losers to their cheap thrills," he said. "How about we go find a weed café?"

We walked out into the street and instantly I felt like I could breathe easier. We wandered to a spot a couple of streets away. Sat down with our ready-rolled joints.

He leaned forward. "You all right, mate?"

"Yeah . . . fine." I inhaled greedily, hungry for the weed haze to descend.

"What freaked you out so much?" he asked, a moment later, "about that place back there?"

"I don't know," I said. "It's not something I want to talk about. If that's OK."

We'd started with the weaker stuff. It didn't seem to do all that much at first. But as it kicked in I felt something shift.

Actually, now I think about it, maybe it wasn't so much the weed. It was Ben.

"Look," he said. "I get that you don't want to talk. But if you need to get anything off your chest, you know?" He put up his hands. "No judgment here."

I thought of that place, the girls. I'd kept it inside me for so long, my grim little secret. Maybe it would be a kind of catharsis. I took a deep breath. A long pull of my joint. And then I started talking. Once I started I didn't want to stop.

I told him about my sixteenth birthday present. How my dad had told me it was time for me to become a man. His gift to me. Best of the best, for his son. He wanted to give me an experience I'd never forget.

I remember the staircase leading downward. Opening that door. Telling him I didn't want that.

"What?" My dad had stared at me. "You think you're too good for this? You're going to throw this back in my face? What's wrong with you, boy?"

I told Ben how I stayed. Because I had to. And how I left that place a changed person—barely a man yet. How it left its stain on me.

All of a sudden it was just spilling out of me, all my secrets, shit I had never told anyone, like this putrid waterfall. And Ben just sat listening, in the dark of the café.

"Christ," he said, his pupils large. "That's seriously fucked-up." I remember that, clearly.

"I haven't told anyone else about it," I said. "Don't—don't tell the others, yeah?"

"It's safe with me," Ben said.

After that we started on the stronger stuff. Egging each other on. That was when it really hit. We'd look at each other and just giggle, even though we didn't know why.

"We didn't see all that much of the city," I tell Jess, now. "So I'm not exactly what you'd call an expert. If you want a good weed café I could probably tell you that much."

If only the night had ended there. Without what came next. Without the darkness. The black water of the canal.

Jess

"HANG ON," I SAY. "YOU told me you and Ben hadn't seen each other for over a decade when you guys bumped into each other again?"

"Yes."

"And that was after that trip, right?"

"Yeah. I hadn't seen him since then."

I let it sit a little, wait for him to continue, to explain the long stretch of time. Silence.

"I have to ask," I say, "what on earth happened in Amsterdam?" I mean it as a joke—mainly. But it feels like there's something there. The way his voice changed when he spoke about it.

For a moment Nick's face is a mask. Then it's like he remembers to smile. "Ha. Just boys being boys. You know."

A gust of icy wind hits us, ripping leaves from the shrubs and tossing them into the air.

"Jesus!" I say, wrapping my arms around myself.

"You're shivering," Nick says.

"Yeah, well—this jacket's not really designed for the cold. Primarni's finest." Though I highly doubt Nick knows what Primark is.

He stretches a hand out toward me, such a sudden motion that I jerk backward.

"Sorry!" he says. "I didn't mean to startle you. You've got a leaf caught in your hair. Wait a second, I'll get it out."

"There's probably all sorts in there," I say, casting around for a joke. "Food, cigarette butts, the lot." I can feel the warmth of his breath on my face, his fingers in my hair as he untangles the leaf.

"Here—" he plucks it out and shows it to me: it's a dead brown ivy leaf. His face is still very close to mine. And in the way you do just know with these things, I think he might be about to kiss me. It's a very long time since I've been kissed by anyone. I find myself letting my lips open slightly.

Then we're plunged into darkness again.

"Shit," Nick swears. "It's the sensors—we've been too still."

He waves an arm and they come back on. But whatever was just happening between us has been shattered. I blink spots of light from my eyes. What the hell was I thinking? I'm trying to find my missing brother. I don't have time for this.

Nick takes a step away from me. "Right," he says, not meeting my eyes. "Shall we go back down?"

We climb back down into the apartment. "Hey," I say. "I think I'll just find a bathroom." I need to pull myself together.

"You want me to show you the way?" Nick asks. Clearly he's familiar with this apartment, I note, despite what he says about not doing this often.

"No, I'm good," I tell him. "Thanks."

He goes back to join the others. I wander down a dimly lit corridor. Thick carpet beneath my feet. More artworks hanging on the walls. I push open doors as I go: I don't know exactly what I'm looking for, but I do know I've got to find something that might tell me more about these people, or what Ben had to do with any of them.

I find two bedrooms: one very masculine and impersonal, like I imagine a room in a swanky business hotel might be, the other more feminine. It looks as though Sophie and Jacques Meunier sleep in different rooms. Interesting, though maybe not surprising. Off Sophie's bedroom is a room-sized wardrobe, with rows of high heels and boots in sensible shades of black and tan and camel, hanging racks of dresses and silk shirts, expensive-looking sweaters with tissue interleaved between them. In one corner is an ornate dressing table with a spindly antique-looking chair and a big mirror. I thought only the Kardashians and people in films had rooms like this.

I find the bathroom too, big enough to hold a yoga class in, with a huge sunken bath encased in marble, his-and-hers sinks. The next door opens onto the toilet: if you're rich I suppose you probably don't wee in the same place that you bathe in your scented oils. A quick poke around in the cabinets, but I don't find much beyond some very posh-looking wrapped soaps from somewhere called Santa Maria Novella. I pocket a couple.

The room opposite the toilet seems to be some sort of study. It smells like leather and old wood. A huge antique-looking desk with a burgundy leather top squats in the center. There's a big black and white picture opposite it which I think is some abstract image at first but then suddenly—like a magic eye— realize is actually a photograph of a woman's torso: breasts, belly button, vee of pubic hair between her legs. I stare at it for a moment, taken aback. It seems like quite an odd thing to hang in your study, but then I suppose you can do what you like if you work from home.

I try the drawers to the desk. They're locked, but these kinds of locks are pretty easy to pick. I've got the first open in a minute or so. The first thing I find is a couple of sheets of paper. It looks like the top sheet must be missing, because these are numbered "2" and "3" at the bottom. Some sort of price list, it looks like. No: accounts. Wines, I think: I see "Vintage" at the top of one column. The number of bottles bought—never more than about four, I notice. A price next to each wine. Jesus. Some of these single bottles seem to be going for more than a thousand euros.

And then what looks like a person's name next to each of these entries. Who spends that much money on wine?

I reach right to the back of the drawer, to see if there's anything else in there. My fingers close around something small and leathery. I pull it out. It's a passport. A pretty old one, by the looks of things. On the front it has a gold circular design and some foreign-looking letters. Russian, maybe? It looks pretty old, too. I open it up and there's a black and white photograph of a young woman. I have the same feeling I did when I looked at that portrait over the fireplace. That I know this person from somewhere . . . though I can't place her. Her cheeks and lips full, her hair long and wild and curling, her eyebrows plucked into thin half-moons. All at once it hits me. Something about the set of the mouth, the tilt of the chin. It's Sophie Meunier, only about thirty years younger. I look at the front cover again. So she's actually Russian or something—not French. Odd.

I shut the drawer. As I do, something falls with a thud off the desk and onto the floor. Shit. I snatch it up: not broken, thank God. A photograph in a silver frame. A posh, formal-looking one. I don't know how I didn't notice it before: I must have been so focused on the drawers. There are several people in it. I recognize the man first. It's Jacques Meunier, Sophie's husband: the guy in the painting. And there's Sophie Meunier next to him, somewhere between the age she is now and in that passport photo, wearing what's probably meant to be a smile on her face instead of a chilly grimace. And then three kids. I frown, squinting at the faces, then tilt the photograph toward me, try and see it better under the dim lights. Two teenagers—boys—and a little girl.

The younger-looking boy, with his mop of golden hair. I've seen him before. And then I remember. I saw him in a photograph in Nick's flat, next to a sailing boat, a man's hand on his shoulder. The younger boy is Nick.

Hang on. Hang on, this doesn't make any sense. Except it does, suddenly, make a terrible kind of sense. That older boy with the darker hair and the scowl, nearly a man—I think that's Antoine. This tiny girl with the dark hair . . . I peer at it more closely. There's something about the startled expression that's familiar. It's Mimi. The people in this photograph are—

It's then I hear my name being called. How long have I been in here? I put the photograph down with a clatter, my hands suddenly clumsy. I scuttle across the room to the door, peek out through the crack into the corridor. The door at the end is still closed but as I watch it begins to open. While there's still time not to be seen I scurry across the hallway, into the toilet.

I hear Nick's voice saying, "Jess?"

I open the door to the toilet again and step into the corridor with my best expression of innocent surprise. My heart is hammering somewhere up near my throat.

"Hey!" I say. "All good?"

"Oh," Nick says. "I just—well, Sophie wanted me to make sure you hadn't got lost." He smiles that nice guy smile and I think: I do not know this person at all.

"No," I say. "I'm fine." My voice, incredibly, sounds almost normal. "I was just coming back to join you."

I smile.

And all the time I'm thinking: *they're a family, they're a family.* Nice guy Nick and frosty Sophie and drunken Antoine and quiet, intense Mimi.

What the actual fuck.

Sophie

PENTHOUSE

THEY'VE ALL LEFT. MY JAW is stiff with the effort of maintaining a mask of serenity. The girl turning up here completely derailed my plans for the evening. I haven't managed to achieve anything I wanted to with the others.

The bottle of wine is left open on the table. I have drunk far more than I would have had Jacques been here. He would be appalled to see me have much more than a glass. But then I have also spent many evenings alone here over the years. I suppose I'm not unlike other women of my social standing. Left to rattle around in their huge apartments while their husbands are away—with their mistresses, caught up in their work.

When I married Jacques I understood it as an exchange. My youth and beauty for his wealth. Over the years, as is the way with this particular kind of contract, my worth only diminished as his increased. I knew what I was getting into, and for the most part I do not regret my choice. But maybe I hadn't reckoned with the loneliness, the empty hours. I glance over at Benoit, sleeping in his bed in the corner. Small wonder that so many women like me have dogs.

But being alone is better than the company of my stepsons. I see how they look at me, Antoine and Nicolas.

I reach for the bottle and pour the remainder into a glass. The liquid reaches to the very rim. I drink it down. It's a very fine burgundy but it doesn't taste good like this. The acid stings the back of my throat and nostrils like vomit.

I open a new bottle and start drinking that too. I drink it straight from the neck this time, tipping the bottle vertical. The wine rushes out too fast for me to gulp it down; I cough. My throat is burning, raw. The wine pours over my chin, down my neck. The cool of it is strangely refreshing. I feel it sinking into the silk of my shirt.

I SAW HIM in the courtyard the morning after our drinks, talking to Mimi's flatmate, Camille, in a puddle of sunlight. Jacques once told me he approved of that girl living with our daughter. A good influence. Nothing to do with that little pink pout, the delicate upturned nose, the small high breasts, I am sure.

She was leaning toward Benjamin Daniels as a sunflower in a Provençal field tilts toward the sun, Vichy-check top slipping off brown shoulders, white shorts so brief that half a bronzed buttock was visible beneath each hem. The two of them together were beautiful, just as he and Dominique had been beautiful; impossible not to see it.

"*Bonjour Madame Meunier*," Camille trilled. A little wave as she shifted her weight from one leg to the other. The "Madame" calculated, no doubt, to make me feel all the cruel power of her youth. Her phone trilled. She read whatever had arrived, a smile forming as though she were reading some secret message from a lover. Her fingers went to her lips. The whole thing was a display for him, perhaps: meant to entice, intrigue. "I have to go," she said. "*Salut* Ben!" She turned and blew him a kiss.

And then it was just me and Benjamin Daniels in the courtyard. And the concierge, of course. I was certain she would be watching all of this from her cabin.

"You've made it beautiful out here," he said.

How did he know it was all my work? "It's not looking its best," I told him. "This time of year—everything is almost over."

"But I love the rich colors," he said. "Tell me, what are those—over there?"

"Dahlias. Agapanthus."

He asked me about several of the borders. He seemed genuinely interested, though I knew he was just humoring me. But I didn't stop. I was enjoying telling him—telling somebody—about the oasis I had created. For a moment I almost forgot my suspicion of him.

And then he turned to face me. "I've been meaning to ask you. Your accent intrigues me. Are you originally from France?"

"Excuse me?" I fought not to lose control of my expression, felt the mask slipping.

"I noticed that you don't always use the definite article," he said. "And your consonants: they're a little harder than a native speaker's." He made a pinch with his thumb and forefinger. "Just a little. Where are you from originally?"

"I—" For a moment, I couldn't speak. No one had ever commented on my accent, not even the French—not even the Parisians, who are the worst snobs of all. I had begun to flatter myself that I had perfected it. That my disguise was complete, foolproof. But now I realized that if he had guessed, and he wasn't even French, it meant others would have done too, of course they would. It was a chink, an opening in the shell through which my former self might be glimpsed. Everything I had carefully put in place, all I had worked so hard at. With that one question he was saying: *you don't fool me.*

* * *

"I DON'T LIKE him," I told Jacques, later. "I don't trust him."

"What on earth do you mean? I was impressed by him last night. You can feel the ambition coming off him. Perhaps he'll be a good influence on my wastrel sons."

What could I tell him? *He made a comment about my accent? I don't like the way he seems to watch all of us? I don't like his smile?* It sounded so weak.

"I don't want him here," I said. It was all I could think to say. "I think you should ask him to leave."

"Oh really?" Jacques said, quite pleasantly. Too pleasantly. "You're going to tell me, now, are you, who I may and may not have in my own house?"

And that was that. I knew not to say anything more on the matter. Not for the time being. I would just have to think of another way to rid this place of Benjamin Daniels.

THE NEXT MORNING a new note arrived.

I know you, Sophie Meunier. I know the shameful secrets hiding beneath that bourgeois exterior. We can keep this between us, or the rest of the world can learn them too. I ask just a small fee for my service of silence.

The amount my blackmailer was asking for had doubled.

I suppose a few thousand euros should sound like small fry to someone living in an apartment worth several million. But the apartment is in Jacques' name. The money tied up in Jacques' accounts, his investments, his business. Ours has always been an old-fashioned arrangement; at any given time I have only had what has been handed out to me for housekeeping, for my wardrobe. I did not realize before I became a part of this world how invisible the grease—the money—that moves its wheels really is. It is all squirreled away, invested, liquid or fixed, so little of it available in ready cash.

Still, I did not tell Jacques. I knew how badly he would react, which would only make things worse. I knew that by telling him I would make this thing real, would dredge up the past. And it would only further underscore the imbalance of power that existed between my husband and me. No, instead I would find a way to pay. I still felt able to handle it on my own. Just. I chose a diamond bracelet, this time: an anniversary gift.

The next morning, I dutifully left another wedge of grubby notes in a cream-colored envelope beneath the loose step.

NOW, I LOOK at myself in the mirror across the room. The spreading crimson stain of the wine. I'm transfixed by the sight of it. The red sinking into the pale silk of the shirt. Like spilled blood.

I rip the shirt from me. It tears so easily. The mother of pearl buttons explode from the fabric, skitter to the corners of the room. Next, the trousers. The fine soft wool is tight, clinging. A moment later I am on the ground, kicking them from me. I am sweating. I am panting like an animal.

I look at myself in my lingerie, bought at great expense by my husband but so seldom seen by him. Look at this body, denied so much pleasure, still so well-honed from the years of dieting. The xylophone of my décolletage, the wishbone of my pelvis. Once my body was all curves and ripeness. A thing to provoke lust or contempt. To be touched. With a great effort I changed it into something to be concealed, upon which to hang the garments made for a woman of my standing.

My lips are stained by the wine. My teeth, too. I open my mouth wide.

Holding my own gaze in the mirror I let out a silent scream.

Jess

I MADE MY EXCUSES TO leave the penthouse as quickly as I could. I just wanted to get out. There was a moment, sensing them all watching, when I wondered if one of them might try and stop me. Even as I opened the door I thought I might feel a hand on my shoulder. I walked back down the stairs to Ben's apartment quickly, the back of my neck prickling.

They're a family. They're a family. And this isn't Ben's apartment: not really. Right now I'm sitting here inside someone's family home. Why on earth didn't Ben tell me this? Did it not seem important? Did he somehow not know?

I think of how impressed I was with Nick's fluent French in the police station. Of course he's bloody fluent: it's his first language. I'm trying to think back to our first conversation. At no point, as far as I can recall, did he actually tell me he was English. That stuff about Cambridge, I just assumed—and he let me.

Although he *did* lie to me about something. He pretended his surname was Miller. Why pick that in particular? I remember the results I got when I searched for him online: did he simply choose it because it's so generic? I march to Ben's bookshelf, pull out his dog-eared French dictionary, flip through to "M." This is what I find:

meunier (mønje, jɛR) **masculine noun**: miller

Miller = Meunier. He gave me a translation of his surname.

One thing I can't work out, though. If Nick has got some other, hidden agenda, why was he so keen to help? Why did he come to the police station with me, speak to Commissaire Blanchot? It doesn't fit. Maybe he has another more innocent reason for keeping all of this from me. Maybe they're just a really private family as they're so rich. Or maybe I've been taken for a complete fool . . .

A chill goes through me as I think of them tonight at the drinks party. Observing me like an animal at the zoo. I think how it didn't make sense that such a random group of people should choose to hang out together. That they seemed to have nothing in common. But a family . . . that's different. You don't have to have anything in common with your family; the thing that binds you is your shared blood. I mean, I assume that's how it is. I've never had much of a family. And I wonder whether that's why I didn't spot the truth. I couldn't read the signs, the important little clues. I don't know how families work.

I go to put the dictionary back on the shelf. As I do, a sheet of paper comes loose and falls out onto the floor. I think it's one of the pages of the book at first, because it's such a ratty old thing, until I pick it up. It takes me a moment to work out why I recognize it. I'm sure it's the top sheet of those accounts I found in the desk drawer in the penthouse apartment. Yes: there's a "1" at the bottom of the page. The same sort of thing: the vintages, the prices paid, the surnames of the people who have bought them, all with a little "M." in front of them. But what *is* interesting is what's printed at the top of the sheet of paper. The symbol of a firework exploding, in raised gold emboss. Just like the strange metal card Ben had in his wallet: the one I've lent to Theo, yesterday. And what's also interesting is that Ben—in the same scrawl he'd used in his notebook—has written something in the margin:

Numbers don't make sense. Wines surely worth much less than these prices.

Then, underneath, underlined twice: *ask Irina*.

My heart starts beating a little faster. This is a connection. This is something important. But how on earth am I going to work out what it means? And who the hell is Irina?

I take out my phone, snap a photo. Piggybacking off Nick's Wifi again, I send it to Theo.

Found this in Ben's stuff. Any ideas?

I think of our meeting in the café. I'm not sure I entirely trust the guy. I'm not even convinced I'll hear back from him. But he's literally the only person I've got left—

My thumb freezes on the phone. I go very still. I just heard something. A scratching sound, at the apartment's front door. I wonder briefly if it's the cat, before I realize it's lying stretched out on the sofa. My chest tightens. There's someone out there, trying to get in.

I get up. I feel the need for something to defend myself with. I remember the very sharp knife in Ben's kitchen, the one with the Japanese characters on it. I go and get it. And then I approach the door. Fling it open.

"You."

It's the old woman. The concierge. She takes a step back. Puts her hands up. I think she's holding something in her right fist. I can't tell what it is, the fingers are clenched too tightly.

"Please . . . Madame . . ." Her voice a rasp, as though it's rusty from lack of use. "Please . . . I did not know you were here. I thought—"

She stops abruptly, but I catch her involuntary glance upward.

"You thought I was still up there, right? In the penthouse." So she's been keeping an eye on my movements around this place.

"So you thought . . . what? You'd come and have a snoop around? What's that in your hand? A key?"

"No, Madame . . . it's nothing. I swear." But she doesn't open her fingers to show me.

Something occurs to me. "Was that *you* last night? Sneaking in here? Creeping around?"

"Please. I do not know what you are talking about."

She is cringing backward. And suddenly I don't feel good about this at all. I might not be big, but she's even smaller than me. She's an old woman. I lower the knife: I hadn't even realized I was pointing it at her. I'm a little shocked at myself.

"Look, I'm sorry. It's OK."

Because how harmless can she be, really? A little old lady like that?

ALONE AGAIN, I think about my options. I could confront Nick about all this, see what he says. Ask him what the hell he thought he was doing, giving me a fake name. Get him to explain himself. But I reject this pretty quickly. I have to pretend to know nothing. If he knows I've discovered his secret—their secret—that will make me a threat to him and to whatever else he might be trying to hide. If he thinks I still don't know anything, then perhaps I can keep digging—invisible in plain sight. When I look at it like this, my new knowledge gives me a kind of power. From the beginning, from the moment I stepped foot in this building, the others have held all the cards. Now I've got one of my own. Just one, but maybe it's an ace. And I'm going to use it.

Mimi

WHEN I GET BACK TO the apartment I just want to go to my room and pull the covers over my head, crawl deep down into the darkness with Monsieur Gus the penguin and sleep for days. I'm exhausted by the drinks upstairs, the effort it all took. But when I try to open the front door I find my way blocked with crates of beer, bottles of spirits and MC Solaar blaring out of the speakers.

"*Qu'est-ce qui se passe?*" I call. "What's going on?"

Camille appears in a pair of men's boxers and lace camisole, dirty blond hair piled up on top of her head in an unraveling bun. A lit spliff dangles from one hand. "Our Halloween party?" she says, grinning. "It's tonight."

"Party?"

She looks at me like I'm crazy. "Yeah. Remember? Nine thirty, down in the *cave*, for the spooky atmosphere—then maybe bring a few people up here for an afterparty. You said before that your papa would probably be away this week."

Putain. I totally forgot. Did I really agree to this? If I did it feels like a lifetime ago. I can't have people here, I can't cope—

"We can't have a party," I tell her. I try to sound firm, assertive. But my voice comes out small and shrill.

Camille looks at me. Then she laughs. "Ha! You're joking, of course." She strides over and ruffles my hair, plants a kiss on my cheek, wafting weed and Miss Dior. "But why the long face, *ma petite chou?*" Then she stands back and looks at me properly. "Wait. *Es-tu sérieuse?* What the *fuck*, Mimi? You think I can just cancel it now, at what, eight thirty?" She's staring now, looking at me properly—as though for the first time. "What's wrong with you? What's going on?"

"*Rien,*" I say. *Nothing.* "It's fine. I was only joking. I'm—uh—really looking forward to it, actually." But I'm crossing my fingers behind me like I did as a little kid, hiding a lie. Camille is looking closely at me now; I can't hold her gaze.

"I just didn't sleep well last night," I say, shifting from one foot to the other. "Look, I . . . I have to go and get ready." I can feel my hands trembling. I clench them into fists. I want to stop this conversation right now. "I need to get my costume together."

This distracts her, thank God. "Did I tell you I'm going as one of the villagers from *Midsommar?*" She asks. "I found this amazing vintage peasant dress from a stall at Les Puces market . . . and I'm going to throw a load of fake blood over it too—it'll be super cool, *non?*"

"Yeah," I say, hoarsely. "Super cool."

I rush into my room and close the door behind me, then lean against it and breathe out. The indigo walls envelop me like a dark cocoon. I look up at the ceiling, where when I was small I stuck a load of glow-in-the-dark stars and try to remember the kid who used to stare at them before she fell asleep. Then I glance at my Cindy poster on the opposite wall and I know it is only my imagination but suddenly she looks different: her eyes wild and frightened.

I've always loved this time of year, Halloween especially. The chance to wallow in darkness after all the tedious cheerfulness and heat of the summer. But I've never been into parties, even at the best of times. I'm tempted to try and hide up here. I glance at the shadowy space under the bed. Maybe I could climb under there like I did as a child—when Papa was angry, say—and just wait for it all to be over . . .

But there's no point. It will only make Camille more suspicious, more persistent. I know I don't have any other option except to go out there and show my face and get so drunk I can't remember my own name. With a stubby old eyeliner I try to draw a black spiderweb on my cheek so Camille won't say I've made no effort but my hands are shaking so much I can't hold the pencil steady. So I smudge it under my eyes instead, down my cheeks, like I've been crying black tears, rivers of soot.

When I next look in the mirror I take a step back. It's kind of spooky: now I look how I feel on the inside.

Concierge

SHE CAUGHT ME. IT'S NOT like me to be so sloppy. Well. I'll just have to watch and wait and try again when the opportunity presents itself.

I'm back in my cabin. The buzzer for the gate goes again and again. Each time I hesitate. This is my tiny portion of power. I could refuse them entry if I wanted. It would be so easy to turn the party guests away. Of course, I do not. Instead I watch them streaming into the courtyard in their costumes. Young, beautiful; even the ones who aren't truly beautiful are gilded by their youth. Their whole lives ahead of them.

A loud whoop—one boy jumps on another's back. Their actions show they are children, really, despite their grown bodies. My daughter was the same age as them when she came to Paris. Hard to believe, she seemed so adult, so focused, compared to these youths. But that's what being poor does to you; it shortens your childhood. It hardens your ambition.

I talked to Benjamin Daniels about her.

At the height of the September heat wave he knocked on the door of my cabin. When I answered, warily, he thrust a cardboard box toward me. On the side was a photograph of an electric fan.

"I don't understand, Monsieur."

He smiled at me. He had such a winning smile. "*Un cadeau*. A gift: for you."

I stared at him, I tried to refuse. "*Non, Monsieur*—it's too generous. I cannot accept. You already gave me the radio . . ."

"Ah," he said, "but this was free! I promise. A two-for-one offer at Mr. Bricolage—I bought one for the apartment and now I have this second, going spare. I don't need it, honestly. And I can tell it must get pretty stifling in there"—with a nod to my cabin. "Look, do you want me to set it up for you?"

No one ever comes into my home. None of the rest of them have ever been inside. For a moment I hesitated. But it *was* stifling in there: I keep all the windows shut for my privacy, but the air had grown stiller and hotter until it was like sitting inside an oven. So I opened the door and let him in. He showed me the different functions on the fan, helped me position it so I could sit in the stream of air while I watched through the shutters. I could see him glancing around. Taking in my tiny bureau, the pull-down bed, the curtain that leads through to the washroom. I tried not to feel shame; I knew at least that it was all tidy. And then, just as he was leaving, he asked about the photographs on my wall.

"Who's this, here? What a beautiful child."

"That is my daughter, Monsieur." A note of maternal pride; it had been a while since I had felt that. "When she was younger. And here, when she was a little older."

"They're all of her?"

"Yes."

He was right. She had been such a beautiful child: so much so that in our old town, in our homeland, people would stop me in the street to tell me so. And sometimes—because that's the way in our culture—people would make the sign against the evil eye, tell me to take care: she was too beautiful, it would only bring misfortune if I wasn't careful. If I was too proud, if I didn't hide her away.

"What's her name?"

"Elira."

"She was the one who came to Paris?"

"Yes."

"And she still lives here too?"

"No. Not any more. But I followed her here; I stayed after she had gone."

"She must be . . . what—an actress? A model? With looks like that—"

"She was a very good dancer," I said. I couldn't resist. Suddenly, hearing his interest, I wanted to talk about her. It had been such a long time since I had spoken about my family. "That was what she came to Paris to do."

I remembered the phone call, a month in. Not much email, back then, or texting. I would wait weeks for a call that would be cut short by the bleeping that would tell us she was running out of coins.

"I found a place, Mama. I can dance there. They'll pay me good money."

"And you're sure it's all right, this place? It's safe?"

She laughed. "Yes, Mama. It's in a good part of town. You should see the shops nearby! Fancy people go there, rich people."

NOW I WATCH as one of the partygoers staggers over to the nearby flowerbed, the one that has just been replanted, and relieves himself right there on the soil. Madame Meunier would be horrified if she knew, though I suspect she has rather more pressing matters to concern herself with at the moment. And usually the thought of her precious border being soaked with urine would give me a dark kind of pleasure. But this is not a normal time. Right now I am more anxious about this invasion of the building.

These people shouldn't be here. Not now. Not after everything that has happened in this place.

Jess

I'M PACING THE APARTMENT. WONDERING: are the rest of them still up there, in the penthouse, drinking wine? Laughing at my stupidity?

I open the windows to try and draw in some fresh air. In the distance I can hear the faint wailing of police sirens—Paris sounds like a city at war with itself. But otherwise it's eerily quiet. I can hear every creak of the floorboards under my feet, even the scuttle of dry leaves in the courtyard.

Then a scream rips through the silence. I stop pacing, every muscle tensed. It came from just outside—

Then another voice joins it and suddenly there's loads of noise coming from the courtyard: whoops and yells. I open the shutters and see all these kids piling in through the front gate, streaming across the cobbles and into the main building, carrying booze, shouting and laughing. Clearly there's some sort of party going on. Who the hell is having a party, here? I take in the pointed hats and flowing capes, the pumpkins carried under their arms, and the penny drops. It must be Halloween. It's kind of hard to believe there's a world, time passing, outside the mystery of this apartment and Ben's disappearance. If I were still in Brighton I'd be dressed as a "sexy cat" right now, serving Jägerbombs to stag dos down from London. It's not much over forty-eight hours since I left that life but already it feels so far away, so long ago.

I see one bloke stop and pee in one of the flowerbeds while his friends look on, cackling. I slam the shutters closed, hoping that'll help block out some of the noise.

I sit here for a moment, the sounds beyond the windows muffled but still audible. Something has just occurred to me. There's a chance someone going to that party might know Ben; he's been living here for a few months, after all. Maybe I can learn more about this family. And frankly anything is better than sitting here, feeling surrounded and spied upon, not knowing what they might be planning for me.

I don't have a costume, but surely I can make use of something here. I stride into the bedroom and while the cat watches me curiously, sitting tucked into its haunches on top of Ben's chest of drawers, I tug the sheet off the bed. I find a knife in the drawer, stab some eye-holes into it and then chuck the thing over my head. I march into the bathroom to have a look, trying not to trip over the edges of the sheet. It's not going to win any prizes, but now I've got an outfit and a disguise in one, and frankly it's a hell of a lot better than a sodding sexy cat, the basic bitch of Halloween costumes.

I open the door to the apartment, listen. It sounds as though they're heading into the basement. I creep down the spiral staircase, following the music and the stream of guests down the stairwell into the *cave*, the thump of the bass getting louder and louder until I can feel it vibrating in my skull.

Nick

I'M ON MY THIRD CIGARETTE of the evening. I only took up smoking when I came back here; the taste disgusts me but I need the steadying hit of the nicotine. All those years of clean living and now look at me: sucking on a Marlboro like a drowning man taking his last breaths. I look down from my window as I smoke, watch the kids streaming into the courtyard. I almost kissed her this evening, up on the terrace. That moment, stretching out between the two of us. Until it seemed like the only thing that made sense.

Christ. If the lights hadn't gone off and shocked me out of my trance, I would have done. And where would I be now?

His sister. His *sister.*

What was I thinking?

I wander into the bathroom. Stub out the cigarette in the sink where it fizzles wetly. Look in the mirror.

Who do you think you are? my reflection asks me, silently. More importantly, *who does* she *think you are?*

The good guy. Eager to help. Concerned about his mate.

That's what she sees, isn't it? That's what you've let her believe.

You know, I read somewhere that sixty percent of us can't go more than ten minutes without lying. Little slippages: to make ourselves sound better, more attractive, to others. White lies to avoid causing offense. So it's not like I've done anything out of the ordinary. It's only human. But, really, the important thing to stress is I haven't actually lied to her. Not outright. I just haven't told her the whole truth.

It's not my fault she assumed I was British. Makes sense. I've honed my accent and my fluency pretty well over the years; made a big effort to do so when I was at Cambridge and didn't want to be known as "that French guy". Flattening my vowels. Hardening my consonants. Perfecting a kind of London drawl. It's always been a point of pride for me, a little thrill when Brits have mistaken me for one of them—just like she did.

The second thing she assumed was that the people in this building are nothing more than neighbors to one another. That was all her, honestly. I just didn't stand in the way of her believing it. To tell the truth, I liked her believing in him: Nick Miller. A normal guy, nothing to do with this place beyond the rent he paid on it.

Look. Can anyone say they've really never wished their family were less embarrassing, or different in some way? That they've never wondered what it might be like to be free of all those familial hang-ups? That baggage. And this family has rather more baggage than most.

I've heard from Papa this evening, incidentally. *Everything OK, son? Remember I'm trusting you to take care of things there.* The "son" was affectionate for him. He must really want me to do his bidding. But then my father excels at getting others to do his bidding. The second part is classic Papa, of course. *Ne merdes pas.* Do not mess this up.

I think of that dinner, during the heat wave. All of us summoned up to the roof terrace. The light purplish, the lanterns glowing among the fig trees, the warm scent of their leaves. The streetlamps coming on below us. The air thick as soup, like you had to swallow it rather than inhale.

Papa at one end of the table, my stepmother beside him in eau-de-nil silk and diamonds, cool as the night was hot, profile turned toward the skyline as though she were somewhere else entirely—or wished she were. I remember the first time Papa introduced us to Sophie. I must have been about nine. How glamorous she seemed, how mysterious.

At the other end of the table sat Ben: both guest of honor and fatted calf. Papa had invited him personally. He had made quite an impression at the drinks party.

"Now Ben," my father said, walking over with a new bottle of wine. "You must tell me what you think of this. It's clear you have an excellent palate. It's one of those things that cannot be learned, no matter how much of the stuff you drink."

I looked over at Antoine, well into his second bottle by now and wondered: had he caught the barb? Our father never says anything accidentally. Antoine is his supposed protégé: the one who's worked for him since he left school. But he's also Papa's whipping boy, even more so than I am—especially because he's had to take all the flak in the years I've been absent.

"Thank you, Jacques." Ben smiled, held out his glass.

As Papa poured a crimson stream into one of my mother's Lalique glasses he put a paternal hand on Ben's shoulder. Together they represented an ease that Papa and I had never had, and looking at them I felt a kind of ridiculous envy. Antoine had noticed, too. I saw his scowl.

But maybe this could work to my advantage. If my father liked Ben this much, someone I had invited into this house, into our family, perhaps there was some way he would finally accept me, his own son. A pathetic thing to hope, but there you have it. I've always had to hunt for scraps where paternal affection's concerned.

"I see that peevish expression of yours, Nicolas," my father said—using the French word, *maussade*—turning to me suddenly in that unnerving way of his. Caught out, I swallowed my wine too fast, coughed and felt the bitterness sting my throat. I don't even particularly like wine. Maybe the odd biodynamic variety— not the heavy, old-world stuff. "Quite incredible," he went on. "Same look exactly as your sainted dead mother. Nothing ever good enough for her."

Beside me I felt Antoine twitch. "That's her fucking wine you're pouring," he muttered, under his breath. My mother's was an old family: old blood, old wine from a grand estate: Château Blondin-Lavigne. The cellar with its thousands of bottles was part of her inheritance, left to my father on her death. And since her death, my brother, who has never forgiven her for leaving us, has been working his way through as many of them as possible.

"What was that, my boy?" Papa said, turning to Antoine. "Something you'd care to share with the rest of us?"

A silence expanded, dangerously. But Ben spoke into it with the exquisite timing of a first violin entering into his solo: "This is delicious, Sophie." We were eating my father's favorite (of course): rare fillet, cold, sautéed potatoes, a cucumber salad. "This beef might be the best I've ever tasted."

"I didn't cook it," Sophie said. "It came from the restaurant." No fillet for her, just cucumber salad. And I noticed that she didn't look at him, but at a point just beyond his right shoulder. Ben hadn't won her over, it seemed. Not yet. But I noticed how Mimi snatched furtive glances at him when she thought no one was looking at her, almost missing her mouth with her fork. How Dominique, Antoine's wife, gazed at him with a half-smile on her face, as though she'd prefer him to the meal before her. And all the while Antoine gripped his steak knife like he was planning to ram it between someone's ribs.

"Now, of course you've known Nicolas since you were boys," my father said to Ben. "Did he ever do any work at that ridiculous place?"

That ridiculous place meaning: Cambridge, one of the top universities in the world. But the great Jacques Meunier hadn't needed a college education, and look where he'd got himself. A self-made man.

"Or did he just piss away my hard-earned cash?" Papa asked. He turned to me. "You're pretty good at doing that, aren't you, my boy?"

That stung. A short while ago I invested some of that "hard-earned cash" in a health start-up in Palo Alto. Anyone who knew anything was buzzed about it: a pin-prick of blood, the future of healthcare. I used most of the money Papa had settled on me when I turned eighteen. Here was a chance to prove my mettle to him; prove my judgment in my own field was just as good as his . . .

"I can't speak for how hard he worked at uni," Ben said, with a wry grin in my direction—and it was a relief to have him cut the tension. "We took different courses. But we pretty much ran the student paper together—and a group of us traveled all over one summer. Didn't we, Nick?"

I nodded. Tried to match his easy smile but I had the feeling, suddenly, of sighting a predator in the long grass.

Ben went on: "Prague, Barcelona. Amsterdam—" I don't know if it was a coincidence, but our eyes met at that moment. His expression was impossible to read. Suddenly I wanted him to shut the fuck up. With a look I tried to convey this. *Stop. That's enough.* This was not the time to be talking about Amsterdam. My father could never find out.

Ben glanced away, breaking eye contact. And that was when I realized how reckless I had been, inviting him here.

Then there was a sound so loud it felt like the building itself might be collapsing under us. It took me a couple of seconds to realize it was thunder, and immediately afterward a streak of lightning lit the sky violet. Papa looked furious. He might control everything that happens in this place, but even he couldn't order the weather what to do. The first fat drops began to fall. The dinner was over.

Thank Christ.

I remembered to breathe again. But something had shifted.

Later that night, Antoine stormed into my room. "Papa and your English pal. Thick as thieves, aren't they? You know it would be just like him, right? Disinherit us and leave it all to some random fucking stranger?"

"That's insane," I said. It was. But even as I said it I could feel the idea taking root. It would be just like Papa. Always telling us, his own sons, how useless we were. How much of a disappointment to him. But would it be like Ben?

What had always made my mate intriguing was his very unknowability. You could spend hours, days, in his company—you could travel across Europe with him—and never be sure you'd got to the real Benjamin Daniels. He was a chameleon, an enigma. I had no idea, really, who I had invited under this roof, into the bosom of my family.

I REACH INTO the cabinet under the sink and grab the bottle of mouthwash, pour it into the little cup. I want to wash away the rank taste of the tobacco. The cabinet door is still open. There are the little pots of pills in their neat row. It would be so easy. So much more effective than the cigarettes. So helpful to feel a little less . . . present right now.

The fact of the matter is that while I've been pretending to Jess, I could almost pretend to myself: that I was a normal adult, living on his own, surrounded by the trappings of his own success. An apartment he paid the rent on. Stuff he'd bought with his own hard-earned cash. Because I want to be that guy, I really do. I've tried to be that guy. Not a thirty-something loser forced back to his father's house because he lost the shirt off his back.

Trust me—as much as I've tried to kid myself, it doesn't make a difference having a lock on the front door and a buzzer of your own. I'm still under his roof; I'm still infected by this place. And I regress, being here. It's why I escaped for a decade to the other side of the world. It's why I was so happy in Cambridge. It's why I went straight to meet Ben in that bar when he got in touch, despite Amsterdam. Why I invited him to live here. I thought his presence might make my sentence here more bearable. That his company would help me return to a different time.

So that's all it was, when I let her think I was someone and something else. A little harmless make-believe, nothing more sinister than that.

Honest.

Jess

THE VOICES ARE A ROAR of sound over the top of the music. I can't believe how many people are packed into the space down here: it must be well over a hundred. Fake cobwebs have been draped from the ceiling and candles placed along the floor, illuminating the rough walls. The scent of the burning wax is strong in the tight, airless space. The reflection of the dancing flames gives the impression that the stone is moving, wriggling like something alive.

I try to blend into the crowd. My costume is by far the worst one I can see. Most of the guests have gone all out. A nun in a white habit drenched in blood is kissing a woman who has painted her entire semi-naked body red and is wearing a pair of twisted devil horns. A plague doctor dressed from head to toe in a black cloak and hat lifts up the long, curved beak of his mask to take a drag from a cigarette and then lets the smoke blow out of the eyeholes. A tall tuxedo-clad figure with a huge wolf's head sips a cocktail through a straw. Everywhere I look there are mad monks, grim reapers, demons and ghouls. And a strange thing: the surroundings make all these figures seem more sinister than they would up above ground, in proper lighting. Even fake blood somehow looks more real down here.

I'm trying to work out how to insert myself into one of these groups of people and start a conversation about Ben. I also desperately need a drink.

Suddenly I feel my sheet wrenched off my head. A dead cowboy puts up his hands: "Oops!" He must have tripped over the trailing fabric. Crap, it's already grimy from the ground, wet with spilled beer. I scrunch it up into a dirty ball. I'll just have to do it without the disguise. There are so many people here I'm hardly going to stand out.

"Oh, *salut*!"

I turn to see a stupidly pretty girl wearing a huge flower crown and a floaty white peasant dress splattered with blood. It takes me a moment to place her: Mimi's flatmate. Camille: that was it.

"It's you!" she says. "You're Ben's sister, right?" So much for trying to blend in.

"Um. I hope this is OK? I heard the music—"

"*Plus on est de fous, plus on rit*, you know? The more the merrier! Hey, such a shame Ben isn't here." A little pout. "That guy seems to love a party!"

"So you know my brother?"

She wrinkles her tiny freckled nose. "Ben? *Oui, un peu*. A little."

"And they all like him? The Meuniers, I mean? The family?"

"But of course. Everyone loves him! Jacques Meunier likes him a lot, I think. Maybe even more than his own children. Oh—" She stops, like she's remembered something. "Antoine. He doesn't like him."

I remember the scene in the courtyard that first morning. "Do you think there might have been something . . . well, between my brother and Antoine's wife?"

The smile vanishes. "Ben and Dominique? *Jamais*." A fierceness to the way she says it. "They flirted. But it was nothing more than that."

I try a different tack. "You said you saw Ben on Friday, talking to Mimi on the stairs?"

She nods.

"What time was that? What I mean is . . . did you see him after that? Did you see him that night at all?"

A tiny hesitation. Then: "I wasn't here that night," she says. Now she seems to spot someone over my shoulder. "*Coucou Simone!*" She turns back to me. "I must go. Have fun!" A little wave of her hand. The carefree party girl seems to be back. But when I asked her about the night Ben disappeared, she didn't seem quite so happy-go-lucky. She suddenly seemed very keen to stop talking. And for a moment I thought I saw the mask slip. A glimpse of someone totally different underneath.

Mimi

FOURTH FLOOR

BY THE TIME I GET down to the *cave* there are already so many people crammed inside. I'm never good with crowds at the best of times, with people invading my space. Camille's friend Henri has brought his decks and a massive speaker and is playing "La Femme" at top volume. Camille's greeting newcomers at the entrance in her *Midsommar* dress, the flower crown wobbling on her head as she jumps up and throws her arms around people.

"Ah, *salut* Gus, Manu—*coucou* Dédé!"

No one pays me much attention even though it's my place. They've come for Camille, they're all her friends. I pour ten centimeters of vodka into a glass and start drinking.

"*Salut* Mimi."

I look down. *Merde*. It's Camille's friend LouLou. She's sitting on some guy's lap, drink in one hand, cigarette in the other. She's dressed as a cat; a headband with black lace ears, silk leopard-print slip dress falling off one shoulder. Long brown hair all tangled like she just got out of bed and her lipstick smudged but in a sexy way. The perfect Parisienne. Or like those Instagram cretins in their Bobo espadrilles and cat-eye liner doing fuck-me eyes at the lens. That's how people think French girls should look. Not like me with my home-cut mullet and pimples round my mouth.

"I haven't seen you for so long." She waves her cigarette—she's also one of those girls who lights cigarettes outside cafés but doesn't actually inhale, just holds them and lets the smoke drift everywhere while she gestures with her pretty little hands. Hot ash lands on my arm. "*I* remember," she says, her eyes widening. "It was at that bar in the park . . . August. *Mon Dieu*, I've never seen you like that. You were *crazy*." A cute little giggle for weirdo Mimi.

At this moment the music changes. And I can barely believe it but it's that song. "Heads Will Roll," by the Yeah Yeah Yeahs. It feels like fate. And suddenly I'm back there.

IT WAS TOO hot to be inside so I suggested to Camille we go to this bar, Rosa Bonheur, in the Parc des Buttes-Chaumont. I hadn't told Camille but knew Ben might be there. He was writing a piece on the bar; I'd heard him talking to his editor through the apartment's open windows.

Since he lent me that Yeah Yeah Yeahs record I'd Googled the lead singer, Karen O. I'd tried dressing like her and when I did I felt like someone else. I'd spent the afternoon cutting my hair into her short, jagged style. And that evening I put on my Karen O outfit: a thin white tank top, painted my lips red, ringed my eyes in black eyeliner. At the last moment I took off my bra.

"*Waouh!*" Camille breathed, when I came out. "You look so . . . different. Oh my God . . . I can see your *nénés*!" She grinned. "Who's this for?"

"*Va te faire foutre.*" I told her to fuck off because I was embarrassed. "It's not *for* anyone." And it was hardly anything compared to what she was wearing: a loose-knit gold mesh dress that stopped just below her *chatte*.

Outside the streets were so hot you could feel the burning pavement through the soles of your shoes and the air was shimmering with dust and exhaust fumes. And then the most horrible coincidence: just as we were leaving through the front gate there was Papa, coming in the other direction. Despite the heat I felt cold all over. I wanted to die. I knew the exact moment when he saw me; his expression shifting dangerously.

"*Salut*," Camille said, a little wave. He smiled at her—always a smile for Camille; like every other guy on earth. She was wearing a jacket buttoned over her dress so you couldn't see that she was pretty much naked beneath. I've noticed that she has this way of being exactly what men want her to be. With Papa she has always been so demure, so innocent, all "*oui Monsieur*" and "*non Monsieur*" from beneath her lowered eyelashes.

Papa turned from Camille to me. "What are you wearing?" he asked, his eyes glittering.

"I . . ." I stammered. "It's so hot, I thought . . ."

"*Tu ressembles à une petite putain.*" That's what he said. I remember it so clearly because I felt the words like they were being burned into me: I can still feel the sting of them now. *You look like a little slut.* He'd never spoken to me like that before. "And what have you done to your hair?"

I put my hand up, touched my new Karen O fringe.

"I'm ashamed of you. Do you hear me? Never dress like this again. Go and change."

His tone scared me. I nodded. "*D'accord, Papa.*"

We followed him back into the building. But as soon as he had disappeared into the penthouse, Camille grabbed my hand and we ran out of there and along the street to the Metro and I tried to forget about it, tried to be just another carefree nineteen-year-old out for the night.

The park felt like a jungle, not part of the city: steam rising up off the grass, the bushes, the trees. A big crowd around the bar. This buzz, this wild energy. I could feel the beat of the music deep

THE PARIS APARTMENT   193

under my rib cage, vibrating through my whole body. There were people wearing way less than me, less than Camille even: girls in tiny bikinis who'd probably spent the day sunbathing on the Paris Plages, those artificial beaches by the river they construct in the summer. The air smelled like sweat and suntan lotion and hot, dry grass and the sticky sweet of cocktails.

I drank my first Aperol Spritz like it was lemonade. I still felt sick about the look on Papa's face. *A little slut.* The way he spat out the words. I drank the second one quickly too. Then I didn't care so much.

The girl at the decks turned the music up and people started dancing. Camille took my hand and dragged me into the crowd. There were some friends of ours—no, hers—from the Sorbonne. There were pills going round from a little plastic baggie. That's not me. I drink but I never take drugs.

"*Allez Mimi,*" LouLou said, after she'd placed the tab on her tongue and swallowed it. "*Pourquoi pas?*" *Come on, Mimi. Why not?* "Just a half?"

And maybe I really had turned into someone else because I took the little half of the tab she held out to me. I kept it on my tongue for a second, let it dissolve.

After that it got blurry. Suddenly I was dancing and I was right in the middle of the crowd and I just wanted to carry on forever in the middle of all those sweaty bodies, these strangers. It seemed like everyone was smiling at me, love just pouring out of them.

People were dancing on tables. Someone lifted me up onto one. I didn't care. I was someone different, someone new. Mimi was gone. It was wonderful.

And then the song came on: "Heads Will Roll." At the same moment I looked over and I saw him. Ben. Down there, in the middle of the crowd. A pale gray T-shirt and jeans, despite the heat. A bottle of beer in his hand. It was like something from a film. I'd spent so much time watching him in his apartment, watching him across the table at dinner, it felt so weird to see him in the real world, surrounded by strangers. I had started to feel like he belonged to me.

And then he turned, like the pressure of my eyes had been enough for him to know I was there, and he raised a hand and smiled. There was a current running through me. I went to step toward him. But suddenly I was falling; I had forgotten about the table, and the ground was rushing up to meet me—

"Mimi. Mimi? Who are you here with?"

I couldn't see the others. All the faces that had seemed to be smiling before weren't now. I could see them looking and I could hear laughter and it seemed like I was surrounded by a pack of wild animals, teeth gnashing, eyes staring. But he was there; and I felt like he would keep me safe.

"I think you need some air." He put out his hand. I grasped hold of it. It was the first time he had touched me. I didn't want to let go, even after he had pulled me up. I didn't ever want to let go. He had beautiful hands, the fingers long, elegant. I wanted to put them in my mouth, to taste his skin.

The park was dark, so dark, away from the lights and sounds of the bar. Everything was a million miles away. The farther we went the more it felt like none of the rest of it was real. Just him. The sound of his voice.

We went down to the lake. He made to go and sit on a bench but I saw a tree right next to the water, roots spreading beneath the surface. "Here," I said. He sat down beside me. I could smell him: clean sweat and citrus.

He passed me an Evian bottle. Suddenly I was thirsty, so thirsty. "Not too much," he said. "Steady on—that's enough." He

took the bottle away from me. We sat there for a while in silence.
"How do you feel? Want to go back and find your friends?"

No. I shook my head. I didn't want that. I wanted to stay here
in the dark with the hot breeze moving the tall trees above us and
the lapping of the lake water against the banks.

"They're not my friends."

He took out a cigarette. "You want one? I suppose it might
help . . ."

I took one, put it between my lips. He went to pass me the
lighter. "You do it," I said.

I loved watching his fingers working the lighter, like he was
casting some spell. The tip lit, glowed. I sucked in the smoke.

"*Merci*," I said.

Suddenly the shadows under the next tree along seemed to
move. There was someone there. No . . . two people. Tangled
together. I heard a moan. Then a whisper: "*Je suis ta petite pute.*"
I'm your little whore.

Normally I would have looked away. I would have been so
embarrassed. But I couldn't take my eyes off them. The pill, the
darkness, him sitting so close—that most of all—it loosened
something inside me. Loosened my tongue.

"I've never had that," I whispered, looking toward the couple
under the tree. And I found myself telling him my most embarrassing secret. That while Camille brought back different guys
every week—sometimes girls, too—I'd never actually had sex
with anyone. Except right then I didn't feel embarrassed; it felt
like I could say anything.

"Papa's so strict," I said. I thought of how he had looked at me
earlier. *A little slut.* "He said this horrible thing this evening . . .
about how I looked. And sometimes I get this feeling, like he's
ashamed, like he doesn't really like me that much. He looks at
me, talks to me, like I'm an . . . an imposter, or something." I

didn't think I was explaining very well. I'd never said any of this to anyone. But Ben was listening and nodding and, for the first time, I felt heard.

Then he spoke. "You're not a little girl any longer, Mimi. You're a grown woman. Your father can't control you anymore. And what you just described? The way he makes you feel? Use it, to drive yourself. Use it for inspiration in your art. All true artists are outsiders." I looked at him. He'd spoken so fiercely. It felt like he was talking from experience. "I'm adopted," he said then. "In my opinion, families are overrated."

I looked toward him, sitting so close in the darkness. It made sense. It was part of that connection between us, the one I'd felt since the first time I saw him. We were both outsiders.

"And you know what?" he said—and his voice was still different than usual. More raw. More urgent. "It's not about where you came from. What kind of shit might have happened to you in the past. It's about who *you* are. What you do with the opportunities life presents to you."

And then he put his hand gently on my arm. The lightest touch. The pads of his fingertips were hot against my skin. The feeling seemed to travel straight from my arm right to the very center of me. He could have done anything to me right there in the dark and I'd have been his.

And then he smiled. "It looks good, by the way."

"*Quoi?*"

"Your hair."

I put my hand up to touch it. I could feel where the hair was sticking to my forehead with sweat.

He smiled at me. "It suits you."

And that was the moment. I leaned over and I grabbed hold of his face in both hands and kissed him. I wanted more. I half-clambered on top of him, tried to straddle him.

"Hey," he laughed, pulling back, pushing me gently away, wiping his mouth. "Hey, Mimi. I like you too much for that."

I got it, then. Not here; not like this: not for the first time. The first time between us had to be special. Perfect.

Maybe you could say it was the pill. But that was the moment I felt myself fall in love with him. I thought I had been in love once before but it didn't work out. Now I knew how false the other time had been. Now I understood. I'd been waiting for Ben.

THE SONG ENDS and the spell is broken. I'm back in the *cave*, surrounded by all these idiots in their stupid Halloween costumes. They're playing Christine and the Queens now, everyone howling along to the chorus. People shoving past me, ignoring me, like always.

Wait. I've just spotted a face in the crowd. A face that has no business being at this party.

Putain de merde.

What the hell is *she* doing here?

Jess

I MOVE THROUGH THE *CAVE*, deeper into the crowd of masked faces and writhing bodies. The party's getting wild; I'm pretty sure I spot a couple up against a wall having sex or something close to it and a little way on a small group doing lines. I wonder if the room full of wine has been locked. I reckon this many people could put quite a dent in those racks of bottles.

"*Veux-tu un baiser de vampire?*" a guy asks me. I see that he's dressed as Dracula in a plasticky cape and some fake fangs—it's almost as crap a costume as my ghost outfit was.

"Erm . . . sorry, what?" I say, turning toward him.

"A Vampire's Kiss," he says in English, with a grin. "I asked if you want one?" For a moment I wonder if he's suggesting we make out. Then I look down and realize he's holding out a glass swimming with bright red liquid.

"What's in it?"

"Vodka, grenadine . . . maybe some Chambord." He shrugs. "Mostly vodka."

"OK. Sure." I could do with some Dutch courage. He hands it over. I take a sip—Jesus, it's even more grim than it looks, the metallic hit of the vodka beneath the sticky sweet of the syrup and raspberry liqueur. It tastes like something we might have served at the Copacabana, and that's not a good thing. But it's worth it for the vodka, even if I'd really prefer to take it neat. I take another long glug, braced this time for the sweetness.

"I've never met you before," he says, sounding almost more French now he's speaking English. "What's your name?"

"Jess. You?"

"Victor. *Enchanté.*"

"Er . . . thanks." I get straight to the point. "Hey, do you know Ben? Benjamin Daniels. From the third floor?"

He makes a face. "*Non, désolé.*" He looks genuinely sorry to have let me down. "I like your accent," he adds. "It's cool. You're from London, *non?*"

"Yup," I say. It's not exactly true, but then where am I from, really?

"And you're a friend of Mimi's?"

"Er—yes, I suppose you could say that." As in: I've met her precisely twice and she's never seemed exactly delighted to see me, but I'm not going to go into particulars.

He raises his eyebrows in surprise, and I wonder if I've made some sort of mistake.

"It's just . . . most people here are friends of Camille. No one really knows Mimi. She—how do you say it in English?—keeps herself to herself. Kind of intense. A bit—" He makes a gesture that I take to mean: "cuckoo."

"I don't know her *that* well," I say, quickly.

"Some people don't get why Camille's friends with Mimi. But I say—you just have to look at Mimi's apartment to know why. Mimi's got rich parents. You know what I'm saying?" He points up toward the apartment. "In this part of town? Seriously expensive. That is some *sick crib.*" He attempts to do the last two words in a kind of American accent.

In other circumstances I could almost feel sorry for Mimi. That people would assume someone's only friends with you because of your money: that's rough. I mean, it's never a problem I've had to deal with, but still.

"So what are you?" he asks.

"What?" A beat, and then I realize he means my costume.

"Oh—right." Shit. I look down at my outfit: jeans and old bobbly sweater. "Well, I was a ghost but now I'm just an ex-barmaid who's sick of everyone's shit."

"*Quoi?*" He frowns.

"It's—er, a British thing," I tell him. "It might not translate."

"Oh right." He nods. "Cool."

An idea hits me. If Camille and Mimi are down here then no one is up there, in the apartment. I could take a look around.

"Hey," I say, "Victor—could you do me a favor?"

"Tell me."

"I really need to pee. But I don't think there's an, er—*toilette*—down here?"

He looks suddenly uncomfortable: clearly French boys get as embarrassed about such matters as their British counterparts.

"Could you ask Camille if we can borrow the key to the place?" I smile my most winning smile, the one I'd use on the big tippers at the bar. Little hair flip. "I'd be *so* grateful."

He grins back. "*Bien sûr.*"

Bingo. Maybe Ben's not the only one with the charm.

I sip my drink while I wait: it's growing on me, now. Or maybe that's the vodka kicking in. Victor comes back a few minutes later, holds up a key.

"Amazing," I say, holding out my hand.

"I'll come with you," he says, with a grin. Crap. I wonder what he thinks is going to come out of this. But maybe it helps me look less suspicious if we go together.

I follow Victor up out of the *cave*, up the dark staircase. We take the lift—his suggestion—and we end up pressed against each other as there's barely room for one person. I can smell his breath—cigarettes and vodka, not a totally unappealing combination. And he's not bad-looking. But too pretty for my liking; you could cut a lemon on his jawline. Besides, he's basically a child.

I have a sudden flashback to Nick and me a couple of hours ago on the roof terrace. That moment, after he'd taken the leaf out of my hair—when he didn't move away as quickly as he should have. That snatched piece of time, just before the lights went out, when I was convinced he was going to kiss me. What would have happened if it hadn't suddenly gone dark? If I hadn't gone sneaking into the rest of the apartment and found that photograph? Would we have gone back to his apartment, fallen into his bed together—

"You know, I've always wanted to be with an older woman," Victor says, earnestly, jolting me back into the real world.

Steady on, mate, I think. And besides, I'm only twenty-eight.

The lift grinds to a halt on the fourth floor. Victor unlocks the door to the apartment. There are a load of bottles and crates of beer stacked in the main room—must be extra party supplies.

"Hey," I say. "Why don't you fix us a couple more drinks while I go and pee? This time big on the vodka please, less of the red stuff."

There's a corridor leading off the main room with several doors. The layout reminds me a little of the penthouse flat, only everything here is more cramped and instead of original artworks on the walls there are peeling posters—CINDY SHERMAN: CENTRE POMPIDOU and a tour list for someone called DINOS. The first room I come to is an absolute tip: the floor scattered with clothes, lace lingerie in bright sorbet colors and shoes—bras and thongs tangled around the sharp points of heels. A dressing table covered in makeup, about twenty mashed lipsticks all missing their lids. The air's so heavily scented with perfume and cigarette smoke it gives me an instant headache. A huge poster on one wall of Harry Styles in a tutu and, on the opposite, Dua Lipa in a tux. I think of Mimi and her scowl, her jagged, grungy fringe. I'm pretty sure this isn't her vibe. I close the door.

The next room has to be Mimi's. Dark walls. Big black and white angry prints on the walls—one of a freaky, blank-eyed woman—lots of serious-looking arty tomes on the bookshelf. A record player with a load of vinyls in a special case next to it. The one on the turntable is by the Yeah Yeah Yeahs: *It's Blitz!*

I creep across to the window. It turns out that Mimi's got a perfect diagonal view into the main living space of Ben's apartment, across the courtyard. I can see his desk, the sofa. Interesting. I think of her dropping her wine glass earlier when I spoke about Ben. She's hiding something, I know it.

I open the cupboard, search through drawers of clothes. Nothing to note. It's all so neat, almost anally so. But the problem is I don't know what I'm looking for—and I suspect I don't have much time before Victor starts wondering why I'm taking so long.

I get on my knees and grope around under the bed. My hand connects with what feels like material wrapped around something harder, wood maybe, and I just know I've found something significant. I get a hold of the whole lot, pull it toward me. A piece of gray material falls open to reveal a ragged pile of artists' canvases, slashed and torn into pieces. So much mess and chaos compared to the rest of the room.

I look more closely at the material they were wrapped in. It's a gray T-shirt with Acne on the label, an exact match for the ones in Ben's cupboard. I'm sure it's one of his. It even smells like his cologne. Why has Mimi been keeping her art stuff in one of Ben's T-shirts? More importantly: why has she got one of Ben's T-shirts at all?

"Jessie?" Victor calls. "Are you OK, Jessie?"

Shit. It sounds like he's getting closer.

I start trying to fit some of the scraps of canvas back together as quickly as I can. It's like doing a really messy jigsaw puzzle. Finally I've pieced enough pieces of the first one together to see the picture. I stand back. It's a really good likeness. She's even managed to get his smile, which others have called charming but I'd definitely tell him makes him look like a smarmy git. Here he is, right in front of me. Ben. Just as he is in life.

Except for one terrible, terrifying difference. I lift a hand to my mouth. His eyes have been removed.

"Jessie?" Victor calls again, "*où es-tu,* Jessie?"

I fit the next image together, and the next. Jesus. They're all of him. There's even one of him lying down and—Christ alive, that's way more of my brother than I ever needed to see. In every single one the eyes have been destroyed, punched or torn out with something.

I had a feeling Mimi was lying about knowing him the first time I met her. I suspected she was hiding something as soon as her wine glass hit the floor in Sophie Meunier's apartment. But I never expected anything like this. If these are anything to go by—if that nude painting is any clue—she knows Ben very well indeed. And feels strongly enough about him to have done some pretty serious damage to these paintings: those tears in the fabric could only have been made with something really sharp, or with a lot of force—or both.

I stand up but as I do a strange thing happens. It's like the whole room tilts with the movement. Whoa. I go to steady myself against the nightstand. I try to blink away the dizziness. I take a step backward and it happens again. As I stand, trying to get my balance, it feels like the ground is rolling around under my feet and everything around me is made of jelly, the walls collapsing inward.

I stagger out of the bedroom, into the corridor. I have to keep a hand out on both sides to stop myself from keeling over. And then Victor appears, at the end of the passage.

"Jessie—there you are. What were you doing?" He's walking toward me down the dark corridor. He smiles and his teeth are very white—just like a real vampire. My only way out is past him; he's blocking my escape. Even with my brain turned to syrup I know what this is. You don't work in twenty different divey bars and not know what this is. The drink some guy's offered to buy you, the freebie that is anything but. I never, ever fall for that shit. What the hell was I thinking? How could I have been so stupid? It's always the pretty ones, the seemingly harmless ones, the so-called nice guys.

"What the fuck was in that drink, Victor?" I ask.

And then everything goes black.

Mimi

FOURTH FLOOR

MORNING. I'M SITTING ON THE balcony watching the light seep into the sky. The joint I stole from Camille hasn't helped me relax: it's just making me feel sick and even more jittery. I feel . . . I feel like I'm trapped inside my own skin. Like I want to claw my way out.

I hurry out of the apartment and run down the twisting stairway to the *cave*, not wanting to meet anyone on the way. It's full of the detritus from the party last night: broken glass and spilled drinks and dropped accessories from people's costumes—wigs and devil's forks and witches' hats. I normally like it better down here, in the dark and the quiet: another place to hide away. But right now I can't be here either because his Vespa is there, leaning against the wall.

I don't—can't—look at it as I pull my bicycle from the rack beside it.

He always went out on that Vespa. I wanted to know about his life, I wanted to follow him into the city, see where he went, what he did, who he met with, but it was impossible because he used that bike to go everywhere. So one day I went down into the *cave* and I stabbed a small hole into the front wheel with the very sharp blade of my canvas-cutting knife. That was better.

He wouldn't be able to use it for a few days. I only did it because I loved him.

That afternoon I saw him leave on foot. My plan had worked. I went after him, followed him into the Metro and got onto the next carriage. He got off in this really shitty part of town. What the hell was he doing there? He went and sat down in this greasy-looking kebab place. I sat in a shisha bar across the road and ordered a Turkish coffee and tried to look like I fitted in among all the old guys puffing away on their rose-scented tobacco. Ben was making me do things I never normally would, I realized. He was making me brave.

Ten minutes or so later a girl came and joined Ben. She was tall and thin, a hood up over her head, which she only took down once she was sitting opposite him. I felt my stomach turn over when I saw her face. Even from across the street I could see that she was beautiful: dark chocolate hair with a sharp fringe that looked so much better than my home-cut one, a model's cheek-bones. And young: probably only my age. Yes, her clothes were bad: a fake-looking leather jacket with that hoodie underneath and cheap jeans, but they somehow made her seem even more beautiful by contrast. As I watched them together I could actually feel my heart hurting, a hot coal burning behind my rib cage.

I waited for him to kiss her, to touch her face, her hand, to stroke her hair—anything—waited for the worse pain I knew would come when I saw him do it. But nothing happened. They just sat there talking. I realized it seemed quite formal. Like they didn't actually know each other that well. There was defi-nitely nothing between them to suggest they might be lovers. Finally he passed her something. I tried to see. It looked like a phone or a camera, maybe. Then she got up and left, and he did too. They went in different directions. I still couldn't work out why he'd been talking to her, or what he might have given her, but I was so relieved I could have cried. He hadn't been unfaithful to me. I knew I shouldn't have doubted him.

Later, back in my room, I thought of that night in the park, how we'd shared that cigarette. The two of us in the dark by the lake. The taste of his mouth when I'd kissed him. I thought about it when I lay in bed at night, fingers exploring. And I whispered those words I heard in the darkness by the lake. *Je suis ta petite pute.* I'm your little whore.

This was it, I knew it. This was why I'd waited so long. I was different from Camille. I couldn't just screw around with random guys. It had to be something real. *Un grand amour.* I had thought I'd been in love before. The art teacher, Henri, at my school—Les Soeurs Servantes du Sacré Coeur. I'd known we had a connection from the beginning. He'd smiled at me in that first lesson, told me how talented I was. But later, when I sent him the paintings I had made of him, he took me aside and told me they weren't appropriate—even though I'd worked so hard on them, on getting the proportions right, the tone: just like he'd taught us. And when I sent them to his wife instead, but cut up into little pieces, they made some kind of formal complaint. And then—well, I don't want to go into all that. I heard they left for another school abroad.

I didn't know where this part of me had been hiding. The part that could fall in love. Actually: I did. I'd been keeping it locked away. Deep down inside me. Terrified that sort of weakness would make me vulnerable again. But I was ready now. And Ben was different. Ben would be loyal to me.

DOWN IN THE *cave*, I tear my eyes away from his Vespa. I feel like there's a metal band around my ribs stopping me from taking in enough air. And in my ears still this horrible rushing sound, the white noise, the storm. I just need to make it stop.

I yank my bike free and haul it up the stairs. I can feel the pressure building inside me as I wheel it across the courtyard, as I push it along the cobbled street . . . all the way down to the main road where the morning rush-hour traffic is roaring past. I jump onto the saddle, look quickly in each direction through the tears blurring my eyes, push straight out into the street.

There's a screech of brakes. The blare of a horn. Suddenly I'm lying on my side on the tarmac, the wheels spinning. My whole body feels bruised and torn. My heart's pounding.

That was so close.

"You stupid little bitch," the van driver screams, hanging out of his open window and gesturing at me with his cigarette. "What the fuck were you doing? What the hell were you think-ing, pulling out into the road without looking?"

I yell back, my language even worse than his. I call him *un fils de pute*, son of a whore, *un sac a merde*, a bag of shit . . . I tell him he can go fuck himself. I tell him he can't drive for shit.

Suddenly the front door of the apartment building clangs open and the concierge is running out. I've never seen that woman move so fast. She always seems so old and hunched. But maybe she moves more quickly when you're not looking. Because she's always there when you least expect to see her. Appearing around corners and out of shadows, lurking in the background. I don't know why we even have a concierge. Most places don't have them any longer. We should have just installed a modern intercom sys-tem. It would be much better than having her around, snooping on everyone. I don't like the way she watches. Especially how she watches me.

Without saying anything she puts out her hands, helps me to stand up. She's much stronger than I ever would have guessed.

Then she looks at me closely; intensely. I feel like she's trying to tell me something. I look away. It makes me think she knows something. Like maybe she knows everything.

I throw off her hand. "*Ça va*," I say. *I'm OK.* "I can get up on my own."

My knees are still stinging like a kid's who has taken a tumble in the playground. And my bike chain has come off. But that's the worst of it.

It could have ended so differently. If I hadn't been such a coward. Because the truth is, I *was* looking. That was the point.

I knew exactly what I was doing.

It was so close. Just not close enough.

Sophie

I DESCEND THE STAIRCASE WITH Benoit trotting at my heels. As I pass the third floor I pause. I can feel her there behind the door, like something poisonous at the heart of this place.

It was the same with him. His presence upset the building's equilibrium. I seemed to see him everywhere after that dinner on the terrace: in the stairwell, crossing the courtyard, talking to the concierge. We never talk to the concierge beyond issuing instructions. She is a member of staff, that sort of divide must be respected. Once I even saw him following her into her cabin. What could they be speaking about in there? What might she be telling him?

When the third note came, it wasn't left in the letterbox. It was pushed beneath the door of the apartment, at a time when I suppose my blackmailer knew Jacques would be out. I had returned from the boulangerie with Jacques' favorite quiche, which I have bought for him every Friday for as long as I can remember. When I saw the note I dropped the box I was holding. Pastry shattered across the floor. It sent a thrill through me that I knew had to be fear but for a moment felt almost like excitement. And that was just as disturbing.

I had been invisible for so long, any currency spent long ago. But these notes, even as they frightened me, felt like the first time in a very long while that I had been seen.

I knew I could not stay in the building for a moment longer.

Outside the streets were still white with heat, the air shimmering. At the cafés tourists clustered at pavement tables and sweated into their *thé glacés* and *citron pressés* and wondered why they didn't feel refreshed. But in the restaurant it was dim and cool as some underwater grotto, as I had known it would be. Dark paneled walls, white tablecloths, huge paintings upon the walls. They had given me the best table, of course—Meunier SARL has supplied them with rare vintages over the years—and the air-conditioning sent an icy plume down the back of my silk shirt as I sipped my mineral water.

"Madame Meunier." The waiter came over. "*Bienvenue.* The usual?"

Every time I have eaten there with Jacques I have ordered the same. The endive salad with walnuts and tiny dabs of Roquefort. An aging wife is one thing; a fat wife is another.

But Jacques was not there.

"*L'entrecôte,*" I said.

The waiter looked at me as though I had asked for a slab of human flesh. The steak has always been Jacques' choice.

"But Madame," he said, "it is so *hot*. Perhaps the oysters—we have some wonderful *pousses en Claire*—or a little salmon, cooked *sous vide . . .*"

"The steak," I repeated. "Blue."

The last time I ate steak was when a gynecologist, all those years ago, prescribed it for fertility; doctors here still recommend red meat and wine for many ailments. Months of eating like a caveman. When that didn't work came the indignity of the treatments. The injections into my buttocks. Jacques' glances of vague disgust. I had inherited two stepsons. What was this obsession with having a child? I could not explain that I simply wanted someone to love. Wholehearted, unreserved, requited. Of course, the treatments didn't work. And Jacques refused to adopt. The paperwork, the scrutiny into his business affairs—he would not stand for it.

The steak came and I cut into it. Watched as the blood ran thin and palest pink from the incision. It was then that I looked up and saw him, Benjamin Daniels, in the corner of the restaurant. He had his back to me, though I could see his reflection in the mirror that ran along the wall. Something elegant about the line of his back: the way he sat, hands in his pockets. The posture of someone very comfortable in their own skin.

I felt my pulse quicken. What was he doing here?

He glanced up and "caught" me watching him in the mirror. But I suspected he knew I was there all along, had been waiting for me to notice him. His reflection raised the glass of beer.

I looked away. Sipped my mineral water.

A few seconds later, a shadow fell across the table. I looked up. That ingratiating smile. He wore a crumpled linen shirt and shorts, legs bare and brown. His clothes were entirely inappropriate for the restaurant's formality. And yet he seemed so relaxed in the space. I hated him for it.

"Hello Sophie," he said.

I bristled at the familiarity, then remembered I had asked him not to call me "Madame." But the way he said my name: it felt like a transgression.

"May I?" He indicated the chair. To do anything other than agree would have been rude. I nodded, to show I didn't care either way what he did.

It was the first time I had been so close to him. Now I saw that he wasn't handsome, not in the traditional sense. His features were uneven. His confidence, charisma: that was what made him attractive.

"What are you doing here?" I asked.

"I'm reviewing the place," he said. "Jacques suggested it at dinner. I haven't eaten yet but I'm already impressed by the space—the atmosphere, the art."

I glanced at the painting he was looking at. A woman on her knees: powerfully built, almost masculine. Strong limbs, strong jaw. Nothing elegant about her, only a kind of feral strength. Her head thrown back, howling at the moon like a dog. The splayed legs, the skirt rucked . . . it was almost sexual. If you could get close enough to sniff it, I imagined it wouldn't be paint you smelled but blood. I felt suddenly very aware of the sweat that might have soaked into the silk beneath my arms on the walk over here, hidden half-moons of damp in the fabric.

"What do you think?" he asked. "I love Paula Rego."

"I'm not sure I agree," I said.

He pointed to my lip. "You have a little—just there."

I put the corner of the napkin up to my mouth and dabbed. Took it away and saw that the thick white linen was stained with blood. I stared at it.

He coughed. "I sense—look, I just wanted to say that I hope we haven't got off on the wrong foot. The other day—when I commented on your accent. I hope I didn't seem rude."

"*Mais non*," I said. "What would make you think that?"

"Look, I took French studies at Cambridge, you see, I'm just fascinated by such things."

"I was not offended," I told him. "*Pas du tout.*" *Not at all.*

He grinned. "That's a relief. And I enjoyed the dinner on the roof terrace so much. It was kind of you to invite me."

"I didn't invite you," I said. "That dinner was all Jacques' idea." Perhaps it sounded rude. But it was also true. No invitation would be offered without Jacques' say-so.

"Poor Jacques, then," he said, with a rueful smile. "The weather that night! I've never seen anyone so furious. I actually thought he was going to try and take the storm on, like Lear. The look on his face!"

I laughed. I couldn't help it. I should have been appalled, offended. No one made a joke at my husband's expense. But it was the surprise of it. And he'd pulled such an accurate impression of Jacques' outraged expression.

Trying to regain my composure I reached for my water, took a sip. But I felt lighter than I had in a very long time.

"Tell me," he said, "what is it like being married to a man like Jacques Meunier?"

The sip caught in my throat. Now I was coughing, my eyes watering. One of the waiters ran forward to offer assistance: I waved him away with a hand. All I could think was: what did Ben know? What could Nicolas have told him?

"Sorry." He gave a quick smile. "I don't think my question came out quite right. Sometimes I can be so clumsy in French. What I meant was: being married to such a successful businessman. What's it like?"

I didn't answer. The look I gave him by way of reply said: *you don't frighten me.* Except I was frightened. He was the sender of the notes, I was certain of it now. He was the one collecting those envelopes of cash I left beneath the loose step.

"I just meant," he said, "that should you ever want to give an interview, I'd be so interested to talk to you. You could talk about what it is to run such a successful business—"

"It's not my business."

"Oh, I'm sure that isn't true. I'm sure you must—"

"No." I leaned across the table to emphasize the point, tapped out each word with a fingernail on the tablecloth. "The business is nothing to do with me. *Comprenez-vous?* Do you understand?*

"OK. Well." He looked at his watch. "The offer still stands. It could be . . . more of a lifestyle piece. On you as the quintessential Parisienne, something like that. You know where I am." He smiled.

I just looked at him. *Perhaps you don't understand who you're dealing with, here. There are things I have had to do to get to where I am. Sacrifices I have had to make. People I have had to climb over. You are nothing compared to all that.*

"Anyway," he stood. "I better be going. I have a meeting with my editor. I'll see you around."

When I was sure he had gone I called the waiter over. "The 1998."

His eyes widened. He looked as though he was about to offer an alternative to such a heavy red in that heat. Then he saw my expression. He nodded, scurried away, returned with the bottle.

As I drank I remembered a night early in my marriage. The Opéra Garnier, where we watched *Madame Butterfly* beneath Chagall's painted ceiling and sipped chilled champagne in the bar in the interval and I hoped Jacques might show me the famous reliefs of the moon and the sun painted in pure gold on the domed ceilings of the little chambers at each end. But he was more interested in pointing out people, clients of his. Ministers for certain governmental departments, businessmen, significant figures from the French media. Some of them even I recognized, though they didn't know me. But they all knew Jacques. Returning his nod with tight little nods of their own.

I knew exactly what sort of man I was marrying. I went into the whole thing clear-eyed. I knew what I'd be getting out of it. No, our marriage would not always be perfect. But what marriage is? And he gave me my daughter, in the end. I could forgive anything for that.

* * *

NOW, I PAUSE for a moment on the landing outside the third-floor apartment. Stare at the brass number 3. Remember standing in this exact spot all those weeks ago. I'd spent the rest of the afternoon at the restaurant, drinking my way through the 1998 vintage as all the waiters no doubt watched, appalled. *Madame Meunier has gone mad.* As I drank I thought about Benjamin Daniels and his impertinence, about the notes, the horrible power they had over me. My rage blossomed. For the first time in a long time I felt truly alive. As though I might be capable of anything.

I came back to the apartment as dusk was falling, climbed the stairs, stood on this same spot and knocked on his door.

Benjamin answered it quickly, before I had a chance to change my mind.

"Sophie," he said. "What a pleasant surprise."

He was wearing a T-shirt, jeans; his feet were bare. There was music playing on the record player behind him, a record spinning round lazily. An open beer in his hand. It occurred to me that he might have someone there with him, which I hadn't even considered.

"Come in," he said. I followed him into the apartment. I suddenly felt as though I was trespassing, which was absurd. This was my home, he was the intruder.

"Can I get you a drink?" he asked.

"No. Thank you."

"Please—I have some wine open." He gestured to his beer bottle. "It's wrong—my drinking while you don't."

Somehow he had already managed to wrong-foot me, by being so gracious, so charming. I should have been prepared for it.

"No," I said. "I don't want any. This is not a social visit." Besides, I could still feel my head swimming from the wine I had drunk in the restaurant.

He grimaced. "I apologize," he said. "If this is about the

restaurant—my questions—I know that was presumptuous of me. I realize I crossed a line."

"It's not that." My heart was beating very fast. I had been carried here by my anger, but now I felt afraid. Voicing this thing would bring it into the light, would finally make it real. "It's you, isn't it?"

He frowned. "What?" He hadn't expected this, I thought. Now it was his turn to be on the back foot. It gave me the confidence I needed to go on.

"The notes."

He looked nonplussed. "Notes?"

"You know what I'm talking about. The notes—the demands for payment. I have come to tell you that you do not want to threaten me. There is little I will not do to protect myself. I will . . . I will stop at nothing."

I can still hear his awkward, apologetic laugh. "Madame Meunier—Sophie—I'm so sorry but I have literally no idea what you're talking about. What notes?"

"The ones you have been leaving for me," I said. "In my letter-box. Under my door."

I watched his face so carefully, but I saw only confusion. Either he was a consummate actor, which I wouldn't have put past him, or what I was saying really didn't mean anything to him. Could it be true? I looked at him, at his bemused expression, and I realized, in spite of myself, that I believed him. But it didn't make sense. If not him, then who?

"I—" The room seemed to tilt a little: a combination of the wine I had drunk and this new realization.

"Would you like to sit down?" he asked.

And I did sit, because suddenly I wasn't sure that I could stand.

He poured me a glass of wine without asking, this time. I needed it. I took the offered glass and tried not to hold the stem so tightly that it snapped.

He sat down next to me. I looked at him—this man who had been a thorn in my side since he arrived, who had occupied so much space in my thoughts. Who had made me feel seen—with all the discomfort that came with that—just when I thought I had become invisible for good. Invisible had been safe, if occasionally lonely. But I had forgotten how exciting it could feel to be seen.

I was in a kind of trance, perhaps. All the wine I had drunk before coming here to face him. The pressure that had been building in me for weeks as my blackmailer taunted me. The loneliness that had been growing for years in secrecy and silence.

I leaned over and I kissed him.

Almost immediately I pulled away. I could not believe what I had done. I put a hand up to my face, touched my hot cheek.

He smiled at me. I hadn't seen this smile before. This was something new. Something intimate and secret. Something just for me.

"I—I need to leave." I put my wine glass down and as I did I knocked his beer bottle to the ground. "Oh, *mon Dieu*. I'm sorry—"

"I don't care about the beer." And then he cradled my head in his hands and pulled me toward him and kissed me back.

The scent of him, the foreignness of it, the alien feel of his lips on mine, the loss of my self-control: these were all a surprise. But not the kiss itself, not really. In some part of myself I had known I wanted him.

"Ever since that first day," he said, as though he were echoing my own thoughts, "when I saw you in the courtyard, I've wanted to know more about you."

"That's ridiculous," I said, because it was. But what made it feel less so was the way he was looking at me.

"It's not. I've been hoping to do that ever since that night at your drinks party. When it was just the two of us in your husband's study—"

I thought of the outrage I had felt, finding him in there looking at that photograph. The fear. But fear and desire are so tangled up in one another, after all.

"That's absurd," I said. "What about Dominique?"

"Dominique?" He seemed genuinely confused.

"I saw you two together at the drinks."

He laughed. "She could eye-fuck a statue. And it was convenient for me to be able to distract your husband from the fact that I was lusting after his wife."

He reached out and pulled me toward him again.

"This can't happen . . ."

But I think he heard my lack of conviction because he grinned. "I hate to say it. But it already *is* happening."

"We have to be careful," I whispered a few minutes later as I began unbuttoning my shirt. As I revealed the lingerie that had been bought at great expense but hardly ever seen by eyes other than my own. Revealed my body, denied so much pleasure, kept and kempt for a man who barely glanced at it.

He dropped to his knees in front of me, as though worshipping at my feet. Pushed down the tight wool of my trousers, finding the thin lace of my knickers with his lips, opening his mouth against me.

Nick

I DIDN'T SLEEP WELL LAST night, and not just because of the bass from the party in the *cave* thumping up the stairwell all night. In the bathroom I shake two more little blue pills into my hand. They're about the only thing keeping me functioning right now. I toss them back.

I wander out into the apartment. As I pass the iMac the screen flickers to life. Did I jolt it? If so I didn't notice. But there it is. The photograph of Ben and me. I stand frozen in place in front of it. Drawn to it in the same way, I suppose, that a self-harmer is drawn to run the razor blade over the skin of their wrist.

After that dinner on the rooftop everything was different. Something had shifted. I didn't like the way Papa had favored Ben. I didn't like the way Ben's eyes slid away from mine when he talked about our Europe trip. I also very much didn't like the fact that every time I suggested we go for a drink, he was too busy. Had to rush off to see his editor, to review some new restaurant. Avoiding my calls, my texts, avoiding my eye when we met on the stairs.

This wasn't how it was supposed to be. It wasn't what I'd planned when I had offered him the apartment. He had been the one to get in touch with me. His email had blown open the past. I had taken a huge risk, inviting him here. I had assumed we had an unspoken agreement.

I walk across to the wall behind my iMac, run my hands over the surface. Feel the thin crack in the plaster. There's a second staircase here. A hidden one. Antoine and I used to play in it when we were kids. Used it to hide from Papa, too, when he was in one of his dangerous moods. I am ashamed to admit this, but there were a couple of times when I used it to watch Ben, peering into his apartment, into his life. Trying to work out what he was up to. Wondering what he could be writing so busily on his laptop, who he was calling on his mobile—I strained to hear the words, but caught nothing.

Though he snubbed me, it seemed he did have time for the other residents of this place. I found them in the *cave* one afternoon when I came down to do my washing. Heard the laughter, first. Then Papa's voice: "Of course, when I inherited the business from their mother it was a mess. Had to make it profitable. Have to be creative now, with a wine business. Especially when the estate's no longer producing and it'll all turn to vinegar soon. Have to find ways to diversify."

"What's going on?" I called. "A private tasting?"

They stepped out of the wine cellar like two naughty schoolboys. Papa holding a bottle in one hand, two glasses in the other. Ben's teeth when he smiled were tinted from the wine he'd drunk. He held one of the few remaining magnum bottles of the 1996 vintage. A gift from my father, it seemed.

"Nicolas," Papa drawled. "I suppose you've come to break up the party?"

Not: *Would you like to join us, son? Care for a glass?* In all the time I have lived under his roof my father has never suggested the two of us do anything like their cozy little wine tasting. It was salt in the wound. The first proper betrayal. I'd told Ben what sort of man my father really is. Had he forgotten?

* * *

BEN GRINS OUT at me from the photograph on the screensaver. And there I am grinning away next to him, like the fool that I was. July, Amsterdam. The sun in our eyes. Talking to Jess has brought it all back. That evening Ben and I spent in the weed café. Telling him all about my birthday, the "gift" from Papa. How it was like a catharsis. How I felt cleansed, purged of it all.

Afterward, Ben and I wandered out into the darkening streets. Just kept walking, chatting. I wasn't sure where we were going; I don't think he had a clue either. Somewhere along the way we'd left the touristy part of town and the crowds behind: these canals were quieter, more dimly lit. Elegant old houses with long windows through which you could see people inside: talking over glasses of wine, eating dinner, a guy typing at a desk. This was somewhere people actually lived.

You couldn't hear anything other than the lapping of the water against the stone banks. Black water, black as ink, the lights from the houses dancing on it. And the smell, like moss and mold. An ancient smell. No queasy clouds of weed to walk through, here. I was sick of the reek of it. Sick, too, of the crush of other people's bodies, the chatter of other people's conversation. I was sick even of the two other guys: their voices, the stink of their pits, their sweaty feet. We'd spent too long together that summer. I'd heard every joke or story they had to tell. With Ben it was different, somehow—though I couldn't put my finger on why.

This quiet: I felt like I wanted to drink it in like a cold glass of water. It felt magical . . . And telling Ben all that stuff about my dad—you know when you've eaten something bad and after you vomit you feel empty but also kind of cleansed, almost better than before in some indefinable way?

"Thanks," I said again. "For listening. You won't tell anyone, will you? The other guys?"

"No, of course not," he said. "This is our secret, mate. If you like."

We were walking along a part of the canal now that was even darker; I think a couple of the lamps had stopped working. It was deathly quiet.

You know those moments in life that seem to happen so smoothly it feels like they've been scripted in advance? This was like that. I don't remember any conscious decision to move toward him. But the next thing I knew, I was kissing him. It was definitely me that made the first move, I know that—even if it was like my body moved before my brain had worked out what it was going to do.

I'd kissed plenty of people. Girls, I mean. Only ever girls. At house parties, or drunk after a formal, a college ball. Fooled around. And it wasn't unpleasant. But it had never felt any more intimate or exciting than, I don't know, a handshake. It didn't disgust me, exactly, but the whole time it was happening I'd found myself thinking about the logistical things—like whether I was using my fingers and tongue right, feeling a little queasy about how much saliva was being passed back and forth between us. It felt like a sport I was practicing, maybe trying to get better at. It never felt like something exciting, something that made my pulse quicken.

But this—this was different. It was as innate as breathing. It was strange how firm his mouth seemed after the softness of the girls' I'd kissed—I wouldn't have thought there would be a difference. And it seemed so right, somehow. Like it was the thing I had been waiting for, the thing that made sense.

I took hold of the chain around his neck, the one I had watched so many times appear and disappear beneath the line of his shirt, the one with the little figure of the saint hanging from it. I gave it a little tug, pulled him closer to me.

And then we were moving backward into the darkness—I

was pushing him into some secret corner, falling to my knees in front of him, again every movement so fluid, like it had all been written out in advance, like it was meant to be. Unzipping his fly and taking him in my mouth, the warmth and hardness, the secret scent of his skin. My knees stung where I knelt on the rough cobblestones. And even though I had never allowed myself to think about this, I must have thought about it, somewhere in my subconscious, somewhere in my deepest thoughts hidden even from myself, because I knew exactly what I was doing.

He smiled, afterward. A sleepy, lazy, stoned smile.

But for me, after that rush of euphoria, there was an immediate descent. I've never had a comedown like it. My knees hurt, my jeans were damp from something I'd knelt in.

"Fuck. Fuck—I don't know what happened there. Shit. I'm just . . . I'm so wasted." Which was a lie. I had been stoned, yes. But I'd never felt more clear-headed in my life. I'd never felt more alive, either—electric, wired—so many different things.

"*Mate*," he said, with a smile. "It's nothing to be worried about. We were a bit pissed, a lot stoned." He gestured around us, shrugged. "And it's not like anyone saw."

I couldn't believe how relaxed he was about it. But maybe at the back of my mind I'd known this about him; this side of him. I'd once heard someone at Cambridge describe him as an "omnivore"; wondered what that meant.

"Don't tell anyone," I told him. I was light-headed with fear, suddenly. "Look, you don't understand. This—it has to stay just between us. If it somehow got back . . . look, my dad, he wouldn't get it." The thought of him finding out was like a punch to the gut, it winded me just thinking about it. I could see his face, hear his voice. Could still remember what he'd said when I told him I didn't want that birthday gift, what was in that room: *What's wrong with you, son? Are you a* faggot*?* The disgust in his voice.

He actually might kill me, I thought. If he suspected. He'd probably prefer that to having a son like me. At the very least, he'd disinherit me. And while I didn't know how I felt about taking his money, I wasn't ready to give it up just yet.

AFTER AMSTERDAM I decided I never wanted to see Benjamin Daniels again. We drifted apart. I had a string of girlfriends. I left for the States for nearly a decade, didn't look back. Yeah, there were a couple of guys there: the freedom of thousands of miles of land and water—even if I still always seemed to hear my father's voice in my head. But nothing serious.

It doesn't mean I didn't think about that night later. In a way, I know I've been thinking about it ever since; trying not to. And then, all those years later: Ben's email. It had to mean something, him getting in touch like that, out of the blue. It couldn't just be a casual catch-up.

Except after that dinner on the terrace, when he'd so impressed Papa, I barely saw or spoke to him other than in passing. He even had time for the concierge, for God's sake, but not me—his old friend. He was ensconced here practically rent-free. He'd taken what he needed and then cut loose. I began to feel used. And when I thought about how shifty he was each time I approached him I felt a little frightened, too, though I couldn't put my finger on why. I thought of Antoine's words about Papa disinheriting us on a whim. It had seemed like madness at the time. But now . . . I began to feel that I didn't want Ben here after all. I began to feel that I wanted to take back the invitation. But I didn't know how to do it. He knew too much. Had so much he could use against me. I had to find another way to make him leave.

THE COMPUTER'S TIMER must have run out; the screen of my iMac goes black. It doesn't matter. I can still see the image. I have been haunted by it for over a decade.

I think about how I nearly kissed his sister last night. The sudden, shocking, wonderful resemblance to him when she turned her head just so, or frowned, or laughed. And also the resemblance of the moment: the darkness, the stillness. The two of us held apart from the rest of the world for just a beat.

That night in Amsterdam. It was the worst, most shameful thing I had ever done.

It was the best thing that had ever happened to me. That was how I used to see it, anyway. Until he came to stay.

Jess

I WAKE IN DARKNESS. THERE'S a heavy weight on my chest, a horrible taste in my mouth, my tongue dry and heavy like it doesn't belong to me. For a few long moments, everything that happened to me before now is a total blank. It feels like peering forward and staring into a black hole.

I grope around, trying to make out my surroundings. I seem to be lying on a bed. But which bed? Whose?

Fuck. What happened to me?

Gradually I remember: the party. That disgusting drink. Victor the vampire.

And then I see something I recognize. Some little green digits, glowing in the blackness. It's Ben's alarm clock. Somehow I'm back here, in the apartment. I blink at the numbers. 17:38. But that can't be right. That's the afternoon. That would mean I've been asleep for—Jesus Christ—the whole day.

I try to sit up. I make out two huge, glowing, slit-pupiled eyes a few inches from my nose. The cat is sitting on me—so that's the weight on my chest. It starts kneading its claws into my throat in painful little darts. I push it away: it hops off the bed. I look down at myself. I'm fully clothed, thank God. And I remember now, in flashes of memory: Victor was the one who got me down here after I blacked out in Mimi's apartment. Not the date-raping predator I suddenly thought he might be. In fact he'd seemed scared by the state I was in—left as quick as he could. I suppose at least he tried to help.

A flicker of memory. I found something last night. Something that felt important. But at first everything that happened only comes back to me in hazy, disjointed fragments. There are big missing patches like holes in a jigsaw. I know my dreams were really trippy. I recall an image of Ben shouting at me through a pane of glass; but I couldn't see his face clearly, the glass seemed warped. He was trying to warn me of something—but I couldn't hear what he was saying. And then suddenly I could see his face clearly but that was much, much worse. Because he didn't have any eyes. Someone had scratched them out.

Now I remember the paintings under Mimi's bed. Jesus Christ. That's what I found last night. Those tears in the canvas, like she'd ripped them all apart in some kind of frenzy. The slashes, the holes where the eyes should have been. And Ben's T-shirt, wrapped around them.

I haul myself out of bed, stumble into the main room. My head throbs. I might be small, but I'm not a cheap date—one drink is not enough to get me in that much of a state. It might not have been Victor, but I'm pretty sure of one thing: someone did this to me.

A loud trilling, so loud in the silence it makes me jump. My phone. Theo's name flashes up on the screen.

I pick up. "Hello?"

"I know what that card is." No niceties, no preamble.

"What?" I ask. "What are you talking about?"

"The card you gave me. The metal one, with the firework on it. I know what it is. Look, can you meet me at quarter to seven? So—in about an hour? The Palais Royal Metro station; we can walk from there. Oh, and try and look as smart as possible."

"I don't—"

But he's already hung up.

Mimi

FOURTH FLOOR

I PUT THE STUFF IN her drink last night. It was so easy. There was ketamine going around and I got hold of some, shook the powder into her glass until it dissolved and asked one of Camille's friends to give it to the British girl with the red hair. He seemed only too pleased to do it: she's quite pretty, I suppose.

I had to do it. I couldn't have her there. But that doesn't mean I don't feel bad about it . . . I've been so careful my whole life about drugs—apart from that night in the park. And then to inflict them on someone else without them even knowing. That wasn't cool. It's not her fault she made the mistake of coming to this place. That's the worst part. She's probably not even a bad person.

But I know I am.

Camille comes out of her room wearing a silk slip, black rings of smudged makeup around her eyes. This is the first time she's surfaced all day.

"Hey. Last night was craaaazy. People really enjoyed it, don't you think?" She looks at me closely. "*Putain*, Mimi, you look like shit. What happened to your knees?" They still hurt from where I hit the tarmac in front of that van; the concierge insisted on dabbing some antiseptic onto the grazes. She grins. "Someone had a good night, *non*?"

I shrug. "*Oui*. I suppose so." Actually it was probably one of the worst nights of my life. "But I didn't . . . sleep well." I didn't sleep at all.

She looks at me more closely. "Ohhh. Was it *that* kind of no sleep?"

"What do you mean?" I wish she'd stop looking at me so intently.

"You know what I mean! Your mystery guy?"

My heart's suddenly beating too fast in my chest. "Oh. No. It wasn't anything like that."

"Wait," she grins at me. "You never told me. Did it work?"

"What do you mean, did it work?" I feel like she's crowding me, the smell of Miss Dior and stale cigarette smoke suddenly overpowering. I need her out of my space.

"The stuff we picked out. Mimi!" She raises her eyebrows. "You can't have forgotten? It was only, like, two weeks ago!"

ALREADY IT FEELS like it happened to someone else. I see myself like a character in a film, knocking on the door to Camille's room. Camille sitting on the bed painting her toenails, the room stinking of nail polish and weed.

"I want to buy some lingerie," I told her.

Maman always bought all my underwear. We went together, every season, to Eres and she would buy me three simple sets: black, white, nude. But I wanted something different. Something I had picked myself. Only I didn't have any idea where to go. I knew Camille would.

Camille's eyebrows shot up. "Mimi! What's happened to you? That new look and now . . . *lingerie*? Who is he?" She smiled slyly. "Or she? *Merde*, you're so mysterious I don't even know if you actually prefer girls." A smirk. "Or maybe you're like me and it depends what mood you're in?"

Could she really not know who it was? To me it seemed so obvious. Not just that I was into him, but that he and I had a special connection. It felt like it was obvious to the outside world, to everyone who saw us.

"Come," she said, jumping up, throwing her foam toe dividers to one side. "We're going now."

She dragged me into Passage du Desir in Châtelet. It's a sex shop—one of a chain—on a big busy shopping street alongside shoe and clothes shops because, I guess, this is France and screwing is, like, a thing of national pride. You see couples coming out carrying bags over their arms, smiling secret smiles at each other, women striding in there on their lunch breaks to buy vibrators. I'd never gone into one before. In fact every time I'd passed one of their stores I'd blushed at the window displays and looked away.

I felt like everyone in there was looking at me, wondering what this blushing loser virgin was doing among all that latex fetish wear and lube. I lowered my head, trying to hide behind my new fringe. I had horrific images of Papa walking past and somehow spotting me inside, dragging me out by my hair: calling me *une petite salope* in front of the whole street.

Camille dug out boxes with things called "love kits" in: whole lingerie and suspender sets for ten euros. But I shook my head; they weren't sophisticated enough. She grabbed a huge, bright pink dildo with obscene protruding veins, waved it in front of me. "Maybe you should get one of *these* while we're here."

"Put it back," I hissed, ready to die of shame. Yeah, we have that expression in French too: *mourir de honte.*

"Masturbating is healthy, *chérie*," Camille said, way louder than she needed to. She was enjoying this, I could tell. "You know what's not healthy? *Not* masturbating. I bet that school your papa sent you to told you it's a sin."

I've told Camille about the school, just not why I had to leave. "*Va te faire foutre*," I said, giving her a shove.

"Ah, but that's exactly what you need to do. Go fuck *yourself*."

I dragged her out of there. We went into a classier place where the shop assistants with their chignons and their perfect red lipstick looked at me sideways. My men's shirts, my big boots, my home-cut fringe. A security guard tailed us. That would be enough normally. I'd leave. But I needed to do this. For him.

"I want to pick out something too," Camille told me, holding a silk harness up against herself.

"You own more stuff than this entire shop."

"*Oui*. But I want something more sophisticated, you know?"

"Who's it for?" I asked her.

"Someone new." She gave a secretive smile. That was weird. Camille's never mysterious about anything. If she has a new fuck-buddy on the scene the whole world has normally heard about it about thirty minutes after their first screw.

"Tell me," I said. But still she refused to say. I didn't like this new, mysterious Camille. But I felt too high with the thrill of my purchase to think much about it. I couldn't wait.

Next to shelves of designer sex toys we browsed through racks of lace and silk, felt the fabric between our fingers. The lingerie had to be perfect. Some of it was too much: crotchless, buckles and straps, leather. Some of it Camille rejected as "stuff your maman would buy": flowers and silk in pastel colors—pink, pistachio, lavender.

Then: "I've found it, the one for you." She held it up to me. It was the most expensive set of all the ones we'd looked at. Black lace and silk so fine you could hardly feel it between your fingers. Chic but still sexy. Grown-up.

In a changing room with velvet drapes I tried the set on. I held up my hair and half closed my eyes. I was feeling less embarrassed now. I'd never looked at myself like this before. I thought I'd feel stupid, gauche. I thought I'd worry about my small tits, my slight pot belly, my bow legs.

But I didn't. Instead I imagined revealing myself to him. I pictured the look on his face. Saw him sliding it off me.

Je suis ta petite pute.

After I'd changed I took it over to the desk and told the shop assistant to ring it up. I liked how she tried to hide her surprise as I took out my credit card. *Yeah: fuck you, bitch. I could buy everything in here if I wanted.*

All the way back to the apartment I thought about the bag over my arm. It weighed nothing, but suddenly it was everything.

For the next few nights I watched him through the windows. They'd got later and later, these writing sessions: fueled by the pots of coffee he'd make on his stove and drink looking out of the windows onto the courtyard. It was something important, I could tell. I could see how fast he typed, hunched over the keyboard. Maybe he'd let me read it one day soon. I'd be the first person he shared it with. I watched him bend down and stroke the cat's head and I imagined I was that cat. I imagined one day I would lie there on his sofa with my head in his lap and he would stroke my hair like he did that cat's fur. And we'd listen to records and we'd talk about all the plans we'd make. I saw the image of us there together in his apartment so clearly it was like I was watching it. So clearly that it felt like a premonition.

Nick

A HAMMERING ON THE DOOR of my apartment. I jump with shock.

"Who is it?"

"*Laissez-moi entrer.*" *Let me in.* More hammering. The door shudders on its hinges.

I go to open it. Antoine shoves his way past me into the room in a cloud of booze and stale sweat. I take a step back.

He pushed his way in here like this only two weeks ago: "Dominique's cheating on me. I know she is. The little slut. She comes back smelling of a different scent. I called her yesterday in the stairwell and I heard her ringtone coming from somewhere in this building. Second time I rang she'd switched it off. She'd told me she was having a pedicure in Saint-Germain. It's him, I know it. It's that English *connard* you invited to live here . . ."

And me thinking: could it be true? Ben and Dominique? Yes, there had been flirtation at that drinks, on the roof terrace. I hadn't read anything into it. Ben flirted with everyone. But could this be an explanation for why he had been avoiding my eye, avoiding my calls? Why he had been *so busy*?

Now Antoine snaps his fingers in front of my face. "Wakey wakey, *petit frère*!" He doesn't say it affectionately. His eyes are bloodshot, breath rank with wine. I couldn't believe the change when I came back after those years away. When I left, my brother was a happy newlywed. Now he's an alcoholic mess whose wife has left him. That's what working for our father does to you. "What are we going to do about her?" he demands. "The girl?"

"Just calm down—"

"*Calm down?*" He stabs the air in front of me with a finger. I take another step back. He may be a mess but I'll always be the younger brother, ready to duck a punch. And he's so like Papa when he's angry. "You know this is all your fault, don't you? All your mess? If you hadn't invited that cunt to live here. Coming here and thinking he could just . . . just help himself. You know he used you, right? But you couldn't see that, could you? You couldn't see any of it." He frowns, mock-thoughtful. "In fact, now I think about it, the way you looked at him—"

"*Ferme ta gueule.*" *Shut your mouth.* I take a step toward him. The anger is sudden, blinding. And when I'm next aware of what I'm doing I realize my hand is around his throat and his eyes are bulging. I loosen my fingers—but with an effort, as though some part of me resists the instruction.

Antoine puts up a hand, rubs at his neck. "Hit a nerve there, didn't I, little bro?" His voice is hoarse, his eyes a little frightened, his tone not as flippant as he'd probably like it. "Papa wouldn't like that, would he? No, he wouldn't like that at all."

"I'm sorry," I say. Ashamed. My hand aches. "Shit, I'm sorry. This isn't helping anything, us fighting like this."

"Oh look at you. So grown-up. Embarrassed about your little hissy fit because you like pretending that you're sorted, don't you? But you're just as fucked-up as I am." When he says the word "fucked"—a harsh *foutu* in French—a huge gob of spit lands on my cheek. I put my hand up, wipe it off. I want to go and wash my face, scrub at it with hot water and soap. I feel *infected* by him.

When Jess spoke about Antoine last night I saw him through a stranger's eyes. I was ashamed of him. She's right. He is a mess.

But I hated her saying it. Because he's also my brother. We can do our family members down as much as we like. But the second an outsider insults them our blood seethes. At the end of the day I don't like him—but I love him. And I see my own failures in him. For Antoine it's the booze, for me it's the pills, the self-punishing exercise. I might be a little more in control of my addictions. I might be less of a mess—in public anyway. But is that really something to boast about?

Antoine's grinning at me. "Bet you wish you'd never come back here, huh?" He takes another step closer. "Tell me, if it was all so great rubbing shoulders with the high-flyers in Silicon Valley, why did you come back? Ah, *oui* . . . because you're no better than the rest of us. You try and pretend you are, that you don't need him, his money. But then you came crawling back here, like we all do, wanting to suck a little more from the paternal teat—"

"Just shut the fuck up!" I shout, hands forming fists.

I take a long breath: in for four, out for eight, like my mindfulness app tells me. I'm not proud of myself losing my temper like this. I'm better than this. I am not this guy. But no one can get under my skin like Antoine. No one else knows exactly what to say and how to say it for maximum impact. Except my father, of course.

But the worst part is that my brother's right. I came back. Back to the paterfamilias like some seasonal bird returning to the same poisoned lake.

"You've come home, son," Papa told me, as we sat together up on the roof terrace on my first night back. "I always knew you would. We'll have to make a trip to the Île de Ré, take the boat out one weekend."

Maybe he'd changed. Mellowed. He didn't taunt me over the money I'd lost on the investment—not yet. He even offered me a cigar, which I smoked, though I loathe the taste. Maybe he'd missed me.

It was only later that I realized it wasn't that at all. It was just more proof of his power. I had failed at finding a life apart from him.

"If you want any more of my money," he told me, "you can come back under my roof so I can keep an eye on you. There'll be no more gallivanting around the world. I want a return on my investment. I want to know you're not pissing it all up the wall. *Tu comprends?* Do you understand?"

Antoine is pacing up and down in front of me. "So what are we going to do about her?" he asks, with drunken belligerence.

"Keep your voice down," I say. "She might understand something." The walls have ears in this place.

"Well what the fuck is she still doing here?" He kicks at the doorframe. "What if she goes to the police?"

"I've handled that."

"What do you mean?"

"It helps to have friends in high places."

He understands. "But she needs to go." He's muttering to himself now: "We could lock her out. It would be so easy. All we'd need to do is change the combination on the front gate—she wouldn't be able to get in then."

"No," I say, "that wouldn't—"

"Or we could make her leave. Little girl like that? Wouldn't be hard."

"No. If anything we'd just force her into going to the police again on her own . . ."

Antoine lets out something between a roar and a groan. He's a total liability. Family, huh? Because blood is always thicker than water, in the end. Or, as we say in French: *la voix du sang est la plus forte.* The voice of blood is the strongest. Summoning me back here to this place.

"It's better that she stays here," I say, sharply. "You must see that. It's better that we can keep an eye on her. For the time being we simply have to hold our nerve. Papa will know what to do."

"Have you heard from him?" Antoine says. "Papa?" His tone has changed. Something needy in it. When he said "Papa" for a second he sounded like the little boy he once was, the little boy who sat outside his mother's bedroom as Paris' best physicians came and went, unable to make sense of the illness eating away at her.

I nod. "He got in touch this morning."

I hope you're holding the fort there, son. Keep Antoine under control. I'll be back as soon as I can.

Antoine scowls. He's Papa's right-hand man in the family business. But right now, for the time being, I'm the trusted one. That must hurt. But that's the way it's always been, our father pitting the two of us against each other in a struggle for scraps of parental affection. Except on the few occasions we unite against a common enemy.

Seventy-Two Hours Earlier

SHE WATCHES THROUGH THE SHUTTERS as he is carried from the building. Just as she watches everything in this place. Sometimes from her cabin in the garden, sometimes from the recesses of the building where she can spy on them unnoticed.

The body in its improvised shroud is visibly heavy. Already stiffening perhaps, unwieldy. A dead weight.

The lights in the third floor apartment have been on up until now, blazing out into the night. Now they are extinguished and she sees the windows become dark blanks, masking everything inside. But it will take more than that to expunge the memory of what has occurred within.

Now the light in the courtyard snaps on. She watches as they set to work, hidden from the outside world behind the high walls, doing everything that needs to be done.

Seeing him, she thought she would feel something, but there was nothing. She smiles slightly at the thought that his blood will now be part of this place, its dark secret. Well, he liked secrets. His stain will be here forever now, his lies buried with him.

Something terrible happened here tonight. She won't talk about what she saw, not even over his dead body. No one in this building is entirely innocent. Herself included.

A new light blinks on: four floors up. At the glass she glimpses a pale face, dark hair. A hand up against the pane. Perhaps there is one innocent in this, after all.

Jess

I'M HUNTING THROUGH BEN'S CLOSET in case there's an outfit an old girlfriend left behind, something I could borrow. Before Theo hung up on me I was going to tell him that I don't have anything smart to wear this evening. And no time or money to get something—he's barely given me any warning.

Just for a moment I pause my riffling through Ben's shirts and pull one of them against my face. Try, from the scent, to conjure him here, to believe that I will see him standing in front of me soon. But already the smell—of his cologne, his skin—seems to have faded a little. It feels somehow symbolic of our whole relationship: that I'm always chasing a phantom.

I drag myself away. Choose the one of my two sweaters that doesn't have any holes and brush my hair: I haven't washed it since I arrived, but at least it's less of a bird's nest now. I chuck on my jacket. Thread another pair of cheap hoop earrings through my earlobes. I look in the mirror. Not exactly "smart," but it'll have to do.

I open the door to the apartment. The stairwell's pitch-black. I fumble around for the light switch. There's that whiff of cigarette smoke, but even stronger than usual. It smells almost like someone's smoking one right now. Something makes me glance up to my left. A sound, perhaps, or just a movement of the air.

And then I catch sight of something out of place: a tiny glowing red dot hovering overhead in the blackness. It takes a moment before I understand what it is. I'm looking at the end of a cigarette butt, held by someone hidden in darkness just above me.

"Who's there?" I say, or try to say, because it comes out as a strangled bleat. I fumble around for the light switch near the door and finally make contact with it, the lights stuttering on. There's no one in sight.

MY HEART'S STILL beating double time as I walk across the court-yard. Just as I reach the gate to the street, I hear the sound of quick shuffling footsteps behind me. I turn.

It's the concierge, emerging once more from the shadows. I try to take a step away and when my heel hits metal I realize I'm already backed right up against the gate. She only comes up to my chin—and I'm not exactly big—but there's something threat-ening about her nearness.

"Yes?" I ask. "What is it?"

"I have something to say to you," she hisses. She glances up at the encircling apartment building. She reminds me of a small animal sniffing the air for a predator. I follow her gaze upward. Most of the windows are dark blanks, reflecting the gleam of the streetlamps across the road. There's only one light on upstairs, in the penthouse apartment. I can't see anyone watching us—I'm sure this is what she's checking for—but then I don't think I'd necessarily be able to spot them if they were.

Suddenly she snatches out a hand toward me. It's such a swift, violent action that for a moment I really think she's going to hit me. I don't have time to step away, it's too fast. But instead she grabs a hold of my wrist in her claw-like hand. Her grip's surpris-ingly strong; it stings.

"What are you doing?" I ask her.

"Just come," she tells me—and with such authority I don't dare disobey her. "Come with me, now."

I'm going to be late for meeting Theo now but he can wait.

This feels important. I follow her across the courtyard to her little cabin. She moves quickly, in that slightly stooped way of hers, like someone trying to duck out of a rainstorm. I feel like a child in a storybook being taken to the witch's hut in the woods. She looks up at the apartment building several more times, as though scanning it for any onlookers. But she seems to decide that it's worth the risk.

Then she opens the door and ushers me in. It's even smaller inside than it looks on the outside, if that's possible. Everything is crammed into one tiny space. There's a bed attached to the wall by a system of pulleys and currently raised to allow us to stand; a washstand; a minuscule antique cooking stove. Just to my right is a curtain that I suppose must lead through to a bathroom of some sort—simply because there's nowhere else for it to be.

It's almost scarily neat, every surface scrubbed to a high shine. It smells of bleach and detergent—not a thing out of place. Somehow I would have expected nothing less from this woman. And yet the cleanness, the neatness, the little vase of flowers, somehow make it all the more depressing. A little mess might be a distraction from how cramped it is, or from the damp stains on the ceiling which I'm fairly sure no amount of cleaning could remove. I've lived in some dives in my time, but this takes the biscuit. And what must it feel like to live in this tiny hovel while surrounded by the luxury and space of the rest of the apartment building? What would it be like to live with the reminder of how little you have on your doorstep every day?

No wonder she hated me, swanning in here to take up residence on the third floor. If only she knew how out of place I am here too, how much more like her than them I really am. I know I can't let her see my pity: that would be the worst insult possible. I get the impression she's probably a very proud person.

Behind her head and the tiny dining table and chair I see several faded photographs pinned to the wall. A little girl, sitting on a woman's lap. The sky behind them is bright blue, olive trees in the background. The woman has a glass in front of her of what looks like tea, a silver handle. The next is of a young woman. Slim, dark-haired, dark-eyed. Maybe eighteen or nineteen. Not a new photograph: you can tell from the saturated colors, the fuzziness of it. But at the same time it's definitely too recent to be of the old woman herself. It must be a loved one. Somehow it's impossible to imagine this elderly woman having a family or a past away from this place. It's impossible, even, to imagine her ever having been young. As though she has always been here. As though she is a part of the apartment building itself.

"She's stunning," I say. "That girl on the wall. Who is she?"

There's a long silence, so long that I think maybe she didn't understand me. And then finally, in that rasping voice, she says: "My daughter."

"Wow." I take another look at her in light of this, her daughter's beauty. It's hard to see past the lines, the swollen ankles, the clawed hands—but maybe I can see a shadow of it, after all.

She clears her throat. "*Vous devez arrêter,*" she barks, suddenly, cutting into my thoughts. *You have to stop.*

"What do you mean?" I ask. "Stop what?" I lean forward. Perhaps she can tell me something.

"All your questions," she says. "All of your . . . *looking.* You are only making trouble for yourself. You cannot help your brother now. You must understand that—"

"What do you mean?" I ask. A chill has gone right through me. "What do you mean, I cannot help my brother now?"

She just shakes her head. "There are things here that you cannot understand. But I have seen them, with my own eyes. I see everything."

"What?" I ask her. "What have you seen?"

She doesn't answer. She simply shakes her head. "I am trying to help you, girl. I have been trying since the beginning. Don't you understand that? If you know what is good for you, you will stop. You will leave this place. And never look back."

Sophie

THERE'S A KNOCK ON THE door. I go to answer it and find Mimi standing there on the other side.

"Maman." The way she says the word. Just like she did as a little girl.

"What is it, *ma petite*?" I ask, gently. I suppose to others I may seem cold. But the love I feel for my daughter; I'd challenge you to find anything close to it.

"Maman, I'm frightened."

"Shh." I step forward to embrace her. I draw her close to me, feeling the frail nubs of her shoulder blades beneath my hands. It seems so long since I have held her like this, since she has *allowed* me to hold her like this, like I did when she was a child. For a time I thought I might never do so again. And to be called "Maman." It is still the same miracle it was when I first heard her say the word.

I have always felt she is more mine than Jacques'. Which I suppose makes a kind of sense: because in a way she was Jacques' greatest gift to me, far more valuable than any diamond brooch, any emerald bracelet. Something—someone—I could love unreservedly.

ONE EVENING—ROUGHLY A week after the night I had knocked on Benjamin Daniels' door—Jacques was briefly home for supper.

I presented him with the quiche Lorraine I had bought from the boulangerie, piping hot from the oven.

Everything was as it should be. Everything following its usual pattern. Except for the fact that a few nights before I had slept with the man from the third-floor apartment. I was still reeling from it. I could not believe it had happened. A moment—or rather an evening—of madness.

I placed a slice of quiche on Jacques' plate. Poured him a glass of wine. "I met our lodger on the stairs this evening," he said as he ate, as I picked my way through my salad. "He thanked us for supper. Very gracious—gracious enough not to mention the disaster with the weather. He sends you his compliments."

I took a sip of my wine before I answered. "Oh?"

He laughed, shook his head in amusement. "Your face—anyone would think this stuff was corked. You really don't like him, do you?"

I couldn't speak.

I was saved by the ringing of Jacques' phone. He went into his study and took a call. When he returned his face was clouded with anger. "I have to go. Antoine made a stupid mistake. One of the clients isn't happy."

I gestured to the quiche. "I'll keep this warm for you, for when you come back."

"No. I'll eat out." He shrugged on his jacket. "Oh, and I forgot to say. Your daughter. I saw her on the street the other night. She was dressed like a whore."

"*My* daughter?" I asked. Now that she had done something to displease him she was "my" daughter?

"All that money," he said, "sending her to that Catholic school, to try and make her into a properly behaved young woman. And yet she disgraced herself there. And now she goes out dressed like a little slut. But then, perhaps it's no surprise."

"What do you mean?"

But I didn't need to ask. I knew exactly what he meant.

And then he left. And I was all alone in the apartment, as usual.

For the second time in a week, I was filled with rage. White hot, powerful. I drank the rest of the bottle of wine. Then I stood up and walked down two flights of stairs.

I knocked on his door.

He opened it. Pulled me inside.

This time there was no preamble. No pretense of polite conversation. I don't think we spoke one word. We weren't respectful or gentle or cautious with one another now. My silk shirt was torn from me. I gasped against his mouth like someone drowning. Bit at him. Tore the skin of his back with my nails. Relinquished all control. I was possessed.

Afterward, as we lay tangled in his sheets, I finally managed to speak. "This cannot happen again. You understand that, don't you?"

He just smiled.

Over the next few weeks we became reckless. Testing the boundaries, scaring ourselves a little. The adrenaline rush, the fear—so similar a feeling to the quickening of arousal. Each seemed to heighten the other, like the rush of some drug. I had behaved so well for so long.

The secret spaces of this building became our private playground. I took him in my mouth in the old servants' staircase, my hands sliding into his trousers, expert, greedy. He had me in the laundry room in the *cave*, up against the washing machine as it thrummed out its cycle.

And every time I tried to end it. And every time I know we both heard the lie behind the words.

* * *

"MAMAN," MIMI SAYS now—and I am jolted, abruptly, guiltily, out of these memories. "Maman, I don't know what to do."

My wonderful miracle. My Merveille. My Mimi. She came to me when I had given up all hope of having a child. You see, she wasn't always mine.

She was, quite simply, perfect. A baby: only a few weeks old. I did not know exactly where she had come from. I had my ideas, but I kept them to myself. I had learned it was important, sometimes, to look the other way. If you know that you aren't going to like the reply, don't ask the question. There was just one thing I needed to know and to that I got my answer: the mother was dead. "And illegal. So there's no paper trail to worry about. I know someone at the *mairie* who will square the birth certificate." A mere formality for the grand and powerful house of Meunier. It helps to have friends in high places.

And then she was mine. And that was the important thing. I could give her a better life.

"Shh," I say. "I'm here. Everything will be OK. I'm sorry I was stern last night, with the wine. But you understand, don't you? I didn't want a scene. Leave it all with me, *ma chérie.*"

It was—is—so fierce, that feeling. Even though she didn't come out of my body, I knew as soon as I saw her that I would do anything to protect her, to keep her safe. Other mothers might say that sort of thing casually. But perhaps it is clear by now that I don't do or say anything casually. When I say something like that, I mean it.

Jess

I COME UP OUT OF the Palais Royal Metro station. I almost don't recognize the tall, smartly dressed guy waiting at the top of the steps until he starts walking toward me.

"You're fifteen minutes late," Theo says.

"You didn't give me any time," I say. "And I got caught up—"

"Come on," Theo says. "We can still make it if we're snappy about it." I look him over, trying to work out why he looks so different from the last time I met him. Only a five o'clock shadow now, revealing a sharp jawline. Dark hair still in need of a cut but it's had a brush and he's swept it back from his face. A dark blazer over a white shirt and jeans. I even catch a waft of cologne. He's definitely scrubbed up since the café. He still looks like a pirate, but now like one who's had a wash and a shave and borrowed some civilian clothes.

"That's not going to cut it," he says, nodding at me. Clearly, he's not having the same charitable thoughts about my outfit.

"It's all I had to wear. I did try to say—"

"It's fine, I thought that might be the case. I've brought you some stuff."

He thrusts a Monoprix bag-for-life toward me. I look inside: I can see a tangle of clothes; a black dress and a pair of heels.

"You *bought* this?"

"Ex-girlfriend. You're roughly the same size, I'd guess."

"Ew. OK." I remind myself that this might all somehow help me find out what's happened to Ben, that beggars can't be choosers about wearing the haunted clothes of girlfriends past. "Why do I have to wear this sort of stuff?"

He shrugs. "Them's the rules." And then, when he sees my expression: "No, they actually are. This place has a dress code. Women aren't allowed to wear trousers, heels are mandatory."

"That's nice and sexist." Echoes of The Pervert insisting I keep the top four buttons of my shirt undone "for the punters": *You want to look like you work in a kindergarten, sweetheart? Or a branch of fucking McDonald's?*

Theo shrugs. "Yeah, well, I agree. But that's a certain part of Paris for you. Hyper-conservative, hypocritical, sexist. Anyway, don't blame me. It's not like I'm taking you to this place on a date." He coughs. "Come on, we don't have all night. We're already running late."

"For what?"

"You'll see when we get there. Let's just say you're not going to find this place in your Lonely Planet guide."

"How does this help us find Ben?"

"I'll explain it when we get there. It'll make more sense then."

God, he's infuriating. I'm also not completely sure I trust him, though I can't put my finger on why. Maybe it's just that I still can't work out what his angle is, why he's so keen to help.

I hurry along next to him, trying to keep up. I didn't see him standing up at the café the other day—I'd guessed he was tall, but now I realize he's well over a foot taller than me and I have to take two steps for every one of his. After a few minutes of walking I'm actually panting.

To the left of us I catch sight of a huge glass pyramid, glowing with light, looking like something that's just landed from outer space. "What is that thing?"

He gives me a look. It seems I've said something stupid. "That's the Pyramide? In front of the Louvre? You know . . . the famous museum?"

I don't like being made to feel like an idiot. "Oh. The *Mona Lisa*, right? Yeah, well, I've been a bit too busy trying to find my missing brother to take a nice tour of it yet."

We push through crowds of tourists chattering in every language under the sun. As we walk, I tell him about what I've discovered: about them all being a family. One united front, acting together—and probably against me. I keep thinking about stumbling into Sophie Meunier's apartment, all of them sitting together like that—an eerie family portrait. The words I'd heard, crouching outside. *Elle est dangereuse.* And Nick discovering that he wasn't the ally I thought he was—that part still stings.

"And just before I left to come here the concierge gave me a kind of warning. She told me to 'stop looking.'"

"Can I tell you something I've learned in my long and not especially illustrious career?" Theo asks.

"What?"

"When someone tells you to stop looking, it normally means you're on the right track."

I CHANGE QUICKLY in the underground toilet of a chi-chi bar while Theo buys a *demi* beer upstairs so the staff don't chuck us out. I shake out my hair, study my reflection in the foxed glass of the mirror. I don't look like myself. I look like I'm playing a part. The dress is figure-hugging but classier than I'd expected. The label inside reads *Isabel Marant*, which I'm guessing might be a step up from my usual Primark. The shoes—*Michel Vivien* is the name printed on the footbed—are higher than anything I'd wear but surprisingly comfortable; I think I might actually be able to walk in them. So I guess I'm playing the part of Theo's ex-girlfriend; not sure how I feel about that.

A girl comes out of the stall next to me: long shining dark hair, a silky dress falling off one shoulder underneath an over-sized cardigan, wings of black eyeliner. She starts outlining her lips in lipstick. That's what I need: the finishing touch.

"Hey." I lean over to her, smile my most ingratiating smile. "Could I borrow some of that?"

She frowns at me, looks slightly disgusted, but hands it over. "*Si tu veux.*"

I put some on a finger, dab it onto my lips—it's a dark vampiric red—and pass it back to her.

She puts up a hand. "*Non, merci.* Keep it. I have another." She tosses her gleaming hair over one shoulder.

"Oh. Thanks." I put the lid back on and it closes with a satisfying magnetized click. I notice it has little interlocking "C"s stencilled on the top.

Mum had a lipstick like this, even though she definitely didn't have spare cash to spend on expensive makeup. But then that was Mum all over: blow it on a lipstick and be left with nothing for dinner. Me, sitting on a chair, legs dangling. Her pressing the waxy stub of it against my lips. Turning me to face the mirror. *There you go, darling. Don't you look pretty?*

I look at myself in the mirror now. Pout just like she asked me to do all those years—a million years, a whole lifetime—ago. There; done. Costume complete.

I HEAD BACK upstairs. "Ready," I tell Theo. He downs the dregs of his stupidly tiny glass of beer. I can feel him running a quick eye over the outfit. His mouth opens and for a moment I think he might say something nice. I mean, part of me wouldn't know what to do with a compliment right now, but at the same time it might be nice to hear. And then he points to my mouth.

"Missed a bit," he says. "But yeah, otherwise that should do."

Oh fuck off. I rub at the edge of my lips. I hate myself for even having cared what he thought.

We leave the bar, turn onto a street thronged with very well-dressed shoppers. I could swear the air around here smells of expensive leather. We pass the glittering windows of rich people shops: Chanel, Celine, and aha!—Isabel Marant. He leads me away from the crowds into a much smaller side street. Gleaming cars flank the pavements. In contrast to the crowded shopping boulevard there's no one in sight and it's darker here, fewer streetlamps. A deep hush over everything.

Then Theo stops at a door. "Here we are." He looks at his watch. "We're definitely a little late. Hopefully they'll let us in."

I look at the door. No number, but there's a plaque with a symbol I recognize: an exploding firework. Where *are* we?

Theo reaches past me—a trace of that citrus cologne again—and presses a doorbell I hadn't noticed. The door swings open with a click. A man appears, dressed in a black suit and bow tie. I watch as Theo fishes a card from his pocket, the same one I found in Ben's wallet.

The doorman glances at the card, nods his head toward us. "*Entrez, s'il vous plaît.* The evening is about to start."

I try and peer past the doorman to get a glimpse of what lies beyond. At the end of the corridor I see a staircase leading downward, dimly lit by sconces with real candles burning in them.

Theo plants a hand in the small of my back and, with a little push, steers me forward. "Come on," he says. "We don't have all night."

"*Arrêtez*," the doorman says, barring our entry with a hand. He looks me over. "*Votre mobile, s'il vous plaît.* No phone allowed—or camera."

"Er—why?" I glance back at Theo. It occurs to me again that I know absolutely nothing about this guy beyond what it says on his business card. He could be anyone. He could have brought me anywhere.

Theo gives a tiny nod, gestures: *don't make a fuss. Do what the guy says.* "O—K." I hand my phone over, reluctantly.

"*Vos masques.*" The man holds up two pieces of material. I take one. A black mask, made of silk.

"Wha—"

"Just put it on," Theo murmurs, near my ear. And then louder: "Let me help, darling." I try to act natural as he smooths down my hair, ties the mask behind my head.

The doorman beckons us through.

With Theo close behind me, I begin to descend the stairs.

Jess

AN UNDERGROUND ROOM. I SEE dark red walls, low lighting, a small crowd of dimly lit figures sitting in front of a stage veiled by a wine-colored velvet curtain. Masked faces turn to look as we descend the final few steps. We're definitely the last to turn up at the party.

"What the hell is this place?" I whisper to Theo.

"*Shh.*"

An usher in black tie meets us at the bottom of the stairs, beckons us forward. We pass walls decorated with stylized gold dancing figurines, then weave among little booths with masked figures sitting behind tables, more faces turning in our direction. I feel uncomfortably exposed. Luckily the table we're taken to is tucked into a corner—definitely the worst view of the stage.

We slide into the booth. There really isn't very much room in here, not with Theo's long legs, which he has to pull up against himself, his knees hard against the wooden surround. He looks so uncomfortable that in different circumstances it might give me a laugh. The tiny amount of seat left means I have to sit with my thigh pressed right up against his.

I look about. It's hard to tell whether this place is actually old or just a clever imitation. The others around us are all very well-heeled; judging by their clothes they could be out for an evening at the theatre. But the atmosphere is wrong. I lean back in my chair, trying to look casual, like I fit in here among the tailored suits, the jewel-encrusted earlobes and necks, the rich person hair. A weird, hungry hum of energy is coming off them, coiling through the room—an intense note of excitement, of anticipation.

A waiter comes over to take our drinks order. I open the leather-bound menu. No prices. I glance at Theo.

"A glass of champagne for my wife," he says, quickly. He turns to me wearing a smile of fake adoration—so convincing it gives me a chill. "Seeing as we're celebrating, darling." I really hope he's paying. He looks down the menu. "And a glass of this red for me."

The waiter is back in a minute, brandishing two bottles in white napkins. He pours a stream of champagne into a glass and passes it to me. I take a sip. It's very cold, tiny bubbles electric on the tip of my tongue. I can't think when I've ever had the real stuff. Mum used to say she was "a champagne girl" but I'm not sure she ever had it either: just cheap, sweet knock-offs.

As the waiter pours Theo's red the napkin slips a little and I notice the label.

"It's the same wine," I whisper to Theo, once the waiter's left us. "The Meuniers have that in their cellar."

Theo turns to look at me. "What was that name you just used?" He sounds suddenly excited.

"The Meuniers. The family I was telling you about."

Theo lowers his voice. "Yesterday I submitted a request to see the *matrice cadastrale*—that's like the Land Registry—for this place. It's owned by one Meunier Wines SARL."

I sit up very straight, everything sharpening into focus. A feeling like a thousand tiny pin-pricks across the surface of my skin.

"That's them. That's the family Ben's been living with." I try to think. "But why was Ben interested in this place? Could he have been reviewing it? Something like that?"

"He wasn't reviewing it for me. And I'm not sure, being so exclusive, that it's the sort of place that exactly courts press coverage."

The lights begin to dim. But just before they do a figure in the crowd catches my eye, oddly familiar despite the mask they're wearing. I try to shift my gaze back to the same spot but the lights are dimming further, voices lowering and the room falling into darkness.

I can hear the smallest rustle of people's clothing, the odd sniff, their intakes of breath. Someone coughs and it sounds deafening in the sudden hush.

Then the velvet curtain begins to roll back.

A figure stands on the stage against a black background. Skin lit up pale blue. Face in shadow. Completely naked. No—not naked, a trick of the light—two scraps of material covering her modesty. She begins to dance. The music is deep, throbbing—some sort of jazz, I think . . . no melody to it, but a kind of rhythm. And she's so in sync with it that it feels almost as if the music is coming from her, like the movements she is making are creating it, rather than following it. The dance is strange, intense, almost menacing. I'm torn between staring and tearing my eyes away; something about it disturbs me.

More girls appear, dressed—or undressed—in the same way. The music gets louder and louder, beating until it's so overpowering that the pulse of it is like the sound of my own heartbeat in my ears. With the blue light, the shifting, undulating bodies on stage, I feel as though I'm underwater, as though the outlines of everything are rippling and bleeding into one another. I think of last night. Could there be something in the champagne? Or is it just the effect of the lighting, the music, the darkness? I glance over at Theo. He shifts in his seat next to me; takes a sip of wine, his eyes locked on the stage. Is he turned on by what's happening on stage? Am *I*? I'm suddenly aware of how close we are to each other, of how tightly my leg is pressed up against his.

The next act is just two women: one dressed in a close-fitting black suit and bow tie, the other in a tiny slip dress. Gradually they remove each other's clothes until you can see that without them they're almost identical. I can feel the audience sitting forward, drinking it in.

I lean toward Theo. Whisper: "What *is* this place?"

"A rather exclusive club," he murmurs back. "Its nickname, apparently, is La Petite Mort. You can't get in unless you have one of those cards. Like the one you found in Ben's wallet."

The lights dim again. Silence falls on the crowd. Another nearly naked girl—this one wearing a kind of feathered head-dress rather than a mask—is lowered from the ceiling on a sus-pended silver hoop. Her act is all confined to the hoop: she does a somersault, a kind of backflip, lets herself fall and then catches herself with the flick of an ankle—the audience gasps.

Theo leans in close. "Careful now, but look behind you," he whispers, breath tickling my ear. I start to swivel round. "No—Jesus, more subtly than that."

God, he's patronizing. But I do as he says. Several times I take small, sly glances behind me. And as I do I notice a series of booths hidden in the shadows at the back, their occupants shielded from the view of the regular punters by velvet curtains and attended by a constant flow of waiters carrying bottles of wine and trays of canapés. Every so often someone leaves or enters, and I notice that it always seems to be a man. All of a similar type and age: elegant, suited, masked, an air of wealth and importance about them.

Theo leans over, as though he's whispering another sweet nothing. "Have you noticed?"

"How they're all men?"

"Yes. And how every so often one of them goes through that door over there."

I follow the direction of his gaze.

"But I'd stop looking now," he murmurs. "Before we start to draw attention to ourselves."

I turn back to the stage. The girl has stepped off the hoop. She smiles out at the audience, taking us all in in a sweeping glance. When she gets to me, she stops. I'm not imagining it: she freezes. She is staring at me in what looks like horror. I feel a thrill go through me. The sharp brown fringe, the height, even the little mole beneath her left eye which I can make out now under the spotlight. I know her.

Sophie

THEY FILE INTO THE APARTMENT. Nicolas, Antoine, Mimi. Take up the same positions on the sofas they occupied last night, when the girl interrupted us. Nick's foot is tapping a frantic rhythm on the Ghom rug. As I watch I am certain I can make out a tiny black scorch mark just beneath his toe. One of several burned into the priceless silk. But you'd only spot them if you knew what you were looking for.

Suddenly I am assaulted by memories. It was my greatest transgression, inviting him up here. We stole a bottle from Jacques' cellar: one of the finest vintages. Had each other there on the rug, Paris glittering nosily in at us through the vast windows. We lay tangled together afterward, warmed by the cashmere throw I had pulled around our naked bodies. If Jacques had come back unexpectedly . . . But wasn't there some part of me that wanted to be caught? Look at me, who you have left here alone all these years. Wanted. Desired.

As we lay there I stroked his hair, enjoying the dense velvety softness of it between my fingers. He lit a cigarette that we passed back and forth like teenage lovers, hot ash scattering, sizzling into the silk of the rug. I didn't care. All that mattered was that with him here the apartment suddenly seemed warm, full of life and sound and passion.

"My mum used to stroke my hair."

I pulled my hand away, sharply.

"I didn't mean it like that," he said, quickly. "I just meant I hadn't realized how much I missed it." And when he turned to look across at me I saw in his expression something undefended and frail, something that had hidden beneath all the charm. I thought I saw my own loneliness reflected there. But in the next moment he smiled and it had vanished.

A minute or so later he sat up, taking in the empty apartment around us. "Jacques is away a lot in the evenings, isn't he?"

I nodded. Was he already planning our next encounter? "He's very busy."

His gaze seemed to sweep over the paintings on the walls, the furnishings, the richness of the place. "I suppose that must mean business is flourishing."

I froze. He'd said it lightly. Too lightly? It brought me back to myself: the madness of what we were doing, all that was at stake. "You should go," I told him, suddenly angry at him . . . at myself. "I can't do this." This time I really believed I meant it. "I have too much to lose."

I close my eyes. Open them again and focus on my daughter's face. She does not meet my eye. All the same, it has brought me back to myself. To what is important. I take a steadying sip of my wine. Force down the memories. "So," I say to them all. "Let us begin."

Nick

MY STEPMOTHER HAS CALLED US all to order. We're sitting upstairs in the penthouse apartment. A dysfunctional little family conference. Like the one we'd been going to have last night before Jess turned up unannounced and set the cat among the pigeons. I was always a keen student of English idioms. We have a French one like it, actually: *jeter un pavé dans la mare*—throw a paving stone in the pond. And maybe that's a more accurate description of what happened when she arrived here. She has displaced everything.

I look at the others. Antoine knocking back the wine—he might as well have picked up the whole bottle. Mimi white-faced and looking ready to bolt from the room. Sophie sitting rigid and expressionless. She's not looking quite herself, my stepmother. I can't work out what's different about her at first. Her shining black bob doesn't have a strand out of place, her silk scarf is knotted expertly at her throat. But there's something off. Then it hits me: she's not wearing lipstick. I don't know if I've ever seen her without it. She looks diminished, somehow. Older, frailer, more human.

Antoine speaks first. "That stupid little cunt is at the club." He turns to me. "Still suggest we do nothing, little bro?"

"I . . . I think the important thing is we all pull together," I say. "A united front. As a family. That's the most important thing. We can't fall apart now."

But I realize, looking at their faces, that they're all unknown quantities to me. I don't feel like I know these people. Not really. I was away for so long. And we're all so estranged from one another that we don't look and feel like the real thing. Even to one another.

"Yes, because you've been such a key player in this family up until now," Antoine says, making me feel even more of an imposter, a fraud. He gestures toward Sophie. "And you're not going to catch me playing the adoring stepson to that *salope*."

"Hey," I say. "Let's just—"

"Watch your mouth," Sophie says caustically, turning to Antoine. "You're sitting in my apartment."

"Oh it's your apartment, is it?" He gives a mock bow. "I'm so sorry, I hadn't realized. I thought you were just a parasite living off Papa's money—I didn't know you'd *earned* any of it yourself."

I was only eight or nine when Papa married the mysterious new woman who had materialized in our lives but Antoine was older, a teenager. Maman had been an invalid for so long, languishing in her rooms on the third floor. This newcomer seemed so young, so glamorous. I was a little besotted. Antoine took it rather differently. He's always had it in for her.

"Just stop it," Mimi says suddenly, her hands over her ears. "All of you. I can't take any more—"

Antoine turns to Mimi with a horrible smile on his face. "*Ah*," he slurs at her now, "and as for you, well you're not really part of this family, are you, *ma petite soeur*—"

"Stop that," Sophie says to Antoine, her voice ice-cold: the lioness protecting her cub.

At her feet the whippet startles and gives a sharp bark.

"Oh, I think she can give as good as she gets," Antoine says. "What about all that stuff at her school, with the teacher? Papa had to make a pretty hefty donation and agree to remove her to keep that one quiet. But perhaps it's no surprise, huh?" He turns to Mimi. "When you consider where she comes from."

"Don't you dare speak to her like that," Sophie says. Her tone is dangerous.

I glance over at Mimi. She's just sitting there, staring at Antoine, her face even paler than usual.

"OK," I say. "Come on, let's all just—"

"And can I just say," Antoine says, "that it's just typical that our darling père has decided to fuck off for all of this. Isn't it?"

All of us glance instinctively at the portrait of my father on the wall. I know it must be my imagination or a trick of the light, but it looks as though his painted frown has deepened slightly. I shiver. Even when he's miles away you can still feel his presence in this apartment, somehow, his authority. The all-seeing, all-powerful Jacques Meunier.

"Your father," Sophie says to Antoine now, sharply, "has his own business to be taking care of. As you well know. It would only complicate things further if he returns. We must all hold the fort for him in his absence."

"What a surprise, he's not here when the shit hits the fan." Antoine gives a laugh, but there's no humor in it.

"He trusts you to be able to handle the situation on your own," Sophie says. "But perhaps that is simply too much to ask. Look at you. You're a forty-year-old man still living under his roof, leeching off his money. He has given you everything. You've never had to grow up. You've had everything handed to you by your father on a silver platter. You're both useless hothouse flowers, too weak for the outside world. Unable to fly the nest." That stings. "For God's sake," she says. "Show your father some respect."

"Oh yeah?" Antoine gives her a nasty smile. "Are you really going to talk to me about respect, *putain*?" The last word hissed under his breath.

"How dare you speak to me like that?" She rounds on him, a surge of real anger breaching the icy façade.

"Oh, how dare I?" Antoine gives her a sly-looking grin. "*Vraiment?* Really?" He turns to me. "You know what she is? You know what our very elegant stepmother really is? You know where she comes from?"

I've had my suspicions. As I grew older, they grew too. But I've barely even allowed myself to think them, let alone voice them aloud, for fear of my father's wrath.

Antoine stands up and walks out of the room. A few moments later he comes back carrying something in a large frame. He turns it around so that all of us can see it. It's a black and white photograph, a large nude: the one from my father's study.

"Put that back," says Sophie, her voice dangerous. Her hands are clenched into fists. She looks over at Mimi who is sitting stock still, her eyes wide and scared.

Antoine sits back in the chair looking pleased with himself, propping the photograph beside him like a child's science project. "Look at her," he says, gesturing to the image, then at Sophie. "Hasn't she done well? The Hermès scarves, the trench coats. *Une vraie bourgeoise.* You'd never know it, would you? You'd never know that she was really a—"

A crack, loud as a pistol shot. It happens too quickly to understand what's going on: she moved so fast. Then Antoine is sitting there holding his hand to his face and Sophie is standing over him.

"She hit me," Antoine says—but his voice is small and scared as a little boy's. It isn't the first time he's been hit like this. Papa always was pretty free with his fists and Antoine, the eldest, seemed to get the worst of it. "She fucking hit me." He takes his hand away and we all see the mark of her hand on his cheek, the imprint of it a livid pink.

Sophie continues to stand over him. "Think what your father would say if he heard you talking to me like that."

Antoine looks up at Papa's portrait again. Tears his eyes away with an effort. He's a big guy but he seems almost to shrink into himself. We all know that he would never dare speak to Sophie like this in Papa's presence. And we all know that when Papa gets back there'll be hell to pay if he hears about it.

"Can we please just focus on what's important?" I say, trying to gain some control. "We have a bigger problem to focus on here."

Sophie gives Antoine another venomous stare, then turns to me and nods, tightly. "You're right." She sits back down and in a moment that chilly mask is back in place. "I think the most important thing is that we can't let her find out any more. We have to be ready for her, when she returns. And if she goes too far? Nicolas?"

I nod. Swallow. "Yes. I know what to do. If it comes to it."

"The concierge," Mimi says suddenly, her voice small and hoarse.

We all turn to look at her.

"I saw that woman, Jess, going into the concierge's cabin. She was on her way to the gate and the concierge ran out and grabbed her. They were in there for at least ten minutes." She looks at all of us. "What . . . what could they have been talking about for all that time?"

Jess

I STARE AT THE GIRL on the stage. It's her, the girl who followed me two days ago, the one I chased onto the Metro train. She stares back. The moment seems to stretch. She looks as terrified as she did when that train pulled away from the platform. And then, as if she's coming out of a trance, she swings her gaze back to the audience, smiles, climbs back onto the hoop as it starts to rise upward—and is gone.

Theo turns to me. "What was that?"

"You saw it too?"

"Yeah, I saw it. She was staring right at you."

"I met her," I say. "Just after I spoke to you for the first time at the café." I explain it all: catching her following me, chasing her into the Metro. My heart is beating faster now. I think of Ben. The family. The mystery dancer. They all feel like parts of the same puzzle . . . I know they are. But how do they all fit?

After the show ends the audience members drain the remainders from their glasses and surge up the staircase, heading out into the night.

Theo gives me a nudge. "Come on then, let's go. Follow me."

I'm about to protest—surely we're not just going to leave?—but I stop when I see that rather than continuing up the stairs with the rest of the paying customers, Theo has shoved open a door on our left. It's the same one we noticed earlier, during the performance, the one through which those suited men kept disappearing.

"Let's try and talk to your friend," he murmurs.

He slips through the door. I follow close behind. Beneath us is a dark, velvet-lined staircase. We begin to descend. I can hear sounds coming from below, but they're muted, like they're coming from underwater. I hear music, I think, and the hum of voices and then a sudden, high-pitched cry that might be male or female.

We have almost reached the bottom of the stairs. I hesitate. I thought I heard something. Another set of footsteps beside our own.

"Stop," I say. "Did you hear that?"

Theo looks at me questioningly.

"I'm sure I heard footsteps."

We listen for a couple of moments in silence. Nothing. Then a girl appears at the bottom of the stairs. One of the dancers. Up close she's so made-up it looks like she's wearing a mask. She stares at us. For a moment I have the impression that there's a scared little girl looking out at me behind the thick foundation, fake eyelashes, and glossy red lips.

"We're looking for a friend," I say, quickly. "The girl who did that act on the swing? It's about my brother, Ben. Can you tell her we're looking for her?"

"You cannot be here," she hisses. She looks terrified.

"It's OK," I say, trying to sound reassuring. "We're not going to stay for long."

She hurries past us, up the stairs, without a backward glance. We keep going. At the end of the corridor there's a door. I put my shoulder against it but there's no give. I suddenly have a sense of how far underground we are: at least two floors deep. The thought makes it harder to breathe. I try to swallow down my fear.

"I think it's locked," I say.

The sounds are louder now. Through the door I hear a kind of groan that sounds almost animal.

I try the handle again. "It's definitely locked. You have a go—"

But Theo doesn't answer me.

And I know, before I turn, that there's someone behind us. Now I see him: the doorman who met us at the entrance, his huge frame filling the corridor, his face in shadow.

Shit.

"*Qu'est-ce qui se passe?*" he asks, dangerously, quietly, as he begins moving toward us. "What are you doing down here?"

"We got lost," I say, my voice cracking. "I . . . was looking for the toilets."

"*Vous devez partir,*" he says. And then he repeats it in English: "You need to leave. Both of you. Right now." His voice is still quiet, all the more menacing than if he were shouting. It says, *absolutely do not fuck with me.*

He takes a hold of my upper arm in one of his huge hands. His grip burns. I try to pull away. He grips tighter. I get the impression he's not even putting much effort in.

"Hey, hey—that's not necessary," Theo says. The doorman doesn't answer, or let go. Instead he takes hold of Theo's arm too, in his other hand. And Theo, who up until now I'd thought of as a large guy, looks suddenly like a child, like a puppet, held in his grip.

For a moment the doorman stands stock-still, his head cocked to one side. I look at Theo and he frowns, clearly as confused as I am. Then I hear a tinny murmur and realize that he is listening. Someone is feeding him instructions through an earpiece.

He straightens up. "Please, Madame, Monsieur." Still that scarily polite tone, even as his hand tightens further around my bicep, burning the skin. "Do not make a scene. You must come with me, now." And then he is steering us, with more than a little force, along the corridor, back up the first flight of stairs, back into the room with the tables, the stage. Most of the lights have been turned off and it's completely empty now. No, not completely. Out of the corner of my eye I think I catch sight of a tall figure standing quite still, watching us from the shadowy recesses in one corner. But I don't manage to get a proper look because now we're being manhandled up the next flight of steps, up to ground level.

Then the front door is opened and we're thrust out onto the street, the doorman giving me such a hard shove in the back that I trip and fall forward onto my knees.

The door slams behind us.

Theo, who has managed to keep his balance, puts out a hand and hauls me up. It takes a long time for my heartbeat to return to normal. But as I manage to gain some control over my breathing I realize that though my knees hurt and my arm feels badly bruised, it could have been so much worse. I feel lucky to be back out here gulping freezing lungfuls of air. What if the voice in the doorman's ear had given different instructions? What might be happening to us now?

It's this thought rather than the cold that makes me shiver. I pull my jacket tighter around me.

"Let's get away from here," Theo says. I wonder if he's thinking along the same lines: *let's not give them a chance to change their minds.*

The street is almost silent, completely deserted: just the blink of the security lights in shop windows and the echo of our feet on the cobblestones.

And then I hear a new sound: another pair of feet, behind us and moving quickly, quicker, growing louder as my heart starts beating faster. I turn to see. A tall figure, hood pulled up. And as the light catches her face just so, I see that it's her. The girl who followed me two nights ago, the girl on the hoop, who stared at me in the audience this evening like she'd come face to face with a nightmare.

Concierge

THE LOGE

I AM DUSTING, UP ON the top floor. Normally I do the hallways and staircases at this time of day—Madame Meunier is very particular about that. But this evening I have trespassed onto the landing. It is the second risk I have taken; the first was speaking to the girl earlier. We might have been seen. But I was desperate. I tried to put a note under her door yesterday evening, but she caught me there, threatened me with a knife. I had to find another way. Because I saw who she was the first night she arrived, coming to that woman's aid, helping her put the clothes back into her suitcase. I could not stand back and let another life be destroyed.

They are all in there, in the penthouse: all apart from him, the head of the family. I could have taken the back staircase—I use it sometimes to keep watch—but the acoustics are much better from here. I can't hear everything they're saying but every so often I catch hold of a word or a phrase.

One of them says his name: Benjamin Daniels. I press a little closer to the door. They are talking about the girl now, too. I think about that hungry, interested, bright way about her. Something in her manner. She reminds me of her brother, yes. But also of my daughter. Not in looks, of course: no one could match my daughter in looks.

* * *

ONE DAY, WHEN the heat had begun to dissipate I invited Benjamin Daniels into my cabin for tea. I told myself it was because I had to show my gratitude for the fan. But really I wanted company. I had not realized how lonely I had been until he showed an interest. I had lost the shame I had felt at first about my meager way of living. I had begun to enjoy the companionship.

He glanced again at the photographs on the walls as he sat cradling his glass of tea. "Elira: have I got that right? Your daughter's name?"

I stared at him. I could not believe he had remembered. It touched me. "That's correct, Monsieur."

"It's a beautiful name," he said.

"It means 'the free one.'"

"Oh—in what language?"

I paused. "Albanian." This was the first thing I trusted him with. From this detail he might have been able to guess my status here, in France. I watched him carefully.

He simply smiled and nodded. "I've been to Tirana. It's a wonderful city—so vibrant."

"I have heard that . . . but I don't know it well. I'm from a small village, on the Adriatic coast."

"Do you have any pictures?"

A hesitation. But what harm could it do? I went to my tiny bureau, took out my album. He sat down in the seat across from me. I noticed he took care not to disturb the photographs as he turned the pages, as though handling something very precious.

"I wish I had something like this," he said, suddenly. "I don't know what happened to the photos, from when I was small. But then again I don't know if I could look—"

He stopped. I sensed some hidden reservoir of pain. Then, as though he had forgotten it—or wanted to forget it—he pointed at a photograph. "Look at this! The color of that sea!"

I followed his gaze. Looking at it I could smell the wild thyme, the salt in the air.

He glanced up. "I remember you said you followed your daughter to Paris. But she isn't here any longer?"

I saw his gaze flicker around the cabin. I heard the unspoken question. It wasn't as though I had left poverty at home for a life of riches here. Why would a person abandon their life for this?

"I did not intend to stay," I said. "Not at first."

I glanced up at the wall of photographs. Elira looked out at me—at five, at twelve, at seventeen—the beauty growing, changing, but the smile always the same. The eyes the same. I could remember her at the breast as an infant: dark eyes looking up at me with such brightness, an intelligence beyond her years. When I spoke it was not to him but to her image.

"I came here because I was worried about her."

He leaned forward. "Why?"

I glanced at him. For a moment I had almost forgotten he was there. I hesitated. I had never spoken to anyone about this. But he seemed so interested, so concerned. And there was that pain I had sensed in him. Before, even when he had shown me the little kindnesses and attentions, I had seen him as one of them. A different species. Rich, entitled. But that his pain made him human.

"She forgot to call when she said she would. And when I eventually heard from her she didn't sound the same." I looked at the photographs. "I—" I tried to find a way to describe it. "She told me she was busy, she was working hard. I tried not to mind. I tried to be happy for her."

But I knew. With a mother's instinct, I knew something was wrong. She sounded bad. Hoarse, ill. But worse than that she sounded vague; not like herself. Every time we had spoken before I felt her close to me, despite the hundreds of miles between us. Now I could feel her slipping away. It frightened me.

I took a breath. "The next time she called was a few weeks later."

All I could hear at first were gasps of air. Then finally I could make out the words: "I'm so ashamed, Mama. I'm so ashamed. The place—it's a bad place. Terrible things happen there. They're not good people. And . . .' The next part was so muffled I could not make it out. And then I realized she was crying; crying so hard she could not speak. I gripped the phone tight enough that my hand hurt.

"I can't hear you, my darling."

"I said . . . I said I'm not a good person, either."

"You are a good person," I told her, fiercely. "I know you: and you're mine and you're good."

"I'm not, Mama. I've done terrible things. And I can't even work there any longer."

"Why not?"

A long pause. So long that I began to wonder if we had been cut off. "I'm pregnant, Mama."

I thought I hadn't heard her properly at first.

"You're . . . pregnant?" Not only was she unmarried; she hadn't mentioned any partner to me; anyone special. I was so shocked I couldn't speak for a moment. "How many months?"

"Five months, Mama. I can't hide it any longer. I can't work."

After this, all I could hear was the sound of her crying. I knew I had to say something positive.

"But I'm—I'm so happy, my darling," I told her. "I'm going to be a grandmother. What a wonderful thing. I'll start getting some money together." I tried not to let her hear my panic, about how I would do this quickly enough. I would have to take on extra work—I would have to ask favors, borrow. It would take time. But I would find a way. "I'll come to Paris," I told her. "I'll help you look after the baby."

I looked at Benjamin Daniels. "It took some time, Monsieur. It was not cheap. It took me six months. But finally I had the money to come here." I had my visa, too, which would allow me to stay for a few weeks. "I knew that she would already have had the baby, though I hadn't heard from her for several weeks." I had tried not to panic about this. I had tried, instead, to imagine what it would be like to hold my grandchild for the first time. "But I would be there to help her with the care; and to care for her: that was the important thing."

"Of course." He nodded in understanding.

"I had no home address for her, when I arrived. So I went to her place of work. I knew the name; she had told me that much. It seemed such an elegant, refined place. In the rich part of town, as she had said.

"The doorman looked at me in my poor clothes. "The entrance for the cleaners is round the back," he said.

"I was not offended, it was only to be expected. I found the entrance, slipped inside. And, because I looked the way I did, I was invisible. No one paid me any attention, no one said I should not be there. I found the women—the girls—who had worked with my daughter, who knew her. And that was when—"

For a moment I could not speak.

"When?" he prompted, gently.

"My daughter died, Monsieur. She died in childbirth nineteen years ago. I came to work here and I have stayed ever since."

"And the baby? Your daughter's baby?"

"But Monsieur. Clearly you have not understood." I took the photograph album from him and shut it back in the bureau with my relics, my treasures. The things I have collected over the years: a first tooth, a child's shoe, a school certificate. "My granddaughter is here. It's why I came here. Why I have worked here for all these years, in this building. I wanted to be close to her. I wanted to watch her grow up."

A WORD, FROM behind the penthouse door, and suddenly I am wrenched back into the present. I have just distinctly heard one of them say: "Concierge." I step backward into the gloom, treading carefully to avoid the creaking floorboards. An instinct: I should not be here. I need to get back to my cabin. Now.

Mimi

I BURST BACK INTO THE apartment. I go straight to my room, straight to the window, stare out through the glass. It was hell, sitting up there with all of them. Talking, shouting at each other. I just wanted it to stop. I wanted so badly to be alone.

Mimi. Mimi. Mimi.

It takes a moment for me to work out where the sound is coming from. I turn around and see Camille standing there in my doorway, hands on her hips.

"Mimi?" She walks toward me, clicks her fingers in front of my face. "Hello? What are you doing?"

"*Quoi?*" *What?* I stare at her.

"You were just staring out of the window. Like some sort of zombie." She does an impression: eyes wide, jaw hanging open. "What were you looking at?"

I shrug. I hadn't even realized. But I must have been looking into his apartment. Old habits die hard.

"*Putain*, you're scaring me, Mimi. You've been acting so . . . so weird." She pauses. "Even weirder than normal." Then she frowns, like she's working something out. "Ever since the other night. When I came back late and you were still up. What is it?"

"*Rien*," I say. *It's nothing.* Why won't she just leave me alone?

"I don't believe you," she says. "What happened here, before I got back that night? What's going on with you?"

I shut my eyes, clench my fists. I can't cope with all these questions. All this probing. I feel like I'm about to explode. With as much control as I can manage, I say: "I just . . . I need to be on my own right now, Camille. I need my own space."

She doesn't take the hint. "Hey—was it something to do with that guy you were being so mysterious about? Did it not work out? If you'd just tell me, maybe I could help—"

I can't take any more. The white noise is buzzing in my head. I stand up. I hate the way she's looking at me: the concern and worry in her expression. Why can't she just get it? I suddenly feel like I don't want to see her face any more. Like it would be much better if she weren't here at all.

"Just shut up! *Fous le camp!*" *Fuck off.* "Just—just leave me alone."

She takes a step back.

"And I'm sick of you bugging me," I say. "I'm sick of all your mess around the place, everywhere I look. I'm sick of you bringing your, your . . . fuck-buddies back here. I might be a weirdo— yes, I know all of your friends think that—but you . . . you're a disgusting little slut."

I think I've done it now. Her eyes are wide as she steps farther away from me. Then she disappears from the room. I don't feel good, but at least I can breathe again.

I hear sounds coming from her bedroom next door, drawers being pulled open, cupboard doors slamming. A few moments later she appears with a couple of canvas bags over each arm, stuff spilling out of them.

"You know what?" she says. "I might be a disgusting little slut, but you are one crazy bitch. I can't be bothered with this any more, Mimi, I don't need this. And Dominique's got her own place now. No more sneaking around. I'm out of here."

There's only one person I know with that name. That doesn't make any sense. "Dominique—"

"Yeah. Your brother's ex. And all that time he thought she was flirting with Ben." A little smile. "That was a good decoy, right? Anyway. This is different. This is the real deal. I love her. It's one woman for me now. No more Camille the—what was it you called me?—disgusting little slut." She hoists her bag higher on her shoulder. "*Bof.* Whatever. I'll see you around, Mimi. Good luck with whatever the fuck is going on with you."

A couple of minutes later she's gone. I turn back to the window. I watch her striding across the courtyard, bags over her arm.

For a moment I actually feel better, calmer, freer. Like maybe I'll be able to think more clearly with her gone. But now it's too quiet. Because it's still here; the storm in my head. And I don't know whether I'm more frightened of it—or of what it's drowning out.

I lift my gaze from the courtyard. I look back into his apartment. A few days ago, I let myself in there with the key I stole from the concierge's cabin. I've been going into that cabin since I was a little girl, sneaking in while I was sure the old woman was on one of the top floors cleaning. It used to fascinate me: it was like the cabin in the woods from a fairytale. She has all these mysterious photographs on the walls, the proof she actually had another life before she came here, as hard as it is to believe. A beautiful young woman in so many of them: like a princess from the same fairytale.

Now I'm older, of course, I know that there's nothing magical about the cabin. It's just the tiny, lonely home of a poor old lady; it's depressing. But I still remembered exactly where she kept the master set of keys. Of course, she's not allowed to use them. They're in case of emergencies, if there was a flood in one of the apartments, say, while we're away on holiday somewhere. And she doesn't have a set for my parents' apartment: that's off-limits.

It was early evening, dusk. I waited, watched him go out

through the courtyard, like I watched Camille just now. He was only in a shirt and it was cold, so I didn't think he was going far. Perhaps just a few streets over to buy some cigarettes from the *tabac*, which still gave me enough time to do what I needed.

I ran down the single flight of steps and let myself into the third-floor apartment.

Underneath my clothes I was wearing the new lingerie I had bought with Camille. I could feel the secret, rustling slipperiness of it against my skin. I felt like someone braver. Bolder.

I was going to wait for him until he came back. I wanted to surprise him. And this way I would be the one in control of the situation.

I'd watched him so many times from my bedroom. But to stand in his apartment was different, I could *feel* his presence there. Smell the scent of him beneath the strange, musty, old-lady odor of the place. I wandered around for a while, just breathing him in. The whole time his cat stalked after me, watching me. Like it knew I was up to no good.

I opened his fridge and I riffled through his cupboards. I looked through his records, his collection of books. I went into his bedroom and lay down on his bed, which still had the imprint of his body in it, and I inhaled the scent of him on the pillows. I looked through the toiletries in his bathroom, opened the caps. I sprayed his lemon-scented cologne down the front of my shirt and in my hair. I opened his closet and buried my face in his shirts, but better were the shirts in his laundry basket—the ones he'd worn, the ones that smelled like his skin and sweat. Better even than that were the short hairs I found around the sink where he'd shaved and hadn't managed to wash them all away. I collected several on a finger. I swallowed them.

If I'd watched myself, I might have said I looked like someone in the grip of an *amour fou*: an obsessive, mad love. But an *amour fou* is usually unrequited. And I *knew* that he felt the same way: that was the important thing. I just wanted to become a part of it, this world, his world. I'd had thousands of conversations with him in my head. I'd told him about my brothers. How horrible Antoine has always been to me. How Nick is really just a big loser who lives off Papa's money and I honestly didn't get why Ben was friends with him. How the second I graduated, I'd be out of here. Off to travel the world. We could go together.

I found a glass in the kitchen and poured myself some of his wine, drank it down like it was a glass of grenadine. I needed to be drunk enough to do this. Then I took off my clothes. I lay down on his bed: waiting like a present left there on the pillow. But after a while I felt stupid. Maybe the wine was wearing off. I was a little too cold. This wasn't how I'd planned it in my head. I'd thought he'd have come back sooner.

Half an hour ticked by. How long was he going to be?

I wandered over to his desk. I wanted to read what he was writing so late into the night—scribbling notes, typing on his laptop.

I found a notebook. A Moleskine, just like I use for my sketching. Another sign that we were meant to be: twinned souls, soulmates. The music, the writing. We were so similar. That was what he was telling me that night when we sat in the darkened park together. And before that, when he gave me the record. Outsiders, but outsiders together.

The book was full of notes for restaurant reviews. Little doodles in between the writing. Cards for restaurants tucked between the pages. It made me feel so close to him. His handwriting: beautiful, clever, a little spiky. Exactly as I would have imagined. Elegant like the fingers that had touched my arm that night in the park. I fell a little deeper in love, seeing that writing.

And then, on the last page, there was a note that had my name written there. A question mark after it, like this:

Mimi?

Oh my God. He'd been writing about me.

I had to know more, had to find out what this meant. I opened his laptop. It asked me for the password. *Merde*. I hadn't a chance of getting in. It could be literally anything. I tried a couple of things. His surname. His favorite football team—I'd found a Manchester United shirt hanging in his closet. No luck. And then I had an idea. I thought of that necklace he always wore, the one he said came from his mum. I typed in: StChristopher.

No: it bounced back at me. It was just a blind guess, so I wasn't surprised. But just because I could I tried again, with numbers substituted for some of the letters, a tighter encryption: 5tChr1st0ph3r.

And this time, when I pressed enter, the password box closed and his desktop opened up.

I stared at the screen. I couldn't believe I had guessed it. That *had* to mean something too, didn't it? It felt like a confirmation of how well I knew him. And I know writers are private about their work, in the same way that I'm private about my art, but it now felt almost like he wanted whatever was on here to be found and read by me.

I went to his documents; to "Recent." And there it was at the top. All the others had the names of restaurants, they were obviously reviews. But this one was called: *Meunier Wines SARL*. According to the little time stamp this was what he had been working on an hour ago. I opened it.

Merde, my heart was beating so fast.

Excited, terrified, I began to read.

But as soon as I did I wanted to stop; I wished I had never seen any of it.

I didn't know what I had expected, but this was not it.

It felt like my whole world was caving in around me.

I felt sick.

But I couldn't stop.

Jess

THE GIRL STEPS FORWARD INTO the light of the streetlamp. She appears totally different from how she did in her act. She wears a cheap-looking fake-leather jacket and jeans with a hoodie underneath—but it's also that she's taken off all that thick makeup. She looks a lot less glamorous and at the same time much more beautiful. And younger. A *lot* younger. I didn't get a proper look at her in the darkness near the cemetery that time—if you'd asked me I might have guessed late twenties. But now I'd say somewhere closer to eighteen or nineteen, the same sort of age as Mimi Meunier.

"Why did you come?" she hisses at us, in that thick accent. "To the club?"

I remember how she turned and sprinted away the first time we met. I know I have to tread very carefully here, not spook her.

"We're still looking for Ben," I say, gently. "And I feel like you might know something that could help us. Am I right?"

She mutters something under her breath, the word that sounds like "*koorvah*." For a moment I think she might be about to turn and sprint away again, like she did the first time we met. But she stays put—even steps a little closer.

"Not here," she whispers. She looks behind her, nervous as a cat. "We must go somewhere else. Away from this place."

AT HER LEAD we walk away from the posh streets with the fancy cars and the glitzy shop windows. We walk through avenues with red-and-gold-fronted cafés with wicker seats outside, like the one I met Theo in, signs advertising *Prix Fixe* menus, groups of tourists still mooching about aimlessly. We leave them behind too. We walk through streets with bars and loud techno, past some sort of club with a long queue snaking around the corner. We enter a new neighborhood where the restaurants have names written in Arabic, in Chinese, other languages I don't even recognize. We pass vape shops, phone shops that all look exactly the same, windows of mannequins wearing different style wigs, stores selling cheap furniture. This is not tourist Paris. We cross a traffic intersection with a bristle of flimsy-looking tents on the small patch of grass in the middle, a group of guys cooking stuff on a little makeshift stove, hands in their pockets, standing close to keep warm.

The girl leads us into an all-night kebab place with a flickering sign over the door and a couple of small metal tables at the back, rows of strip lights in the ceiling. We sit down at a greasy little Formica table in the corner. It's hard to imagine anywhere more different from the low-lit glamor of the club we've just left. Maybe that's exactly why she's chosen it. Theo orders us each a carton of chips. The girl takes a huge handful of hers and dunks them, all together, into one of the pots of garlic sauce then somehow crams the whole lot hungrily into her mouth.

"Who's he?" she mumbles through her mouthful, nodding at Theo.

"This is Theo," I say. "He works with Ben. He's helping me. I'm Jess. What's your name?"

A brief pause. "Irina."

Irina. The name is familiar. I remember what Ben had scribbled on that sheet of wine accounts I found in his dictionary. *Ask Irina.*

"Ben said he would come back," she says suddenly, urgently.

"He said he would come back for me." There's something in her expression I recognize. Aha. Someone else who has fallen in love with my brother. "He said he would get me away from that place. Help find a new job for me."

"I'm sure he was working on it," I say cautiously. It sounds quite like Ben, I think. Promising things he can't necessarily deliver. "But like I said before, he's disappeared."

"What has happened?" she asks. "What do you think has happened to him?"

"We don't know," I tell her. "But I found a card for the club in his stuff. Irina, if there's anything you can tell us, anything at all, it might help us find him."

She sizes both of us up. She seems confused by being in this unfamiliar position of power. And frightened, too. Glancing over her shoulder every few seconds.

"We can pay you," I say. I look across at Theo. He rolls his eyes, pulls out his wallet.

When we've agreed on an amount of cash Irina is happy with—depressingly small, actually—and after she's finished the chips and used up both of our pots of garlic sauce, she draws one leg up against the table protectively, the skin of her knee pale and bruised in one spot through the ripped denim. For some reason this makes me think of playground scrapes, the child she was not so long ago.

"You have a cigarette?" she asks Theo. He passes her one and she lights up. Her knee is juddering against the table, so hard that the little salt and pepper shakers are leaping up and down.

"You were really good by the way," I say, trying to think of something safe to begin with. "Your dancing."

"I know," she says, seriously, nodding her head. "I'm very good. The best at La Petite Mort. I trained as a dancer, before, where I come from. When I came for the job, they said it was for dancing."

"It seemed like the audience really enjoyed it," I say. "The show. I thought your performance was very . . ." I try and think of the right word. "Sophisticated."

She raises her eyebrows, then makes a kind of *ha* sound without any humor in it.

"The show," she mutters. "That's what Ben wanted to know about. It seemed like he knew some things already. I think someone told him some of it, maybe."

"Told him some of what?" I prompt.

She takes a long drag on her cigarette. I notice that her hand is shaking. "That the show, all of it: it's just—" She seems to be searching for the right words. "Window . . . looking. No. Window shopping. Not what that place is really about. Because afterward they come downstairs. The special guests."

"What do you mean?" Theo says, sitting forward. "Special guests?"

A nervous glance out through the windows at the street. Then suddenly she's fumbling the roll of notes Theo gave her back out of her jacket pocket, thrusting it at him.

"I can't do this—"

"Irina," I say, quickly, carefully, "we're not trying to get you in any trouble. Trust me. We won't go blabbing to anyone. We're just trying to find out what Ben knew, because I think that might help us find him. Anything you can tell us might be useful in some way. I'm . . . really scared for him." As I say it my voice breaks: it's no act. I lean forward, begging her. "Please. Please help us."

She seems to be absorbing all this, deciding. I watch her take a long breath. Then, in a low voice, she begins to talk.

"The special guests pay for a different kind of ticket. Rich men. Important men. Married men." She holds up her hand for emphasis, touches her ring finger. "We don't know names. But we know they are important. With—" she rubs her thumb and forefinger together: *money.* "They come downstairs. To the other rooms, below. We make them feel good. We tell them how handsome they are, how sexy."

"And do they," Theo coughs, "buy . . . anything?"

Irina stares at him blankly.

I think his delicacy might have been lost in translation.

"Do they pay for sex?" I ask, lowering my voice to a murmur— wanting to show we have her back. "That's what he means."

Again she glances at the windows, out at the dark street. She's practically hovering in her seat, looking like she's ready to leg it at any moment.

"Do you want more money?" I prompt. I kind of want her to ask for more. I'm sure Theo can afford it.

She nods, quickly.

I nudge Theo. "Go on then."

A little reluctantly he pulls another couple of notes out of his pocket, slides them across the table to her. Then, almost like she's reading from some sort of script, she says: "No. It is illegal in this country. To pay."

"Oh." Theo and I look at each other. I think we must both be thinking the same thing. *In that case, then what . . . ?*

But she hasn't finished. "They don't buy *that.* It's clever. They buy wine. They spend *big* money on wine." She spreads her hands to demonstrate this. "There's a code. If they ask for a 'younger' vintage that's the kind of girl they want. If they ask for one of the 'special' vintages it means they'd like . . . extras. And we do everything they want us to. We do whatever they ask. We're theirs for the night. They choose the girl—or girls—they want, and they go to special room with a lock on the door. Or we go somewhere with them. Hotel, apartment—"

"Ah," Theo says, grimacing.

"The girls at the club. We don't have family. We don't have money. Some have run from home. Some—many—are illegal." She sits forward. "They have our passports, too."

"So you can't leave the country," I say, turning to Theo. "That's fucking dark."

"I can't go back there anyway," she says, suddenly, fiercely. "To Serbia. It wasn't—it wasn't a good situation back home." She adds, defensively: "But I never thought—I never thought that would be where I'd end up, a place like that. They know we won't go to the police. One of the clients, some girls say he *is* police. Important police. Other places get shut down all the time. But not that place."

"Can you actually prove that?" Theo asks, sitting forward.

At this, she checks over her shoulder and lowers her voice. Then she nods. "I took some photos. Of the one they say is police."

"You've got photos?" Theo leans forward, eagerly.

"They take our phones. But when I started speaking to Ben he gave me a camera. I was going to give this to your brother." A hesitation. Her eyes dart between us and the window. "More money," she says.

Both of us turn to Theo, wait as he finds some more cash and puts it on the table between us.

She fumbles her hand into the pocket of her jacket, then takes it back out, fist clenched, knuckles showing white. Very carefully, like she's handling something explosive, she places a memory card on the table and pushes it toward me. "They're not such good photos. I had to be so careful. But I think it's enough."

"Here," Theo says, reaching out a hand.

"No," Irina says, looking at me. "Not him. You."

"Thank you." I take it, slide it into my own jacket pocket. "I'm sorry," I say, because it seems suddenly important to say it. "I'm sorry this has happened to you."

She shrugs, hunches into herself. "Maybe it's better than other things. You know? At least you're not going to end up murdered at the end of an alley or in the Bois de Boulogne, or raped in some guy's car. We have more control. And sometimes they buy us presents, to make us feel good. Some of the girls get nice clothes, jewelry. Some go on dates, become girlfriends. Everybody's happy."

Except she looks anything but happy.

"There's even a story—" She leans closer, lowers her voice.

"What?" Theo asks.

"That the owner's wife came from there."

I stare at her. "What, from the club?"

"Yes. That she was one of the girls. So I guess it worked out OK for some."

I'm trying to process this. Sophie Meunier? The diamond earrings, the silk shirts, the icy stare, the penthouse apartment, the whole vibe of being better than everyone else . . . she was one of *them*? A sex worker?

"But it's not rich husbands for everyone. Some guys—they refuse to wear anything. Or they take it off when you're not looking. Some girls get, you know . . . sick."

"You mean STIs?" I ask.

"Yes." And then in a small voice: "I caught something." She makes a face, a grimace of disgust and embarrassment. "After that, I knew I had to leave. And some girls get pregnant. It happens, you know? There's a story too, about a girl a long, long time ago—maybe it's just a rumor. But they say she got pregnant and wanted to keep it, or maybe it was too late to do something . . . anyway, when she went into—" She mimes doubling over with pain.

"Labor?"

"Yes. When that happened she came to the club; she had no other place to go. When you're illegal, you're scared to go to hospital. She had the baby *in* the club. But they said it was a bad birth. Too much blood. They took her body away, no one ever knows she existed. No problem. Because she wasn't official."

Jesus Christ. "And you told all this to Ben?" I ask her.

"Yes. He said he would make sure I was safe. Help me out. A new start. I speak English. I'm clever. I want a normal job. Waitressing, something like that. Because—" Her voice wavers. She puts up a hand to her eyes. I see the shine of tears. She swipes at them with the heel of her hand, almost angrily, like she doesn't have time for crying. "It's not what I came to this country for. I came for a new life."

And even though I never cry I feel my own eyes pricking. I hear her. Every woman deserves that. The chance of a new life.

Mimi

I SIT HERE ON MY bed, staring into the darkness of his apartment, remembering. On his laptop, three nights ago, I read about a place with a locked room. About what happened in that room. About the women. The men.

About how it was—is—connected to this place. To this family.

I felt sick to my stomach. It couldn't be right, what he'd written. But there were names. There was detail. So much horrible detail. And Papa—

No. It couldn't be true. I refused to believe it. It had to be lies—

And then I saw my own name, like I had in his notebook, when it had been so exciting. Only now it filled me with fear. Somehow I was connected to that place, too. There were horrible things my older stepbrother had said. I had always thought they were just random insults. Now I wasn't sure. I didn't think I could bring myself to read it, but I knew I had to.

What I saw next . . . I felt my whole life fall apart. If it was true, it would explain exactly why I had always felt like an outsider. Why Papa had always treated me the way he had. Because I wasn't really theirs. And there was more: I glimpsed a line, something about my real mother, but I couldn't read it because my eyes had blurred with tears—

I froze. Then I heard footsteps outside, approaching the door. *Merde.* I slammed the laptop closed. The key was turning in the lock. He was back.

Oh God. I couldn't face him. Not now. Not like this. Everything was changed between us, broken. Everything I believed in had just been shattered. Everything I had ever known was a lie. I didn't even know who I was any more.

I ran into the bedroom. There was no time . . . The closet. I yanked the doors open, slipped inside, crouched down in the darkness.

I heard him put a record on the player in the main room and the music streamed out, just like the music I had heard every hot summer night, floating to me across the courtyard. As though he had been playing it for me.

It felt like my heart was breaking.

It couldn't be true. It couldn't be true.

Then, over the sound of my own breathing, I heard him entering the room. Through the keyhole I saw him moving around. He pulled off his sweater. I saw his stomach, that line of hair I had noticed on the first day. I thought about that girl I had been, the one who had watched him from the balcony. I hated her for being such a clueless little idiot. A spoiled brat. Thinking *she* had issues. She had no idea. But at the same time I was grieving for the loss of her. Knowing I could never go back to her.

He paced close to the closet—I cringed back into the shadows—and then moved away again, stepping into the bathroom. I heard him turn on the shower. All I wanted, now, was to get out of there. This was my moment. I pushed the door open. I could hear him moving around in the bathroom, the shower door opening. I began to tiptoe across the floor. Quiet as I could. Then there was a knock on the front door to the apartment. *Putain.*

Back I ran, back to the closet, crouching down in the darkness.

I heard the shower stop. I heard him go to answer it, greeting whoever it was at the door.

And then I heard the other voice. I knew it straightaway, of course I did. They talked for a while, but I couldn't hear what they were saying. I opened the closet door a crack, trying to hear.

Then they were coming into the bedroom. Why? What were they doing in the bedroom? Why would those two come in here? I could just make them out through the keyhole. Even in those snatched glimpses I could see there was something strange about their body language—something I couldn't quite work out. But I knew that something was wrong . . . something was not how it should be.

And then it happened. I saw them move together, the two of them. I saw their lips meet. It felt like it was happening in slow motion. I was digging my nails so hard into my palms I thought I might be about to draw blood. This couldn't be happening. This couldn't be real. I sank down into the darkness, fist in my mouth, teeth biting into my knuckles to stop myself from screaming.

A few moments later I heard the shower start again. The two of them going into the bathroom, closing the door. Now was my chance. I didn't care about the risk, that they might catch me. Now nothing mattered as much as getting out of there. I ran like I was running for my life.

BACK IN MY room, back in the apartment, I fell to pieces. I was sobbing so hard I could hardly breathe. The pain was too much; I couldn't bear it. I thought of all the plans I had made for the two of us. I knew he had felt it too, what had been between us in the park that night. And now he'd broken it. He'd ruined it all.

I took out the paintings I'd made of him and forced myself to look at them. Grief became rage. Fucking bastard. Fucking lying *fils de pute*. All those horrible, twisted, lying words on his computer. And then he and Maman, the two of them together like that—

I stopped, remembered what I'd seen on his computer. I had called her Maman, but after everything I had read I wasn't even sure what she was to me now—

No. I couldn't think about that. I wouldn't, couldn't believe it. It was all too painful. I could only focus on my anger: that was pure, uncomplicated. I took out my canvas-cutting knife, the blade so sharp you can cut yourself just by touching it to your thumb. I held it to the first canvas and I sliced through it. All the time I felt like he was watching me with those beautiful eyes, asking what I was doing, so I punched holes through them so I couldn't see his eyes any longer. And then I ripped into all of them, stabbing through the canvas with the blade, enjoying hearing it tear. I pulled at the fabric with my hands, the canvas rasping as his face, his body, was torn to pieces.

Afterward I was trembling.

I looked at what I'd done, the mess, the violence of it. Knowing that it had come from me. I felt like I had an electric current running through me. A feeling that was kind of like fear, kind of like excitement. But it wasn't enough.

I knew what I had to do.

Jess

"I HAVE TO GO," IRINA says. A nervous glance out at the dark, empty street beyond the windows. "We've been too long, talking like this."

I feel bad just letting her wander off into the city on her own. She's so young, so vulnerable.

"Will you be OK?" I ask her. She gives me a look. It says: I've been looking after myself for a very long time, babe. I trust myself to do that better than anyone else. And there's something proud about her as she walks away, a kind of dignity. The way she holds herself, so upright. A dancer's posture, I suppose.

I think how Ben promised to take care of her. I could make promises, too. But I don't know if I can keep them. I don't want to lie to her. But I make a vow to myself, in this moment, that if I can find a way, I will.

AS THEO AND I walk toward the Metro I'm reeling, running through everything Irina told us. Do they all know? The whole family? Even "nice guy" Nick? The thought makes me feel nauseous. I think of how he told me that he was "between jobs," how it clearly didn't make much odds to him. I suppose it wouldn't if you don't need an income, if your lifestyle is being bankrolled by a load of girls selling themselves.

And if the Meunier family knew that Ben had found out the truth about La Petite Mort, what might they have done to prevent a secret like that from getting out?

I turn to Theo. "If Ben's story had printed the police would have to act, wouldn't they? It wouldn't matter if the Meuniers have some high-up contacts. Surely there'd be public pressure to investigate."

Theo nods, but I sense he's not really listening. "So he really was onto something, after all," he mutters quickly, almost to himself. He sounds very different from his usual sardonic, downbeat self. He sounds . . . I try to put my finger on it. Excited? I glance at him.

"It's going to be a huge scoop," he says. "It's big. It's really big. Especially if establishment figures are involved. It's like the President's Club but way, way darker. It's the sort of thing that wins awards . . ."

I stop dead. "Are you taking the piss?" I can feel anger pulsing through me. "Do you even care about Ben at all?" I stare at him. "You don't, do you?" Theo opens his mouth to say something but I don't want to hear another word. "Ugh. You know what? Fuck you."

I march away from him, as fast as I can in these ridiculous heels. I'm not completely sure where I'm going, and of course my stupid phone ran out of data, but I'll work it out. Far better than having to spend literally another second in his company.

"Jess!" Theo calls.

I'm half jogging now. I turn left onto another street. I can't hear him anymore, thank God. I think this is the way. But the problem is that all the crappy phone shops look exactly the same, especially with their lights off and grilles down, no one about. There's an odd smell coming from somewhere, acrid, like burning plastic.

What a bastard. I seem to be crying. Why the hell am I crying? I always knew I couldn't trust him, really; I suspected he'd had some angle the first time we met. So it's not like it's a big surprise. It must be everything, the stress of the last few days. Or

Irina: the horror of everything she just told us. Or simply the fact that, even though I half saw it coming, I'd kind of hoped I was wrong, just this once.

And now here I am alone, again. Like always.

I turn onto a new street. Hesitate. I don't think I recognize this. But there seem to be Metro stops everywhere in this city. If I walk for another couple of blocks I'm sure I'll find one. Over the churn of angry thoughts in my head I'm vaguely aware of some sort of commotion nearby. Yelling and shouting: a street party? Maybe I should head in that direction. Because I've just realized there's a lone guy walking in my direction from the other end of the street, hands in his pockets, and I'm sure he's fine, but I don't really want to test it.

I turn off, head toward the noise. And way, way too late I realize this is no street party. I see a mass of people surging in my direction, some of them wearing balaclavas and swim goggles and ski masks. Huge plumes of black smoke are mushrooming into the air. I can hear screaming, shouting, the sound of metal being struck.

Heat roars toward me in a powerful wave and I see the fire in the middle of the street: the flames as high as the second-floor windows of the buildings opposite. In the middle you can just make out the blackened skeleton of a police van that has been turned on its side and lit ablaze.

Now I can make out the police approaching the protestors in riot gear, helmets and plastic visors, waving batons in the air. I hear the whiplash crack of the batons as they make contact. And mixing with the black smoke is another kind of vapor: grayish, spilling in all directions—coming toward me. For a moment I stand, frozen, watching. People are running in this direction, slaloming around me. Pushing, yelling, desperate, holding scarves and T-shirts over their mouths. A guy next to me turns and lobs something—a bottle?—back in the direction of the police.

I turn and follow, trying to run. But there are too many bodies and the gray vapor is catching up with me, swirling all around. I start coughing and can't stop; I feel like I'm choking. My eyes are stinging, watering so much I can hardly see. Then I collide—smack!—into another body, someone who's just standing still in the middle of the stampede. I ricochet back, winded by the impact. Then look up, squinting through the tears.

"Theo!"

He grabs hold of the arm of my jacket and I cling onto him. Together we turn and half-run, half-stumble, coughing and wheezing. Somehow we find a side street, manage to break free from the torrent of people.

A few minutes later we shove through the door of a nearby bar. My eyes are still streaming: I look at Theo and see his are red-rimmed too.

"Tear gas," he says, putting his forearm up to rub at them. "Fuck."

People are turning on their bar stools to stare at us.

"We need to wash this stuff out of our eyes," Theo says. "Straightaway."

The barman points us wordlessly in the right direction.

It's a single, largish bathroom. We get the tap running and splash water onto our faces, leaning together over the small sink. I can hear ragged breathing. I'm not sure if it's mine or his.

I blink. The water has helped to ease the stinging a little. It's now, as my pulse returns to normal, that I remember: I don't want to be in this guy's company at all. I grope for the door.

"Jess," Theo says. "About before . . ."

"No. Nope. Fuck off."

"Please, hear me out." He does, at least, look a little ashamed. He puts up a hand, mops his eyes. The fact that the tear gas makes him look like he's been crying is an odd addition. He starts speaking, quickly, like he's trying to get it all out before I can cut him off: "Please let me explain. Look. This job is a total pain in the arse, it pays absolutely nothing, it broke up my last relationship—but every so often something like this comes along and you get to expose the bad guys and suddenly it all seems worthwhile. Yeah—I realize that's no excuse. I got carried away. I'm sorry."

I look down at the floor, my arms crossed.

"And if I'm truthful, no, I didn't really care about your brother. One key skill as a journalist is being able to read people. And can I be really, brutally honest now? Ben always seemed totally self-interested. Always out for numero uno."

I hate him for saying it, not least because there's a part of me that suspects he may be right. "How dare—"

"No, no. Let me speak. When he initially told me about his big scoop, I was skeptical. He's also a bit of a bullshit merchant, no? But when you played me that voicemail, I thought: yeah, actually there might be a story here. Maybe he did get tangled up in something nasty. It might be worth seeing where this all leads after all. So no, I didn't care about your brother. But you know what, Jess? I want to help you."

"Oh f—"

"No, listen. I want to help you because I think you deserve a break and I think you're pretty bloody brave and I also think you don't have a bad bone in your body."

"Ha! Then you *really* don't know me at all."

"Christ, does anyone really know anyone? But I'm not a bad guy, Jess. To be fair, I'm not an entirely good one, either. But—" He coughs, looks down at the floor.

I glance at him. Is he bullshitting me? My eyes have started streaming again: I really don't want him to think they're tears.

"Ow. Jesus," I wince as I rub at them.

He steps toward me. "Hey. Can I take a look?"

I shrug.

He reaches out a hand and tilts my chin upward. "Yeah— they're still pretty red. But I think we only got a little of it, thank God. It should wear off soon."

His face is very close to mine. And I'm not quite sure how it happens, but one moment he's holding my jaw and peering at me, his touch surprisingly gentle; the next I appear to be kissing him and he tastes like cigarettes and the wine from the club, which is suddenly one of the better tastes I can imagine, and he's a lot taller than me so my neck is cricked but actually I don't care, in fact I kind of like it, because this is hot—it's really fucking hot— and also wrong in so many different ways, not least because I'm wearing his ex-girlfriend's clothes.

And even though he's so much bigger than me I'm the one pushing him back against the sink and he's letting me and one of his big hands is tangling in my hair and then I'm taking his other hand and pulling it under this stupid, tiny dress. And it's only now that we remember we should probably lock the door.

Sophie

PENTHOUSE

THE OTHERS HAVE LEFT THE penthouse. I sent Mimi to her apartment, to wait. I don't want her to witness any of what's to come. My daughter is so fragile. Our relationship, too. We have to find a new way of being with one another.

I walk into the bathroom, gaze at myself in the mirror, grip the sides of the sink. I look pale and drawn. I look every one of my fifty years. If Jacques were here right now he would be appalled. I smooth my hair. I spray scent behind my ears, on the pulse points of my wrists. Powder the shine off my forehead. Then I pick up my lipstick and apply it. My hand falters only once; otherwise I am as precise as ever.

Then I walk back to the main room of the apartment. The bottle of wine is still there on the table. Another glass, just to help me think—

I start as I realize I am not alone. Antoine stands by the floor-to-ceiling windows, watching me: a malignant presence. He must have stayed behind after the other two left.

"What are you doing here?" I ask him. I try to keep my voice controlled, even though my pulse is fluttering up somewhere near my throat.

He steps forward, under the spotlights. The mark of my hand is still pink on his cheek. I'm not proud of myself for that loss of restraint. It happens so rarely; I have become good at keeping my emotions in check over the years. But on those very rare occasions when the provocation is great enough, I seem to lose all sense of proportion. The rage takes over.

"It's been fun," he says, coming nearer still.

"What has been fun?"

"Oh." The grin he gives me now makes him look quite deranged. "But surely you have guessed by now? After that whole thing with the photograph in Papa's study? You know. Leaving those little notes for you in your postbox, under your door. Waiting to collect my cash. I really do like how you package it up like that for me. Those nice cream envelopes. Very discreet."

I stare at him. I feel as though everything has just been turned on its head. "*You?* It's been you all along?"

He gives a little mock-curtsy. "Are you surprised? That I got it together enough? A 'useless hothouse flower' like me? I even managed to keep it all to myself . . . up till now. Didn't want my darling brother to try and get in on the action too. Because, as you well know, he is just as much of a—what was the word you used again?—*leech* as I am. He's just more hypocritical about it. Hides it better."

"You don't need money," I tell him. "Your father—"

"That's what you think. But you see, I had an inkling a few weeks ago that Dominique might be about to try and leave. Just as I suspected, she's trying to fleece me for everything I've got. She's always been a greedy little bitch. And darling Papa is so fucking tight-fisted. So I've wanted a little extra cash, you know? To squirrel away."

"Did Jacques tell you?"

"No, no. I worked it all out on my own. I found the records. Papa keeps very precise notes, did you know that? Of the clients, but also of the girls. I always had my suspicions about you, but I wanted proof. So I went deep into the archives. I found the details of one Sofiya Volkova, who used to "work"—he puts the word in air quotes—"at the club nearly thirty years ago."

That name. But Sofiya Volkova no longer exists. I left her back there, shut up in that place with the staircase leading deep underground, the velvet walls, the locked room.

"Anyway," Antoine says. "I'm more switched on than people realize. I see a great deal more than everyone thinks." That manic grin again. "But then you knew that part already, didn't you?"

Jess

THEO AND I WALK TO the Metro together. Funny, how after you've slept with someone (not that you'd call what we just did up against the sink "sleeping") you can suddenly feel so shy, so unsure of what to say to each other. I feel stupid, thinking about the time we might have just wasted. Even if, admittedly, neither of us took that much time. It also feels almost like it just happened to someone else. Especially now I've changed back into my normal clothes.

Theo turns to face me, his expression solemn. "Jess. You obviously can't go back to that place. Back into the belly of the beast? You'd be bloody mad." His tone no longer has that drawling, sardonic edge to it: there's a softness there. "Don't take this the wrong way. But you strike me as the kind of person who could be a little . . . reckless. I know you probably think it's the only way you can help Ben. And it's really . . . commendable—"

I stare at him. "*Commendable*? I'm not trying to win some kind of bloody school prize. He's my brother. He's literally the only family I have in the entire world."

"OK," Theo says, putting his hands up. "That was clearly the wrong word. But it's way, way too dangerous. Why don't you come to mine? I have a couch. You'd still be in Paris. You'll be able to keep looking for Ben. You could speak to the police."

"What, the same police who supposedly know about that place and haven't done anything about it? The same police who might well actually be in on it? Yeah, fat lot of good that would do."

We head down the steps to the Metro together, down onto the

platform. It's almost totally empty, just some drunk guy singing to himself on the opposite side. I hear the deep rumble of a train approaching, feel it behind my breastbone.

Then I have a sudden, definite feeling that something is wrong, though I can't work out what. A kind of sixth sense, I suppose. Then I hear something else: the sound of running feet. Several pairs of running feet.

"Theo," I say, "look, I think—"

But before I've even got the words out it's happening. Four big guys are tackling Theo to the ground. I realize that they're in uniform—police uniforms—and one of them is triumphantly holding a baggie full of something white in the air.

"That's not mine!" Theo shouts. "You've planted that on me— fuck's s—"

But his next words are muffled, then replaced by a groan of pain as one policeman slams his face into the wall, while another clips cuffs on him. The train is pulling into the platform: I see the people in the nearest carriage staring from the windows.

Then I see that another man is approaching us from the stairs onto the platform: older, wearing a smart suit beneath an equally smart gray coat. That cropped steel-gray hair, that pitbull face. I know him. It's the guy Nick took me into the police station to meet. Commissaire Blanchot.

Now, thinking wildly back, I make another connection. The figure I thought I recognized in the audience at the club, just before the lights went down. It was him. He must have been following us all night.

The two policemen who aren't so preoccupied with holding Theo start toward me now: it's my turn. I know I only have a few seconds to act. The train doors are opening. Suddenly a whole crowd of protestors are pouring from the carriage, carrying signs and makeshift weapons.

Theo manages to turn his head toward me. "Jess," he calls through a split lip, his voice slurred. "Get on the bloody train." The guy behind him knees him in the back; he crumples onto the platform.

I hesitate. I can't just leave him here . . .

"Get on the fucking train, Jess. I'll be fine. And don't you dare go back there."

The nearest policeman lunges for me. I step quickly out of his way, then turn and shove my way through the oncoming crowd. I leap up into the carriage just before the doors close.

Sophie

"WELL," ANTOINE SAYS. "MUCH AS I have enjoyed our little chit-chat, I'd like my cash now, please." He puts out his hand. "I thought I'd come and collect it in person. Because I've been waiting for three days now. You've always been so prompt in the past. So diligent. And I've let a day go by for extenuating circumstances, you know . . . but I can't wait forever. My patience does have limits."

"I don't have it," I say. "It is not as easy as you think—"

"I think it's pretty fucking easy." Antoine gestures about at the apartment. "Look at this place."

I unclasp my watch and hand it to him. "Fine. Take this. It's a Cartier Panthère. I'll—I'll tell your father it has gone for mending."

"Oh, *mais non*." He puts up a hand, mock-affectedly. "I'm not getting my hands dirty. I'm Papa's son, after all, you must know that about me, surely? I would like another pretty cream-colored envelope of cash, please. It's so very like you, isn't it? The elegant exterior, the cheap grubby reality inside."

"What have I done to make you hate me so much?" I ask him. "I've done nothing to you." Antoine laughs. "You're telling me that you really don't know?" He leans in a little closer and I can smell the stink of the alcohol on his breath. "You are nothing, *nothing*, compared to Maman. She was from one of the best families in France. A truly great French line: proud, noble. You know the family thinks he killed her? Paris' best physicians and they couldn't work out what was making her so sick. And when she died he replaced her with what—with you? To be honest I didn't need to see those records. I knew what you were from the moment I met you. I could *smell* it on you."

My hand itches to slap him again. But I won't allow another loss of control. Instead I say: "Your father will be so disappointed in you."

"Oh, don't try with the 'disappointment' card. It doesn't work for me any longer. He's been disappointed in me ever since I came out of my poor mother's *chatte*. And he's given me fucking nothing. Nothing, anyway, that hasn't been tied up with guilt and recrimination. All he's given me is his love of money and a fucking Oedipal complex."

"If he hears about this—you threatening me, he'll . . . he'll cut you off."

"Except he won't hear about it, will he? You can't tell him because that's the whole point. You can't let him find out. Because there's so much I *could* tell. Other things that have gone on inside these apartment walls." He pulls a thoughtful expression. "How does that saying go, again? *Quand le chat n'est pas là, les souris dansent . . .*" *While the cat's away, the mice dance.* He takes out his phone, waves it back and forth in front of my face. Jacques' number, right there on the screen.

"You wouldn't do it," I say. "Because then you wouldn't get your money."

"Well isn't that exactly the point? Chicken and egg, *ma chère belle-mère*. You pay, I don't tell. And you really don't want me to tell Papa, do you? About what else I know?"

He leers at me. Just as he did when I left the third-floor apartment one evening, and he emerged out of the shadows on the landing. Looked me up and down in a way that no stepson should look at their stepmother. "Your lipstick, *ma chère belle-mère*," he said, with a nasty smile. "It's smudged. Just there."

"No," I tell Antoine, now. "I'm not going to give you any more."

"Excuse me?" He cups a hand behind his ear. "I'm sorry, I don't understand."

"No, you're not getting your money. I'm not going to give it to you."

He frowns. "But I'll tell my father. I'll tell him the other thing."

"Oh no, you won't." I know that I am in dangerous territory. But I can't resist saying it. Calling his bluff.

He nods at me, slowly, like I'm too stupid to understand him. "I assure you, I absolutely will."

"Fine. Message him now."

I see a spasm of confusion cross his face. "You stupid bitch," he spits. "What's wrong with you?" But suddenly he seems uncertain. Even afraid.

I TOLD BENJAMIN Daniels about Sofiya Volkova. That was my most reckless act. More than anything else I did with him. We had showered together that afternoon. He had washed my hair for me. Perhaps it was this simple act—far more intimate than the sex, in its way—that released something in me. That encouraged me to tell him about the woman I thought I had left behind in a locked room beneath one of the city's better-heeled streets. In doing so I felt suddenly as though I was the one in control. Whoever my blackmailer was, they would no longer hold all of the cards. I would be the one telling the story.

"Jacques chose me," I said. "He could have had his pick of the girls, but he chose me."

"But of course he chose you," Ben said, as he traced a pattern on my naked shoulder.

He was flattering me, perhaps. But over the years I had also come to see what the attraction must have been for my husband. Far better to have a second wife who could never make him feel inferior, who came from somewhere so far beneath him that she would always be grateful. Someone he could mold as he chose. And I was so happy to be molded. To become Madame Sophie Meunier with her silk scarves and diamond earrings. I could leave that place far behind. I wouldn't end up like some of the others. Like the poor wretch who had given birth to my daughter.

Or so I thought. Until that first note showed me that my past hung over my life like a blade, ready at any moment to pierce the illusion I had created.

"And tell me about Mimi," Ben murmured, into the nape of my neck. "She's not yours . . . is she? How does she fit into all this?"

I went very still. This was his big mistake. The thing that finally shocked me out of my trance. Now I knew I wasn't the only one he was speaking to. Now I realized how stupid I had been. Stupid and lonely and weak. I had revealed myself to this man, this stranger—someone I still didn't really know, in spite of all our snatched time together. In hindsight, perhaps even as he had told me about his childhood he had been selecting, editing—part of him slipping away from me, ever unknowable. Giving me choice morsels, just enough that I would unburden myself to him in return. He was a journalist, for God's sake. How could I have been so foolish? In talking I had handed him the power. I hadn't just risked everything I had built for myself, my own way of life. I had risked everything I wanted for my daughter, too.

I knew what I had to do.

Just as I know what I have to do now. I steel myself, give Antoine my most withering stare. He may be taller than me but I feel him cringing beneath it. I think he has just understood that I am beyond bullying.

"Message your father or not," I say. "I don't care. But either way, you aren't getting another euro from me. And at this moment I think we all have more important matters to focus on. Don't you? You know Jacques' position on this. The family comes first."

Jess

I'M BACK HERE. BACK IN this quiet street with its beautiful build-ings. That familiar feeling settles over me: the rest of the city, the world, seems so far away.

I think of Theo's words: *"You strike me as the kind of person who could be a little . . . reckless."* It made me angry, when he said it, but he was right. I *know* there is a part of me that is drawn to danger, even seeks it out.

Maybe it's madness. Maybe if Theo hadn't just been arrested, I'd have gone back to his place like he said I should. Crashed on his sofa. Maybe not. But as it stands I don't have anywhere else to go. I know I can't go to the police. I also know that if I want to find out what happened to Ben, this place is the only option. The building holds the key, I'm sure of it. I won't find any answers running away.

I had a gut feeling that day with Mum, too. She was acting weirdly that morning. Wistful. Not herself. Her smile dreamy, like she was already somewhere else. Something told me I shouldn't go to school. Fake a sick note, like I had before. But she wasn't sad or frightened. Just a little checked out. And it was sports day and once upon a time I was good at sports and it was summer and I didn't want to be around Mum when she was like that. So I went to school and completely forgot Mum even existed for a few hours, that anything existed except my friends and the three-legged race and the sack race and all that stupid stuff.

When I got home at ten to four I knew. Before I even got to the bedroom. Before I even unpicked that lock and opened that door. I think maybe she'd changed her mind, remembered she had kids who needed her more than she needed to leave. Because she wasn't lying peacefully on the bed. She was lying like a snapshot of someone doing a front crawl, frozen in the act of swimming toward the door.

I'll never ignore a gut feeling again.

If they've done something to Ben, I know I've got the best chance of finding it out. Not the police in their pay. No one but me. I've got nothing to lose, really. If anything, I feel a kind of pull toward this place now. To crawl, as Theo put it, back into the belly of the beast. I'd thought it sounded melodramatic when he said it but, when I stand at the gate and look up at it, it feels right. Like this place, this building, is some huge creature ready to swallow me whole.

THERE'S NO SIGN of anyone about when I enter the apartment building, not even the concierge. All the lights are off in the apartments up above. It seems as deathly quiet as it did the night I arrived. It's late, I suppose. I tell myself it must just be my imagination that lends the silence a heavy quality, like the building has been waiting for me.

I move toward the stairwell. Strange. Something draws my eye in the dim light. A large, untidy pile of clothes at the bottom of the stairs, strewn across the carpet. What on earth is that doing there?

I reach for the light switch. The lights stutter on.

I look back at the pile of old clothes. My stomach clenches. I still can't see what it is but in an instant I know, I just know. Whatever is there at the bottom of the stairs is something bad. Something I don't want to see. I move toward it as though I'm pushing through water, resisting, and yet knowing I have to go and look. As I get closer I can make it out more clearly. There's a solid shape visible inside the softness of the material.

Oh my God. I'm not sure if I whisper this out loud or if it's only in my head. I can see now with horrible clarity that the shape is a person. Lying face down, spread-eagled on the flagstones. Not moving. Definitely not moving.

Not again. I've been here before. The body in front of me, so horribly still. *Oh my God oh my God.* I can see little spots dancing in front of my eyes. *Breathe*, Jess. *Just breathe.* Every part of me wants to scream, to run in the opposite direction. I force myself to crouch down. There's a chance she could still be alive . . . I bend down, put out a hand—touch the shoulder.

I can feel bile rising in my throat, gagging me. I swallow, hard. I roll the concierge over. Her body moves as though it really is just a loose collection of old clothes, too fluid, too senseless. A couple of hours ago she was warning me to be careful. She was frightened. Now she's—

I put a couple of fingers to her neck, sure there'll be nothing . . .

But I think I feel something. Is that?—yes, beneath my fingertips: a stuttering, a pulse. Faint, but definite. She is still alive, but only just.

I look up at the dark stairwell, toward the apartments. I know this wasn't an accident. I know one of them did this.

Jess

"CAN YOU HEAR ME?" CHRIST, I realize I don't even know the woman's name. "I'm going to call an ambulance."

It seems so pointless. I'm sure she can't hear me. But as I watch her lips begin to part, as though she's trying to say something.

I reach into my pocket for my phone.

But there's nothing there. My jacket pocket is empty. What the hell—

I scrabble in my jeans pockets. Not in there either. Back up to my jacket. But it's definitely not here. No phone.

And then I remember. I handed it over to that doorman in the club, because he wouldn't let us in otherwise. We got thrown out before I had a chance to collect it—and I'm certain he wouldn't have handed it over anyway.

I close my eyes, take a deep breath. OK, Jess: think. *Think.* It's fine. It's fine. You don't need your phone. You can just go onto the street and ask someone else to call an ambulance.

I shove open the door, run through the courtyard to the gate. Pull at the handle. But nothing happens. I pull harder: still nothing. It doesn't move a millimeter. The gate is locked; it's the only explanation. I suppose the same mechanism that allows it to be opened with the key code can also be used to lock it shut. I'm trying to think rationally. But it's difficult because panic is taking over. The gate is the only way out of this place. And if it's locked, then I'm trapped inside. There is no way out.

Could I climb it? I look up, hopefully. But it's just a sheet of steel, nothing to get a toehold on. Then there are the anti-climb spikes along the top and the shards of glass along the wall either side that would shred me to pieces if I tried to climb over.

I run back into the building, into the stairwell.

When I return I see the concierge has managed to sit up, her back against the wall near the bottom of the staircase. Even in the gloom I can make out the cut at her hairline where she must have hit her head on the stone floor.

"No ambulance," she whispers, shaking her head at me. "No ambulance. No police."

"Are you mad? I have to call—"

I break off, because she has just looked up at the staircase behind me. I follow her gaze. Nick is standing there, at the top of the first flight of stairs.

"Hello Jess," he says. "We need to talk."

Nick

"YOU ANIMAL," SHE SAYS. "YOU did this to her? Who the fuck are you?"

I put up my hands. "It—it wasn't me. I just found her."

It was Antoine, of course. Going too far, as usual. An old woman, for God's sake: to shove her like that.

"It must have been a . . . a terrible accident. Look. There are some things I have to explain. Can we talk?"

"No," she says. "No, I don't want to do that, Nick."

"Please, Jess. Please. You have to trust me." I need her to stay calm. Not do anything rash. Not force me to do something I'll regret. I'm also still unsure whether or not she has a phone on her.

"Trust you? Like I trusted you before? When you took me to meet that shady cop? When you hid from me that you were a family?"

"Look, Jess," I say, "I can explain everything. Just—come with me. I don't want you to get hurt. I really don't want anyone else to get hurt."

"What," she gestures to the concierge. "Like her? And Ben? What have you done to Ben? He's your friend, Nick."

"No!" I shout it. I've been trying to be so calm, so controlled. "He was not my friend. He never my friend." And I don't even try to keep the bitterness at bay.

* * *

THREE NIGHTS AGO my little sister Mimi came and told me what she had found on his computer.

"It said . . . it said our money doesn't come from wine. It says . . . it says it's girls. Men buying girls, not wine . . . this horrible place, this club—*ce n'est pas vrai* . . . it can't be true, Nick . . . tell me it's not true." She was sobbing as she tried to speak. "And it says . . ." she fought for breath, "it says I'm not really theirs . . ."

I suppose we always knew about Mimi, Antoine and I. I suppose all families have these kind of secrets, these commonly agreed deceptions that are never spoken of aloud. Frankly, we were too afraid. I remember how, when we were little more than kids, Antoine made some comment that our father overheard—some insinuation. Papa backhanded him across the room. It has never properly been mentioned again. Just another skeleton thrown to the back of the closet.

Ben had clearly been very, very busy. It sounded as though he had discovered more about Papa and his business than I even knew myself. But then I haven't wanted to know all the deplorable particulars. I've kept as much distance, as much ignorance, as possible over the years. Still, it was all tied up with the thing I had told him in strictest confidence ten years before in a weed café in Amsterdam. The confession he had promised me, hand on heart, never to share with another soul. The secret at the very heart of my family. My main, terrible, source of shame.

I can still remember my father's words when I was sixteen, outside that locked door at the bottom of the velvet staircase. Taunting: "Oh, you think this is something you can just turn your nose up at, do you? You think you're above this? What do you think really paid for that expensive school? What do you think paid for the house you live in, the clothes you wear? Some dusty old bottles? Your sainted mother's precious inheritance?

No, my boy. *This* is where it comes from. Think you're immune now? Think you're too good for all of it?"

I knew all too well what Mimi had felt, reading about it on Ben's computer. Learning about the roots of our wealth, our identity. Discovering it was sullied money that had paid for everything. It's like a disease, a cancer, spreading outward and making all of us sick.

But at the same time you can't choose your blood. They are still the only family I have.

When Mimi told me what she had read, all of it—Ben's casual text message months ago, our meeting in the bar, the move into this building—suddenly revealed itself to be not the workings of happy coincidence, but something far more calculated. Targeted. He had used me to fulfil his own ambitions. And now he would destroy my family. And in the process, he apparently didn't care that he would also destroy me.

I thought again of that old French saying about family. *La voix du sang est la plus forte*: the voice of blood is the strongest. I didn't have a choice.

I knew what I had to do.

Just as I know what I have to do now.

Jess

"PLEASE JESS," NICK SAYS IN a reasonable tone. "Just hear me out. I'll come down there and we can chat."

For a moment I think: just because they're a family, it doesn't mean they're all responsible for what's happened here. I remember how Nick briefly referred to his father as "a bit of a cunt": clearly they don't all see eye to eye. Maybe I've jumped to conclusions—maybe she really did fall. An old woman, frail, slipping on the stairs late at night . . . no one to hear her because it's late. And maybe the front gate is locked because it's late, too—

No. I'm not going to take my chances. I turn to look back at the concierge, slumped on the floor and grimacing in pain. And as I do, I see the door to the first-floor apartment opening. I watch as Antoine steps out onto the landing to stand next to his brother—the two of them so much more alike than I had realized. He smiles down at me, a horrible grin.

"Hello, little girl," he says.

Where to run? The front gate is locked. I refuse to be the girl in the horror film who flees into the basement. Both brothers are advancing toward me down the stairs now. I don't have any time to think. Instinctively I step into the lift. I press the button for the third floor.

The lift clanks upward, the mechanism grinding. I can hear Nick running up the stairs below: through the metal grille I can see the top of his head. He's chasing me. The gloves are off now.

Finally I reach the third floor. The lift clanks into place agonizingly slowly. I open the metal gate and dash across the landing, shove the keys into the door to Ben's apartment and fling it open, slam it shut behind me, lock the door, my chest heaving.

I try to think, panic making me stupid, just when I need my thoughts to be as clear as possible. The back staircase: I could try and use that. But the sofa's in the way. I run to it, start trying to tug it away from the door.

Then I hear the unmistakable sound of a key beginning to turn in the lock. I back away. He has a key. Of course he has a key. Could I pull something in front of the door? No: there's no time.

Nick starts advancing toward me across the room. The cat, seeing him, streaks past and jumps up onto the kitchen counter to his right, mewing at him—perhaps hoping to be fed. Traitor.

"Come on, Jess," Nick says, coaxingly, still that chillingly reasonable tone. "Just, just stay where you are—"

This new menace in Nick is so much more frightening than if he hadn't worn that nice-guy mask before. I mean, his brother's violence has always seemed to simmer just beneath the surface. But Nick—this new Nick—he's an unknown quantity.

"So what?" I ask him. "So you can do the same thing to me that you've done to Ben?"

"I didn't do anything—"

There's a strange emphasis on the way he says this. A stress on the "I": "*I* didn't."

"Are you saying someone else did? One of the others?" He doesn't answer. Keep him talking, I tell myself, play for time. "I thought you wanted to help me, Nick," I say.

He looks pained now. "I did want to, Jess. And it's all my fault. I set this whole thing in motion. I invited him here . . . I should have known. He went digging into stuff he shouldn't have . . . fuck—" He rubs at his face with his hands and when he takes them away I see that his eyes are rimmed with red. "It's my fault . . . and I'm sorry—"

I feel a coldness creeping through me. "What have you done to Ben, Nick?" I meant it to sound tough, authoritative. But my voice comes out with a tremor.

"I haven't . . . I didn't . . . I haven't done anything." Again that emphasis: "*I* didn't, *I* haven't."

The only way out is past Nick, through that front door. Just by the door is the kitchen area. The utensil pot's right there; inside it is that razor-sharp Japanese knife. If I can just keep him talking, somehow grab the knife—

"Come on, Jess." He takes another step toward me.

And suddenly there's a streak of movement, a flash of black and white. The cat has leapt from the kitchen counter onto Nick's shoulders—the same way it greeted me the very first time I entered this apartment. Nick swears, puts his hands up to tear the animal away. I sprint forward, yank the knife out of the pot. Then I lunge past him for the door, wrench it open, and slam it behind me.

"Hello little girl."

I turn: fuck—Antoine stands there, he must have been waiting in the shadows. I lunge the knife toward him, slashing so violently at the air with the blade that he staggers backward and falls down the flight of stairs, collapsing in a heap on the next landing. I peer at him through the gloom, my chest burning. I think I hear a groan but he's not moving.

Nick will be out any moment. There's only one way to go.

Up.

I'm clearly outnumbered here, one of me: four of them. But perhaps there's somewhere I can hide, to try and buy some time.

Come on, Jess. Think. You've always been good at thinking yourself out of a tight spot.

Mimi

"WHAT'S GOING ON OUT THERE? Maman?" After everything I have learned the word still feels strange, painful.

"Shh," she says, stroking my hair. "Shh, *ma petite*."

I'm crouched on the bed, trembling. She came down to check on me. I've allowed her to sit beside me, to put an arm around my shoulders.

"Look," she says. "Just stay in here, yes? I'm going to go out there and see what's going on."

I grab hold of her wrist. "No—please don't leave me." I hate the neediness in my voice, my need for her, but I can't help it. "Please," I say. "*Maman*."

"Just for a couple of minutes," she says. "I just have to make sure—"

"No. Please—don't leave me here."

"Mimi," she says, sharply. "Let go of my arm, please."

But I keep hanging onto her. In spite of everything I don't want her to leave me. Because then I'd be left alone with my thoughts—like a little girl afraid of the monsters under the bed.

Jess

I SPRINT UP THE STAIRS, taking them two at a time. Fear makes me run faster than I've ever done in my life.

Finally I'm on the top floor, opposite the door to the penthouse apartment, the wooden ladder up to the old maids' quarters in front of me. I begin to climb, ascending into the darkness. Maybe I can hide out here long enough to gather my thoughts, work out what the hell I'm going to do next. I'm already pulling the hoop earrings from my ears, bending them into the right shape, making my rake and my pick. I grab for the padlock, get to work. Normally I'm so quick at this but my hands are shaking—I can feel that one of the pins inside the lock is seized and I just can't get the pressure right to reset it.

Finally, finally, the lock pops open and I wrench it off and push open the door. I close it again quickly behind me. The open padlock is the only thing to give me away; I'll just have to pray they won't immediately guess I've come in here.

My eyes start to adjust in the gloom. I'm looking into a cramped attic space, long and thin. The ceiling slopes down sharply above me. I have to crouch so I don't knock my head on one of the big wooden beams.

It's dark but there's a dim glow which I realize is the full moon, filtering in through the small, smeared attic windows. It smells of old wood and trapped air up here and something animal: sweat or something worse, something decaying. Something that stops me from breathing in too deeply. The air feels thick, full of dust motes which float in front of me in the bars of moonlight. It feels as though I have just pushed open a door into another world, where time has been suspended for a hundred years.

I move forward, looking around for somewhere to hide.

Over in the dim far corner of the space I see what looks like an old mattress. There appears to be something on top of it.

I have that feeling again, like I did downstairs when I found the concierge. I don't want to step any closer. I don't want to look.

But I do, because I have to know. Now I can see what it is. Who it is. I see the blood. I understand.

He's been up here all along. And I forget that I am meant to be hiding from them. I forget everything apart from the horror of what I'm looking at. I scream and scream and scream.

Mimi

FOURTH FLOOR

A SCREAM TEARS THROUGH THE apartment.

"He's dead. He's dead—you've fucking killed him."

I let go of my mother's arm.

The storm in my head is growing louder, louder. It's a swarm of bees . . . then like being crashed underwater by the waves, now like standing in the middle of a hurricane. But it still isn't loud enough to shut out the thoughts that are beginning to seep in. The memories.

I remember blood. So much blood.

You know how when you're a kid you can't sleep because you're afraid of the monsters under the bed? What happens if you start to suspect that the monster might be you? Where do you hide?

It's like the memories have been kept behind a locked door in my mind. I have been able to see the door. I have known it's there, and I have known that there is something terrible behind it. Something I don't want to see—ever. But now the door is opening, the memories flooding out.

The iron stink of the blood. The wooden floor slippery with it. And in my hand, my canvas-cutting knife.

I remember them pushing me into the shower. Maman . . . someone else, too, maybe. Washing me down. The blood running dilute and pink into the drain, swirling around my toes. I was shivering all over; I couldn't stop. But not because the shower was cold; it was hot, scalding. There was a deep coldness inside me.

I remember Maman holding me like she did when I was a little girl. And even though I was so angry with her, so confused, all I wanted, suddenly, was to cling to her. To be that little girl again.

"Maman," I said. "I'm frightened. What happened?"

"Shh." She stroked my hair. "It's OK," she told me. "I'm not going to let anything happen. I'll protect you. Just let me take care of all of this. You aren't going to get into any trouble. It was his fault. You did what had to be done. What I wasn't brave enough to do myself. We had to get rid of him."

"What do you mean?" I searched her face, trying to understand. "Maman, what do you mean?"

She looked closely at me then. Stared hard into my eyes. Then she nodded, tightly. "You don't remember. Yes, yes, it's best like that."

Later, there was something crusted under my fingernails, a reddish-brown rust color. I scrubbed at it with a toothbrush in the bathroom until my nail beds started bleeding. I didn't care about the pain; I just wanted to be rid of whatever it was. But that was the only thing that seemed real. The rest of it was like a dream.

And then she arrived here. And the next morning she came to the door. She knocked and knocked until I had to open it. Then she said those terrible words:

"My brother—Ben . . . he's . . . well, he's kind of disappeared."

That was when I realized it could have been real, after all.

I think it might have been me. I think I might have killed him.

Sophie

PENTHOUSE

"HE'S DEAD. HE'S DEAD—YOU'VE FUCKING killed him."

"I have to go, *chérie*," I tell Mimi. "I have to go and deal with this." I step onto the landing, leaving her in the apartment.

I look upward. It has happened. The girl is in the *chambres de bonne*. She's found him.

I remember pushing open the door to his apartment that terrible night. My daughter, covered in blood. She opened her mouth as though to speak, or scream, but nothing came out.

The concierge was there, too, somehow. But then of course she was: she sees, knows, everything—moving around this apartment building like a specter. I stood looking at the scene before me in a state of utter shock. Then a strange sense of practicality took over.

"We need to wash her," I said. "Get rid of all this blood." The concierge nodded. She took Mimi by the shoulders and led her toward the shower. Mimi was muttering a stream of words now: about Ben, about betrayal, about the club. She knew. And for some reason she had not come to me.

When she was clean the concierge took her away, back to her apartment. I could see my daughter was in a state of shock. I wanted to go with her, comfort her. But first I had to deal with the consequences of what she had done. The thing, in all honesty, that I had considered doing myself.

I found and used every tea towel in the apartment. Every towel from the bathroom. All of them, soaked through crimson. I wrenched the curtains down from the windows and wrapped the body in them, tied it carefully with the curtain cords. I hid the weapon in the dumbwaiter, in its secret cavity inside the wall, and wound the handle so it traveled up to a space between the floors.

The concierge brought bleach; I used it to clean up after I'd washed the blood away. Breathing through my mouth so as not to smell it. I pressed the back of my hand to my mouth. I couldn't vomit, I had to stay in control.

The bleach stained the floor, leached the varnish out of the wood. It left a huge mark, even larger than the pooling blood. But it was the best I could do, better than the alternative.

And then—I don't know how much later—the door opened. It wasn't even locked, I had forgotten that in the face of the task ahead of me.

They stood there. The two Meunier boys. My stepsons. Nicolas and Antoine. Staring at me in horror. The bleach stain in front of me, blood up to my elbows. Nick's face drained of all color.

"There's been a terrible accident," I said.

"Jesus Christ," Nicolas said, swallowing hard. "Is this because—"

There was a long pause, while I tried to think of what to say. I would not speak Mimi's name. I decided that Jacques could take the blame, as a father should. This was, after all, really his mess. I settled on: "Your father found out what Ben had been working on—"

"Oh Jesus." Nick put his face in his hands. And then he howled, like a small child. A sound of terrible pain. His eyes were wet, his mouth gaping. "This is all my fault. I told Papa. I told him what Mimi had found, what Ben had been writing. I had no idea. If I'd known, oh Jesus—"

For a moment, he seemed to sway where he stood. Then he rushed from the room. I heard him vomiting, in the bathroom.

Antoine stood there, arms folded. He looked equally sickened, but I could see he was determined to tough it out.

"Serves him right, the *putain de bâtard*," he said, finally. "I'd have done it myself." But he didn't sound convinced.

A few minutes later, Nick returned, looking pale but determined.

The three of us stood there, staring at one another. Never before had we been anything like a family. Now we were oddly united. No words passed between us, just a silent nod of solidarity. Then we got to work.

Jess

EVEN IN MY DARKEST MOMENTS over the last couple of days, even learning what Ben had got himself into, I haven't allowed myself to imagine it. Not finding my brother like this, how I found Mum.

I sink to my knees.

It doesn't look like my brother, the body on the mattress. It isn't just the pale, waxy color of the skin, the sunken eye-sockets. It's that I've never seen him so still. I can't think of my brother without thinking of his quick grin, his energy.

I take in the dark, rusted crimson color of his T-shirt. I can see that elsewhere the fabric is pale. It's a stain. It covers his entire front.

He must have been up here all along, all this time, while I've been scurrying around following clues, tying myself in knots. Thinking I was helping him somehow. And to think I'd seen that locked attic door on my first morning here.

Crouched here beside him, I rock back and forth as the tears begin to fall.

"I'm so sorry," I say. "I'm so bloody sorry."

I reach down to take a hold of his hand. When was the last time we held hands, my brother and I? That day in the police station, maybe. After Mum. Before we went our separate ways. I squeeze his fingers tight.

Then I almost drop his hand in shock.

I could have sworn I felt his fingers twitch against mine. I know it's my imagination, of course. But for a moment, I really thought—

I glance up. His eyes are open. They weren't open before . . . were they?

I get to my feet, stand over him. Heart thundering.

"Ben?"

I'm sure I just saw him blink.

"Ben?"

Another blink. I didn't imagine it. I can see his eyes attempting to focus on mine. And now he opens his mouth, but no sound comes out. Then—"Jess." It's little more than an exhalation, but I definitely heard him say it. He closes his eyes again, as though he's very, very tired.

"Ben!" I say. "Come on. Hey. Sit up." It suddenly seems very important to get him upright. I put my arms under his armpits. He's almost a dead weight. But somehow I manage to haul him into a sitting position. He half slumps forward and his eyes are cloudy with confusion, but they are open.

"Oh, Ben." I take hold of his shoulders—I don't dare hug him in case he's too badly hurt. Tears are streaming down my face now; I let them fall. "Oh my God, Ben: you're alive . . . you're alive." I hear a door slam behind me. It's the door to the attic. For a moment I had genuinely forgotten about anything and anyone else.

I turn around, slowly.

Sophie Meunier stands there. Behind her: Nick. And even though I'm reeling from everything that's just happened, I'm still able to make out that there's a big difference in their expressions. Sophie's face is an intense, terrifying mask. But Nick's, as he looks at Ben, shows surprise, horror, confusion. In fact, Nick looks—and this is the only way I can think to describe it—as though he has seen a ghost.

Nick

SECOND FLOOR

I FEEL DREAD CREEPING THROUGH me as I take in the scene in the attic. I ran up here when I heard the screaming, after dragging Antoine, semi-conscious, to the sofa in my apartment.

He's here. Ben is here. He doesn't look well, but he is sitting up. And he is alive.

This can't be right. It doesn't make any sense. It's not possible.

Ben is dead. He's been dead since Friday night. My one-time friend, my old university mate, the guy I fell for on that warm summer night in Amsterdam over a decade ago and have been thinking about ever since.

He died and it was my fault and in the days since I have been trying to live with the guilt and the grief of it: walking around feeling only barely alive myself.

I look to my stepmother, expecting to see my own shock reflected in her expression. It isn't there. This doesn't seem to have come as a surprise to her. She knows. It's the only explanation. Why else would she be so calm?

Finally I manage to speak. "What is this?" I ask, voice hoarse. "What is this? What the fuck is happening?" I point to Ben. "This isn't possible. He's dead."

You see, I know it for a fact. I had plenty of time to take it all in: the unspeakable horror of that lifeless shape in its makeshift shroud. The undeniable fact of it. Of the blood, too, spilled across the floorboards and soaked into the towels: far more blood than anyone could lose and live. But it's more than that. Three nights ago, Antoine and I carried his body down the stairs and dug a shallow trench and buried him in the courtyard garden.

Mimi

IT HAS ALL GONE SO quiet now, after the scream up above. What is going on? What has she found?

This is the part I remember. After this there is nothing, until the blood.

It was late and I was tired from all the thoughts whirring around my brain, but couldn't sleep. I couldn't stop thinking about what I had read. What I saw. Ben—and my mother. I'd destroyed my paintings of him. But it didn't feel like enough. I could see him over there in his apartment, working away at his computer. But it was all different now. I knew what he was writing about and the thought of it made me feel sick, all over again. I could never un-know it. Even if I tried not to believe it. But I think I do. I think I do believe it. The hushed tones everyone uses when they talk about Papa's business. Things I've heard Antoine say. It was all beginning to make a horrible kind of sense.

Ben came to the window and looked out. I ducked out of sight, so he wouldn't spot me. Then I went back to watching.

He moved back to his desk, looking at his phone, holding it to his ear. But then he looked up. Turned his head. He began to stand. The door was opening. Someone was stepping into the room.

Oh—merde.

Putain de merde.

What was he doing there?

It was Papa.

He wasn't meant to be home.

When did he get back? And what was he doing in Ben's apartment?

Papa had something in his hands. I recognized it: it was the magnum of wine he had given Ben as a present only a few weeks earlier.

He was going to—

I couldn't bear to keep looking. But at the same time I couldn't look away. I watched as Ben crumpled to his knees. As Papa raised the bottle again and again. I watched as Ben staggered backward, as he collapsed onto the floor, as blood began to soak into the front of his pale T-shirt, turning the whole thing red. And I knew it was all my fault.

Ben crawled toward the window. I watched as he raised his hand, hit his palm against the glass. And then he mouthed a word: *Help*.

I saw my father raise the bottle again. And I knew what was going to happen. He was going to kill him.

I had to do something. I loved him. Ben had betrayed me. He had destroyed my whole world. But I loved him.

I reached for the nearest thing at hand. And then I ran down the stairs so quickly it felt as though my feet weren't even touching the ground. The door to Ben's apartment was open and Papa was standing over him and I just had to make him stop—I had to make him stop and at the same time maybe there was a little voice inside me saying: he's not really your papa, this man. And he's not a good man. He's done some terrible things. And now he's about to become a killer too.

Ben was on the ground and his eyes were closed. And then I was behind Papa—he hadn't seen me, hadn't heard me creep into the room—and I had my canvas cutting knife in my hand and it's small but the blade is sharp, so very sharp, and I raised it above my head . . .

And then nothing.

And then the blood.

Later, I thought I heard the sound of voices in the courtyard. I heard the scrape of shovels. It didn't make any sense. Maman likes to garden, but it was dark, nighttime. Why was she doing it now? It couldn't be real: it had to be a dream. Or some kind of nightmare.

Nick

I REMEMBER LEAVING PAPA'S STUDY after I had told him what Ben had been up to, what he was writing about. I had called him home, told him there was something he needed to hear. As I descended the staircase I thought about the look on his face. The barely controlled rage. A charge of fear that returned me to childhood; when he wore that expression it was time to make yourself scarce. But at the same time I felt a frisson of perverse pleasure, too. At bursting the Benjamin Daniels bubble. At showing Papa that his famous judgment wasn't always as sound as he thought, tarnishing the golden boy he had briefly seemed to hold closer than his own sons. I had betrayed Ben, yes, but in a much smaller way than he had betrayed me and my family's hospitality. He had it coming.

Any feeling of triumph soured quickly. Suddenly I wanted to be numb. I went and took four of the little blue pills and lay in my apartment in an oxycodone haze.

Maybe I was aware of some kind of commotion upstairs, I don't know—it was like it was happening in another universe. But after a while, as the pills began to wear off, I thought perhaps I should go and see what was going on.

I met Antoine on the stairs. Could smell the booze on him: he must have been passed out in yet another drunken stupor.

"What the fuck's happening?" he asked. His tone was gruff, but there was something fearful in his expression.

"I have no idea," I said. This wasn't quite true. Already, an unnameable suspicion was forming in my mind. We climbed to the third floor together.

The blood. That was the first thing I saw. So much of it. Sophie in the middle of it all.

"*There's been a terrible accident.*" That was what she told us.

I knew in an instant that this was my fault. I had set all of this in motion. I knew what kind of man my father was. I should have known what he might be driven to do. But I had been so blinded by my own anger, my sense of betrayal. I had told myself I was protecting my family. But I also wanted to lash out. To hurt Ben somehow. But this . . . the blood, that terrible, inert form wrapped in the curtain shroud. I could not look at it.

In the bathroom I vomited as though I could expel the horror like something I had eaten. But of course it did not leave me. It was part of me now.

Somehow I pulled myself together. Ben was beyond help. I knew I had to do this, now, for the survival of the family.

The terrible weight of the body in my arms. But none of it felt real. Part of me thought that if I looked at Ben's face it would make it real. Perhaps that was important, for some sort of closure. But in the end I couldn't bring myself to do it. To undo all that tight binding, to confront what lay beneath.

So you see, this is what happened. Three nights ago Ben died—and we buried him.

Didn't we?

Sophie

FROM THE MOMENT I SAW her, covered in blood—my husband's blood—I acted so quickly, almost without thought. Everything I did was to protect my daughter. It is possible that I was in shock too but my mind seemed very clear. I have always been single-minded, focused. Able to make the best out of a bad situation. It's how I ended up with this life, after all.

I knew that if I were to have the cooperation of his sons, their help in this, Jacques would have to be alive. I knew that it had to be Benjamin who had died. Before I wrapped the body I had held Jacques' phone up to his face, unlocked it, changed the passcode. I have kept it on me ever since, messaging Antoine and Nicolas as their papa. The longer I could keep Jacques "alive," the more I could get out of his sons.

After I had done what I could for Benjamin—stemming the blood with a towel, cleaning the wounds—the concierge and I brought him up here to the *chambres de bonne*. He was too concussed to struggle; too badly injured to try and free himself. Here I've been keeping him alive—just. I've been giving him water, scraps of food: the other day a quiche from the boulangerie. All until I could decide what to do with him. He was so badly wounded that it might have been easier to let nature take its course. But we had been lovers. There was still that reminder of what we had briefly been to each other. I am many things: a whore, a mother, a liar. But I am not a killer. Unlike my beloved daughter.

"Jacques has gone away for a while," I told my stepsons, when they arrived. "It is best that no one knows he was here in Paris tonight. So as far as you know, should anyone ask, he has been away the entire time on one of his trips. Yes?"

They nodded at me. They have never liked me, never approved of me. But in their father's absence they were hanging on my every word. Wanting to be told what to do, how to act. They have never really grown up, either of them. Jacques never allowed them to.

I think of the gratitude that I'd felt to Jacques in the beginning, for "rescuing" me from my previous life. I didn't realize at the time how cheaply I had been bought. I didn't free myself when I married my husband, as I'd thought. I didn't elevate myself. I did the exact opposite. I married my pimp: I chained myself to him for life.

Perhaps my daughter did the very thing I hadn't had the courage to do.

Jess

I GRIP THE KNIFE, READY to defend Ben—and myself—should either of them come closer. Strangely, they don't seem so threatening right now. The air feels less charged with tension. Nick is looking from Sophie to Ben and back; his eyes wild. Something else is going on here, something I can't understand. And yet still I grip the knife. I can't let my guard down.

"My husband is dead," Sophie Meunier says. "That is what happened." At these words I watch Nick stagger backward. *He didn't know?*

"*Qui?*" he says, hoarsely. "*Qui?*" I think he must be asking who.

"My daughter," Sophie Meunier says, "she was trying to protect Ben. I have been keeping your brother here," she gestures in our direction, "I have kept him alive." She says it like she thinks she deserves some sort of credit. I can't find the words to answer.

I look from one to the other, trying to work out how to play this. Nick is a shrunken figure: crouched down, head in his hands. Sophie Meunier is the threat here, I'm sure. I'm the one with the knife but I wouldn't put anything past her. She steps toward me. I raise the knife but she barely seems fazed.

"You are going to let us go," I say: trying to sound a lot more assertive than I feel. I might have a knife, but she has us trapped here: the outside gate is locked. I'm quickly realizing there's no way we're getting out of this place unless she agrees to it. I doubt Ben can stand without a lot of help and there's the whole building between us and the outside world. She's probably thinking the same thing.

She shakes her head. "I cannot do that."

"Yes. You have to. I need to take him to a hospital."

"No—"

"I won't tell them," I say, quickly. "Look . . . I won't say how he got the injuries. I'll . . . I'll tell them he fell off his moped, or something. I'll say he must have come back to his apartment—that I found him."

"They won't believe you," she says.

"I'll find a way to convince them. I won't tell." I can hear desperation in my voice now. I'm begging. "Please. You can take my word for it."

"And how can I be sure of that?"

"What other choice do you have?" I ask. "What else can you do?" I take a risk here. "Because you can't keep us here forever. People know I'm here. They'll come looking." Not exactly true. There's Theo, but he's presumably banged up in a cell right now and I never told him the address: it would take him some time to find out. But she doesn't need to know this. I just need to sell it. "And I know you aren't a killer, Sophie. As you say, you kept him alive. You wouldn't have done that if you were."

She watches me levelly. I have no idea if any of this is working. I sense I need something more.

I think of how she said, "My daughter," the intensity of feeling in it. I need to appeal to that part of her.

"Mimi is safe," I say. "I promise you that much. If what you're saying is true, she saved Ben's life. That means a lot—that means everything. I will never tell anyone what she did. I swear to you. That secret is safe with me."

Sophie

CAN I TRUST HER? DO I have any other choice?

"I will never tell anyone what she did." Somehow she has managed to guess my greatest fear.

She is right: if I wanted to kill them, I would have done so already. I know that I cannot trap the two of them here indefinitely. Nor do I want to. And I don't think my stepsons will cooperate with me now. Nicolas appears to be falling apart at the realization of his father's death; Antoine has helped so far only because he thought he was doing his father's bidding. I dread to think what his reaction will be when he learns the truth. I will have to work out what to do with him, but that's not my main problem now.

"You will not tell the police," I say. It isn't a question.

She shakes her head. "The police and I don't get along." She points to Nicolas. "He'll back me up on that." But Nicolas barely seems to hear her. So she keeps talking, her voice low and urgent. "Look. I'll tell you something, if it helps. My dad was a copper, actually. A real fucking hero to everyone else. Except he made my mum's life hell. But no one would believe me when I told them about it: how he treated her, how he hit her. Because he was a 'good guy,' because he put bad guys in jail. And then . . ." she clears her throat, "and then one day it got too much for my mum. She decided it would just be easier to stop trying. So . . . no. I don't trust the police. Not here, not anywhere. Even before I met your guy—Blanchot. You have my word that I am not going to go and tell them about this."

So she knows about Blanchot. I had wondered about calling him for help here. But he has always been Jacques' man, I do not know if his loyalties would extend to me. I cannot risk him learning the truth.

I size the girl up. I realize that, almost in spite of myself, I believe her. Partly because of what she's just told me, about her father. Partly because I can see it in her face, the truth of it. And finally, because I'm not sure I have any other choice but to trust her. I have to protect my daughter at all costs: that is all that matters now.

Nick

I AM NUMB. I KNOW that feeling will return at some point, and that no doubt when it does the pain will be terrible. But for now there is only this numbness. There is a kind of relief in it. Perhaps I do not yet know what to feel. My father is dead. I spent a childhood terrorized by him, my whole adult life trying to escape him. And yet, God help me, I loved him, too.

I am acting on pure instinct, like an automaton, as I help to lift Ben, to carry him down the stairs. And though I am numb I am still aware of the strange and terrible echo of three nights ago, when I carried another body, so stiff and still, out into the courtyard garden.

For a moment, our eyes meet. He seems barely conscious, so perhaps I am imagining it . . . but I think I see something in his expression. An apology? A farewell? But just as quickly it is gone, and his eyes are closing again. And I know I wouldn't trust it anyway. Because I never knew the real Benjamin Daniels at all.

Jess

WE SIT IN SILENCE ACROSS the Formica table, my brother and I. Ben knocks back the espresso in its little paper cup. I tear one end from my croissant and chew. This may be a hospital café but it's France, so the pastries are still pretty good.

Finally, Ben speaks. "I couldn't help myself, you know? That family. Everything we never had. I wanted to be part of it. I wanted them to love me. And at the same time, I wanted to destroy them. Partly for living off women who might have been Mum, at one stage in her life. But also, I suppose, just because I could."

He's looking bloody awful: half his face covered in dark green bruising, the skin above his eyebrow stapled together, his arm in a cast. When we sat down the woman next to us gave a little start of shock and glanced quickly away. But knowing Ben he'll have an attractive scar to show for it soon enough, one he'll work into his charm offensive.

I brought him to the hospital in a taxi: with cash from his wallet, naturally. Explained that he'd had a fall on his moped near his apartment, got a pretty bad head injury. Said he'd made it back to his place and collapsed there, totally out of it, until I turned up and saved the day. It raised a few eyebrows—crazy English tourists—but they've treated him.

"Thanks," he says, suddenly. "I can't believe what you went through. I knew I should have told you not to come and stay—"

"Well, thank God you didn't, right? Because I wouldn't have been able to save your life."

He swallows. I can tell he doesn't like hearing it. It's uncomfortable, acknowledging that you need people. I know this.

"I'm sorry, Jess."

"Well, don't expect me to rescue you next time."

"Not just for that. For not being there when you needed me. For not being there the one time it really mattered. You shouldn't have had to find her alone."

A long silence.

Then he says, "You know, in a way I've always been jealous of you."

"For what?"

"You got to see her one last time. I never got to say goodbye." I can't think of anything to say to this. I couldn't have imagined anything worse than finding her. But maybe a part of me understands.

Ben glances up.

I follow his gaze and see Theo in a dark coat and scarf, hand raised, on the other side of the windows. I might have lost my phone but luckily I still had his business card in my stuff. With his split lip he now looks like a pirate who's been in some sort of duel. He looks good, too.

I turn back to Ben. "Hey," I say. "Your article. You still have it, right?"

He raises his eyebrows. "Yes. Christ knows what they did to my laptop, but I'd already backed it up to my Cloud. Any writer worth their salt knows that."

"It needs to come out," I say.

"I know, I was thinking the same thing—"

"But," I hold up a finger. "We have to do it right. If it publishes, the police will have to look into the club. And those girls who work there—most of them will get deported, right?"

Ben nods.

"So it'll be even worse for them than it is now,' I say. I think of Irina. *I can't go back . . . it wasn't a good situation.* I think of how she spoke about wanting a new life. I promised that if I found Ben, I would find a way to help her. I'm definitely not going to be responsible for her being sent home. If we get this wrong, only the vulnerable will get screwed, I know this.

I look at Ben and then at Theo as he crosses the room to join us. "I have an idea."

Sophie

THE CREAM-COLORED ENVELOPE TREMBLES IN my grip. Hand-delivered to the apartment building's postbox this morning.

I tear it open, slide out a folded letter. I have never seen this handwriting before—a rather untidy scrawl.

Madame Meunier,
There was something we didn't get a chance to discuss. I think we both had other things on our minds? Anyway, I made you a promise: I haven't talked to the police and I won't. But Ben's article about La Petite Mort *will publish in two weeks' time, whether you do anything or not.*

I catch my breath.

But, if you help, it'll have a different emphasis. Either you can be part of the story, take its starring role. Or he'll make sure you aren't named, that you're left out of it as far as possible. And your daughter won't be mentioned at all.

I grip the letter tighter. Mimi. I've sent her away to the South of France, to paint, to recuperate. This went against every maternal instinct; I didn't want to be separated from her, knowing how vulnerable she was, how angry. But I knew she couldn't stay here, with the shadow of death hanging over this place. But before she left I explained it all to her, in my own words. How much she was wanted when she came into my life. How much she is loved. How I have never thought of her as anything other than my very own. My miracle, my wondrous girl.

I have also tried to make her see that in the circumstances she did the only thing she could that night. That she saved a life as well as taking one. That she, too, acted out of love. I did not tell her I might have done the same. That for a brief time he was almost everything to me, too. But I suspect she knows, somehow, about the affair—if that is what one can call those snatched few weeks of selfish, reckless, glorious insanity.

I know that things may never again be the same between my daughter and I. But I can hope. And love her. It is all I can do.

I, too, would leave this place and join her—given the choice. But my late husband is buried in the garden. I have to stay. It is something I have made my peace with. This may be a gilded cage, but it is the life I have chosen.

I keep reading.

Nick won't be mentioned either. Maybe he's not a bad guy, underneath it all. I think he just made some questionable choices. (P.T.O.)

Nicolas has also left, along with the few possessions he kept here. I don't think he'll be back. I think it will be good for him to leave this place. To stand on his own two feet.

My other stepson remains here and while he isn't the most congenial of neighbors it is better having him where I can keep an eye on him. And he is a less threatening presence now. I don't think I'll be receiving any more of his little notes. He seems diminished by everything, by the grief he feels for a father who was rarely anything other than cruel to him. In spite of myself I feel for him.

I turn the letter over. Read on:

Here's what I'm asking you to do. Those girls? The ones at the club? The ones who are your daughter's age, who are being screwed by rich, important guys so that all of you can live in that place? You're going to do right by them. You're going to give every one of them a nice big chunk of cash.

I shake my head. "There's no way—"

I suppose you'll say the building, all that, is in your husband's name. But what about those pictures on the walls? What about those diamonds in your ears, that cellar of wine downstairs? I'm not exactly an expert, but even by my modest estimate you're sitting on quite a fortune. I'm telling you now that you should sell it to someone who doesn't want a paper trail. Someone who pays cash.

I'll give you a couple of weeks. It'll give the girls a chance to sort themselves out, too. But then Ben's story has to go to print. He's got an editor who's expecting it, after all. And that place needs to disappear. La Petite Mort needs to die its own little death. The police will have to investigate, then. Maybe not as hard as they might do, considering they're probably tied up in it.

I'm asking you to do all of this as a mother, as a woman. Besides, something tells me you wouldn't mind being completely free of that place yourself. Am I right?

I fold the letter again. Slide it back into the envelope.
And then I nod.
I glance up, feeling watched. My gaze goes straight to the cabin in the corner of the courtyard. But there's no one inside. I looked for her that night. I searched the building from top to

bottom, thinking that she couldn't possibly have gone far with her injuries. I even looked in her cabin. But there was no sign. Along with the photographs on the wall, several of the smallest and yet most valuable items from the apartment—that little Matisse, for example—and also my silver whippet, Benoit, the concierge was gone.

AN ARTICLE IN THE *PARIS GAZETTE*

It would appear that the owner of La Petite Mort, Jacques Meunier, has vanished in the wake of the sensational allegations about the exclusive nightclub. The police are now attempting to conduct a full-scale investigation, though this is reportedly hampered by the fact that there are no witnesses available for questioning. Every dancer formerly employed by the club has apparently disappeared.

This may come as something of a relief for the former patrons of the club's alleged illegal activities. However, an anonymized website has recently published what it claims is a list of accounts from La Petite Mort's records, listing dozens of names from the great and good of the French establishment.

In addition, a high-ranking police official, Commissaire Blanchot, has tendered his resignation following the circulation of explicit images purporting to show him *in flagrante* with several women in one of the club's basement rooms.

As has previously been reported, Meunier's son, Antoine Meunier (allegedly his father's right-hand man), shot himself with an antique firearm at the family property in order to avoid being taken into custody.

EPILOGUE

Jess

I TRUNDLE MY SUITCASE ACROSS the concourse at Gare de l'Est, the broken wheel catching every few steps; I really do need to get it fixed. I look up at the screen to find my train.

There it is: the night service to Milan, where I'll change before going on to Rome. In the early hours of the morning we'll travel along the shore of Lake Geneva and apparently when it's clear you can see the Alps. Sounds pretty good to me. I thought it was time for my own European tour, of sorts. Ben's staying here to make a name for himself as an investigative journalist. So for perhaps the first time ever, I'm the one leaving him. Not running from anything or anyone. Just traveling, in search of the next adventure.

I've even got a place waiting for me. A studio, which is actually a fancy word for a tiny room where you can reach everything from the bed. Funnily enough, it's a conversion of an old maids' quarters at the top of an apartment block. And apparently it has a view of St. Peter's, if you squint. It probably won't be much bigger than the concierge's cabin. But then I don't have that much to put in it: the contents of one broken suitcase.

Anyway, it's all mine. No, not *mine* mine . . . I didn't buy it— are you crazy? Even if I did somehow have the cash, I wouldn't want my name on the deeds for anything. Wouldn't want to be tied down. But I did put down the deposit on it and paid the first month in advance. I took a cut of the money the girls at the club were getting. A kind of finder's fee, if you like. I'm not a saint, after all.

As for the girls—the women, I should say—of course I couldn't hold each of their hands and make sure it was all going to be OK. But it's nice to know that they've been given the same thing I have. That it'll buy them time. A little breathing room. Maybe even the opportunity to do something else.

Twenty minutes before my train leaves. I look around for somewhere to grab a snack. And as I do I glimpse a figure moving through the crowd. Small, with a familiar, crouching, shuffling gait. A silk headscarf. A silver whippet on a lead. Joining the queue of people waiting to board a train—I look up at the screen above the platform—to Nice, in the South of France. And then I glance away, and don't look again until the train is pulling out of the platform. Because we're all entitled to that, aren't we?

The chance of a new life.

ACKNOWLEDGMENTS

I LOVED WRITING THIS BOOK. At the same time, it was the hardest of my books to write: partly because it was the most complicated structure and premise I've attempted yet . . . and partly because it was written first while I was very pregnant and then with a new baby in tow. *And* during a pandemic, though on that score I know how lucky I am to have a job where I can easily work from home, unlike so many, especially those incredibly brave key workers.

Anyway, I'm so proud of this book and of releasing it into the world. It's not very British to say it, but I am! At the same time, it feels so, so important to stress that none of it would have been possible without the hard work of some very kind, dedicated, and talented people. There really should be multiple names on that front cover: this book has been a huge team effort!

Thank you to the phenomenal Cath Summerhayes, for your endless wit and wisdom and sage counsel, and for being such fun to work with and to go for lunch with and for cocktails with . . . and for always being there on the end of the phone. I am so lucky to have you and so grateful for everything you do.

Thank you to the incredible Alexandra Machinist, for your unfailingly excellent advice and unbelievable negotiating skills. And though for the time being our planned Parisian adventures have fallen foul of the winter vomiting virus, I know we'll be having a glass of champagne on the *terrasses* soon—I can't wait to toast your brilliance!

Thank you to Kim Young, for being the most patient and supportive of editors, for championing this book from its first inception and (frankly fairly ropey) first draft. You always know how to coax my best work from me—you inspire me with your belief in me and my writing! Thank you for holding my hand throughout this whole process—and for always being ready to jump on the phone to discuss a mad new plot idea!

Thank you to Kate Nintzel, for your masterly editorial counsel—for your razor-sharp eye and overall publishing wizardry. I still can't quite believe what you have achieved with *The Guest List* in the U.S., bringing my dark little British book to well over a million readers! I am so lucky to have you as my champion.

Thank you to the utterly brilliant Charlotte Brabbin. You are such a talented, dedicated editor. I am so grateful for all your hard work and advice, tact and creativity, and for always being ready and willing for a brainstorm—however small or silly the query, whatever time of day or night!

Thank you to Luke Speed, for all your kindness and wisdom . . . and for your endless patience in explaining the magical and mystifying world of film to me! And thank you at the same time for being such fun to work with. You and Cath are the dream team! May there be many more lunches . . . and cinema dates!

Thank you to Katie McGowan, Callum Mollison, and Grace Robinson, for your incredible work in finding my books so many publishers around the world. It's such a thrill to think of them being translated into other languages and finding so many new readers globally. I'm in awe of what you do.

Thank you to the fabulous Harper Fiction family: to Kate Elton, Charlie Redmayne, Isabel Coburn, Abbie Salter, Hannah O'Brien, Sarah Shea, Jeannelle Brew, Amy Winchester, Claire Ward, Roger Cazalet, Izzy Coburn, Alice Gomer, Sarah Munro, Charlotte Brown, Grace Dent, and Ben Hurd. I am so lucky to be published by you all. I'm so hoping we all get to raise a glass together soon!

Thank you to the brilliant team at William Morrow: Brian

Murray, Liate Stehlik, Molly Gendell, Brittani Hilles, Kaitlin Harri, Sam Glatt, Jennifer Hart, Stephanie Vallejo, Pam Barricklow, Grace Han, and Jeanne Reina. Thank you so much for your tireless work and dedication and for championing my books stateside. I can't wait to visit you all in New York and celebrate together!

Thank you to the wonderful wider Curtis Brown A-Team: to Jonny Geller, Jess Molloy, and Anna Weguelin.

Thank you to my darling friend Anna Barrett, for doing such a fantastic early read-through and edit of *The Paris Apartment* when I was too scared to show it to anyone else—for hugely boosting my confidence in the book with your encouragement and suggestions. I highly recommend Anna if you're looking for an independent edit of your novel—she's at www.the-writers-space.com.

Last, but very much not least . . . thank you to my family:

Thank you to the Foley, Colley, and Allen clans, for all your support.

Thank you to my wonderful siblings, Kate and Robbie (again—thank God!—nothing like the siblings in this book!). I'm so proud of you both and so lucky to have you.

Thank you to my parents, for your pride in me and for the endless, unflagging support. Thank you for forgiving me for turning up to stay only to dump the wee man on you with no warning and disappear behind my laptop. For being such kind and loving grandparents, feeding and playing and looking after the little guy so lovingly and uncomplainingly while I've been mired in copyedits and proofreads. Thank you for encouraging me in my storytelling since I was a little girl telling Farmer Pea tales in the back seat!

Thank you to Al, for quite literally making all of this possible. For holding the baby; for putting stuff on hold to help me; for talking me through plot crises at three A.M. and on walks and drives and over dinners we've gone out for and holidays we've taken to *get away* from the book . . . for your wisdom; your support; your belief; your encouragement. For reading through almost as many drafts of this book as I have myself, biro in hand—even when knackered from a day's work or baby wrangling . . . or both. You say twenty percent—I say I owe you everything.

About the author

About the book

Insights,
Interviews
& More . . .

Read on

Meet Lucy Foley

Philippa Gedge

LUCY FOLEY studied English literature at Durham University and University College London and worked for several years as a fiction editor in the publishing industry. She is the author of five novels, including *The Guest List* and *The Hunting Party*. She lives in London. ∽

Literary and Cinematic Inspiration for *The Paris Apartment*

In writing *The Paris Apartment,* as with any of my novels, I was hugely inspired by various books and films. There are far too many to list, but here are some of my favorites . . .

Books

The Wheel Spins by Ethel Lina White

This wonderful book, written in the 1930s, is arguably the original "girl on the train." Iris is on a train hurtling across Europe when she meets a fellow Englishwoman who subsequently disappears midjourney, in suspicious circumstances. No one else on the train will believe Iris when she reports the woman as missing—indeed, a sinister group of characters begins to suggest that Iris is imagining things . . . even that she's mad. This incredibly gripping read—which was turned into a film called *The Lady Vanishes* by Alfred Hitchcock—was a huge source of inspiration to me in writing *The Paris Apartment.* That alienating feeling when you don't speak the language or know the local rules and the desperation of ▶

trying to raise the alarm when no one else believes you: these themes fed into the book and into my depiction of Jess and her quest.

The Talented Mr. Ripley by Patricia Highsmith

This book is one of my all-time favorites—it's one of the few I've read more than once. I'm endlessly fascinated by Ripley: enigmatic, chameleon-like, and highly intelligent, with a profound fragility hinted at beneath the layers of obfuscation. I'm also fascinated by Highsmith's ability to encourage the reader to identify with and perhaps even root for him despite his many, many dislikable traits . . . murderous intentions among them! I was definitely inspired by Highsmith's characterization when developing Ben—and there are even elements of Ripley in Jess: that desire to infiltrate another world and perhaps best its occupants at their own game.

The Inspector Maigret novels by George Simenon

I discovered George Simenon's books while browsing the shelves in Shakespeare & Company and fell in love with his tales of the redoubtable Inspector Maigret solving crimes in Paris. I can't pick a favorite, as each is utterly brilliant in its own way, so I thought I'd mention them all here! I was so inspired by Simenon's depiction of the different facets of the City of Light—the seamy underbelly; the shabby, hand-to-mouth existence of many of its inhabitants; and the glamorous, rarefied rich . . . all hiding their own dark secrets.

Film

Charade

This is one of my favorite films set in Paris. Audrey Hepburn plays a woman who has recently been widowed—and quickly discovers her wealthy husband was not the man she thought he was at all. In fact, there are some fairly nasty (and criminal!) elements after the secret fortune her husband supposedly left behind. With the help of Cary Grant's charming, mysterious stranger, she tries to uncover the truth—all while being tailed by some baddies. It's a wonderful, twisty caper and lots of fun— but it's also really gripping and at times incredibly tense. The tenacious heroine at the center of the story and the quest element fed into my depiction of Jess and her sleuthing.

The Tenant

For me the apartment at the center of this film is the star of the show. The tenant in question moves into a mysterious, increasingly nightmarish old building in Paris that is like a character in its own right . . . even causing the boundaries between reality and imagination to shift and blur as the tenant finds himself becoming infected by the place. The oppressive atmosphere and the sense of the bricks themselves holding secrets and menace were something I wanted to replicate in the building at the heart of *The Paris Apartment*. ▶

Rear Window

I've watched this film more times than I can count (or would like to admit!). The premise is so simple and so clever: the protagonist witnesses a terrible crime from the rear window of his building and attempts to solve it while housebound and at the mercy of the murderer. I love the voyeuristic element, that fascination I think so many of us have with our neighbors and who they might really be beneath the respectable surfaces they present to the outside world, what secrets they might be concealing. This was something I wanted to play with in *The Paris Apartment*, allowing the reader (and Jess!) partial—perhaps misleading—glimpses of the various characters in the building, gradually revealing that nothing is exactly as it meets the eye. ∾

Reading Group Guide

1. Tension seeps through every crack of this book, from the moment that Jess encounters each of the characters until the very last secrets are revealed. How does this feeling of being on edge affect how you understand and empathize with each of the characters?

2. The author includes scenes where we see the same moment repeated through the perspectives of multiple characters. How does this technique contribute to the plot? Specifically, did you recognize the club Nick describes to Ben in Amsterdam when its true location was revealed?

3. Foley masterfully creates a wide band of characters whose unique perspectives draw the reader deeper into the story. How is the concierge—who Sophie described as appearing "from some dark corner as if formed from the shadows themselves"—central to the eerie nature of the mystery? Were you able to guess her true identity before it was revealed?

4. How does the apartment building become a character of its own? How does the physical structure become intertwined with the secrets hiding inside its walls?

5. A refrain in the novel is "*la voix du sang est la plus forte*" ("the voice of blood is the strongest"). What does family mean in this story? How is it a dynamic and complex force at the center of the plot?

6. What is the role of Antoine's character in his family and in Jess's investigation? How does his relationship with Sophie represent the underlying contradictions that characterize his family? ▸

7. Does Nick's desire to re-create himself and distance himself from his family's secrets justify his decision to lie to Jess and lead her astray?

8. How do Mimi's *amour fou,* "obsessive love," and feeling of being an outsider in her family ultimately make her lose control?

9. What are Sophie's motivations for her actions? What does she represent? How does she subvert power dynamics and aim to reclaim her own power?

10. Among this cast of characters, who were you drawn to most and why? Were there any narrators you trusted from the beginning? Any you suspected?

11. Did you find the end satisfying? Were you able to guess what had happened before it was revealed? What did you make of Jess's final letter to Sophie? ∾

An Excerpt from *The Hunting Party*

Read on

If you loved *The Paris Apartment*, read on for an excerpt from Lucy Foley's *The Hunting Party* . . .

1

H E A T H E R

Now
January 2, 2019

I SEE A MAN COMING THROUGH THE falling snow. From a distance, through the curtain of white, he looks hardly human, like a shadow figure.

As he nears me I see that it is Doug, the gamekeeper.

He is hurrying toward the Lodge, I realize, trying to run. But the fallen, falling snow hampers him. He stumbles with each step. Something bad. I know this without being able to see his face. ▶

9

An Excerpt from *The Hunting Party* (continued)

As he comes closer I see that his features are frozen with shock. I know this look. I have seen it before. This is the expression of someone who has witnessed something horrific, beyond the bounds of normal human experience.

I open the door of the Lodge, let him in. He brings with him a rush of freezing air, a spill of snow.

"What's happened?" I ask him.

There is a moment—a long pause—in which he tries to catch his breath. But his eyes tell the story before he can, a mute communication of horror.

Finally, he speaks. "I've found the missing guest."

"Well, that's great," I say. "Where—"

He shakes his head, and I feel the question expire on my lips.

"I found a body."

2

EMMA

Three days earlier
December 30, 2018

NEW YEAR. ALL OF US TOGETHER FOR THE FIRST TIME IN AGES. Me and Mark, Miranda and Julien, Nick and Bo, Samira and Giles, their six-month-old baby, Priya. And Katie.

Four days in a winter Highland wilderness. Loch Corrin, it's called. Very exclusive: they only let four parties stay there each year—the rest of the time it's kept as a private residence. This time of year, as you might guess, is the most popular. I had to reserve it pretty much the day after New Year last year, as soon as the bookings opened up. The woman I spoke with assured me that with our group taking over most of the accommodations we should have the whole place to ourselves.

I take the brochure out of my bag again. A thick card, expensive affair. It shows a fir-lined loch, heather-red peaks rising behind, though they may well be snow-covered now. According to the photographs, the Lodge itself—the "New Lodge," as the brochure describes it—is a big glass construction, über-modern, designed by a top architect who recently constructed the summer ▶

pavilion at the Serpentine Gallery. I think the idea is that it's meant to blend seamlessly with the still waters of the loch, reflecting the landscape and the uncompromising lines of the big peak, the Munro, rising behind.

Near the Lodge, dwarfed by it, you can make out a small cluster of dwellings that look as though they are huddling together to keep warm. These are the cabins; there's one for each couple, but we'll come together to have meals in the shooting lodge, the bigger building in the middle. Apart from the Highland Dinner on the first night—"a showcase of local, seasonal produce"—we'll be cooking for ourselves. They've ordered food in for me. I sent a long list in advance—fresh truffles, foie gras, oysters. I'm planning a real feast for New Year's Eve, which I'm very excited about. I love to cook. Food brings people together, doesn't it?

T HIS PART OF THE JOURNEY IS PARTICULARLY DRAMATIC. WE have the sea on one side of us, and every so often the land sheers away so that it feels as if one wrong move might send us careering over the edge. The water is slate gray, violent-looking. In one cliff-top field the sheep huddle together in a group as though trying to keep warm. You can hear the wind; every so often it throws itself against the windows, and the train shudders.

All of the others seem to have fallen asleep, even baby Priya. Giles is actually snoring.

Look, I want to say, *look how beautiful it is!*

I've planned this trip, so I feel a certain ownership of it— the anxiety that people won't enjoy themselves, that things might go wrong. And also a sense of pride, already, in its small successes . . . like this, the wild beauty outside the window.

It's hardly a surprise that they're all asleep. We got up so early this morning to catch the train—Miranda looked particularly cross at the hour. And then everyone got on the booze, of course. Mark, Giles, and Julien hit the drinks trolley early, somewhere around Doncaster, even though it was only eleven. They got happily tipsy, affectionate, and loud (the next few seats along did not look impressed). They seem to be able to fall back into the easy camaraderie of years gone by no matter how much time has passed since they last saw each other, especially with the help of a couple of beers.

Nick and Bo, Nick's American boyfriend, aren't so much a feature of this boys' club, because Nick wasn't part of their group at Oxford . . . although Katie has claimed in the past that there's more to it than that, some tacit homophobia on the part of the other boys. Nick is Katie's friend, first and foremost. Sometimes I have the distinct impression that he doesn't particularly like the rest of us, that he tolerates us only because of Katie. I've always suspected a bit of coolness between Nick and Miranda, probably because they're both such strong characters. And yet this morning the two of them seemed thick as thieves, hurrying off across the station concourse, arm in arm, to buy "sustenance" for the trip. This turned out to be a perfectly chilled bottle of Sancerre, which Nick pulled from the cool-bag to slightly envious looks from the beer drinkers. "He was trying to get those G-and-Ts in cans," Miranda told us, "but I wouldn't let him. We have to start as we mean to go on."

Miranda, Nick, Bo, and I each had some wine. Even Samira decided to have a small one, too, at the last minute: "There's all this new evidence that says you can drink when you're breastfeeding."

Katie shook her head at first; she had a bottle of fizzy water. "Oh, come on, Kay-tee," Miranda pleaded, with a winning ▶

smile, proffering a glass. "We're on holiday!" It's difficult to refuse Miranda anything when she's trying to persuade you to do something, so Katie took it, of course, and had a tentative sip.

T HE BOOZE HELPED LIGHTEN THE ATMOSPHERE A BIT; WE'D HAD a bit of a mix-up with the seating when we first got on. Everyone was tired and cross, halfheartedly trying to work it out. It turned out that one of the nine seats on the booking had somehow ended up in the next carriage, completely on its own. The train was packed, for the holidays, so there was no possibility of shuffling things around.

"Obviously that's my one," Katie said. Katie, you see, is the odd one out; not being in a couple. In a way, I suppose you could say that she is more of an interloper than I am these days.

"Oh, Katie," I said. "I'm so sorry—I feel like an idiot. I don't know how that happened. I was sure I'd reserved them all in the middle, to try to make sure we'd all be together. The system must have changed it. Look, you come and sit here . . . I'll go there."

"No," Katie said, hefting her suitcase awkwardly over the heads of the passengers already in their seats. "That doesn't make any sense. I don't mind."

Her tone suggested otherwise. For goodness' sake, I found myself thinking. It's only a train journey. Does it really matter?

The other eight seats were facing each other around two tables in the middle of the carriage. Just beyond, there was an elderly woman sitting next to a pierced teenager—two solitary travelers. It didn't look likely that we'd be able to do anything about the mess-up. But then Miranda bent across to speak to the elderly woman, her curtain of hair shining like gold, and worked her magic. I could see how charmed the woman was by her: the looks, the cut-glass—almost antique—accent. Miranda, when she wants to, can exert _serious_ charm. Anyone who knows her has been on the receiving end of it.

Oh yes, the woman said, of course she would move. It would probably be more peaceful in the next carriage anyway: "You young people, aha!"—though none of us are all that young anymore—"And I prefer sitting forward, as it is."

"Thanks, Manda," Katie said, with a brief smile. (She sounded grateful, but she didn't look it, exactly.) Katie and Miranda are best friends from way back. I know they haven't seen as much of each other lately, those two; Miranda says Katie has been busy with work. And because Samira and Giles have been tied up in baby land, Miranda and I have spent more time together than ever before. We've been shopping, we've gone for drinks. We've gossiped together. I have begun to feel that she's accepted me as her *friend*, rather than merely Mark's girlfriend, last to the group by almost a decade.

Katie has always been there to usurp me, in the past. She and Miranda have always been so tight-knit. So much so that they're almost more like sisters than friends. In the past I've felt excluded by this, all that closeness and history. It doesn't leave any new friendship with room to breathe. So a secret part of me is—well, rather pleased.

I REALLY WANT EVERYONE TO HAVE A GOOD TIME ON THIS TRIP, for it all to be a success. The New Year's Eve getaway is a big deal. They've done it every year, this group. They've been doing it for long before I came onto the scene. And I suppose, in a way, planning this trip is a rather pitiful attempt at proving that I am really one of them. At saying I should be properly accepted into the "inner circle" at last. You'd think that three years—which is the time it has been since Mark and I got together—would be long enough. But it's not. They all go back a very long way, you see: to Oxford, where they first became friends.

It's tricky—as anyone who has been in this situation will know—to be the latest addition to a group of old friends. ▶

15

An Excerpt from *The Hunting Party* (continued)

It seems that I will always be the new girl, however many years pass. I will always be the last in, the trespasser.

I look again at the brochure in my lap. Perhaps this trip—so carefully planned—will change things. Prove that I am one of them. I'm so excited. ∾

Praise for *The Hunting Party*

"A ripping, riveting murder mystery—wily as Agatha Christie, charged with real menace, real depth. Perfect for fans of Ruth Ware."
—A. J. Finn, #1 *New York Times* bestselling author of *The Woman in the Window*

"A tense, perfectly paced murder mystery."
—*People*

"An auspicious thriller debut. . . . A cracklingly suspenseful story for a long winter's night."
—*Publishers Weekly*

"Very gripping and so good on the awfulness of some long-history friendships!"
—Sophie Hannah

"Fans of Ruth Ware will likely rip through *The Hunting Party* at warp speed."
—PopSugar

"Anyone who's grown apart from old friends will recognize the yearning depicted here to make everything as it was. . . . Readers are left wondering until the end which guest has died as well as who the killer is; they will be well rewarded by the story's ending."
—*Booklist*

"My favorite kind of whodunit, kept me guessing all the way through, and reminiscent of Agatha Christie at her best—with an extra dose of acid."
—Alex Michaelides, author of the #1 *New York Times* bestseller *The Silent Patient*

"Grab a blanket and read the surprising things that happen when highly educated English people let their hair down."
—Mystery Scene

"*The Secret History* meets *And Then There Were None*, this is a fantastic crime debut.
—Cass Green

"Like a deliciously drawn out game of Clue, this novel brings together a group of Oxford friends at a remote Scottish highlands estate for the Christmas holidays. . . . Foley paints such a vivid hunting-lodge-and-lochs setting that you'll immediately be booking your own highland fling, clandestine killers or no."
—*National Geographic*

THE
HUNTING
PARTY

A NOVEL

LUCY
FOLEY

WILLIAM MORROW
An Imprint of HarperCollinsPublishers

P.S.™ is a trademark of HarperCollins Publishers.

HarperCollins books may be purchased for educational, business, or sales promotional use. For information, please email the Special Markets Department at SPsales@harpercollins.com.

Published in 2019 by HarperFiction, an imprint of HarperCollins UK.

A hardcover edition of this book was published in 2019 by William Morrow, an imprint of HarperCollins Publishers.

FIRST WILLIAM MORROW PAPERBACK EDITION PUBLISHED 2020.

Designed by William Ruoto
Photo courtesy of Denis Belitsky/Shutterstock, Inc.

Library of Congress Cataloging-in-Publication Data has been applied for.

ISBN 978-0-06-286891-6

23 24 25 26 27 LBC 20 19 18 17 16

Should old acquaintance be forgot
And never brought to mind?

1

HEATHER

Now
January 2, 2019

I SEE A MAN COMING THROUGH THE FALLING SNOW. FROM A DIS-
tance, through the curtain of white, he looks hardly human, like
a shadow figure.

As he nears me I see that it is Doug, the gamekeeper.

He is hurrying toward the Lodge, I realize, trying to run. But
the fallen, falling snow hampers him. He stumbles with each step.
Something bad. I know this without being able to see his face.

As he comes closer I see that his features are frozen with shock.
I know this look. I have seen it before. This is the expression of
someone who has witnessed something horrific, beyond the bounds
of normal human experience.

I open the door of the Lodge, let him in. He brings with him a
rush of freezing air, a spill of snow.

"What's happened?" I ask him.

There is a moment—a long pause—in which he tries to catch

his breath. But his eyes tell the story before he can, a mute communication of horror.

Finally, he speaks. "I've found the missing guest."

"Well, that's great," I say. "Where—"

He shakes his head, and I feel the question expire on my lips.

"I found a body."

2

EMMA

Three days earlier
December 30, 2018

N EW YEAR. ALL OF US TOGETHER FOR THE FIRST TIME IN
ages. Me and Mark, Miranda and Julien, Nick and Bo, Samira
and Giles, their six-month-old baby, Priya. And Katie.

Four days in a winter Highland wilderness. Loch Corrin, it's
called. Very exclusive: they only let four parties stay there each
year—the rest of the time it's kept as a private residence. This time
of year, as you might guess, is the most popular. I had to reserve it
pretty much the day after New Year last year, as soon as the bookings opened up. The woman I spoke with assured me that with our
group taking over most of the accommodations we should have the
whole place to ourselves.

I take the brochure out of my bag again. A thick card, expensive affair. It shows a fir-lined loch, heather-red peaks rising behind,
though they may well be snow-covered now. According to the
photographs, the Lodge itself—the "New Lodge," as the brochure
describes it—is a big glass construction, über-modern, designed by

a top architect who recently constructed the summer pavilion at the Serpentine Gallery. I think the idea is that it's meant to blend seamlessly with the still waters of the loch, reflecting the landscape and the uncompromising lines of the big peak, the Munro, rising behind.

Near the Lodge, dwarfed by it, you can make out a small cluster of dwellings that look as though they are huddling together to keep warm. These are the cabins; there's one for each couple, but we'll come together to have meals in the shooting lodge, the bigger building in the middle. Apart from the Highland Dinner on the first night—"a showcase of local, seasonal produce"—we'll be cooking for ourselves. They've ordered food in for me. I sent a long list in advance—fresh truffles, foie gras, oysters. I'm planning a real feast for New Year's Eve, which I'm very excited about. I love to cook. Food brings people together, doesn't it?

THIS PART OF THE JOURNEY IS PARTICULARLY DRAMATIC. WE have the sea on one side of us, and every so often the land sheers away so that it feels as if one wrong move might send us careering over the edge. The water is slate gray, violent-looking. In one clifftop field the sheep huddle together in a group as though trying to keep warm. You can hear the wind; every so often it throws itself against the windows, and the train shudders.

All of the others seem to have fallen asleep, even baby Priya. Giles is actually snoring.

Look, I want to say, *look how beautiful it is!*

I've planned this trip, so I feel a certain ownership of it—the anxiety that people won't enjoy themselves, that things might go wrong. And also a sense of pride, already, in its small successes . . . like this, the wild beauty outside the window.

It's hardly a surprise that they're all asleep. We got up so early this morning to catch the train—Miranda looked particularly cross at the hour. And then everyone got on the booze, of course. Mark,

Giles, and Julien hit the drinks trolley early, somewhere around Doncaster, even though it was only eleven. They got happily tipsy, affectionate, and loud (the next few seats along did not look impressed). They seem to be able to fall back into the easy camaraderie of years gone by no matter how much time has passed since they last saw each other, especially with the help of a couple of beers.

Nick and Bo, Nick's American boyfriend, aren't so much a feature of this boys' club, because Nick wasn't part of their group at Oxford . . . although Katie has claimed in the past that there's more to it than that, some tacit homophobia on the part of the other boys. Nick is Katie's friend, first and foremost. Sometimes I have the distinct impression that he doesn't particularly like the rest of us, that he tolerates us only because of Katie. I've always suspected a bit of coolness between Nick and Miranda, probably because they're both such strong characters. And yet this morning the two of them seemed thick as thieves, hurrying off across the station concourse, arm in arm, to buy "sustenance" for the trip. This turned out to be a perfectly chilled bottle of Sancerre, which Nick pulled from the cool-bag to slightly envious looks from the beer drinkers. "He was trying to get those G-and-Ts in cans," Miranda told us, "but I wouldn't let him. We have to start as we mean to go on."

Miranda, Nick, Bo, and I each had some wine. Even Samira decided to have a small one, too, at the last minute: "There's all this new evidence that says you can drink when you're breastfeeding."

Katie shook her head at first; she had a bottle of fizzy water. "Oh, come on, Kay-tee," Miranda pleaded, with a winning smile, proffering a glass. "We're on holiday!" It's difficult to refuse Miranda anything when she's trying to persuade you to do something, so Katie took it, of course, and had a tentative sip.

THE BOOZE HELPED LIGHTEN THE ATMOSPHERE A BIT; WE'D had a bit of a mix-up with the seating when we first got on.

Everyone was tired and cross, halfheartedly trying to work it out. It turned out that one of the nine seats on the booking had somehow ended up in the next carriage, completely on its own. The train was packed, for the holidays, so there was no possibility of shuffling things around.

"Obviously that's my one," Katie said. Katie, you see, is the odd one out, not being in a couple. In a way, I suppose you could say that she is more of an interloper than I am these days.

"Oh, Katie," I said. "I'm so sorry—I feel like an idiot. I don't know how that happened. I was sure I'd reserved them all in the middle, to try to make sure we'd all be together. The system must have changed it. Look, you come and sit here . . . I'll go there."

"No," Katie said, hefting her suitcase awkwardly over the heads of the passengers already in their seats. "That doesn't make any sense. I don't mind."

Her tone suggested otherwise. For goodness' sake, I found myself thinking. It's only a train journey. Does it really matter?

The other eight seats were facing each other around two tables in the middle of the carriage. Just beyond, there was an elderly woman sitting next to a pierced teenager—two solitary travelers. It didn't look likely that we'd be able to do anything about the mess-up. But then Miranda bent across to speak to the elderly woman, her curtain of hair shining like gold, and worked her magic. I could see how charmed the woman was by her: the looks, the cut-glass—almost antique—accent. Miranda, when she wants to, can exert *serious* charm. Anyone who knows her has been on the receiving end of it.

Oh yes, the woman said, of course she would move. It would probably be more peaceful in the next carriage anyway: "You young people, aha!"—though none of us are all that young anymore—"And I prefer sitting forward, as it is."

"Thanks, Manda," Katie said, with a brief smile. (She sounded grateful, but she didn't look it, exactly.) Katie and Miranda are best friends from way back. I know they haven't seen as much of each other lately, those two; Miranda says Katie has been busy with work. And because Samira and Giles have been tied up in baby land, Miranda and I have spent more time together than ever before. We've been shopping, we've gone for drinks. We've gossiped together. I have begun to feel that she's accepted me as her *friend*, rather than merely Mark's girlfriend, last to the group by almost a decade.

Katie has always been there to usurp me, in the past. She and Miranda have always been so tight-knit. So much so that they're almost more like sisters than friends. In the past I've felt excluded by this, all that closeness and history. It doesn't leave any new friendship with room to breathe. So a secret part of me is—well, rather pleased.

REALLY WANT EVERYONE TO HAVE A GOOD TIME ON THIS TRIP, for it all to be a success. The New Year's Eve getaway is a big deal. They've done it every year, this group. They've been doing it for long before I came onto the scene. And I suppose, in a way, planning this trip is a rather pitiful attempt at proving that I am really one of them. At saying I should be properly accepted into the "inner circle" at last. You'd think that three years—which is the time it has been since Mark and I got together—would be long enough. But it's not. They all go back a very long way, you see: to Oxford, where they first became friends.

It's tricky—as anyone who has been in this situation will know—to be the latest addition to a group of old friends. It seems that I will always be the new girl, however many years pass. I will always be the last in, the trespasser.

I look again at the brochure in my lap. Perhaps this trip—so carefully planned—will change things. Prove that I am one of them. I'm so excited.

3

KATIE

SO WE'RE FINALLY HERE. AND YET I HAVE A SUDDEN LONGING to be back in the city. Even my office desk would do. The Loch Corrin station is laughably tiny. A solitary platform, with the steel-covered slope of a mountain shearing up behind, the top lost in cloud. The signpost, the National Rail standard, looks like a practical joke. The platform is covered in a thin dusting of snow, not a single footprint marring the perfect white. I think of London snow—how it's dirty almost as soon as it has fallen, trodden underfoot by thousands. If I needed any further proof of how far we are from the city, it is this, that no one has been here to step in it, let alone clear it. Toto, I've a feeling we're not in Kansas anymore. We passed through miles and miles of this wild-looking countryside on the train. I can't remember the last time I saw a human structure before this one, let alone a person.

We walk gingerly along the frozen platform—you can see the glint of black ice through the fallen snow—past the tiny station building. It looks completely deserted. I wonder how often the "Waiting Room," with its painted sign and optimistic shelf of books, gets used. Now we're passing a small cubicle with a pane of dirty glass: a ticket booth, or tiny office. I peer in, fascinated by the idea of an office here in the middle of all this wilderness, and feel a small shock as I realize it isn't empty. There's actually someone sitting there, in the gloom. I can only make out the shape of him: broad-shouldered, hunched, and then the brief gleam of eyes, watching us as we pass.

"What is it?" Giles, in front of me, turns around. I must have made a noise of surprise.

"There's someone in there," I whisper. "A train guard or something—it just gave me a shock."

Giles peers through the window. "You're right." He pretends to tip an imaginary cap from his bald head. "Top o' the morning to ya," he says, with a grin. Giles is the clown of our group: lovable, silly—sometimes to a fault.

"That's Irish, idiot," says Samira affectionately. Those two do everything affectionately. I never feel more aware of my single status than when I'm in their company.

The man in the booth does not respond at first. And then, slowly, he raises one hand, a greeting of sorts.

THERE'S A LAND ROVER WAITING TO PICK US UP: SPLATTERED with mud, one of the old kind. I see the door open, and a tall man unfolds himself.

"That must be the gamekeeper," Emma says. "The email said he'd pick us up."

He doesn't look like a gamekeeper, I think. What had I imagined, though? I think, mainly, I'd expected him to be old. He's probably only about our age. There's the bulk, I suppose: the shoulders, the height, that speak of a life lived outdoors, and the rather wild dark hair. As he welcomes us, in a low mumble, his voice has a cracked quality to it, as though it doesn't get put to much use.

I see him look us over. I don't think he likes what he sees. Is that a sneer, as he takes in Nick's spotless Barbour coat, Samira's

Hunter wellies, Miranda's fox-fur collar? If so, who knows what he makes of my city dweller's clothes and wheeled Samsonite. I hardly thought about what I was packing, because I was so distracted.

I see Julien, Bo, and Mark try to help him with the bags, but he brushes them aside. Beside him they look as neat as schoolboys on the first day of the new term. I bet they don't love the contrast.

"I suppose it will have to be two lots," Giles says. "Can't get all of us in there safely."

The gamekeeper raises his eyebrows. "Whatever you like."

"You girls go first," Mark says, with an attempt at chivalry, "us lads will stay behind." I wait, cringing, for him to make a joke about Nick and Bo being honorary girls. Luckily it doesn't seem to have occurred to him—or he's managed to hold his tongue. We're all on our best behavior today, in tolerant holiday-with-friends mode.

It's been ages since we've all been together like this—not since last New Year's Eve, probably. I always forget what it's like. We fit back so quickly, so easily, into our old roles, the ones we have always occupied in this group. I'm the quiet one—to Miranda and Samira, my old housemates, the group extroverts. I revert: we all do. I'm sure Giles, say, isn't nearly such a clown in the hospital where he's a highly respected department head. We clamber into the Land Rover. It smells of wet dog and earth in here. I imagine that's what the gamekeeper would smell like, too, if you got close enough. Miranda is up front, next to him. Every so often I catch a whiff of her perfume: heavy, smoky, mingling oddly with the earthiness. Only she could get away with it. I turn my head to breathe in the fresh air coming through the cracked window.

On one side of us now a rather steep bank falls away to the loch. On the other, though it's not quite dark, the forest is already impenetrably black. The road is nothing more than a track, pitted and very thin, so a false move would send us plunging down toward the water, or crashing into the thickets. We seesaw our way along and then suddenly the brakes come on, hard. All of us are thrown forward in our seats and then slammed back against them.

"Fuck!" Miranda shouts as Priya—so quiet for the journey up—begins to howl in Samira's arms.

A stag is lit up in the track in front of us. It must have detached itself from the shadow of the trees without any of us noticing. The huge head looks almost too big for the slender reddish body, crowned by a vast bristle of antlers, both majestic and lethal-looking. In the headlights its eyes gleam a weird, alien green. Finally it stops staring at us and moves away with an unhurried grace, into the trees. I put a hand to my chest and feel the fast drumbeat of my heart.

"Wow," Miranda breathes. "What was that?"

The gamekeeper turns to her and says, deadpan, "A deer."

"I mean," she says, a little flustered—unusually for her—"I mean, what sort of deer?"

"Red," the gamekeeper says. "A red stag." He turns back to the road. Exchange over.

Miranda twists around to face us over the back of the seats, and mouths, *He's hot, no?* Samira and Emma nod their agreement. Then, aloud, she says, "Don't you think so, Katie?" She leans over and pokes me in the shoulder, a tiny bit too hard.

"I don't know," I say. I look at the gamekeeper's impassive expression in the rearview mirror. Has he guessed we're talking about him? If so, he gives no indication that he's listening, but all the same, it's embarrassing.

"Oh, but you've always had strange taste in men, Katie," Miranda says, laughing.

Miranda has never really liked my boyfriends. The feeling has, funnily enough, generally been mutual—I've often had to defend her to them. "I think you pick them," she said once, "so that they'll be like the angel on your shoulder, telling you: 'She's not a good'un, that one. Steer clear.'" But Miranda is my oldest friend. And our friendship has always outlasted any romantic relationship—on my side, that is. Miranda and Julien have been together since Oxford.

I wasn't sure what to make of Julien when he came on the scene, at the end of our first year. Neither was Miranda. He was a bit of an anomaly, compared to the boyfriends she'd had before. Admittedly, there were only a couple for comparison, both of them projects like me, not nearly as good-looking or as sociable as her, guys who seemed to exist in a permanent state of disbelief that they had been chosen. But then, Miranda has always liked a project.

So Julien seemed too obvious for her, with her love of waifs and strays. He was too brashly good-looking, too self-confident. And those were her words, not mine. "He's so arrogant," she'd say. "I can't wait to hand him his balls next time he tries it on." I wondered if she really couldn't see how closely he mirrored her own arrogance, her own self-confidence.

Julien kept trying. And each time, she rebuffed him. He'd come over to chat to us—her—in a pub. Or he'd just happen to "bump into" her after a lecture. Or he'd casually be dropping into the bar of our college's Junior Common Room, ostensibly to see some friends, but would spend most of the night sitting at our table, wooing Miranda with an embarrassing frankness.

Later I came to understand that when Julien wants something badly enough he won't let anything stand in the way of his getting it. And he wanted Miranda. Badly.

Eventually, she gave in to the reality of the situation: she wanted him back. Who wouldn't? He was beautiful then, still is, perhaps even more so now that life has roughed a little of the perfection off him, the glibness. I wonder if it would be biologically impossible not to want a man like Julien, at least in the physical sense.

I remember Miranda introducing us, at the Summer Ball—when they finally got together. I knew exactly who he was, of course. I had borne witness to the whole saga: his pursuit of Miranda, her throwing him off, him trying and trying—her, finally, giving in to the inevitable. I knew so much about him. Which college he was at, what subject he was studying, the fact that he was a rugby Blue. I knew so much that I had almost forgotten he wouldn't have a clue who I was. So when he kissed me on the cheek and said, solemnly, "Nice to meet you, Katie"—quite politely, despite being drunk—it felt like a big joke.

T HE FIRST TIME HE STAYED AT OUR HOUSE—MIRANDA, SAMIRA, and I all lived together in the second year—I bumped into him coming out of the bathroom, a towel wrapped around his waist. I was so conscious of trying to be normal, not to look at the bare expanse of his chest, at his broad, well-muscled shoulders gleaming wet from the shower, that I said, "Hi, Julien."

He seemed to clutch the towel a little tighter around his waist. "Hello." He frowned. "Ah—this is a bit embarrassing. I'm afraid I don't know your name."

I saw my mistake. He had completely forgotten who I was, had probably forgotten ever having met me. "Oh," I said, putting out my hand, "I'm Katie."

He didn't take my hand, and I realized that this was another mistake—too formal, too weird. Then it occurred to me it might also have been that he was keeping the towel up with that hand, clutching a toothbrush with the other.

"Sorry." He smiled then, his charming smile, and took pity on me. "So. What did you do, Katie?"

I stared at him. "What do you mean?"

He laughed. "Like the novel," he said. "*What Katie Did*. I always liked that book. Though I'm not sure boys are supposed to." For the second time he smiled that smile of his, and I suddenly thought I could see something of what Miranda saw in him.

This is the thing about people like Julien. In an American rom-com someone as good-looking as him might be cast as a bastard, perhaps to be reformed, to repent of his sins later on. Miranda would be a bitchy Prom Queen, with a *dark secret*. The mousy nobody—me—would be the kind, clever, pitifully misunderstood character who would ultimately save the day. But real life isn't like that. People like them don't need to be unpleasant. Why would they make their lives difficult? They can afford to be their own spectacularly charming selves. And the ones like me, the mousy nobodies, we don't always turn out to be the heroes of the tale. Sometimes we have our own dark secrets.

WHAT LITTLE LIGHT THERE WAS HAS LEFT THE DAY NOW. You can hardly make out anything other than the black mass of trees on either side. The dark has the effect of making them look thicker, closer: almost as though they're pressing in toward us. Other than the thrum of the Land Rover's engine there is no noise at all; perhaps the trees muffle sound, too.

Up front, Miranda is asking the gamekeeper about access. This place is truly remote. "It's an hour's drive to the road," the gamekeeper tells us. "In good weather."

"An *hour*?" Samira asks. She casts a nervous glance at Priya, who is staring out at the twilit landscape, the flicker of moonlight between the trees reflected in her big dark eyes.

I glance out through the back window. All I can see is a tunnel of trees, diminishing in the distance to a black point.

"More than an hour," the gamekeeper says, "if the visibility is poor or the conditions are bad." Is he enjoying this?

It takes me an hour to get down to my mum's in Surrey. That's some sixty miles from London. It seems incredible that this place is even in the United Kingdom. I have always thought of this small island we call home as somewhat overcrowded. The way my stepdad likes to talk about immigrants, you'd think it was in very real danger of sinking beneath the weight of all the bodies squeezed onto it.

"Sometimes," the gamekeeper says, "at this time of year, you can't use the road at all. If there's a dump of snow, say—it would have been in the email you got from Heather."

Emma nods. "It was."

"What do you mean?" Samira's voice has an unmistakable shrillness now. "We won't be able to leave?"

"It's possible," he says. "If we get enough snow the track becomes impassable—it's too dangerous, even for snow tires. We get at least a couple of weeks a year, in total, when Corrin is cut off from the rest of the world."

"That could be quite cozy," Emma says quickly, perhaps to fend off any more worried interjections from Samira. "Exciting. And I've ordered enough groceries in—"

"And wine," Miranda supplies.

"—and wine," Emma agrees, "to last us for a couple of weeks if we need it to. I probably went a bit overboard. I've planned a bit of a feast for New Year's Eve."

No one's really listening to her. I think we're all preoccupied by this new understanding of the place in which we're going to spend the next few days. Because there *is* something unnerving about the isolation, knowing how far we are from everything.

"What about the station?" Miranda asks, with a sort of "gotcha!" triumph. "Surely you could just get a train?"

The gamekeeper gives her a look. He is quite attractive, I realize. Or at least he would be, only there's something haunted about his eyes. "Trains don't run so well on a meter of snow, either," he says. "So they wouldn't be stopping here."

And, just like that, the landscape, for all its space, seems to shrink around us.

4

DOUG

F IT WEREN'T FOR THE GUESTS, THIS PLACE WOULD BE PERFECT.
But he supposes he wouldn't have a job without them.

It had been everything he could do, when he picked them up,
not to sneer. They reek of money, this lot—like all those who
come here. As they approached the Lodge, the shorter, dark-haired
man—Jethro? Joshua?—had turned to him in a man-to-man way,
holding up a shiny silver phone. "I'm searching for the Wi-Fi,"
he said, "but nothing is coming up. Obviously there's no 3G: I get
that. You can't have 3G without a signal . . . Ha! But I would have
thought I'd start picking up on the Wi-Fi. Or do you have to be
closer to the Lodge?"

He told the man that they didn't turn the Wi-Fi on unless
someone asked for it specifically. "And you can sometimes catch a
signal, but you have to climb up there"—he pointed to the slope of
the Munro—"in order to get it."

The man's face had fallen. He had looked for a moment almost
frightened. His wife had said, swiftly, "I'm sure you can survive
without Wi-Fi for a few days, darling." And she smothered any further protest with a kiss, her tongue darting out. Doug had looked
away.

HE SAME WOMAN, MIRANDA—THE BEAUTIFUL ONE—HAD SAT up in front with him in the Land Rover, her knee angled close to his own. She had laid an unnecessary hand on his arm as she climbed into the car. He caught a gust of her perfume every time she turned to speak to him, rich and smoky. He had almost forgotten that there are women like this in the world: complex, flirtatious, the sort who have to seduce everyone they meet. Dangerous, in a very particular way. Heather is so different. Does she even wear perfume? He can't remember noticing it. Certainly not makeup. She has the sort of looks that work better without any adornment from cosmetics. He likes her face, heart-shaped, dark-eyed, the elegant parentheses of her eyebrows. Someone who hadn't spent time with Heather might think that there was a simplicity to her, but he suspects otherwise, that with her it is very much a case of still waters running deep. He has a vague idea that she lived in Edinburgh before, that she had a proper career there. He has not tried to find out what her story is, though. It might mean revealing too much of his own.

Heather is a good person. He is not. Before he came here, he did a terrible thing. More than one thing, actually. A person like her should be protected from someone like him.

HE GUESTS ARE NOW IN HEATHER'S CHARGE, FOR THE moment—and that's a relief. It took no small effort to conceal his dislike of them. The dark-haired man—Julien, that was the name—is typical of the people that stay here. Moneyed, spoiled, wanting wilderness, but secretly expecting the luxury of the hotels they're used to staying in. It always takes them a while to process what they have actually signed up for, the remoteness, the simplicity, the priceless beauty of the surroundings. Often they undergo a kind of conversion, they are seduced by this place—who wouldn't be? But he knows they don't understand it, not properly.

They think that they're roughing it, in their beautiful cabins with their four-poster beds and fireplaces and underfloor heating and the fucking *sauna* they can trot over to if they really want to exert themselves. And the ones he takes deer-stalking act as if they've suddenly become DiCaprio in *The Revenant,* battling with nature red in tooth and claw. They don't realize how easy he has made it for them, doing all the difficult work himself: the observation of the herd's activities, the careful tracking and plotting . . . so that all they have to do is squeeze the bloody trigger.

Even the shooting itself they rarely get right. If they shoot badly they could cause a wound that, if left, might cause the animal to suffer for days in unimaginable pain. A misfired head shot, for example (they often aim for the head even though he tells them: *never* go for it, too easy to miss), could cleave away the animal's jaw and leave it alive in deepest agony, unable to eat, slowly bleeding to death. So he is there to finish it off with an expert shot, clean through the sternum, allowing them to go home boasting of themselves as hunters, as heroes. The taking of a life. The baptism in blood. Something to post on Facebook or Instagram—images of themselves smeared in gore and grinning like lunatics.

He has taken lives, many of them in fact. And not just animal. He knows better than anyone that it is not something to boast about. It is a dark place from which you can never quite return. It does something to you, the first time. An essential change somewhere deep in the soul, the amputation of something important. The first time is the worst, but with each death the soul is wounded further. After a while there is nothing left but scar tissue.

He has been here for long enough to know all the different "types" of guests, has become as much of an expert in them as he is in the wildlife. But he isn't sure which variety he hates more. The "into the wild" sort, the ones who think they have in a few short days of luxury become "at one" with nature. Or the other kind, the ones who just don't get it, who think they have been tricked . . . worse, robbed. They forget what it is they booked. They find problems with everything that deviates from the sort of places they are used to staying in, with their indoor swimming pools and Michelin-starred restaurants. Usually, in Doug's opinion, they are the ones who have the most problems with themselves. Remove all of the distractions, and here, in the silence and solitude, the demons they have kept at bay catch up with them.

For Doug, it is different. His demons are always with him, wherever he is. At least here they have space to roam. This place attracted him for a rather different reason, he suspects, than it does the guests. They come for its beauty—he comes for its hostility, the sheer brutality of its weather. It is at its most uncompromising now, in the midst of its long winter. A few weeks ago, up on the Munro, he saw a fox slinking through the snow, the desiccated carcass of some small creature clamped in its jaws. Its fur was thin and scabrous, its ribs showing. When it spotted him it did not bolt immediately. There was a moment when it stared back at him, hostile, challenging him to try to take its feast. He felt a kinship with it, a stronger sense of identification than he has had with any human, at least for a long time. Surviving, existing—just. Not living. That is a word for those who seek entertainment, pleasure, comfort out of each day.

He was lucky to get this job, he knows that. Not just because it suits him, his frame of mind, his desire to be as far from the rest of humanity as possible. But also because it is very likely that no one else would have had him. Not with his past. The man sent to interview him by the boss had seen the line on his record, shrugged, and said, "Well, we definitely know you'll be good for dealing with any poachers, then. Just try not to attack any of the guests." And then he had grinned, to show that he was joking. "I think you'll be perfect for the job, actually."

That had been it. He hadn't even had to try to excuse or explain himself—though there *was* no excuse, not really. A moment of violent madness? Not really: he had known exactly what he was doing.

When he thinks about that night, now, hardly any of it seems real. It seems like something glimpsed on the TV, as though he were watching his own actions from a long way away. But he remembers the anger, the punch of it in his chest, and then the brief release. That stupid, grinning face. Then the sound of something shattering. Inside his own mind? The sense of feeling himself unshackled from the codes of normal behavior and loosed into some animal space. The feel of his fingers, gripping tightly about yielding flesh. Tighter, tighter, as though the flesh was something he was trying to mold with sheer brute force into a new, more pleasing shape. The smile finally wiped away. Then that warped sense of satisfaction, lasting for several moments before the shame arrived.

Yes, it would have been difficult to get a job doing much of anything after that.

5

HEATHER

Now
January 2, 2019

A BODY. I STARE AT DOUG.

No, no. This isn't right. Not here. This is my refuge, my escape. I can't be expected to deal with this, I can't, I just can't . . . With an effort of will, I stopper the flood of thoughts. You can, Heather. Because, actually, you don't have a choice.

Of course I had known it was a possibility. Very likely, even, considering the length of time missing—over twenty-four hours—and the conditions out there. They would be a challenge even to someone who knew the terrain, who had any sort of survival skills. The missing guest, as far as I know, had nothing of the sort. As the hours went by, with no sign, the probability became greater.

As soon as we knew of the disappearance we had called Mountain Rescue. The response hadn't been quite what I'd hoped for.

"At the moment," the operator told me, "it's looking unlikely we can get to you at all."

"But there must be some way you can get here—"

"Conditions are too difficult. We've haven't seen anything like this amount of snow for a long time. It's a one-in-a-thousand weather event. Visibility is so poor we can't even land a chopper."

"Are you saying that we're on our own?" As I said it I felt the full meaning of it. No help. I felt my stomach turn over.

There was a long pause at the other end of the line. I could almost hear her thinking of the best way to respond to me. "Only as long as the snow continues like this," she said at last. "Soon as we have some visibility, we'll try and get out to you."

"I need a bit more than 'try,'" I said.

"I hear you, madam, and we'll get to you as soon as we are able. There are other people in the same situation: we have a whole team of climbers stuck on Ben Nevis, and another situation nearer Fort William. If you could just describe exactly your problem, madam, so I have all the details down."

"The guest was last seen at the Lodge, here," I said, "at . . . about four A.M. yesterday morning."

"And how big is the area?"

"The estate?" I groped for the figure learned in my first few weeks here. "A little over fifty thousand acres."

I heard her intake of breath in my ear. Then there was another long pause on the end of the line, so long that I almost wondered if it had gone dead, whether the snow had cut off this last connection to the outside world.

"Right," she said finally. "Fifty thousand acres. Well. We'll get someone out there as soon as we can." But her tone had changed: there was more uncertainty. I could hear a question as clearly as if she had spoken it aloud: *Even if we get to you, how can we be certain of finding someone in all that wilderness?*

FOR THE PAST TWENTY-FOUR HOURS WE HAVE SEARCHED AS far as we can. It hasn't been easy, with the snow coming down like this, relentlessly. I've only been here a year, so I've never actually experienced a snow-in. We must be one of the few places in the UK—bar a few barely inhabited islands—where inclement weather can completely prohibit the access of the emergency services. We always warn the guests that they might not be able to leave the estate if conditions are bad. It's even in the waiver they have to sign. And yet it is still hard to process, the fact that no one can get in. Or out. But that's exactly the situation we find ourselves in now. Everything is clogged with snow, meaning driving's impossible—even with winter tires, or chains—so our search has all been done on foot. It has just been Doug and me. I am beyond exhausted—both mentally and physically. We don't even have Iain, who comes most days to perform odd jobs about the place. He'll have been spending New Year's Eve with his family: stuck outside with the rest of them, no use to us. The Mountain Rescue woman was at least some help with her advice. She suggested checking first the sites that could have been used for shelter. Doug and I searched every potential hideout on the estate, the cold stinging our faces and the snow hampering our progress at every turn, until I was so tired I felt drunk.

I trudged the whole way to the station, which took me a good three hours, and checked there. Apparently there had been some talk among the guests of getting a train back to London.

"One of the guests has gone missing," I told the stationmaster, Alec. He's a hulk of a man with a saturnine face: low eyebrows. "We're looking all over the estate." I gave him a description of the missing guest.

"They couldn't have got on a train?" I knew it was ridiculous, but felt it had to be asked.

He laughed in my face. "A train? In this? Are you mad, lass? Even if it weren't like this, there's no trains on New Year's Day."

"But perhaps you saw something—"

"Haven't seen anyone," he told me. "Not since I saw that lot arrive a couple a days ago. No. Woulda noticed if there were a stranger pokin' about."

"Well," I said, "perhaps I could have a look around?"

He spread his hands wide, a sarcastic invitation. "Be ma guest."

There wasn't much to search: the waiting room, a single care-taker's closet that appeared at one point to have been a toilet. And the ticket office I could see into through the window: a small, paper-strewn cubicle from which, through the money and ticket gap, came the scent of something sweetish, slightly rotten. Three crushed cans of soda decorated one corner of the desk. I saw Iain in there once with Alec, having a smoke. Iain often takes the train to collect supplies; they must have struck up something of a friend-ship, even if only of convenience.

Just beyond the office was a door. I opened it to discover a flight of stairs. "That," Alec said, "leads up to ma flat. Ma private *residence*"—with a little flourish on "residence."

"I don't suppose—" I began. He cut me off.

"Two rooms," he said. "And a lavvy. Ah think Ah'd know if someone were hidin' themselves away in there." His voice had got a little louder, and he'd moved between me and the doorway. He was too close; I could smell stale sweat.

"Yes," I said, suddenly eager to leave. "Of course."

As I began my tortuous journey back toward the Lodge I turned, once, and saw him standing there, watching me leave.

DOUG AND I FOUND NOTHING, IN ALL THE HOURS OF SEARCH-ing. Not a footprint, not a strand of hair. The only tracks we came across were the small, sharp impressions left by the hooves of the deer herd. The guest, it seemed, had not been active since the snow started coming down.

There's CCTV in one place on the estate: the front gate,

where the long track from the Lodge heads toward the road. The boss had it put up to both deter and catch poachers. Sometimes, frustratingly, the feed cuts out. But the whole lot was there to watch this time: from the evening before—New Year's Eve—to yesterday, New Year's Day, when the guest was reported missing. I fast-forwarded through the grainy footage, looking for any sign of a vehicle. If the guest had somehow left by taxi—or even on foot—the evidence would be here. There was nothing. All it showed me was a documentation of the beginning of this heavy snowfall, as on the screen the track became obliterated by a sea of white.

P ERHAPS A BODY HAD BEGUN TO SEEM LIKE A POSSIBILITY. BUT the confirmation of that is something so much worse.

Doug pushes a hand through his hair, which has fallen, snow-wet, into his eyes. As he does, I see that his hand—his arm, the whole of him—is trembling. It is a strange thing to see a man as tough-looking as Doug, built like a rugby player, in such a state. He used to be in the marines, so he must have seen his fair share of death. But then so did I, in my old line of work. I know that it never quite leaves you, the existential horror of it. Besides, being the one to find a dead person—that is something else completely.

"I think you should come and take a look, too," he says. "At the body."

"Do you think that's necessary?" I don't want it to be necessary. I don't want to see. I have come all this way to escape death. "Shouldn't we just wait for the police to get here?"

"No," he says. "They're not going to be able to make it for a while, are they? And I think you need to see this now."

"Why?" I ask. I can hear how it sounds: plaintive, squeamish.

"Because . . ." He draws a hand over his face; the gesture tugs his eye sockets down in a ghoulish mask. "Because . . . of the body. How it looks. I don't think it was an accident."

I feel my skin go cold in a way that has absolutely nothing to do with the weather.

W HEN WE STEP OUTSIDE, THE SNOW IS STILL COMING DOWN so thickly that you can only see a few feet from the door. The loch is almost invisible. I have shrugged on the clothes that are my de facto outdoor uniform in this place: the big, down Michelin-man jacket, my hiking boots, my red hat. I tramp after Doug, try-ing to keep up with his long stride, which isn't easy, because he's well over six foot, and I'm only a whisker over five. At one point I stumble; Doug shoots out a big, gloved hand to catch my arm, and hefts me back onto my feet as easily as if I were a child. Even through the down of my sleeve I can feel the strength of his fingers, like iron bands.

I'm thinking of the guests, stuck in their cabins. The inactiv-ity must be horrible, the waiting. We had to forbid them from joining us in the search, or risk having another missing person on our hands. No one should be out in these conditions. It is the sort of weather that people die in: "danger to life," the warnings say. But the problem is that to most of the guests, a place like this is as alien as another planet. These are people who live charmed ex-istences. Life has helped them to feel untouchable. They're so used to having that invisible safety net around them in their normal lives—connectivity, rapid emergency services, health and safety guidelines—that they assume they carry it around with them every-where. They sign the waiver happily, because they don't really think about it. They don't believe in it. They do not expect the worst to happen to them. If they really stopped to consider it, to *understand* it, they probably wouldn't stay here at all. They'd be too scared. When you learn how isolated an environment this really is, you realize that only freaks would choose to live in a place like this. People running from something, or with nothing left to lose. People like me.

Now Doug is leading me around to the left shore of the loch, toward the trees.

"Doug?" I realize that I am whispering. It's the silence here, made more profound by the snow. It makes your voice very loud. It makes you feel as though you are under observation. That just behind that thick wall of trees, perhaps, or this pervasive curtain of white, there might be someone listening. "What makes you think it wasn't an accident?"

"You'll see when we get there," he says. He does not bother turning back to look at me, nor does he break his stride. And then he says, over his shoulder, "I don't 'think,' Heather. I know."

6

MIRANDA

O F COURSE, I DIDN'T BOTHER LOOKING AT THE EMAIL EMMA
sent, with that brochure attached. I can never get excited
about a trip in advance—just seeing photos of turquoise seas or
snowcapped mountains doesn't interest me. I have to actually *be*
there to feel anything, for it to be *real*. When Emma mentioned
this place, the Lodge, I'd vaguely imagined something old-timey,
wooden beams and flagstones. So the building itself comes as a bit
of a surprise. Fucking hell. It's all modernist, glass and chrome, like
something out of *The Wizard of Oz*. Light spills from it. It's like a
giant lantern against the darkness.

"Christ!" Julien says, when the blokes finally arrive in the Land
Rover. "It's a bit hideous, isn't it?" He would say that. For all his
intelligence, Julien has zero artistic sensibility. He's the sort of person who'll walk around a Cy Twombly exhibition saying, "I could
have drawn that when I was five," just a *bit* too loudly. He likes to
claim it's because he's a "bit of rough": his background too grim

for anything like the development of aesthetic tastes. I used to find it charming. He was different: I liked that roughness, beside all those clean-behind-the-ears public schoolboys.

"I like it," I say. I do. It's like a spaceship has just touched down on the bank of the loch.

"So do I," Emma says. She would say that—even if she really thinks it's hideous. Sometimes I find myself testing her, saying the *most* outrageous things, almost goading her to challenge me. She never does—she's so keen just to be accepted. All the same, she's reliable—and Katie and Samira have been AWOL of late. Emma's always up for going to the cinema, or a trip shopping, or drinks. I always suggest the venue, or the activity, she always agrees. To be honest, it's quite refreshing: Katie's so bloody busy with work it's always been me going to her, to some lousy identikit city slicker bar, just to grab three minutes of her time.

With Emma it's a bit what I imagine having a little sister would be like. I feel almost as though she is looking up to me. It gives me a rather *delicious* sense of power. Last time we went shopping I took her into Myla. "Let's pick out something that will really make Mark's jaw fall open," I told her. We found exactly the right set—a sweetly slutty bra, open knickers, and suspender combo. I suddenly had an image of her telling Mark that it was me who helped to pick it out, and I felt an unexpected prickle of desire at the thought of him knowing that it was all my work. It's not Mark, of course, never has been. I've always found his unspoken attraction nicely ego-stoking, yes. But never a turn-on.

With Katie absent and Samira busy all the time with Priya—she is a bit obsessed with that child, it can't be healthy to share quite so many photos on social media—I have found myself falling back on Emma's company instead. A definite third choice.

I have been looking forward to this, to catching up with every-one. There's a security to it, how when we're together we fall back into our old roles. We can have been apart for months, and then when we're in each other's company everything is back to how it always was, almost like it was when we were at Oxford, our glory days. The person I most want to catch up with is Katie, of course. Seeing her this morning at the train station with her new hair, in clothes I didn't recognize, I realized quite how long it's been since I last saw her . . . and how much I have missed her.

NSIDE THE LODGE, IT'S BEAUTIFUL—BUT I'M GLAD WE'RE ONLY going to be having meals in here, not sleeping. The glass emphasizes the contrast between the bright space in here and the dark outside. I'm suddenly aware of how visible we would be from outside, lit up like insects in a jar . . . or actors on a stage, blinded by the floodlights to the watching audience. Anyone could be out there, hidden in the blackness, looking in without our knowing.

For a moment the old dark feeling threatens to surface, that sense of being watched. The feeling I have carried with me for a decade, now, since it all began. I remind myself that the whole point is that there *is* no one out there. That we are pretty much completely alone, save for the gamekeeper and the manager—Heather—who's come in to welcome us.

Heather is early thirties, short, prettyish—though a decent haircut and some makeup would make a vast improvement. I wonder what on earth someone like her is doing living alone in a place like this; because she does actually *live* here—she tells us that her cottage is "just over there, a little nearer to the trees." To be here permanently must be pretty bloody lonely. I would go completely mental with only my thoughts for company. Sometimes, on days at home, I turn on the TV *and* the radio, just to drown out the silence.

"And you," she says to us, "have all of the cabins nearest to the Lodge. The other guests are staying in the bunkhouse at the other end of the loch."

"The other guests?" Emma asks. There is a taut silence. "What other guests?"

Heather nods. "Yes. An Icelandic couple—they arrived yesterday."

Emma frowns. "But I don't understand. I was certain we had the place to ourselves. That was what you told me, when we spoke. 'You should have the whole place to yourselves,' you said."

Heather coughs. "I'm afraid there has been a . . . slight misunderstanding. I did understand that to be the case, when we spoke. We don't always rent out the bunkhouse. But I'm afraid I was unaware that my colleague had booked them in and—ah—hadn't yet got around to filling it out in the register."

The mood has definitely been killed. Just the phrase "the other guests" has an unpleasant ring to it, a sense of infiltration, of trespass. If we were in a hotel, that would be one thing, you'd expect to be surrounded by strangers. But the idea of these other people here in the middle of nowhere with us suddenly makes all this wilderness seem a little overcrowded.

"They'll be at the Highland Dinner tonight," Heather says apologetically, "but the bunkhouse has its own kitchen, so otherwise they won't be using the Lodge at all."

"Thank God," Giles says.

Emma looks as cross as I have ever seen her, her hands are clenched into tight fists at her sides, the knucklebones white through the skin.

There's a sudden *Bang!* behind us. Everyone turns, to see Julien, holding a just-opened bottle of champagne, vapor rising from the neck like smoke.

"Thought this would liven up the gloom a bit," he says. The liquid foams out of the top of the bottle and splashes onto the carpet by his feet: Bo holds out a glass to rescue some. "Hey, who knows . . . maybe the other guests will be fun. Maybe they'll want to come and celebrate New Year's Eve with us tomorrow."

I can't think of anything worse than some randoms coming and spoiling our party; I'm sure Julien can't, either. But this is his Mr. Nice Guy act. He always wants so badly to be liked, to seem fun, for other people to think well of him. I suppose that is one of the things I fell in love with.

Heather has helped Emma bring glasses from the kitchen. The others take them, smiling again, drawn by the sense of occasion that has just been created by the champagne. I feel a rush of warmth. It's so good to see them again. It has been too long. It's so special, these days, all being together like this. Samira and Katie are either side of me. I hug them to me. "The three musketeers," I whisper. The innermost ring of the inner circle. I don't even mind when I hear Samira swear softly—my hug has jolted her into spilling a little champagne on her shirt.

I see that Julien's offering Heather a glass, even though you can tell she doesn't want one. For goodness' sake. We had a tiny bit of a disagreement over the champagne yesterday, in the vintner's. Twelve bottles of Dom Pérignon: over a grand's worth of champagne. "Why couldn't you just have got Moët," I asked him, "like a normal person?"

"Because you would have complained. Last time you told me it gave you a headache, because of 'all the sugar' added in the standard brands. Only the finest stuff for Miranda Adams."

Talk about pot calling bloody kettle black. It always has to be a bit extra with him, that's the thing. A bit more extravagance, a bit more cash. A hunger to have more than his fair share . . . and his job hasn't helped with that. If in doubt, throw money at it: that is Julien's go-to solution. Fine . . . mine, too, if I'm being completely honest. I often like to joke that we bring out the worst in each other. But it's probably truer than I let on.

I let him buy the bloody champagne. I know how much he wants to forget the stress of this year.

As I expected, the woman, Heather, isn't drinking it. She's taken one tiny sip, to be polite, and put it back down on the tray. I imagine she thinks it's unprofessional to have more than that, and she's right. So, thanks to Julien's "generosity," we're going to be left with a wasted glass, tainted by this stranger's spit.

Heather runs us through arrangements for the weekend. We're going deer-stalking tomorrow: "Doug will be taking you, he'll come and collect you early in the morning."

Doug. I'm rather fascinated by him. I could tell he didn't like us much. I could also tell that I made him uncomfortable. That knowledge is a kind of power.

G ILES IS ASKING HEATHER SOMETHING ABOUT WALKING routes now. She takes out an ordnance survey map and spreads it across the coffee table.

"You have lots of options," she's saying. "It really depends on what you're looking for—and what sort of equipment you've brought. Some people have arrived with all the gear: ice picks, crampons, and carabiners."

"Er, I'm not sure that's really us," Bo says, grinning. Too bloody right.

"Well, if you want something very sedate, there's the path around the loch, of course." She traces it on the map with a finger. "It's a few miles, completely flat. There are a few waterfalls—but they have sturdy bridges over them, so there's nothing to tax you too much. You could practically do it in the dark. At the other end of the scale you've got the Munro, which you may be interested in if you're planning on 'bagging' one."

"What do you mean?" Julien asks.

"Oh," she says, "like a trophy, I suppose. That's what it's called when you climb one. You claim it."

"Oh yes," he says, with a quick grin. "Of course—maybe I did know that." No, he didn't. But Julien doesn't like to be shown up.

Even if he has no artistic sensibilities to speak of, appearances are important to my husband. The face you present to the world. What other people think of you. I know that better than anyone.

"Or," she says, "you could do something in the middle. There's the hike up to the Old Lodge, for example."

"The *Old* Lodge?" Bo asks.

"Yes. The original Lodge burned down just under a century ago. Almost everything went. So not a *great* deal to see, but it makes a good point to aim for, and there are fantastic views over the estate."

"Can't imagine anyone survived that?" Giles says.

"No," she says. "Twenty-four people died. No one survived apart from a couple of the stable hands, who slept in the stable block with the animals. One of the old stable blocks is still there, but it's probably not structurally sound: you shouldn't go too near it."

"And no one knows what started it?" Bo asks. We're all ghoulishly interested—you could hear a pin drop in here—but he looks genuinely alarmed, his glance flitting to the roaring log fire in the grate. He's such a city boy. I bet the nearest Bo normally gets to a real fire is a flaming sambuca shot.

"No," Heather says. "We don't know. Perhaps a fire left unattended in one of the grates. But there is a theory . . ." Heather pauses, as if not sure she should continue, then goes on. "There's a theory that one of the staff, a gamekeeper, was so damaged by his experiences in the war that he set fire to the building on purpose. A kind of murder-suicide. They say the fire could be seen as far away as Fort William. It took more than a day for help to come . . . by which time it was too late."

"That's fucked up," Mark says, and grins.

I notice that Heather does not look impressed by Mark's grin. She's probably wondering how on earth someone could be amused by the idea of two dozen people burning to death. You have to know Mark pretty well to understand that he has a fairly dark—but on the whole harmless—sense of humor. You learn to forgive him for it. Just like we've all learned that Giles—while he likes to seem like Mr. Easygoing—can be a bit tight when it comes to buying the next round . . . and not to speak to Bo until he's had at least two cups of coffee in the morning. Or how Samira, all sweetness and light on the surface, can hold a grudge like no one else. That's the thing about old friends. You just know these things about them. You have learned to love them. This is the glue that binds us together. It's like family, I suppose. All that history. We know everything there is to know about one another.

Heather pulls a clipboard from under her arm, all business suddenly. "Which one of you is Emma Taylor? I've got your credit card down as the one that paid the deposit."

"That's me." Emma raises a hand.

"Great. You should find all the ingredients you've asked for in the fridge. I have the list here. Beef fillet, unshucked oysters—Iain got them from Mallaig this morning—smoked salmon, smoked mackerel, caviar, endive, Roquefort, walnuts, one hundred percent chocolate, eighty-five percent chocolate, quails' eggs"—she pauses to take a breath—"double cream, potatoes, on-vine tomatoes . . ."

Christ. My own secret contribution to the proceedings suddenly looks rather meager. I try to catch Katie's eye to share an amused look. But I haven't seen her for so long that I suppose we're a bit out of sync. She's just staring out of the big windows, apparently lost in thought.

7

EMMA

CHECK THE LIST. I DON'T THINK THEY'VE GOT THE RIGHT tomatoes—they're not baby ones—but I can probably make do. It could be worse. I suppose I'm a bit particular about my cooking: I got into it at university, and it's been a passion of mine ever since.

"Thank you," Heather says as I hand the list back.

"Where'd you get all this stuff?" Bo asks. "Can't be many shops around here?"

"No. Iain went and got most of it from Inverness and brought it back on the train—it was easier."

"But why bother having a train station?" Giles asks. "I know we got off there, but there can't be many people using it otherwise?"

"No," she says. "Nor have there ever. It's a funny story, that one. The laird, in the nineteenth century, insisted that the rail company build the station, when they came to him with a proposal to put a track through his land."

"It must have been almost like his own private platform," Nick says.

The woman smiles. "Yes, and no. Because there were some . . . unintended consequences. This is whiskey country. And there was a great deal of illegal distilling going on back in the day—and robbery from the big distilleries. The old Glencorrin plant, for example, is pretty nearby. Before the railway, the smugglers around here had to rely on wagons, which were very slow, and very likely to be stopped on the long journey down south by the authorities. But the train was another matter. Suddenly they could get their product down to London in a day. Legend has it that some of the train guards were in their pay, ready to turn a blind eye when necessary. And some"—she stops, poised for the coup de grâce—"say that the old laird himself was in on it, that he had planned it from the day he asked for his railway station." She sits forward. "If you're interested, there are whiskey bothies all over the estate. They're marked on the map. Discovering them is something of a hobby of mine."

Over the top of her head, I see Julien roll his eyes. But Nick is intrigued. "What do you mean?" he asks. "They haven't all been found? How many are there?"

"Oh, we're not sure. Every time I think I must have discovered the last one, I come across another. Fifteen in total at the last count. They're very cleverly made, small cairns really, built out of the rocks, covered with gorse and heather. Unless you're right on top of them they're practically invisible. They disappear into the hillside. I could show you a couple if you like."

"Yes, please," Katie says—at the same time as Julien says, "No thanks." There is a slightly awkward pause.

"Well . . ." Heather gives a small, polite smile, but there's a flash of steel in the look she gives Julien. "It's not compulsory, of course."

I have the impression that she may not be quite as sweet and retiring as she looks. Good on her. Julien gets away with a little too much, as far as I'm concerned. People seem prepared to let him act as he likes, partly because he's so good-looking, and partly because he can turn on the charm like throwing a switch. Often he does the latter after he's just said something particularly controversial, or cruel—so that he can immediately take the sting out of it . . . make you think that he can't really mean it.

This might sound like sour grapes. After all, Mark is always blundering around offending people just by being himself: laughing inappropriately, or making jokes in bad taste. I know who most people would prefer to have dinner with. But at least Mark is, in his way, authentic—even if that sometimes means authentically dull (I am not blind to his faults). Julien is so much *surface*. It has made me wonder what's going on beneath.

My thoughts are interrupted by Bo. "This is incredible," he says, staring about. It *is*. It's better than any of the places anyone else has picked in the last few years, no question. I feel myself relax properly for the first time all day, and allow myself just to enjoy being here, to be proud of my work in finding it.

The room we're standing in is the living room: two huge, squashy sofas and a selection of armchairs, beautiful old rugs on the floor, a vast fireplace with a stack of freshly chopped wood next to it—"We use peat with the wood," Heather says, "to give it a nice smokiness." The upper bookshelves are stuffed with antiquarian books, emerald and red spines embossed with gold, and the lower with all the old board-game classics: Monopoly, Scrabble, Twister, Cluedo.

On the inner wall—the outer wall being made entirely of glass—are mounted several stags' heads. The shadows thrown by their antlers are huge, as though cast by old dead trees. The glass eyes have the effect some paintings have; they seem to follow you wherever you go, staring balefully down. I see Katie look at them and shiver.

You'd think that the modernist style of the building wouldn't work with the homey interior, but, somehow, it does. In fact, the exterior glass seems to melt away so that it's as though there is no barrier between us and the landscape outside. It's as though you could simply walk from the rug straight into the loch, huge and silver in the evening light, framed by that black staccato of trees. It's all perfect.

"Right," Heather says, "I'm going to leave you now, to get settled in. I'll let you decide which of the cottages suits each of you best."

As she begins to walk away she stops dead, and turns on her heel. She smacks a palm against her head, a pantomime of forgetfulness. "It must be the champagne," she says, though I hardly think so; she has only had a couple of sips. "There are a couple of very important safety things I should say to you. We ask that if you are planning on going for a hike beyond our immediate surroundings—the loch, say—you let us know. It may look benign out there, but at this time of year the state of play can change within hours, sometimes minutes."

"In what way?" Bo asks. This all must be very alien for him: I once heard him say he lived in New York for five years with only one trip out of the city, because he "didn't want to miss anything." I don't think he's one for the great outdoors.

"Snowstorms, sudden fogs, a rapid drop in temperature. It's what makes this landscape so exciting . . . but also lethal, if it chooses to be. If a storm should come in, say, we want to know whether you are out hiking, or whether you are safe in your cottages. And"—she grimaces slightly—"we've had a *little* trouble with poachers in the past—"

"That sounds pretty Victorian," Julien says.

Heather raises an eyebrow. "Well, these people unfortunately *aren't*. These aren't your old romantic folk heroes taking one home for the pot. They carry stalking equipment and hunting rifles. Sometimes they work in the day, wearing the best camouflage gear money can buy. Sometimes they work at night. They're not doing it for fun. They sell the meat on the black market to restauranters, or the antlers on eBay, or abroad. There's a big market in Germany. We have CCTV on the main gate to the property now, so that's helped, but it hasn't prevented them getting in."

"Should we be worried?" Samira asks.

"Oh no," Heather says quickly, perhaps realizing for the first time how all of this might sound to guests who have come for the unthreatening peace and quiet of the Scottish Highlands. "No, not at all. We haven't actually had any proper poaching incidents for . . . a while, now. Doug is very much on the case. I just wanted you to be aware. If you see anyone you do not recognize on the estate, let either of us know. Do not approach them."

I can feel how all this talk of peril has dampened the atmosphere slightly. "We haven't toasted being here," I say quickly, seizing my champagne glass. "Cheers!" I clash it against Giles's, with slightly too much force, and he jumps back to avoid the spillage. Then he gets the idea, turns to Miranda, and does the same. It seems to work: a little chain reaction is set off around the room, the familiarity of the ritual raising smiles. Reminding us of the fact that we are celebrating. That it is good—no, wonderful—to be here.

8

KATIE

THERE'S NO POINT IN MY EXPRESSING ANY PREFERENCE OVER which cabin I get. I am the singleton of the group, and it's been tacitly agreed by all that my cabin should be the smallest of the lot. There's a bit of good-natured wrangling over who is going to get which of the others. One is slightly bigger than the rest, and Samira—probably rightly—thinks that she and Giles should have it, because of Priya. And then both Nick and Miranda clearly want the one with the best view of the loch—I suspect for a moment that Nick is saying so just to rile Miranda, but then he defers, graciously. Everyone is on best behavior.

"Let's go for a walk now," Miranda says, once it's all decided. "Explore a bit."

"But it's completely dark," Samira says.

"Well, that will make it even better. We can take some of the champagne down to the loch."

This is classic Miranda. Anyone else would be content simply to lounge in the Lodge until dinner, but she's always looking for adventure. When she first came into my life, some twenty years ago, everything instantly became more exciting.

"I have to put Priya to bed," Samira says, glancing over to

where the baby has fallen asleep in her carrier. "It's late for her already."

"Fine," Miranda says offhandedly, with barely a glance in Samira's direction.

I don't know if she sees Samira's wounded look. For most of today Miranda has acted as though Priya is a piece of excess baggage. I remember, a couple of years ago, her talk of "when Julien and I have kids." I haven't seen her enough lately, so I'm not sure whether her indifference is genuine or masking some real personal suffering. Miranda has always been a champion bluffer.

The rest of us—including Giles—traipse outside into the dark. Samira gives him a look as she stalks off toward their cabin—presumably he, too, was meant to go and help with Priya's bedtime. It's probably the closest I've ever seen them come to a disagreement. They're such a perfect couple, those two—so respectful, so in sync, so loving—it's almost sickening.

We walk, stumbling over the uneven ground, down the path toward the water, Bo, Julien, and Emma using the torches provided in the Lodge to light the way. In the warmth indoors I'd forgotten how brutal it is outside. It's so cold it feels as though the skin on my face is shrinking against my skull, in protest against the raw air. Someone grabs my arm and I jump, then realize it's Miranda.

"Hello, stranger," she says. "It's so good to see you. God I've missed you." It's so unusual for her to make that sort of admission—and there is something in the way she says it, too. I glance at her, but it's too dark to make out her expression.

"You too," I say.

"And you've had your hair cut differently, haven't you?" I feel her hand come up to play with the strands framing my face. It is all I can do not to prickle away from her. Miranda has always been touchy-feely—I have always been whatever the opposite of that is.

"Yes," I say, "I went to Daniel Galvin, like you told me to."

"Without me?"

"Oh—I didn't think. I suddenly had a spare couple of hours . . . we'd closed on something earlier than expected."

"Well," she says, "next time you go, let me know, okay? We'll make a date of it. It's like you've fallen off the planet lately." She lowers her voice. "I've had to resort to Emma . . . God, Katie, she's so nice it does my nut in."

"Sorry," I say, "it's just that I've been so busy at work. You know, trying for partnership."

"But it won't always be like that, will it?"

"No," I say, "I don't think so."

"Because I've been thinking, recently . . . remember how it used to be? In our twenties? We'd see each other every week, you and I, without fail. Even if it was just to go out and get drunk on Friday night."

I nod. I'm not sure she can see, though. "Yes," I say—my voice comes out a little hoarse.

"Oh God, and the night bus? Both of us falling asleep and going to the end of the line . . . Kingston, wasn't it? And that time we went to that twenty-four-hour Tesco and you suddenly decided you had to make an omelet when you got home and you dropped that carton of eggs and it went everywhere—I mean *everywhere*— and we just decided to run off, in our big stupid heels . . ." She laughs, and then she stops. "I miss all of that . . . that *messiness*." There's so much wistfulness in her tone. I'm glad I can't see her expression now.

"So do I," I say.

"Look at you two." Julien turns back to us. "Thick as thieves. What are you gossiping about?"

"Come on," Giles says, "share with the rest of us!"

"Well," Miranda says quickly, leaning into me, "I'm glad we have this—to catch up. I've really missed you, K." She gives my arm a little squeeze and, again, I think I hear the tiniest catch in her voice. A pins-and-needles prickling of guilt; I've been a bad friend.

And then she transforms, producing a new bottle of champagne from under her arm and yelling to the others, "Look what I've got!"

There are whoops and cheers. Giles does a silly dance of delight; he's like a little boy, letting off pent-up energy. And it seems to be infectious . . . suddenly everyone is making a lot of noise, talking excitedly, voices echoing in the empty landscape.

Then Emma stops short in front of us, with a quiet exclamation. "Oh!"

I see what's halted her. There's a figure standing on the jetty that we're heading for, silhouetted by moonlight. He is quite tall, and standing surprisingly, almost inhumanly, still. The gamekeeper, I think. He's about the right height. Or maybe one of the other guests we've just heard about?

Bo casts his torch up at the figure, and we wait for the man to turn, or at least move. And then Bo begins to laugh. Now we see what he has. It isn't a man at all. It's a statue of a man, staring out contemplatively, Giacometti-like.

W E ALL SIT DOWN ON THE JETTY AND LOOK OUT ACROSS the loch. Every so often there's a tiny disturbance in the surface, despite there being very little wind. The ripples must be caused by something underneath, the glassy surface withholding these secrets.

Despite the champagne, everyone suddenly seems a bit subdued. Perhaps it's just the enormity of our surroundings—the vast black peaks rising in the distance, the huge stretch of night sky above, the pervasive quiet—that has awed us into silence.

The quiet isn't *quite* all-pervasive, though. Sitting here for long enough you begin to hear other sounds: rustles and scufflings in the undergrowth, mysterious liquid echoes from the loch. Heather told us about the giant pike that live in it—their existence confirmed by the monstrous one mounted on the wall of the Lodge. Huge jaws, sharp teeth, like leftover Jurassic monsters.

I hear the *shush-shush* of the tall Scots pines above us, swaying in the breeze, and every so often a soft thud: a gust strong enough to disturb a cargo of old snow. Somewhere, quite near, there is the mournful call of an owl. It's such a recognizable yet strange sound that it's hard to believe it's real, not some sort of special effect.

Giles tries to echo the sound: *"Ter-wit, ter-woo!"*

We all laugh, dutifully, but it strikes me that there's something uneasy in the sound. The call of the owl, such an unusual noise for city dwellers like us, has just emphasized quite how unfamiliar this place is.

"I didn't even know there were places like this in the UK," Bo says, as if he can read my thoughts.

"Ah, Bo," Miranda says, "you're such a Yank. It's not all London and little chocolate-box villages here."

"I didn't realize you got outside the M25 much yourself, Miranda," Nick says.

"Oi!" She punches his arm. "I do, occasionally. We went to Soho Farmhouse before Christmas, didn't we, Julien?" We all laugh— including Miranda. People think she can't laugh at herself, but she can . . . just as long as she doesn't come out of it looking *too* bad.

"Come on, open that bottle, Manda," Bo says.

"Yes . . . open it, open it—" Giles begins to shout, and everyone joins in . . . it's almost impossible not to. It becomes a chant, something oddly tribal in it. I'm put in mind of some pagan sect; the effect of the landscape, probably—mysterious and ancient.

Miranda stands up and fires the cork into the loch, where it makes its own series of ripples, widening out in shining rings across the water. We drink straight from the bottle, passing it around like Girl Guides, the cold, densely fizzing liquid stinging our throats.

"It's like Oxford," Mark says. "Sitting down by the river, getting pissed after finals at three P.M."

"Except then it was cava," Miranda says. "Christ—we drank gallons of that stuff. How did we not notice that it tastes like vomit?"

"And there was that party you held down by the river," Mark says. "You two"—he gestures to Miranda and me—"and Samira."

"Oh yes," Giles says. "What was the theme again?"

"*The Beautiful and Damned,*" I say. Everyone had to come in twenties' gear, so we could all pretend we were Bright Young Things, like Evelyn Waugh and friends. God, we were pretentious. The thought of it is like reading an old diary entry, cringe-worthy . . . but fond, too. Because it *was* a wonderful evening, even magical. We'd lit candles and put them in lanterns, all along the bank. Everyone had gone to so much effort with their costumes, and they were universally flattering: the girls in spangled flappers and the boys in black tie. Miranda looked the most stunning, of course, in a long metallic sheath. I remember a drunken moment of complete euphoria, looking about the party. How had little old me ended up at a place like this? With all these people as my friends? And most particularly with that girl—so glamorous, so *radiant*—as my best friend?

As we walk back toward the lights of the Lodge and the cabins, I spot another statue, a little way to our left, silhouetted in the light thrown from the sauna building. This one is facing away from the loch, toward us. It gives me the same uncanny little shock that the other did; I suppose this is exactly the effect they are meant to achieve.

THE PRIVACY OF MY CABIN IS A WELCOME RESPITE. WE'VE SPENT close to eight hours in each other's company now. Mine is the farthest away from the Lodge on this side, just beyond the moss-roofed sauna. It's also the smallest. Neither of these things particularly bothers me. I linger over my unpacking, though I've brought very little with me. The aftertaste of the champagne is sour on my tongue now, I can feel what little I drank listing in my stomach. I have a drink of water. Then I take a long, hot bath in the freestanding metal tub in the bathroom using the organic bath oil provided, which creates a thick aromatherapeutic fug of rosemary and geranium. There's a high window facing toward the loch, though the view out is half obscured by a wild growth of ivy, like something from a Pre-Raphaelite painting. It's also high enough that someone could look in and watch me in the bath for a while before I noticed them—if I ever did. I'm not sure why that has occurred to me—especially as there's hardly anyone here to look—but once the thought is in my mind I can't seem to get rid of it. I draw the little square of linen across the view. As I do I catch sight of my reflection in the mirror above the sink. The light isn't good, but I think I look terrible: pale and ill, my eyes dark pits.

I'll admit, I half-wondered about not coming this year. Just pretending I hadn't seen the email from Emma in my inbox until it was "too late" to do anything about it. A sudden, rebellious thought: Perhaps I've done my part? I could just stay hidden here for the three days, and the others would make enough noise and drama without actually noticing that I had disappeared. Nick and Bo and Samira are loud enough when they get going, but Miranda can make enough noise and drama for an entire party on her *own*.

Of course, it would help that I'm known as the quiet one. The observer, melting into the background. That was the dynamic when we lived together, Miranda, Samira, and me. They were the performers, I their audience.

If you told all this to the people I work with I reckon they'd be surprised. I'm one of the more senior associates at the firm now. I'm hopefully not far off making partner. People listen to what I say. I give presentations, I'm pretty comfortable with the sound of my own voice, ringing out in a silent meeting room. I like the feeling, in fact . . . seeing the faces upturned toward me, listening carefully to what I have to say. I command respect. I run a whole team. And I have found that I like being in charge. I suppose we all carry around different versions of ourselves.

With this group I have always been an also-ran. People have often wondered, I'm sure, what someone like me is doing with a friend like Miranda. But in friendship, as in love, opposites often attract. Extrovert and introvert, yin and yang.

It would be very easy to dislike Miranda. She has been blessed by the gods of beauty and fortune. She has the sort of absurd figure you see held up as a "bad, unrealistic example to young girls"—as though she has been personally Photoshopped. It doesn't really seem fair that someone so thin should have breasts that size; aren't they made up largely of fat? And the thick, infuriatingly shiny blond hair, and green eyes . . . no one in real life seems to have properly green eyes, except Miranda. She is the sort of person you would immediately assume was probably a bitch. Which she can be, absolutely.

The thing is, beneath her occasionally despotic ways, Miranda can be very kind. There was the time my parents' marriage was falling apart, for example—when I had a standing invitation to stay at her house whenever I felt like it, to escape the shouting matches at home. Or when my sixth-form boyfriend, Matt, dumped me un-ceremoniously for the prettier, more popular Freya, and Miranda not only lent me a shoulder to cry on, but put about the rumor that he had chlamydia. Or when I couldn't afford a dress for the college Summer Ball and, without making a thing of it at all, she gave me one of hers: a column of silver silk.

When I opened my eyes at one point on the train journey up here I caught Miranda watching me. Those green eyes of hers. So sharp, so assessing. A slight frown, as though she was trying to work something out. I pretended to sleep again, quickly. Sometimes I genuinely believe that Miranda has known me for so long that somewhere along the way she might have acquired the ability to read my mind, if she looks hard enough.

W E GO BACK EVEN FURTHER THAN THE REST OF THE group, she and I. All the way back to a little school in Sussex. The two new girls. One already golden, the sheen of money on her—she'd been moved from a private school nearby as her parents wanted her "to strive" (and they thought a comprehensive education would help her chances of getting into Oxford). The other girl mousy-haired, too thin in her large uniform bought from the school's secondhand collection. The golden girl (already popular, within the first morning) taking pity on her, insisting they sit next to each other at assembly. Making her her project, making her feel accepted, less alone.

I never knew why it was that she chose me to be her best friend. Because she *did* choose me: I had very little to do with it. But then she has always liked to do the unexpected thing, has Miranda, has always liked to challenge other people's expectations of her. The other girls were lining up to be her friend, I still remember that. All that hair—so blond and shiny it didn't look quite real. Eyelashes so long she was once told off by a teacher for wearing mascara: the injustice! Real breasts—at twelve. She was good at sport, clever but not *too* clever (though at an all-girls' school, academic prowess is not quite the handicap it is at a mixed one).

The other girls couldn't understand it. Why would she be friends with me when she could have them, any of them? There had to be something weird about her, if her taste in people was so "off." She could have ruled that school like a queen. But because of this, her friendship with me, she was probably never quite as popular as she might have been. But that didn't matter to the boys at the parties we began to go to in our teens. *I* never got the invites to houses of pupils from the boys' grammar up the road, or parties on the beach. Miranda could have left me behind then. But she took me with her.

When I think of this, I feel all the more ashamed. This feeling is the same one I used to get when I stayed over at her beautiful Edwardian house and was tempted to take some little trophy home for myself. Something small, something she'd hardly notice: a hair clip, or a pair of lace-trimmed socks. Just so I'd have something pretty to look at in my little beige bedroom in my dingy two-up two-down with stains on the walls and broken blinds.

THERE'S A KNOCK ON THE FRONT DOOR AT ABOUT EIGHT: NICK and Bo, thank God. For a moment I had thought it might be Miranda. Nick and I met in freshers' week, and have been friends ever since. He was there through all the ups and downs of uni.

The two of them come in, checking out the place. "Your cabin is just like ours," Nick says, when I let them in, "except a bit smaller. And a *lot* tidier . . . Bo has already covered the whole place with his stuff."

"Hey," Bo says. "Just because I don't travel with only three versions of the same outfit."

It's not even an exaggeration. Nick's one of those people who have a self-imposed uniform: a crisp white shirt, those dark selvedge jeans, and chukka boots. Maybe a smart blazer, and always, of course, his signature tortoiseshell Cutler and Gross glasses. Somehow he makes it work. On him it's stylish, authoritative—whereas on a lesser mortal it might seem a bit plain.

We sit down together on the collection of squashy armchairs in front of the bed.

Bo sniffs the air. "Smells amazing in here, too. What is that?"

"I had a bath."

"Oh, I thought that oil looked nice. Don't do things by halves here, do they? Emma's really knocked it out of the park. It's awesome."

"Yes," I say, "it is." But it doesn't come out quite as enthusiastically as I'd meant it to.

"Are you all right?" Nick jostles me with his shoulder. "I hope you don't mind my saying this, but you seem a bit . . . off. Ever since this morning. You know, that thing on the train earlier, with you being put in the other carriage, I'm sure it wasn't intentional. If it had been Miranda, that would be a different story . . ." He raises his eyebrows at Bo, and Bo nods in agreement. "I wouldn't necessarily make the same assumption. But it was Emma. I just don't think she's like that."

"I'm not sure she's my biggest fan, though." Emma's so decent, and I've wondered in the past if it's that she's seen something she doesn't like in me and recoiled from it.

Bo frowns. "What makes you say that?"

"I suppose it's just a feeling . . ."

"I really wouldn't take it so personally," Nick says.

"No," I say. "Maybe it's just that I haven't seen everyone in such a long time. And I shouldn't drink in the day—it always makes me feel weird. Especially when I haven't had enough to eat."

"Totally." Bo nods. But Nick doesn't say anything. He's just looking at me.

Then he asks, "Is there something else?"

"No," I say. "No, there isn't."

"You sure?"

I nod my head.

"Well, come on, then," Nick says, "let's go fuel you up at this dinner. There better be at least some combination of bagpipes, venison, and kilts, otherwise I'm going to ask for my money back."

Nick, Bo, and I walk over to the Lodge for the dinner, arm in arm. Nick smells, as ever, of citrus and perhaps a hint of incense. It's such a familiar, comforting scent that I want to bury my face in his shoulder and tell him what's on my mind.

I was a bit in love with Nick Manson at Oxford, at first. I think most of my seminar group was. He was beautiful, but in a new, grown-up way entirely different from every other first-year male—so many of them still acne-plagued and gawky, or completely unable to talk to girls. His was a much more sophisticated beauty to, say, Julien's gym-honed handsomeness. Nick might have been beamed in from another planet, which in a way he had. He'd taken the baccalaureate in Paris (his parents were diplomats), where he had also learned fluent French and a fondness for Gitanes cigarettes. Nick laughs now at how pretentious he was—but most undergraduates were pretentious back then . . . only his version seemed authentic, justified.

He came out to a select few friends in the middle of our second year. It wasn't exactly a surprise. He hadn't gone out with any of the girls who threw themselves at him with embarrassing eagerness, so there had perhaps been a bit of a question mark there. I had chosen not to see it, as I had my own explanation for his apparent celibacy: he was saving himself for the right woman.

It was a bit of a blow, his coming out, I'm not going to pretend otherwise. My crush on him had had all the intensity that one at that age often does. But over time I learned to love him as a friend.

When he met Bo he fell off the radar. Suddenly I saw and heard a lot less of him. It was hard not to feel resentful. Of Nick, for dropping me—because that's how it felt at the time. Of Bo, as the usurper. And then Bo had his issues. He was an addict, or still is, as he puts it, just one who never takes drugs anymore. Nick became pretty much his full-time carer for a few years. I suspect Bo resented me in turn, as a close friend of Nick's. I think now he's more secure of himself and their relationship these days . . . or perhaps we've all just grown up a bit. Even so, with Bo, I sometimes feel as though I'm overdoing things a bit. Being a little too ingratiating. Because if I'm totally honest I still feel that with his neediness—because he *is* needy, even now—he's the reason Nick and I aren't such good friends anymore. We're close, yes. But nothing like we once were.

It's even cooler now; our mingled breath clouds the air. There are ribbons of mist hanging over the loch, but around us the air is very clear, and when I look up it's as though the cold has somehow sharpened the light of the stars. As we stumble along the path to the Lodge, I happen to look over toward the sauna, where I saw the second statue, earlier, the one that had been facing toward us. But, funny thing, though I search for it in the light thrown from the building, assuming it must be hidden in shadow, I can't see it. The statue is gone.

9

HEATHER

Now
January 2, 2019

As I tramp through the snow, trying to step in Doug's big footprints, I'm thinking of the guests, sitting about in their cabins and wondering: not knowing yet.

Unless . . . I push the thought away. I can't let my mind race to conclusions. But if Doug is right, there's something more sinister at play. And something had gone wrong between them all, that was clear. There had been a "disagreement," that was how they all put it when they came to tell me about the disappearance.

It would be easy to say, with hindsight, that I had a sense of foreboding three days ago, when they all arrived. I didn't see this coming. But I did feel *something*.

My Jamie was fascinated by the idea of the "lizard brain." Maybe it was something to do with his job. He saw people on the edge, acting purely on instinct: the father who ran from a burning house before saving his children, or, conversely, the one who shielded his wife and baby from a blaze and suffered third-degree burns over half of his body. It's all down to the amygdala—a tiny nodule, hidden among the little gray cells, the root of our most instinctive actions. It's behind the selfish urge to grab for the biggest cookie, the comfiest seat. It's what alerts you to danger, before you even consciously know of a threat. Without it, a laboratory mouse will run straight into the jaws of a cat.

Jamie believed that people are basically civilized animals. That the essential urges are hidden beneath a layer of social gloss; stifled, controlled. But at times of even fairly minor stress, the animal within has a go at breaking through. Once he was stuck just outside Edinburgh on a train for four hours, because of an electrical fault. "You saw straightaway which people would eat you," he told me, "without any hesitation, if you were stuck on a lifeboat together. There was a man who was hammering on the driver's cabin after only a few minutes, bright red in the face. He was like a caged animal. He looked at the rest of us like he was just waiting for one of us to tell him to shut up . . . then he'd have an excuse to lose it completely."

That's the thing, you see. Some people, given just the right amount of pressure, taken out of their usual, comfortable environments, don't need much encouragement at all to become monsters. And sometimes you just get a strong sense about people, and you can't explain it; you simply know it, in some deeper part of yourself. That's the lizard brain, too.

So I find myself, now, returning to three days ago, the evening they all arrived. My first, animal impressions.

The Highland Dinner on the first night of the stay is one of the promises made by the brochure. But every time we host it, I think the guests would be quite happy to do without. It always seems to take on the atmosphere of an enforced occasion, like a state dinner. I'm sure it's just another means of extracting money from them. The markup on the food, even accounting for the fact that the "best local ingredients" are used, is huge. I've also wondered if it's a way of keeping the community onside, because local lads and lasses are employed as the waiting staff, and all the ingredients are bought from nearby suppliers, save the venison, which comes from here.

I have read the headlines from when the boss first bought the place—from the family who had owned it for generations—articles complaining about the "elitist prices," the "barring of local people from their own land"—there's a right to roam in the Highlands, which the old laird had always upheld, but the boss had fences and threatening signs put up. He claims they are to deter poachers, but, funny thing, apparently that wasn't so much of a problem under the previous owner. Maybe the poachers hadn't got themselves organized, weaponized, hadn't realized the healthy demand for venison and mounted stags' heads. But I think there might be another angle to the deer killings that happen now. In the vein of a lesson taught, something taken back.

Once, in our nearest shop in Kinlochlaggan (still over an hour away), I happened to tell the shopkeeper where it was that I worked. "You seem nice enough, lass," she said, "but it's a nasty place. Foreign money." (By which she meant, I presume, the boss's Englishness, and the fact that the guests often come up from England, or from farther afield.) "One of these days," she told me, "they'll pay the proper price for keeping people from what's theirs." I remembered then the theory I'd heard about the Old Lodge, the one I don't tell guests: that the fire hadn't been started by the gamekeeper, but by a disgruntled local, slighted by the laird.

If the Highland Dinner is meant to stem this ill will toward the place, I'm not sure it has worked. If anything, the waiting staff probably return home with tales of the guests' bad behavior. I remember a stag party where a drunk—but not that drunk—best man groped a very young waitress as she bent to retrieve a dropped napkin. Guests have passed out in their plates, succumbing to too much of the Glencorrin single malt. Some have vomited at the table, in full view of the staff.

The London group of guests would be better behaved than the stag party, I was sure. There was a baby among them, so surely that meant something, even if the parents weren't joining us (the mother had asked for their food to be brought to them in their cabin). That left seven of them. The dark-haired man, the tall blond. Julien and Miranda. A perfectly matched pair, the most beautiful, even the poshest names of the lot. Then there was the thin, sleek, auburn-haired man with the architect's glasses—Nick—and his American boyfriend, Bo. The third couple: Mark and Emma. He might almost have been good-looking, but his eyes were too close together, like a small predator's, and his top half was disproportionately heavy, lending him the unnatural appearance of an action figure. I found myself thinking she was like a budget version of the taller blonde; dark hair at the roots, a roll of flesh showing at the top of her jeans where her top had ridden up. I was surprised at myself. I'm not, as a rule, a judgmental person. But even if you don't have much interaction with other human beings—as I do not—it turns out that the instinct to judge one another, that basic human trait, does not leave us. And the resemblance was un-ignorable. Her hair was dyed the same shade, the clothes were of a type, and she'd even made up her eyes in the same way, little flecks of black at the corners. While they made her friend's eyes look large and catlike, they only served to emphasize the smallness of her own.

Then there was the last one, Katie. The odd one out. I almost missed her at first. She was standing so still, so quiet, in the shadows at the corner of the room—almost as though she wanted to disappear into them. She didn't match the others, somehow. Her skin was sallow, and there were large purple shadows beneath her eyes. Her clothes were too formal, as though she were going on a business trip and had turned up here by mistake.

Normally, though I have to learn the names, I prefer to *think* of the people who stay here as simply the "guests": guest 1, guest 2, etc. I'd prefer not to think of them as individual people with lives outside this place. Perhaps this sounds odd. I suppose I could argue it's a survival tactic. Don't get involved in their lives. Don't let their happiness—or otherwise—touch you. Don't compare yourself to their wholeness, those couples who come for a romantic retreat, the happy families.

The last twenty-four hours has meant a closer acquaintance with this group—a forced intimacy that I could well have done without.

But I suppose, if I'm honest, even from the beginning I was curious about them. Perhaps because they were roughly the same age as me: early to mid-thirties, at a guess. I could have been like them, if I had found a high-paying job in the city, like some friends did after university. This is what you could have had, it felt like the universe was saying to me. This is where you could have been, what you could have been doing, at the loneliest time of the year (because New Year's Eve is, isn't it?).

I might have been envious. And yet I didn't feel it. Because I couldn't put my finger on it, but there was an unease, a discontent, that seemed to surround them. Even as they laughed and jostled and teased one another, I could sense something underneath it—something off. They seemed almost at times like actors, I thought, making a great show of what a wonderful time they were having. They laughed a little *too* hard. They drank a great deal too much. And at the same time, despite all this evidence of merriment, they seemed to watch each other. Perhaps it's hindsight, making this impression seem like more than it was. I suppose there are probably tensions in most groups of friends. But I was struck by the thought that they did not seem completely comfortable in one another's company. Which was odd, as they'd told me right at the beginning that they were very old friends. But that's the thing about old friends, isn't it? Sometimes they don't even realize that they no longer have anything in common. That maybe they don't even like each other anymore.

The other guests, the Icelandic couple, walked in just as the starter was being served—"locally caught salmon with wild herbs"—to a frisson of hostility from the others.

Iain had booked them in. I'd been on one of my rare trips to the local shop, so he'd had to take the call. He could see that the bunkhouse was free on the system, he said, and he'd checked with the boss, who'd okayed it all. I was annoyed he hadn't written their names down in the book: if I had known, I wouldn't have promised the other group they'd have the run of the place.

I wasn't sure what sort of behavior to expect from these two. They weren't the usual, well-heeled sort. Both had windburned complexions, the roughened look of people who spend a lot of time in harsher elements. The man had very pale blue eyes, like a wolf's, and stringy blond hair tied back with a leather thong. The woman had a double-ended stud passing through the septum of her nose and a tangled dark ponytail.

They arrived at the station with huge backpacks, half the size of themselves. They explained that they had caught a passage on a fishing trawler from Iceland to Mallaig farther up the coast—I saw the beautiful blonde wrinkle her nose at this—where Iain collected them and brought them to the estate in his truck. They came with proper gear—Gore-Tex jackets and heavy boots—making the coats and Hunter wellies the other lot wore look slightly ridiculous. They hadn't changed out of their outdoor gear for dinner, so that even Doug and Iain, in their special Loch Corrin kilts, looked rather tarted up next to them, as did the serving staff, the two girls and the boy in their white shirts and plaid aprons. The beautiful blonde looked at the two new arrivals as though they were creatures that had just emerged from the bottom of the loch. Luckily, they were either side of me; she was seated opposite, next to Doug, and fairly quickly seemed to decide that she would waste no more of her attention on them, and give it wholeheartedly to Doug instead. I looked at her, with all that gloss: the fine silk shirt, the earrings set with sparkling—diamond?—studs. She watched him as though whatever he was saying was the most fascinating thing she had heard all evening, her lips curved in a half smile, her chin in her palm. Doug wouldn't go for someone like her—would he? She wouldn't be his type, surely? Then I remembered that I had absolutely no idea what his type would be, because I didn't really know anything about him.

I focused my attention back on the Icelandic guests either side of me. They spoke almost perfect English, with just a slight musicality that betrayed their foreignness.

"You've worked here long?" the woman—Kristin—asked me.

"Just under a year."

"And you live here all by yourself?" This was from the man, Ingvar.

"Well, not quite. Doug . . . over there, lives here, too. Iain lives in town, Fort William, with his family."

"He's the one who collected us?"

"Yes."

"Ah," he said, "he seems like a nice man."

"Yes." Though I thought: Really? Iain's so taciturn. He arrives, does his work—upon orders received from the boss—and leaves. He keeps very much to himself. Of course, he could say exactly the same of me.

Ingvar said, almost thoughtfully, "What makes someone like you come to live in a place like this?" The way he asked it—so knowing—almost as though he had guessed at something.

"I like it here," I told him. Even to my own ears it sounded defensive. "The natural beauty, the peace . . ."

"But it must get lonely for you here, no?"

"Not particularly," I said.

"Not frightening?" He smiled when he said this, and I felt a slight chill run through me.

"No," I said curtly.

"I suppose you get used to it," he said, either not noticing or ignoring my rudeness. "Where we come from, one understands what it is to be alone, you see. Though, if you're not careful, it can send you a little crazy." He made a boring motion with a finger at his temple. "All that darkness in the winter, all the solitude."

Not quite true, I thought. Sometimes solitude is the only way to regain your sanity. But it also got me thinking. If you lived in Iceland—with its long winter nights—wouldn't you go a little farther from the cold and dark than Scotland? For the price of the cabins at this place you could get all the way to the relative warmth of southern Europe. And for that matter, I wondered how two people who got here by hitchhiking on a fishing trawler could have afforded our rates. But perhaps they did it simply for the adventure. We get all sorts, here.

"Should we be worried?" Ingvar asked next. "About the news?"

"What do you mean?"

"You don't know? The Highland Ripper."

Of course I knew. I'd been hoping the guests didn't. I'd seen the pictures in the paper the day before: the faces of the six victims. All youngish, pretty. You might bump into a hundred girls like that walking down Princes Street in Edinburgh—and yet the images had the ominous look of all victim photos, as though there was something about each innocuous smiling snap that would have foretold their fate, if you had known what to search for. They looked, somehow, as though they had been marked for death.

"Yes," I said carefully. "I've seen the papers. But Scotland is a pretty big place, you know, I don't think you've got anything—"

"I thought it was the Western Highlands, where they found the victims?"

"Still," I said, "it's a pretty large area. You'd be as likely to bump into the Loch Ness monster."

I sounded a little more blasé than I felt. That morning, Iain had said, "You should tell the guests to stay indoors at night, Heather. On account of the news." It rather put me on edge that Iain—who hardly ever mentioned the guests—had expressed concern for their welfare.

I didn't think this man, Ingvar, was really scared of anything. I sensed, instead, that he was having a bit of fun with the whole thing; a smile still seemed to be playing around the corners of his mouth. It was a relief when he asked about hunting, and I could escape the scrutiny of those pale blue eyes. I remember thinking that there was something unnerving about them: they didn't seem quite human.

"Oh, you're better off asking Doug about hunting," I said. "That's definitely his side of things. Doug?"

Doug glanced over. The blonde looked up, too, clearly annoyed at the interruption.

"Do you ever shoot the animals at night," Ingvar asked, "using lamps and dogs?"

"No," Doug said, very quickly and surprisingly loudly.

"Why not?" Ingvar asked, with that odd smile again. "I know it's very effective."

Doug's reply was bald. "Because it's dangerous and cruel. I'd never use lamping."

"Lamping?" the blond guest asked.

"Spotlights," he said, barely glancing in her direction, "shining them at the deer, so they freeze. It confuses them—and it terrifies them. Often it means you shoot the wrong deer: females with young calves, for example. Sometimes they use dogs, which tear the animal apart. It's barbaric."

There was a rather taut silence, afterward. I reflected that it might have been the most I had ever heard Doug say in one go.

The two Icelandic guests have been very eager to help with the search. They're probably the only two that I'd trust in these conditions: they must see similar weather all the time. But they are still guests, and I am still responsible for their well-being. Besides, I know nothing about them. They are an unknown quantity. All of the guests are. So my lizard brain is saying, loud and clear: *Trust no one.*

I wonder what the guests all make of me. Perhaps they see someone organized, slightly dull, absolutely in charge of everything. At least, that is what they will have seen if I have pulled it off, this clever disguise I have built for myself, like a tough outer shell. Inside this shell, the reality is very different. Here is a person held together by tape and glue and prescription-strength sleeping pills—the only thing I can be persuaded to make a foray into civilization for, these days. Washed down sometimes, often, with a *little* too much wine. I'm not saying that I have a drinking problem; I don't. But I don't ever drink for pleasure. I do it out of necessity. I use it as another painkiller: to blunt the edge of things, to alleviate the chronic, aching torment of memory.

10

MIRANDA

Dinner is served in the big dining room in the lodge, off the living room, which has been lit with what appear to be hundreds of candles, and staffed by a few spotty teenagers in plaid aprons. We're two short: Samira and Giles are having supper in their cabin. Samira said she's heard too many stories about parents "just leaving their kids for an hour or so" when everything goes horribly wrong. Yes, I told her, patiently—but not in the middle of nowhere. Besides, Priya's hardly going to be wandering off on her own at six months, for God's sake. Still, Samira wasn't having any of it.

I almost can't believe this woman is Samira, who at one party in our early twenties decided to jump the two-foot gap between the house building and the building next to it, just for a laugh. She was always one of the wild ones, the party girl, the one you could rely on to raise the tempo of things on a night out. If Katie's the one who I go way back with, Samira's probably much more like me: the one I've always felt most akin to. Now I feel I hardly recognize her. Perhaps that's just because she's been so busy with Priya. I'm sure the real Samira is in there somewhere. I'm hoping this will be our chance to catch up, to remember that we're partners in crime. But honestly, when some people have kids it's like they've had a personality transplant. Or a lobotomy. Maybe I should count myself lucky that I don't seem to be able to get pregnant. At least I'll remain myself for Christ's sake.

I've got the gamekeeper, Doug, on one side of me and the other guy, Iain, on the other. Both of them are wearing identikit green kilts and sporrans. Neither looks particularly happy about it. As you might imagine, the gamekeeper wears his outfit best. He really *is* quite attractive. I am reminded of the fact that, before Julien, I was sometimes drawn to men like this. The reticent, brooding sort: the challenge of drawing them out, making them care.

I turn to him and ask: "Have you always been a gamekeeper?"

He frowns. "No."

"Oh, and what did you do before?"

"The marines."

I picture him with a short back and sides, in uniform. It's an appealing image. He looks good scrubbed up, even if I'm sure his hair hasn't seen a brush anytime in the last five years. I'm glad I made an effort: my silk shirt, undone perhaps one button lower than strictly necessary, my new jeans.

"Did you have to kill anyone?" I ask, leaning forward, putting my chin in my hand.

"Yes." As he says it his expression is neutral, betraying no emotion whatsoever. I experience a small shiver of what might be disquiet . . . or desire.

Julien is sitting directly opposite us, with a front and center view of things. There is nothing like stirring a bit of jealousy to fire things up in a relationship—especially ours. It could be an overfamiliar waiter in a restaurant, or the guy on the next sun lounger who Julien's convinced has been checking me out (he's probably right). "Would you want him to do this to you?" he'd pant in my ear later, "Or this?"

If I'm honest, sex has become, lately, a mechanism for a specific end rather than pleasure. I've got this app that Samira told me about, which identifies your most fertile days. And then, of course, there are certain positions that work best. I've explained this to Julien so many times, but he doesn't seem to get it. I suppose he's stopped trying, recently. So yes, we could do with things being spiced up a little.

I turn back to Doug, keeping Julien in my peripheral vision. He's talking to the Icelandic woman, so I touch a hand against Doug's, just for fun. I've had a couple of glasses too many, maybe. I feel his fingers flinch against mine.

"Sorry," I say, all innocence. "Would you mind passing me the *jus*?" I think it's working. Certainly Julien's looking pretty pissed off about something. To all intents and purposes he might be having a whale of a time—always so important to present the right face to the world—but I know him too well. It's that particular tension in the side of the neck, the gritting of the teeth.

I glance over to where poor Katie, across the table from me, is seated next to the Icelandic man with the strange eyes, who seems to have taken a bit of a shine to her. It's a bloody nightmare, them being here, too. Are we going to have to share the sauna with them? Judging by the state of the clothes they're wearing I'd have to disinfect myself afterward.

The man, now, is leaning toward Katie as though he has never seen anything so fascinating or beautiful in his life. Clearly—judging by his partner—he has *unconventional* taste.

Though . . . there is definitely something different about Katie. She looks tired and pale, as per, but there's that new haircut for a start. At the place she normally goes to, they style her hair à la Mrs. Williams, our old school hockey teacher. You would have thought that with her corporate lawyer's salary, she might try a bit harder sometimes. I've been telling her to go to Daniel Galvin for ages—I go for highlights every six weeks—so I don't know why I feel so put out about her finally having listened to me. Perhaps because she hasn't given me any credit for it, and I feel I deserve some. And perhaps because I had sort of imagined we might go together. Make a morning of it, the two of us.

I still remember the girl she was back then: flat-chested when everyone else was starting to develop. Lank-haired, knock-kneed, the maroon of the school uniform emphasizing the sallowness of her complexion.

I have always liked a project.

Look at her now. It's difficult to be objective, as I've known her so long that she's practically a sister, but I can see how some men might find her attractive. Sure: she'll never be pretty, but she has learned to make the best of herself. That new hair. Her teeth have been straightened and whitened. Her clothes are beautifully cut to make the most of her slight frame (I could never wear a shirt like that without my boobs creating the kind of shelf that makes you look bigger than you really are). She had her ears pinned back as a present to herself when she qualified at her law firm. She looks almost . . . chic. You might think she was French: the way she's made the best of those difficult features. What's that expression the French have for it? *Jolie laide*: ugly beautiful.

Katie would never be wolf-whistled at by builders or white-van men. I never understand why some people think you might be flattered by that. Look, okay, I *know* I'm attractive. Very attractive. There, I've said it. Do you hate me now? Anyway, I don't need it confirmed by some potbellied construction workers who would catcall anyone with a short skirt or tight top. If anything, they cheapen it.

They wouldn't shout at Katie, though. Well, they might shout at her to "Smile, love!" But they wouldn't fancy her. They wouldn't understand her. I'm *almost* envious of it. It's something that I'll never have, that look-twice subtlety.

Anyway. Maybe now we're finally together, I can find out what's been going on in her life—what it is that has prompted this mysterious change in her.

11

EMMA

I T'S HARD NOT TO SPEND THE WHOLE OF THE MEAL LOOKING around the table, checking that everyone's enjoying themselves. I really wish I'd opted us out of this dinner when I'd booked—it seemed like a great idea at the time, but with the Icelandic couple here as well there's an odd dynamic. And this close proximity to the other guests just emphasizes the mess-up over our not having the place to ourselves. I know I should be able to let it go: *que será será,* and all that, but I so wanted it to be perfect for everyone. It doesn't help that the other guests are so weird-looking and un-kempt: I can see how unimpressed Miranda, in particular, is by them. Katie's sitting next to the man, Ingvar—who is looking at her as though he wishes she were on the plate in front of him, not the overscented meat.

I, meanwhile, am sitting next to Iain. He doesn't say very much, and when he does his accent is so thick it's hard to understand everything.

"Do you live here, too?" I ask him.

"No," he says. "Fort William—with my wife and kids."

"Ah," I say. "Have you worked here long?"

He nods. "Since the current owner first bought the place."

"What do you do?"

"Whatever needs doing. Odd jobs, here and there: working on the pumphouse, at the moment, down by the loch. I bring the supplies in, too: food, the bits for the cabins."

"What's the owner like?" I ask, intrigued. I imagine a whiskery old Scottish laird, so I'm a bit surprised when Iain says, "He's all right, for an Englishman." I wait for him to say more, but he either doesn't have anything to add, or is reluctant to do so.

I seem to have run out of questions, so it's a relief when the Icelandic man asks about the deer-stalking, and the whole table's attention is turned to that. It's as if the idea of a hunt, a kill, has exerted a magnetic pull upon everyone's attention.

"We don't hunt the deer just for the sake of it," the gamekeeper says. "We do it to keep the numbers down—otherwise they'd get out of control. So it's necessary."

"But I think it's necessary for another reason," the man—Ingvar—says. "Humans are hunters, it's in our very DNA. We need to find an outlet for those needs. The *blood lust*." He says the last two words as though they have a particularly delicious flavor to them, and there's a pause in which no one quite seems to know what to say, a heightening of the awkward tension that's plagued this meal. I see Miranda raise her eyebrows. Perhaps we can all laugh about this later—it'll become a funny anecdote. Every holiday has these moments, doesn't it? "Well, I don't know about all that," says Bo, spearing a piece of venison, "but it's delicious. Amazing to think it came from right here."

I'm not so sure. It's not terrible, exactly, but I could have done so much better. The venison is overly flavored with juniper, you can hardly taste the meat, and there isn't nearly enough jus. The vegetables are limp: the Tuscan kale a slimy oversteamed mush.

I'll make up for it tomorrow evening. I have my wonderful feast planned: smoked salmon blinis to go with the first couple of bottles of champagne, then beef Wellington with foie gras, followed by a perfect chocolate soufflé. Soufflés, as everyone knows, are not easy. You have to be a bit obsessive about them. The separation of the eggs, the perfect beating of the whites—the timings at the end, making sure you serve them before the beautiful risen crest falls. Most people don't have the patience for it. But that's exactly the sort of cooking I like.

It's a relief, to be honest, when the dessert (a rather limp raspberry pavlova) is finally cleared away.

As everyone is readying to leave, Julien motions us all to sit back down. He's had a bit too much to drink; he sways slightly as he stands.

"Darling," Miranda says, in her most silken tones, "what are you doing?" I wonder if she's remembering last New Year—in the exclusive environs of Fera at Claridge's restaurant—when he stood up out of his seat without looking, only to send a waiter's entire tray of food crashing to the ground.

"I want to say a few words," he says. "I want to thank Emma"— he raises his glass at me—"for picking such a fantastic place—"

"Oh," I say, "I haven't really done anything . . ."

"And I want to say how special it is to have everyone here, together. It's nice to know that some things never change, that some friends are always there for you. It hasn't been the easiest year—"

"Darling," Miranda says again, with a laugh, "I think everyone gets the idea. But I absolutely agree. Here's to old friends . . ." She raises her glass. Then she remembers, and turns to me. "And new, of course. Cheers!"

Everyone echoes her, including Ingvar—though of course she did not mean him. But even his interjection doesn't spoil it. The toast has rescued the atmosphere, somehow—it's brought a sense of occasion to the meal. And I feel, again, that special little glow of pride.

12

DOUG

ABOUT AN HOUR AFTER THE DINNER THERE'S A KNOCK ON his door. The dogs, Griffin and Volley, go crazy at this unexpected excitement: no one *ever* comes to his cottage. He checks his watch: midnight.

"What the—"

It's the beautiful one, the tall blonde who sat next to him at the meal. Who touched her hand to his, which was, as it happens, the first time anyone has touched his skin in a long time. She smiles, her hand lifted, as though ready to knock again. He can smell trouble coming off her.

Griffin barrels past him and leaps up at her even as Doug roars, "Down!" She throws her arms up, and as she does her sweater lifts, exposing a taut sliver of stomach, the tight-furled bud of her navel. The dog's nose leaves a wet slick across the skin.

She seems embarrassed by her reaction of fear; she bends to caress Griffin's head, a show of bravado. "Pretty girl," she says, sounding less than completely convinced. She grins up at him, all her white teeth. *Look at me,* the grin says, *look how relaxed I am.* "Hi. Hope you don't mind my interrupting you like this."

"What is it?"

Her smile falters. Too late, he remembers that this is a guest, that he owes her a service, even if it is ridiculously late for her to be asking anything of him. He attempts some damage limitation with the next question. "How can I help?"

"I was wondering if you could help us make a fire," she says, "in the Lodge."

He stares at her. He cannot imagine how nine people might not have the skills between them to set a fire.

"We've been trying to make one," she says, "but without much luck." She leans one arm against the doorpost, slouching her hip. Her jumper has ridden up again. "We're Londoners, you see. I know you'd make it *much* better than we ever could."

"Fine," he says, curtly, and then remembers again that she is a customer. A *guest*. "Of course."

He senses that she is the sort of woman who is used to getting her way. He can feel her trying to peer into the interior of the cottage. He is not used to this: he blocks her view with his body and closes the door behind him so quickly that he only just avoids Griffin's eager nose.

She crooks her finger at him, inviting him to follow. Just toward the Lodge, to light the bloody fire . . . but still. He knows what she is offering up to him. Not the act itself, perhaps, but the whisper, the hint, the wink of it.

How long has it been? A long time. More than a year—maybe a lot more.

As he follows he catches that scent of her perfume again, the church-like smokiness of it. It smells to him like trouble.

He follows her back to the Lodge. As he kneels in the grate, the big guy—Mark?—comes over and says in a man-to-man way, "Waste of your time, mate. She insisted on going and getting you. But I practically had it going. The wood's just a bit damp, that's all."

THE HUNTING PARTY **73**

He looks at the haphazard arrangement of logs in the grate, the twenty or so burned matches scattered around, and says nothing.

"Want some help?" the man asks.

"No, thanks."

"Suit yourself, *mate*." The man's face has reddened in a matter of seconds with either embarrassment, or, Doug suspects, anger. Short fuse on that one, he thinks. Takes one to know one.

13

HEATHER

Now
January 2, 2019

Normally the water of the loch reflects the land-scape as perfectly as if the mountains and trees and lodge were peering into a mirror. Sometimes in this reflection they look some-how more crisp, more perfect than they do in reality. But today the surface is clouded, blind, scarred by ice. Please, I think, following Doug around the bend of the path beside the water, don't let it be the loch. Don't let him have found the body there.

The loch is my sanctuary, my church.

The first time I wandered into those freezing depths I didn't intend on coming back out. It was in the early days here, when I realized that I hadn't been able to outrun everything. But some-thing happened, as my clothes became weighed down, and the cold surrounded me in its terrible grip. Some essential urge, beyond my control, to kick, to fight. Here was life, suddenly: inside me, powerful, insuperable. The feeling was—is—addictive. It is one of the few times that I do not feel that I am drowning.

I have my routine down pat now. I get myself up and get straight into my swimming costume, a chaste one-piece like those we used to wear for swimming lessons at school. I'm not trying to impress anyone, and it's the most coverage I can get for warmth without resorting to a full wet suit. I go every morning of the year. I do it especially when it is below freezing—like now—and when I have to break the ice on the surface of the loch. When the water is so cold that it grips you like a vise and squeezes all thoughts from your mind, and your heart seems to be beating so hard it might explode. That's when I am most myself, without the weight of everything upon me. The one time these days when I really feel alive.

Afterward I dry off and go back to my cottage. By then every nerve ending in my body is tingling pleasantly. I suppose you could say it's the next best thing to sex.

I saw Doug swimming in the loch, just once. I have an uninterrupted view of the water from my cottage. He went right to the edge and stripped off down to his boxers, revealing powerful shoulders, skin pale as milk. When he swam—not a moment's hesitation at the cold—it looked as though his body was a machine specifically designed to cut through the water with the greatest possible speed. When he stepped out his face was grim.

As I watched I felt a powerful sense of shame, as though I had intruded upon some private moment of his, even though all it took was a glance from the window. And shame, too, because it felt like a disloyalty. Because I had looked, and kept on looking, and had not been immune to the sight of my coworker's body. Because I had held the image of it in my mind when I took a bath, later, and gave myself the first orgasm I had had in more than a year.

Now Doug turns around, to check I'm following, and I feel the heat rise instantly to my cheeks. Hopefully the sting of the cold will be enough to justify it.

WE ARE ABOUT TO PLUNGE INTO THE THICKET OF TREES that ring the loch on this side. A fringe of dark pines. Some of them aren't native; they're Norwegian imposters, planted after the war. They're much denser than the local Scots pine, and when you're among them all sound from the outside world seems to be muffled. Not that there are many sounds here, beyond the occasional cawing of the birds.

On my good days, I persuade myself that I love these trees: their glossy needles, the cones that I collect to keep in bowls around the house, the warm, green Christmas scent of the resin when you walk among them. On my bad days I decide they look funereal, like sinister black-cloaked sentinels.

We are out of sight of the Lodge now. Completely alone. I am suddenly reminded that though I've worked alongside this man for a year I know almost nothing about him. This is definitely the most time I have ever spent in his company—and quite possibly the most we have ever spoken to each other.

I'm not sure he speaks to *anyone*. Early on, I kept expecting him to ask me if he could use the Internet: to send an email, perhaps, or check up on friends and family on Facebook. But he never did. Even I check in with friends and family every so often. "Your mam worries about you," my dad said, at the beginning. "Stuck in a place like that all on your own, after everything you've been through. It's not right." So I try to go back every few months or so to put her mind at rest, though the experience of reentering the outside world is not one I particularly relish.

But Doug *never* seems to leave the estate unless he has to: taking guests into town to visit the shops, for example. I made the mistake of mentioning him to my mum, the lonely existence he leads. Of course, in true parental style, she was worried for me.

"He could be anyone," she told me. "What's his background? Where does he come from?"

I told her the one thing I did know, that he'd been in the marines. This did not reassure her in the slightest. "You need to goggle him, Heather," she told me.

"Google, Ma."

"Whatever it is. Just promise me you'll do it. You need to know who this man is . . . I can't sleep for worrying about you, Heather. Running off and leaving us all behind just when you need your family about you most. Not letting us help you like we want to. No word for days, weeks. I need to know that you're safe at least. Who you're working with. It's not fair, Heaths." And then she seemed to check herself. "Of course—I know it must sound awful, me saying that. What happened to you . . . that was the most unfair thing that could happen—"

"All right, Ma," I said, not wanting to hear any more. "I'll do it, I'll google him." But I didn't, not then. Truthfully, the thought of it felt like a betrayal.

Of course, when my mum asked me what I had found—I could tell it was one of those things that she wouldn't give up on, a terrier with a bone—I reassured her. "It's fine," I said. "I looked. There's nothing there. You can stop worrying about me now."

There was a pause. "I never stop worrying about you, pet." I put the phone down.

The truth is, she's right. I don't know anything about Doug. Just what the boss hinted at during my interview, that his background made him well suited to the job—particularly seeing off any poachers. When he was asked to take his pick of the cottages he chose the one farthest from anything—at the bottom of the flank of the Munro, with no sheltering trees, with no view of the loch. It's unquestionably the worst of all of them, which would suggest he chose it purely for its position. I understand the need to be alone. But the need for even further isolation within this remote wilderness makes me wonder exactly what it is he is trying to distance himself from.

WHERE ARE WE GOING, DOUG?"

"Just a little way now," he says, and I feel a leap of trepidation, a powerful urge to turn and start in the other direction again, back toward the Lodge. Instead I follow Doug as we tramp farther into the trees, the only sound the squeak of our boots in the snow.

Up ahead of us I see the first of the waterfalls, the small wooden bridge that spans it, the pumphouse building a little way farther up. Normally it would take us only ten minutes to get here. But in these conditions it has taken the best part of half an hour.

I see the big impressions of Doug's boots in the snow on the bridge, where he apparently stood the first time, looking down. There are no other footprints, I notice. But then there wouldn't be. This snow has been falling for hours. Any other tracks—including those of the dead guest—will have long ago been obscured.

"There," he says, pointing.

I step warily onto the bridge. At first I can't see anything. It's a long way down to the bottom, and I'm very aware of Doug standing just behind me. It would only take a little push, I find myself thinking, to send me over. I grip the chain rail hard, though it suddenly seems very flimsy in my grasp.

There is a moment of incomprehension as I stare into the void. All I can make out is a lot of snow and ice gathered in the ravine.

"Doug," I say, "I can't see anything. There's nothing there."

He frowns, and points again. I follow his finger.

Suddenly, peering down among the rocks, the great pillows of fallen snow, it appears below me like the slow emergence of a magic eye image.

"Oh God." It's more an exhalation of air, like a punch to the gut, than a word. I have seen dead bodies before in my time, in my old line of work. A greater number than the average person, definitely. But the horror of the experience never leaves you. It is always a shock—a profound, existential shock—to be confronted with the inanimate object that was once a person. A person so recently thinking, feeling, seeing, reduced to so much cold flesh. I feel the long-ago familiar swoop of nausea. At medical school they told us it would go away, after our first few. "You get used to it." But I'm not sure I ever really did. And I am unprepared, despite knowing what I have come to see. I have been ambushed, here in this place, by death. I thought that I could outrun it.

It almost looks like part of the landscape now: I think that is partly what helped it to blend in. But now I can see it, I can't believe I missed it before. The corpse has a kind of dark power, drawing the eye. The lower half of it is covered modestly by fallen snow, though the shield of the bridge has protected the top half of the body. The skin is a grayish blue, leached of all blood and human color. That hair, too, spilling behind the head, might just be more dead weed, such as those that poke obstinately through the snow in places.

There seems to be a great deal of skin, in fact. This is not the corpse of a person who came out dressed for the elements. The cold would have killed in an hour—less—if nothing else had. Or *someone* else had.

I see now, looking harder, the halo of blood about the head: rust-colored, covering the rocks beneath like a peculiar species of lichen. There is a lot of it. A fall onto rock. That could have been the thing that did the killing, in itself.

But I can see that it is more complicated than that. There is an unmistakable necklace of darkness about the neck. The skin there, even from this distance away, looks particularly blue and bruised-looking. I know very little about forensics—barely more than someone with no background in medicine. My old vocation was in saving life, not examining the evidence left after its loss. But you would not need to be an expert in the field to see that something has compressed the skin there, injured it.

The face . . . no, I don't want to think about the face.

I turn back to Doug. His gaze is a blank; as though there is no one behind his eyes. I take a step back, involuntarily. Then I get a grip of myself.

"I see it," I say. "I see what you mean. Yes."

We must wait for the police to arrive, to make their judgments, of course. But I know now why Doug wanted me to come and take a look. This does not look like an accident.

14

EMMA

Three days earlier
December 30, 2018

W E'RE BACK IN THE LIVING ROOM OF THE LODGE, ALL A BIT
tipsy. Tired from the day, too—but no one wants to go to
bed, because it's a novelty to be together like this. Samira and Giles
have joined us now—Priya's finally fallen asleep apparently, though
Samira keeps holding the baby monitor up to her ear as though
worried it has stopped working. There's a lot of laughter and hilarity, the booze loosening us.

"So what did we miss?" Giles asks.

"Not a lot," Nick says. "Though clearly I should have brought
a kilt. De rigueur here, it seems."

"I think it's a good look," Miranda says, with a glance in the direction of the gamekeeper, who's kneeling in the grate to make our
fire. "Oh," she says mysteriously, "and we met the other guests . . ."

"What are they like?" Samira asks.

Bo does a heavily accented impression of the man, Ingvar.

"Ze blood lust," he says, gesticulating, "don't you feel it stirring in you in a place like zis, ze urge to keeeeeell?"

Miranda snorts with laughter. "Yes, yes—that's it exactly!"

He's a good mimic—he would be, being an actor. But he's also slurring a bit, drunker than everyone else. He had some problems with drugs in the past, apparently, but alcohol doesn't seem to be off-limits. At the dinner he was knocking back the glasses of wine like water.

"God," Samira says, "he sounds like a bit of a freak. But presumably . . . you know, a harmless one?"

"He liked you, Katie!" Miranda says.

"*Did* he, Katie?" Giles asks, grinning.

Katie colors. She's curled up on one of the sofas next to Nick, feet tucked under her, as though she's attempting to take up as little room as possible. "I don't think so," she says.

"Oh yes he did," Mark says, "I think he wanted to drag you off into the woods and have his way with you."

Again, I'm aware of the gamekeeper's presence. But he's hardly going to tell the other guests what he's overheard, is he? I watch as he makes a tepee of the wood and kindling: there's something satisfying about his efficiency. Giles and Mark were peeved that Miranda thought it necessary to go and get him, but their first few attempts fizzled out within minutes. He doesn't look particularly impressed about being asked, either—I suppose it is pretty late. I wonder if anyone other than Miranda would have been able to summon him at this time of night.

Miranda, speaking of, is now at the cocktail cabinet making us "boulevardiers," her specialty: a negroni, with the gin swapped out for bourbon. She had them served at her wedding.

"Want one?" she asks the gamekeeper.

"No," he says, looking at the floor. "I've got to be getting back."

"Suit yourself."

He stands up, wipes the soot from his hands on his jacket, and makes for the door. "Good night!" Miranda calls as it closes.

"Good riddance," Mark says. "He's hardly a barrel of laughs, is he?"

"Not everyone has your wit and charm, Marky-Mark," Miranda says as she brings the cocktails over to us, then huffs down onto the sofa, kicking off her pumps in one fluid motion. Her toenails are painted a perfect dark blood red. I love that color, really chic. I'll have to remember to ask her what shade it is.

"I want a smoke," she announces. "I always want a smoke with one of these." She takes out her packet. They're Vogue lights. I know, because I smoke the same ones—I haven't smoked anything else since I took up the habit, at nineteen.

"I don't think you can smoke in here," Nick says.

"Of course I can. Fuck that. We've paid enough for the privilege, haven't we? Besides"—she points at the giant fire in the grate, which is sending up clouds of peat-scented smoke—"that thing stinks enough to mask the smell."

But someone could look in and see you, I think. Heather, or the gamekeeper, Doug. When you look at the windows now you can mainly just see the reflection of us, the room, the fire. And then just beyond, the very faint outline of the nighttime landscape: the darker black of the trees and the gleam of the loch. But we're pretty blind to anything else out there.

It said it on the form, I remember. Quite clearly: no smoking indoors, please. If someone sees her, we'll be charged the damage deposit. But I won't say anything, not now at least. The last thing I want to be is a killjoy. I just want everyone to have a good time.

"For fuck's sake," Miranda says, "where's my lighter? I thought I'd left it right there on the coffee table. It's a special one: it was my grandfather's. It has our crest on it."

Miranda always finds little ways to remind people of the grand stock she comes from. But I don't think she does it in a mean way, really. It's just how she is.

Mark fumbles in a pocket, finds his lighter. Miranda leans forward into the flame, so far that we can all see the raspberry lace of her bra.

"Perhaps your stalker took it?" Nick says teasingly, leaning back and taking a sip of his whiskey—he refused a cocktail.

"Oh God," Miranda says, widening her eyes. "I swear . . . every time I lose something, I half find myself blaming it on him first. It's rather convenient."

"What stalker?" I ask.

"Oh," Miranda says, "I always forget how new you are, Emma."

No she doesn't. She's always reminding me how new I am to the group. But I suppose I don't mind.

"Manda had this stalker," Samira says. "It started in Oxford, but it carried on in London for several years, didn't it, Manda?"

"You know," Miranda says, airily, "sometimes I could almost believe that there never really was one. That it was someone playing a joke on me, instead."

"Funny sort of joke," Julien says. "And I don't remember you being that blasé about it at the time. It was fucking creepy—you must remember how much it frightened you?"

Miranda frowns. I suspect she doesn't like the implication that it had worried her. Playing the victim is not her style. "Anyway," she says, "he used to take stuff from me. Weird things, little things—but often with some sentimental value. To be honest, it took me a while to work it out. I'm so disorganized that I'm always losing things and never finding them again."

"He'd return them, too," Katie says, over the top of the magazine she's reading. She's been so quiet for the last hour or so—while everyone else has been making so much noise—that I'd almost forgotten she was there. "Later on, he'd return them."

"Oh yes," Miranda says. For a moment I think I see a shadow

of something in her expression—some fear or disquiet—but if the memory unnerves her, she conceals it quickly. "At Oxford he used to leave the things he'd taken in my locker at college, with a little typed note. And then when we were in London, I'd get stuff posted to me—also with a note. Little things: an earring, a jumper, a shoe. It was like he was just keeping them for a while."

"It was horrible," Samira says. "Especially when we lived in that gloomy little house in second year next to the railway tracks—do you remember? I always thought you must have been so scared. *I* was scared, just thinking that he was lurking around."

"I think I actually found it quite funny, more than anything," Miranda says.

"I'm not sure you did at the time," Katie says. "I remember, in college, you coming to my room in the middle of the night with your duvet over your shoulder, saying you felt like someone had been in your room, watching you. You used to come and sleep on my floor."

Miranda frowns. I suppose that's the problem with old friends; they have long memories. It's as if Katie's not playing by the rules—her comment has cut through the fun.

"You know," Julien says, "I always thought it was someone you knew. It had to have been someone who was always there, near you—close enough to take those things."

I see Katie dart a look at Mark, and then quickly glance away again. I'm sure I know what she's thinking. I bet her pet theory is that he was the stalker. He has always had a crush on Miranda. Yes, I know about it. No, it doesn't bother me. It's harmless, I know it is. Mark is, at heart, a fairly simple soul. He has a temper, yes, but he lacks the calculating nature needed for such behavior.

I see the pity in the way Katie looks at me sometimes. It irks me. I do not need her pity. I wish I could tell her that, without sounding like I am protesting too much.

15

MIRANDA

PEOPLE HAVE ALWAYS BEEN ENTERTAINED BY TALES OF MY stalker. I know how to dress them up to give that little ghost-story shiver down the spine. And it's such a *bizarre* thing, isn't it? A real-life stalker. Everyone seems to think it only happens to celebrities: actresses, singers, breakfast TV hosts. Sometimes I'll catch the person I'm telling looking at me: squinting, head on one side, as though they're assessing me. Do I really deserve to be stalked? Am I really *that* interesting?

I often bring up my stalker as a piece of dinner party conversation. At times it feels like he's an exotic and fascinating pet, or a particularly gifted child. It starts conversations. It can stop them, too: the idea of someone watching you, knowing everything about you. And then I'll segue neatly into my whole routine—about how, when you think about it, in the times we live in we are *all* stalkers. All of us knowing so much about one another's lives. Even people we haven't seen in years. Old childhood friends, old schoolmates. I'll talk about how we all submit to being stalked. How we think that we're in control, sharing what we think we choose to share, but really putting a lot more out there than we're aware of.

"So really," I'll say, at this point in my performance, "my stalker was just a bit ahead of the game! A trendsetter, of sorts. He was just analog. Although having probably been a student at Oxford, too"—little pause to let that settle, let it glimmer and impress for a moment—"for all I know he's probably behind some social media app anyway. Sharing his expertise with the world!"

Cue: wry laughter. Cue: an ongoing discussion about privacy, and what we should submit ourselves to and where we should draw the line . . . and how privacy is the true battleground of the twenty-first century. Cue: an exchange of various weird experiences people have had: private messages from strangers on Instagram, trolling on Twitter, a creepy friend request on Facebook from someone they've never met. None of it, however, nearly as strange and *special* as my own experience.

I will sit back, feeling a little glow. As though I've just performed some well-practiced routine, and pulled it off with even more sparkle than before. My own little social gymnastics display. Julien will probably be rolling his eyes at this point. He's heard the whole thing—what, maybe fifty, a hundred, a thousand times before? And he's never been able to see the interesting, or amusing, side of it. He was the one who thought, all those years ago, that I should get the police involved. He used to look annoyed when I brought up the subject, because he thought I shouldn't make light of something "so fucking creepy," as he put it. Now I think he's mainly just a bit bored with hearing it.

But the truth I don't tell anyone is that I was—am—frightened of my stalker. There are things the stalker knows about me, secret, shameful things, that I have told no one. Not even Katie, not even back then when we were thick as thieves, not Julien.

The stalker knew, for example, that every so often I liked to dabble in a bit of recreational shoplifting at Oxford. Only at times of high stress: exam season, or before a big paper had to be in. My therapist (the only one I've told about this little habit) thinks it was a control thing, a bit like my dieting and exercising: something

I had power over, and was good at. She thinks it's in the past, though—she doesn't know that sometimes I'll still snaffle the odd lipstick, a pair of cashmere gloves, a magazine. There's the thrill of getting away with it, too; my therapist hasn't worked that part out.

I stole a pair of earrings from the Oxford Topshop. Gold hoops with a little painted parrot sitting on each one. A few days after I'd lifted them they disappeared from my room. They were returned a few weeks later in my cubbyhole, with a note: *Miranda Adams: I'd have expected better from you. Sincerely, a concerned friend. xxx.* The kisses were the worst fucking part of it.

He must have been *right* next to me in the shop when I did it. It had been crowded, I remembered: and there had been men in there as well as women, trailing after girlfriends, or making their way down to Topman. No particular face stood out, though. I had no memory of anyone looking at me—more than normal—or acting weirdly.

While the earrings were missing I remember seeing a bespectacled girl in the Bodleian in that exact pair—and almost chased after her into Short-Term Loans. Until I realized that anyone could have bought them. They were from Topshop, for Christ's sake. There might have been twenty—fifty—girls in the city with them. This was how paranoid my stalker had made me, bringing me to the point of chasing down a complete stranger.

Then there was the essay that I bought from a student in the year above, with the intention of plagiarizing it for my own. Both had been sitting on the desk in my room—the original, and my poorly disguised copy. I'd gone out for a drink at the pub and returned to find them both gone. I'd had to cobble something together, drunk, in the hours before the deadline, and ended up getting a bare pass, my worst mark yet—though not ever. A week later they were returned to me. The note: *I don't think you want to go down that path, Miranda.* And yet, a week later, when a few students got held up for their own acts of plagiarism, I was almost oddly grateful.

And there was the time, very early on with Julien, when I cheated on him. A drunken shag with a guy in my tutor group. As luck would have it, my period didn't arrive that month. I took a pregnancy test—thankfully negative—which was returned a week later with a note that read, *Naughty, naughty, Manda. What would Julien say?*

The casual use of "Manda," which is what only my closest friends call me.

I didn't tell anyone of these particular communications. Not even Katie, or Samira. They revealed aspects of myself that I would have preferred no one know anything about. And I feared that if I did something to displease my stalker he would use all my secrets to destroy me.

Nevertheless, I did go to the police—though, again, I didn't tell anyone. I took along a couple of the notes: the ones I could bring myself to show. I wasn't taken very seriously. "Have there been any threats made in the notes, miss?" the officer I spoke to asked.

"Well, no."

"And you haven't noticed anyone behaving in a threatening manner?"

". . . No."

"No signs of forced entry?"

"No."

"It seems to me"—he picked up one of the notes again and read it—"that one of your mates might be playing a prank on you, my dear." Patronizing arse.

That was that. I regretted ever having gone—and not just because the police were no help. In doing so I had made myself into the victim I refused to be.

But it carried on in London for several years. He worked out where I was living. It's one thing to access a student room on a relatively accessible corridor. It's quite another to gain entry to a London property with three high-security locks on the door. And then we moved, and it *kept* happening. The items that went missing were always of a similar kind. On the surface, valueless, but all with some inner significance. The tiniest doll from the very inside of the beautiful painted *matryoshka* I was given by my beloved godmother, before she died from cancer. The batik scarf I bought in a Greek village on my first holiday with Julien—the summer of our second year. The woven friendship bracelet that Katie gave me in our first year of knowing each other.

I thought I'd always have my stalker. He had begun to feel like a part of my life, a part of me, even. But then, out of the blue, it stopped. A couple of years ago now. At least, I think it stopped. I've received no packages, no notes. But sometimes, when I misplace something, I have that old frisson of fear. There was that silver baby rattle I bought from Tiffany's recently, on a whim as I was walking down Bond Street. I'm sure it will show up somewhere. I'm not the most organized person, after all. I tell myself that it's just paranoia. But I haven't ever shaken that feeling of being watched.

I haven't told anyone—not even Julien, or Katie or Samira, say—of the feeling of creeping horror I get, sometimes. Moments when I am in the middle of a crowd and suddenly convinced that someone is standing right behind me, breathing on my neck . . . only to turn around and see that there is no one there. Or a sudden certainty that someone is watching me with an intensity that isn't normal. You know . . . that prickling feeling you have when you know you are being looked at? It's happened at music festivals and on shopping trips, in supermarkets and nightclubs. On the tube platform I sometimes find myself staggering back away from the edge, convinced that someone is standing right behind me, about to give me a shove.

No, I don't tell anyone these fears. Not Katie, not Julien, certainly not my amused dinner party guests.

I have bad dreams, too. It's worst when Julien is away on business trips. I have to double-check all the locks on the doors, and even then I'll wake in pitch blackness convinced that someone is in the room with me. Similar to the sort of tricks your mind plays on you if you've just watched a horror film. Suddenly you'll see sinister shadows in every corner. Only this is a hundred times worse. Because some of those shadows might be real.

16

KATIE

MIRANDA'S FINALLY COMING TO THE END OF HER LITTLE repertoire. Just at this moment the wind chooses to do a long, melodramatic howl down the chimney. The fire seems to billow out, a scatter of sparks landing just inside the grate. It is perfect, horror-movie timing. Everyone laughs.

"Reminds me of that house we stayed in in Wales," Giles says.

"The one where we kept having blackouts?" Nick asks. "And the heating kept going off at random intervals?"

"It was haunted," Miranda says. "That's what the owner told us—remember. It was Jacobean." That place had been Miranda's choice.

"It was definitely old," says Mark, "but I'm not sure ghosts are an excuse for dodgy plumbing and electrical faults."

"But there had been plenty of sightings," Emma says loyally. "The woman said they'd had people from *Most Haunted* come to visit them."

"Yes," Miranda says, pleased by this. "There was that story about a girl being thrown out of a window by her stepbrothers, because they'd realized she was going to inherit the property. And people had heard her, screaming at night."

"I certainly heard someone screaming at night," Giles says, grinning at her. There had been a lot of hilarity over the thinness of the walls, and certain "noises" keeping everyone up at night. Miranda and Julien had been singled out as the main culprits.

"Oh, stop it," Miranda says, hitting Giles with a cushion. She's laughing, but as the conversation moves on she stops and I see a new expression—wistful?—cross her features. I look away.

Giles's mention of Wales has opened a conversation about other years past. It is a favorite hobby, raking over our shared history together. These are the experiences that have always bound us, that have given us a tribal sense of affiliation. For as long as we have known each other, we have always spent New Year's Eve together. It's a regathering of threads that have become a little looser over the years, as our jobs and lives take us in different directions. I wonder if the others experience the same thing that I do, on these occasions. That however much I think I have changed, however different I feel as a person at work, or with the few non-university friends I have, at times like this I somehow return to exactly the same person I was more than a decade ago.

"I can't believe I drank so much last year . . . while I was pregnant with Priya," says Samira, looking horrified.

"You didn't know at the time," Emma says.

"No, but still—all those shots. I can't even imagine drinking like that now. It just seems so . . . excessive. I feel like an old lady these days."

She certainly doesn't look like one. With her shining black hair and dewy, unlined skin, Samira looks like the same girl we knew at Oxford. Giles, on the other hand, who once sported a full head of hair, looks like a completely different person. But at the same time Samira has changed, perhaps more dramatically than Giles has. She used to be spiky, slightly intimidating, with that razor-sharp intellect and impeccable style. She was involved in everything at Oxford. The Union, several sports, theater, the college orchestra—as well as being a notorious party girl. Somehow she seemed to fit ten times the normal amount of activity into her four years and still emerge with a high First.

She seems softer now, gentler. Perhaps it's motherhood. Or things going so well with her career—apparently the consultancy firm where she works is desperate for her to return from maternity early; it's not hard to imagine the place being on its knees without her. Perhaps it's simply growing older. A sense that she doesn't need to prove herself any longer, that she knows exactly who she is. I envy that.

J ULIEN'S TALKING ABOUT A PLACE WE VISITED IN OXFORD-shire a couple of years ago—Emma's first New Year's Eve with us, I believe.

"Ha!" Mark takes a sip of his drink. "That was the one where I had to show those local oiks who was boss. Do you remember? One of them actually tried to beat me up?"

Not quite how I remember it.

This is what I recall. I remember the group was exactly the wrong size. Fifteen people—not big enough for a party, not small enough for intimacy. The plan was to go to the races on the afternoon of New Year's Eve. I had been expecting something a bit more glamorous, scenes borrowed from *My Fair Lady* and *Pretty Woman*. Not so much. There were girls wearing skirts so short you could see their Ann Summers thongs, and boys in cheap shiny suits and bad haircuts and sun-bed tans, strutting around and getting more and more raucous as the evening went on. The food was less champagne and caviar, more steak and ale pies and bottles of vodka. And yet it was all a bit of fun. They were all just kids, really, those miniskirted girls and those shiny-suited lads, preening and swaggering and hiding their self-consciousness beneath the haze of booze, just as we had all done before them.

And then Mark decided to make some comment about the place being "overrun with pikeys."

Admittedly we were in a deserted bit of the stadium, drinking our alcopops—most people were down at the racetrack, cheering on their horses. But there were still a few people around. A group of *youths,* as the *Daily Mail* might label them. And Mark hadn't made any effort to be quiet. He's like that. Sometimes I think that if Emma weren't so unobjectionable, so ready to muck in, people would tolerate him a lot less.

Two of the booze-fueled teenagers heard him. Suddenly they were squaring up to him. But you could see that they didn't really mean it. It was just something they felt they should do, to protect their slighted honor, like in a nature documentary when the smaller males of the pack can't afford to show any fear, or risk being eaten. Quite understandable, really.

The foremost one was a short, thin guy, with the faintest whisper of teenagerish stubble about his chin, a particularly garish pinstripe number. "Say that again, mate." His voice had an unmistakable adolescent reediness to it; he couldn't have been more than nineteen.

I waited for Mark to apologize, defuse the situation—make light of it somehow. Because that would have been the only sensible, adult thing to do. We were the grown-ups, after all. Mark stood a couple of heads taller than his pinstripe-suited aggressor.

But Mark punched him. Took two steps forward, and punched him full in the face, with one of those meaty hands. So hard that the boy's head snapped back. So hard that he fell like a toppled statue. There was a noise, a crack, a simulacrum of the racecourse starting gun, the way I had thought only really happened in films.

We all just stood there, stunned, including his little gaggle of mates. You might have thought his friends would fight back, try to avenge him. Not so. That was the quality of the violence. It was too sudden, too brutal. You could see: they were terrified.

They bent down to him, and, as he came round, asked if he

was all right. He moaned like an animal in pain. There was a trail of bright red blood coming from his nose, and another—more worryingly, somehow—coming from his mouth. I'd never seen anyone bleed from their mouth before, either, apart from in films. It turned out that he had bitten off the tip of his tongue when his head hit the ground. I read that in an article online, in the local rag, a couple of weeks later. I read, too, that the police were looking for the perpetrator. But there was also some mention of the fact that the guy was a bit of a troublemaker—so perhaps it wasn't a very serious hunt.

What was so odd, I thought, was that Emma didn't even seem particularly shocked. I remember thinking that she must have seen this side of Mark before. She had a clear, immediate idea of what to do—as though she had been waiting for something like this to happen. All practicality. "We need to leave," she said, "now. Before anyone gets wind of this."

"But what if he's not okay?" I asked.

"They're just a load of drunk chavs," Emma said. "And they started it." She turned around to face us all. "Didn't they? Didn't they start it? He was just defending himself."

She was so earnestly convincing—so convinced—that I think we all rather started to believe it. And no one mentioned it again, not for the whole duration of the three-day break. On New Year's Eve, when Mark danced on the table wearing a silly wig and a big, goofy grin, it was even easier to believe that it had never happened. It's almost impossible to imagine it now, looking at him pulling Emma onto his lap, ruffling her hair tenderly as he smiles down at her—the image of the caring boyfriend. Almost, but not quite. Because the truth is I have never quite been able to forget what I saw, and sometimes when I look at Mark I am jolted back to the memory of it, with a little shock of horror.

17

DOUG

TWO A.M. WHEN HE LIFTS THE CURTAIN HE CAN SEE LIGHT blazing from the Lodge, which seems brighter now, almost, a defiance of the darkness surrounding it. He has been lying awake for hours now, like an animal whose territory has been encroached upon, who cannot rest until the threat is gone. He can hear the guests even from here, the music thumping out, the occasional staccato of their laughter. He can even hear the low vibration of their voices. Or is he imagining that part? Difficult to be certain. For someone who was once told at school that he had "an unfortunate lack of imagination" his brain seems to conjure a fair amount from thin air these days.

He chose this cottage specifically because it was the farthest from all the other buildings. The windows predominantly face the bleak grayish flank of the Munro; the loch can only be glimpsed through the window of the toilet, which is almost entirely overgrown with ivy. He can almost imagine himself completely alone here, most of the time. It would be best if he were completely alone. For his own sake, for that of others.

H E VAGUELY RECALLS A MAN WHO WAS SOCIABLE, WHO EN-
joyed the company of others—who had (whisper it) *friends*. Who
could hold court over pints, who had a bit of a rep as a comic, a
raconteur. That man had a life before: a home, a girlfriend—who
had waited for him through three long tours in Afghanistan. She
stuck by him even when he came back from the last tour, broken.
But then the thing happened—or rather he did the thing. And after
that she left him.

"I don't know you anymore," she had said as she piled her
things haphazardly into bin liners, like someone fleeing from a natural disaster. Her sister was waiting in the car, she said, as though
he might try to do something unspeakable to stop her. "The man
I loved—" and there had been tears in her eyes as though she was
grieving someone who had died, "wouldn't do something like
that."

More than that, she was frightened of him. He could see it as
he moved toward her, to try to comfort her—because he hated to
see her cry. She had backed away, thrust the bag she was holding
in front of her like a shield. She moved away; changed her number.
His family, too, retreated. The idea that the man he remembers
was, in fact, himself, seems too absurd to be real. Better to imagine
him as some distant relative.

H E SAW HOW THEY LOOKED AT HIM, THE GUESTS, AS THOUGH
he were a curiosity, a freak show. When he has—rarely—
caught a glimpse of his appearance in a mirror he has some idea of
why. He looks like a wild man, someone on the very margins of
society. This is probably the only profession in which looking the
way he does, the unbrushed hair and battered old clothes, might
actually be considered a kind of prerequisite. Sometimes he wonders whether he should drop this pretense of living like an almost-
normal person, and live fully wild. He could do it, he thinks. He's

definitely tough enough: those first few months of training with the marines quickly sloughed off any softness, and the years since have only toughened him further, like the tempering of steel. The only weak thing about him, the thing he seems unable to control, is his mind.

He has a particular set of skills, knowledge of how to survive in the wild indefinitely. He could take a gun, a rod: shoot and catch his own food. Everything else he could steal, if he needed. He has no qualms about taking a little back. He has given everything, hasn't he? And most people don't realize how much more they have than they need. They are lazy, and greedy, and blind to how easy their lives are. Perhaps it isn't their fault. Perhaps they merely haven't had the opportunity to see how fragile their grip on happiness is. But sometimes he thinks he hates them all.

Except for Heather. He doesn't hate her. But she's different. She doesn't move around in a cloud of blithe obliviousness. He doesn't know her well, true, but he senses that she has seen the dark side of things.

He climbs out of bed. No point in pretending he's ever going to sleep. As he opens the door to the living room he rouses the dogs, who look at him from their bed in sleepy confusion at first, then dawning excitement, leaping up at him, tails wagging furiously. Maybe he will take them for a walk, he thinks. He likes the more profound silence of this place at night. He knows the paths nearest to the Lodge just as well by darkness as he does by day.

"Not yet, girls," he says, reaching for the bottle of single malt and sloshing some—and a bit more—into a glass. Perhaps this will take the edge off things.

18

HEATHER

Now
January 2, 2019

CALL THE POLICE, TO TELL THEM ABOUT THE BODY.

The operator (who can't be older than nineteen or so) sounds ghoulishly animated.

"It doesn't look accidental," I say.

"And how did you work that out, ma'am?" There's a faint but definite note of facetiousness to his tone—I'm half tempted to tell him who I used to be, what I used to do.

"Because," I say, as patiently as I can, "there is a ring of bruising around the neck. I'm . . . no expert, but that would suggest to me a sign of something, some force." *Such as strangulation,* I think, and do not say. I do not want to give him another chance to think I'm getting ahead of myself.

There's a longish pause on the other end of the line, which I imagine is the sound of him working out that this is something above his pay grade. Then he comes back on. His tone has lost all of its former levity. "If you'd wait a few moments, madam, I'm going to go and get someone else to speak to you."

I wait, and then a woman comes on the line. "Hello, Heather. This is DCI Alison Querry." She sounds somehow too assured for a little local station. Her accent isn't local, either: a light Edinburgh burr. "I've been seconded to the station to assist in the investigation of another case." Ah, I think. That explains it. "I understand that what we have is a missing person situation that has now, unfortunately, turned out to be a death."

"Yes."

"Could you describe to me the state of the deceased?"

I give the same description I did to her junior, with a little more detail. I mention the odd angle of the body, the spray of gore across the rocks.

"Right," she says. "Okay. I understand that access is currently proving impossible, due to the conditions and the remoteness of the estate. But we're going to be working hard on a way to get to you, probably via helicopter."

Please, I want to beg her, this Alison Querry with her calm, measured tones, *get out here as quickly as you can. I can't do this on my own.*

"When," I ask, instead, "do you think that will be?"

"I'm afraid we're still not sure. As long as it keeps snowing like this, it's rather out of our hands. But soon, I'm sure of that. And in the meantime, I'd like you to keep all of the guests indoors. Tell them what you need to, obviously, but please keep any of the details you gave to me out of the picture. We don't want to alarm anyone unduly. Who's there at the moment?"

I struggle to count past the tide of tiredness—I haven't slept now for twenty-four hours. I have spent that time veering between exhaustion and surges of adrenaline. Now my thoughts feel treacle-slow. "There are . . . eleven guests," I say, finally, "nine in one group from London, and a couple from Iceland. And the gamekeeper, Doug, and myself."

"Just the two of you, to manage that big place? That must be a bit of a strain, mustn't it?"

She says it sympathetically, but it feels as though there's something behind the inquiry—something sharp and probing. Or maybe it's just my sleep-deprived mind, playing tricks on me.

"Well," I say, "we manage. And, there's one other employee, Iain, but he left on New Year's Eve after finishing his work for the day. He doesn't live here, you see—it's just Doug and me."

"Okay. So as far as you know the only people on the estate that night were you, your colleague the gamekeeper, and the eleven guests? So: thirteen."

Unlucky for some . . . I seem to hear.

"Well, that keeps it simple, I suppose."

Simple how? I wonder. Simple, I realize, because if it really was a murder, the culprit is probably among us. Twelve suspects. Of which presumably, undoubtedly, I must be one. The realization shouldn't surprise me. But it does, because of DCI Querry's easy manner, the sense she has given—the pretense, I realize now—of putting me in charge in her absence.

"So," she says, "to summarize: keep everyone where they are. In the meantime, it would be a great help to me if you could have a good hard think about anything you might have noticed over the last forty-eight hours. Anything that struck you as odd. Maybe you saw something, maybe you heard something—maybe you even noticed someone about the place that you didn't recognize? Any detail could be significant."

"Okay," I say. "I'll think."

"Anything that comes to mind now?"

"No."

"Please. Just take a moment. You might surprise yourself."

"I can't think of anything." But as I say it, I do remember something. Perhaps it's because of where I am standing while I speak to her: at the office window, looking out across the loch to the dark peak of the Munro and the Old Lodge, crouched there like some malignant creature. I get a sudden mental image, almost the same scene I see before me but in blackness, viewed from my window at some ungodly hour in the morning—if you could call it that—of New Year's Day. I shut my eyes, try to clarify the image. Something had woken me: I couldn't work out what at first. Then I heard the guests' baby wail. That might have been it. I staggered to the loo, to splash some water on my face. As I looked out of the little bathroom window there was the towering shape of the Munro like a cutout against the night sky, blotting out the starlight. And then something odd. A light, moving around like a solitary firefly— a wayward star. It was moving in the direction, I thought, of the Old Lodge. Traversing its way slowly across the side of the dark slope.

But I can't tell her this. I'm not even sure it was real. It's all so nebulous, so uncertain. I can't even be sure exactly *when* I saw it, just that it was at some point in the early morning. As I try to sharpen the memory in my mind, interrogate it for anything else I might have forgotten, it fades from me until I'm almost certain it was nothing more than my imagination.

"And one more thing. Just informally, for my picture of things so far. It would be so helpful. Do you remember what you were doing, the night the guest went missing?"

"I was—well, I was in bed." Not quite true, Heather. It isn't a lie, exactly—but it's not the whole truth, either. But as you've just remembered, you were stumbling around at God knows what time of night.

New Year's Eve. The loneliest night of the year, even if you're with people. Even before my life fell apart I remember that. There's always that worry that you're maybe not having quite as much of a good time as you could be. As you should be. And this year, the sound of all the fun the Londoners were having—even if I had told myself I didn't envy any of them—didn't help. So I'd had quite a lot more to drink than usual: forgetting that trying to get drunk to assuage loneliness only ever makes you feel lonelier than before.

When I'd staggered into the bathroom at whatever time it was—five, six?—I was in no fit state to be sure of what I had seen, or even whether I really witnessed anything at all. And I can't tell her any of this. Because then I'd have to admit just how drunk I really was. *And then what?* a little voice asks. *You'd have to admit you aren't the capable, forthright person you're pretending to be? You'd lose her trust?* I am reminded once again that for all her questions about what I might have noticed, her pretense of putting me in a position of responsibility until she arrives, I am one of the thirteen who were here that night. I, too, am a suspect.

"You've gone quiet on me there, Heather," DCI Alison Querry says. "Are you still there?"

"Yes," I say. My voice sounds small, uncertain. "I'm still here."

"Good. Well, let's keep in touch. Any questions, I'm here. Anything that occurs to you, don't hesitate to pick up the phone."

"Of course."

"I will be there as soon as possible. In the meantime, it sounds like you have a very capable grip on things."

"Thank you." Ha. I remember my sister, Fi: "Sometimes it's okay not to put a brave face on things, Heaths. It can do more harm than good, in the end, keeping everything bottled up."

"And I'll be in touch very shortly with an estimate of timings," DCI Querry says, "when we think we'll be able to get the chopper out. We just need this snow to ease off enough for safe flying conditions."

What do we do until then? I wonder. Just wait here in the falling snow with the specter of death just outside the door?

And then I ask it, even though I know I probably won't get an answer. "The case you've been seconded to," I say, "which one is it?"

A short pause. When she next speaks her tone is less friendly, more official. "I'll let you know that information if and when it becomes necessary to do so."

But she doesn't need to tell me. I'm fairly certain I know. The body, the way it looked. I've read about it in the papers. It would have been impossible not to. He has his own chokehold over the nation's imagination. His own title, even. The Highland Ripper.

19

KATIE

Three days earlier
December 30, 2018

IT'S NEARLY TWO THIRTY IN THE MORNING. I'M JUST WONDER-
ing if it's late enough that I could slink away to my cabin without
being called a buzzkill, when Miranda flops down next to me on
the sofa. "Feel like I've hardly had a chance to talk to you this evening," she says. Then she lowers her voice. "I've just managed to
escape Samira. Honestly, I love her dearly, but all she can talk about
these days is that baby. It's actually a bit—well, it's a bit bloody insensitive, to be honest."

"What do you mean?"

She frowns. "I can't even remember if I told you last time I saw
you—it's been ages. But"—she lowers her voice even further, to a
whisper—"we've been trying, you know . . ."

"To get—"

"Pregnant, yes. I mean, it's early days and everything. Everyone
says it takes a while." She rolls her eyes. "Except Samira, apparently—

she says she got magically knocked up the second she came off the pill."

"I suppose it's different for everyone."

"Yes. I mean, maybe it's a blessing in disguise, to be honest. It's the end of everything, isn't it? Life as we know it. Look at those two. But it's like . . . I don't know, suddenly it's a rite of passage. Every single person I know on Facebook seems to have a kid, or has one in the oven . . . it's like this sudden *epidemic* of fertility. Do you know what I mean?"

I nod. "I stopped checking Facebook a while ago, to be honest. It's toxic."

"Yes, toxic!" she says eagerly. "That's it, exactly. God, it's so refreshing talking to you, K. You're out of all of it—single, doing your own thing . . . so far away from even thinking of kids."

"Yup," I say, swallowing past something that seems to be stuck in my throat. "That's me."

"Sorry," she says, with sudden sensitivity, "I meant that as a compliment."

"It's okay," I say—the lump in my throat's still there. "I understand."

"Look—I've got something that will cheer us up." She winks at me, and fishes something from the pocket of her jeans. Then she calls out to the others: "Does anyone want any pudding?"

"You baked?" Nick asks, in mock surprise. "Never remember you being much into your cooking, Miranda." This is an understatement—which I'm sure is his point. Miranda is a *terrible* cook. I remember a particularly awful risotto where half the rice had stuck to the bottom of the pan and burned black.

"But we've had some," Giles says quickly. "That meringue-and-raspberry thing at the dinner."

Miranda grins, wickedly. Now she is the Miranda of university days, the undisputed chief party queen. She has that gleam to her eyes: something between excitement and mania. It sends a jolt of adrenaline through me, just as it did so many years ago. When Miranda is like this she is fun, but also dangerous.

"This is a *bit* different," she says, holding aloft a little plastic Ziploc bag, a rattle of small white pills inside. "Let's call them our 'after-dinner mints.' Like a palate cleanser. And for old time's sake . . . in the spirit of our all being here together."

I know immediately that I can't take one—I can't handle the loss of control. The one time I did it went horribly wrong.

IBIZA. OUR EARLY TWENTIES. A BIG GROUP. I HADN'T ACTUALLY been invited, the organizer was someone I'd never known very well at Oxford (read: he didn't consider me cool enough to invite along to any of the famously debauched parties he held). But the week before the holiday, Miranda's granny had died, and she sold her place to me, for a discount. Julien was going, and Samira and Mark, and lots of others who have long since fallen away. I'm not sure I could remember many of their names even if I particularly wanted to try.

I liked the long, lazy lunches by the pool. The evenings drinking rosé, getting a tan, reading my book. What I wasn't so keen on was the part of the evening when the pills came out, and everyone looked at me—when I refused—like I was a parent who'd come along to spoil everyone's fun. And then they would descend into lesser versions of themselves—hysterical, uninhibited, huge-pupiled: like animals. If only they could have seen themselves, I thought. At the same time, I felt uptight, boring: a poor replacement for Miranda. Samira—always with the "in" crowd—took me to one side and told me: "You just need to loosen up a bit."

By the end of the week, they would hardly get up at all during the day. The house had become disgusting. Everywhere you stood there seemed to be dirty clothes, beer cans, used condoms, even puddles of vomit halfheartedly cleaned up. I was on the point of booking a flight home. This was meant to be a holiday, for God's sake. A respite from the job where I was working eighty-hour weeks. I knew that I would be going back feeling tired, sullied, and angry. But I stuck it out. I found a bit of terrace just out of sight of the main house. I dragged a sun bed there and I spent the last few days reading. At least I'd get a proper tan, finish my book: a simulacrum of what you were meant to do on holiday. At least I'd *look*—to all my colleagues, my family—like I'd had a good time.

On the last night, by some miracle, everyone mastered the energy to put together a barbecue like the ones we'd had at the beginning of the week, before they all ruined themselves. I drank quite a lot of cava, and then some more. In the candlelight, looking at everyone's faces, and the dark turquoise glimmer of the sea, I wondered how I could possibly have decided I wasn't having a good time. This was what it meant to be young, wasn't it?

So when the pills inevitably came out, I took one. The euphoria hit me shortly after, I felt invincible. Freed from the prison of being me: Miranda's less fun, less cool friend.

A lot of what happened after seemed to take place in a liberated, not-quite-real place. I remember the swimming pool, jumping into it fully clothed; someone eventually pulling me out, telling me I'd get cold, even though I kept insisting I just wanted to "stay in the water *forever.*" I remember loving all of it, all of them. How had I not realized how much I loved them?

Later I remember a man, and I remember the sex in the dark pool house, long after everyone else seemed to have disappeared to bed. Almost total blackness, which made all the sensations only the more intense. I was driving it, I was in charge of it. When I came, I felt for a moment as though my whole body had shattered into stars. I was at once the most myself I had ever felt . . . and like someone else completely.

The next morning I couldn't believe it. That daring, sexual

person couldn't have been me, could it? If Miranda had been there I might have asked her: How much of what I thought I remembered had been real? Had she seen me go off with the man to the pool house? Had that actually happened? Or had it, in fact, just been a particularly lurid hallucination? I couldn't bring myself to ask Samira, for fear that she'd laugh at me and tell me to grow up.

It must have happened, I decided: there was a telltale ache between my legs that said it had. I was convinced I could smell him on me. But no one said anything the next day. I checked for any signs of joking or bravado among the boys, but there was nothing.

LUCKILY, THERE ARE SEVERAL OF US ABSTAINING THIS EVENING. Bo—of course, Samira, Nick in support of Bo. I could see how unimpressed Nick was by this addition to the evening in his glare when Miranda proffered the bag to him, practically reaching across Bo to do so. She seemed utterly oblivious, but then she's always given a good impression of shrugging off things, as though nothing can touch her. As her oldest friend, I know that this isn't necessarily the case. Sometimes it takes no small effort to appear so carefree.

Now she's over by the record player in the corner of the Lodge's living room, flicking through a shelf full of old records. Eventually, with a cry of victory, she finds the one she wants—*HITS: STUDIO 54*—and places it on the turntable. As the music spills out, some husky-voiced songstress, Miranda goes to the middle of the room and begins to dance. She is completely at ease, dancing like this with the rest of us watching, sitting still. She's so in tune with her body. I have always longed for that lack of inhibition. Because, really, isn't that what dancing is? It isn't about being particularly talented: not unless it's something you do professionally. It's more an ability to shake off your own self-consciousness. I have never been able to do that. It's not really something you can learn to do. You either have it, or you don't.

I remember our teenage years, blagging our way into night-clubs. Though Miranda didn't have to blag. They always let her in on first sight: she was fifteen going on twenty-five, and already gorgeous. In hindsight, when I think about the looks men would give her, the comments they made to her, it turns the stomach. I'd creep in behind her, hoping no one would notice me. I remember dancing beside her, warmed by the vodka stolen from my mum's limitless supplies. Copying Miranda's moves as faithfully as her own shadow, because I have always been that: her shadow. The darkness to her flaming torch. Feeling almost as though I had shaken off my awkwardness.

Miranda is the sort of friend who makes you bold. Who can make you feel six feet tall, almost as radiant as she is, as though you are borrowing a little of her light. Or she can make you feel like shit. Depending on her whim. Sometimes on those nights out she would compliment me on how I looked—always in something borrowed from her already extensive wardrobe, baggy in the bust and hip region, a bit like a girl playing woman in her mother's clothes. Other times she would say something like: "Oh God, Katie, do you know how serious you look when you're dancing?" then an impression—squint-eyed, grim-mouthed, stiff-hipped—"You look like you have the *worst* case of constipation. I'm pretty sure that isn't how Sean Paul intended people to dance to this." I would feel all my newfound confidence desert me—I would feel worse than ever. I would take a big long swig of whatever vodka-and-something drink I was holding, until I felt the slide, the shift. And I'd understand then why my mother seemed to use alcohol like medicine.

As ever, it is almost impossible not to watch Miranda dance. She is so graceful, so fluid, you could assume that she has had some kind of special training. The only one of us who is not watching her, actually, is Julien. He's looking out of the window at the blackness, frowning, apparently lost in thought.

Miranda gestures to us all to join her. She grabs Mark's hand, pulls him to his feet. At first he looks lumpish and awkward in the middle of the carpet. But as she fits her body to his they begin to move together, and with her he acquires a rhythm, sinuous, even sensual, that he would never find on his own. It seems to be infectious, the thrum of the music exerting a pull over everyone. Samira gets up—she's always been a fantastic dancer. She has that looseness, that sense of ease in her own skin. Giles grabs Emma's hand, pulls her to her feet, and dances her around the room. Giles has no rhythm at all, but he clearly doesn't care—he's like an overgrown, drunken schoolboy. They cannon into one of the deer heads on the wall, knocking it askew. Emma tries to right it, with an anxious grin, but as she does Giles seizes her around the waist and turns her upside down.

"Giles!" Samira shouts, but she's laughing, and she turns away from them with her eyes closed, lost to the music. Emma's laughing, too—though she's perhaps the only self-conscious one of all of them, tugging her top down as Giles sets her back on her feet. Now Nick's standing, too, putting his hand out for Bo, and they're arguably even better dancers than Miranda, they move so well together.

As ever, though, it is Miranda the eye is drawn back to: the sun around which all the others are orbiting planets. Mark is in his element, leaning into the grooves of her body as they dance. Never has his crush on her been more blatant. If you can call it a crush. Sometimes I have wondered if it might be something more.

When Miranda and Julien started going out, I remember thinking it was a bit odd that his mate seemed to be acting as a kind of courier between them, ferrying messages back and forth. Mark would arrive at our college, asking to speak with her. He had something to tell her from Julien. Julien, like a king, sending out an envoy, wanted to invite her to his rugby game that weekend. Or to accompany him to some party. It was pathetic, I thought. It couldn't really be a friendship at all, more like a form of hero wor-

THE HUNTING PARTY 113

ship, or slavery. Who did Julien think he was? And why did Mark put up with it? True, like Miranda, Julien has the sort of looks—and the kind of charisma—that are prone to attracting acolytes. But Mark wasn't unattractive, or awkward and shy. He didn't need to stoop so low. And it was bizarre. We all had mobiles by then. Julien could simply have sent a text.

But when I started to notice how Mark looked at her, I began to suspect that those visits weren't at Julien's instigation, after all. Mark had volunteered. He began turning up not just outside, on the quad below our block, but actually in our very corridor. Someone had let him in, he'd say, when I asked how he'd got past the door code.

Once I ran into him sitting just outside Miranda's room.

"She's out," I said. "She has a meeting with her tutor until four." It would be an hour and a half until she came back.

"It's fine," he said. "I don't have anything else to do." And I realized that he wanted to be there, waiting around for her.

There was one other time that sticks in my mind. Julien and Miranda were properly together by then, the hot new couple. We went for a barbecue at Julien's house on a boiling day after exams—we'd moved into private housing by then—the huge, ramshackle town house where he lived with eight other rugby lads, including Mark. I was the invisible plus one. Admittedly a couple of Julien's friends had tried, halfheartedly, to flirt, but I'd been cold and standoffish with them. I didn't want to be known as Miranda's worse-looking but easy friend.

Julien was at the grill, holding court, his shirt off to show the expanse of his muscled back, tapering into that surprisingly neat waist. Despite the fact that it was only the beginning of the summer, he had somehow managed to acquire an even, golden tan. I couldn't help comparing myself: the angry flare of heat rash across my chest and upper arms, the rest of me pale as milk. Miranda was looking at him, too, in a not dissimilar way to how she'd looked at her glossy new pony, Bert, at sixteen. Then she turned to me, and caught me looking.

So I glanced away, toward Mark. He was wearing try-hard Ray-Bans that didn't particularly suit his broad face. If you glanced quickly at him he might have appeared to be daydreaming, staring into space. But as I continued to look I saw that his sunglasses weren't as opaque as I had thought. And I could see that his eyes were fixed in one prolonged sidelong look at Miranda. He did not look away once. Every time I glanced that way he was looking at her. And when she pulled off her vest to expose her bikini top, I saw his look intensify, indefinably. I saw him shift in his seat.

Later I told Miranda what I had seen. "Seriously, Manda," I told her, "it was weird. He wasn't just looking, he was staring. He looked like he wanted to eat you alive."

She laughed. "Oh, Katie, you're so paranoid. He's harmless. You were like this about Julien, too."

It was almost enough to make me doubt what I had seen. Even to ask myself: Was I just jealous? I was fairly certain it wasn't that. But I *was* humiliated, cross with her for not taking me seriously.

"And you two!" I'm jolted back to the present. Miranda's looking at Julien and me—the two outside the bubble, the only ones not dancing with abandon around the room.

"Julien," she says, "dance with Katie, for God's sake. She won't do it on her own." There is the faintest edge of steel to her tone.

There is nothing I feel less like doing, but Julien gets up, takes my hands in his. I am suddenly reminded of watching them dancing at their wedding. Five, six years ago? Miranda made him take dancing lessons, beforehand, so they could fox-trot their way around in front of us. It was all quite typically Miranda, the wedding. She wanted to do something tiny, she claimed, different. She wanted to elope!

In the end it was at her parents' manor house in Sussex. Two hundred guests. Those spindly gold chairs you only ever see at weddings, the round tables, the "starry night" LED ceiling above the dance floor. And then, the cherry on the tiered, sugar-flowered cake: the couple's dance.

Julien, who up until then looked very much the part of the dashing, handsome groom, had shrunk into himself. He had missed steps, tripped on Miranda's train (almost as long as Kate Middleton's), and generally looked as though he wished himself anywhere but there. He wears the same expression now.

20

MIRANDA

I WATCH KATIE AS SHE DANCES—OR MAKES SOME HALFHEARTED
attempt to do so. She looks as if she's actively trying *not* to have a
good time. She's been off since we got here, now I think about it.
Fine, she's always been a bit quiet, but never such a sullen, mono-
syllabic presence. I have the sudden uncanny feeling that I'm looking
at a stranger.

I've always known exactly what's going on in Katie's life. She
has always known exactly what I've chosen to share of mine. But
lately, I don't have a clue about her. She's made all these excuses
over the last couple of months not to see me. I've told myself they're
genuine: she is always so busy, busy, *busy* with her fucking work.
Busy being a proper grown-up, unlike me. Or having to go down
to Sussex to see her mum, who's been ill (read: all that drinking
has finally caught up with her). I've even offered to go with her to
see Sally; I have known the woman for going on twenty years, for
God's sake. Even if she never liked me—she used to call me Miss
Hoity-Toity to my face, her breath wine-sour—it seemed like the
right thing to do. But Katie shrugged off the suggestion so quickly
it was as if the idea appalled her.

The thing is, I've needed her recently. I know I've always given the impression of being self-sufficient, of not wanting anyone to poke their nose in. But, lately, it's all become a bit much. Katie's the only one I can talk to about the problems we've been having. I can't tell her everything about Julien's issues, because it is so important that no one else finds out about that, but still.

I've told her about the fertility problems now. Or rather, I told her *something*. The truth is that we haven't only just started trying. It's been over a year now—a year and a half, in fact. Two years is enough for the NHS to offer you IVF, isn't it?

I could also have told her about the lack of sex—which isn't exactly conducive to getting pregnant. The sense of distance that seems to have been growing between Julien and I over the last year . . . maybe even longer.

If I'm completely honest with myself, I know the reason I haven't shared is that I enjoy the idea of being the one with the perfect life, the friend who has it all. Always ready to step in and offer advice when needed, from her lofty position. It would take more than a few arguments, a few months of infrequent sex, for me to want to give that up.

Maybe this distance between Katie and me is inevitable, a part of growing up, becoming adults with our own lives. Responsibilities, family, coming in the way of friendship. It is only going to get worse, surely, not better. I suppose I can't blame her. I know that friends grow apart, grow out of enjoying each other's company. I look at Facebook sometimes, those decade-old photos from our time at Oxford, and there are photos of me with people—faces that recur in many of the snaps—who I hardly recognize . . . let alone remember names for. It's slightly unnerving. I'll scroll through the images: parties upon parties, in houses and bars and Junior Common Rooms, my arms draped around people who might as well be complete strangers. The photos from the first year are the most obscure. They say you spend your first year at university trying to shake off all the "friends" you make in your first week, and that was true for me: I made the mistake of chatting with an overly intense girl at interviews; of drunkenly talking to a guy at a freshers' welcome do who then used to "bump into" me in various spots around college so he could suggest we go for coffee.

After uni you spend the next few years winnowing those remaining friends down, realizing that you don't have the time and energy to trek across London or indeed the country to see people who have barely anything in common with you anymore.

I never thought it would happen to Katie and me, though. We've known each other since we were children. It's different. Those friends are always there, aren't they? If you've already stuck together this long?

Still, if I didn't know better, I would say it's like Katie has outgrown me. And at the back of my mind is an insistent little voice. An unpleasant voice, the worst version of myself—saying: *I made you who you are, Katie. You would be nothing without me.*

Anyway. I'm not going to let her spoil my mood. I take a long gulp of my drink, and wait to feel the pill start its work.

In the next hour there's a general loosening. Giles begins tearing through the pile of board games stacked near the fire. He unearths a box of Twister with a cry of triumph.

"Oh, fuck off!" Julien shouts, but he does so with a grin. It's a long time since I've seen him smile properly. It's probably just the pill, but it makes a bubble of something like happiness expand inside me. Maybe it's time to let him out of the doghouse, after all. It's been a year, now. And it's exhausting: him acting so guilty all the time, me feeling disappointed in him.

It takes several attempts and lots of giggling for us to even get the plastic mat laid out. Everyone is suddenly pretty high.

"I'll be caller," Katie says quickly. She didn't have a pill—neither did Samira, but she at least has a good reason: the baby monitor clipped to her chest like a policewoman with a radio. In this moment Katie's face—the expression she wears, of adult exasperation in the face of childish silliness—almost pierces through the bubble of joy inside me. I want to say something, call her out on it, but I can't find the words to do it. Before I can, Mark has grabbed my arm and launched me forward to land: left hand, red. Julien goes next: right foot, green. Then Emma, Giles, Mark. Bo, then Nick: even Nick isn't above Twister, for God's sake. Soon Julien is half straddling me, and through the fuzz in my head I think how curiously intimate it feels. Probably the most intimate we have been for a while, that's for certain. We'll have sex tonight, I think, in that big, draped four-poster bed. Not baby-making sex. Just for the sheer fun of it.

Emma topples and puts herself out of the game. She staggers to her feet, laughing.

A few more moves. Nick staggers a foot outside the mat and goes out, then Giles collapses trying to cross his left leg over his right. It's just Bo, Mark, Julien, and me in the game now.

I become aware of a hand on the side of my torso, just below my right breast, and moving upward. It's on the side that's out of sight of the others. I smile and look around, expecting to see Julien. Instead I find myself following the hand to Mark's arm. We are faced away from Emma, and because Julien is above me I'm fairly certain no one else can see. There is a moment while Mark and I look at each other. His eyes are glazed like a sleepwalker's. My head suddenly feels the sharpest it has since I took the pill, since even before I started drinking. Wrong, is all I can think. This is wrong.

It's like he has forgotten the rules. We flirt, yes, and he fancies me, and I quite enjoy it, and he does things for me, and his reward is looking. But he can't touch. That's different.

I shrug myself out of his grip. As I do I must unbalance him—he sways and crashes to the mat.

"Mark's out!" Emma cries, in glee.

I feel a bit sick, all that rich food and the booze and then the pill. I roll out of my position, amid catcalls of "spoilsport!" and summonses back to the mat, and stumble down the corridor to the bathroom. I want to wash my face—this is the mantra in my head—I want to wash my face with cold water.

I look at myself for a while in the mirror. In the bright light, despite all my efforts, I look older than thirty-three. It's not lines— I've made sure there are as few of those as possible—it's something intangible, something strained and tired about my face. I feel a strange sense of disconnection between the person looking back at me and my internal self. This isn't me, is it? This woman in the mirror? What was I thinking, getting that stuff? I forgot how after the hilarity and the ease it can quickly make me feel so off. But then who am I kidding? I've been feeling like this more and more recently, pills or not.

It used to be enough. Just to be me. To look the way I do, and to be a bloody Oxbridge graduate, and to be able to talk with fluency about current affairs or the state of the economy and the new trend for bodycon or slip dresses.

But I woke up one morning and realized I was supposed to have something more: to be something more. To have, specifically, "A Career." "What do you do?": that's the first question at any drinks gathering or wedding or supper. It used to sound so pretentious when someone asked this—in our early twenties, when we were all just playing at being adults. But suddenly it wasn't enough to be Miranda Adams. People expected you to be "Miranda Adams: *insert space for something high-powered.*" An editor, say, or a lawyer, or a banker or an app designer. I tried for a while to say casually that I was writing a novel. But that only led to the inevitable questions: "Have you got an agent? A publisher? A book deal?" Then, "Oh." (Silently) So, you're not really a writer, are you?

I stopped bothering.

Sometimes, for shock value, I'll say, "Oh, you know, I'm a housewife. I just like to keep things nice at home for Julien, and look after him, make sure he's comfortable." And I'll pretend to myself that I am very amused by the appalled silence that follows.

That was why you flirted with Mark. To prove you've still got it. To prove you're not a . . . whisper it . . . has-been.

It was stupid. I mean, I flirt with pretty much everyone: something Katie pointed out when we were first at university. But I know it's different with Mark—that I shouldn't lead him on.

I hear footsteps in the corridor. Perhaps it's Julien, come to check I'm all right. Or Katie, like in the olden days. But when the door opens, slowly, it is the last person I want to see.

He's so tall; I always forget this. He's blocking the doorway with his frame.

"What the fuck, Mark?" I hiss. "What was that? You groping me out there?"

I wait for him to plead with me not to tell Emma, claim he was too out of it to realize what he was doing.

Instead, he says, "He doesn't deserve you, Manda."

"What?" I glare at him. "And you do, I suppose?" I feel filled with righteous anger and shove out at him. "Let me past."

He moves aside. But as he does he reaches out, quick as a flash, to grab my upper arm. I try to twist away from him, but his fingers only tighten, gripping me so hard it stings. I feel a shot of adrenaline and pure fear. He wouldn't try anything, would he? Not here, with the others only in the next room?

"Get the fuck off me, Mark," I say, my voice low and dangerous. He's never been like this before—not with me, anyway. I try to tug my arm away, but his grip is vise-like. I think of all those useless body combat sessions I've done in the gym: I am so weak compared to him.

He bends down to my ear. "All this time, I've been there for him. Since Oxford. Looking out for him, covering for him if necessary. And does he look out for me? Does he help me out when I ask him to? To have something of my own, for once? No. I'm sick of it. I'm not lying for him any longer."

He sounds completely sober, his words clear-cut. It's as if the pill hasn't affected him at all. In comparison I feel fuggy and confused. Except for the pain in my arm, anchoring me.

"What do you mean?" I ask him. I feel as if I'm several minutes behind.

"I know about him. I know his little secret. Shall I tell you what he's been up to?"

I'm shaking, with a mixture of fear and anger. It's important, here, to pretend I don't know anything—don't *want* to know anything.

"Whatever it is," I say, "I don't want to hear it. I don't want anything to do with it."

He looks momentarily taken aback. His grip slackens, and I wrench my arm away. "I . . . ," he fumbles, "you mean—you really don't want to know?"

Does he really imagine that my own husband wouldn't have let me in on his shameful little secret? Still, definitely best to play dumb. Just in case there comes a time when I need to distance myself from it all, to insist on my own innocence.

"No," I say. "I don't want to know."

"Fine," he says, looking genuinely astonished, all the bluster gone out of him. He steps back. "If that's really what you want."

I stumble on unsteady legs back into the dining room, sure that someone will notice the expression on my face and ask me what the matter is—I'm not sure whether I want their attention right now, or not.

No one sees me at first. There's another game of Twister going on, and they're all cackling with laughter as Giles tries to straddle Bo. The atmosphere is exactly the same as it was before—everyone joyful, riding the high of booze and pills. But suddenly I'm on the outside looking in, and it all seems ridiculous . . . false even, like they're all trying too hard to show what a good time they're having.

Emma turns and sees me standing in the doorway. "Are you okay, Manda?" she asks.

"We thought you'd got stuck in there," Giles says, with a stupid, goofy grin. "So Mark went to check you were all right."

"Oh God," Emma says, "Manda—do remember that time someone had a house party and you got stuck in the loo?"

"No," I say. But even as I do I realize that I do remember it, vaguely. The feeling of humiliation when someone had to crowbar me out. God—mortifying. I could swear it happened at least a decade ago. But if Emma remembers it, it must have been much more recently. "When was that?"

"Hmm," Emma says, "it must have been in London at some point. The days when everyone actually had house parties—when we were fun, you remember? So recent, and yet it feels like centuries ago."

I nod, but something about the mention of it has given me an odd, uneasy feeling. But I cannot work out why.

"*Are* you all right?" Emma asks again.

Her tone's so maternal, so caring . . . so fucking patronizing. "Yes," I say, "why wouldn't I be?"

Perhaps it comes out as sharply as I meant it: she looks stung.

I sit it out for an hour or so. I've done better than Katie—she must have gone back to her cabin while I was in the bathroom. And yet she's the one I want to talk to about what just happened—more so than my own husband, somehow. I could go and find her . . . she might still be awake. But if I leave I might show Mark that he has me rattled, and I don't want that. The effects of the pill have completely worn off for me, and I look enviously at the others, blissed out, beaming at each other.

Finally, when I decide I've stuck it out long enough, I turn to Julien. "I'm tired," I say. He nods, vaguely, but I think he has barely registered the fact that I've spoken. Pills have always affected him strongly. I'd half meant it as an invitation to walk me back to the cabin, but I'm not going to embarrass myself in front of the others by making that clear now.

WHEN I STEP OUTSIDE, THE MOON SHINES FULL AND THE loch is lit up silver. It's a clear night, except for a band of cloud on the horizon where the light of the stars disappears, as though a shroud has been pulled over them.

I think about Mark, and what just happened. The top of my arm still aches where he grabbed me. I'm sure there will be bruises in the morning: the reminders of his fingers.

I fish the iPhone from my pocket and turn on the torch. It casts a weak stream of light in front of me; a small comfort, a lantern against the dark. Several times I have to turn around and look behind me to check that no one is following. It's silly, probably—but I'm on edge, and the silence out here feels watchful, somehow. I am reminded of dark, drunken walks home in London in the early clubbing days, keys between my knuckles. Just in case. But here I'm in the middle of nowhere, with no one except my closest friends. The silence here, the expanses, seem suddenly hostile. That's a ridiculous thought, isn't it? In the morning, it will all seem different, I tell myself.

Or we could leave in the morning. I could tell Julien, and we could leave. He wouldn't like it—I'm sure he's been looking forward to this trip. We both have, actually—perhaps me even more so. I think he would agree, if I explained everything. We could go back to the house and have champagne and maybe order something in and watch the Westminster fireworks over the rooftops. I realize that when I think of this I'm not imagining our current home: the grown-up, stuccoed house. I'm actually thinking of our first flat in London: before I failed to do anything interesting with my life, became an also-ran. Before Julien got so busy with making money.

It might be fun.

But it would also be giving up. It should be Mark who is ashamed, who has to leave. Not me. The thought fills me with rage. Then I think of that moment, looking at myself in the mirror— seeing more than I wanted to, beyond the effects of the pill. Even before that, even before Mark groped me during Twister, I'd been feeling like I wasn't enjoying myself quite as much as I should have done. There was Samira, talking my ear off about sleep schedules and breast pumps, showing me the stains on her baggy old T-shirt. This, from the girl whose nickname at Oxford was "Princess Samira," because she was always so perfectly coiffed, glamorously tailored, even at nineteen. I loved what a stir we'd cause going into a pub or bar together, or even just the Junior Common Room, the two of us roughly the same height, one dark, one blond, dressed in the best clothes. Birds of a feather.

Then there's Katie—so distant since we got here, probably thinking of something much more important, something at work. Acting like she is better than all of us: the successful lawyer. I'd had this sudden, rushing sense of being left behind. That was why I'd got everyone dancing. It was why I'd brought the pills out when I did. I'd been saving them for tomorrow, in fact, for New Year's Eve. But suddenly I needed to be the one in control again, dictating the order of things.

As I round the corner I see in the distance three rectangles of bright light, blazing out into the dark. It's the gamekeeper's cottage, of course. When I walked there earlier I didn't realize quite how far away it is from the other buildings, almost at the foot of the mountain. As I continue to look, a dark figure appears in the central window, haloed in light. It must be the gamekeeper, Doug, still up. But from this distance he is featureless and spectral. I take a step back, which is ridiculous: even if he can see the tiny pinprick of light from my phone, he can't see me. But it feels as though he is looking straight at me. And it's nothing like earlier, when I went and knocked on his door. Right now, with what just happened, I feel vulnerable, displaced, the landscape so vast and alien and silent around me. I long for the noise and lights and bustle of the city.

I half run the rest of the way along the path. Inside the cabin I feel safe for a moment. But only briefly, because when I go to bolt the door I realize that there is no lock.

GET READY FOR BED, AND WHEN I NEXT LOOK OUT OF THE windows I can see that lights have gone on now in the other cabins. Everyone must have chosen to go to bed shortly after me. So where is Julien? Presumably on his way back along the path—but he's taking his time about it.

Half an hour passes, then an hour. My arm aches where Mark grabbed it. I pull on a jumper, some big silly fluffy slippers that Julien hates because they make me look "like a suburban sixties housewife," and yet I have never got rid of because they're too bloody comfortable. My teeth are chattering, I realize—even though I'm not really cold.

WAKE AT 4 A.M. I DON'T KNOW WHERE I AM. THE FIRST THING I see are the numbers blinking on the little alarm beside the bed. At first I think I'm at home, but then I realize it's too quiet for that: in the city there'd be that background music of sirens and car engines, however late at night. I'm not sure what has woken me. I don't actually remember falling asleep. I'm still in the jumper and slippers, I realize, lying on top of the coverlet. The light is on, in the hallway. Did I leave it on? I can't remember.

Then I see a figure standing in the dark by the doorway. I scrabble backward, away from him. Then he steps forward and I see that it's Julien. His cheeks are red from the cold. His eyes are oddly blank.

I sit up. "Julien?" My voice comes out small and reedy; it does not sound like my own. I see him start at the sound of my voice. "Where have you been?"

"Sorry," he says. "I went for a walk."

"In the middle of the night?"

"Well, yes—to clear my head. Those fucking pills—and then I got the comedown, started worrying about everything. I walked the whole way around the loch." He runs a hand through his hair. "Oh, and I saw that weirdo, the gamekeeper."

"You did?" I remember now how unnerved I was by his silhouette in the lit-up window on my walk back.

"He was creeping around the edge of the loch—coming out of the really dense bit of forest. He had dogs with him. What on earth could he have been doing? Honestly, I think he might be a bit of a nutjob. I think you should stay away from him."

I am both touched and irritated by this chauvinistic display of protection. At least it shows he cares, I think, then I catch myself. Have I become so uncertain of his affection recently that I have become that needy?

"He's not the one to worry about," I say.

"What do you mean?"

"Mark. He came on to me in the loo. He grabbed my arm. Here." I pull up the sleeve of the jumper to show him. "He said he knew your *dirty little secret.* Yes, that's how he put it."

I see him flinch.

"Does he mean what I think he does?" I ask. "Did you tell him? We've gone over this before, Julien, you can't tell anyone. It would destroy everything. And don't tell me I'm being paranoid. The moment you decided to use me you made *me* part of it, like it or not."

There is a longish pause. Then, "Look, Manda," Julien says, pushing his hand through his hair and sighing, "we all had a lot to drink . . . and then the pills—"

I feel a flush of anger. "Are you saying I'm making this up? That you don't believe me?"

"No—no. What I'm saying is that he might not have really meant it, to hurt you, that is. He's a big guy, sometimes he just throws his weight around a bit too much. I mean, how long have we known him?"

"Hang on a second," I say. "It sounds to me like you're defending him."

"I'm not, I promise I'm not. But . . . look, is it really worth spoiling everything for ourselves because of his stupidity? He's one of my oldest friends. Don't you think we should give him the benefit of the doubt?"

I suddenly see what he's doing. He isn't protecting Mark. He's protecting himself. Because if Mark really does know his—our—secret, and Julien challenges him, Mark might use it against him.

I should be outraged. But suddenly I just feel very tired.

He's undressed now. He takes out his pajamas. They're very chic ones, a present from my mother, who likes to be up on any new style trend: a Christmas purchase from Mr. Porter. Nevertheless, there was a time—not so long ago—when he wouldn't have worn anything in bed, not even boxers. We liked to lie skin to skin.

"Don't," I say as he goes to shrug the trousers on. He stands for a minute looking particularly naked and confused. "It's cold," he says.

"Yes," I say. "But you can put them on . . . afterward." I suddenly want the comfort of his arms around me, his weight on top of me, his mouth on mine: I want to obliterate that odd, creeping feeling I've had since this evening.

For emphasis I pull the jumper over my head. I'm naked underneath. I lie back and let my legs fall open, so he can be in no doubt about what I have in mind. "Come here," I say, beckoning him.

But he makes a kind of grimace, his mouth pulling down at the edges. "I'm really tired, Manda."

I feel my skin prickle with the chill of his rejection.

In the first few years of knowing each other, of being together, it was always me who turned him down. Perhaps just twice in eight years it was the other way around: the exception that proved the rule, when he had the flu, say, or an interview the next day. But lately I've been keeping count. The last ten times, perhaps more, it has been him.

I have two separate underwear drawers at home. One is for everyday: my Marks & Spencer undies and bras, made exclusively for comfort. Julien used to cringe in horror at my beige T-shirt bras as they came out of the wash. Then another drawer: froths of Agent Provocateur and Kiki de Montparnasse, Myla, and Coco de Mer. Hundreds, perhaps even thousands of pounds' worth of silk and lace. The sort of lingerie that is not meant to be worn under clothes, that is meant only to grace your flesh for a few minutes before it is whipped off. I realized, packing for this trip, that I had not worn any of those pieces for as long as I could remember. I was half tempted to chuck them out: they seemed to be mocking me. Instead, I gathered the whole lot into my arms and dumped them into the suitcase. Armor, for a desperate—last-ditch?—offensive.

I suppose it makes a kind of sense that Julien's gone off sex. He has a lot on his plate—though most of it's his own fault—and there's been my insistence on getting pregnant. But here, in this beautiful wilderness, fueled by champagne and pills, I thought it would be different. I feel a tiny tremor of fear as he lies down next to me and rolls away to face the wall.

I move toward him, to borrow some of his warmth. I reach out a hand to touch the back of his head. My palm comes away damp. "Your hair," I say.

"What?" His voice doesn't even sound sleepy. I wonder if he's been pretending, lying there awake, like me.

"It's damp, here, at the back."

"Oh, well—it started raining on the way over."

As I lie there I think of the clear sky and my walk to the cabin, and think the clouds must have come over very quickly for it to have started raining. It's too cold to rain anyway, surely. It would have been snow. I'm suddenly sure he's lying. Though what about, and why, I have no idea. I tell myself that there's no point in worrying. I already know his worst secret, after all.

I T WAS ABOUT A YEAR AGO THAT JULIEN SAID, VERY CASUALLY, one evening, "I've got a friend. He'd love you to design a website for him. He's left the City and he's trying to set up a business. What do you reckon?"

Did I know, even then, that there was something off about it? It's only with hindsight that I can see the way he asked it was a little too casual. That he was drumming his fingers against the kitchen counter: a direct contrast to his tone. That he would hardly look at me as he spoke. There was also the fact that he had never up to that point seemed to think much of my skills in website design, or my little business idea: to set it up as a company, seek out commissions. He had called it my "project," as though I were making a quilt.

It would only be my second commission to date—the first had been for a friend's baby shower. But I decided to overlook my misgivings. I assumed that the reason for his shiftiness was that this was clearly a bit of a pity project, whatever else he claimed. He earned enough money for the two of us put together, more than we needed, but I think he knew that my pride had been hurt by my own lack of success. So, to tell the honest truth, I didn't look too closely into it. Not then. And it would be a useful showcase, I thought. It would be helpful simply to have another happy client under my belt: to share on my website, via my social media. You have to have a bit of a body of work to entice others. A bit chicken and egg, but there it is.

"Should I send him a quote?" I asked Julien. "Because I hope he knows I'm not going to work gratis." I didn't want this guy to think that just because I was his mate's wife I would do him a freebie. I might give mates' rates, certainly, but I was a professional. My time was valuable. It had been a long time since I had felt really useful to anyone professionally, if ever, and I was going to savor the feeling. That was my biggest worry at the time. That I might be humiliated by working for free.

"Don't worry about the money," Julien said. "He's already reassured me that he'll pay you handsomely." He grinned. "Some in cash, some in a bank transfer—so you don't have to declare it all to the taxman if you don't want to." Well, that wasn't exactly a concern. The company hadn't made any money yet—it was unlikely it would be in profit by the end of the tax year. Surely Julien knew that?

Even then I didn't feel any particular suspicion. Should I have done? He was my husband, for God's sake.

It was only when a payment of £50,000 arrived in my bank account, and when Julien returned home from "watching rugby at the pub," with the same amount in fifties, that I became suspicious. "Julien," I asked him, "what the fuck is going on?" He grinned awkwardly, spread his hands wide. "This is just what he wants to pay you," he said. "He was so pleased with the work. He has absolutely pots of money, so this is just like loose change to him."

I might even have believed him, if I hadn't seen his eyes.

"Julien," I said sharply, so he knew there was no bullshitting me, "this money is in my account. So whatever else, I am now involved in whatever the fuck is happening here. And I am your wife. So I think you need to tell me everything, right now."

"It will be good for us, in the end," he said blusteringly. "I . . . I suppose you could say I saw an opportunity."

"What sort of opportunity? Outside work?"

"Well . . ." He gripped the back of the chair in front of him, hard. "I suppose you could say it is connected to work. Loosely . . ."

He seemed to gather himself. "Look, it was just—sitting there, right in front of me. There was some information that I was aware of, and it would have been completely stupid not to use it."

It was then, finally, that it struck me. "Oh my God, Julien. Oh my God. Do you mean insider trading? Is that what you're saying to me? Is that where this money comes from?"

I knew the truth less from anything he said then than from the way his face drained immediately of all color. "I wouldn't call it anything as formal as that," he said. "No, it's nothing like that. I've just given a couple of people a bit of a nudge. Friends. Nothing really big. This sort of thing happens all the time."

I couldn't believe what he was telling me. "I think what you mean, Julien, is that people get arrested all the time."

Only the other week I had been reading about Ray Yorke, a partner at one of the big investment banks who was serving time for trading secrets with his golf buddy. As they made their way around the course he'd casually dropped in tidbits of information—supposedly not realizing that his mate was trading on the information, and making millions in the process. He claimed he didn't realize even when he started accepting the gifts his friend pressed on him: a Rolex watch, jewelry for his wife, parcels of cash. When he was caught, his life had ended. He'd lost his job, he'd gone to prison, his wife had divorced him, he'd never work in finance again. CNN had shown an interview of him outside the courthouse practically weeping: offering himself up as a cautionary tale. And of course, in the process, he'd had to give it all back—and then some.

I'd had zero sympathy for the guy. Who, I had thought, could be that fucking stupid? It had seemed so obvious to me. Of course you get found out for something like that, in the end.

As it turned out, my husband could be exactly that fucking stupid. "What on earth is wrong with you, Julien?" I said. "You're like a gambler, always in for one more hand."

"I'm sorry, Manda, I don't know what to—" And then suddenly his face had changed, hardened. He stopped the expansive inno- cent guy routine, he called off the cringing, hand-wringing mea culpa. "Well, I suppose it's easy for you to say, Miranda," he said. "But you seem to forget quite how much you enjoy this life. The holidays—Tulum, the Maldives, St. Anton—they don't come for free, you know. Half the time you seem to be sitting around read- ing some kind of brochure for holidays that cost more than some people earn in a year. Or the boxes that turn up from Net-a-Porter every season, or the five hundred pounds you pay every month to your fucking nutritionist. Yes, I earn a lot. But we have practically no savings. And now you're talking talking talking about having children—do you know how much private school costs these days? Because of course the children of Miranda Adams couldn't go anywhere so lowly as a *free* school, like I did. And university, now they've hiked the fees? And with only one of us working . . ." He looked me straight in the eye. "My job isn't as secure as you think it is, Miranda. The financial crisis wasn't all that long ago. And then we'd have been screwed."

I couldn't believe it. "You can't put this on me, Julien. This is your fuckup."

Perhaps I should have seen it coming. Because this is how he has always been. He didn't grow up in a well-off household, like me, with a solid family unit. His mum was a single parent. It cost her everything to put him through university. Though you would never know it, from the way he acted there. He has a profound shame of the fact that he used to be—not even poor—from a lower-income family. He has a fear of looking bad—which is what poor is, in his mind. It's like he has always felt the deficit. Perhaps if it weren't this, it would be something else. It would be an affair, for instance, or a gambling addiction. Maybe I should even be grateful that it isn't something more, something worse: though it's difficult to imagine what that would be, right now.

21

DOUG

I T IS DARK, LATE. THIS IS HIS FAVORITE TIME. HE HAS THE WHOLE place to himself—finally. Or at least he thought he did, until he came across that idiot guest, the one who had pestered him about the Wi-Fi, the one with the handsome, punchable face. Julien. When the torch beam passed over him he was walking along the track that led from the Lodge to the cottage where he and his wife were staying. But it was about an hour after all that awful noise from the Lodge had stopped—and after the lights had gone off.

The man had started in surprise when he caught him with the torch. He had looked like an animal, like one of the herd, fixed in the Land Rover's beam. His face had worked, as though he were wrestling with himself as to whether he should explain what he was doing out so late. But in the end he had settled for a grimace and a nod, and continued on his way without turning back. He looked as guilty as a man could look. He had the hunched shoulders, the stiff, mincing walk, of someone who had been up to no good. Doug would bet that the man had not expected to see anyone else on his way. And in whatever he was doing, he had been caught out.

That, at least, had made up for the interruption to his peace. Thinking about it now, he smiles.

He has taken the dogs out with him. Griffin and Volley: Griffin a beautiful flat-coated retriever with a mouth as soft as velvet, and Volley an Australian shepherd, beautiful, too, but also strange-looking, with one milky-blue eye and a marbled coat like ink dropped into water. They actually seem to like him, seem not to sense the darkness in him in the same way that people do.

Both of the dogs are skittish, excited, this evening. It's the promise of the snow in the air, he's sure—the scent sharpening, metallic, strange. There has been nothing in the forecast, but in a place like this you learn to trust what you can see and smell over any supposed science.

He'll have to go and warn the bloody guests about it tomorrow. There could be a lot of it coming. If they need any groceries for the next few days they'll have to let him know by this evening. If it's a bona fide dump, the track will be impossible to navigate, even in the Land Rover—even with the snow tires on. No one will be able to get back in here. Or out.

He picks up a stick from the path and throws it. It disappears outside the beam of his head-torch, beyond his vision. Both dogs hurtle after it, their sight keener than his. They are almost a match for speed, though Griffin is getting old, and slackens her pace first. Volley bounds ahead, true to his name, and takes the prize, tail wagging furiously, an unmistakable air of triumph in the proud way he holds his head.

At times like this Doug breathes easier.

Now Volley has dropped the stick, and begun to whine. "What is it, boy? Hey, what is it?"

Griffin has caught the scent, too. They begin to follow it, muzzles down. A rabbit, perhaps, or a fox. Maybe even a deer, though they don't tend to come around the side of the loch as regularly. Then Doug hears something a little way off: the noise of a large animal passing through the undergrowth beside the path. "Who's there?" he calls.

No answer, but the unmistakable noise of snapping and tearing continues, at a greater pace. Something—or someone—is running from them.

The dogs tear ahead, after the sound. He calls them back. They turn and trot back to him, reluctant, but obedient. If it's another of the guests, the dogs could terrify them.

Doug flashes the beam of his torch on the earth around him and illuminates a man's footprint a few feet ahead. Just one; apparently this is the only part of the path soft enough to take an impression. A large foot. He places his own inside it: roughly the same size. Might be one of the guests, of course, though he would be very surprised if they'd got this far from the Lodge in their evening explorations. He'd heard them down by the lake before supper, but he doubts they would have ventured much farther in the dark. And this boot has a good tread on it. The London guests all turned up wearing city people's idea of rugged outdoor wear—Dubarry boots and Timberlands.

The Icelanders then, perhaps, with their proper boots. But the question remains: Why would any of the guests have run away, when he called?

H E OFTEN COMES OUT AT THIS TIME TO CHECK FOR ANYTHING untoward. Some of his nighttime forays, however, are not so intentional.

Once he woke up and discovered himself lying in the damp heather a little way from the other end of the loch, near the deserted Scout camp. It was the middle of the night, but luckily there was enough of a moon for him to see where he was. He had no memory of how he had got there, but his legs ached as though he had been running. His hands stung. Later, in the light of the cottage, he would discover that they were lacerated by cuts and grazes, in a couple of places very deeply.

He could not remember anything that had happened before this point. Once, as a boy, he had a general anesthetic. It had been a black curtain coming down upon his consciousness, a light switched off, the time lost like the blink of an eye. These were like that. Great mouthfuls of time swallowed, leaving voids in their place. He could have been anywhere. He could have done anything.

It had happened to him in the city, too. That was worse: then he had ended up on the other side of town, had come around wandering in unknown streets, or lying in a children's playground, or stumbling his way down a railway siding.

There is a word for it, a word that sounds like a piece of music: fugue. A beautiful word for something so terrifying. They were brought on by the trauma, the psychiatrist said. They were a symptom, not a condition in and of themselves. The first thing he had to do was start talking about what had happened to him. He understood that, didn't he? Because this problem, while so far it hasn't caused any great harm other than a few confusing nights—well, it could be dangerous. For himself. For others around him. After all, there was already the incident in question: the very reason he was having the sessions.

"Yes," he had said, looking the psychiatrist right in the eye. "But that didn't happen in a *fugue* state. I knew exactly what I was doing then."

The psychiatrist had coughed, looked uncomfortable. "Still: I think we have established that both the incident and these episodes, directly or less so, stem from the same trauma."

There had been an enforced number of sessions, though the psychiatrist wrote in her report that she believed they needed more. He double-checked: this was only advisory, not mandated. He was free to ignore her advice. He couldn't quite believe that he had got off so easily, and he suspected that she couldn't, either. It had stuck with him, though, the idea that he could hurt someone: not intentionally, as the other thing had been, but without even knowing what he was doing. So instead of getting to the bottom of the issue—because he didn't think he could ever talk about that day, even if it were to save his life—he has come somewhere where there are very few people that he could hurt.

HE WAITS FOR A WHILE LONGER AT THE EDGE OF THE TREES, his ears prickling for any further movement. But there's nothing, and the dogs seem to have lost interest, too. He turns and tramps back along the path in the direction he has come.

When he returns to the cottage he lies back on his bed, fully clothed. Allows himself, finally, to hope for the possibility of sleep.

The room is Spartan. Here there are no pictures upon the walls, no knickknacks on the shelves, which hold only a couple of slim volumes: a book of short stories, a collection of poems. He never reads these days, but they are clues, tethers to the person he used to be. There is nothing here to tell you about the man who inhabits the room, unless the nothing is in itself a clue to something. It has the anonymity of a prison cell. This, if one knew him, which no one does well, is no coincidence.

He turns onto his side and closes his eyes. It is a mimicry of sleep. If he is lucky he will get perhaps an hour—maybe even two—of rest. He has learned to exist on this, to drink enough coffee to combat the dizziness, to take enough painkillers to mask, as much as possible, the migraines. There was a time when he used to sleep the deep, untroubled sleep of an animal. He cannot imagine it now. That life belonged to a different man. Now every time he closes his eyes he sees their faces. With pleading eyes they ask him: *Why us? What did we do to deserve it?* Their hands grope for him, catch at his hair, his clothes. He can feel them on him—he has to fight them off. Even when he opens his eyes he can feel the ghost traces of their fingertips upon his skin: cobweb memories.

22

HEATHER

Now
January 2, 2019

AFTER I CALL THE POLICE, I DIAL THE BOSS'S NUMBER, IN LON-don. I don't get through to him first, of course: it's a silken-voiced PA. "How can I help?"

I tell her everything. There's a stunned silence on the line, then: "I'll put you through to him," she says, in a much more ordinary voice, as though she has quickly decided that the husky purr isn't appropriate here.

He comes on the line quickly. "Hello, Heather," he says, as fa-miliarly as if we talk every day on the phone like this. From the one time I met him, I remember him being quite handsome (though difficult to say whether that was just the effect of good grooming, and all that charm), with the smile of a politician.

"It's bad," I say. "We found a body."

"Oh," he says. "Oh God." But he doesn't sound particularly shocked. Instead, I am certain I can hear him thinking—just like the politician he resembles—of how to manage this, of how to protect the estate.

"And I'm afraid it doesn't look like an accident."

"Hmm," he says. "You've called the police, of course?"

"Yes," I say, "just before I called you."

"I'd come up," he says, "but I'm not sure that would help matters."

"It's likely you wouldn't be able to get here anyway." I explain the situation with the weather, the fact that we're essentially snow-bound here.

"It was Doug who found the body, you say?"

"Yes."

"Where?" He asks it with a new sharpness in his tone. Maybe he's wondering if there's any way he could be sued for this.

"In the waterfall near the old watermill."

"Okay. And did you see anything? Did Doug?"

"No—nothing in particular."

"Does Iain know, too?"

"Er . . . no, not yet. He would have left on New Year's Eve, once he'd finished his work for the day."

"Well, he'll still need to know, of course. Important that you put him in the loop, too."

"Yes," I say. "Of course. I'll try him now."

"Do. And keep me posted with any updates, please."

"Of course." I tried for something assertive, but it came out as little more than a whisper. He sounds so businesslike, so removed. Perhaps it's possible to be so where he is, far away in London . . . untouched by the atmosphere of death that has permeated every inch of this place.

I try Iain next. I only have a mobile for him, no home number. It goes straight to voice mail. The problem with only being con-tactable by mobile in this part of the world is that most of the time you don't have enough signal to be reached. I'll leave him a voice mail. I'm sure he'd be touched by the boss's concern, but frankly he's the least of my worries at the moment.

I'm about to leave a quick message when there's a knock on the door.

It's Doug. "They're here," he says. "The guests." While I've been on the phone, he's gone and rounded up the others from their cabins, shepherded them into the Lodge.

Doug looks awful—I'd noticed it earlier, but not really *seen* it, being too distracted by the immediate disaster. His eye sockets are a dark, bruised purple, as though he hasn't slept for a week. It looks almost as though the guest's death has affected him personally. His hand, I notice, is bandaged, a thick gauze covering most of the skin. I hadn't seen it when we were outside, of course, because he had been wearing gloves.

"What happened to your hand?" I ask.

"Oh," he says. He holds it up and looks at it as though he's never seen it before. "I suppose I injured it."

"When? It looks bad."

"Don't know," he says. He scratches the back of his head with his other hand. "A few days ago, I suppose." But that's not true— it can't be. He hadn't been wearing a bandage at the Highland Dinner . . . I'm sure of that; I would have noticed it. And the injury beneath must be bad for him to have used the bandage: I've seen Doug with terrible cuts and bruises before, and he hasn't even bothered with a plaster.

"Shall I tell them you're coming out to talk to them?" he asks. I notice that he has hidden the bandaged hand in the pocket of his jacket.

Somehow the role of telling the guests has fallen to me: we seem to have agreed upon that without even discussing it. Trying to swallow down my mounting dread, I nod, and follow him out of the office.

THE GUESTS ARE ASSEMBLED JUST DOWN THE CORRIDOR IN the living room, waiting for the news. Just the London guests: the Icelandic pair are back at their bunkhouse. Doug and I decided to tell the group of friends first: the death, after all, will be a much more devastating revelation for them.

When I go into the living room they all look up at me. I have been on this side before, in my old job. All those anxious families waiting for news, me having to tell them the very last thing they want to hear. *It was not successful. There was an unforeseen complication. We did everything we could.*

I dig my nails into the skin of my palms. I have also been on the other side of this. I know exactly how it feels. Their faces swim before me, upturned, expectant, utterly intent on what I am about to say. I feel a lurch of nausea in the pit of my stomach. What I am about to tell them is going to change their lives forever.

"We have found her," I say. The questions begin almost at once; I put up a hand for silence. The important thing is to get the terrible news to them as quickly as possible now, to extinguish any lingering hope. Hope is a great thing, when there is still a chance of everything being okay. But in cases that are quite literally hopeless it can do much more damage than good. Though: I don't think any of them really have hope anymore. They know already. But the confirmation of that knowledge is something else.

"I'm afraid it's very bad news," I say. You could suddenly cut the atmosphere with a knife. The horrible power of being in this situation hits me with full force. I hold all of the cards, ready to lay them down in front of the guests—they will make of them what they will.

"I'm very sorry to tell you that she's dead."

There's the shock at first: they are united in that. They stare at me as though they are waiting for me to deliver the punch line. And then each begins to process the information and their grief in different ways: hysterics, mute incomprehension, anger.

I know that none of these reactions are any more or less valid. I saw all of these on the ward, whenever I had to inform next of kin. And as any paramedic will tell you, it's often the quiet ones you need to worry about after a disaster: not those who wail and scream about their pain. But those who wail and scream are still in pain. Grief can be as different in the way it displays itself as the people who experience it. I know this all too well.

But the thought goes through me, all the same: Is it possible that one of these displays is just that? A display? A performance? As they ask me questions about the body, how I found it, how it looked when I found it, I wonder: Does one of them know all of this already? Does someone know more than he or she is letting on?

B ACK IN THE SANCTUARY OF THE OFFICE MY PHONE RINGS. I seize it, expecting the boss again, or the police—perhaps with an update on when they expect to be able to get here. It's not the police.

"I can't talk right now, Mum."

"Something bad's happened. I can tell."

How can she tell from six words? I clench my jaw. Then un-clench. "I can't talk now. I'm fine, that's all you need to know at the moment. I'll tell you about it later. Okay?"

"You didn't call yesterday, like we agreed you would. So I knew something had happened." Her voice is ragged, frayed at the edges with worry. "Oh, Heather, I knew I shouldn't have let you go and live in that place."

S HE HAS NEVER UNDERSTOOD IT. WHY, HAVING SUDDENLY found myself all alone in the world for the first time in fifteen years, I would choose to compound that loneliness by moving to such a place. But what she couldn't understand—because it wasn't really something I could explain, only something I felt—was that I felt much more alone surrounded by people. All our friends, however much they were trying to help, and sympathize, reminded me of him. And the city we had lived in together. Around every corner was a café where we had eaten brunch, or a bookshop we had browsed, or even a branch of Sainsbury's where we had picked up a ready meal curry and a bottle of wine. Our apartment was worst of all, of course. I could hardly bring myself to be inside it before it was sold. Here were all the memories of a life together, of growing up together: the place we had lived in practically since we left university. My whole adult life.

And being around people—people carrying on with their lives, busy and messy, settling down, having children, getting married—just emphasizes how much my own has stalled, indefinitely. Perhaps forever.

So yes, sometimes, I get lonely here. But at least this landscape has always seemed suited to loneliness, and I am not confronted, every day, by all that I have lost, by the echoes of my old life, whole and happy and filled with love. And yes, sometimes, as I had in the city, I have found myself almost unable to get out of bed, and have had to force myself to get dressed, eat my breakfast, make the short walk to the office in the Lodge. But it is a lot easier to face the day when you know you won't have to face other people and their happiness.

Here, I have been able to go and howl my misery and my anger—yes, there's a lot of that—at the mountains and the loch, and feel the vast landscape soak up something of my grief. Here, loneliness is the natural state of things.

When it happened, part of me wondered if I had been simply waiting for it, that I had always known it would come. I had always felt, ever since Jamie and I got together, that it was too good, that we were too lucky. That happiness like this couldn't possibly last: we were using up more than our allotted quota of the stuff, and at some point someone had to notice. Fate decided to prove me right. The expression that Jamie's boss, Keith, wore when he came to tell me. I knew before he opened his mouth. Smoke inhalation. No one realized, in the chaos, that Jamie hadn't reappeared. He'd been trapped, in the burning house. The other firemen had done everything they could. Had been hunkered down there with the paramedics.

Keith had done CPR on Jamie for a full forty-five minutes before they could get there. When he began to cry I had had to look away, because it was such a terrible, unexpected sight. Seeing a man like Keith cry. And because that, more than anything, made it all real.

Jamie was a fireman. He could have been many things, with that brain of his: a scientist, a lawyer, a professor. But he wanted to do something that he really felt mattered, he told me—like I did. The thing that made him one of the best was that he always went the extra mile. As Keith said, at the service, when others had given up on a lost cause, Jamie would try that little bit harder, risk that little bit more. He had seemed, at times, almost invincible. But he wasn't. He was just a man. A bighearted, brave, self-sacrificing man—but definitely mortal.

What they don't tell you is that when someone you love dies you might be angry with him. And that was true, I was so angry with Jamie. Before, life had meaning. Everything about us was meant to be. The way we met—him deciding at the last minute to come to a house party thrown by a friend of a friend. The beautiful light-filled apartment we found in Edinburgh's Old Town, which the owner decided to rent for a song to anyone who would also dog-sit for him when he went away traveling. Even just the way we fitted together, he and I—two pieces of a very simple jigsaw that, when combined, made the picture complete.

When he died, nothing made sense anymore. A world in which he could be taken from me had to be a cruel, chaotic place. And I thought—briefly, but definitely—about ending it all. In the end it wasn't any desire to survive that stopped me from doing it; it was the knowledge of what it would do to my family.

Coming here was the next best thing, you see. It was a way of escaping from life as I had known it, from everything that tied me to the past. Sometimes I think it's a little like dying—a slightly more palatable option than the pills and the jump from the Forth Bridge that I had contemplated in the weeks after Jamie's death. So in an odd way this landscape has been a sanctuary. But now, with this new horror and the falling snow trapping us in and keeping help out, it has become, in the space of twenty-four hours, a prison.

23

EMMA

Two days earlier
New Year's Eve 2018

LAST NIGHT, MARK AND I HAD SOME PRETTY GREAT SEX. HE threw me onto the bed. There was an intensity to his features, a dark cast to them. He looks quite similar when he is turned on as when he's really angry.

I don't know what got into him. It might have been the stuff we all took (which I shouldn't have had, looking back, because I say stupid things—things I don't mean to say aloud). But his intensity might also have had something to do with the thing he's just told me, too—the thing he's found out—that strange, almost erotic delight we sometimes take in someone else's messing up.

I know people wonder about Mark and me. "How did you two meet?" they ask. Or "What drew you to him?" and "When did you know he was 'the one'?" Sometimes I'll tell them it was his dance moves to Chesney Hawkes in the middle of Inferno's dance floor that got me, and that will normally get a laugh. But that's only a temporary measure to stall the questions that will undoubtedly follow, the deeper, more probing inquiries.

They're looking for the romance, the chemistry, the vital spark that drew us together, that keeps us together. Normally, I think they probably end up disappointed in their search. Because, the truth is, there is no great romance between us. There was no grand passion. There wasn't ever that—even in the first place. I don't mind admitting it. It wasn't the thing I was looking for.

There are people who hold out for love, capital letters *LOVE,* and don't stop until they've found it. There are those who give up because they don't find it. Boom or bust—all or nothing. And then, perhaps in the majority, there are those who settle. And I think we're the sensible ones. Because love doesn't always mean longevity.

I'm happy with what we've got. Mark, too, I think. People seem to comment a lot on the fact that we're not that similar. "Opposites attract," they say with a knowing look. "Isn't that right?" The important thing is for a couple to have certain interests or hobbies in common, that's how I see it. A few areas—or even just one area—for which you share the same degree of interest. Which we do. There's one thing in particular. And no, it's not that, though we do have good, even great sex.

So no, we don't have the huge chemistry of a couple like Miranda and Julien . . . though something, now I come to think of it, seems to be off between them—I wonder if I'm the only one to notice it. And yes, I do know Mark has a whopping crush on Miranda, in case you were wondering. I'm not an idiot. In fact, I see quite a bit more than most people give me credit for. I don't mind. I really don't. I can almost *hear* the incredulity. But I promise it's the case. You're just going to have to take my word for it, I'm afraid.

So no, when I saw Mark in that sweaty nightclub just off Clapham High Street, I didn't necessarily think: Here is the man of my dreams, this must be the thing great literature and film is made of; true love, love at first sight. It wasn't like that.

What I saw was at once more and less than that. I saw a life. A new way of being. I saw the thing I had always wanted.

Mark and I both had difficult childhoods. I was moved from school to school every few years and never managed to find any proper friends. This pales in comparison to Mark's experience. His dad beat him. Not a couple of ill-advised slaps for being naughty. Proper, old-fashioned, barbaric beating. Once, he told me, his mother put concealer on him to go into school, to cover the bruising around his eye. She didn't stop his father. She couldn't. Not as frequently—but every so often—she was the victim of one of his fits of temper herself. When he was younger, Mark was small for his age, and used to get pummeled on the rugby pitch, to his dad's disdain. Then he began to grow. He drank protein powder shakes and hit the gym. The beatings finally stopped, as though his father had suddenly come to the realization that his son might be able to fight back: and win.

Mark has inherited something of his dad's temper. He throws his weight around. He has never been violent with me . . . though there have been just a couple of times in the midst of a particularly explosive argument when I have felt he's on the edge. A door slammed with such force that the wood fractured, a picture we'd disagreed about, smashed against a wall. But he's not the unfeeling bonehead that people might assume. Last night he may have joked about that incident at the races, but I remember the remorse afterward, his horror at what he had done . . . how he was almost in tears hearing that boy had been taken to hospital. I had to stop him from going and turning himself in.

Mark desperately does not want to turn out like his father. But I also know that, at times, he is frightened that he is becoming him.

24

MIRANDA

WAKE EARLY. JULIEN IS CURLED AWAY FROM ME BENEATH THE sheet. Immediately memories of last night arrive, all looped together and unclear, like a tangled ball of wool. Mark—in the bathroom. The way he had towered over me, the threat of his grip upon my upper arm.

I get up and dress. I'll go for a run, try to breathe the weirdness of last night from my lungs. I like running now. I've come to like it—it hasn't always been the case. I didn't like it at fourteen, when I suddenly went up a couple of sizes and my darling mother got me a gym membership for my birthday.

I sprint past the other cabins and the Lodge as quickly as I can. I really don't want to see any of the others yet. I haven't got my face on—and I don't mean makeup. I mean tough, fun, up-for-anything Miranda. When I reach the dark shelter of the trees that edge the loch and there has been no call of "Where are you off to?" I breathe a sigh of relief.

Mark: How *dare* he? I'm tempted to tell Emma, today. But I can tell how hard she's worked to bring this all together, how much pride she takes in having found such an awesome place—I'm not *quite* as insensitive to that sort of thing as people think. So maybe

I should wait until afterward, broach it over drinks with her in London. She must have seen that side of him, mustn't she? If he was like that with me, how does he behave with her? She seems so capable, so in charge of her life, but—as I well know—the face we present to the world can be misleading.

The air is noticeably colder today. Some of the puddles of rainwater seem to have frozen overnight. There's an edge, a rawness, to this cold that is unfamiliar. A chilly day in London is always offset by the warm blasts from overheated shops, the stickiness of the tube, the press of other bodies. But here the cold has a chance to get you properly in its grip. It feels a little like I'm trying to outrun it.

I've taken my phone with me so I can listen to music—I find it always helps to relax me, drowns out all the other noise in my head. Much better than the "mindful silence" my therapist is so bloody keen on. As promised, the little signal indicator is empty. Funny, that we live in a world now where a lack of connectivity might be advertised as a feature in itself.

A few yards ahead, the path forks off toward another jetty. It's a perfectly beautiful, melancholy spot. I jog down toward it. There are canoes stacked here, presumably from the summer season—one is on its bottom, and has filled with a winter's worth of rainwater, now frozen solid. I stand over it, and as I look inside it's as if my reflection is trapped beneath the surface of ice—as though I am trapped in there. I shiver, though I'm well wrapped up against the cold. I head back to the path.

I've run perhaps two hundred yards along the rutted track we drove along last night, the forest on one side of me, the loch on the other, when I come to a bridge spanning one of the waterfalls that feeds the loch. The waterfall itself is overlooked by a small, derelict-looking building. I wonder what on earth it is. I hang over the edge of the bridge—there's just three lines of chain between myself and the void—and look down at the waterfall itself, now mainly frozen into icicles, and the black, moss-covered rocks.

Beyond this, the path is uneventful for a stretch. But at one point I come to a small patch of burned ground, a circle, as though someone has lit a fire here. Nearby are a couple of burned, rusted beer cans. I remember what Heather told us about poachers.

STEP OFF THE PASS ONTO THE BANK THAT SHEARS DOWN TO the water, ducking my way through the branches of the trees at the lochside, stumbling and slipping over ancient moss-covered roots, twigs snagging at my hair, face, and jacket. At one point I almost lose my footing entirely and begin slithering toward a small inlet of water to my right, only just regaining my balance at the last minute. As I do I catch sight of something gleaming beneath the surface. Shocking white, so much brighter than the brownish rocks surrounding it. I peer closer, and realize what it is. A bone. Quite a large one, half concealed by rotted leaves. As I look about me I see another—and another, scattered about the grassy bank. Some are even larger than the one in the water, as long as my own femur. They are animal bones, I know this. I tell myself this as I search for the skull that will confirm it. An animal killed by another animal, or dead from old age. But some of them, I see, have scorch marks. And there is no skull to be seen. Again, I remember the warning about poachers trespassing; perhaps they've taken the heads away for mounting. I shudder. The killing of something this size must have involved a certain amount of violence, and intent.

I need to put some space between myself and this place. The grisly discovery sits queasily on my empty stomach. So I push myself going up the slight incline until I can focus only on the burn in my lungs and legs. I remind myself of what a beautiful place this is. The bones have sent a chill through me, put a dark cast on things. But there is nothing sinister here. It is just different, I remind myself. Remote, wild.

Now I'm almost at the opposite end of the loch from the Lodge: it glitters strange and magnificent on the other bank. There's a gap in the trees that ring the loch here, leaving a bald-looking stretch with a lot of rocks and some dead-looking heather. There's a building here, too, low-slung and timbered like the cabins. This must be the bunkhouse where the Icelanders are staying. All the windows are dark, no sign of life within. Perhaps they're still asleep.

I carry on my way, picking up the pace for the second half of the lap as I always do when I run. As I plunge back into the trees again I hear a sound, high and keening, like an animal in pain. I think inevitably of the bones on the other bank. It's difficult to tell exactly where the sound is coming from, but I peer in the vague direction of the noise into the dark thicket. And now I see them—I can't believe I didn't originally. Jesus. So much naked skin. The woman crouches on the mossy ground on her hands and knees, the man mounting her from behind, hips flexing powerfully, his hand tangled in her black hair. Her head is thrown back, or possibly pulled back by the force of his grip. Both of them are making a lot of noise, and the noises are bestial, uninhibited. There is something horrifyingly compelling about the sight. My feet are rooted to the spot, I'm unable to glance away.

And then the man turns his head and looks straight at me. With two fingers he makes a kind of beckoning motion with his hand. "Come," he calls, "join us." Then he laughs, a kind of cackle. He's mocking me. The woman looks up, to see who he's speaking to. She, too, grins at me: the half-drugged expression of someone in the throes of lust. Their exposed skin is very white in the stark light. Her knees are almost black with dirt.

And though I have always liked to think of myself as *very* open-minded, sexually liberated, once my limbs decide to work again I find myself stumbling backward, then turning and running away as fast as my legs will carry me, branches snagging at my ankles and whipping my cheeks. I feel as though I can still hear his laughter ringing out, though worryingly I'm not absolutely sure that it isn't in my head.

B ACK AT THE LODGE, I GO TO MAKE MYSELF A COFFEE FROM THE Nespresso machine. My fingers don't seem to work properly. They're trembling. I'm sure it's just the cold, but it would be a lie to say that scene in the woods didn't rattle me. It was the animal nature of it, the violence of it, in the middle of all that wildness. I hear the door open behind me. I do not turn around. I'm already certain—from the lack of greeting—that it's Mark. Oh, for God's sake. I could really do without seeing him now.

Finally, I wrestle the little gold capsule into the slot and clunk the lever down. Press the button and wait for something to happen. I hear the capsule fall into the cavity at the back. "Fuck!" I seem to have become completely uncoordinated.

Suddenly Mark is next to me. "Here," he says, "you have to turn it on before you put the capsule in." He shows me, and a perfect stream of velvet brown pours into the cup.

"Thanks," I say, without looking at him.

"Miranda," he says. "Manda . . . I want to apologize for last night. I don't know what came over me. I'd had too much to drink, and then those pills—what even were they?"

"That's no excuse," I say.

"No," he says quickly. "No excuse, I know that. I behaved unforgivably. Did I hurt you?"

I push up my sleeve to show him the bruise, which has turned a rather impressive purple.

He hangs his head. "I'm sorry. I can't believe I did that. Sometimes—I don't know, I let my anger get the better of me. It's like something takes over . . . again, it's unforgivable. And it wasn't even you I was angry at—of course it wasn't. It was Julien.

That's one thing I won't, can't, take back. He doesn't deserve you, Miranda. He never has. But especially recently—"

"No." I put up a palm. "Whatever you think you know about his 'little secret,' or whatever you call it, I want you to keep it to yourself. For my sake, if you won't do it for his. Do you understand?"

"I think so, but . . ." He looks dumbfounded. "I just—I'm thinking of you, Miranda. I feel like you have a right to know what he's been up to. You're sure?"

"Yes," I say, nodding my head for emphasis. "Absolutely sure."

I sip my coffee. It's too hot, and scalds my tongue, but I won't wince in front of him. "Oh, and Mark?"

"Yes?"

"Touch me again like that—either like you did on the Twister mat, or in the bathroom—and I'll *fucking* kill you. Have you got that?"

25

KATIE

I DIDN'T SLEEP WELL LAST NIGHT. I DON'T THINK I'VE SLEPT PROP-
erly for months. It feels like years.

When I come in for breakfast, Emma is standing in the kitchen
of the Lodge, making preparations for tonight's supper. Her hair is
scraped off her face, no makeup. I'm not sure when I've ever seen
her without makeup, actually. It's odd, sometimes, seeing someone
barefaced for the first time. Especially someone fair, like Emma,
who is usually equipped with the punctuation of mascara, eyeliner;
she looks almost featureless.

She has planned a big feast for this evening, she tells me. The
fridge is packed with smoked salmon and the finest beef fillet, and
she's whipping up a batter for blinis. She makes her own blinis, for
God's sake. "The shop-bought ones taste like rubber," she says.
"And it's so easy to do them." She is in her element, humming
away to herself. She has me cutting tiny triangles of salmon with
much more care than I normally would. It's actually nice to have
something to focus on. Though try as I might, my thoughts keep
wandering. I carry on until Emma cries out, "Katie, oh my God!
You're bleeding! Didn't you notice?" And in a slightly irritated
tone, "Oh, you've got blood all over the salmon."

"Have I?" I look down at my hand. "Oh." She's right, I've cut quite far into the flesh of my forefinger. A bright red gash. The fish is slick with it, made suddenly gory.

Emma stares at me. "How did you not notice?" She takes my hand, a little roughly. "Oh, you poor thing. That must have hurt. It's quite deep."

She is trying to sound sympathetic, but it doesn't quite conceal a note of irritation.

All at once the pain arrives. Sharp, bringing tears to my eyes. But I find myself almost enjoying the sting of it. It feels right, like what I deserve.

LATER, WE EAT BRUNCH IN THE DINING ROOM AT THE LODGE, all of us around the big table in the center, apart from Samira and Giles, who haven't arrived yet. They're awake, though—when I passed their cabin I heard raised voices and a shriek of infant rage.

The atmosphere is subdued this morning—the conversation around the table stilted, everyone picking listlessly at their fry-ups. There are the hangovers from last night, of course, but maybe there's something else, too. Something slightly strained . . . as though everyone's somewhat exhausted their quota of niceness on yesterday's reunion. Only Emma is all brightness and bustle, checking everyone has enough bacon, enough coffee.

"For Christ's sake," Julien says, "sit down, Emma! We're all *fine*." I'm sure he was going for a light, teasing tone, but he doesn't quite manage it.

Emma sits, a flush stealing up the side of her neck.

"Katie." Miranda pulls out the seat next to her. "Sit by me."

I take the seat and reach for a cold piece of toast to butter. Miranda's wearing a lot of perfume this morning, and, as I chew, it's like the toast has taken on the heavy, fragrant flavor of it. My stomach churns. I take a swig of coffee, but this, too, tastes off.

When I finally look up, I realize Miranda has turned in her seat to look directly at me, her head on one side. I see rather than feel the piece of toast tremble in my hand. Those X-ray eyes of hers. "You've got a new man, haven't you?" she asks. She's grinning at me . . . but it occurs to me that it's more a grimace than a smile. I know her too well not to guess when something is off. If I were a good friend I'd ask her about it . . . but I can't quite bring myself to. Besides, I reason, it's too public a forum here, with everyone around us. "What makes you say that?" I ask.

"I can tell. You look different. The hair, the clothes." I move an inch or so away; her breath is a little stale, which is unlike her. She once told me that she brushes before *and* after breakfast in accordance with some fascist rule of her mother's. She must have forgotten. "And," she says, "you've been so elusive recently. Even more so than normal. You've always done this when there's a new guy on the scene. Ever since I've known you." Everyone else suddenly seems to be listening. I feel the eyes of the room upon me. Nick's eyebrows are raised. Because if I am seeing someone, I know he's thinking, I would have told him, wouldn't I?

I take a bite of toast, but it sticks in my gullet and it takes several attempts to swallow it. My throat feels raw, wounded.

"No," I say, hoarsely. "I don't have time at the moment—I'm far too busy with work."

"God," she says. "All work and no play, Katie—have you ever heard that one? You're completely obsessed. I don't understand it."

But then she wouldn't. Miranda has tried and failed to make a go at several different careers, with no real success. She crashed out of Oxford with a Third, in the end. She didn't care, she told me. But I know better. She had been arrogant enough to think that she could just breeze through as she had always done. The thing is, Miranda is clever, but she isn't necessarily Oxford clever. Her mum hired a tutor to help her get those four A's at A level, and I'm sure she dazzled them in the interview. But still. Once in, she was in a different league entirely. She somehow managed to blag the first and second years of university, and she ignored the warning signs in our third year that she wasn't on the right track, even though I tried to point them out. I swear I wasn't pleased when she opened that envelope and saw her result. But I must confess that perhaps I did feel a little—a tiny *tiny* bit—as though justice had been done.

That Third was an insult. It smarted. It stung her pride. If you look at all of us, now, she's the odd one out. All of us have good jobs. Samira's a management consultant, I'm a lawyer, Julien works for the hedge fund, Nick's an architect, Giles is a doctor, Bo works for the BBC, Mark for an advertising firm. Emma works for a literary agency—I remember when Miranda learned that one. "I don't understand," she said. "How did you get that job in the first place? I thought that agency *only* picked from redbrick, and usually Oxbridge."

Emma was unfazed. "I don't know," she said, with a shrug. "I suppose I must just give good interview."

Miranda herself had had a crack at getting into the publishing industry. Then a go at advertising. Mark gave her a much bigger leg up than he probably should have done, persuading one of his colleagues to interview her for an assistant position. She got it, but left after only two months. She was bored of it, she said. But I met a girl who used to work there at a wedding and she told me that it was a little more complicated.

"They let her go," she told me. "She was unbelievably lazy. She seemed to think she was above things. Once, stuffing envelopes, she actually refused to lick them to seal them shut. She said she hated the taste and it was below her pay grade to do it. Said she hadn't been to Oxford just to do that. Can you imagine?"

Yes, bad friend that I am, of course I could.

Giles and Samira have arrived now. They look several degrees more shattered than everyone else. Samira flops into a chair and puts her head in her hands with a groan as Giles tries to lift Priya into the high chair. She grizzles, fighting this restraint. As the pitch rises to a shrill whine I see Nick sneak his fingers into his ears. "Oh God," Samira groans. "Priya woke us up at five, and then again at six."

"I can't even imagine," Bo says. "I couldn't dress myself this morning, let alone a little person. Nick had to point out my T-shirt was on backward, didn't you?" Nick smiles wanly.

"Well, I suppose it's a life choice, isn't it?" Miranda says breezily, pouring herself an orange juice. "It's not like you're forced to have kids, is it?"

Even for Miranda—who miraculously often manages to get away with such comments—this is a cattiness too far. But then there's definitely something about her this morning. Her brightness has a brittle edge.

I haven't seen Samira angry for a long time, but now I remember that it's a terrifying spectacle. There's a proper temper hidden under that calm, groomed exterior. She has gone absolutely rigid in her chair. We all watch her, silently, waiting to see what she will do next. Then she seems to give a sort of shiver, and reaches for the *cafetière*. Her hand shakes only a little as she pours. She does not look at Miranda once. For the sake of group harmony, perhaps, she has evidently decided to rise above it.

With a bit of a stutter, the conversation around the table moves on. We're going stalking today, because apparently this is a "must-do" if you're staying on an estate in Scotland.

"I suppose you two won't be coming stalking, will you?" Mark asks, indicating Nick and Bo.

"Why not?" Nick asks.

"Well . . ." Mark's mouth curls a little at the corner. "Because—you know."

"No. I don't know."

"Just didn't think you'd be into that sort of thing."

"Hang on a sec, Mark," Nick says. "If I've got this correct, it sounds as though you've decided we won't be coming because we're gay. Is that really what you're saying?"

Spoken aloud, it sounds so ridiculous that even Mark must be able to see it.

"It's not a disability, Mark. Just want to make that clear."

Mark makes a noncommittal noise at the back of his throat. Nick's knuckles are white about his coffee mug. For all Mark's muscle, I'm not sure that I would back him in a fight between the two.

"It's true," Nick goes on, "that like most sensible people, I don't particularly like the idea of killing animals for pure sport"—Mark assumes an aha! expression—"but, from what I hear, the deer numbers get out of control if they aren't managed. So I'm at peace with the idea. I'm also a pretty good shot: the last time I went to shoot clays I hit eighteen out of twenty. Thanks, though, for your concern."

After this, no one, not even Miranda, seems to be able to think of anything to say.

26

HEATHER

Now
January 2, 2019

HAVE MADE ENDLESS CUPS OF TEA, SO MUCH SO THAT I HAVE begun to feel like an extension of the kettle. No one seems to actually be drinking them, but every time I ask, they all nod, vaguely, and then sit holding the cups as the hot tea slowly cools, untasted. Beyond the windows the snow shows no sign of stopping. It is difficult to imagine a time when it was not there, this moving curtain of white.

Normally, after a body has been found, I am sure it is all flashing lights, men in white hazmat suits, and commotion. But this is no ordinary place. And in this case the landscape has had its own ideas. The weather has forced us to bend to its own whims. I realize, for one of the first times since I moved here, quite how alien this place is, how little I really know of it. It might as well be another planet. I am certain that there are secrets here beyond the whiskey bothies, beyond the monster pike deep in the loch. Those are just the small things the landscape chooses to reveal.

There is a loud wail from the next room, cacophonous in the silence, startling me so much that I spill water from the kettle onto the floor. It's just the baby, of course. I remember the sound of the baby crying on New Year's Eve when I woke to go to the toilet, and when I saw—or thought I saw—that strange light, up on the flank of the Munro. And I wonder now whether it's possible that the sound could have concealed any other noises out there.

I think of all the sounds in this place that have come to seem normal, that I choose not to question. As I wait for the kettle to boil I'm remembering one of my very first nights at the Lodge. I'd moved into the cottage, and was focusing on not thinking too much about anything. It was the week of the terrible anniversary. I'd had quite a lot of wine—a medicinal quantity, a bottle and a half, perhaps. I remember sinking into the bed and pulling the duvet up over me. One thing I have learned about "silence"—at least this sort of silence, that of the wilderness—is that it is surprisingly loud. The building is old, it creaked around me. Outside in the night were the sounds of animals; two owls conversed in long mournful calls. The wind was moving through the tops of the great Scots pines just beyond my window. It sounded like a moan. It could be soothing, I remember telling myself. Perhaps I would get used to it. (I have never quite got used to it.)

Then there was a sound that ripped through everything else. A scream, high-pitched, desperate: horrible, the sound of a person in terrible pain. The air rang with the echo of it for several seconds afterward. I sat up in bed, all the drowsiness from the wine leaving me. My ears felt sensitive as an animal's, the whole of me prickling, waiting for another scream. None came.

I waited for a response: surely someone else must have heard it? Then I remembered that it was just me and the gamekeeper: no one else for miles around . . . apart from, presumably, whoever it was that had screamed. I imagined Doug pulling on those big boots of his, taking one of the rifles from the barn. He would be the right person to go, I told myself. Not five-foot-two drunk me. But the night seemed even quieter now than before.

I pulled the shutter open a little way and looked out. I couldn't see any lights. I checked my watch. Two A.M. The hours had blurred; I had not realized how much time had passed. Wine does that, I suppose. It began to occur to me that Doug might be sleeping. That I might be the only one of the two of us awake to have heard the scream.

I started to believe that I had imagined it. Perhaps I had dropped off to sleep for those two minutes, without realizing. I couldn't even quite remember how it sounded, though there was still the reverberation of it in my ears.

Then, as if to remind me, it came again, and this time it was more terrible than the last. It was the sound of purest agony, something almost animal in it. I climbed out of bed, felt for my slippers. I had to go and see—I could not pretend now. Someone out there was in trouble.

I crept downstairs, shrugged on my coat and boots, took the cast-iron poker from the fireplace and the torch from the window-sill.

The night outside was black and still. I remember noticing that above me the sky had a depth I had never seen before, how at that moment it looked sinister, like a void.

I peered into the shadows, trying to discern any sign of movement. "Hello?" I called. My hands were shaking so much that the light from my torch bounced everywhere, illuminating indifferent patches of earth. The silence around me felt like a held breath. "Hello?"

Perhaps it was inevitable that I felt I was being watched, haloed as I was by light from the door. I realized that in calling out I had exposed myself, made myself visible and audible. I might just have put myself in danger.

I took a few steps. And somewhere in the direction of the loch

I caught a movement. Not with the torch beam, rather with some animal sense I didn't know I had: a mixture of sight and sound. "Who's there?" Fear had stifled my voice—it came out as a tiny, strangled squeak. I directed the torch beam toward where I thought I had caught the movement. Nothing. Then another flicker, much closer at hand.

"Heather?"

I swung my arm and illuminated a face. In the torchlight the figure was ghoulish, and I almost shrieked; was glad as realization dawned that I did not. It was Doug.

"Are you all right?" he asked. There was no urgency in his voice, just the deep, unhurried tone he always spoke in.

"I heard someone scream. Did you hear it?"

But he frowned. "A scream?"

"Yes. Very high-pitched. Whoever it was sounded terrified. I came out to see . . ." In the face of his evident incredulity I faltered. "You didn't hear it?"

"Was it," he asked, "like this?" And then, to my amazement, he mimicked the sound almost perfectly. I felt the same cold flood of dread down the backs of my legs.

"Yes. That's it exactly."

"Ah. In that case, you heard a fox. A vixen, to be precise."

"I don't understand. It sounded like a woman."

"It's a terrible sound—and an easy mistake to make. You certainly aren't the first to have done so. There was a story, quite recently, about a man killing himself on a train track outside Edinburgh trying to help what he thought was a woman in distress." He raised his eyebrows. "You didn't hear that story, living in the city?"

"No," I said. I was beginning to be embarrassed by the tremor in my voice, and wished I could bring it under my control.

"It's when they're . . ." He grimaced. "The male's . . . you-know-what, is barbed. So it's not exactly a pleasant experience for the female."

I couldn't prevent my wince.

"Exactly. So not pleasant. But not someone being murdered, either." He paused. "You're sure you're okay?"

"Yes." Even to my own ears it didn't sound quite convincing. I tried to bolster it by saying, "Honestly, I'm fine."

"In that case, I'll let you get back to bed."

I remember that his eyes swept over me then, so quickly that I might almost have imagined it. But not quite. I was wearing pajamas. But I felt more exposed, suddenly, than if I had been standing there completely naked.

"Thank you," I said.

He doffed an imaginary cap. "You're welcome."

I closed the door, stepped inside, and pressed a hand to my chest. My brain did not seem to have told my heart that the danger had passed. It was beating so hard and fast it seemed to be trying to leap out of my rib cage. It was only when I finally climbed back into bed, and pulled the duvet over myself, that it occurred to me to think properly about what had just happened. If it wasn't the scream that had woken Doug, as it had me, then what on earth was he doing wandering the grounds in the dead of night?

THINK OF HIS HAND; HOW HE'S BEEN SO VAGUE ABOUT THE WAY in which he injured it. I think of the boss's mention of how good he would be at fighting off any poachers, the intimation of violence. It isn't enough that I don't want him to have had anything to do with any of this. *And that's just because you fancy him,* a little voice says. *Just because you made yourself come thinking about him.* With some effort, I mute this train of thought.

I remember my mother's words about googling him. It suddenly seems important, necessary.

With a quick step I move to the door of the office and lock it. If Doug tries to come in I'll pretend I've done it accidentally, "force of habit." Still, I don't have long, unless I want to raise suspicion. I open the doors to the cabinet where I keep all the filing. The two personnel files: my own, Doug's. Iain's only a contractor, and I think he worked for the boss before, so he didn't need to apply for his job the way Doug and I did ours.

I open Doug's file. There's a short CV, detailing a period in the marines: six years. Nothing more. What exactly am I looking for? I move to the computer, plug Doug's full name into the search engine, and wait for the results to load via the creakingly slow Internet connection. It is only when my chest starts to burn that I realize I have been holding my breath. There won't be anything, I think. There won't . . . and I'll feel terrible for doing it, because I'll have breached his trust without him ever knowing, but it will stop there. He will never know. And I will be able to lay any suspicions—if that is even what they are—to rest.

Finally, the page blinks into life.

I can see immediately that there are a lot of hits. For a normal person, someone who isn't a celebrity or notorious in some other way, you'd expect to get, what? Three hits, at most? A few social media profiles, including those of anyone sharing the same name, perhaps the odd mention of a sporting achievement or a part in the college play. But Doug's unusual name takes up the entire first page of hits. And none of it is very nice. In fact, it's all pretty horrible.

I wish I hadn't looked. I wish I had never seen any of this.

27

MIRANDA

W E TRAIPSE AFTER DOUG TO THE YARD BEHIND THE LODGE, where his Land Rover sits parked next to a big old red truck—maybe that's what Heather gets around in. The thought of her, all five-foot-nothing, behind the wheel of that big old vehicle makes me laugh.

Doug opens the barn for us with a state-of-the-art keypad that looks completely bizarre against the old wood. I suppose they need it, if there are guns in here. As he yanks the heavy wooden door back I enjoy his muscles move beneath the old shirt he wears (just a shirt—in this weather!). He would make, I think, an excellent candidate for Lady Chatterley's lover, so tall and broad and tousled. Bit of an unflattering contrast for Julien, I can't help thinking, whose various ointments and tinctures jostle for space on the bathroom shelf beside my own.

He kits us up in the barn: over-trousers and jackets, even walking boots for Katie, who has failed to bring anything remotely sensible. Mark asks for one of the hats, which are ridiculous Sherlock Holmes affairs.

"If you want one, mate," Doug says, with something that might be mistaken for a sneer.

Beside the jackets and the trousers hang ten rifles. There is something lethal-looking about just the shape of the weapons, as though they could somehow kill you without ever being fired.

Then there's a long talk on safety, and on where we're going today: up the steep hillside past the Old Lodge, because apparently that's where the deer have been congregating lately: though we're only looking for the hinds, the females, because it's the wrong time of year for shooting stags. At the end, I say, "So, let me get this right. We might well not actually get a deer today. And even if we do shoot a deer it won't have antlers, because it's not the right season. But we're paying hundreds of pounds for the privilege."

"Yep." Doug nods. "That's pretty much the size of it." His tone is direct, but I notice he can't quite make eye contact. I feel a little thrill of triumph. I recognize *that* particular symptom, you see. I have always been faithful to Julien—well, with that one exception, right at the beginning. But it would be a lie to say I do not enjoy flexing my power, dropping a lure. My own sort of hunting, I suppose. Much more fun than freezing-wet heather and hideous waterproof over-trousers.

Doug locks the door behind him with a seamless click of metal. Now he has us lie on the ground to shoot at a box with a target. Julien, Giles, Bo, and Mark are terrible, laughably so. With the exception of Bo, who is always so lighthearted (though surely, with that druggie past, he can't always have been?), they aren't finding it at all funny. Mark—I can just about bring myself to watch him— wears his mouth in a snarl as he shoots. When Julien has his sixth attempt, I see that muscle in the side of his jaw draw tight in the way that it does when he's angry about something, and with each report his eye twitches. He cares, I realize. They all care. Even mild-mannered Giles seems to have undergone a personality trans-plant. Perhaps they're imagining themselves in some action film or video game. I'm sure that's it: men reverting to little boys. All the same, it's a bit weird.

Katie is *awful*, too, but I'm not sure she's even bothering to try—just as she seems to have stopped bothering to pretend she's having a good time. Samira—who, after much persuading, left Priya with the manager, Heather, for a couple of hours—is not great, but she makes up for it with lots of intensity. I'm reminded of her rowing blue past. Give her a week with this and she'd probably be Olym-pian standard. It's a glimmer of the old Samira, the girl I knew before, and I'm glad of it. This, after all, is the woman who once set fire to the dining table in our house, in imitation of a bar in Ibiza, and had a formal reprimand from the college dean for her behavior.

I'm not bad, but I'm not quite as good as I had thought I would be: I've always had a knack for sports. Doug tells me I'm being too "vigorous" with the trigger. "You just need to coax it with your finger," he says. He's straight-faced—but . . . is it just me, or does that sound a bit filthy?

Nick is pretty good, as he'd told us he would be. No surprise there, funnily enough. He was always good at sport, and he's so precise about things, so intense, sometimes. But it's Emma, of all people, who excels. Doug says she is a "natural," and she smiles and shakes her head, typically modest. "Women are often better," he says. "They're more accurate, more deadly. This sport isn't about testosterone or brute strength."

I wish I didn't mind so much that it's not me earning his praise.

We begin our ascent up the hillside. We're walking toward the Old Lodge, the building Heather pointed out to us yesterday after-noon. I hate walking. It's so boring, and purposeless. Give me a run any day, something that burns double the number of calories in half the time. Mark, Julien, and Nick jostle for position at the front, as though each is determined that they will be the one to take the shot. Katie, meanwhile, is a few feet ahead of me, talking to Bo. I feel slighted that she hasn't chosen to walk with me. I could go and join them, but I'm not going to grovel for her to pay me attention. It seems like I offended her at breakfast, asking if she had a new man. Fine, I could have been a little more subtle about it—she's intensely private about that sort of thing—but I was only trying to show an interest. And, frankly, after all this time apart it wouldn't fucking kill her to ask me about my life. That's not like her: in the past she's always been such a good listener. Julien once—not too kindly— joked it was a lucky thing that I'd found a friend who likes to listen as much as I like to talk. But he wasn't totally wrong. I've always thought of her as my opposite, my complementary part.

The path has melted away now, so we're just trekking upward through the heather, and it's hard, hard work. Every so often it tangles around an ankle, yanking me back as though reminding me who's in charge. Because this landscape is definitely in charge. It's brutal. The temperature has dropped even more, and the air is raw, stinging any exposed flesh. Even my teeth hurt when I open my mouth to speak. It feels like the cold has got inside the jacket I've been lent, and the beautiful—and I'd thought very warm— cashmere jumper I'm wearing under it, and is pressing against my skin.

The ground is boggy in places, too; there must be streams under the soil. Every so often I step into a particularly soft patch, and freezing water comes up over my boots, soaking my socks. They'll be ruined. They're cashmere, too—a present in the autumn from Julien. There was a period when every week he seemed to come home with some sort of gift—guilt over what he'd made me a part of, I'm sure, though he claimed he just wanted to spoil me.

Nick, Mark, and Julien can't go fast enough. They're almost elbowing each other in their haste to get ahead, to be first up the hill. That can't be very safe while carrying loaded rifles, can it? At one point Mark turns and seems to shove Julien. Lightly, but unmistakably. He makes a joke of it, and I see Julien force a laugh . . . but I can see he's not really amused.

It's a relief when we pause at the Old Lodge: a sad, fire-blackened old ruin. Doug gets out a hip flask and passes it around. When he hands it to me I let my fingertips touch his, for just a moment too long. His eyes are such a dark brown that you can hardly make out the pupils. I want Julien to see this, to register this man desiring me.

I'm not a big fan of whiskey but somehow it feels right here, in this wild place. And the warmth of it helps, too, seems to soothe this weird mood I seem to have found myself in since last night. I take another swig, and when I pass it back to Doug I see that my mouth has left a pleasing stain of lipstick around the neck.

It looks as though someone might have been up here before us. It's just the remains of a few cigarettes, scattered here and there. But Doug picks up one of the stubs and looks at it, intently, as though there might be a secret message written on the side. I notice that he pockets it. Bizarre. Why would you pick up someone's old cigarette butt? Then I look at his battered jacket, his worn boots, and feel an unexpected tug of pity. Perhaps, I realize, he's going to keep it and smoke it later.

28

KATIE

THE OLD LODGE, WHEN WE GET TO IT, IS A HORRIBLE PLACE. IT'S probably the only ugly thing in this landscape, a burned shell, with just one blackened building still standing. It's somehow colder here than anywhere else, perhaps because it's so exposed to the elements. Why on earth would you build something here? So far from shelter, and from help. I think of the fire. It must have been seen for miles around—like the beacons they lit for the millennium up and down the country.

There is a silence here that is different from the silence on the rest of the estate. It's like a held breath. It feels—as clichéd as this might sound—as though we are not alone. As though something, someone, is watching us. The stones are like old bones: a skeleton of someone who has died and been left out in the open, denied the dignity of a burial. When we get near enough I am sure the air smells of burning. That's impossible, isn't it? Or could there be some way in which the smoke has gone deep within the stone, remained locked in there? It wouldn't be hard to believe that the fire happened a few years ago, not nearly a century in the past.

The stable building—the bit that survived because the flames couldn't make the leap—is almost obscene in its wholeness. They've put a keypad lock on it, too, I realize—like the one on the barn—presumably to stop guests just wandering in, if it's not safe. The sky is a very pale violet. Doesn't that mean snow? What would we even do if it did start to snow, properly, while we're stuck out here? We're completely exposed here, on the flank of a mountain. The Lodge—the New Lodge, I suppose—looks like a small shard of glass from here, beside the loch, which looks gray and opaque as lead in the strange light, the trees ringing it a charcoal bristle. The station, roughly the same distance from us here as the Lodge is on the other side, looks like a toy town model.

"I don't know why we're doing this," Miranda says suddenly, "when we could be back at the Lodge getting stuck into the champagne." She complained on the climb up here, too: about the boggy ground and the icy water seeping over the top of her boots. It's because she wasn't any good at the target practice—I'm sure of it. If she had turned out to be a crack shot, it would be a different story—she'd be leading the charge. Miranda hates being bad at anything. I could practically see her lip curl as Doug praised Emma, as though she didn't believe someone like Emma had any right to be a good shot.

"It's so fucking cold," she adds, "I'm sure the deer will be hiding somewhere out of sight, if they have any sense. Surely we're not going to catch anything now?"

Nick wheels suddenly on his heel to face her. "Hey!" the gamekeeper shouts. "Careful, man, you're carrying a loaded weapon."

"Sorry." Nick looks slightly abashed. "But to be honest, I'm pretty tired of hearing about how bored you are, Miranda. Why don't you go back to the Lodge, if you're so keen for that? We're never going to surprise anything if you keep moaning about what a terrible time you're having."

There's a resounding silence in the aftermath, the freezing air seems to drop another few degrees. Miranda looks as if she has just been slapped. Everyone has been a little more tense on this excursion, but this is the first openly hostile thing that anyone has actually said. Perhaps it's no surprise that it's between Nick and Miranda. Nick, after all, has never been Miranda's greatest fan. I don't think he's ever really forgiven her.

WHEN NICK CAME OUT TO A FEW OF US, IN OUR FIRST YEAR at Oxford, he hadn't yet told his parents, who were then serving an ambassadorship in Oman. It wasn't that he was afraid of doing so, he told me. "They're pretty liberal, and they might have guessed already—there were a couple of guys, when we were in Paris, who I got close to."

But he wanted to choose the right moment, because it was an important milestone, an affirmation of who he was.

Miranda claimed that she knew none of this when Nick's parents came up for reading week, and Nick introduced them to everyone in the JCR. There was some discussion about end-of-year exams, and Miranda said—in a nudge-nudge wink-wink tone—"Don't worry, Mr. and Mrs. M, we'll make sure Nick has his nose to the grindstone and doesn't just go off chasing after all the prettiest boys."

She wasn't even supposed to know, that was the worst of it. The select group Nick had confided in had not included Miranda. I had not been proud of myself for telling her. I was very good, normally, at keeping secrets. But I had been drunk, and Miranda had been teasing me about my crush on Nick, and it had just come out. Of course, I had begged her not to say that she knew. And yet she claimed to have no memory of this at all. She claimed, too, afterward, that she assumed Nick's parents "just knew."

I was sure that Nick would never forgive me. So I was relieved by his reaction. He was furious, that was true. But not, thankfully, with me. He told me that he had thought of several unpleasant ways in which to exact his revenge on Miranda, but couldn't find anything that matched the scale of what she'd done to him.

"I know it shouldn't really matter," he told me. "I was going to tell them this week anyway . . . over a nice lunch or something. But it was the principle of it. I *know* it wasn't an accident. I think she did it because she liked having that power. And to cause trouble between the two of us, of course."

"What do you mean?" I asked, surprised.

"I'm pretty sure she resents your being friends with me."

"That's rubbish," I told him. "Miranda has loads of other friends, and I have . . . a few."

"Yes, but she doesn't have any other *close* friends—have you noticed that, Katie? She's only got you and Samira at a pinch. And I don't think she likes sharing her toys."

Now, of course, that's all water under the bridge. Or, at least, Nick has done a good job of suggesting as much. I wonder, though, whether he still thinks of it. Wounds inflicted at that sort of raw, unformed time in our lives tend to cut the deepest—and leave the worst scars.

EY," SAMIRA SAYS SHARPLY. "LET'S ALL JUST CHILL OUT, okay? We're here on holiday."

Funny, I don't remember Samira being quite so sanguine in the past about things. And I recall her struggle with herself at brunch, how she managed to bite back whatever rejoinder she might have made to Miranda then.

Miranda mutters something under her breath, defiantly. But I can see that she's really stung. She can give it out, you see, Miranda—but she can't always take it. Underneath that tough, glossy exterior she's softer than she looks. And I think she's always secretly admired Nick, sees him as an equal.

I see her glance at Julien. I wonder if she's waiting for him to stick up for her. If so, she's disappointed, but perhaps not surprised.

She has always said that he hates confrontation, likes to try to please everybody—never wanting to be seen as the bad guy.

I don't want to take sides, either. I can't afford to. I have enough of my own issues to deal with. I feel as though I've been catapulted into the past: Miranda causing drama, me having to mediate between her and the unlucky opponent—feeling that each of them is asking me to choose. I'm not going to do it now. I walk away from the group, around to the other side of the ruin, and stand in the full force of the wind for a few minutes, my eyes closed.

I clench my fingernails into my palms until they sting. I have to stop. I have to stop this thing, this compulsion, once and for all. But every time I have tried I find that I can't bring myself to. When it really comes to doing it, I'm never strong enough. I can't believe I've got myself into the mess that I have. I take a few deep breaths, open my eyes, and try to distract myself with the view.

I have been to some beautiful places in my life, but nowhere quite like this. It's the wildness of the landscape, perhaps: raw, untouched by human hand other than the small cluster of dwellings below us, the tiny station on the other side, and the old ruin behind us. It is bleak and brutal, and its charm, if it can be called that, lies in this. The colors are all muted: slate blue, the old bruise yellow of the sky, the rust red of the heather. And yet they are just as mesmerizing as any turquoise sea, any white sandy beach.

As I watch, a huge clump of the heather seems to lift up and move, and I realize that it is deer, running as one, their sleekness only offset by the comedy flashes of their white tails. Perhaps it's this movement that draws my eye to another flash of movement, lower down the slope. I don't think I would have seen it otherwise. Seen him, that is. He is some fifty yards away, wearing camouflage gear, a large backpack on his back. I can't make out his face, or even his height—because he's up to his waist in heather. He appears to be making an effort not to be seen, keeping low down, close to the heather as he moves. It must have been him that scared the deer and set them sprinting off.

I don't think he's seen me yet. I can feel my heartbeat somewhere up near my throat. There's something menacing about the way he moves, like an animal. Then, like a predator catching my scent on the breeze, he looks up and sees me. He stops short.

I can't make sense of what happens next. It defies all logic. In the next couple of seconds he seems to sink from view; to disappear into the heather itself. I blink, in case something has actually happened to my vision. But when I open my eyes there is still no sign of him.

I think of the manager's instructions. "Tell the gamekeeper or me if you see anyone you don't recognize on the estate." So should I tell them? But I'm not even completely sure of what I have seen. A person doesn't just dissolve in plain sight, do they? It's true that my eyes are full of tears from the rawness of the wind, and I'm still a bit groggy from the sleeping pills I took last night. The others will think I'm simply making it up, or imagining things. I'm too weary to try to explain what I saw. If I were Miranda, I'd make this into a big drama, a ghost-story anecdote. But I'm not. I'm Katie: the quiet one, the watcher. Besides, there can't be any real harm in not saying anything. Can there?

29

DOUG

THERE'S A CHANGE IN THE GROUP. HE NOTICED IT EVEN BE-
fore the argument between the man with the glasses and the
beautiful blonde. He has seen it happen before, this shift. It starts
with the rifles. Each of them is suddenly invested with a new, terrible power. At first, during the target practice, they flinched with
each report, at the jump of the device as it punched bruises into the
flesh beneath their shoulders. But quickly—too quickly, perhaps—
it became natural, and they were leaning into each shot: focused,
intent. They began enjoying themselves. But something else crept
in, too. A sense of competition. More than that . . . something
primeval has been summoned. The "buck fever" felt by all nov-
ice hunters before their first trophy. The blood lust. Each of them
wants to be the one that makes the kill. And yet they don't even
know what it is they're yearning for. Because they have never killed
before—not beyond the odd swatted fly, or trapped mouse. This is
something completely different. They will be changed by it. An
innocence they did not know they possessed will be forsaken.

There is the landscape, too. It has made them edgy. Up here
the harsh, skeletal lines of the land are revealed, granite peeking
like old bone through the rust red fuzz of heather. Up here they

become aware of quite how alone they are in this place—not another human soul for a very long way indeed.

Except . . . his fingers now find the cigarette stub in his pocket. He doesn't like it. It shows that someone has been up here, recently. Heather doesn't smoke, as far as he knows—and she certainly doesn't go anywhere near the Old Lodge if she can help it. Iain smokes, he thinks, but he has no need to come up here: he's been working down by the loch, on the pumphouse. It could also have been the Icelandic couple—but he saw them smoking rollies the other evening, after the dinner.

He'll mention it to Heather, later. Just to check whether she's noticed anything.

Poachers? But there would have been some other evidence of them, surely? In the past he has found blood-smeared grass where they have dragged their illegal bounty, or the cartridge shells with which they killed it. He has found the remains of fires they've made to attempt to burn the rest of the body (it's the heads they're after, in general) and the blackened bones that remain. Sometimes he's even found the kill before they've come back to claim it—they'll take the head, the most valuable part, and leave the headless corpse hidden in the grass until there's an opportune time to come and collect it.

It could merely have been dropped by a hiker—there's still a right to roam, though they're no doubt discouraged by the (probably illegal) "Private Property" signs. He can't remember the last time he saw a walker. Besides, hikers are all bright windbreakers and cellophane-wrapped lunches and earnestness, not the sort to callously litter the landscape they've come to enjoy.

No, he doesn't like it one bit.

HE'S PLEASED TO PUT THE OLD LODGE BEHIND HIM. ITS STORY parallels his own ghosts. The gamekeeper haunted by his own war, burning the place down. He knows the sorts of forces that might drive a man to such an act.

They find the hinds in the stretch of land beyond the Lodge. There is a stain of darkness in the sky already—the sun, invisible behind cloud, must be readying to set. They need to be quick. He has the guests lie in the heather and crawl toward the deer, so as not to alarm them.

One has got separated from the others, an old doe, with a hobble to her walk. Perfect. You only shoot the old, the limp. Despite what the poachers might think, this is not about magnificent trophies.

When they are close enough, he turns to the shorter, not-beautiful blonde. "You," he says. "Want to try her?"

She nods solemnly. "All right."

He helps her sight it. "The largest part of the chest," he says, "not the head. Too much room for error with the head. And not too low, or you'll shatter her leg. And *squeeze* the trigger, remember, gently does it."

She does as he says. The gun discharges, a flat thunderclap of noise, ringing in the ears. The other deer scatter in fright, fleeing at astonishing speed. There are exclamations from the other guests behind him, sharp intakes of breath.

There is a beat, as always, when it seems that the bullet must have misfired, or disappeared completely. Then the doe jerks as though passed through with an electric current. There is the belated thud of the bullet's impact, the metal entering flesh. A bellow, the sound as much like rage as pain. She staggers a couple of steps, swaying on her feet. And then finally, down she goes—quite gently, as though she is being careful with herself, her legs folding underneath her. Her chest is, suddenly, a mass of red. A perfect shot.

He walks the hundred yards or so to the dying beast. She's still there, just: her breath mists in the cold. There is a moment when her eyes seem to meet his. Then he takes his knife and shoves it in, clean, to that place at the base of the skull. Now she is gone. He feels little remorse, other than for the grace that once was, now stilled. Unlike other deaths for which he has been responsible, he knows this one is right, necessary. Unchecked, the population would get out of control; resources would be so thin that the whole herd would begin to starve.

He bends, and dips a hand into the wound, coating his fingers with gore. Then he walks back to the woman, Emma, and—in time-honored tradition—anoints her forehead and cheeks with the blood.

30

EMMA

THE GAMEKEEPER TOLD ME I'D HAVE TO WAIT FOR THE FILLET from the deer I shot. It needs to be hung for a few days—apparently in the first twenty-four hours rigor mortis really sets in and it would be inedible until the tissues start to soften again. But they've got some properly aged meat that I can use if I want. I was going to do a beef Wellington tonight, but I've realized I could make it with venison instead. That would be perfect, wouldn't it—a reminder of our day?

I've come over to the barn to collect it. I've washed my face first, of course. Apparently there's some old wives' tale about not cleaning it off until midnight or bad luck will befall you, but that's just nonsense and superstition. Besides, it had dried and crusted into a very unsightly mess.

When I get to the barn there's no sign of anyone, but the door is slightly ajar. I give it a push with one hand and it swings open.

I can hear the murmur of voices, low and urgent. At the sound of my footsteps, they cease. It's gloomy inside, and I have to squint to adjust my eyes. When I do I take a step back. At one end of the room hang two huge, grisly, bloody pendants of meat next to the carcass of the deer I shot, skinned, its eyes still glossy black and staring. There's a distinctive smell, impossible to mistake: heavy, metallic.

Behind the carcasses I make out the odd-job man I sat next to at the dinner, Iain, wielding a large cleaver in one hand, and wearing a butcher's apron soaked in blood. He raises his other hand in greeting; his palm is stained red. Next to him are the two Icelandic guests.

I wonder what these three strangers could have been talking about so fervently.

"Got your venison ready for you," Iain says. He reaches toward the counter behind him and lifts up a parcel wrapped in stained greaseproof paper.

"Thank you," I say, taking it from him gingerly. It's heavy, cold.

"These two"—he points to the two other guests—"were just asking me if they could have the heart from your kill, as that's best fresh. I hope you don't mind them taking that?"

"No . . . ," I say, trying to conceal my distaste, as a good chef should. "Not at all."

The man, Ingvar, grins at me. "Thank you. You know, you should try it sometime. It's the tastiest part."

31

HEATHER

Now
January 2, 2019

STARE AT THE COMPUTER SCREEN. I SIT WITH MY HAND OVER my mouth like a pantomime of shock. But I am genuinely stunned by what a simple search of Doug's full name has brought up. It's bad. Really bad. It's far worse than probably even my mother could have guessed in her most lurid imaginings.

I can see that even from the brief précis of each article on the Google results page. He almost killed someone. I've been living in this place alone with a man who has served time in jail. Who was convicted of, as the official line has it: "causing grievous bodily harm with intent."

The *Daily Mail* article is the first hit. I click it open. There is a photo of Doug, hollow-eyed, mouth a grim line, hair shorn to the scalp. Another of him in an ill-fitting suit, being shepherded out of a car into the courthouse, his teeth bared at the photographers in a snarl. He *looks* like a criminal; he looks violent, dangerous. The article that follows is a lurid attack on every aspect of his character.

Educated at a private school; university dropout; time in the marines, the only one to survive an attack by the Taliban in "murky circumstances." Strongly insinuating, if not stating outright, that some foul play or cowardice was involved on his part.

And then a "brawl in a bar."

As I read on, it only gets worse. The form of "bodily harm"? *Attempted strangulation.* I look for anything in the article that might exonerate Doug's behavior in some way: something I could latch on to. I want him to be exonerated. Not just because the idea of having lived with someone capable of cold-blooded murder (or at least the attempt of it) is horrifying, but because, despite his taciturn ways, I have come to rather like Doug. I genuinely believed what I said when I told my mum he was "harmless."

There is nothing to excuse him, though. I discard the *Daily Mail,* click on the BBC News link, which should give me an account without bias or sensationalism. That article contains a quote from an eyewitness: "It just happened out of nowhere. One moment they were talking, I think—just two blokes having a quiet chat in the corner of the pub, the next that man was trying to strangle him. People tried to pull him off, and he fought them all, until finally there were enough of them to overpower him. It was terrifying."

My skin prickles with cold, even though the heating in the Lodge is turned right up. Attempted *strangulation.* I remember the bruising around the guest's neck, the black-and-blue collar.

And yet what possible reason could Doug have had to kill the guest? She had only been here for two days. She was a complete stranger.

Maybe, a little voice says, he didn't need a reason. The man in the pub, according to these articles, was also believed to be a complete stranger.

There is at least one thing that doesn't fit, I tell myself. Doug's discovery of the body. Why show me the whereabouts of the body, rather than conceal it somehow? In order to control the situation?

Maybe . . . but then it would only make sense to do that if it were still possible to make it look like an accident. It is fairly obvious, even to someone who is not a doctor, that she was strangled.

There's a knock on the door. I freeze, then slam the laptop closed. With a few swift steps I'm at the door, have unlocked it. When I open it, on the other side—as I had somehow known he would be—is Doug.

32

KATIE

Two days earlier
New Year's Eve 2018

EVERYONE IS HEADING TO THEIR OWN CABINS TO GET READY for the evening. Miranda wants us all to dress up. "It's ridiculous," Samira muttered to Emma and me, "we're in the middle of nowhere, in the countryside. Funnily enough, I have other priorities besides tarting myself up—I thought we all came here to relax?"

"Oh, but I suppose it'll give it all a sense of occasion," Emma said loyally.

Besides, in matters like this there is no point in putting up any resistance. Miranda *will* get what she wants.

I don't spend the time before supper getting ready, however. I spend it in my bathroom, crouched over a little plastic stick, and then pacing the length of my cabin, wondering what I am going to do. I want to scream. But this place is so bloody quiet they'd all hear me.

Maybe, I tell myself, trying to breathe, the test was faulty somehow. I wish I had got a spare. I was too flustered in the Boots at King's Cross, though, too afraid that one of the others would see me buying it. Besides, the little sheet of instructions suggests that while it's possible for the test *not* to pick up on a positive result, the reverse pretty much never happens.

It's eight o'clock before I know it, and I pull on a black dress I just remembered to throw in the case, an old office-to-cocktails affair, and pull a brush through my hair, so hard I hurt myself.

I am not sure whether it is my imagination or not, but the dress feels tighter than it was at the office Christmas party, and when I study my reflection sideways in the mirror, I am certain that I can see a tiny protuberance where I have had nothing before. Oh God. I turn, this way and that. It's definitely there. Dread rises in me.

Now that I have noticed it, it seems unmistakable; I'm amazed that Miranda hasn't commented on it. Add this to the fact that I've noticed a little more tenderness in my breasts—and that my appetite has been up and down. And yet: How the hell did this happen? I thought I'd been so careful. Clearly not careful enough. And I don't know what I am going to do about it.

I sit back on the bed. I don't want to go. I can't do this—I can't go out there and face them all. I sit for maybe half an hour. Wondering . . . hoping . . . maybe they've forgotten all about me?

There's a knock on the door. For a moment I can almost pretend I imagined it.

"Katie? What are you doing in there? I can see you sitting on the bed!"

I go to the door and open it—what choice do I have? I feel like an animal, routed in its den. Miranda stands there, a hand on one hip. She looks incredible, of course: she's gone for a skintight gold sheath dress; the sort of thing you can only get away with if you look like Miranda, and even then probably only on New Year's Eve.

"Well . . ." She looks me up and down. *Can she see it? I'm standing front on, so probably not.* "Not very festive," she says. Then she opens the little evening bag she has slung over one arm. "Here, this will help." In a kind of daze I feel her press the lipstick onto my lips, the waxy scent of it almost overpowering.

She stands back. "There. That's better. Come on, then." She grasps my wrist, her nails grazing my skin—half drags me through the open doorway, forces my arm through hers.

I can't take this close contact right now. I extract my arm from hers. "I'm fine, thanks," I say—it comes out sharper than I had intended. "I think I can just about manage to walk there on my own."

Miranda stares at me, as shocked as if I'd just yelled at her. You see, I never answer back. She likes to tell people that, as friends, "we just don't fight." But that's not down to her, for God's sake. It's because I've never, in the past, put up any resistance.

"Look," she says, her voice low, dangerous, "I don't know what's up with you, Katie. You've been a total misery ever since we got here. It's like you're too *good* for us suddenly. Like you can't be bothered to take part. But, well, tonight you're going to. You're bloody well going to have a good time." She turns on her heel. And I find myself following her as meekly as if she had a rope around my neck, as I have done so many times before. What other choice do I have?

THERE'S A DIFFERENT FEELING THIS EVENING. LAST NIGHT IT was high spirits, a sense of camaraderie, togetherness. Tonight, the atmosphere carries a dangerous edge. It's as though that time out there, in all that wilderness, has put us on our guard. I wonder if the others can still see the deer, like me: buckling to her knees. It has become a dark thing between us, with the freighted quality of a guilty secret. We killed something together. We were all complicit, even if Emma was the one who took the shot. We did it for "fun."

Everyone—apart from me—seems to have fractured into their proper pairs, drawing back into their primary allegiances: Nick and Bo, Emma and Mark, Miranda snaking an arm around Julien's waist. At a little remove, Giles and Samira stand talking to each other in a low murmur. Miranda has persuaded them to leave Priya in the cabin tonight so we could "all be grown-ups" this evening, but judging by Samira's mutinous expression, she isn't exactly happy about it.

There's some enforced jollity as Julien carries a bottle of champagne around, pouring liberally, but everyone seems to be gulping it down, hardly tasting it, as though they are trying to drink themselves into the spirit of things. Of course, perhaps I'm imagining this: projecting onto them a tension that really exists only in my own mind. But I'm not so sure. Because I see the quick, animal, darting looks they are all giving one another—I am not alone in that. We are looking for something in each other's faces. But what is it? Familiarity? A reassuring reminder of all that holds us close? Or are we fearfully searching for some new element, glimpsed out there on that bleak mountainside? Something new and strange and violent.

D INNER IS SERVED!" EMMA CALLS FROM THE KITCHEN. IT'S A relief to have a new focus, not to have to stand around making small talk—that suddenly feels as strained and difficult as it might with complete strangers.

It's venison Wellington: although not made with the deer from earlier, I'm relieved to hear. Emma is a wonderful cook. It goes hand in hand with her incredible organization, I suppose. She has planned this whole trip, down to the very last detail. And she at least seems unchanged by whatever strange spirit has possessed everyone else: brisk and energetic as she carries the dish to the table with a flourish.

"God," Miranda says, "I'm in awe of you, Emma. Half the time, if you look in our fridge, you'll just find a bottle of champagne and half a jar of olives. It's like you're a proper adult."

Emma flushes with pleasure. Except . . . I don't think it was a compliment. It makes her look homey, sort of dull. Whereas Miranda comes out of it looking glamorous, in an unpredictable, rock-'n'-roll way.

It's not even true. Yes, she's not a good cook, but she does *do* it. But she'll never let an opportunity slip to look superior to Emma in some way.

What a bitch. I catch myself, stifle the thought. What has got into me? And, after all, *I* am a fine one to talk.

We all applaud and exclaim over the venison: the golden sheen of the pastry, the neatness of the compact parcel of meat.

I cut a morsel. It's perfectly cooked: the pastry flaky, the venison miraculously pink in the middle. But, as I prod it with my fork, a little bloody stream seeps out. I think of that deer today, staggering to her knees, the terrible groan that seemed to echo from the surrounding peaks as she went down, and I feel my stomach turn over. I take a bite, anyway, and sit there struggling to swallow. For a brief, panicked moment the food seems to catch at the back of my throat, and I think I might really choke. It takes a big gulp of my water to send it on its way, and I find myself coughing hoarsely in the aftermath.

Samira, next to me, gives me a nudge. "Are you all right?"

I nod. Emma, I see, has turned to look at me. "I hope it's okay?" she asks.

"Yes," I say, my throat raw, "it's absolutely delicious."

She gives a very small nod of her head. But she doesn't smile. I wonder if she saw the difficulty I had forcing it down: worse, my grimace of slight disgust at the sight of the bloodied meat. But I think it's more than that. Emma has never really seemed to like me much. I've tried so hard with her—perversely I've tried much harder than I might have done if she had seemed to like me. And, it should be the other way around, shouldn't it? She should make the effort with me. She should be the one looking for some kind of acceptance with Mark's oldest friends. She's certainly made the effort with Miranda, despite Miranda being an absolute bitch to her, at times.

I definitely felt a bit sorry for Emma when she joined our group. There was so much to catch up on, so many in-jokes, so much history. It was different for Bo. His Americanness, somehow, set him apart. He was exotic—a New Yorker—and besides, he studied at Stanford, so there wasn't exactly going to be an inferiority complex there. Whereas Emma went to Bath, and Miranda has always seemed determined to find little ways to lord Oxford over her, to show her up as not being quite as good as the rest of us. I don't think she wants Emma to feel bad, per se, she just wants a kind of serf-like acknowledgment of her superiority.

To her credit, Emma barely seems to notice when Miranda has a go at her. She has a robustness about her, a self-containment. I feel like she's one of those people it's easy to be friends with, because she has no baggage . . . but she's not the kind of person who would be my *best* friend. She doesn't seem to have a deeper layer; or if she does, she hides it well. Refreshing, yes, but also perhaps just a tiny bit dull. God, I'm starting to sound like Miranda.

"You know," I'd told Emma, two New Years ago, when she was very new to the group, "you really shouldn't put up with Miranda's crap."

"What do you mean?" she asked, wide-eyed.

"The way she talks to you. She's like it with all of us, to be honest. I sometimes think she has this idea that everyone was put on earth to serve her." I knew how that felt, well enough. "I love her dearly, because she has her many good qualities, too—but it's definitely one of her less admirable ones. You don't want to play up to her idea of her own superiority."

Emma frowned. "I really don't mind, Katie." There was a sharpness to her tone that I had never heard before.

"Oh," I said, "I only thought—"

"You don't need to worry about me," she repeated, "I really don't mind."

And she genuinely doesn't seem to. I watch her now, grinning away at everyone, asking Miranda where she bought her dress. Maybe I'm being oversensitive, but I have sometimes got the impression that she is just barely tolerating me, for the sake of group harmony. That under the surface, there might be real dislike. Or as close as someone like Emma comes to dislike.

It's quite upsetting, to feel yourself disliked by someone as straightforward and good—"good," yes, that's exactly the word—as Emma. Sometimes, in my more paranoid moods, I have wondered if she recognizes that there is something "off" about me. That she saw the destructiveness and the selfishness in me even before I recognized them myself.

MIRANDA IS PICKING THROUGH HER MEAL, CAREFULLY SEParating the fillet from the pastry, and then only eating half of that. She has always been very careful about her weight. Which is ridiculous, because she has pretty much the perfect figure, at least according to the glossies and the *Daily Mail*. But I remember meals at her house, and her mother taking away her plate before she had finished. "A lady," she would say, "leaves her plate unfinished and keeps her waist under twenty-five inches." And I thought I came from a dysfunctional family. For a couple of years Miranda went vegan, then she did the 5:2 for a while. And on top of that every Pilates, ballet barre, and soul cycle class offered at her upscale gym. She's obviously gorgeous, but if you ask me she'd look better with a little more weight, more softness. Already, in her thirties, she's starting to get that brittle ageing Hollywood starlet look. Oh, and I'm certain she's had Botox. You would imagine, as her best friend, I might know this for a fact either way. But she's oddly private about such things. The fact that she gets regular fake tans, for example: she'll turn up to a wedding looking as though she's spent three weeks in St. Barts. But when I comment on it she'll say something like, "Oh yes, I spent a lot of time in the sun recently—I tan so easily" and abruptly change the subject.

"He's so hot, isn't he," she's saying now, "that gamekeeper? The strong and silent type . . . Like something from a Mills and Boon novel. So skilled. I didn't realize stalking a deer was so difficult. And so *tall*. Couldn't you just climb that?"

"God yes," Samira says, to a wounded "Oi!" from Giles.

But Miranda hardly seems to notice that she's spoken. She is looking at Julien. The "tall" part seems a particularly pointed barb. Julien is many things; the one thing he is not, and never will be, is tall. "Such a *masculine* sort of man," Miranda adds. "There's something almost dangerous about him . . . But that makes him all the more attractive. You just know he'd be able to fix anything, or build you a shelter in the middle of a wood. No one has those sorts of skills anymore."

"You know what you two sound like?" Giles says. His tone is light, but I think he's a bit pissed off, too.

"What?" Miranda says playfully.

"A couple of desperate old spinsters."

I do not miss the glances at me—even Nick, for God's sake. Because if anyone is a desperate old spinster here, then it is, well: yours truly. I concentrate on getting a perfect morsel of venison and pastry onto the end of my fork.

"I think," Miranda says, undeterred, "on behalf of women everywhere, that you should try and seduce him, Katie." She says it playfully, but there's an edge to it, and I wonder what it means. She seems slightly *too much* this evening: the gold dress, her hair piled into a kind of warrior's headdress, the gleam in her eyes, her laugh just a fraction too loud.

"And get herself murdered?" Giles says, laughing. "Well, you've got to wonder, haven't you? What's a chap like that doing all alone somewhere like this? I mean, it's beautiful and tranquil and everything for a few days, but it would be pretty creepy living here all the time on your own. You'd go mad even if you weren't already."

"He's not on his own," I say. "There's that woman in the office, Heather."

"Yes," Miranda says, "but they're not together, are they? And she's probably a bit cuckoo, too. If you've chosen this life you're obviously a bit of a weirdo, or you have something to run away from."

"I think she seems perfectly normal," I say. I don't know why I'm defending them. It isn't a good idea to disagree with Miranda when she's in this sort of mood. "And he seemed perfectly harmless. And yes, I suppose he is good-looking."

"I see," Julien says, in the unconvincing manner of a kindly uncle. "That's your type is it, Katie?"

I can feel them all peering at me, as though I am a specimen at the bottom of a jar. I swallow the morsel of venison Wellington, take a long draft of my water, though I long for the wine. "Maybe it is."

AFTER WE'VE EATEN SUPPER IT'S STILL QUITE EARLY. EMMA IS doing her best to keep everyone well lubricated. She keeps insisting on getting up and topping up glasses—which is faintly embarrassing, as though she's our waitress for the evening. In spite of her efforts, conversation around the table seems to have run dry. There's a strange pause. What to do, what to fill the time with? With the ease of last night mysteriously vanished, it doesn't seem enough to sit around and reminisce together. I remind myself it always feels like this on New Year's Eve, because of all the enforced celebration. Midnight—not particularly late on any given night—suddenly seems like a faraway milestone.

"I was wondering," Samira says, "and I know it's a bit teenage . . . But we could play Truth or Dare?"

There are mingled groans.

"We're in our thirties, Samira," Nick says, raising an eyebrow. "I think we're a bit beyond Truth or Dare."

"Oh, come on," Miranda says. "Some of us here like to consider ourselves as young."

"And it could be fun?" Emma says. She's the only one whose mood doesn't seem to have changed from yesterday morning: she's all enthusiasm, flushed with pleasure from the meal's success. She's made a proper effort this evening—she can't match Miranda's glamour, but her off-the-shoulder gunmetal dress has a bit of a shimmer to it, and she's colored her lips in bright red. It's almost a perfect match for the tiny smear of blood that she's missed, up above her ear next to the hairline, a leftover from this afternoon's hunt.

In the absence of another suggestion, everyone seems to accept that this is what we are doing now: playing Truth or Dare. There's a palpable relief, in fact, that we have a structure for the next part of our evening, something to keep us occupied.

We sit down around the table. Emma grabs an empty wine bottle and spins it. It lands on Bo. "Dare," he says.

"Kiss Mark," Miranda says.

Bo wrinkles his nose. "Do I have to?"

Mark looks, frankly, terrified. But Bo leans over, matter-of-factly, and plants his mouth on Mark's. And for a moment—blink-and-you'd-miss-it—I think Mark responds, his mouth moving sensually under Bo's. It's kind of hot. I see Nick frown. He's noticed it, too.

Everyone's laughing. But there is a new tension in the air, now, a frisson of sex.

Bo spins the bottle. It lands on Miranda. "Truth," she says, with a slightly vacant smile. Between this, and the lazy, sleepy look of her eyes, I can tell she's already had quite a lot to drink.

"Okay," Nick says, "I've got one. Have you ever slept with anyone else around this table?"

Miranda giggles. "Have I ever slept with anyone else?" she says—and there's a slight slur on the "slept." "I suppose you mean apart from my *husband*?"

"Yes," Nick says. There's an intensity in the way he's looking at her: it reminds me of a cat watching a bird.

"Um . . ." She puts a finger up to her lips—though the first time she misses and catches her chin—in a pantomime of thought. "I suppose in that case I would have to say . . . yes."

There's a stunned silence. That can't be true, can it? If so, I've never heard anything about it. How do *I* not know? I glance at Julien, but he doesn't look particularly surprised. Does he know? Who can it have been? I study all the faces around the table, but no one's expression seems to give anything away. Mark? He's the most likely, I suppose, but I feel that would have come out, somehow, before now. Still, I think of him spending all that time hanging around college, waiting to give Miranda some message from Julien. There would have been opportunity.

Miranda shrugs at us all. "I'm not going to tell you anything else, so you might as well spin again."

"Come on," Samira says, "you *have* to tell us."

"Yes," Bo says, "you can't tell us that and not say any more."

"Yes I can," Miranda says, with a sly smile. "I've answered the question. I've told my truth."

Giles hands Miranda the bottle. "Right. Next."

The gleam in Miranda's eye has grown brighter. After her revelation, the stakes feel higher, the air charged. She spins, and it lands on Mark.

"Dare," he says, almost before it has even fully stopped.

"Okay." Miranda thinks for a moment. "Drink this." She holds out a bottle of Dom Pérignon.

"The whole thing?" Emma stares. "You can't do that."

"It used to be my party trick," Mark says. "Have I never told you? A whole bottle in ten minutes."

I remember. I also remember the mess afterward. Mark is one of those people who shouldn't drink. It makes some people emotional, some belligerent, others angry—you can guess which group Mark falls into.

"I'll do it," Miranda says, getting to her feet. She pops the cork with an air of ceremony, making sure to do it carefully so that none spills. Then she walks toward Mark. "Kneel down," she says, half seductress, half sergeant major. "Open wide." He does what she says, and she upends the bottle, with no warning and very little gentleness, shoving the neck between his parted lips. He makes a kind of gagging sound, but she doesn't relent. If anything, I think I see her give the base a further thrust with one manicured hand.

Mark gulps the liquid, his throat working hard and his eyes streaming, red, almost bloodied-looking. Julien and Giles are egging him on: "Get it down you!" and "Chug, chug, chug . . ."—remnants of chants from rugby socials, no doubt. The rest of us just watch.

His nose is running with snot, like a crying child's. He makes more of those gagging sounds, and beneath them there is a kind of low, animal whine that makes the hairs on my arms stand to attention. For all that, most of the booze is frothing over his chin and soaking into his smart shirt, the crotch of his suit trousers.

"Oh God," Samira says, "he's probably had enough."

"For fuck's sake," Miranda barks, completely ignoring her. "Drink it. You're not drinking it."

I think of how dense the bubbles are in champagne, how painful it is to down even a glass of the stuff.

It's horrible to watch, a grotesque imitation of a sexual act. But for some reason it is both impossible to look away and to do anything to stop it. The guys have stopped cheering him on now, their chants dwindling to an uneasy silence. Even Emma doesn't move, doesn't make a sound to help her boyfriend. We sit watching as though stunned, mesmerized by this obscene spectacle.

Finally, it's drained. Slowly, almost reluctantly, Miranda withdraws the bottle. She gives it a slap with the flat of one hand, and a few more drops fall out, one of them splashing into Mark's eye in a final indignity, the punctuation to the insult.

Mark is wheezing, retching, doubled over, his hands on his knees for support. For a horrible moment it looks as if he's going to vomit. Samira, nearest to him, puts a reassuring hand on his back. He shrugs her off with a violent jerk of his shoulders. We wait, silent, no one saying a word, to see how this will play out. Finally, after what feels like a long time, Mark raises his head. He gives us a weak, unconvincing grin, and puts one hand into the air like a victor. He must know, surely, that whatever we just witnessed was in no way *his* victory. Still, there's a collective sigh of relief. The others cheer. It was a game! Ha, ha—Miranda, you're so brutal. Mark—well done, chap!

When Mark goes to spin the bottle, his hand shakes.

It lands, as I had somehow known it would, on me.

"Dare," I say. I don't want to do one: Miranda's dares have always been notoriously horrible. But I'd take pretty much any dare over a truth right now.

"Mark?" Samira asks, turning to him. "Got any ideas?"

Mark puts a hand to his throat, and tries to speak, but only a hoarse kind of wheeze comes out. He shakes his head, and defers his choice.

"Fine," Miranda says, matter-of-fact, apparently unconcerned by the fact that she's the cause of this indignity. She steeples her fingers, then goes to Emma, whispers in her ear. Jesus Christ, it's like something from school. How can Emma be so friendly with Miranda, after what she just inflicted on her boyfriend? But perhaps we really are pretending it was just fun and games, no harm meant or done.

Emma is nodding. "Or," she says, and whispers something in Miranda's ear in return.

Bo laughs. "Going to share with us?"

Emma shakes her head at him playfully. Miranda doesn't even bother glancing in his direction. She is looking straight at me. I feel a chill go through me.

"Into the loch," she says. "Ten seconds, fully submerged. Then out."

I stare at her. She can't be serious. "Miranda, it's below freezing out there. There's ice on the surface."

"Yes," Nick cuts in. "Miranda—she'll freeze to death."

I expect Samira to have my back, too. But she's frowning into space as though her mind is somewhere else completely.

Miranda smiles, blithely, and shakes her head. "The manager told me she swims in there most days, even in winter. Besides, we'll be ready for you with a towel. You'll be fine, Katie."

I stare at her. I can't believe she's actually going to make me do this. But her eyes are blank, expressionless. "Go on," she says, with a little nod of encouragement. "Strip."

So often, at school, Miranda was my vanquisher: belittling the girls who tried to have a go at me. But there was another side, too. Miranda, the bully. When she wanted to be she could be far crueler than any of the classroom bitches. It was rare, but it did happen. The flicking of a switch, the flexing of her muscles. Just to remind me who was in charge.

I have one particular memory—one of those you just can't shake, however much you try. Year nine. In the changing room before hockey. One of the girls—Sarah—was complaining about the fact that Miss wouldn't let her sit it out, despite it being the first day of her period. "She says it's supposedly 'good for' me. Says it will make it better. But I know it won't. It's not fair." The others: nodding and murmuring in sympathy.

I remembered the packet of paracetamol in my rucksack: dug it out and offered it to her. Sarah was one of the less terrible ones. Sometimes we sat together in class: the ones I didn't have with Miranda, of course. She looked up at me and smiled as she took the pills. "Thanks, Katie." I felt a little warmth, spreading through my chest.

And then Miranda's voice, clear as a bell. "But I suppose Katie wouldn't understand. Seeing as she hasn't even got hers yet." All the other girls turned to me in shock, in fascination. Looking at me as though I were exactly what I felt: a freak show. It had been a sign, I was sure of it—that there was something definitely, definitively wrong with me. Fourteen and no period to speak of. I had confided in Miranda in the strictest confidence. At the time she had reassured me, said she was certain fourteen wasn't that late, in the grand scheme of things.

And then she had used it to humiliate me. As a way of keeping me in check.

She's doing this now.

This is absurd. I'm thirty-three years old. I have people who respect and depend on me at work. I have responsibilities. I'm a brilliant lawyer, in fact—I know that—I never let the other side win. I will not allow myself to be humiliated like this.

Fine, I think, looking at Miranda. I see you. I raise you. As though it is nothing at all in the world, I wriggle out of my dress, so I'm standing in front of them all in my underwear. I've somehow managed to wear good underwear, in fact: yellow silk, lace trimmed. New. I see Miranda's eyebrows rise a fraction. She was expecting some greige overwashed horrors, I suspect, in order to compound my humiliation. I wonder if they have noticed my belly. Perhaps it can be explained away by post-dinner bloat. I hunch over, all the same, as I walk across the room without a single look at any of them, open the front door.

Fuck. It is even colder than earlier, if that is possible. It's so cold that it actually hurts. I can feel my skin shrinking. I can't think about it, or I won't be able to do it. I have to be steely, my best, strongest self. The water is only a few yards away, down the path. It looks black as ink. But I can see small pale fragments of ice, gossamer thin, on its surface. I walk toward it and simply keep going as the water covers my ankles, my calves, my stomach, then I plunge downward, up to my neck. Unbelievable cold. It feels as if I'm drowning, though my head is above the surface. The cold is forcing all the air from my lungs; I'm breathing too quickly, but I can't seem to draw any breath in. And then, finally, I get myself under control. I turn and look at them all, watching me now, from the bank. All of them cheering and whooping, except Miranda. She's just watching me.

I look straight back at her, as I tread water. I hate you, I think. I hate you. I don't feel bad anymore. You deserve everything that is coming to you.

33

EMMA

FIND KATIE A TOWEL FROM THE LOO IN THE LODGE. SHE'S SO cold that her teeth are chattering with a sound like someone shaking dice. In the light of the living room her lips are bluish. But it's her eyes that are most disturbing. I know this look, it is that of someone on the edge. I've seen it in Mark. I saw it that day at the racecourse.

"I hate her," she says, in a hiss. "I actually hate her. I can't believe she just made me do that. You don't know her properly, Emma—so perhaps you can't understand. You don't know what she's capable of."

Actually, I think, I know her a lot better than you're always trying to make out. Who has been there for her recently, when you've dropped off the planet? And I certainly know what *you're* capable of, Katie Lewis.

I don't say this, of course. Instead I grit my teeth and say, "How about a glass of champagne? That will warm you up, won't it?"

"No. I don't want a glass of champagne. Besides, hasn't your boyfriend drunk it all?" She's spitting the words out. I stare at her. I've never seen her like this. I'm not sure I've ever actually seen Katie angry.

"Look, Katie, I'm sure she didn't mean it. She's just had a lot to drink, and she thought it would be funny."

"It was fucking dangerous," she growls. "Do you have any idea how cold that water is?"

"Come on, Katie. It's about to be a new year: 2019. A *whole new year*. Try and forget about it? I'm sure we've all done things we aren't proud of, recently." I fix her with a look, just enough to give her pause. She swallows, and then bows her head, as though she is conceding something.

"I just really want everyone to have a good time," I say. "I've been planning this for so long."

"Yes," she says, chastened. "I know. Sorry, Emma."

I usher her into the loo, persuade her to change back into her clothes. Suddenly she is obedient as a child.

I find a record at random and put it on the player, cranking it up to full volume. It's Candi Staton, "You Got the Love." My favorite song. It's like it was meant to be.

And it has the required effect. Everyone starts dancing. Even Katie—albeit somewhat halfheartedly.

Miranda is pretty drunk now. But she's still a better dancer than anyone else here, swaying in the middle of the room, her gold dress incandescent with light. I stand up to dance with her, mirroring her moves, and she gives me a big grin. Then her smile wavers, falters.

"What is it?"

"Sho weird . . ." (She's slurring her words now, using Sean Connery *S*'s.) She squints at me. "But I feel like this has all happened before. Do you ever get that? When you could swear that you remember this exact moment happening in the past?"

Typical of Miranda, bless her, to think déjà vu is an experience unique to herself. "Yes," I say, "sometimes."

"It's this song . . ." She frowns. "I really mean it. I know we've danced to it somewhere before. Don't you feel like this has all already happened?" She's looking at me, questioningly. I don't know what to say, so I laugh. If I'm honest, she's scaring me a little bit. I'm relieved when she spots Julien over my shoulder.

"Julien," she says. "Dance with me." She reaches for him, her hands groping at his shoulders.

He humors her for a few minutes, swaying obediently to the music, his hands on her hips, but there is a curious lack of intimacy about the pose. He looks bored, if anything. But it all makes sense now, of course.

E VERYONE SUDDENLY SEEMS VERY DRUNK. I FEEL LIKE THE only one still in control of my faculties—apart from Katie, perhaps. Mark has seized the deer's head from the wall and is parading around with it, wearing it like a mask, pretending to charge at people. I can see how drunk he is after downing that bottle, his movements uncoordinated. Samira shrieks—something between laughter and real terror—and ducks away from him, falling back onto one of the sofas.

"Mark," I shout, "put that back." But he doesn't hear me—or he ignores me. There is no reasoning with him when he's like this.

Giles, meanwhile, is strolling around the room, drinking straight from an open bottle of champagne. As though struck by sudden inspiration, he puts his thumb in the end and begins to shake it, furiously—like a Formula 1 driver. Then he lets go, aiming for Julien. Julien cowers beneath the spray—a fountain of champagne—as it soaks the front of his shirt, his groin. A good deal of it missed him, though. I see it flooding onto the sheepskin rug, the rich fabric of the sofa . . .

"Stop—" I shout, running toward them. "Stop!" But they're completely oblivious to me. In their drunkenness they seem somehow outsized, their actions bigger, more dramatic. Now Julien leaps at Giles, catching him by the front of his shirt and yanking down, the shirt ripping open, buttons spraying everywhere, landing with little pinging sounds. Mark turns and sees them. He drops the deer's head, like a child who has caught sight of others playing with better toys. He cannons toward them as though not wanting to be left out, tackling both of them about the necks. The three of them lurch, struggle, and then topple. There's a crash as they come down, straight into the glass coffee table in the middle of the room. The dancers—Miranda, Nick, Bo, and Samira—stop what they're doing and look over. I watch as the glass cracks down the middle, slowly, almost ponderously, and then shatters into fragments, which skid everywhere. The three of them surface, blearily.

"Oh, fuck," Giles says. Then he giggles.

"Doesn't matter," Julien slurs. "Don't worry, Emma"—he looks about for me—"I'll pay for it." He stretches out both his arms. "I'll pay for all of it." He puts out a hand to Mark, who has somehow managed to clamber to his feet. "Help me up, mate."

Mark takes it. He begins to pull Julien to his feet. Then, just as he's almost lifted him to full height, he lets go, so that he crashes back to the floor. I wonder if I'm the only one who saw that it wasn't an accident.

"Sorry, mate," he says.

Julien is looking up at him, and he's trying to laugh. But his eyes, I see, are intense, almost black.

It's all going horribly wrong. I look about me at the wreckage of the room, to the beautifully dressed dining table beyond—which seems to be mocking me. This is not anything like what I had planned. Then, on the wall clock, I see the time. I could weep with relief.

"Hey," I shout, making a funnel of my hands over my mouth, knowing this might just catch their attention like nothing else, "it's nearly midnight!"

34

MIRANDA

WE STUMBLE OUTSIDE TO THE EDGE OF THE LOCH. JULIEN IS hunched over himself—I think he might have hurt himself a bit when he was messing around with Giles and Mark just now. They broke a table, for Christ's sake—they're like children. Katie is still wrapped in one of the big woolen blankets, over the top of her clothes. She can't *still* be cold, can she? She's always been so bloody fragile. Still, I feel quite bad about my behavior. Not for Mark—he had that coming, ever since last night. But Katie hasn't done anything to me, really, beyond being a bit distant and not much fun. Sometimes these impulses overtake me—the urge to push things a bit further . . . even the urge to wound. I can't stop myself, it's like a compulsion.

I'd like to say something to Katie, to apologize, maybe, but I can't find the words. The champagne has hit me really hard. My breath is misting in the air, but I can't actually feel the cold, wrapped as I am in my own little blanket of booze. I feel numb. I'd forgotten I had so much wine before the champagne. My thoughts are jumbled, my mind fuggy. Maybe it would be better if I were sick.

The countdown to midnight begins. "A minute!" Emma shouts, looking at her watch.

I stare up at the stars. The new year. What is it going to bring for me?

"Thirty seconds!"

I look around at the others. They're all grinning, but their faces, in the light thrown from the Lodge, look strange, spectral, and their smiles look like snarls.

Mark stands poised with a new bottle of champagne. He hasn't glanced in my direction once, since the game. I'm used to having his eyes on me. I don't miss it, of course I don't. But at the same time, as I stand here in the dark, I have this feeling of being invisible . . . untethered . . . like a balloon that might suddenly float up into that starlit sky.

"Twenty seconds . . ." The others are chanting now. "Nineteen, eighteen . . ."

I don't like it, all of a sudden. It feels like the countdown to something terrible . . . the explosion of a bomb. I imagine the little red lights blinking down.

"Five, four, three, two . . ."

"Happy New Year!" The rest of us parrot it in response. Giles is fumbling with a lighter at the shoreline.

"Be careful!" Samira calls, her voice high and shrill.

"Come on!" I shout, trying to shake off the bad feeling. "We're all waiting!"

Finally, Giles seems to manage to light the thing. He staggers backward. Then there's a promising fizz, and then a whoosh, and a big red rocket erupts from the ground with a sound like a scream and explodes over the loch. The water reflects it: a thousand tiny fragments of fire. It's beautiful. I try to focus on it, but everything is spinning. The silence afterward is so . . . heavy. The dark around us is so thick, like I could reach out . . . touch it. If we were in London—or anywhere near civilization, for that matter—we would be able to see all the other firework displays going off around us. Reminding us of other people, other life. But here we are absolutely alone.

I can still hear the scream of the firework inside my head. But it no longer sounds the same, it sounds like a person. And I have this thought . . . that it wasn't like a firework at all. More like one of those safety flares. SOS. Fired from the deck of a sinking ship.

Julien comes back over to us. "It's not quite Westminster fireworks," he says.

"But who wants Westminster—all those sweaty bodies pressed together—when you can have this?" Emma asks. "This place"— she spreads her arms wide—"and best friends." She links her arm with mine, and smiles at me, a proper, warm smile. I want to hug her. Thank fuck for Emma.

And then she begins to sing—her voice is surprisingly good. I try and join in.

> Should old acquaintance be forgot,
> and never brought to mind?
> Should old acquaintance be forgot,
> and days of auld lang syne?

OK, I know I've had a lot to drink but together, out here in the dark and silence, our voices sound beautiful, and there's something vulnerable about the noise. The trees around us are so thick and black. Anyone could be watching us, going through this little ritual together.

It must be all the booze, I think, that is making me feel so . . . strange. There's a loud bang, and I jump with shock. But it's just Nick opening another bottle of Dom. He pours it into glasses. As he passes one to Katie, I see her face, and it makes me shiver. What's wrong with her? It can't all be due to her dunk in the loch, can it? She doesn't even look at the glass of champagne being passed to her, and it slips from her grasp. "Whoops!" Bo says, catching it. "That was nearly a goner!"

Nick raises his glass. "To old friends!" he says. He looks straight at me while he says it. I don't know why, but I have to look away. I down my glass.

There's a strange pause, now. No one seems to know what to do next. The landscape around us is so quiet in the lapse. I feel my stomach do an unpleasant somersault; the ground beneath me seems to shift under my feet. Wow. I'm *definitely* drunk.

"We should kiss," Samira says. "Where's the kissing?" She reaches up and smacks a kiss on Julien's cheek. "Happy New Year!"

Mark turns to me. I don't want him to kiss me. When he leans in, I duck so that his lips barely graze my ear. I catch the flash of annoyance, even anger, in his expression. I think of his eyes last night, the menace of his tone.

I turn to Julien. His face is completely in shadow from this angle. I cannot make out his features, or his expression: just the dark gleam of his eyes. When I lean in to kiss him—on the mouth, of course—I have this . . . feeling that he, too, is a stranger. This man with whom I have spent so much of my life, with whom I have shared a house and a bed, beside whom I have slept most nights. How little it takes, I think, just some shadows, really, to make ourselves unknown to each other. Wow. Alcohol always makes me think deep thoughts.

"Happy New Year," I say.

"Happy New Year," he says. And I'm not sure, but I think he turns slightly as I reach up to him, so that my lips land on the very corner of his mouth. Just like I did, with Mark.

Nick is on my other side. "Nick!" I say, with forced jollity. "Happy New Year again! Come here." I put out my arms; he lets me hug him. He smells amazing, like the cologne counter at Liberty. "Why have we never been better friends, Nick?" I ask. It comes out sounding pretty fucking needy. I didn't quite mean to say it out loud.

He steps back, his hands on either side of my shoulders: to everyone else he might be holding me in an affectionate embrace.

He looks straight into my eyes as he says, "Oh, Miranda, I think you know the answer to that."

It's the way he says it: so quiet, under his breath, so that no one else can hear. I suddenly feel cold in a way that I don't think has anything to do with the freezing air. I take a step back.

I drink a bit more. Then *much* more, as the others go on partying around me. I want to get back into the swing of things. I want to get rid of this feeling. A kind of fear, deep in my belly, deeper, somehow, than anything I felt last night, in the bathroom. I feel I am clinging to a cliff edge and slowly, slowly, my fingers are loosening their grip. That beneath me is . . . nothing, the loss of everything . . . everything important.

Bo slides up to me. "You all right?" He's always been the one to notice when someone isn't okay. It's because he's quiet—he observes, while the rest of us are busy making lots of noise. And he's kind. He's so unlike Nick, with all his sharpness.

"Yes," I say.

"Want to go have a drink of water?"

I know he's saying I need it because I'm drunk, but actually I do feel a bit weird. "All right." I follow him into the kitchen and watch dumbly while he runs me a glass from the tap. When he hands it to me I say, "Thanks. I might just sit by myself for a bit, if that's okay."

"Okay . . . ," he says, hovering.

"Go!" I shoo him away.

"All right," he says, and then, with a teacher-like waggle of his finger: "But I'm coming back in a little while if you haven't reappeared."

"Fine." And then I remember to say, "Thank you, Bo."

"Forget it, darling. The number of times someone helped me out like this—I owe the universe a great deal."

"But, Bo," I say, before I can stop myself, "I'm not a junkie. I've

THE HUNTING PARTY 213

just had a bit too much champagne." Oops. I didn't quite mean to say that.

Something in his face changes, his eyes going all narrow. I've never seen Bo look like this before. I've always thought there must be someone else in there: someone darker. And, from what Katie told me once, someone capable of some fairly out-there behavior. It's like he's been wearing this . . . mask, and I've just seen behind it. I suddenly feel a bit more sober.

"I'm sorry, Bo," I say. "I didn't mean it—I don't know what's wrong with me. I've had too much to drink. Please . . ." I reach out a hand to him.

"It's okay," he says, his tone light. But he doesn't take my out-stretched hand.

I WAIT UNTIL HE'S GONE, AND THEN I CLICK OFF THE LIGHT AND let my legs collapse under me like a folding chair, so I'm sitting on the floor. I'll just rest here a bit, until I sober up . . . What the fuck is wrong with me? How could I have said that to *Bo* of all people, when he was trying to help me?

Katie once told me I was "careless." "You say things off-the-cuff," she said, "without thinking. The only problem is people who don't know you might think you mean them."

She knows me so well. But I'm not sure even she knows how I hate myself, later on, after making one of these so-called careless remarks. The way, at Oxford, I'd lie in my bed the morning after a night out and think, think, think about how I'd behaved: everything I'd said and done.

"Everyone falls in love with you," Samira told me, once. "They can't bloody help it."

But, I have often wondered, do they actually like me?

I'll just let my eyes close here, just for a little bit . . .

'M WOKEN BY THE SOUND OF A VOICE: LOW, URGENT.

"Miranda?" It's a man's voice, little more than a hoarse whisper, as though he doesn't want to be heard. Who is it? "Julien?" I squint through the gloom. I'm confused by the dark. In the distance I can hear the rumble of voices . . . the others, I realize. My head's swimming.

He steps forward, and finally, I see who it is. I've never seen him like this. There's a strange, almost threatening, expression on his face.

35

DOUG

H E'S SITTING IN THE ONE ARMCHAIR IN HIS COTTAGE. EVERY so often he reaches over and pours a little more from the bottle of single malt. His aim is to get so drunk that he simply passes out, or anesthetizes himself, but his mind is still obstinately clear.

New Year's Eve. Another year clicking over. They say that time is the greatest healer, but it hasn't done much good in his own experience. Events from six months ago are a blur—the days run into one another here, with little to differentiate them other than the slowly changing seasons. But that day in his past—three years now—is as clear as if it happened yesterday, an hour ago.

Beyond the window there is an explosion. He feels his whole body go rigid with shock; he almost drops to the floor, his heart feels like it's going to punch its way out through his chest. Then he realizes what it is. A firework. He fucking hates fireworks. Still, after all these years, they have this effect on him.

T HE DAY YOUR LIFE CHANGES FOREVER. DOES ANYONE SEE IT coming? He definitely didn't. It had been an uneventful few weeks. Things had settled into a pattern, had started to feel as normal as you can get in a place like Helmand Province. All the men had relaxed, perhaps got a bit sloppy. It's impossible not to, even though you're trained in how to keep yourself alert. But when you have to be more "on" than the human body is ever meant to be, for four days in a row, it's impossible not to switch off when the threat level lessens.

It was a routine excursion. As usual as a police officer's beat. Just to check that everything was as it should be. The men making a patrol of the street, him up above as cover. Doug was one of two snipers; they had to take turns, shifts, to make sure that they were really focused, and this one was his watch.

The men were just below him, coming around the corner in the armored trucks, when the spotter shouted out to him. A small child—a little boy—running from the other end of the street. Everything froze, apart from the small running figure. Doug realized the boy looked bulky. He was wearing a jacket several sizes too big for him. And he was running straight toward the men. He was only about five years old. Hardly even a proper little boy yet, hardly older than a toddler. But immediately Doug was thinking: bomb. He knew what he had to do. He took aim through the viewfinder. Tracked the boy. His finger was on the trigger. He was ready. But he wanted to get a better visual. He couldn't see any proper evidence of a device, other than that bulky jacket.

He had perhaps ten seconds. Then nine, then five, then three. The spotter was screaming at him, but it was as if he was underwater: his brain and body seemed to have slowed. He could not shoot.

And then everything exploded. The men. The trucks. Half the street. All in the same second that he finally managed to exert the required pressure on the trigger.

The therapist he saw told him that his reaction had been completely understandable—that the situation had been an impossible one. And yet this didn't help him explain it to himself, or to the families of the dead men who visited him at night. This is why he does not sleep: because as long as he is awake, he does not have to see their faces, and answer to their silent interrogation. Though lately, they have begun arriving even in his waking hours. He sees them approaching in the middle of the landscape. So real that he swears he could reach out and touch them.

This is why he is lucky to have this job. In any other, he might not be able to hide it. Someone would notice that he was acting oddly, and report it, and that would be it. But here there is no one to notice. There's Heather, in the office, but she gives him a wide berth. And perhaps she has some hiding of her own to do. Why else would a young, thirtysomething, attractive woman come and live in a place like this on her own? He doesn't ask her her reasons, and she in turn doesn't ask him his. It's an unspoken, mutual agreement.

He was lucky that the boss didn't care about the other thing, even though he had to declare it on his application. "The boss," said the suit who interviewed him, "doesn't mind about all that. He wants you to feel you have a clean slate here." A clean slate. If only.

HE SWITCHES ON THE TV AND IMMEDIATELY REGRETS IT. ALL it shows, of course, are thousands of happy faces: families snug together on the bank of the Thames, eyes lit with red and gold flames as they watch the display. He wonders what Heather is doing, over in her cabin. He has seen her lights on, late at night. He knows she does not sleep well, either.

He could go around, with the bottle of whiskey, as he has thought of doing on more nights than he would care to admit. He recalls that night, when she opened her door to him—when she had heard the sound. He remembers everything about it, a picture clear in his mind: the flush of her cheeks, her dark hair mussed about her head, the giant pajamas swamping her. She had invited him in—and then she had blushed, as she realized how it sounded. He had refused, of course. But he has imagined following her in. He has imagined a lot more, too, in the lurid, sleepless small hours of the night, when he has glimpsed the light on in her cottage. He has imagined pushing her up against the wall, her wrapping her legs around his waist, how her mouth might taste on his . . . He will not go around there. Not tonight, not any night. Someone like him has a duty to stay away from someone like her. She does not deserve the catastrophe that he represents.

That sort of life is closed to him, now. He leans over, toward the fire. He raises a hand, and, with the dispassionate regard of a scientist, holds it in the flames, so that the skin sears like steak.

36

HEATHER

Now
January 2, 2019

DOUG STANDS IN THE DOORWAY, FROWNING AT ME.

"Come in, Doug," I say. "Close the door." He comes to stand in front of the desk, towering over me.

"Doug," I say. "I shouldn't have done this. But I have something to confess. I googled your name. I found out about the court case."

He says nothing. His eyes are on the floor.

"What happened?" *Explain it to me,* I think. *What you did. The violence. Make me understand.* Although I'm not sure that he can. I can't see how there can be any way he could explain it.

He takes a breath, and begins.

He had been in a bar in Glasgow, he says, with friends, about three months after returning home from his tour. "Tour of Afghanistan, six months." He'd had one too many, or rather several too many, but he was feeling loose and relaxed for the first time in as long as he could remember. And then this bloke swaggered over to him. "Hey," he said. "I recognize your face. I know you from somewhere."

"I doubt it." He'd barely glanced at the guy.

"No," the man said, "I do." He took out his phone, did something on it. He held the screen up. Facebook, a photograph, it was him. It was in Helmand. "My best mate, Glen Wilson. I knew it. This is you, isn't it? In the photo with him. I know it's you."

He could hardly bring himself to look at the photograph. "Then I'm sure you're right," he'd said, feeling the beer sour in his stomach, still just trying to brush the guy off. Maybe this would placate him. "It must be me."

"So you were there?" The man was standing too close.

"Yes, I was there. I knew Glen. He was a great guy." He wasn't, actually. Not one of the best—always picking fights—but you didn't speak ill of the dead. And he knew so very many dead.

"You were in his regiment?" The man's face, beer-stale, was squared up to his own. He was speaking too loudly. There was a pugnacious twist to his face, his shoulders set. Doug could sense the interest of those surrounding them quickening in the background, the irresistible lure of confrontation. *Something's going on.*

"Yes," he said, trying to stay measured, to speak calmly, to counteract the man's tone. The therapist had taught him some breathing exercises—he could try those. "I was."

"But I don't understand," the bloke said, smiling, except it wasn't a smile at all, it was more like a snarl. "I thought everyone in that regiment was killed. I thought they were all surrounded, and blown up by the Taliban."

Doug closed his eyes. *It was al-Qaeda, actually.* "They were. Most of us . . ."

"Then how did you manage to get away, eh, mate? Look at me, I'm talking to you. How are you standing here, alive and well, drinking a fucking beer, *mate*? While my best friend is lying dead in Durka Durkistan? Can you explain that to me?"

He could feel something rising inside him. Something dangerous, rapidly growing outside his control. "I don't have to explain it to you. Mate." He tried breathing in through his nose, out through his mouth. It didn't seem to be working.

The man took another step forward. "I think you do, actually. And we've got all night. I'm not going anywhere until you explain it all to me, piece by fucking piece. Because I loved that guy like a brother. And from where I'm standing, shall I tell you what it looks like?"

"What?" he managed—he was still fighting it, the thing rising in him. "What does it look like?"

The bloke prodded him, hard, in the center of his chest. "It looks like you're a fucking coward."

That was when the mist had come up over him: the red mist they talk about—though it was more like a flood. If anything, he was most purely himself in that moment—more than he had been in months. More so than he had been since the good days at the beginning of the tour.

He had lunged forward and grabbed the man by the front of his shirt. "What's your name?"

The man gulped, but didn't speak.

"What's your name, *laddie*? Forgotten how to speak?"

The man had made a kind of garbled noise in his throat, and Doug had realized then he was actually holding his collar too tightly for him to get any words out. He relaxed his grip infinitesimally, and roared in the bloke's face: "What's your fucking name?"

The man's friends, it seemed, weren't interested in helping him out. "Some mates you've got, eh?" He looked at them. He felt as though he could take all of them on, if necessary, and he wondered if they knew it, too.

"It's—it's Adrian."

"Well. Let me tell you, *Adrian*. I don't think you should go meddling in things you don't understand, got it? I don't have to explain myself to anyone—especially not a little dipshit like you. What do you do for a living?"

"I'm—ah—ah—an accountant."

"Right. An accountant." He gave the bloke a shake, and he whimpered. He couldn't be bothered, he realized; suddenly he just felt tired, and very sober. The flood was ebbing away. This man wasn't worth his energy. He let him go. "Do yourself—do everyone—the favor, and stop meddling in things you can't possibly understand. Yeah?"

There was no answer. The man was massaging his throat. But he nodded, twice.

Doug's hand ached. He flexed it. He wasn't proud of what he had done, but at least he had stopped himself. Then he heard, sotto voce, "Fucking coward."

That was when he had lost it properly, according to the eyewitnesses, of which there were many: it was a crowded bar, after all. They said they thought he was trying to kill the bloke. The police had to drag him off him. Adrian Campbell. That was his full name. There had been extenuating circumstances, to a degree. Campbell had a history of involving himself in brawls, and generally disrupting the peace. There was the nature of the insult—put in context with his own, previously undiagnosed condition: Post Traumatic Stress Disorder, making him not fully in charge of his own actions.

He knew otherwise. Unsurprisingly, his lawyer advised him not to mention this in court. The sentence was two hundred and fifty hours' community service, and the sessions with the psychiatrist. He thought, when it came to the latter, that he probably would have preferred to stay in prison.

OKAY," I SAY, WHEN DOUG FINISHES. BUT IT'S NOT REALLY okay. I'm not okay. I don't know what to feel about it. On the one hand there is the fact that, for all its violence, the story has a strange kind of logic to it. He was suffering from PTSD, and he was viciously provoked. From what he says, that man was trying to get a rise out of him, pushing all his buttons. I suppose it at least provides some context for the horror I read on the Internet. But there's a small voice that's also saying: *You are drawn to this man, in spite of yourself—therefore you are trying to excuse the inexcusable.* Because his blunt, even dispassionate, account of the incident has illustrated exactly what he is capable of. Far more graphically, somehow, than any of those lurid column inches could.

What exactly the boss thought he was doing employing me here with a man who had done such a thing as my sole other co-worker, I don't know, but that's another matter. The important question is, does it make him capable of killing that guest? No, of course it doesn't. At least . . . probably not. Hopefully not.

Unless, of course, she provoked him.

37

EMMA

One day earlier
New Year's Day 2019

THE PARTY BY THE LOCH HAS SUDDENLY DIMINISHED. GILES told us he was going to check on Priya, Katie has gone to get another jumper. It's too cold to sit out here much longer.

"Crap," Bo says, "Miranda still hasn't come back. I bet she's passed out. She told me to leave her . . . and to be honest, she isn't her best self right now."

"Leave her," says Nick. "She could do with sleeping a bit of it off."

"I don't know," Bo says, "she was in a pretty bad way—"

"I'll go," I say.

It's dark and very quiet when I step into the Lodge, so much so that I assume Miranda can't be here at first. Then I hear the voices. Something makes me stop; there's an intimacy to the darkened room that makes me feel I shouldn't disturb them. One voice is low, hoarse, almost a whisper. The other drunken, belligerent. "I had to tell the truth. Duh. It was Truth or Dare."

"No you didn't. You know you didn't. You were doing it to wind me up."

A laugh, sharp and mean. "Believe it or not, Giles, I didn't think of you *once*."

"Fine—exactly. You didn't think. You don't. And what about Julien?"

"Oh . . . he won't think anything of it. I told him I slept with Katie once, to turn him on. He has this whole little fantasy about us—slutty schoolgirls. Chill out. She's *never* going to guess it was you, Giles."

"If you hadn't noticed, there aren't that many candidates here. It wouldn't take a genius. Samira knows we were in the same tutor group together."

"Oh, for fuck's sake. I don't know why you're getting your knickers in such a twist. It happened a million fucking years ago."

"Except not so much so that you could helpfully forget about it for one stupid bloody game. If Samira found out about us—even though it happened a long time ago—it would be really, really bad. She had a lot of trouble, after Priya was born, more than you know. And she's always had this suspicion, this idea that something might have happened. That I have a thing about you. Which is completely ridiculous, of course."

"Is it?" Miranda says now. "Is it, Giles? What about that party—"

"For God's sake, yes. What are you trying to say? Don't look at me like that. Look . . . we've all had a lot to drink. I think it's probably time we all went to bed. I *know* you're not going to say anything to her. I just got worried, for a second . . . when we were playing that stupid game."

"No. I don't think so. Can't promise anything, though. Might be good for your marriage—a little test. Might be refreshing for us all. Show you aren't quite as bloody perfect as you think you are."

"For God's sake, Miranda." He's practically hissing now. "You know what? One of these days you're going to go too far."

Then, suddenly, there's a groan: a deep, animal sound.

"Oh, for God's sake," Giles says again.

Miranda is hunkered over in her gold dress, on her hands and knees, vomiting onto the ground.

Giles watches her, impassive. He doesn't seem at all like the man I have come to know, the caring husband and father—the man who saves people's lives on a ward. I would have expected that man to kneel down, to hold back her hair. I've seen another side of him, this evening.

Then he turns, suddenly, before I have time to hide myself. His eyes meet mine.

38

MIRANDA

WHEN I WAKE IT'S VERY DARK, AND QUIET. FOR A MOMENT I have absolutely no idea where I am. I grope about with one hand to get my bearings. My first impression is of feeling absolutely disgusting, like my insides and my throat have been scoured with wire wool. The taste in my mouth is sour, acrid. What's wrong with me? Am I ill? I grope for a switch, blink it on.

Oh. The light returns me to my surroundings. With a horrible inevitability the events of the evening come back to me. Drinking far too much. Having to prove myself as the Life and Soul of the Party. Giles accosting me with his paranoia. Well, maybe he's not being *totally* paranoid. I know Samira's always had her suspicions. And I didn't feel good about it at the time . . . it was after a boozy night in the pub for our tutor group, and I already knew she liked him. But for God's sake—it was before they even started going out. If you let something like *that* upset you, you're frankly too bloody thin-skinned. If anyone needs to be worried, it's me. I *was* with Julien at the time, after all.

Oh God, and now I remember vomiting while Giles looked on, eyes on me the whole time, like he half wanted me to choke on it. When Julien appeared he just looked tired, vaguely disgusted. No: I wasn't so drunk that I don't remember that.

I glance in the mirror hanging above the dressing table. I thought I looked amazing in the gold dress. No, I *knew* I looked amazing. But it's like I've woken up in a parallel universe. Now the fabric is rumpled and stained, and my makeup (I was wearing quite a lot of it—I need to wear more of it these days) has sunk into the creases of skin about my eyes and mouth that I could swear weren't as deep yesterday. I move away from the light, thinking of Blanche DuBois, cringing away from lamps. Is that what I'm going to become? Is there anything sadder than a once-beautiful woman who has lost her looks?

For some reason there's a song going around and around in my head. Candi Staton's "You Got the Love." And there's something about it that niggles at me, though I can't put my finger on it. It's like last night, when someone said that disconcerting thing. Who was it? And what did they say?

At least I'm feeling a bit less drunk now. I must have got rid of most of the booze from my system. I have no idea what time it is. But Julien isn't back yet—so the party must be continuing. I feel a sudden sense of FOMO, at the idea of them carrying on without me. I can't believe I managed to pass out. I've got to rally myself, get back out there. This is what is expected of me, after all. I stagger into the bathroom, drag a comb through my hair, splash some water on my face, and attempt to tidy the makeup smeared around my eyes, with little effect. I brush my teeth: that's something, at least. What time is it? I check the clock. Four in the morning. Wow, the others have really made a night of it, then. I feel that sting again, at the knowledge of the fun I must've missed. I have always been—prided myself on being—the life and soul of the party. That was what Julien said at our wedding: "I love you," looking at me, looking into my eyes, "because you are the life and soul of the party." "And a few other reasons, I hope," I had said, laughing.

He had grinned. "Of course." But it has stuck with me, that phrase. I remember the way he looked at me as he said it, and I can never let it go, that aspect of myself. Well, I'm going to show him now.

I open the door of the cabin. The cold hits me like a slap. I steel myself against it. There are lights on, coming not from the Lodge building, as I had first thought, but from the sauna. I feel a little sting of resentment—they could have come and got me, asked if I wanted to join them. I've been wanting to try out the sauna.

I slip and slide my way there along the frozen path, past the Lodge. All the lights in there are off bar a single lamp in the living room. I can just make out Mark, sleeping on one of the sofas. Another casualty of this evening, then. I feel a little better for knowing that I'm not the only one.

There is a smell in the air that I recognize from skiing trips: a freshness, almost metallic. I remember Doug's warning. Wouldn't it be wonderful if we were all sitting in the sauna, looking out toward the loch, and it started to snow? So picturesque. Give us a good memory of tonight, one that would erase my messiness.

As I get nearer, I hear a strange sound that literally stops me in my tracks. Something animal. Somewhere between a cry and a groan. It sounded as though it came from the direction of the sauna, the woods behind. I feel my skin wash with goose bumps as I hurry toward the sauna: it represents a haven now from the great, wild outdoors.

Only a couple of feet from the door I hear the sound again, and this time I hesitate. Because now I'm almost certain it came not from the trees behind the sauna, but from inside the sauna itself.

39

HEATHER

Now
January 2, 2019

I GO TO THE LITTLE TOILET NEXT TO MY OFFICE TO SPLASH SOME cold water on my face, in an attempt to try to clear my mind after everything I've just discovered about Doug.

I'm just drying my face when I hear something, a murmuring of voices. A man and a woman. It's two of the guests, I'm certain, but I can't work out which ones. Part of the problem is that they all have the same voices to my ear: southern, middle class, entitled.

The man, first: "If they find out—I'm screwed."

"Why would they find out?" The woman, answering.

"There's a note."

I freeze, and move closer to the wall, as quietly as I can. Of course—the corridor to the back door wraps around beside my office. Someone could go there wanting to have a private conversation and never know that there's a room here, because the loo is only accessible through the office.

"The note?" the woman says, with a tremor of incredulity. "You didn't destroy it?"

"No—I didn't think. I was too panicked, with everything else. I don't even know where it is now . . ."

There is a long silence, during which I am fairly sure the woman is trying to think of ways not to berate him. What sort of note? I wonder. A suicide note? That seems unlikely, the last time I checked it was pretty difficult to strangle yourself.

"The important thing," the woman says, calmly, at last, "is that you didn't have anything to do with her death. That's what counts. They'll be able to see that."

"But will they, though?" he says. His voice rises to a shrill, panicked pitch. Then it sinks to a murmur again, quieter than before: I think she's shushed him. I press my head closer to the wall.

"When the other stuff comes out about me—when they decide what sort of person they think I am . . ."

There's a sudden crash. I jump back, confused, and realize that in my eagerness to hear I've managed to dislodge the little hunting scene on the wall next to me. It has fallen to the ground with an impressive explosion of broken glass.

The voices, of course, have gone quiet. I can almost feel them, standing there rigid with shock, on the other side of the wall— hardly breathing. As quietly as I can, I creep my way back into the office.

40

MIRANDA

One day earlier
New Year's Day 2019

THE SIGHT CONFRONTING ME INSIDE THE SAUNA IS ABSURD. I am so stunned that I feel a strange urge to laugh. I remember when our cat got run over when we were children, how when my mum told us, my brother's first reaction was, "Ha!" I was so shocked I slapped him. But my mum explained that it was a simple reaction to the trauma. The brain short-circuiting, unable to make sense of something.

This is what I see: my husband, crouched on the floor of the sauna. Above him I see Katie. My best friend, my oldest friend. Completely nude. Her legs open, his head buried between them. My plain, flat-chested, thick-thighed friend. Her head thrown back in ecstasy. He grips her calves. She has her feet locked around his back. And as I watch, he reaches up and takes the nipple of one of her fried egg breasts in one hand. This, finally, is too much. It's torn out of me. "Ugh."

They freeze. Then both, slowly, turn to look at me. Julien—oh,

Christ—wipes his mouth with the back of his hand. Their expressions are blank at first, as they make sense of what they are seeing. I feel a tide of horror flooding through me, like a poison entering the bloodstream. I glance over at the scuttle of hot coals, and for a second I am tempted—really tempted—to pick up the shovel and chuck a load of the burning rocks at them.

It is all completely absurd. My husband and my best friend. It can't be possible. I almost expect them to both suddenly crack grins and congratulate themselves on pranking me, as they did at the surprise party for my thirtieth birthday. This would be rather difficult to explain away as a prank, though.

"Oh," Katie says. "Oh God."

"I thought you were asleep," Julien says. "I left you at the cabin. You were passed out . . ." And then, apparently, realizing the ridiculousness of accusing his wife of not being where he thought she was while he cheated on her, he says, "Oh God, Miranda. Oh, fuck. I'm so sorry. It's not—it's not what it seems."

And now I do laugh, a mad-witch cackle that only makes them look more afraid. Good. I want them to be afraid.

"Don't you dare come back to the cabin," I say to Julien. "I don't care where you stay, frankly. You can be with her, for all it matters to me now. But I don't want to see your face. So don't come anywhere near me." I'm rather amazed by how calm I sound: at the contrast between my internal and external selves.

"We need to talk—"

"No, we don't. I don't want to speak or look at you for a long time. Perhaps never again." As I say it, I realize I mean it. I was furious at him for the insider trading—at first I thought, briefly, about walking away. But I never *truly* considered it. Now this, this is different.

He nods mutely. I can't bring myself to look at Katie. "I can't believe I wasted so much time on you. Either of you."

And then something occurs to me, something almost too horrible to vocalize. But I have to say it, have to know. I turn to Katie, still not looking at her, but in her vague direction. "You didn't drink anything," I say. "On the train. I saw. You had a glass of wine, but you didn't drink it. You haven't been drinking at all, actually."

Silence. She's going to make me say it out loud. I can see even now how she crouches over in her nakedness. Trying to hide it from me: what I saw earlier when she was in her underwear, but couldn't understand at the time, because I was too drunk, because it made no sense. It's no Christmas paunch. Katie isn't the sort of person to get a Christmas paunch.

"You're pregnant." When she doesn't respond, I say it again, louder. "You're pregnant. Say it, for fuck's sake. You're pregnant; it's his. Oh my God."

I see Julien's mouth fall open. So he doesn't know yet. It's a small victory, at least, to see how appalled he looks.

"Manda," Katie says, "It was an accident . . . I'm s—"

I put up a hand to stop her. I will not cry in front of them. That's all I can think. Miranda Adams never cries.

"You're welcome to each other," I say, while the grief and rage courses through me like acid. The pregnancy is so much worse than the affair, somehow. The sense of the theft is so much greater. It's like Katie has stolen it directly from me. That thing inside her should be *my* baby.

"I'm getting the early morning train back to London," I say, and I'm proud that there's only the hint of a catch in my voice. "There are some things I need to do. Something I need to set right—a secret I've kept for far too long. Julien, I think you know what I'm talking about?"

His eyes widen. "You wouldn't, Miranda. You wouldn't do that."

But I would. "Oh, wouldn't I?" I smile—I know it will unnerve him even more. "You think you know me so well? Well, until just a few minutes ago I thought I knew you. But it would appear that I was wrong. What's to say you know me so well, in return? Want to find out how little you understand me?"

"It would destroy you, too."

I put a hand to my lips, a pantomime of deliberation. I am almost enjoying this, making him squirm. It is a very tiny compensation. "I don't think it will, actually. I'll explain it all to them, how you even tried to trick me, at first. It will be a bit embarrassing, yes, and I suppose there might be some small penalty for not doing it sooner. But I won't be the one losing my job. I won't be the one going to prison. That will be you, just in case you're unclear. You will be the one going to prison."

His mouth is set, grim.

"It's a pretty big offense, isn't it? Especially in this post-credit-crunch world. You think any jury would hesitate to convict you? You're a Fat Cat Wanker Banker. They'd take one glance at your smug face and tell the judge to throw away the key."

I'm not even sure insider trading cases have a jury, but it is enough to see the look on Julien's face: the fear. Katie looks completely baffled. So this is one intimacy he has not shared with her. Lucky girl.

He comes toward me again, and this time I put my hands up, to stop his words landing on me, affecting me. To show him that I will not be swayed.

"It would ruin both of us, Manda."

The short, affectionate version of my name—as though he thinks it might soften me.

"Don't you ever call me that again," I say. "And yes, when I divorce you, I suppose there will be less coming my way, once they finish with you. If that's what you're referring to. But at least I'll have a clear conscience."

And I'll have got my revenge.

41

KATIE

S O THIS IS THE TRUTH. THE ONE I COULD NEVER HAVE TOLD
in that game.

It had been a really long week. I'd had two nights of sleeping
in the office. They actually have these little rooms called "sleeping
pods" where you can grab a couple of hours' rest. No—in case
you're wondering—that's not the company looking after its employees, it's simply in order to keep them close, to wring as much
work out of them as possible. My mind felt numb. The case was
over, I was going home—except that nothing was waiting for me
there beyond a fridge with some curdled milk in it, if I was lucky,
and a prime but utterly uninspiring view of the very square mile
I slaved away in daily. And silence. The silence of a single woman
with nothing for company but a bottle, or two, of wine.

It was ten o'clock. Too late to call anyone, scare up some plans.
In my early twenties there would have been more of a chance of
that. People might have been busy, but invariably it would have
been something I could join at late notice. A house party—Samira
was always throwing them—or a night out clubbing with Miranda,
a big dinner with the gang. Now everyone had plans that took
place in smaller numbers, usually twos or fours, and were arranged

in advance, didn't welcome a last-minute interloper. Maybe I could have called Miranda, but I wasn't sure I had the energy for her. For all that perfection. For her to make me her project, as she always did—has always done—and tell me what was wrong with my life.

So I could go home and sit with my bottle of wine in my empty flat, or I could do it in a bar, and perhaps pick someone up to bring home. This was my replacement strategy, you see, for the nights out and house parties and dinners of our twenties. I suppose in a way it was more efficient: at least you didn't have to make conversation.

Of the two options open to me, the second was infinitely more appealing. I could take someone home, and for a couple of hours the flat would have life and noise in it. So I walked into one of my regular spots in the shadow of St. Paul's. The barman knows me so well that he started pouring me a large glass of Pouilly-Fumé before I'd even sat down—which is either thoughtful or depressing, depending on which way you look at it.

I sat down on the stool and waited for someone to approach me. It usually didn't take too long. I'll never be Miranda-beautiful, of course. This used to depress me. It's not easy growing up in the shadow of a friend like her. But of late, perhaps only really since I turned thirty, I have learned that I have something that seems to intrigue men—my own particular attraction for them.

There were a few people around the bar: groups of coworkers, probably, and a scattering of Tinder dates—but it wasn't packed. Only Tuesday evening, so not a proper night out. Perhaps I had been overly confident about my chances. There was only one man sitting along the other bar, perpendicular to me. I'd vaguely noticed him as I sat down, though he hadn't glanced up, and I hadn't actually looked properly at him. I could tell even from the hazy outline in my peripheral vision that he was "youngish" in the way that I am "youngish," and attractive. I don't know how I knew this without properly looking, it must have been some animal sense.

And that same sense told me that there was something despondent about him, hunched over.

And then both of us looked up at the same time, to get the barman's attention. I saw, with a shock, who it was.

"Julien?"

He looked surprised to see me, too. I suppose perhaps it shouldn't have been all that shocking, considering we both work in the City. But there are still thousands of bars and thousands of people, and I would have assumed Julien was at home with Miranda, anyway. This was one of the first things I mouthed to him. "Where's Miranda?"

We had never had that much to do with each other, that was the thing, unless it was through Miranda.

"She's at home," he mouthed back to me. And then he mimed: he was coming to sit next to me. I was half pleased, half put out. Now I definitely wouldn't be going home with anyone; by the time Julien and I had had our conversation and he'd headed off to Miranda I'd be too tired to start up anything with someone new.

He came to sit next to me. As he leaned down to pull the stool toward him I caught the scent of his aftershave, a gin-and-tonic freshness, and I remembered how twenty minutes ago, when I thought him a stranger, I'd had the sense that he was probably good-looking. And he *was* good-looking. I had known this—I'd realized it when he and Miranda first started dating, of course— but at some point I had stopped noticing. Now it was as if I was seeing him clearly again. It was an odd feeling.

"What are you doing here?" I asked.

"I might ask the same of you," he said. Which, of course, was not an answer.

I told him about finishing the case. "So I suppose you could say I'm celebrating."

"Where are the others? Your colleagues? Are they here?"

I couldn't exactly say, *They've gone to another bar, I never socialize with them if I can help it.* So I said, "Home—all too knackered to think about going out."

"So you decided to celebrate all on your own?"

"Something like that."

"Isn't that a bit lonely?"

There was a strange tension between us. I think it was the knowledge of having known each other for ten years and yet suddenly being aware that we did not know each other at all. We were really little more than friendly strangers. We needed Miranda there to make sense of the connection between us. Both of us were drinking quite fast, in an attempt to dissipate this awkwardness. I hadn't even realized that I had finished my drink before he asked, "Have another?"

"Oh, all right, then." I was rather flattered. He was enjoying my company.

"Where's Miranda?" I asked again.

"You've already asked me that." The way he said it was a little teasing.

"Yes, but then why are you here all on your lonesome?" My reply was equally teasing. Oh my God, was I flirting with my best friend's husband?

"Just thought I'd have a quick one."

The alcohol dared me to say it: "So we're here, drinking—her best friend and her husband? We're like kids playing truant or something." It was meant to be silly, off-the-cuff, but it had the inevitable effect of making what we were doing into a conspiracy from which Miranda was excluded. I drank a big slug of my wine.

"If she knew, she'd definitely be jealous," he said. And then quickly, "I know that she misses you." He smiled, but there was something sad and tired about his eyes; they didn't participate in the smile. "Look," he said, more seriously, "if I'm honest, I needed a bit of time to myself."

"What's up?" I asked. I was worried—but with the very tiniest tinge of amusement that we sometimes get, hearing of our friends' problems. Everything about Miranda and Julien's life seemed flawless, golden.

I said as much to him. "What could possibly be the problem? You guys are perfect."

"Oh yes," he said, with a smile that somehow went down at the corners rather than up. "Perfect. That's exactly what we are. So bloody perfect."

There was an awkward pause. I couldn't think what to say. "You mean . . ." I looked for a way to put it. "You mean—things aren't great between you guys? Miranda hasn't said anything."

That was true enough. She hadn't said anything to me. But then we hadn't seen each other for quite a while. We'd chatted briefly a couple of times, but I am hopeless on the phone: something that always made my teenage years rather difficult. Besides, I hardly had any free time with work—and even if I did it was late at night, or early morning, times when I doubt Miranda would have relished a phone call. I felt a twist of guilt. She had asked me several times in the last month if I was free, and we had made a date, but I had to blow her off at the last minute because of a sudden crisis with the case.

"It isn't problems with us exactly," he said. "It's a bit more complicated. I suppose it would be more accurate to say it's a problem with me. Something like that. I have done something bad." He saw my raised eyebrows. "No . . . Not like that. I haven't cheated. I got myself involved in something bad. And now I can't get out of it."

"And Miranda doesn't know?"

"No . . . She does know. I had to tell her, because it involved both of us. She's been"—he frowned—"I suppose she's been quite good about it. Understanding. All things considered. Except sometimes I catch her looking at me, and she seems so disappointed. Like this isn't what she signed up for. It's just a bit of a mess."

He pronounced mess as "mesh," and I wondered quite how much he had been drinking before we started chatting.

"Do you want to talk about it?"

He shook his head. "No. I mean—I'd like to, actually, but I can't."

"Why not?" I caught myself. "Sorry—I've had too much to drink. That was rude of me. Just tell me to shut up."

"Please don't." He gave me that funny downward smile again, so different from the expansive, charming gleam of his usual expression. I preferred this one; it was more real. "I like talking to you," he said. "Isn't it funny—we've known each other all these years. What is it, ten?"

"Eleven," I said. June 2007. That was when I had run into him coming out of our bathroom.

"And yet you and I have never really talked properly, have we?"

"I suppose not."

"Well, have another drink, and let's talk. Properly."

"Well—I . . ."

"Come on. Please. Otherwise I'm going to be here drinking on my own, and that's perhaps the saddest thing ever." He caught himself, evidently remembering that was exactly what I had been doing. "Sorry, I didn't mean—"

"It's okay," I said. He was right. But drinking at home was worse. My empty flat, with the empty fridge, and the empty view: the sea of office blocks, the City—the place that ate all of my time, and meant that my life was empty, too.

The thought of going back there suddenly made my skin crawl. I'd prefer to have another drink with him, I thought. But there was something strange about it, being here in a bar with Miranda's husband, when she didn't know. And . . . strangely enjoyable, too, which was perhaps the worst thing about it.

"All right," I said. *What the hell.*

"Good." He grinned at me, and I felt something inside me

somersault. "What will you have?" And then, before I could answer: "I know—let's have whiskey. Do you like whiskey?" Without waiting for my answer, he turned to the barman. "We'll get the Hibiki." He smiled. "You'll like it. It's Japanese—twenty-one years old."

I never drink whiskey. I hardly ever drink spirits, to be honest—I can sink a bottle of wine and hardly feel it, but spirits are another matter entirely.

The whiskey went straight to my head. That is no excuse for what happened next.

Miranda was obviously a sore subject. So we ended up talking about everything else. I realized that Julien was a much better conversationalist than I had ever appreciated before. I had always thought of him as all charm, all surface, concealing some inner lack. We reminisced about Oxford, how easy life had been then, even though, back then, we thought we were working the hardest we would ever work in our lives.

We talked about my work—he'd read a little about the case I had been working on. For once, I didn't find myself second-guessing, assuming he was asking out of politeness, while he waited for Miranda to rescue him, or for someone more stimulating to come along. He was turned toward me on his stool, his knees pointing toward mine. A body language expert would have said that all the signs were very good. Or very bad, depending upon which way you looked at it. But I didn't think anything of it, still. Or, if I did, I pushed those thoughts away. They were ridiculous, weren't they?

We talked about the first time we'd met (he didn't remember the previous occasion, at the Summer Ball, and I was too proud to correct him), when he had come out of the bathroom clutching his towel.

"There I was," he said, "half naked, and there you were, looking so elegant."

I was surprised by this; I had always just assumed he thought I was Miranda's uglier, more boring friend. Elegant. I realized that I would be turning that word over in my mind for a while.

"This is so nice," he said to me at one point. "Isn't it nice? Just chatting, like this? How have we never done this before?" His breath was laced with whiskey, true, but I still felt his words warm me. And I realized he wasn't quite as arrogant as I had always thought—and also, clearly, not so perfect. Perhaps the years had rubbed some of the shine off him, and I hadn't stopped to notice. Or perhaps he had always been like this. Either way, he seemed much nicer, more humble, than I had ever appreciated. The sober me might have been able to point out that this was probably just Julien's famous charisma at work. But the drunk me liked it very much.

Because at some point I realized that we were both very drunk. "I should go home," I said. Though I realized that I didn't want to, and not just because of the depressing thought of the sterile single-person flat that awaited me. It was because I was actually having fun. I was enjoying his company. But I made a big show of finishing my glass, and getting down from my seat. As I slid from my seat and wobbled on my heels, I discovered that I was even drunker than I had thought. He got down from his stool, and I saw him sway on his feet, too.

"You can't go home on your own," he said. "I'll walk you back. It's not safe."

For some reason I didn't bother to tell him that I walked home alone every night and that I'd been more drunk than this before when I did, sometimes with a complete stranger in tow. I think we both knew, even then, that it was mainly an excuse to keep the conversation going, to stay in each other's company.

I don't remember which of us made the first move. I just recall that suddenly we were standing in an empty alleyway, and all I could hear was the sound of our breathing. Just beyond that alleyway was the thoroughfare of Cheapside and cars and people, and beyond that the whole city, lit up, chaotic, with all its millions of inhabitants. But in that dark passage it was just the two of us, and we were both breathing very loudly. And neither of us was suddenly quite so drunk. That flash of desire had sobered us. And then there was the light pressure of his thumbs on my hipbones, and I could feel the greater pressure of him between my legs, how hard he was. And I took his hand and guided it up, beneath my skirt, and he groaned against my neck.

The sex was quick: it had to be, in that public place. Anyone could have come across us, at any moment. It was also very good. I came embarrassingly quickly. But he, despite the alcohol and the awkwardness of our position (he had to hold me up against the wall), followed soon after. It was the strangeness of it, I think, the illicitness of it, that made it incredibly exciting. Afterward, we stayed glued together for several seconds, his face in my neck. I couldn't believe what we had done.

He said it out loud. "I can't believe that just happened."

"I know," I said. "Let's . . . Let's just pretend it didn't." A small secret part of me was thinking: *Would anyone have done?* Was I just some girl in a bar, the right place, the right time? Or was it me?

These things should not have mattered, I knew. And yet they did. Because for so long I had assumed he saw me as the colorless, uninteresting counterpart, and that was why he had hardly bothered to speak to me. Now, here, was a new, thrilling possibility. That in fact he had desired me.

42

MIRANDA

TURN AT THE SOUND OF FOOTSTEPS BEHIND ME ON THE PATH. It's Julien, clutching a towel about his waist, his feet skidding on the mud.

"I've made a big mistake," he says in a let's-all-be-adults tone. "I know I've made a big mistake. But I've been under a lot of stress."

"Sorry," I say, "you've been under a lot of stress?"

"Yes," he says. "It's—a deal went bad. And I'd cut Mark in on it. He wasn't happy."

I think back to what Mark said on the first night, when he grabbed me. The reference to Julien's "dirty little secret." The choice of words had struck me as odd at the time. I'd thought he was talking about the insider trading, but now I understand. "He knew," I say, "didn't he? About you and"—I can't bring myself to say her name—"her."

"I let something slip, when I was very drunk. I felt so guilty . . . I wanted his advice. He is—was—my best mate. And now he's threatening me, Manda."

He looks ridiculously sorry for himself. I really, truly detest him, in this moment. Not just for what he has done, but for his cowardice, his pathetic self-pity. "All of this," I say, "has been brought on by you, you fucking idiot. All of it because you always want a little bit more. You always think you're entitled to a bigger share. I should have seen this coming a mile off. Of course you were going to have an affair. Though I would never in a million years have thought of Katie. I thought you might have better taste than that."

He grimaces then, a little quirk of the mouth, and for a surreal moment I actually think he might be about to defend her to me. Clearly, he thinks better of it. I know him too well; he's more worried about saving his own bacon.

"She seduced me, Manda."

My skin crawls. "Don't fucking call me that," I hiss.

"Sorry. But I want to make that clear. It was all her. I think . . . I think she had a plan, from the moment she saw me sitting there in that bar. I think she knew, looking at me, at the state I was in—that I would have been incapable of resisting. I didn't have a chance. It was like that time in Ibiza."

"What time in Ibiza?"

"Oh God." He looks as though he immediately regrets having said anything. He rubs his face with a hand. "You might as well know. That holiday we all went on. The last night. She came on to me. It was . . . crazy. I was a bit out of it, and I was missing you . . . She was like a woman possessed, Manda—sorry. She was all over me."

I stare at him, bile rising in my throat. Ibiza. While I was at my grandmother's funeral . . . he was sleeping with my best friend. It wasn't that long after we'd first started going out, well before we were married—all of which makes it worse, means that that disgusting secret has been there between us for all that time. Julien is clearly regretting having revealed any of this to me. He makes a kind of desperate sweeping gesture with his hand, as though trying to brush it from view, and says, "But . . . what I want to say is, I didn't mean any of it."

It would almost be amusing, I think. To watch him falter, to continue to dig himself into this particular grave. Amusing if, that is, he weren't my husband, the man to whom I have given over a decade—all my youth—and if I weren't really the butt of this particular joke.

"Anyway," Julien hurries on—he must see the disgust and utter incredulity on my face—"when we bumped into each other in that bar . . . I think she saw I was at a low point. You'd been treating me like a second-class citizen. Barely speaking to me. I felt like an utter failure, a disappointment. She made me feel . . . desired, desirable. I tried to call a stop to it. I went around to her apartment the next day, to tell her to call it off. But she wouldn't let me do it. I was so weak, I see that. She was like a drug habit I couldn't shake—"

I hold up a hand. "What script are you reading from, Julien? Do you have so little respect for me that you think I'm really going to buy any of this pathetic, clichéd crap?"

He makes a pleading, feeble gesture with his hands. "I just wanted to try to explain."

"Well. It's not going to do any good. Can't you see that? I'm not buying any more of your utter bullshit." I think that if I had a weapon now I would kill him. If I knew the combination to that store with the rifles I think there would be very little stopping me from taking one, going back to the sauna, and shooting both of them dead. Do people still get lighter sentences for crimes of passion? Any sentence, right now, seems worthwhile. No one screws Miranda Adams over like this.

I don't have a rifle. But perhaps the weapon I do have is more powerful than any gun.

The insider trading. I've been involved, of course. But I could get a good lawyer. My parents would help me out. And however bad it might be for me, it would be a tiny fraction of the shit that would descend on Julien. In this moment, it seems worth it.

"Actually," I say, "I do know what I'm going to do. I'll log on to your precious bloody Wi-Fi and send a sodding email right now. It will take a click of a button. Just one fucking click. I may not have a career, but I have friends, Julien—you know them, too. Olivia, you know she's now at the *Times*? Or Henry, my ex from before uni? He's at the *Mail* now—I can just *imagine* the headline they'll dream up for you. And you know what? I reckon I could do pretty well from it myself."

He takes a step back. His face is in shadow. I can hardly make out his features, let alone his expression. And, not for the first time—but with much better reason now—I think: *I do not know this person at all. I do not know what he is capable of.*

43

HEATHER

Now
January 2, 2019

I WALK BACK INTO THE OFFICE. DOUG'S SITTING THERE—AND I'M about to tell him what I heard just now in the bathroom, when the phone rings. I pick it up. "Yes?"

"Hello, Heather, it's DCI Alison Querry here."

"Have you found a way to get here?" I can feel Doug's eyes on me.

"Well," Querry says, "we're still working hard on that, of course. The forecast suggests that the snow should be easing off in the next few hours, then we can make an attempt with a chopper. But there's something else. I just wanted to let you know that unfortunately I'm being called away: DCI John MacBride is going to take my place. He's extremely capable, I need not add. I'll put you on the phone to him now."

My brain is racing. Alison Querry is the lead on the Highland Ripper investigation. If she's been called away from this one, that means . . .

As DCI John MacBride introduces himself I am hardly listening. I am googling with one hand, *Highland Ripper,* then the NEWS tab. The headlines triumph out at me from the screen: "Suspect Arrested in Glasgow Hideaway," "Raid on Glasgow Lair of the Ripper," "Ripper Routed?" They've found someone. Glasgow is over two hours' drive from here, more in bad conditions. This can only mean one thing. If they have indeed found the man who killed those other women, he can have had nothing to do with this particular murder. It was someone else. It was someone here.

4 4

KATIE

One day earlier
New Year's Day 2019

JULIEN COMES BACK INTO THE SAUNA. DIMLY, I REGISTER HOW
absurd he looks: completely naked, his cock curled up from the
cold, his feet covered in mud. And just for a moment, with perhaps
the greatest force since we first started seeing each other, I ask myself, *What am I doing?*

Has it all been about Julien? The secret longing I have harbored
for him for all these years? Or has it also been about Miranda? I
could never have admitted this to myself, not before. But for all the
remorse I felt, looking at her standing there, staring in horror, for
all the shame . . . was there not something else? The tiniest hint of
schadenfreude? About, for once, having one up on her?

I'd like to point out that I originally went to the sauna just to
try and warm up from that horrible icy bath in the loch, not with
an assignation in mind. I'd probably been in there for about ten
minutes when there was a knock on the door.

I opened it, and saw Julien. He grinned at me, came in, quickly, furtively. Immediately he began to shrug out of his clothes.

In spite of myself I felt a shiver of excitement. Of anticipation.

"It's okay," he said. "I've put her to bed—she's completely out of it. And Mark's passed out in the Lodge, and Emma's back at her cabin. It's just us. I was actually on my way to your cabin when I saw the light on here and thought . . . well, what a good idea."

"What if Miranda wakes up and finds you gone?"

"She's going nowhere. So it'll be like last night. I'll just tell her I've been for a walk."

Sometimes it has made me uneasy, the speed at which the lies come to him. "And you think she'd believe you? Julien, it's three in the morning."

"Yes, I know. But you see . . . she knows I've had a lot on my mind recently."

"The thing you'd like to share with me but can't possibly tell me about?"

"Yes. That."

I don't know why it stung, that he had persistently refused to talk about it. "We seem to have shared quite a bit recently," I said. "I suppose I just can't understand why you wouldn't talk about this particular thing."

"I don't want to burden you with it," he said. "There's no need for you to know. Like I've said, if I told you, too, it would make you guilty by association—complicit."

"But I am guilty," I said.

"I know," he said, and reached for me—but not without a backward glance, as though anyone could possibly see anything through the locked shutters. "So deliciously guilty."

"Julien," I said. "What are you . . . I thought we had agreed—"

He silenced my protest with his mouth. He ran his hands up and down my arms, then down my back, cupping my ass, lifting me up so that I had no choice other than to lock my legs around his back. All my resistance had melted, instantly.

"That was before," he said. "We agreed that before."

"Before what?"

"Before I realized that I'm completely obsessed with you. These last few weeks, not seeing you—Christmas at Miranda's parents . . ."

"I've felt sick with guilt," I said. "Physically sick, Julien. I literally was—on the train, I had to go and throw up in the toilet."

Although, actually, that might have been due to the thing I discovered this morning.

"Poor Katie-did."

"No, don't give me that. We can't go on like this. It isn't fair on Miranda."

He nodded. "It isn't fair on Miranda," he said, "and that's why I think we should tell her." I opened my mouth to protest, but he shook his head. "Hear me out. We were just kids when we got together. She seemed so certain of herself. She was dazzling. I wanted a bit of that. And yes, I fancied the pants off her. But then, over the years . . . all that drive seemed to go. Everything she wanted changed. She didn't want to do or be something amazing. She just wants *things* now, all the time: holidays and clothes and a new car and, well, a baby. But she hates kids. I'm not even sure she doesn't want a baby just because everyone else has one—because it's 'Life Goals.'

"And with you, Katie-did . . . it's different. It's more complex. It's deeper. It's so much . . . freer."

I thought of that little plus on the stick. I'd wait, I thought. I'd find the right moment.

"You know who you are. You have a career, a life. You don't need me to validate who you are."

I felt a strange, unexpected wave of sympathy for Miranda: over ten years, they have been together. In what world could that not be called deep? But beneath the sympathy, despite all the guilt . . . yes, I realized there was some dark, complex pleasure. All those years of playing the wing woman, the second fiddle, the understudy. Now, finally, I had bested her at something.

45

DOUG

SOMETHING HAS WOKEN HIM. HIS BODY IS ALERT, PRICKLING with awareness—his mind struggling to catch up. He has been wrenched out of his whiskey-soaked stupor agitated, his heart going double time. He looks about himself. He is surrounded by broken glass. But now he remembers . . . before he passed out he'd thrown his tumbler at the television, enjoyed the sound of it shattering the screen. Enjoyed how it briefly drowned out the sound of the guests partying over at the Lodge, the music turned up full blast. Making a mockery of his own "celebrations"—a bottle of single malt and the depressing spectacle of others' happiness on the screen. Then he had drained the last drops straight from the bottle and sunk finally, gratefully, into unconsciousness.

But now something has roused him. A knock on the door. Loud as a rifle shot.

He stills, listening like an animal.

It comes again.

He didn't imagine it. He gropes for his watch. It's four in the morning. Who could need him at four in the morning? Heather, he thinks, incoherently. She might need his help, somehow.

He opens the door, looks out with bleary eyes. It's her, the guest, the beautiful one. Except she looks . . . terrible. Still beautiful, in a long golden gown, but with a wrecked quality to everything: the fabric of her dress ripped, her face stained with makeup. Her lipstick is a long smear across one cheek.

"Hi," she says, swaying slightly on her feet. "Sorry, I hope it's not an imposition." He is drunk, but she is drunker. The realization sobers him.

She peers beyond him. "Wow," she says. "It's really empty in here. Very . . . minimalist."

"You can't come in here," he says. He tries to block her entry with his body; she wriggles past.

"But I brought champagne!" She holds up an open bottle. Dom Pérignon, the really posh stuff. "You wouldn't let me drink the rest on my own, would you?" As she steps nearer he realizes that the now familiar smokiness of her perfume is tainted by something sour and rank.

He feels like an animal, routed out in its cave, its safe and private space. She takes a step forward and takes his head in her hands, and kisses him. Her mouth is a concentration of sourness, but also that perfumed smokiness, which seems to wrap itself around him. And her tongue is deft, and she has fitted her body to his. It has been so long. He feels desire rise up in him—mixing uncomfortably with the anger he still feels at the interruption. She is reaching for his fly, unzipping him, reaching her hand inside. Her fingers are tangling in his hair.

"No," he says, his mind clearing.

She steps back from him. Her lip curls. "Pardon?"

"No," he says again.

"Fuck you! Don't tell me you don't want it. I can *see* that you do."

"I can . . . make you a cup of tea," he says, though he has no idea whether he currently has the wherewithal to complete this task.

She laughs, staggers on her glittery heels, and then scowls at him. "I don't think so," she says. And then she points at him. "I know you want it. I've seen how you look at me. At that dinner . . . yesterday, on the shoot. You don't fool me." She is furious, wrathful, her finger stabbing at his chest. "But you're too scared. Do you know what you are? You're a *fucking coward*."

Those words. He feels the rage and grief rising inside him, like that other time. He feels the red flood of his anger come down over everything, and something inside himself loosen, loosen . . . and break.

46

HEATHER

Now
January 2, 2019

T HAT WAS THE POLICE," I TELL DOUG. "THEY'VE FOUND THE
Highland Ripper. Miles away from here, so it doesn't look like
he's anything to do with us. It must have been someone here."

As I say it, I hear the truth of it for the first time. It becomes
real. They are here. "And I just heard something, while I was in
the bathroom—" I stop, catching sight of the look on Doug's face.

"Doug?" I stare at him. "Are you all right?" He's pacing in
front of my desk, rubbing his jaw back and forth—so vigorously
that the skin beneath his stubble is raw and red, though the rest of
his face seems to have drained of all color. His eyes are black and
fathomless. It is as though he is taking all of this unusually personally. He has looked bad since the morning, I realize; I've noticed it,
but I haven't really had a chance to properly consider it. It seemed
natural, what with him finding the body, and everything.

"Doug?"

He turns toward me, but he hardly seems to have heard the question.

"Doug!" I snap my fingers in front of his face, force him to focus on me. "What is it? What now?"

He shakes his head, for several seconds. And then he says, in a rush, "There's something more. I didn't tell you all of it."

Oh God. I brace myself. "What is it?"

"That night, close to when you'd first got the job here," he says, "when you heard the scream . . . do you remember?"

"Yes," I say. The sound is still imprinted upon my memory.

"Well, that wasn't a fox." He grimaces. "It was a scream. It was me."

I think of my first impressions on hearing the noise—that it was a sound made by a person in profoundest agony. "Oh, Doug."

"I have these—episodes—I suppose, when I can't remember what I have been doing. I find myself in strange places, without knowing how I have got there. That night, for example . . . I wasn't aware of making any noise. I came round, in the trees beside the loch, and I realized it had to be me."

I don't want to hear any more. But there is more—he keeps going, unstoppable. "On New Year's Eve . . ." He runs his uninjured hand through his wild hair, in that nervous gesture I have seen him make so many times in the last few hours. "I'd been drinking a lot . . . I remember that. And . . ." He blows out his cheeks. He doesn't meet my eyes. "I was angry. So I drank some more. I think I passed out. And then there's a whole period of time that's just . . . a blank."

A blank.

Finally, he meets my eyes. The expression in his is that of a drowning man.

47

KATIE

One day earlier
New Year's Day 2019

'VE GOT TO GO AND SPEAK TO MIRANDA. NO, THIS ISN'T A LATE
crisis of conscience. There's no point in apologizing now, it is
far too late for that. If I was really sorry, I would have stopped a
long time ago. It's only now that I have seen Julien's reaction to
all of this—his cowardice in scuttling straight after Miranda, and,
I'm sure, pleading with her, then coming back here and pretending
he hadn't—that I have properly regretted it for the first time. The
scales, as they say, have fallen from my eyes.

But I want a chance to explain. I want her to understand that I
didn't plan any of it, that I didn't do it on purpose, to hurt her . . .
not consciously, at least. That the affair—because that's what it
became—swept me along with it, strong as an undertow. This is
not to excuse myself, as I know there is no excuse. Not for doing
something this terrible to one of your oldest friends. But it seems
important to say these things.

I'm also slightly worried for her. She seemed so wild, so drunk,

standing there in her stained and ripped gold dress, like some vengeful fallen goddess. It's so cold now—I hadn't realized it could get any
colder, and she was wearing nothing more than a thin layer of silk,
and her feet were practically bare, except for those ridiculous heels.
She wouldn't do anything stupid, would she? No. I'm fairly certain
that isn't Miranda's way. She would want to harm *us,* not herself.

I suddenly feel exposed out here. The dark surrounds me, fathomless, inscrutable. The only movement I can see is my breath
leaving me in little huffs of vapor. It has just occurred to me that
Miranda could be out here somewhere with me, watching from
some hiding place. I think of that room from earlier, with the rifles.
I must keep my wits about me. I wouldn't put that much past her
at this point. As a friend she can be bad enough. The thought of
having her as an enemy is frankly terrifying.

I knock on the door of her cabin. No answer. I look up at the
dark windows, and imagine her looking out, seeing me, smiling
to herself.

"Miranda," I call, "we need to talk." The cabin looks back at
me blankly, mocking me.

"I need to explain everything to you," I call. My voice seems
to echo in the silence, reverberations coming back at me from far
away, from the encircling mountains. "I'll be waiting, in my cabin,
if you want to talk."

There's no answer. Silence, like a held breath.

BACK IN MY CABIN JULIEN IS SITTING WRAPPED IN A TOWEL,
huddled on the sofa, sipping neat from a bottle of Scotch. I think
it might have been the complimentary one provided by the estate.
I hadn't touched it at all, but it is now more than half empty.

"Julien." I try to pry it out of his grasp. He clings on to it, like a
child to a toy. "Julien, you need to stop. You're going to kill yourself if you drink any more."

He shakes his head. "She'll kill me first. She'll take everything I've worked for. She'll destroy me . . . you don't understand."

He looks completely pathetic, curled in the towel. Suddenly I'm almost repulsed by him. His broad, muscled chest looks ridiculous. Who has a body like that unless they're incredibly vain? Before it had seemed exotic, so different to the men I had been with. And the flattery of him wanting me—that had been perhaps the biggest turn-on of all. Over the last six months I have been able to overlook the little things that rankled with me: his selfishness after we'd had sex, always running to the shower first, or always demanding that we did things his way, or failing to respond to any of my messages for several days and then becoming irate if I left one of his unreplied to for more than an hour. The excitement of it all—the subterfuge, the illicit rendezvous, and yes, the quality of the sex, had made them palatable.

Was that all it was? I ask myself, now. The real source of the excitement, beyond any chemistry, or physical attraction? The sheer disbelief that he wanted me, and not Miranda? Did I really envy her that much? *Yes,* a little voice says. Maybe I did.

48

HEATHER

Now
January 2, 2019

DOUG IS RIGHT. IT DOESN'T LOOK GOOD FOR HIM. IT SEEMS
that he may have been the last person here to see the guest alive.
But I now feel oddly invested in his innocence. I just don't think
he did it.

It's funny, a couple of days ago I knew so little of him. I wouldn't
have known whether I could trust him. Seeing those news results
load, the horror of the headlines about him, had briefly seemed as
good as a guilty sentence. But for some reason, since the vulner-
ability and honesty of his confessions about himself, I feel differently. He has bared his innermost, most shameful secrets to me, and
yet, somehow, I find I can't judge him too harshly for it.

And then there was that conversation overheard in the hallway.
Two of the guests, at least, may not be as innocent in this as they
appear. I only wish I hadn't dislodged that sodding picture, that I
had been able to hear more.

I enter the living room, and they all look up.

"Are the police here yet?" the woman called Samira asks, jostling the baby on her lap. Could it have been her in the corridor, the woman's voice? I'm not sure. She was the one who alerted us to the disappearance in the first place. But that doesn't necessarily mean anything.

"No," I say, "though they're hoping it may be clearer by this afternoon."

She nods sullenly. They are all watching me, I know. I'd give a good deal to have the situation be reversed, so that I could observe them instead, watch them for any betraying anomalies, flickers of guilt. I go to the kettle, on autopilot, to make more tea, and I see we've run out already. At a rough calculation, that's some fifty tea bags in a day. There are more in the store. I shrug on my down jacket, my red hat, my hiking boots, and tramp out into the world of white, the snow squeaking with each step.

I unlock the big doors of the barn, unleashing a scent of dust and wood shavings and turpentine. On one side are all of our supplies: bottled water in case of a supply fault (it has happened more than once), sugar and packs of Nespresso pods and loo rolls and crates of beer. Life's little necessities, even in this place.

Out here's also where we have the feed from the CCTV camera on the gate, humming away on an ancient TV screen. There's much better technology out there nowadays—I could get it all streamed to my computer in the office—but the boss is oddly stingy about some things. I glance at the display: the familiar image of the track. There's so much snow that there's barely any definition to the picture—everything it shows is white.

On the other side is all the stalking equipment: the camouflage gear, the walking boots, the binoculars. The neat row of hunting rifles. Doug's military precision.

Except . . .

I blink, look again. Recount.

. . . Except that one of the rifles seems to be missing. One of the brackets is empty. I think there are normally ten. And now there are only nine.

I turn on the radio, still in the pocket of my jacket. My hand hovers over the transmit button—I'm about to call Doug, to ask him if there's any reason for this absence. Has he, say, taken one of the rifles for something? Then I stop and think: *Can I trust him? Should I really draw his attention to what I've noticed? Because perhaps he already knows. Perhaps he was the one who took it.*

After all, whoever took the rifle must have had access to the store, which pretty much rules out one of the guests. There are only two other people who know the passcode. And the other left the estate on the afternoon of New Year's Eve to spend it with his family.

I'm trying to decide what to do with this new knowledge. It's not a reassuring thought, precisely, but it occurs to me that I'm not sure Doug would even need to take a rifle from here—I think he has his own. And maybe there have only ever been nine rifles. I rub my eyes, which are sore, gritty with tiredness. I'm so, so tired. Maybe I'm simply conjuring chimeras out of my own mind.

I grab the big box of tea. I won't say anything to Doug, I decide. But I'll keep it in mind, too. Just in case. As I pass the old CCTV monitor I glance at the screen displaying its unchanging snowy scene: the view from the gates. Our recordings might well be the most uneventful in the UK. It might as well be showing me a fixed image, if it weren't for the flakes of snow falling listlessly past the lens, the seconds ticking over in the top-right-hand corner. An identical scene to when I checked it for any sign of the missing guest, seeing nothing more than a time lapse of the snow. I remember fast-forwarding through the frames: nothing, nothing, nothing, dizzy with the sameness of it all. And yet . . . a sudden quickening of my heartbeat, my body seeming to understand something even before my mind does. *Nothing.* But shouldn't there have been . . . something? Shouldn't I have seen, for example, a red truck—Iain's truck—leaving the property on New Year's Eve? He left on New

Year's Eve: this is what I've assumed the whole time. This is what I told the police.

But if I didn't see him leave . . .

. . . Then he must be here. Somewhere, on the estate. It's the only explanation.

My radio crackles. It's Doug. "Where are you?" he asks.

I think of that light I saw on New Year's Eve, traveling up the flank of the Munro, toward the Old Lodge.

I think of the one other viable shelter on the estate, which Doug and I didn't even bother checking because no one goes in there, because it's locked. I suddenly know where I have to go. I think of how emphatically Iain has always told me *never to go near it* because of the danger. I think, too, of how he told me not to let the guests outside at night.

"Heather, are you there?" Doug's voice echoes in the silence of the barn. There is, I think, genuine concern in his voice. "Are you all right?"

"Yes," I say. "I'll—I'll be back in a bit." I slip the radio back into my pocket.

THIS IS PROBABLY A VERY STUPID IDEA. I KNOW THE SENSIBLE thing would be staying put, in the warmth and safety of the Lodge. But I'm sick of doing nothing. And I don't mean simply these last few days. Because, really, I've been doing nothing for so long, running away, hiding from everything. Here is a chance to prove something to myself.

I've kitted myself out from the storeroom. Even sturdier hiking boots, a pair of binoculars, a multi-tool. I have my mobile in my pocket, which is only really useful as a torch, unless I can get any signal up on the peak. I didn't bother with the camo gear, of course—it would be almost as visible as anything else against the white of the landscape. Oh, and I sling a rifle over my shoulder. I've only shot once, and I wouldn't say it exactly came easily to me. But it's better than nothing. It will act as a deterrent, if not a weapon.

As I walk, I summarize what I know of Iain. Not much, is the answer. I don't even know his surname. He's mentioned his "missus" to me a couple of times, but I've never met her. I can't recall, trying to summon a mental image of him, whether he wears a wedding ring—but then I can't even precisely recall the features of his face. On the whole, when he has been here, he has seemed part of the landscape. He has gone about his work without any consultation with me, on—I have always assumed—instructions direct from the boss.

If anything, the snow is thicker still on the flank of the Munro. I slip and fall several times—the gradient is almost too much for my hiking boots, even this low down. This is exactly the sort of behavior we would counsel the guests against. Do not go out without the proper equipment. At least I've got the radio in my pocket, if necessary.

I take a deep breath. I haven't come up here for a long time.

The ruins, and the standing stable building, look particularly dark against the fresh-fallen snow. I hate this place. I can smell the burn on it, and it smells like death. It smells like everything that I have run away from. Well, I'm not running anymore.

EATHER? HEATHER—WHERE ARE YOU? IT'S BEEN ALMOST AN hour." My radio is crackling. It's Doug, of course.

It's the faint note of panic in his voice—something I've never heard, even when he was telling me about his past—that compels me to answer.

"I'm . . . outside."

"Why? What are you doing?" He sounds angry.

"I just wanted to do a bit more exploring, that's all—I've had an idea about something."

"For Christ's sake, Heather—are you mad? Tell me exactly where you are. I'm coming to find you."

"No," I tell him. "You have to keep an eye on the guests."

Before he can reply, I cut him off. I need to concentrate.

The door of the stable building is locked, just as it has always been, the little screen of the passcode panel blinking. It looks so incongruous against the old stone. Iain told me once, right at the beginning, that the building isn't structurally sound. It could fall down at any point. And then we'd end up with a horror of a lawsuit on our hands. "The big man wants to make sure it's really secure," he said. "Don't go anywhere near it. We don't want any guests going in there and killing themselves when the roof falls in on them."

I have always been very happy to give the place the widest berth possible. I have never come near the Old Lodge unless I can help it. When we were searching for the missing guest, we came up here. I tried the door, felt the unyielding resistance of the lock against my hand, and hurried away again. So now is the first time that it has occurred to me to wonder why I have never been given the passcode. At the time I had simply seen the locked door and assumed that meant that there was no way the guest could be within.

It feels, suddenly, like a secret that has been under my nose the whole time and which I've never stopped to see, so wrapped up have I been in my inner world, the long legacy of my grief. If I hadn't been, would that guest have died? I push the thought away. It is not worth thinking about now.

There is no way I can force the door: it's an ancient, heavy, oak affair, and there's no give against the lock when I push it. And if I shove too hard, I'm worried I really might bring the building down on my head. So I walk around to the back. All the windows are boarded up, impenetrable.

Ah, but now that I'm looking, I can see that one of the boards higher up is a little loose. There's a dark gap showing through a chink between it and the next one. If I stand on one of the rocks below I might just be able to reach it. I clamber onto one of the fallen stones, I take the multi-tool from my pocket, open up the pliers, and use them to grip one end of the plank. The stone I'm standing on rocks beneath my weight ominously, and the rifle knocks against me. I take it off my shoulder. I'm sure the safety is on, but I have a sudden vision of myself slipping and discharging the gun.

I work the pliers back and forth, using all my strength, until I feel the board begin to give. With a *pop!* a nail springs free, and the board swings downward to expose a gap the length of my arm. After that it's easy to wrench the neighboring boards away to expose a square foot of space. I peer inside, gripping the ledge of the plank below with my hands, feeling the rock tilt dangerously beneath me. There's a musty smell—and yes, just discernible—the century-old smell of burned things. Can that be possible, or is it just my imagination? I can make out very little—but what I can see is that the space is not empty. There is something in the middle of the room, a pile of something. I climb down and take out my phone, flip it onto the torch function. For a moment I have the strongest impression of being watched. I check in every direction, but see just the undisturbed sugar shell of snow—save the track of my own footprints. It is probably just the silence up here. The Old Lodge does that to you. It has a presence all of its own.

I cast the beam toward the object in the middle of the room. I can see it now, but can't quite work it out. It isn't one object, but a collection: a teetering stack of packages, tightly wrapped with clear film, each individual package roughly the size of a bag of sugar.

Actually, whatever is within, bulging through the clear wrapping, looks a little like sugar: some whitish substance. And then the penny drops. I'm suddenly fairly certain that whatever is inside those packages is something very different from and far more valuable than sugar.

As in a nightmare, I hear the footsteps behind me.

"What are you doing up there?" Almost polite, conversational.

I drop down in shock, my hands catching the rough wood on the way down, splinters tearing into my flesh. My legs hardly support me; they are suddenly weak with fear. I reach for the rifle and hear rather than feel the loud crack of something hitting the back of my skull. My sight is snuffed out like a blown candle.

WHEN I COME TO IT TAKES SEVERAL SECONDS FOR MY VI-sion to clear. When it does, I make out a figure standing over me. At first I don't even recognize him, through the haze of pain in my head, and because of what he's wearing: a huge down jacket, even bigger than mine, that makes him look almost double his normal size. His face is pinched with cold, blue about the lips. He looks like someone who has been sleeping rough. But it is Iain.

"I don't understand," I say stupidly. "I thought you were at home. Where have you—" I stop, because I see that he is carrying a gun. He holds it loosely, at the moment, but he hefts it in his hands. The gesture, I am sure, is to show his ease with it—and how simple it would be to lift it and aim it at me.

"I told you not to come up here," he says. "I told you to keep away."

"Because you said it wasn't safe," I say.

"Precisely. It isn't safe, as you see."

"You told me it was because of the building, because it might fall down. Not because—" I don't know how to express it, whether it's safe to do so: *Not because there is something in here you don't want me to see.*

"Yes. You're either less stupid than I had banked on you being—or a lot *more* stupid. I'm trying to work out which. I think it's probably the latter."

Why—why—did I not just wait for the police, voice my suspicions to them? I *am* stupid. More than that, I didn't even tell Doug where I was going. *Because you knew he would stop you.* I have been a complete idiot. This whole thing, suddenly, looks like a suicide mission. And the thought occurs to me . . . *was* it a suicide mission? I think of the oblivion I have contemplated in the past: the pills, the bridge. I have spent a long time thinking that perhaps dying wouldn't be such a bad thing after all. But now—and perhaps it's just some deep-rooted animal instinct—I suddenly discover I want to live.

"Look," I say, trying to sound calm, reasonable. "Let's pretend I didn't see any of this. I'll just go away, and it will be like it never happened."

He actually laughs. "No, I don't think we can do that."

I stare at him. If it weren't so horrifying it might almost be fascinating, the change that has come over this man, who, from what I gleaned, seemed a simple, uncomplicated sort, if a bit taciturn. But then it isn't a change, I realize. This is the real him. He's just worn the other persona like a cloak.

He steps forward, reaching with his spare arm, and I flinch away. "Fine," he says. "We'll do it like this." He raises the rifle. I go rigid, my skin tightening, my throat closing up in terror. I think: *This is it. He's going to kill me.*

"Start walking," he says. "What are you waiting for?"

He directs me around the other side of the stable building. Keeping the rifle vaguely trained in my direction, he reaches for the passcode. This is my opportunity, I think. This is the bit where I could try and run. But run to where? There is just gaping whiteness, all around. He couldn't hope for a clearer target. So I can only wait while he opens the door and ushers me inside, into the darkness.

Immediately, I realize that it's much warmer in here than I expected. In the corner of the room, I see, he has set up a generator.

"How nice of you," I say, trying to sound less afraid than I feel. "To think of me."

He sneers.

"And what have you got there?" I ask. "Brown paper packages tied up with string?"

I am talking, because the talking—the effort of not screaming, of forming the words—seems to be keeping me calm.

"Exactly," Iain says. "And you definitely *don't* need to worry your little head about what's inside."

But I need to keep him talking. I have to find a way to stay alive—and at the moment, distracting him from the business of killing me is the only card I have up my sleeve. There's no point in promising him I won't tell anyone about what I've seen. He won't believe me. He would probably be right.

So instead, I ask, "Is this what you've been doing the whole time? The jobs about the estate—were they just a ruse? I can imagine this is probably a bit more lucrative."

"Wouldn't you like to know?" he says. And then he gives a sort of "why not?" shrug—which cannot be good. If he's deciding it's okay to tell me things, he has also decided that I won't have an opportunity to tell them to anyone else. No point in thinking like that. Just buy yourself time. Time is life.

"If you must know," he says, "I like to think of this as just another one of my jobs. I build a mean drystone wall. I can re-grout a windowpane in ten minutes. And I make a pretty good . . . deliveryman."

"I see," I say slowly, as though I am fascinated by his genius. "You bring it in on your truck from—"

"Let's just say from *somewhere*," he says, faux-patient.

"And then you keep it here and then—" I try to think beyond the wailing panic alarm in my head. What would be the point in bringing it here, one of the remotest places in the UK, with no way of getting it anywhere else?

And then I think of the history of the place. The old laird, insisting they build him his station. "Then you put it on the train."

He doffs an imaginary cap to me with his free hand. "Straight down to London." He smiles, and the expression makes him look all the more sinister. I wonder how I could ever have thought he was a normal, simple-living guy. He looks like a maniac. He looks more than capable of strangling that woman. I won't ask him about that yet, though. I'll keep him talking on this.

The radio, I think. If I could just get my hand to the transmit button, I might be able to get through to Doug. I could keep my finger on the button so there won't be any giveaway feedback. He'd hear everything. Perhaps I could even say something that would let him know exactly where I am.

"Straight down to London," I say. "How very clever. Like the whiskey, in the old days. Of course—they think the laird himself was in on that, did you know?"

Iain doesn't say anything. But he does give me a look. *Duh.*

"Oh." The realization hits me like a punch to the gut. "The boss is in on this, too?"

Iain doesn't answer—he doesn't need to.

It's just like the old times: the laird taking a cut from the smuggled whiskey. And I've spent the last year blithely going about my business in the office—wondering, would the boss like to advertise the Lodge a bit more widely? Of course he didn't want to. The business must have been a nice blind for him—but too many visitors, and people might start noticing things.

I have been a complete fool. They must have been laughing at me, all this time. The idiot in the office, not seeing what was going on under her very nose.

"And how do you get it on the train?" I ask. "Without anyone noticing?"

He gives me another look. Of course: that station guard, Alec. I think of how he behaved when I went to look around the station, the way he stood in front of the door up to his flat. Because he had something to hide.

Doug, I think. Does *he* know? Am I the only one here who has been kept in the dark? It might have been a kind of quid pro quo: turn a blind eye to the goings-on here, and we'll turn a blind eye to your criminal record.

If I radio him, now, will he simply ignore me? He wouldn't want me to die, though, would he? I think of how open, how vulnerable he was with me back at the Lodge. But that could all have been an act. Because the truth is, I realize, it was all a brief fantasy. I don't actually know him at all.

I have to try; it's my only chance. In incremental movements, so as not to draw attention, I inch a hand up my body, toward my pocket. Iain doesn't seem to notice. He's studying the gun as though it were a particularly fascinating pet.

I slide my hand into my pocket, slowly, slowly. My fingers brush the antenna of the radio, feeling for the hard body of it.

"What the fuck are you doing?"

His face is dark with anger. He strides over to me in a couple of steps. "N-nothing."

"Take your hand out of your fucking pocket." He reaches roughly into my jacket and grabs hold of the radio. He looks at it for a couple of seconds, in mute rage, and then throws it at the wall with more force than I would have thought a man of his size capable of. It falls to the stone floor with a clatter, and in two pieces.

Now he comes at me with a roll of gaffer tape, and roughly binds my wrists, so hard that the bones bruise against one another, and my ankles. While he's down by my feet I test the bonds around my hands. I can't move them at all. He might as well have bound them together with a metal chain for all the give the gaffer tape has. I could try to kick him in the head, I think, while he's crouched there. But I'm not sure I could get enough force into my legs. He's not a big man, Iain, but he's strong enough: all the work he does on the estate. And if I just hurt him slightly, not enough to hinder him—which is the most likely outcome of this—he will only kill me quicker.

Iain stands up, looking proud of his work. Then there is a sudden, deafening bang. He pitches forward, with a look of slack-jawed surprise, and lands on top of me, the rifle clattering to the floor. I can't make sense of what has just happened. I can't see anything, either, because he's on top of me. And then I realize that the front of my gray jacket is wet with dark red blood.

49

MIRANDA

One day earlier
New Year's Day 2019

I CAN'T BELIEVE THE GAMEKEEPER REJECTED ME. THE HUMILIA-
tion of it, when I had thought it might make me feel a bit better
about myself.

The pain of it all winds me. I fold over on myself as if someone has actually punched me in the gut, and let myself sink to the
ground. The sting of the sharp pebbles beneath my knees feels
oddly right, so does the cold on my skin—though it doesn't feel
cold, it feels like fire. I must look completely absurd, kneeling here
in my gold dress and stiletto heels. And perhaps it's just because
I'm aware of what a state I must appear . . . but I have the sudden
strange, animal feeling that I'm not alone.

As I look about me I catch a shiver of movement in the trees near
the loch. I could have sworn I saw the dark shape of something—
someone—in the darkness of the pines. I'm certain now. Someone
else is out here with me. Oh, whatever. I don't care. Normally, I

might be unnerved. But *nothing* can shock me as much as what I just saw, in that sauna.

No doubt my observer, in the trees, is very much enjoying my little display. I think of the Icelandic man's grin when I spotted them in the woods, his beckoning hand.

"Go on," I shout, into the silence. "Get a good long look. See if I fucking care."

MMA, I THINK. I'LL GO AND SEE EMMA. I NEED TO TALK TO someone. With any luck, Mark is still passed out on the couch in the sitting room of the Lodge. I check through the windows. Yes, he's there, spread-eagled on his back.

I knock on the door of their cabin. Silence. It's after four in the morning, after all. I try again. Finally, the door swings open. Emma stands there frowning, looking groggy. She's in pajamas: silk, piped ones, not dissimilar to my own set.

"Oh," she says. "Hi, Manda."

I normally flinch when she calls me that. It sounds too try-hard. Only Julien and Katie really use it, the two people closest to me. No, the irony of that is not lost on me.

"Can I come in?" I ask.

"Sure." No questions, no hesitation. I feel a sharp stab of guilt for the way I've been with her. She has only ever been nice to me, while, at times, I've behaved like such a bitch—showing her up in front of the others, excluding her. Well, from now on everything is going to be different. I'm going to be different.

I follow her inside. It's almost the same design as ours: the one large room, the armchairs and fireplace, the big four-poster, the dressing table—even the stag's head mounted on the wall. The major difference is that it's pin neat, like stepping into an alternative reality. Our belongings are scattered everywhere, we've always been such slobs. *Our,* I think, *we.* No more: it's all going to change. The house we bought together, all our plans. All that history. My legs suddenly don't feel capable of supporting me.

I stagger over to the nearest chair, which happens to be the little stool at the dressing table.

"Do you want a drink?" Emma gestures to the cocktail cabinet in the corner. She hasn't asked me what this is all about yet, but the gesture suggests that she knows something is wrong.

"Yes, please."

She pours me a whiskey. "More please," I say, and she raises an eyebrow a fraction, then slugs another inch into the glass. I thought I'd had a lot to drink last night, but suddenly I feel far too sober, my mind painfully clear, the images in it unforgettable, sharp-focused. I want to stop seeing them. I want to be numbed, anesthetized.

Beyond the window the light in the sauna is still on. How could they have been so stupid? It's almost like they wanted to be found. Perhaps they genuinely hadn't appreciated how conspicuous it looks out there in the dark, like a lantern against the night. A beacon. I wonder—even though I know I shouldn't think about it—what they're doing, now. Are they discussing next steps, like co-conspirators? Have they even put their clothes back on? I can't get that image out of my head: her paleness against the tan of his skin, their dark heads together. I take a gulp of the whiskey, letting it burn its path down my throat, focusing on the pain of it. But I'm not sure all the whiskey in the world will help me to forget how strangely, horribly beautiful they were together.

"Emma," I say, "do you have any paper?"

She raises her eyebrows only a fraction. "Er . . . I think so." She produces a pad from somewhere—Basildon Bond. It's so Emma, somehow, to have a pad of writing paper on hand.

Now my mind is oddly clear. As though some other power is guiding me, I go to the dressing table beside the bed, sit down, and write a note to Julien. I'll give it to Emma, make sure she passes it on.

All I want is to do as much damage as possible, to make him feel the sense of powerlessness that I do. My hand is shaking so much I have to press the pen to the paper to control my writing; twice it rips the whole way through. Good. He'll see that I mean business. With one fell stroke, he has just destroyed everything I thought I knew. Well, now I will destroy him.

50

HEATHER

Now
January 2, 2019

D OUG DRAGS IAIN OFF ME, AS THOUGH HE WERE A SACK OF sand, and leaves him where he lies, moaning like an animal. Then he hunkers down in front of me, and grips my shoulders with both hands.

"Are you all right? Heather? What the fuck were you thinking? I followed your footsteps, through the snow—" and then, "What did he do to you? Jesus Christ, Heather—" Something about the expression on his face, the concern in it—the care—is almost too much. So, too, is the feel of his hand—now cupping my jaw, his fingertips callused but his touch light, brushing the hair back from my forehead, assessing for damage with infinite care. I would not have known such a big man could be so gentle.

"I'm fine," I say. "No—he didn't hurt me."

"He did." He takes his hand away from the side of my head and shows me his palm, slick with blood. "That fucking—"

He gets up and lifts a foot, as if to kick Iain, who whimpers below him on the ground, his hand pressed to his shoulder, where the blood is seeping through his down jacket in a dark brown stain. He looks as though he might be about to pass out.

It's hard to watch. "Don't, Doug." It seems the old paramedic instinct is still in me: to preserve life.

"Why? Look what he did to you, Heather. I won't let him get away with it."

"But . . . we don't want him to die." That's a lot of blood. When Doug still doesn't look convinced I say, "And he might know something—we have to find out."

He wavers. "Fine."

He doesn't look convinced, but he lowers his foot. And at my insistence he makes a dressing, ripping a piece of fabric from the bottom of his own shirt, pressing it to Iain's shoulder beneath the jacket, to stop the bleeding.

Iain watches him with dull eyes, unresisting. His skin is grayish, his body is slumped. Doug keeps a foot on him, just above his groin, in case he were to try for an escape . . . though he hardly seems capable of that.

"You'll be all right," Doug tells him matter-of-factly, as if he can hear my thoughts. "It's just torn your shoulder. I've seen worse. It'll sting like a bitch of course, but then . . . well, you deserve it, don't you, *mate*?"

"Why did you kill her?" I ask Iain.

"What?" He frowns, and then grimaces again, against the pain.

"The guest. Did you push her into that gully because she saw something? Because she was on to you?"

"I didn't kill her," he moans.

"I don't believe you," I say.

"I've never killed anyone," he says, breathing heavily between each word, as though running up a hill. I hope Doug's right about the wound not being that bad. "I've done some bad things in my time, but I've never *killed* a person."

There seems to be a genuine repugnance about the way he says "killed"—as though it really is something he sees as beyond the pale. But then he's done a fairly good job of acting the innocent up until now.

"I didn't kill that woman. Why would I?"

"If she saw something," I say. "Like I saw something—you were prepared to kill me. You were going to shoot me."

"No," he says, "no—I wasn't. I hardly even know how to use that thing." He gestures to the rifle, where it lies on the floor. Doug hefts his own rifle in his hand—a warning. *I do,* the movement says. I know how to use it. Iain sees this, swallows.

"But you took it from the storeroom," I say, "so you must have thought you might use it."

He looks genuinely perplexed. "No," he says, weakly, "no, I didn't."

"What do you mean, you didn't? You've had it pointed at my head for the last hour."

He looks at me as if I'm going mad. "That's the rifle *you* had when you came up here. I pointed it at you to stop you from going anywhere." He moves slightly, and winces against the pain. He is sweating horribly. "Look, *I* was the one that saw something. That was why I moved the stash—from the pumphouse to up here."

I'm caught by those words. *I saw something.* "What do you mean?" I ask urgently. "What did you see?"

"I saw her get killed. The girl. And then I thought, Oh, fuck, the police are going to be all over this by the morning. They'll be searching the whole place. They'll find everything. I knew I had to move the stuff farther away from the Lodge, and get it off the estate by the time they arrived. But I hadn't realized about the snow. They couldn't get here—but we couldn't get away, either. The train—" He stops, as though he knows he's given too much away. That *we* interests me, but there isn't time to ponder it now.

"You've been using the trains?" Doug asks at the same time as I say, "How did she die? The woman. You said you saw it. I suppose you're going to say she fell?"

"No." He shakes his head. "Of course not. She was murdered. I saw it all. I was there, near the pumphouse. Early in the morning, about four A.M., checking on the stuff, like I told you. *She* killed her."

"She?" I ask.

"Yes. The other woman. One of the guests. They had an argument, I think—I couldn't hear what about, exactly. But I did hear her saying, 'You were never really my friend. Friends don't do that to each other.' And I thought, oh, classic woman's tiff, about some love affair or something. Inconvenient, but no matter. I'll lie low, I thought, wait for it to blow over, wait for them to get out of the area. But then I saw the other one grab her by the neck, like she was trying to choke the words out of her. And then push her, right in the center of the chest. Just watched as she fell. Cold as anything."

51

MIRANDA

One day earlier
New Year's Day 2019

THIS IS THE ONLY THING THAT BRINGS ME SOME RELIEF: THE thought of Julien's horror at the idea of me telling the world about him. He'll be thinking, *I won't try her yet. I'll try in an hour or so, when she's had a chance to calm down.* But he'll be too late. I'm going to hide out until I can get the first train down to London. I think of Julien going to the cabin, finding it empty, panic setting in properly. My note, left for him: *There is nothing you can say. I should never have kept your secret for you in the first place.*

"There." I put the pen down, satisfied by my work. The dressing table is neatly ordered. A hairbrush, a small wooden box, a couple of lipsticks. One of them is Chanel. I turn it upside down, read the little label. *Pirate:* the same shade I wear. I thought I'd recognized it on Emma last night, but it's so difficult to tell: everyone wears color differently.

"I have this one," I say. "It's my favorite." Actually, I need to buy another. I've lost my old one somewhere, probably in the lining of one of my handbags.

"Oh yeah," Emma says. "I love it." I open it up, and focus on applying it perfectly to my mouth in the mirror, a waxy crimson bow. I read somewhere once that sales of lipsticks go up when times are tough. I pout at myself in the mirror. Never has "war paint" seemed like a more appropriate term. My face is pale, sunken-eyed, but the lipstick transforms it. It gives my face resolution, context, like a piece of punctuation. I try a smile, and quickly stop. I look deranged, like Heath Ledger's Joker.

"Lipstick looks so good on you," Julien told me once. "On other women it always looks like they're trying a bit too hard. But you're—what's that saying— you're born to wear it."

I take a tissue from the dispenser, wipe it off. Now my mouth just appears raw-looking, bloody.

"Look," Emma says now. "Shall we go over to the Lodge? It's more comfortable there. Mark's passed out in the living room, but still . . ."

"Oh," I say, "no thanks. I don't want to see anyone else. I'm getting the first train in the morning, and that's going to be it. I don't ever want to see Julien or Katie again, if I don't have to."

Her eyes go wide. "Manda—oh my God . . . what's happened?"

I have an idea of myself delivering the news with the cool panache of a thirties movie star. But to my horror, I realize that the tears are coming; I can feel them rising within me, like an unstoppable tide. I haven't cried in so long—not since I got my Third, while just across from me Katie opened her envelope to reveal a big, shiny First.

I clench my hands into fists, dig my nails into the soft flesh of my palms. "Julien and Katie have been sleeping together." I still can't bring myself to say: *having an affair.* Not yet. It sounds so intimate, so sordid.

"Oh my God." She puts a hand to her mouth. But she's not quite meeting my eyes. The whole performance rings false.

I don't believe it. Emma, of all people, knew that my husband was screwing around while I didn't? What the fuck? "You *knew*?"

"Only since yesterday night, I swear, Miranda. Mark told me."

Mark, I think—the little secret of Julien's he'd warned me about. This was it. This is what he was trying to tell me. No wonder he looked confused when I told him I wasn't interested in hearing.

"I didn't want to just tell you, you know," she says. "I suppose I wanted to give Katie or Julien a chance to tell you themselves. I didn't want to presume I had any right."

"What, to tell me my husband and my best friend are fucking?"

"I'm so sorry, Manda. I should have told you . . . I'll never forgive myself—"

She looks so tragic that I wave her away with a hand—I can't be bothered. "You know what . . . whatever. It isn't about you. I know now. And I know what I'm going to do about it." I hand her the note. "Look," I say, "I want you to make sure Julien gets this. I can't bring myself to give it to him."

"Okay," she says, taking it. "But why—"

"Could I have another?" I say, at the same time, holding out my glass.

"Of course." She smiles. "It's medicinal, you know."

She turns away and busies herself with pouring the measures, the ice.

For something to do, more than anything, I pick up the little box on the dressing table. It's a pretty, painted thing, one of those Chinese puzzle boxes. My granny used to have one. I turn it upside down. It's the same style, I think, as hers. I used to play with it—once she showed me the secret, the way to open it, I was obsessed. Can I still remember? I'm not sure. Tentatively, I push at one of the bottom panels; it doesn't budge. I turn it around and do the same on the other side. It moves. I feel a sense of simple satisfaction. What's the next bit? Oh yes, the panel on the shorter side. My fingers move of their own accord, pushing, twisting. Almost there—I just need to find that lever, pull it out. If it's the same, it will spring open. Aha! Here it is.

"Oh," Emma says, in a strange voice. She's turned toward me, holding both whiskeys. "Oh no—don't do that!"

It's too late. The box has sprung open, disgorging its contents onto the floor with a clatter. There's so much, it's amazing to think it's all been inside there, that little box.

I hear the crash of breaking glass and look up, confused. Emma has dropped both of the whiskeys. Shards of broken glass scatter the floorboards, the liquid spilling around her feet.

"Oh shit," I say, "I'm such an idiot."

But she hardly seems to hear. She hardly seems to notice the whiskey. Instead she's on the ground, scrabbling at the fallen objects among the shards of glass, half shielding the mess with her body.

"Careful," I say, "you'll—" and then the words leave me.

She does not want me to see. But I have seen. Several items I recognize. An earring, lost at the Summer Ball some eleven years ago: the evening I finally got together with Julien. I remember him reaching up to my earlobe, giving it a tug. "Is this a new look? The single earring? Only you could pull it off." It feels now as if it happened to someone else.

A pendant. A present from Katie for my twenty-first. It had given me such a pang to lose it, because it was the one she knew I really wanted from Tiffany's, and it must have cost her so much money.

A Parker fountain pen. I don't recognize that. Oh no, wait, I think I do. I'd lost it somewhere, in the first few weeks of university. I wasn't very good with my belongings, but I had been sure one morning it had been in my bag, and by the afternoon it was missing. I spent a few fruitless hours retracing my steps. Someone must have picked it up, I thought. Well: someone had.

Even my lighter—the one with the crest, lost only the other night.

"Emma," I say. "Why do you have all this stuff? It's all my stuff. Why is it here?" I'm thinking of the little notes left in my cubbyhole. The odd item being returned. But not these: these were clearly considered too precious for that.

"I don't know," Emma says, not looking up at me. "I don't know why all this is here. I had no idea what was in that box—it's Mark's."

Set aside the fact that I can't for a moment imagine Mark owning such a thing. I'm looking at the way she's cradling the things to her chest—the pen, the earring, the necklace. I'm thinking of the look on her face—the sheer terror, that's what it was—when she saw me playing with the box, just before I pulled it open. Her shouted warning. The dropped whiskey glasses.

I'm thinking, too, of the other night.

"Manda," she says, "it's so silly. I can explain."

"No, Emma. I don't think you can."

I'm just working out what it was that unsettled me so much, in what she said the other night. When she talked about that party— the one where I got stuck in the toilet. When she claimed it must've happened in London, when she was there, or that one of the others must have told her. But none of them could have. None of them were there. Because it didn't happen in London; it happened in Oxford.

It was the very first week. Now I remember it very clearly. That's why I was so mortified by it—I needed to make a good impression on everyone—and why I never told any of the others. But Emma, somehow, was in Oxford. At that party. There is no other explanation for it.

I take my phone out of my pocket.

"What are you doing?" she asks, looking up from where she's scrabbling on the floor.

"Finding proof."

For a moment an expression flashes across her face—something violent and urgent—and I think she's about to lunge forward and knock the phone out of my hands. Then she seems to get herself under control.

"What proof?" she asks. She might be faking calm, but her voice is strange—high, shrill.

I don't answer. I'm briefly almost grateful to Julien for insisting that the Lodge's Wi-Fi be switched on. Still, it takes a while to open Facebook, and all the while I can see Emma, looking ready to lunge for my mobile. Eventually, when it loads, I click on "photos of you." I scroll through the photographs. I can't believe how many there are, and how many terrible ones, as I plumb the depths. After all this, when I'm starting afresh, I will have a cull. As I scroll, my face gets younger and younger—my cheeks are fuller, my eyes seem larger. I can't believe how much I've changed; I didn't realize. How much all of us have changed. There is Julien, the beautiful boy I fell in love with, the boy who became the man who has just ruined my life. But I don't have time for that. I'm looking for something else. I must have swiped through hundreds of photographs, half of them failing to load. It doesn't matter. It's further back than this. And then, finally, I'm in the right territory. First-year freshers' week. A week of strangers, of trying to pick among them the people who might be your friends. Every face unknown, so that it would be difficult to remember any one face in particular. This is how she has hidden from me. I'm suddenly certain of what I'm going to find. And there, there it is: a photograph from that very party, I'm certain now, the one where I got stuck in the loo. A sea of milling almost-adults. Terrible quality, but it will do. Because there is a face among them, looking right at me, that I would never have noticed had Emma not given me her prompt. Mousy-haired, rounder-cheeked, the features less decided, the eyes obscured by Harry Potter glasses. Much younger-looking, much dowdier-looking. I look up and compare her to the woman in front of me. And despite all of the changes, it is her, it is unmistakably her.

"It wasn't Mark," I say. "It was you, Emma. You took these things." I can't work out how, but this much is clear. "My lighter," I say, seeing it gleam in her fingers. "Give me my fucking lighter, Emma."

She hands it to me, wordlessly. Now she is looking at me— intently, as though trying to read my mind, work out what I'm going to do next.

Again, I think, I'd quite like to be cool in this moment. To light a fag with this very lighter, and sit back, and ask her to explain it all. How she, Emma, Mark's drippy little girlfriend, who I've only known for three years, came to be my stalker. But I can't. Two revelations in one night. It's too much. I feel, suddenly, like everything I thought I knew has been ripped from under me.

52

EMMA

SO. MIRANDA AND I DO GO BACK QUITE A WAY, AFTER ALL. NO, not as long as Miranda and Katie, her utterly false "best" friend. But further than Julien or Mark, certainly. To explain, I have to take you back more than a decade.

Oxford interviews. Autumn. The academic interview I'd be fine on, I knew. No worries there. I knew the slight concern, held by my parents, certainly, was the personal interview. What if they had in some way got hold of my record: the trouble at my previous school? If so, I had been drilled. It had all been a terrible misunderstanding, you know how teenage girls can be—etc. No mention of the psychiatrist (it wasn't their right to ask about that, apparently), or his diagnosis.

Would they, essentially, see past the brilliance of my academic record, and see the real me (whoever that was)? And would that be a problem? Because, in actual fact, you don't get seven A's at A level without having certain—one could say—obsessive qualities. The academic output was the positive manifestation of it. The other thing, with that stupid girl, was the negative.

When it came to the dreaded interview I got away with it. I got the "interests" question, of course. As I answered—tennis, French cinema of the Nouvelle Vague period (all borrowed from interviews with various film directors and learned, rote), cooking—I wondered what they would make of it if I told them my real hobbies. Observation, close study, collection. The only issue was that the things I had liked to collect were rather unusual. I liked to collect personalities.

HERE'S THE THING. I HAVE NEVER REALLY FELT LIKE A REAL person. Not in the proper sense, the way other people seemed to feel it. From quite a young age I had discovered I was very good at certain things—particularly learning, academia. But a machine can learn. What I seemed to lack was a personality of my own. I lacked any sense of "me." But that's okay. What you don't have you can always borrow, or steal.

So I was always on the lookout for particularly colorful personalities, like a parasite searching for a host. There was the girl at the first school, which ended in a rather unfortunate way when she told her parents that I followed her home from school and sometimes sat in the tree house opposite her window, watching her. This was rather unfair. I was only doing my homework, just like any other child. I could do all of my real homework on the short bus journey from school. The real swotting for me was in learning her habits, studying the way she was when she was on her own, what her bedroom looked like, what music she listened to. Then I would go home and emulate these tastes and habits: buy the same CDs, the same clothes.

I was moved to a different school, after the meeting with the headmistress. Then another, when the same thing happened at the next. "Oh," I said blithely, in the interview, "my father's job changed a lot, so we moved around the country following him." She gave me an unconvinced look at this, but—as I suspected—my academic performance far outweighed any other concerns.

T WAS IN THE JUNIOR COMMON ROOM OF THE COLLEGE THAT I met Miranda. She seemed lit up from within. Had absolute confidence in who she was. She drank a beer with some of the guys, and played pool with them, and then seemed to get bored—perhaps it was the slavish adoration with which they were looking at her. Then her gaze landed, incredibly, on me.

She came and sat down next to me in the empty seat across the table. "Hi. How did your interviews go?"

I was so stunned I couldn't speak for a second. Looking at her was like looking directly at the sun. It wasn't just that she was beautiful. It was that she was so very much herself—complex and contradictory and multilayered, as I would learn—but absolutely, uniquely, triumphantly her own person.

"I have the same feeling," she says. "I mean, I think the first went really well, of course"—I remember the fabulous arrogance of that, even now!—"but I'm not at all sure about the second one. There were some horrible questions about the use of metaphors in Donne's Holy Sonnets and I totally froze up—I don't think they seemed very impressed. But maybe I winged it. That happens sometimes, doesn't it?"

I nodded, though I wasn't even really sure of the question. The question, really, was immaterial. Because I would have found it absolutely impossible not to agree with her.

"Look," she said, "I really need a drink. No more beer for me; I want something stronger. Do you want a drink?"

I nodded, still numb with blissful surprise. We had another academic interview in the morning, but that seemed completely meaningless now.

She bought us two Jim Beam and Cokes, which at the time seemed the most sophisticated thing I had ever experienced: the sly, sticky warmth of the bourbon beneath all the sweetness of the soda. She drank hers with a straw, and somehow made it look cool. I kept waiting for her to really *see* me, or rather the lack of me, the thing that was missing, the void inside. She'd be appalled, she'd be disgusted—she'd realize her mistake and go off with any of the other bright young things who were so much more her type. But it never happened. What I hadn't come to appreciate then was that Miranda is—was—someone who spends so much time negotiating the various disparate parts of herself that she doesn't have very much time to properly see anyone else. To notice any discrepancy, or lack. And that has always suited me just fine. In addition to this, Miranda likes a project. She doesn't like to go for the expected thing. She has eclectic taste, is a collector in her own way. Before anything else we had that much in common.

It didn't seem to matter to her what I said—or indeed what I didn't say, as I sat there, dazzled. She was happy to have a mirror, a sounding board.

ALREADY SHE MADE ALL THE OTHERS, THE ONES BEFORE, THE causes of so much heartache and shame, seem like paper cutouts of people. Here, finally, was something to emulate. Here was a proper project, worthy of all my resources and attention. Or, as other people, normal people, might have put it: here was someone who could be my friend.

We went dancing in a club she'd learned about from a third year who was meant to be supervising us, but spent most of the evening trying to chat her up. As soon as we got in there, she shook him off with an "as if" roll of her eyes, and grabbed my hand. We danced on a little retro multicolored dance floor, sticky with spilled drinks. For once I wasn't aware of my fatness, or my weirdness, or—briefly, joyously—the absence inside, because I was borrowing from her light: I was like the moon to her sun, and it was meant to be.

I didn't believe I would see her again when I got accepted to Oxford. It would be too perfect, and I wasn't used to the things

I wanted happening. Besides, for all her brilliance, I wasn't sure that she would have been bright enough—in the Oxford sense—to have got in. But there she was, at registration. My Best Friend to Be. My inspiration, my living mood board. The fount from which I might draw in the hopes of constructing a personality of my own.

I stood in line and waited for her to notice me. The moment would come, of course, I just had to be patient. It was impossible that she wouldn't notice me, we'd had that electric connection. Best friends at first sight. I imagined precisely how it would happen. She'd slouch along the row of freshers, all so raw and shufflingly awkward, already looking like she'd been there for years, like she owned the place. Her hair a gleaming sheet of gold, her leather bag of books pre-battered, her silk scarf trailing almost to the ground. Dazzling. And then she'd stop and do a double take when she saw me. "It's you! Thank *God,* I haven't met anyone else I've wanted to chat to. Fancy going for a coffee?"

And all the others in the queue who had seen only a fat, be-spectacled shell of a person would suddenly see something else—someone who was worthy of the attention of this goddess. I waited for that moment as a priest might await the visitation of the divine presence, tingling with anticipation. She was turning, she was coming toward me—a lazy catch of the silk scarf, a toss of it over her right shoulder. And still I waited, almost trembling now. For a moment I was so overwhelmed I actually shut my eyes, one long blink. And when I opened them she was gone. I turned, in disbelief. She had walked past me. Straight by, without even stopping, let alone saying hello.

I saw that she was turning to talk to the girl behind her: dark-haired, too thin, dowdy. Her clothes almost conspicuously unfashionable—as unstylish as Miranda's were chic. And I understood: she already had a project, a hopeless case. This girl, whoever she was, had usurped me.

Still I had hope. I waited for her to notice me. I went to the

Junior Common Room and sat at the same table and watched her at the bar, drinking her Jim Beam and Coke. I'd sit close enough that I could hear all the things she talked about. I heard once that she hated the food in the canteen—but couldn't cook herself, so supposed she was stuck with it. So that was when I learned to cook, of course. I'd spend hours in the kitchen on her hallway, making elaborate meals as good as any you could find in Oxford's restaurant scene. I'd wait for her to come past and loiter outside the door and say something like, "Oh my God, that smells incredible." Then I'd offer her some of it—because of course it was all for her—and we'd sit down and eat it together and we'd become the best of friends. And I could once again borrow a little of her light.

But it never happened; she never noticed me. The few times she did pass, she was too busy texting on her phone, or chatting with her awful friend, or later, chatting with her equally awful boyfriend. They deserve each other, Katie and Julien. They never deserved her.

THINK OF THE SAD, LONELY GIRL WHO USED TO SIT SIX SEATS behind her in lectures—who remembered the first day she walked into the lecture hall. As with the others, I couldn't decide what I wanted more: to be her, or simply to be close to her. But I could see immediately that neither would be possible. Her friends were nothing like me. None of them were as pretty as she was, but they had the same gloss of cool—even awkward, lank-haired Katie, absorbing some of her allure. They would reject me, as a foreign body.

I had made no impact on her life at all, I began to realize. While she had defined the last few months for me, ever since that interview. So I began to follow her, everywhere. She would—did—call it "stalking." I just thought of it as close observation. And when that didn't satisfy, I began to take things. Sometimes items that I suspected were of sentimental value. Other times things that I knew had high significance—such as the essay she had plagiarized, or the earrings she had stolen. I wore those earrings for a week, the little painted parrots. With them hanging from my ears I felt a little more her, a little less myself, as though they contained some essence of her power, her personality. I actually smiled at baristas in coffee shops, and handed an essay in a day late, and sat in the sun beside the Isis to tan my legs. I waited for her to notice, to challenge me about them. She never did. There was a moment, in the street, when I saw her catch sight of them and stop short. Her mouth formed a small O of surprise. Then she shook her head, as though reprimanding herself about something, and carried on her way, and I knew that she had only seen the earrings. She had not even seen *me*.

That's when I realized that I could force her to pay attention. I could send the items back. I could let her know that it wasn't just her imagination, or that she hadn't suddenly become even more clumsy, more forgetful. Some things, though, the most special things, I did not send back. They were my talismans, like the holy relics of a religion. When I carried them about with me, I felt transformed. I became her guardian angel.

She was so careless. Perhaps it was just that she had so many nice things, they didn't mean that much to her. A cashmere cardigan casually discarded on the edge of the dance floor, or a hair band poking out of the top of the bag she left on a café table while she went to the loo, or a heeled sandal after she'd taken them off at a ball and was too drunk to remember where she left them. I was her Princess Charming. I'd return each item with a carefully thought-out note. I imagined the little frisson she would get, knowing that she had a secret admirer out there. It would be better than not having lost the thing in the first place.

BEGAN TO DRESS MORE AND MORE LIKE SHE DID. I WENT ON A
diet, I had my hair straightened and dyed. Sometimes, if I caught
a fleeting glimpse of myself in a shop window, it was almost like
she was there instead of me. I got a Second, rather than the First
my tutors had predicted. But I didn't mind. I'd got top marks in
studying, and becoming, her.

I followed her to London. I knew where they liked to drink, she
and her friends, where they went out. The ironically divey bar on
the high street, and then to the even more divey club on Clapham
High Street, Inferno's. And that was where, while I was sipping my
lemonade at the bar, Mark approached me.

Of course I knew who he was. At first I was petrified, I thought
he'd come to challenge me, ask why I was there. Then he said, "Can
I buy you a drink?" and a whole new world of possibility opened
up to me. I suddenly realized that he didn't see me as weirdo Em-
meline Padgett. He saw me as a desirable woman he'd met in a club,
wearing her Miranda-esque leather skirt and silk shirt. So when he
asked me my name, I said, "Emma." My favorite Austen heroine, of
whom Miranda had always reminded me a little.

Something magical happened. As Emma, I became someone
new. It was acting, the same beautiful dislocation from myself that
I had known on stage in a school production, when I briefly managed to become a different person entirely. Emma could be capable
and cool, sexy, clever, but not too much so, not the kind of clever
that scared people. She would be a social creature, she would be
someone without layers, without darkness. She would be everything that I was not.

And I would be legitimately close to her. Would be called, even,
a friend.

THAT BLOODY PHOTOGRAPH. I'VE THOUGHT ABOUT IT BEFORE,
many times. Of course I knew it was there, I have an encyclo-

pedic knowledge of Miranda's Facebook account. But it wasn't my photograph, I didn't even know the person taking it—so there was nothing I could do about it. I could have reached out, asked him to take it down, but Miranda knew him, so that might only have drawn attention to it . . . It might have been worse than leaving it up. I wasn't tagged in it or anything—of course, no one would have known my name. And I looked so different. You'd have to have looked very hard, and known exactly what it was you were looking for. Why would anyone study a photograph from fourteen years ago, and some thousand photos back? I thought I had been safe. I had been safe.

T IS YOU," SHE SAYS. "I'VE ALWAYS BEEN GOOD AT FACES." SHE shakes her head, as though she's trying to clear it. "It all makes sense. But wow, you have changed. You've lost weight. You've dyed your hair. But it is definitely you."

"No," I say, "you've got it wrong. It can't have been me. I was at Bath." I've always prided myself on my game face and my acting abilities, but suddenly everything I say sounds false, sounds like the lie it is. I shouldn't have said that, I realize. I should have just said I didn't know what she was talking about. In denying her accusations I have confirmed that she is right.

I make one more attempt to save myself. "Oh," I say, "perhaps I came up to visit a couple of weekends. I had friends at Oxford, of course."

But it is all too late. I can hear it in the background like a Greek chorus: *lie, lie, lie.*

It doesn't seem to matter, anyway. It's like she hasn't even heard me. She is saying, "I can see it all now. The stalker stopped almost around the time you and Mark got together. I thought it was him for a bit—I thought so again recently. He's always had a bit of a thing for me, but then I'm sure you know that. Now I understand."

She pauses, then says, "You know I used to feel sorry for you? I thought Mark was just using you, for your passing resemblance to me. Katie pointed it out—I would never have noticed it myself. But it was the other way around, wasn't it?"

"I just want to be your friend." I know how it sounds—I can hear it. Desperate . . . pathetic. But there's no point in lying. She knows it all now. It might as well all come out.

53

HEATHER

Now
January 2, 2019

WHAT DID SHE LOOK LIKE?" I ASK. "YOU'RE SURE IT WAS A woman?"

Iain screws up his eyes. He has gone very pale. I hope it's just the pain, not the loss of blood—but I suspect it is the latter. I've seen too many people die in an ambulance from wounds not much worse.

"Iain, what did she look like?"

"Just a woman," he says. "Just two women."

"You must have seen more than that," I say. "What color was her hair? The killer?"

"Don't know," he says, and gives another groan. ". . . I suppose it was light-colored. Maybe blond. Not sure. Difficult to see properly. But definitely not dark." He seems certain of this. The other two female guests—Samira and Katie—have unmistakably dark hair. He might not know the exact shade of the woman's hair, but neither of theirs could be described as "light."

And then something else occurs to me. "Iain, are you telling the truth when you say you didn't take the rifle?"

"Why would I lie?" he groans. "You know everything else now. Why would I lie about that?"

He has a point. But I don't want it to be true. Because, if it is, she has the rifle. And in coming up here, we've made a horrible mistake.

54

MIRANDA

One day earlier
New Year's Day 2019

SHOVE MY WAY OUT OF THE CABIN. I CAN HEAR THE CLATTER of Emma's feet on the steps behind me. "Miranda," she says, "please—please listen. I never meant any of it to upset you."

I don't answer. I can't look at her, or speak to her. I have no idea where I'm headed. Not to my own cabin, not to the Lodge. Instead I realize that I'm running in the direction of the path that stretches around the side of the loch. I have the dim idea of getting to the train station, waiting for a train. What time did Heather say they leave? Six A.M. That can't be too far from now. I'm aware that I'm still drunk, drunker than I thought, and that there are probably a number of problems with this plan, but my brain is too fuzzy to think of them. I'll work them out when I get there. For now, I just have to get away.

I plunge into the trees. It's darker here, but the gleam of the moon penetrates the branches, flickering over me like a strobe light. *It's a long way to the station,* says a little sober voice, from somewhere deep in the recesses of my brain. I push it away. I could run like this forever. Nothing hurts when you're drunk.

The only obstacle—I see it looming in front of me—is the bridge over the waterfall. I'll have to be careful there.

And then, suddenly, there's a black figure on the path just ahead. A man. He looks like something that has just uncut itself from the fabric of the night. He has a hood pulled up, like death personified. Inside I can just make out the white gleam of his eyes. Then he is scrambling away from me, up the side of the slope above the path into the trees, disappearing into a little building that is almost hidden there.

I teeter for a second, on the edge of the bridge. Is he going to rush out and attack me? He didn't like being seen, I know that much. I suddenly feel much more sober than before. It's the fear that has done it.

"Manda."

I turn. Oh Christ. Emma is just rounding the bend in the path. My hesitation has given her time to catch up with me.

"Manda," she says breathlessly, walking toward me. "I just wanted to be your friend. Is that such a terrible thing?"

55

EMMA

"YOU WERE NEVER REALLY MY FRIEND," SHE SAYS NOW. "Friends don't do that to each other."

"Don't say that."

"And you were only my friend before because of your connection to Mark. I would never have chosen you as a friend. I've always thought you're a bit dull, to be honest. I always thought you lacked depth. And I always thought you were trying too hard. It all makes sense now."

There is a terrible pain beneath my rib cage, as if she has reached into the cavity with her bare hands and is squeezing, crushing. "You don't mean that," I say.

"No?" she says. "No—I do." She is actually smiling. Her face is beautiful and cruel. "I prefer this version of you. Much more interesting. Even if you are a fucking weirdo."

That stings. "Don't call me that."

"What?" Her manner is playground bully now. "A fucking weirdo?"

Memories are surfacing from some dark, long-buried place, a classroom, the most popular girl in a year who looks—yes, I can see it now, rather like Miranda. I hadn't realized it before. The two faces: the remembered one and the one in front of me, seem to converge upon one another. Back then I gave that girl a shove, a hard shove in the middle of her chest, and she toppled back into the sandpit.

"God," Miranda says, "we call ourselves the inner circle. The best friends—the ones who remained while all the other ones fell away. But those other people were the sensible ones. They saw that the only thing holding us together was some tenuous history. Well, I'm going to get on the train, and start a new life—one in which I don't have to see any of you lot again. Especially not you."

"Don't say that, Manda."

"Don't call me that. You have no right to call me that. Can you get off the bridge, please? I don't think it's meant for two people at the same time."

I don't move. "You can't mean that, Manda. All I have ever wanted is to be close to you, to be part of your life."

She puts out her hands, as if to fend off my words. "Just leave me alone, you fucking psychopath."

That word. It's the action of a moment. I put out my own hands, and grab her neck. She's taller than me, stronger, probably—from all that boxercise and Pilates. But I have the element of surprise. I've got there first.

I don't have any particular plan. I just want her to stop talking, to stop her from saying these horrible things that I know she can't mean. I am so disappointed in her. How can she see those little gifts—the well-thought-out notes—as the work of a psychopath?

She's like one of them, one of the adults who tried to diagnose me, so long ago. Not a psychopath, actually. Personality disorder. That's the "official" term for what I supposedly have.

But I know the real definition. The feeling behind all that effort. All those little thefts and returns, all that work in tracking her down, in getting Mark to like me, to become part of the gang.

Love. That's all it is.

I don't know when it is that I realize there's no longer any sound coming from her. She has become strangely heavy, limp, in my arms, slumped forward on me so that I am bearing all her weight. It is with a kind of unthinking horror that I push her away from me, with quite a lot of force. Like I once pushed that girl, at the first school—the one who taunted me for dressing like her, for following her back home. No real damage done, just a shattered elbow. Enough, though, for the headmistress to call my parents into the office and for them to announce I was leaving before she could even utter the word: "expulsion." Better for everyone's reputation if no one made too much fuss about the whole thing.

Except, that time she fell backward into a sandpit.

I had forgotten. I swear it. I had forgotten that we were standing on the edge of the bridge, some forty feet above the frozen waterfall. When she fell, her head went back and her limbs were loose like a rag doll's—almost comical, windmilling. Then she disappeared into thin air and there was a long silence.

"Manda?" I call softly. But I think I already knew there was no way she would answer. "Manda?"

Only silence.

When I look, there she is. She might almost be sleeping. Except for the fact that her legs are at funny angles, splayed-looking—and she is so graceful, my Miranda. And there is the red bloom around her head where it has struck the rocks—a starburst, a supernova of red—and something else, paler, mixed in with the blood, that I don't want to think about.

LOOK ABOUT ME. HAS ANYONE SEEN? THE LANDSCAPE IS COMpletely deserted. There is no one, anywhere. I don't like the look of the little building, perched just above the waterfall. But there is no one in there, of course, it is just the way it has looked all weekend: the dark windows like blank eyes.

The snow continues to fall, like the curtain coming down after the final act. Or a white shroud—to cover the beautiful broken body in the waterfall below. It covers my footprints, filling them as I step away, as though they had never been.

I begin to cry. For her, for myself, for what I have lost.

56

HEATHER

Now
January 2, 2019

DOUG," I SAY, "I'VE GOT TO GET BACK TO THE LODGE, NOW. YOU stay here, make sure he's all right."

"No chance," he says. "I'm not going to let you go haring off to try to kill yourself again. We're going together."

His choice of words stalls me. Kill yourself. It summons an idea that has been on the edge of thought. Because, when I decided to go up to the Old Lodge, I knew I would be in danger. At that point, I was fairly certain Iain had a gun. I knew that there was a chance I might be killed. I was gambling on that chance. Yes, it was as bad as a suicide mission. And no, I don't want to examine too closely what that means.

Doug helps me to my feet. The sudden movement makes everything lurch—I'd forgotten about the head injury—and I stagger against him. He wraps an arm about me, to prop me up. I can feel the warmth of his body, even through our clothes. I take a step back.

"What about him?" I motion to Iain.

"He's all right. Let's leave him here to think about what he's done."

"He doesn't look so good, Doug." He doesn't—though it's also true that he's not looking much worse. The bleeding seems, largely, to have been stanched by Doug's homemade gauze.

"I'm not," Iain says. "I'm not doing so well. Take me with you."

"If it were that bad," Doug says brutally, "you'd have lost consciousness half an hour ago. You can stay here until we come back to find you, guarding your precious stash."

It occurs to me that there might be a chance to get a signal on my phone. Every so often, up on the peaks, it flickers into life. I take it out, wave it in the air, turn airplane mode off and on—and finally, with a cry of triumph, I manage to raise a solitary bar.

"Who are you calling?" Doug asks.

"The police."

Iain shudders, as though someone has just prodded the wound in his shoulder.

In the time we've been in here, I notice, it has stopped snowing. The police helicopter can reach us now. But they are not aware of the new urgency of the situation.

"Please," I say to the operator, "put me through to DCI John MacBride. I have something very important to tell him."

57

EMMA

WHO DID YOU THINK TOOK THAT RIFLE FROM THE STORE-room? Me, of course! Ta-da!

I've become pretty adept at noticing things, over the years. And I have a memory that might as well be photographic. That passcode was stored in the neat little filing cabinet inside my mind from the second that big oaf of a gamekeeper punched it in.

Seriously, what did Miranda see in him? She always did have terrible taste in men.

There is a phone ringing incessantly in the office across the hall-way from the living room.

"Why doesn't she pick it up?" Mark asks. "Or him? It could be something important. It could be the police, or something."

We wait, as the ringing stops, only to pick up again a minute later.

"I'm going to go and have a look," I say, "see what's going on."

THE REST OF THE LODGE SEEMS PARTICULARLY QUIET. IT IS THE silence of emptiness. Even before I push open the door to the office I'm sure that the knock I give is redundant. They're not here.

Not Heather, not the idiot gamekeeper. The phone is on the desk, still ringing. The sound is so loud it almost seems to vibrate in the silence.

I lift the receiver. "Hello?"

"Is that Heather Macintyre?" The voice on the other end is almost prepubescently youthful. "DCI John MacBride asked me to give you a call. I've been trying your mobile, too, but it's just going through to voice mail."

Some instinct now persuades me to say, modulating my voice to a gentle, Edinburgh burr (I told you I've always been a good actress): "Yes. It's Heather here. How can I help?"

"The DCI is on his way to you, in the chopper." There is an unmistakable delight in the way he says this, like he's enjoying the drama of it.

"Finally," I say. "Well, that's excellent news." They have no way of tracing it to me, I think. Even if they can work their CSI magic with DNA and fibers—well, I was wearing Mark's coat, and our DNA will be all over each other. There would be nothing strange about Miranda having flakes of my own skin on hers, or my hairs on her person. We've traveled on a train together, eaten together, danced and hugged over the last few days. I owe it to Miranda not to get myself caught, you see. Because I still have my chance to avenge her.

"He also . . . ." The operator coughs. I swear I hear a squeak in his voice, as if it's only just breaking (God, if they're practically employing children to man their phones I have even less to fear from these goons than I thought), "he also asked that you do nothing to alarm the . . . suspect."

"The suspect?" I ask.

"Yes . . . well, of course"—he's speaking quietly, anxiously now, as though he knows he's made a mistake—"she won't *officially* be that until we have assessed the situation. But the one you say was seen, that night, with the victim."

She.

I want to ask him to repeat himself, just to be certain . . . even though I know what I heard. To do so, though, would be to arouse suspicion.

But no one saw. I just stop myself from saying it. My shock is a momentary lapse of control. They might be talking about Katie, I think, wildly. Yes—that must be it. Perhaps Julien dropped her in it to save his own bacon, or something to that effect . . .

Except, I'm not sure I can afford to think that way.

It's not prison I'm afraid of. I deserve to pay for what I have done. Though no punishment will be worse than the one I have already had meted upon me, the loss of Miranda: my idol, my lodestar. What I fear is not having time to take revenge on her behalf. Well, I'll just have to speed things up.

58

KATIE

KATIE," EMMA SAYS. "CAN I HAVE A WORD, OUTSIDE?" THERE'S an odd urgency to her tone. I wonder what it was about that phone call she just took. Miranda's death seems to have hit her, if possible, the hardest of any of us. I suppose Julien and I have our guilt to contend with, which complicates things. I haven't yet been able to work out which of the two emotions I feel more strongly: grief, or self-hatred. Somehow, this has all felt like our fault. But Emma has spent the day staring at the floor, hardly saying anything. She rushed to that phone as if she was hoping it was someone ringing to say there'd been a terrible misunderstanding: that Miranda had been found alive, after all—that everything else has been a big mistake.

"Please," she says, "it's important."

"Okay." I get up and follow her. She leads me along the corridor, out toward the front of the Lodge, where the snow lies pristine and white as an eiderdown beside the loch. It has stopped falling, I notice. That's good news, isn't it?

"Who was that on the phone?" I ask Emma. "Was it the police?"

"Yes," she says. "It turns out they have a suspect."

"Who?" I ask.

"Come over here," she says. Her face is contorted with some powerful emotion that I can't quite read. She beckons with a hand. "I don't want one of the others to overhear us."

This can only mean one thing. It's one of us. *Mark,* I think. I know it can't be Julien—when I woke up from a fitful sleep he was beside me on the sofa, his mouth hanging open. I actually had to double-check he was alive. It has to be Mark. Oh God, that explains Emma's weird expression.

"Emma," I say, walking toward her. "Is it . . . is it who I think it is?" He has always been obsessed with her. I warned Miranda, and she laughed it off. She always thought she could handle herself.

Now Emma does something odd. She bends and sweeps her hand through the snow, as though she is searching for something.

"What are you doing?" I ask.

When she stands up she is holding something. It takes me a beat to work out what it is. My body seems to have done so before my mind has caught up: suddenly my limbs are frozen, my spine rigid.

"Emma. What are you doing with that?"

She doesn't seem to register the question. Her entire face has changed. She looks like a stranger, not the woman I have known for three years. "It's your fault," she hisses. "Everything that happened to her. If she hadn't found out about you two, and your disgusting affair, she wouldn't have been so upset. She wouldn't have said the terrible things she did. It wasn't her fault. It wasn't mine. It was yours."

At first, when I try to speak, I can only form the words silently with my mouth, releasing nothing but a bubble of air. I am aware of a strange thundering noise, staggeringly loud, all around us— the sound of something drumming, *whoomp, whoomp, whoomp,* like a giant heartbeat. I can't see anything to make sense of it, though. And perhaps, after all, it is only the rushing of the blood in my ears.

"I don't understand, Emma. I don't understand what you're saying."

"Of course not," she says. "Because you're too stupid." She spits the word. "You never deserved her for a friend."

I see something change in her expression, a spasm of pain. I understand. "It was you," I say.

She doesn't answer. She just raises her eyebrows, and does something to the rifle, making an ominous clicking sound. It is raised, level with my sternum.

Don't shoot for the head, I can hear the gamekeeper saying. Shoot for the body, where all the internal organs are clustered together. A shot like that is much more likely to be fatal.

I see Emma's face as it was after she shot the deer, anointed in gore, marked out as a killer.

I don't have time to do anything before I hear the sound of the report, familiar from before. I feel something shunt into me with terrible force. As I hit the ground, everything goes black.

59

DOUG

I T SEEMS AN INCREDIBLE DISTANCE BACK TO THE LODGE, MUCH farther down than it had seemed, perversely, on the way up. Beneath the snow are tangles of heather that snag at their ankles and threaten to trip them with every step. But it is also the new knowledge they now possess, the new understanding of how dangerous the situation at the Lodge might prove to be. They have made a huge mistake, leaving the guests to their own devices. But knowing what Iain could have done to Heather had Doug not shown up, he cannot be sorry he chose as he did.

Finally they are on the path back to the Lodge. And then above them a vast metal bird begins to descend from the clouds, blades whirring with a deafening throb. For a moment Doug is thrown back nine years to a place of fear and darkness—in spite of the blinding desert light—and the helicopter becomes an instrument of war: an Apache circling overhead, trying to pick out enemy positions. He reminds himself that it is the police, that this is a good thing. The great Scots pines are shedding their covering of snow, thrashing in the draft created by the blades.

Then Heather gives a horrified cry and picks up her pace. Incredibly, it is he who is struggling to keep up with her. Now he sees what she has seen. The two women, one blond, one dark, stand facing one another in front of the Lodge. The blonde is stooping to unearth something in the snow. He knows what it is even before he sees it emerge in her hand. The long, elegant barrel, lethal from some distance—but from three meters, the gap between the two figures: catastrophic.

They have finally reached flat ground. And before he can tell her to stop, Heather is sprinting toward them. Neither of the women sees her, so intent are they on each other. He is running, too, toward the one with the rifle. He is too late. As the gun discharges he sees Heather leap toward the dark-haired woman, knocking her out of the way.

He sees an explosion in a faraway place, that terrible moment— the men, his friends, all dead because of his hesitation. He wrenches himself back to the present. He throws himself down next to her, where the snow is splattered with her blood.

EPILOGUE

60

HEATHER

WHEN I FIRST CAME ROUND FROM AN OPIATED SLEEP I HAD no idea who I was, let alone where. The first person I saw was Doug.

"Hello," he said. "I hope you don't mind me being here."

Before the nurse left the room she said, "You've got a great man here. He's been sitting in that same spot the whole time you were in surgery, waiting for you to come round."

I looked at Doug. He seemed embarrassed, as though he had been caught out in something. "I had to tell them we were together," he said, in an undertone. "Otherwise they would have sent me away. I hope you don't mind."

His hand was only a few centimeters from mine, resting on the sheet. I lifted mine, with some effort, to cover his. It seemed miraculously warm and alive. It was the first time I had touched another human being, in any significant way, in a long, long time.

OVER THE NEXT COUPLE OF HOURS THEY ALL ARRIVED AF-ter the long drive from Edinburgh: the friends whose happiness and wholeness I have been avoiding for a year. And, of course, my family: my mum repeating that she "knew that place had something bad in it." And what I realized was: I am loved. I love. I have lost the great love, the one that for years defined me, that had come to be the sum total of who I was. So much so that when it was gone, I was certain there was nothing left to salvage.

I'm not sure what compelled me to do what I did. I saw the whole scene playing out before me, as though at half the speed, and I realized that there was time, and that I had the element of surprise. I *could* do something. I didn't even really think about the danger to myself, there wasn't time for it. I didn't even think about it as the bullet entered my abdomen. It was only when I lay on the ground, winded, and the pain arrived in a wave so intense that I was convinced I had to be dying. But now I'm wondering if it was some memory of Jamie always putting the lives of strangers before his own that impelled me.

Iain is all right. In fact, apparently he's on the same ward as me, somewhere. With a police escort, naturally. According to Doug he was in so much pain that he sobbed out his confession when Doug brought the police up to the Old Lodge. It seems he was a cog in a much larger machine: the drugs came from a lab in Iceland. Ingvar and Kristin? Not their real names, obviously. Those backpacks had been filled with something much more valuable than hiking equipment. The train guard at the station was paid more than double his own salary to turn a blind eye. A few innocuous suitcases unloaded at the other end, delivered to the boss's members' clubs. And New Year's Eve the best time to do it: everyone distracted, emergency services stretched to capacity.

The one turning these cogs, of course, was the boss. It turned out he and Iain went a long way back. As a young man, Iain had served a long sentence in prison for car theft, and had come out without any options. Finally he had managed to get a job as the bouncer of a rather upmarket club in London. The owner of the club had approached him with an offer: a cushy job, better pay, a new start. The drugs, it turned out, had been the boss's main source of money all along. Not the members' clubs, nor the Lodge—though both had provided a nice blind, and both were integral to the product's journey from Icelandic lab to the well-heeled end users. They caught him sipping an orange juice in the first-class lounge at Heathrow, en route to skipping the country.

Quite a coup for the Fort William police station. A murder *and* a drugs bust, all from the same serene almost-wilderness. A wilderness that, I've decided (and not just because of the murder and the drugs bust), isn't for me. I'll miss my morning swim in the loch, of course. And—a surprise even to me, this—I'll miss my taciturn coworker. Doug's agreed to come and spend the weekend with me once I've settled back into life in Edinburgh and bought myself a guest sofa bed, which may or may not be used. He has his own stuff to work out first, his own journey to go on. Both of us, I think, have been living in limbo. Both of us running from death, and in so doing fleeing from everything else. Now it is time to get on with the difficult business of living.

61

KATIE

'M DUE TO GIVE BIRTH IN A FEW WEEKS. THERE WAS A WORRY
that I might lose the baby, after being tackled to the ground like
that—but she was fine. She: I'm going to have a girl. I'm working
right up to my due date. I've been working hard, putting in longer
hours and operating on less sleep than I should have had in my
condition. But it's been a distraction. My whole pregnancy has been
tangled up with my grief for Miranda. Yes, grief. I know it might
be almost hard to believe, considering what a terrible friend I had
been to her of late. And the way she could be with me. It's true, I
didn't always like Miranda. Sometimes I positively hated her. But I
did love her. That's what happens when you have known someone
for such a long time. You see all their faults, yes, but you know
their best qualities, too—and Miranda had so many of those. No
one could light up a party like her. No one would offer her best
dress to borrow at the drop of a hat. And there aren't many popular girls of thirteen who will stake all their social credit on the
rescue of an outsider. She was, in her way, utterly unique. No one
could be a fiercer ally. And yes, no one could be a more formi-
dable enemy.

Apart from, perhaps, one person.

Emma was spectacular at the trial, very contrite and grief-stricken and very—though not *too*—well dressed. Gone was the resemblance to Miranda, the seductive blonde, the femme fatale. I suppose you don't particularly want to go for the fatale look when you're on trial for murder. Her hair had been dyed back to a very modest shade of mouse, she wore a high-necked, almost Victorian piecrust blouse: she looked like something between a choir girl and a schoolteacher. She wept as she explained that Miranda had started taunting her about her condition, despite her attempts to explain. Oh, she hadn't meant to strangle Miranda, she said. There had been a tussle, yes, after Miranda had said some terrible—unforgivable—things. It was self-defense. Miranda had been drunk and vengeful, had come at her fighting tooth and nail. She'd shoved her away, and then, realizing the consequences of the push, had tried to save Miranda by grabbing on to the nearest thing within reach . . . her neck.

No, doesn't sound very likely to me—and the prosecution didn't think so, either. It should be impossible *not* to convict on the basis of so much evidence. But we live in a post-truth world. The jury lapped it up. They simply could *not* convict her of murder. Not this well-spoken, quiet, meek person who looked just like the daughter of a friend, or a girl they remembered from school. People like her didn't commit murder. Not proper *murder*. They simply had unfortunate accidents.

The papers compared it to the case of that other Oxford alumnus, a few years ago, who stabbed her boyfriend with a bread knife. People like them just don't serve time. The defense, meanwhile, gleefully painted a picture of Miranda as an unhappy person: someone whose life was falling apart beneath a glossy facade. A big drinker. A drug taker—she, after all, had supplied our group with drugs on the first night of the holiday. Emma, importantly, had abstained from taking anything. And Miranda was prone to erratic, bullying behavior, the defense claimed: the way she'd forced

Mark to drink that champagne, coerced me into the freezing loch. Controlling, manic, unstable—she'd been seeing a psychotherapist, hadn't she?

Manslaughter, that was the charge. And a four-year sentence. She—this woman who pushed my oldest friend to her death and who tried to kill me—will be out in four years' time. I try not to think about it.

As for the rest of them—apart from Nick and Bo, of course—I was right in suspecting we had nothing in common. Miranda had really been the link. And history, I suppose: the laziness of habit. I am not here to try to acquit myself. I behaved no better than any of them, and far worse than some. But isn't that just part of the problem? Old friends don't challenge us on our faults. I have not been a good person. I needed something to show me that. I just wish it hadn't been this.

The group has fragmented now. The inner circle has imploded from within. There is no center to it, no high priestess. Samira and Giles are, I imagine, getting along very happily in Balham with all their right-thinking friends, who don't take drugs or down bottles of champagne, or, for that matter, kill each other.

Nick and Bo are moving back to New York. Mark has already— make of this what you will—met another almost-but-not-quite Miranda substitute at the agency where he works. Julien's path has been the most radical. He has gone off for a detox in Goa for a month—though with the lithe yoga instructor at the City gym he used to visit, so perhaps there's more to it than a desire to become a Zen master. He's told me he'll be back in time for my due date . . . worse luck. If I could have this baby without ever having to see him again I don't think I'd particularly mind. I'll be linked to him, now. My child's father. Not quite the clean break I would have wanted—from him, and, by association, from the whole group. Still, at least I never have to go on another bloody holiday with any of them.

I'd like, now, to get to know people who know me for *me*—not for who I used to be. Who won't expect me to step back into a role that I don't quite fit into anymore. Who won't see me as a project, to be worked on . . . but will see me as whole, fully formed.

Last week, when we concluded our latest case at the firm, I decided to go for a rare drink (elderflower for me) with my colleagues. They actually aren't all that bad—they might even be normal people when they're not inside the fetid air of the office, hamster-wheeling their way through contracts. There is one guy, Tom, from the litigation team, who doesn't actually look all that bad without his crumpled suit jacket, glasses, and the fear of God in his eyes.

Perhaps it's time to make some new friends.

ACKNOWLEDGMENTS

To Al—for taking me to the spot that first inspired the book, and for those long walks in the snow plotting and evenings reading . . . Twenty percent definitely earned!

To my dear Hoge—thank you for all your time and wise editorial input. This book would not be the same without you!

To my fabulous agents, Cath Summerhayes and Alexandra Machinist, who were highly supportive of this move to the dark side! And huge thanks to Luke Speed, Melissa Pimentel, and Irene Magrelli.

To Kim Young, editor extraordinaire, and her fantastic team at HarperCollins—thank you for all the passion and imagination you are bringing to publishing this book: Charlotte Brabbin, Emilie Chambeyron, Jaime Frost, Ann Bissell, Abbie Salter, Eloisa Clegg.

To Katherine Nintzel, and her William Morrow stateside dream team: Vedika Khanna, Liate Stehlik, Lynn Grady, Nyamekye Waliyaya, Stephanie Vallejo, Aryana Hendrawan, Eliza Rosenberry, Katherine Turro, Kaitlin Harri.

To Jamie Laurenson and Patrick Walters at See-Saw—I'm so excited by your vision for bringing the book to life on-screen!

About the author

About the book

Read on

Insights,
Interviews
& More . . .

Meet Lucy Foley

Philippa Gedge

LUCY FOLEY studied English literature at Durham University and University College London and worked for several years as a fiction editor in the publishing industry. She is the author of *The Book of Lost and Found* and *The Invitation*. She lives in London. ❧

About the author

From the World of *The Hunting Party*: *The Getaway*

I look across the expanse before me:
the rust-colored moorland patched with
fallen snow, a heavier covering of white
on the peaks that sheer up behind.
An ancient landscape, sculpted by the
vast mass of ice that once forced its way
through it. There isn't another soul
in sight and despite all this space the
presence of just one other would be an
affront, somehow. This place feels like
the end of the world. Certainly, the end
of the line—the estate has its own tiny
railway station, an incongruous nod
to civilization in the midst of all this
wilderness. Fifty thousand acres of it,
to be precise.

It's perfect. For my purposes, anyhow.
As unlike London as anywhere I could
imagine. In the city, I see reminders
of our life everywhere, what we built
together from memories, friends, shared
joys, and love. She was a mistake, he told
me. Harmless sounding. Like filling in
the wrong box on a form, wearing odd
socks. One that he kept on repeating.
We never came to Scotland together.
He doesn't like the cold.

The gamekeeper, Doug, picked me
up from the train in his Land Rover.
They have a deer herd here, which
he manages. He told me they have
problems with poachers who hunt
at night, blinding and stunning their ▶

prey with bright lamps, killing before the animals' instincts have a chance to protect them. "They terrify the deer before they shoot them," he told me. "They enjoy it. The sport of it. It's barbaric." The only other person I've met is the estate manager, Heather— a young woman. Imagine that—working all alone in this vast, wild place, with only your thoughts for company. I know I wouldn't be able to stand it. It would send you mad, wouldn't it?

For a week or so, however, it's perfect. Space to organize my thoughts. I've brought some work with me; stuff I just haven't been able to focus on back home. It may be just after Christmas but there's no rest for the wicked—or freelancers. My cottage is set a little way away from the other few dwellings, but even if it weren't, I wouldn't be disturbed: there are no guests staying here, apart from me. The other buildings have an eerie look about them: dark and shuttered. They've got a party—also Londoners— coming here next week, to celebrate Hogmanay, apparently. But right now we are in that listless dead time between Christmas and New Year's Eve, when everyone is supposed to be spending time with their loved ones, hunkered down amidst wrapping paper and leftovers, feeling fat and happy and loved. Everyone apart from Doug, Heather, and I, it would seem.

I'm out on a walk now, after a solid day's work. I set out without any particular direction in mind, just a need to get some of the pure Highland air into my lungs. I've gone further than I'd planned to, rather enjoying the ache in my legs, the focusing sting of the cold, the crunch of the old frozen snow beneath my soles. *Earth stood hard as iron*, I think, *water like a stone*. If you asked me how long I've been walking, I'm not sure I'd be able to tell you. I know that a while ago I climbed up and over a ridge and then picked my way across a long expanse of tussocky, spongy moorland, bisected by a deep-cut, half-frozen stream. It's only now, feeling myself tiring, realizing it's getting dark, that I think about turning back. I look behind me.

The ridge I came over stretches across the horizon. I realize, with a prickle of unease, that I don't recall where I crossed it. I don't remember any distinguishing features—in this weakening, shifting light I don't think I would be able to make them out anyway. I don't know if I've been walking in a straight line, or a diagonal, or, most likely, wandering hither and thither as I tried to find the best footing across the rough ground. The ridge must be several miles across. If I crossed back over the wrong point, I could find myself completely lost. It seems astonishing that I am suddenly so unaware of my bearings. How long have I been walking? Two hours? Three? It could take me much longer to get back. I'll . . . use Google maps. I take my mobile out of my pocket. But of course, there's no signal—they told me this—anywhere on the estate.

When I look up from my screen, it appears to have got even darker. The light seems to be seeping from the landscape even as I've stood here. Colder, too, the bite of the chill air through all my layers of clothes. And a light snow has begun to fall: I feel it in the tiny ice-wet kisses upon my skin and sense it in the diminishment of all sound, that strange vacuum that it creates about it. My own breathing sounds louder in the absence of any other noise.

I flick on my mobile's torch, cast the weak beam ahead of me, catching the pale flecks in the beam. The snow's growing heavier: the flakes like white down now, coming thick and fast and silent, curtaining me off from my surroundings. I have no choice but to turn back in the direction I think I came and start walking. But it's harder going not being able to see through the dark and the falling snow, as if the landscape is resisting me, my feet snaring in invisible patches of grass. I try not to panic, to measure my breathing—even as twilight gives way to total darkness. To focus on putting one foot in front of the other.

And then I become aware of a source of light, somewhere behind me, the deep guttural snarl of an engine. I turn and in the near distance see two headlights, moving in my direction. Where on earth have they come from? I didn't realize there was a track out here. As they get closer my first, instinctive, thought is that there is something menacing about them: the lantern eyes of some night-time beast advancing on me, keeping me in its sights. Then, more rationally, I think: *thank Christ*. It must be the gamekeeper—perhaps he realized I was still out in this. I turn, blinking, and raise a hand.

I expect some signal from the vehicle: a flash of the lights or toot of the horn, to acknowledge that they've seen me. ▶

But there's nothing. Then I hear the engine gun, a diesel growl. Whoever it is, they aren't slowing down. In fact, if I'm not mistaken, they appear to be speeding up. The lights advance on me rapidly toward the curtain of snow. If I don't do something, they'll be on top of me in moments. And without further pause for thought, I turn and begin to run. I am stumbling over hidden hillocks, my legs feeling heavy and stupid, the nightmare sense that I'm hardly moving as the headlights gain on me, seemingly swinging round to follow me as I change direction. My breath comes loud and fast and rough, like a hunted animal's. Like prey. I *am* prey.

Then suddenly the ground seems to disappear from beneath me and I find myself pitching forward. I'm falling, my arms flailing and grasping at air before I land hard on my hands and knees in stinging, freezing wetness. I'd forgotten about the stream. I am winded by the cold of it, heart racing and lightheaded, the icewater beneath the frozen layer soaking me to my thighs. I scrabble about for purchase, encountering rocks too glazed with ice to hold me.

Then I'm being hauled bodily to my feet. "You alright there, lassie?"

I'M SITTING IN the vehicle. There's an odd smell in here: heavy, metallic, oddly familiar. It doesn't help my sense of unease. Because I think I know what it is. I remind myself of what Doug told me about the necessary culls of the herd on the estate, the export of venison. It must be that, I tell myself. At some point the back of the truck will no doubt have contained the grisly cargo of several deer carcasses. It somehow doesn't provide much reassurance: some animal part of me is deeply troubled by it.

I sneak glances at my rescuer. He's oldish, I think, but I can't get a proper glimpse of his face—just a whitish beard and the dark gleam of his eyes beneath a flat cap. There's a rifle propped up beside his seat on the other side. That, too, draws my eyes. The silent menace of it.

The quiet in the dark cab of the truck is broken only by the swish of the wipers sloughing snow from the windscreen, which covers the glass as quickly as it is cleared. Then he revs up the engine and we begin to rattle and seesaw over the rough ground.

"So you're a gamekeeper, too?" I ask him, to break the silence.

"Yes, lass. Suppose I am." He doesn't look at me, though, keeps his eyes forward. I wonder how he can possibly see where we're going through the chaos of white flakes, dense now as a screen of static on an old TV set. "I suppose you must be one of the guests from the estate?" he asks. I wonder whether I am imagining the mocking emphasis on the word *guests*.

"Yes," I say.

"Got yourself in a wee bit of bother there, didn't you?"

"I just went for a walk," I say. "I had no idea it would turn so quickly . . ."

He tells me he can't understand what I was doing, running off like that. I'm too embarrassed to tell him that I thought he was chasing me. I don't want him to feel any more disdain for me than he no doubt already does. I know how I must seem to him: the idiotic Londoner who got herself lost in a snowstorm, who sprinted away in terror as he tried to rescue her. It seems ridiculous now. But I had been so sure of it at the time—the way the engine gunned, how the vehicle seemed to accelerate toward me, how I was certain that it wasn't going to stop.

"You don't want to be caught out at night, lassie," he says now. "Want to get yourself tucked up warm indoors. Not a place for one such as you, after dark. You could find yourself in a whole heap of trouble."

Normally I'd laugh at such an ominous-sounding pronouncement. But when I think of the predicament I just found myself in, how much trouble I would be in right now if he hadn't rescued me, I realize he might be right. I'll be more careful tomorrow. No twilit excursions for me.

We drive over the ridge and enter the forest on the other side. The dense pines hold a still-deeper darkness, the falling snow has yet to properly penetrate their midst. Then I see the lights of the lodge glimmering through the trees, their reflection upon the gleaming black water of the loch. I am weak with relief. I think of the hot bath I'm going to run when I get back ▶

to the cabin, to soak the cold from my bones, the stiff drink I will make to calm my nerves after this strange ordeal.

"Thank you—" I'm about to say that this will be fine, that I can walk myself back from here. Then I realize that he has turned the wheel. That we are moving in a different direction. Into the forest, deeper into the trees, the lights disappearing behind us.

The words die in my throat. ∾

Reading Group Guide

1. The members of the friend group all fit a certain mold: the new parents, the quiet one, the city boy, and so on. How did these tropes serve the story?

2. How does the stark setting impact the storytelling? How different would this book have been if it took place during a different time of year, assuming the characters still ended up stuck at the estate?

3. The idea that perception is reality is brought up by several characters. Do you think this is true? How does this belief impact the group dynamic?

4. Do you think any of the point-of-view characters are reliable narrators? What made them more reliable or less reliable to you? How did they influence your opinions of the other characters?

5. Lucy Foley intentionally tried to make it seem like practically any of the characters could have committed murder. Were you able to guess who the real culprit was before the reveal? Who were the biggest red herrings?

6. What role does class and socioeconomic standing play in the book? How does the act of hunting relate to it?

7. In chapter 52, Emma says that Miranda was "happy to have a mirror, a sounding board." How successfully do Emma, Julien, and Katie mirror Miranda? What does Miranda reflect to each of them?

8. What kinds of imagery does Foley use to create a feeling of trepidation and dread in readers?

9. All of the POV characters except for Doug are women. Why do you think Foley made this choice? What effect does it have on how the other male characters are perceived and portrayed? ▶

About the book

10. *The Hunting Party* is a closed-room thriller, in that there is a limited set of characters and they're all trapped in one location. What effect does this have on the story? What are the advantages and disadvantages of this sort of thriller?

11. Though the novel focuses on the friend group, how do the characters outside the group impact the friends' dynamic? How does Foley use them to reveal more about the characters and push the plot forward?

12. Doug mentions "buck fever" during the hunt, and the blood lust and competition of the expedition. How does this concept apply to the friends, and to the book as a whole?

13. At the end of the novel, Katie says "we live in a post-truth world." Do you think that's true? How big a role does the truth play in *The Hunting Party*? ∽

An Excerpt from
The Guest List

Chapter 1: The Wedding Night

THE LIGHTS GO OUT.
In an instant, everything is in darkness.
The band stop their playing. Inside the
marquee the wedding guests squeal
and clutch at one another. The light
from the candles on the tables only adds
to the confusion, sends shadows racing
up the canvas walls. It's impossible to see
where anyone is or hear what anyone is
saying: above the guests' voices the wind
rises in a frenzy.

Outside a storm is raging. It shrieks
around them, it batters the marquee.
At each assault the whole structure
seems to flex and shudder with a loud
groaning of metal; the guests cower
in alarm. The doors have come free
from their ties and flap at the entrance.
The flames of the paraffin torches that
illuminate the doorway snicker.

It feels personal, this storm. It feels as
though it has saved all its fury for them.

This isn't the first time the electrics
have shorted. But last time the lights
snapped back on again within minutes.
The guests returned to their dancing,
their drinking, their pill-popping, their
screwing, their eating, their laughing . . .
and forgot it ever happened. ▶

An Excerpt from *The Guest List* (continued)

How long has it been now? In the dark it's difficult to tell. A few minutes? Fifteen? Twenty?

They're beginning to feel afraid. This darkness feels somehow ominous, intent. As though anything could be happening beneath its cover.

FINALLY, THE BULBS flicker back on. Whoops and cheers from the guests. They're embarrassed now about how the lights find them: crouched as though ready to fend off an attack. They laugh it off. They almost manage to convince themselves that they weren't frightened.

The scene illuminated in the marquee's three adjoining tents should be one of celebration, but it looks more like one of devastation. In the main dining section, clots of wine spatter the laminate floor, a crimson stain spreads across white linen. Bottles of champagne cluster on every surface in testament to an evening of toasts and celebrations. A forlorn pair of silver sandals peeks from beneath a tablecloth.

The Irish band begin to play again in the dance tent— a rousing ditty to restore the spirit of celebration. Many of the guests hurry in that direction, eager for some light relief. If you were to look closely at where they step you might see the marks where one barefoot guest has trodden in broken glass and left bloody footprints across the laminate, drying to a rusty stain. No one notices.

Other guests drift and gather in the corners of the main tent, nebulous as leftover cigarette smoke. Loath to stay, but also loath to step outside the sanctuary of the marquee while the storm still rages. And no one can leave the island. Not yet. The boats can't come until the wind dies down.

In the center of everything stands the huge cake. It has appeared whole and perfect before them for most of the day, its train of sugar foliage glittering beneath the lights. But only minutes before the lights went out the guests gathered around to watch its ceremonial disemboweling. Now the deep red sponge gapes from within.

Then from outside comes a new sound. You might almost

mistake it for the wind. But it rises in pitch and volume until it is unmistakable.

The guests freeze. They stare at one another. They are suddenly afraid again. More so than they were when the lights went out. They all know what they are hearing. It is a scream of terror.

Chapter 2: The Day Before

AOIFE
The Wedding Planner

Nearly all of the wedding party are here now. Things are about to crank into another gear: there's the rehearsal dinner this evening, with the chosen guests, so in that sense the wedding really begins tonight.

I've put the champagne on ice ready for the pre-dinner drinks. It's vintage Bollinger: eight bottles of it, plus the wine for dinner and a couple of crates of Guinness—all as per the bride's instructions. It is not for me to comment, but it seems rather a lot. They're all adults, though. I'm sure they know how to restrain themselves. Or maybe not. That best man seems a bit of a liability—all of the ushers do, to be honest. And the bridesmaid— the bride's half-sister—I've seen her on her solitary wanderings of the island, hunched over and walking fast like she's trying to outpace something.

You learn all the insider secrets, doing this sort of work. You see the things no one else is privileged to see. All the gossip that the guests would kill to have. As a wedding planner you can't *afford* to miss anything. You have to be alert to every detail, all the smaller eddies beneath the surface. If I didn't pay attention, one of those currents could grow into a huge riptide, destroying all my careful planning. And here's another thing I've learned— sometimes the smallest currents are the strongest.

I move through the Folly's downstairs rooms, lighting the ▶

blocks of turf in the grates, so they can get a good smolder on
for this evening. Freddy and I have started cutting and drying
our own turf from the bog, as has been done for centuries past.
The smoky, earthy smell of the turf fires will add to the sense of
local atmosphere. The guests should like that. Besides, it may be
midsummer but it gets cool at night on the island. The Folly's
old stone walls keep the warmth out and aren't so good at holding
it in.

Today has been surprisingly warm, at least by the standards
of these parts, but the same's not looking likely for tomorrow.
The end of the weather forecast I caught on the radio mentioned
wind. We get the brunt of all the weather here; often the storms
are much worse than they end up being on the mainland, as if
they've exhausted themselves on us. It's still sunny out but this
afternoon the needle on the old barometer in the hallway swung
from FAIR to CHANGEABLE. I've taken it down. I don't want
the bride to see it. Though I'm not sure that she is the sort
to panic. More the sort to get angry and look for someone
to blame. And I know just who would be in the firing line.

"Freddy," I call into the kitchen, "will you be starting on
the dinner soon?"

"Yeah," he calls back, "got it all under control."

Tonight they'll eat a fish stew based on a traditional
Connemara fisherman chowder: smoked fish, lots of cream.
I ate it the first time I ever visited this place, when there were
still people here. This evening's will be a more refined take on
the usual recipe, as this is a refined group we have staying.
Or at least I suppose they like to *think* of themselves as such.
We'll see what happens when the drink hits them.

"Then we'll be needing to start prepping the canapés for
tomorrow," I call, running through the list in my head.

"I'm on it."

"And the cake: we'll be wanting to assemble that in good time."

The cake is quite something to behold. It should be. I know
how much it cost. The bride didn't bat an eyelash at the expense.
I believe she's used to having the best of everything. Four tiers
of deep red velvet sponge, encased in immaculate white icing
and strewn with sugar greenery, to match the foliage in the

chapel and the marquee. Extremely fragile and made according to the bride's exact specifications, it travelled all the way here from a very exclusive cake-makers in Dublin: it was no small effort getting it across the water in one piece. Tomorrow, of course, it will be destroyed. But it's all about the moment, a wedding. All about the day. It's not really about the marriage at all, in spite of what everyone says.

See, mine is a profession in which you orchestrate happiness. It is why I became a wedding planner. Life is messy. We all know this. Terrible things happen—I learned that while I was still a child. But no matter what happens, life is only a series of days. You can't control more than a single day. But you can control *one* of them. Twenty-four hours can be curated, managed. A wedding day is a neat little parcel of time in which I can create something whole and perfect to be cherished for a lifetime, a pearl from a broken necklace.

Freddy emerges from the kitchen in his stained butcher's apron. "How are you feeling?"

I shrug. "A wee bit nervous, to be honest."

"You've got this, love. Think how many times you've done this."

"But this is different. Because of who it is—" It was a real coup, getting Will Slater and Julia Keegan to hold their wedding here. I worked as an event planner in Dublin, before. Setting up here was all my idea, restoring the island's crumbling, half-ruined folly into an elegant ten-bedroom property with a dining room, drawing room, and kitchen. Freddy and I live here permanently but use only a tiny fraction of the space when it's just the two of us.

"Shush." Freddy steps forward and enfolds me in a hug. I feel myself stiffening at first. I'm so focused on my to-do list that it feels like a diversion we don't have time for. Then I allow myself to relax into the embrace, to appreciate his comforting, familiar warmth. Freddy is a good hugger. He's what you might call "cuddly." He likes his food—it's his job. He ran a restaurant in Dublin before we moved here.

"It's all going to work out fine," he says. "I promise. It will all be perfect." He kisses the top of my head. I've had a great ▶

deal of experience in this business. But then I've never worked on an event I've been so invested in. And the bride is very particular—which, to be fair to her, probably goes with the territory of what she does, running her own magazine. Someone else might have been run a little ragged by her requests. But I've enjoyed it. I like a challenge.

Anyway. That's enough about me. This weekend is about the happy couple, after all. The bride and groom haven't been together for very long, by all accounts. Seeing as our bedroom is in the Folly too, with all the others, we could hear them last night. "Jesus," Freddy said as we lay in bed. "I can't listen to this." I knew what he meant. Strange how when someone is in the throes of pleasure it can sound like pain. They seem very much in love, but a cynic might say that's *why* they can't seem to keep their hands off each other. Very much in lust might be a more accurate description.

Freddy and I have been together for the better part of two decades and even now there are things I keep from him and, I'm sure, vice versa. Makes you wonder how much they know about each other, those two.

Whether they really know all of each other's dark secrets. ❧

OUTSTANDING PRAISE FOR
THE GUEST LIST

"Lucy Foley has done it again."
—GOOD HOUSEKEEPING

"Lucy Foley has honed her unique brand of reverse-whodunit suspense down to a science— and thank goodness for that."
—HARPER'S BAZAAR

"Easily my favorite book of 2020 so far. . . . Will keep you guessing until the very end."
—BETTER HOMES & GARDENS

"This juicy murder mystery is a perfect Agatha Christie–esque summer read."
—AFAR MAGAZINE

"Yes, there's a murder, but there's *so much more* than that. (The twists, I admit, are pretty good too.)"
—MARIE CLAIRE

"RSVP AT YOUR OWN RISK." —E! ONLINE

ONCE YOU'VE MADE IT OFF THE ISLAND, HEAD TO AN ISOLATED LODGE IN SCOTLAND FOR . . . *THE HUNTING PARTY*

Praise for *The Guest List*

"Evoking the great Agatha Christie classics *And Then There Were None* and *Murder on the Orient Express*, Lucy Foley's clever, taut new novel, *The Guest List*, takes us to a creepy island off the coast of Ireland. . . . Foley builds her suspense slowly and creepily, deploying an array of narrators bristling with personal secrets. . . . Pay close attention to seemingly throwaway details about the characters' pasts. They are all clues."

—*The New York Times Book Review*

"I didn't think Lucy Foley could top *The Hunting Party*, but she did! I loved this book. It gave me the same waves of happiness I get from curling up with a classic Christie. A remote, atmospheric island, a wedding no one is particularly happy to be at, old secrets—and a murder. The alternating points of view keep you guessing, and guessing wrong. I can't wait for her next book."

—Alex Michaelides, #1 *New York Times* bestselling author of *The Silent Patient*

"Lucy Foley gets better with every book. . . . The characters leap off the page, the twists are darker and more unexpected, and the setting is straight out of a Gothic novel. . . . Yes, there's a murder, but there's *so much more* than that. (The twists, I admit, are pretty good too.)"

—*Marie Claire*

"An updated *Murder on the Orient Express*."

—*Booklist*

"Wedding season means a thrilling web of mystery in *The Guest List*."

—*Parade*

"[Foley's] puzzle is solid, she plays fair with the reader, and overall her story is swift and entertaining."

—*Seattle Times*

"No one may have come to the island intending to murder, but this destination wedding spirals into mayhem when it's slowly revealed that most everyone in attendance is capable of becoming a lusting-for-revenge killer."

—*Washington Post*

"This thrilling page turner will have you guessing until the very end."   —*OK!* magazine (UK)

"An Agatha Christie–like thriller."   —Huffington Post

"Foley delivers another atmospheric, Agatha Christie–style whodunit with *The Guest List*. The multiple points of view will keep you guessing right until the end."   —BuzzFeed

"[There are] clues on nearly every page, but no spoilers here. Needless to say, you'll be up late flipping through your Kindle until all is revealed."   —Mashable

"With a dizzying array of suspects, this delicious thriller has all the elements for the perfect whodunit."   —*Columbus Dispatch*

"Foley expertly peels back the layers of eight highly suspicious members of the wedding party, and all with murderous secrets. This summer best seller, a Reese's Book Club pick, will keep you transfixed to the end."   —*AARP The Magazine*

"The one thing you can expect from Foley's novels? That you'll probably never guess the twist . . . or should we say twists when it comes to her latest bestseller. . . . You'll never see the ending coming."   —E! Online

"A delightfully suspenseful thriller. . . . Set in such an isolated location, with a fairly small cast of characters, *The Guest List* feels a bit like a modern Agatha Christie novel. It is a fast-paced, intriguing mystery."   —Shelf Awareness

"Clever."   —PopSugar

"Lucy Foley's latest doesn't disappoint. . . . Told from varying perspectives throughout as details unfold, it's a slow build and burn—and totally worth the wait."   —*Condé Nast Traveler*

"Gloriously escapist thrills from an Agatha Christie for the Instagram age."   —*The Guardian* (UK)

THE
GUEST
LIST

ALSO BY **LUCY FOLEY**

The Hunting Party

Last Letter from Istanbul

The Invitation

The Book of Lost and Found

wm

WILLIAM MORROW

An Imprint of HarperCollins*Publishers*

THE GUEST LIST

A NOVEL

LUCY FOLEY

P.S.™ is a trademark of HarperCollins Publishers.

THE GUEST LIST. Copyright © 2020 by Lost and Found Books Ltd. Excerpt from THE HUNTING PARTY © 2019 by Lost and Found Books Ltd. All rights reserved. Printed in the United States of America. No part of this book may be used or reproduced in any manner whatsoever without written permission except in the case of brief quotations embodied in critical articles and reviews. For information, address HarperCollins Publishers, 195 Broadway, New York, NY 10007.

HarperCollins books may be purchased for educational, business, or sales promotional use. For information, please email the Special Markets Department at SPsales@harpercollins.com.

Published in 2020 by HarperFiction, an imprint of HarperCollins UK.

A hardcover edition of this book was published in 2020 by William Morrow, an imprint of HarperCollins Publishers.

FIRST WILLIAM MORROW PAPERBACK EDITION PUBLISHED 2021.

Designed by Elina Cohen

Library of Congress Cataloging-in-Publication Data has been applied for.

ISBN 978-0-06-286894-7

23 24 25 26 27 LBC 21 20 19 18 17

FOR KATE AND ROBBIE, THE MOST SUPPORTIVE
SIBLINGS A GIRL COULD HOPE FOR . . . LUCKILY
NOTHING LIKE THE ONES IN THIS BOOK!

THE WEDDING NIGHT

THE LIGHTS GO OUT.

In an instant, everything is in darkness. The band stop their playing. Inside the tent the wedding guests squeal and clutch at one another. The light from the candles on the tables only adds to the confusion, sends shadows racing up the canvas walls. It's impossible to see where anyone is or hear what anyone is saying: above the guests' voices the wind rises in a frenzy.

Outside a storm is raging. It shrieks around them, it batters the tent. At each assault the whole structure seems to flex and shudder with a loud groaning of metal; the guests cower in alarm. The doors have come free from their ties and flap at the entrance. The flames of the paraffin torches that illuminate the doorway snicker.

It feels personal, this storm. It feels as though it has saved all its fury for them.

This isn't the first time the electric has shorted. But last time the lights snapped back on again within minutes. The guests returned to their dancing, their drinking, their pill-popping, their screwing, their eating, their laughing . . . and forgot it ever happened.

How long has it been now? In the dark it's difficult to tell. A few minutes? Fifteen? Twenty?

They're beginning to feel afraid. This darkness feels somehow ominous, intent. As though anything could be happening beneath its cover.

FINALLY, THE BULBS FLICKER BACK on. Whoops and cheers from the guests. They're embarrassed now about how the lights find them: crouched as though ready to fend off an attack. They laugh it off. They almost manage to convince themselves that they weren't frightened.

The scene illuminated in the three adjoining tents should be one of celebration, but it looks more like one of devastation. In the main dining section, clots of wine spatter the laminate floor, a crimson stain spreads across white linen. Bottles of champagne cluster on every surface; testament to an evening of toasts and celebrations. A forlorn pair of silver sandals peeks from beneath a tablecloth.

The Irish band begins to play again in the dance tent—a rousing ditty to restore the spirit of celebration. Many of the guests hurry in that direction, eager for some light relief. If you were to look closely at where they step you might see the marks where one barefoot guest has trodden in broken glass and left bloody footprints across the laminate, drying to a rusty stain. No one notices.

Other guests drift and gather in the corners of the main tent, nebulous as leftover cigarette smoke. Loath to stay, but also loath to step outside its sanctuary while the storm still rages. And no one can leave the island. Not yet. The boats can't come until the wind dies down.

In the center of everything stands the huge cake. It has appeared whole and perfect before them for most of the day, its train of sugar foliage glittering beneath the lights. But only minutes before the lights went out the guests gathered around to watch its ceremonial disemboweling. Now the deep red sponge gapes from within.

Then from outside comes a new sound. You might almost mistake it for the wind. But it rises in pitch and volume until it is unmistakable.

The guests freeze. They stare at one another. They are suddenly afraid again. More so than they were when the lights went out. They all know what they are hearing. It is a scream of terror.

AOIFE

The Wedding Planner

N EARLY ALL OF THE WEDDING PARTY ARE HERE NOW. THINGS ARE about to crank into another gear: there's the rehearsal dinner this evening, with the chosen guests, so the wedding really begins tonight.

I've put the champagne on ice ready for the predinner drinks. It's vintage Bollinger: eight bottles of it, plus the wine for dinner and a couple of crates of Guinness—all as per the bride's instructions. It is not for me to comment, but it seems rather a lot. They're all adults, though. I'm sure they know how to restrain themselves. Or maybe not. That best man seems a bit of a liability—all of the ushers do, to be honest. And the bridesmaid—the bride's half sister—I've seen her on her solitary wanderings of the island, hunched over and walking fast like she's trying to outpace something.

You learn all the insider secrets, doing this sort of work. You see the things no one else is privileged to see. All the gossip that the guests would kill to have. As a wedding planner you can't *afford* to miss anything. You have to be alert to every detail, all the smaller eddies beneath the surface. If I didn't pay attention, one of those currents could grow into a huge riptide, destroying all my careful planning. And here's another thing I've learned—sometimes the smallest currents are the strongest.

I move through the Folly's downstairs rooms, lighting the

blocks of turf in the grates, so they can get a good smolder on for this evening. Freddy and I have started cutting and drying our own turf from the bog, as has been done for centuries past. The smoky, earthy smell of the turf fires will add to the sense of local atmosphere. The guests should like that. It may be midsummer but it gets cool at night on the island. The Folly's old stone walls keep the warmth out and aren't so good at holding it in.

Today has been surprisingly warm, at least by the standards of these parts, but the same's not looking likely for tomorrow. The end of the weather forecast I caught on the radio mentioned wind. We get the brunt of all the weather here; often the storms are much worse than they end up being on the mainland, as if they've exhausted themselves on us. It's still sunny out but this afternoon the needle on the old barometer in the hallway swung from FAIR to CHANGEABLE. I've taken it down. I don't want the bride to see it. Though I'm not sure that she is the sort to panic. More the sort to get angry and look for someone to blame. And I know just who would be in the firing line.

"Freddy," I call into the kitchen, "will you be starting on the dinner soon?"

"Yeah," he calls back, "got it all under control."

Tonight they'll eat a fish stew based on a traditional Connemara fisherman's chowder: smoked fish, lots of cream. I ate it the first time I ever visited this place, when there were still people here. This evening's will be a more refined take on the usual recipe, as this is a refined group we have staying. Or at least I suppose they like to *think* of themselves as such. We'll see what happens when the drink hits them.

"Then we'll be needing to start prepping the canapés for to-morrow," I call, running through the list in my head.

"I'm on it."

"And the cake: we'll be wanting to assemble that in good time."

The cake is quite something to behold. It should be. I know

how much it cost. The bride didn't bat an eyelid at the expense. I believe she's used to having the best of everything. Four tiers of deep red velvet sponge, encased in immaculate white icing and strewn with sugar greenery, to match the foliage in the chapel and the marquee's tents. Extremely fragile and made according to the bride's exact specifications, it traveled all the way here from a very exclusive cake-maker's in Dublin: it was no small effort getting it across the water in one piece. Tomorrow, of course, it will be destroyed. But it's all about the moment, a wedding. All about the day. It's not really about the marriage at all, in spite of what everyone says.

See, mine is a profession in which you orchestrate happiness. It is why I became a wedding planner. Life is messy. We all know this. Terrible things happen, I learned that while I was still a child. But no matter what happens, life is only a series of days. You can't control more than a single day. But you can control *one* of them. Twenty-four hours can be curated. A wedding day is a neat little parcel of time in which I can create something whole and perfect to be cherished for a lifetime, a pearl from a broken necklace.

Freddy emerges from the kitchen in his stained butcher's apron. "How are you feeling?"

I shrug. "A little nervous, to be honest."

"You've got this, love. Think how many times you've done this."

"But this is different. Because of who it is—" It was a real coup, getting Will Slater and Julia Keegan to hold their wedding here. I worked as an event planner in Dublin, before. Setting up here was all my idea, restoring the island's crumbling, half-ruined folly into an elegant ten-bedroom property with a dining room, drawing room and kitchen. Freddy and I live here permanently but use only a tiny fraction of the space when it's just the two of us.

"Shush." Freddy steps forward and enfolds me in a hug. I feel myself stiffening at first. I'm so focused on my to-do list that it feels like a diversion we don't have time for. Then I allow myself to relax into the embrace, to appreciate his comforting, familiar warmth. Freddy is a good hugger. He's what you might call "cuddly." He likes his food—it's his job. He ran a restaurant in Dublin before we moved here.

"It's all going to work out fine," he says. "I promise. It will all be perfect." He kisses the top of my head. I've had a great deal of experience in this business. But then I've never worked on an event I've been so invested in. And the bride is very particular—which, to be fair to her, probably goes with the territory of what she does, running her own magazine. Someone else might have been run a little ragged by her requests. But I've enjoyed it. I like a challenge.

Anyway. That's enough about me. This weekend is about the happy couple, after all. The bride and groom haven't been together for very long, by all accounts. Seeing as our bedroom is in the Folly too, with all the others, we could hear them last night. "Jesus," Freddy said as we lay in bed. "I can't listen to this." I knew what he meant. Strange how when someone is in the throes of pleasure it can sound like pain. They seem very much in love, but a cynic might say that's *why* they can't seem to keep their hands off each other. Very much in lust might be a more accurate description.

Freddy and I have been together for the best part of two decades and even now there are things I keep from him and, I'm sure, vice versa. Makes you wonder how much they know about each other, those two.

Whether they really know all of each other's dark secrets.

HANNAH
The Plus-One

THE WAVES RISE IN FRONT OF US, WHITECAPPED. ON LAND IT'S A beautiful summer's day, but it's pretty rough out here. A few minutes ago we left the safety of the mainland harbor and as we did the water seemed to darken in color and the waves grew by several feet.

It's the evening before the wedding and we're on our way to the island. As "special guests," we're staying there tonight. I'm looking forward to it. At least—I *think* I am. I need a bit of a distraction at the moment, anyway.

"Hold on!" A shout from the captain's cabin, behind us. Mattie, the man's called. Before we have time to think the little boat launches off one wave and straight into the crest of another. Water sprays up over us in a huge arc.

"Christ!" Charlie shouts and I see that he's got soaked on one side. Miraculously I'm only a little damp.

"Would you be a bit wet up there?" Mattie calls.

I'm laughing but I'm having to force it a bit because it was pretty frightening. The boat's motion, somehow back and forth and side to side all at once, has my stomach turning somersaults.

"Oof," I say, feeling the nausea sinking through me. The thought of the cream tea we ate before we got on the boat suddenly makes me want to hurl.

Charlie looks at me, puts a hand on my knee and gives a squeeze. "Oh, God. It's started already?" I always get terrible motion sickness. Anything sickness really; when I was pregnant it was the worst.

"Mm-hmm. I've taken a couple of pills, but they've hardly taken the edge off."

"Look," Charlie says quickly, "I'll read about the place, take your mind off it." He scrolls through his phone. He's got a guidebook downloaded; ever the teacher, my husband. The boat lurches again and the iPhone nearly jumps out of his grasp. He swears, grips it with both hands; we can't afford to replace it.

"There's not that much here," he says, a bit apologetically, once he's managed to load the page. "Loads on Connemara, yeah, but on the island itself—I suppose it's so small . . ." He stares at the screen as though willing it to deliver. "Oh, here, I've found a bit." He clears his throat, then starts to read in what I think is probably the voice he uses in his lessons. "Inis an Amplóra, or Cormorant Island, in the English translation, is two miles from one end to the other, longer than it is wide. The island is formed of a lump of granite emerging *majestically* from the Atlantic, several miles off the Connemara coastline. A large bog comprised of peat, or 'turf' as it is called locally, covers much of its surface. The best, indeed the only, way to see the island is from a private boat. The channel between the mainland and the island can get particularly choppy—"

"They're right about that," I mutter, clutching the side as we seesaw over another wave and slam down again. My stomach turns over again.

"I can tell you more than all that," Mattie calls from his cabin. I hadn't realized he could overhear us from there. "You won't be getting much about Inis an Amplóra from a guidebook."

Charlie and I shuffle nearer to the cabin so we can hear. He's got a lovely rich accent, does Mattie. "First people that settled the place," he tells us, "far as it's known, were a religious sect, persecuted by some on the mainland."

"Oh, yes," Charlie says, looking at his guide. "I think I saw a bit about that—"

"You can't get everything from that thing," Mattie says, frowning and clearly unimpressed by the interruption. "I've lived here all my life, see—and my people have been here for centuries. I can tell you more than your man on the internet."

"Sorry," Charlie says, flushing.

"Anyway," Mattie says. "Twenty years or so ago the archeologists found them. All together in the turf bog they were, side by side, packed in tight." Something tells me that he is enjoying himself. "Perfectly preserved, it's said, because there's no air down in there. It was a massacre. They'd all been hacked to death."

"Oh," Charlie says, with a glance at me, "I'm not sure—"

It's too late, the idea is in my head now: long-buried corpses emerging from black earth. I try not to think about it but the image keeps reasserting itself like a glitch in a video. The swoop of nausea that comes as we ride over the next wave is almost a relief, requiring all my focus.

"And there's no one living there now?" Charlie asks brightly, trying for a change of conversation. "Other than the new owners?"

"No," Mattie says. "Nothing but ghosts."

Charlie taps his screen. "It says here the island was inhabited until the nineties, when the last few people decided to return to the mainland in favor of running water, electricity and modern life."

"Oh, that's what it says there, is it?" Mattie sounds amused.

"Why?" I ask, managing to find my voice. "Was there some other reason they left?"

Mattie seems to be about to speak. Then his face changes. "Look out for yourselves!" he roars. Charlie and I manage to grab the rail seconds before the bottom seems to drop out of everything and we are sent plunging down the side of one wave, then smashed into the side of another. Jesus.

You're meant to find a fixed point with motion sickness. I train my gaze on the island. It has been in view the whole way from the mainland, a bluish smudge on the horizon, shaped like a flattened anvil. Jules wouldn't pick anywhere less than stunning, but I can't help feeling that the dark shape of it seems to hunch and glower, in contrast to the bright day.

"Pretty stunning, isn't it?" Charlie says.

"Mm," I say noncommittally. "Well, let's hope there's running water and electricity there these days. I'm going to need a nice bath after this."

Charlie grins. "Knowing Jules, if they hadn't plumbed and wired the place before, they'll have done so by now. You know what she's like. She's so efficient."

I'm sure Charlie didn't mean it, but it feels like a comparison. I'm *not* the world's most efficient. I can't seem to enter a room without making a mess and since we've had the kids our house is a permanent dump. When we—rarely—have people round I end up throwing stuff in cupboards and cramming them closed, so that it feels like the whole place is holding its breath, trying not to explode. When we first went round for dinner at Jules's elegant Victorian house in Islington it was like something out of a magazine; like something out of *her* magazine—an online one called *The Download*. I kept thinking she might try and tidy me away somewhere, aware of how I stuck out like a sore thumb with my inch of dark roots and off-the-rack clothes. I found myself trying to smooth out my accent, even, soften my Mancunian vowels.

We couldn't be more different, Jules and I. The two most important women in my husband's life. I lean over the rail, taking deep breaths of the sea air.

"I read a good bit in that article," Charlie says, "about the island. Apparently it's got white sand beaches, which are famous in this part of Ireland. And the color of the sand means the water in the coves turns a beautiful turquoise color."

"Oh," I say. "Well, that sounds better than a peat bog."

"Yep," Charlie says. "Maybe we'll have a chance to go swimming." He smiles at me.

I look at the water, which is more of a chilly slate green than turquoise, and shiver. But I swim off the beach in Brighton, and that's the English Channel, isn't it? Still. There it feels so much tamer than this wild, brutal sea.

"This weekend will be a good distraction, won't it?" Charlie says.

"Yeah," I say. "I hope so." This will be the closest we'll have had to a holiday for a long time. And I really need one right now. "I can't work out why Jules would choose a random island off the coast of Ireland," I add. It seems particularly *her* to choose somewhere so exclusive that her guests might actually drown trying to get there. "It's not like she couldn't have afforded to hold it anywhere she wanted."

Charlie frowns. He doesn't like to talk about money, it embarrasses him. It's one of the reasons I love him. Except sometimes, just sometimes, I can't help wondering what it would be like to have a tiny bit more. We agonized over the gift registry and had a bit of an argument about it. Our max is normally fifty quid, but Charlie insisted that we had to do more, because he and Jules go back so far. As everything listed was from Liberty's, the £150 we finally agreed to only bought us a rather ordinary-looking ceramic bowl. There was a scented candle on there for £200.

"You know Jules," Charlie says now, as the boat makes another swoop downward before hitting something that feels much harder than mere water, bouncing up again with a few sideways spasms for good measure. "She likes to do things differently. And it could be to do with her dad being Irish."

"But I thought she doesn't get on with her dad?"

"It's more complicated than that. He was never really around and he's a bit of a dick, but I think she's always kind of idolized him. That's why she wanted me to give her sailing lessons all those years ago. He had this yacht, and she wanted him to be proud of her."

It's difficult to imagine Jules in the inferior position of wanting to make someone proud. I know her dad's a big-deal property developer, a self-made man. As the daughter of a train driver and a nurse who grew up constantly strapped for cash, I'm fascinated by—and a little bit suspicious of—people who have made loads of money. To me they're like another species altogether, a breed of sleek and dangerous big cats.

"Or maybe Will chose it," I say. "It seems very him, very Outward Bound." I feel a little leap of excitement in my stomach at the thought of meeting someone so famous. It's hard to think of Jules's fiancé as a completely real person.

I've been catching up on the show in secret. It's pretty good, though it's hard to be objective. I've been fascinated by the idea of Jules being with this man . . . touching him, kissing him, sleeping with him. About to get *married* to him.

The basic premise of the show, *Survive the Night*, is that Will gets left somewhere, tied up and blindfolded, in the middle of the night. A forest, say, or the middle of an Arctic tundra, with nothing but the clothes he's wearing and maybe a knife in his belt. He then has to free himself and make his way to a rendezvous point using his wits and navigational skills alone. There's lots of high drama: in one episode he has to cross a waterfall in the dark; in another he's stalked by wolves. At times you'll suddenly remember that the camera crew is there watching him, filming him. If it were really all that bad, surely they'd step in to help? But they certainly do a good job of making you feel the danger.

At my mention of Will, Charlie's face has darkened. "I still don't get why she's marrying him after such a short time," he says. "I suppose that's what Jules is like. When she's made up her mind, she acts quickly. But you mark my words, Han: he's hiding something. I don't think he's everything he pretends to be."

This is why I've been so secretive about watching the show. I know Charlie wouldn't like it. At times I can't help feeling that his dislike of Will seems a little like jealousy. I really hope it's *not* jealousy. Because what would that mean?

It could also be to do with Will's stag party. Charlie went, which seemed all wrong, as he's Jules's friend. He came home from the weekend in Sweden a bit out of sorts. Every time I even alluded to it he'd go all weird and stiff. So I shrugged it off. He came back in one piece, didn't he?

The sea seems to have got even rougher. The old fishing boat is pitching and rolling now in all directions at once, like one of those rodeo-bull machines, like it's trying to throw us overboard. "Is it really safe to keep going?" I call to Mattie.

"Yep!" he calls back, over the crash of the spray, the shriek of the wind. "This is a good day, as they go. Not far to Inis an Amplóra now."

I can feel wet hanks of hair stuck to my forehead, while the rest of it seems to have lifted into a huge tangled cloud around my head. I can only imagine how I'll look to Jules and Will and the rest of them, when we finally arrive.

"Cormorant!" Charlie shouts, pointing. He's trying to distract me from my nausea, I know. I feel like one of the children being taken to the doctor's for an injection. But I follow his finger to a sleek dark head, emerging from the waves like the periscope of a miniature submarine. Then it swoops down beneath the surface, a swift black streak. Imagine feeling so at home in such hostile conditions.

"I saw something in the article specifically about cormorants," Charlie says. He picks up his phone again. "Ah, here. They're particularly common along this stretch of coast, apparently." He puts on his schoolteacher voice: "'The cormorant is a bird much maligned in local folklore.' Oh, dear. 'Historically, the bird has been represented as a symbol of greed, bad luck and evil.'" We both watch as the cormorant emerges from the water again. There's a tiny fish in its sharp beak, a brief flash of silver, before the bird opens its gullet and swallows the thing whole.

My stomach flips. I feel as though it's me that has swallowed the fish, quick and slippery, swimming about in my belly. And as the boat begins to list in the other direction, I lurch to the side and throw up my cream tea.

JULES
The Bride

I'M STANDING IN FRONT OF THE MIRROR IN OUR ROOM, THE BIGGEST and most elegant of the Folly's ten bedrooms, naturally. From here I only need to turn my head a fraction to look out through the windows toward the sea. The weather today is perfect, the sun shimmering off the waves so brightly you can hardly look at it. It bloody well better stay like this for tomorrow.

Our room is on the western side of the building and this is the westernmost island off this part of the coast, so there is nothing, and no one, for thousands of miles between me and the Americas. I like the drama of that. The Folly itself is a beautifully restored fifteenth-century building, treading the line between luxury and timelessness, grandeur and comfort: antique rugs on the flagstone floors, claw-footed baths, fireplaces lit with smoldering peat. It's large enough to fit all our guests, yet small enough to feel intimate. It's perfect. Everything is going to be perfect.

Don't think about the note, Jules.

I will *not* think about the note.

Fuck. *Fuck.* I don't know why it's got to me so much. I have never been a worrier, the sort of person who wakes up at three in the morning, fretting. Not until recently anyway.

The note was delivered through our letter box three weeks ago. It told me not to marry Will. To call it off.

Somehow the idea of it has gained this dark power over me. Whenever I think about it, it gives me a sour feeling in the pit of my stomach. A feeling like dread.

Which is ridiculous. I wouldn't normally give a second thought to this sort of thing.

I look back at the mirror. I'm currently wearing the dress. *The* dress. I thought it important to try it on one last time, the eve of my wedding, to double-check. I had a fitting last week but I never leave anything to chance. As expected, it's perfect. Heavy cream silk that looks as though it has been poured over me, the corsetry within creating the quintessential hourglass. No lace or other fripperies, that's not me. The nap of the silk is so fine it can only be handled with special white gloves which, obviously, I'm wearing now. It cost an absolute bomb. It was worth it. I'm not interested in fashion for its own sake, but I respect the power of clothes, in creating the right optics. I knew immediately that this dress was a queenmaker.

By the end of the evening the dress will probably be filthy, even I can't mitigate that. But I will have it shortened to just below the knee and dyed a darker color. I am nothing if not practical. I have always, *always* got a plan; have done ever since I was little.

I move over to where I have the table plan pinned to the wall. Will says I'm like a general hanging his campaign maps. But it is important, isn't it? The seating can pretty much make or break the guests' enjoyment of a wedding. I know I'll have it perfect by this evening. It's all in the planning: that's how I took *The Download* from a blog to a fully fledged online magazine with a staff of thirty in a couple of years.

Most of the guests will come over tomorrow for the wedding, then return to their hotels on the mainland—I enjoyed putting "boats at midnight" on the invites in place of the usual "carriages." But our most important invitees will stay on the island tonight and tomorrow, in the Folly with us. It's a rather exclusive guest list. Will had to choose the favorites among his ushers, as he has so many. Not so difficult for me as I've only got one bridesmaid—my half sister, Olivia. I don't have many female friends. I don't have time for gossip. And groups of women together remind me too much of the bitchy clique of girls at my school who never accepted me as their own. It was a surprise to see so many women at the bachelorette party—but then they were largely my employees from *The Download*—who organized it as a not entirely welcome surprise—or the partners of Will's mates. My closest friend is male: Charlie. In effect, this weekend, he'll be *my* best man.

Charlie and Hannah are on their way over now, the last of tonight's guests to arrive. It will be so good to see Charlie. It feels like a long time since we hung out as adults, without his kids there. Back in the day we used to see each other all the time—even after he'd got together with Hannah. He always made time for me. But when he had kids it felt like he moved into that other realm: one in which a late night means 11 P.M., and every outing without kids has to be carefully orchestrated. It was only then that I started to miss having him to myself.

"You look stunning."

"Oh!" I jump, then spot him in the mirror: Will. He's leaning in the doorway, watching me. "Will!" I hiss. "I'm in my dress! Get out! You're not supposed to see—"

He doesn't move. "Aren't I allowed to have a preview? And I've seen it, now." He begins to walk toward me. "No point crying over spilled silk. You look—*Jesus*—I can't wait to see you coming up the aisle in that." He moves to stand behind me, taking ahold of my bare shoulders.

I should be livid. I *am*. Yet I can feel my outrage sputtering. Because his hands are on me now, moving from my shoulders down my arms, and I feel that first shiver of longing. I remind myself, too, that I'm far from superstitious about the groom seeing the wedding dress beforehand—I've never believed in that sort of thing.

"You shouldn't *be* here," I say, crossly. But already it sounds a little halfhearted.

"Look at us," he says as our eyes meet in the mirror, as he traces a finger down the side of my cheek. "Don't we look good together?"

And he's right, we do. Me so dark-haired and pale, him so fair and tanned. We make the most attractive couple in any room. I'm not going to pretend it's not part of the thrill, imagining how we might appear to the outside world—and to our guests tomorrow. I think of the girls at school who once teased me for being a chubby nerd (I was a late bloomer) and think: *Look who's having the last laugh*.

He bites into the exposed skin of my shoulder. A pluck of lust low in my belly, a snapped elastic band. With it goes the last of my resistance.

"You nearly done with that?" He's looking over my shoulder at the table plan.

"I haven't quite worked out where I'm putting everyone," I say.

There's a silence as he inspects it, his breath warm on the side of my neck, curling along my collarbone. I can smell the aftershave he's wearing: cedar and moss. "Did we invite Piers?" he asks mildly. "I don't remember him being on the list."

I somehow manage not to roll my eyes. *I* did all of the invitations. *I* refined the list, chose the stationer's, collated all the addresses, bought the stamps, mailed every last one. Will was away a lot, shooting the new series. Every so often, he'd throw out a name, someone he'd forgotten to mention. I suppose he did check through the list at the end pretty carefully, saying he wanted to make sure we hadn't missed anyone. Piers was a later addition.

"He wasn't on the list," I admit. "But I saw his wife at those drinks at the Groucho. She asked about the wedding and it seemed total madness not to invite them. I mean, why wouldn't we?" Piers is the producer of Will's show. He's a nice guy and he and Will have always seemed to get along well. I didn't have to think twice about extending the invitation.

"Fine," Will says. "Yes, of course that makes sense." But there's an edge to his voice. For some reason it has bothered him.

"Look, darling," I say, curling one arm around his neck. "I thought you'd be delighted to have them here. They certainly seemed pleased to be asked."

"I don't mind," he says, carefully. "It was a surprise, that's all." He moves his hands to my waist. "I don't mind in the least. In fact, it's a *good* surprise. It will be nice to have them."

"OK. Right, so I'm going to put husbands and wives next to each other. Does that work?"

"The eternal dilemma," he says, mock-profoundly.

"God, I know . . . but people do really care about that sort of thing."

"Well," he says, "if you and I were guests I know where I'd want to be sitting."

"Oh, yes?"

"Right opposite you, so I could do this." His hand reaches down and rucks up the fabric of the silk skirt, climbing beneath.

"Will," I say, "the silk—"

His fingers have found the lace edge of my underwear.

"Will!" I say, half-annoyed, "what on earth are you—" Then his fingers have slipped inside my knickers and have begun to move against me and I don't particularly care about the silk anymore. My head falls against his chest.

This is not like me at all. I am not the sort of person who gets engaged only a few months into knowing someone . . . or married only a few months after that. But I would argue that it isn't rash, or impulsive, as I think some suspect. If anything, it's the opposite. It's knowing your own mind, knowing what you want and acting upon it.

"We could do it right now," Will says, his voice a warm murmur against my neck. "We've got time, haven't we?" I try to answer—*no*—but as his fingers continue their work it turns into a long, drawn-out groan.

With every other partner I've got bored in a matter of weeks, the sex has rather too quickly become pedestrian, a chore. With Will I feel like I am never quite sated—even when, in the baser sense, I am more sated than I have been with any other lover. It isn't just about him being so beautiful—which he is, of course, objectively so. This insatiability is far deeper than that. I'm aware of a feeling of wanting to possess him. Of each sexual act being an attempt at a possession that is never quite achieved, some essential part of him always evading my reach, slipping beneath the surface.

Is it to do with his fame? The fact that once you attain celebrity you become, in a sense, publicly owned? Or is it something else, something fundamental about him? Secret and unknowable, hidden from view?

This thought, inevitably, has me thinking about the note. *I will not think about the note.*

Will's fingers continue their work. "Will," I say, halfheartedly, "anyone might come in."

"Isn't that the thrill of it?" he whispers. Yes, yes, I suppose it is. Will has definitely broadened my sexual horizons. He's introduced me to sex in public places. We've done it in a nighttime park, in the back row of a near-empty cinema. When I remember this I am amazed at myself: I cannot believe that it was me who did these things. Julia Keegan does not break the law.

He's also the only man I have ever allowed to film me in the nude—once, even during sex itself. I only agreed to this once we were engaged, naturally. I'm not a fucking idiot. But it's Will's thing and, since we've started doing it, though I don't exactly *like* it—it represents a loss of control, and in every other relationship I have been the one in control—at the same time it is somehow intoxicating, this loss. I hear him unbuckle his belt and just the sound of it sends a charge through me. He pushes me forward, toward the dressing table—a little roughly. I grip the table. I feel the tip of him poised there, about to enter me.

"Hello-hello? Anybody in there?" The door creaks open.

Shit.

Will pulls away from me, I hear him scrabbling with his jeans, his belt. I feel my skirt fall. I almost can't bear to turn.

He stands there, lounging in the doorway: Johnno, Will's best man. How much did he see? *Everything.* I feel the heat rising into my cheeks and I'm furious with myself. I'm furious with him. I *never* blush.

"Sorry, chaps," Johnno says. "Was I interrupting?" Is that a smirk? "Oh—" He catches sight of what I'm wearing. "Is that . . . ? Isn't that meant to be bad luck?"

I'd like to pick up a heavy object and hurl it at him, scream at him to get out. But I am on best behavior. "Oh, for God's sake!" I say instead, and I hope my tone asks: *Do I look like the sort of cretin who would believe something like that?* I raise my eyebrow at him, cross my arms. I am past master at the raised eyebrow game—I use it at work to fantastic effect. I *dare* him to say another word. For all Johnno's bravado, I think he's a little scared of me. People are, generally, scared of me.

"We were going through the table plan," I tell him. "So you interrupted that."

"Well," he says. "I've been such a bellend . . ." I can see that he's a little cowed. Good. "I've just realized I've forgotten something pretty important."

I feel my heart begin to beat faster. Not the rings. I told Will not to trust him with the rings until the last minute. If he's forgotten the rings I cannot be held responsible for my actions.

"It's my suit," Johnno says. "I had it all ready to go, in the liner . . . and then, at the last minute . . . well, I dunno what happened. All I can say is, it must be hanging on my door in Blighty."

I look away from them both as they leave the room. Concentrate hard on not saying anything I'll regret. I have to keep a handle on my temper this weekend. Mine has been known to get the better of me. I'm not proud of the fact, but I have never found myself able to completely control it, though I'm getting better. Rage is not a good look on a bride.

I don't get why Will is friends with Johnno, why he hasn't cut him out of his life by now. It's definitely not the witty conversation that keeps him hanging in there. The guy's harmless, I suppose . . . at least, I assume he's harmless. But they're so different. Will is so driven, so successful, so smart in the way he presents himself. Johnno is a slob. One of life's dropouts. When we collected him from the local train station on the mainland he stank of weed and looked like he'd been sleeping rough. I expected him to at least get a shave and a haircut before he came out here. It's not too much to ask that your groomsman doesn't look like a caveman, is it? Later I'll send Will over to his room with a razor.

Will's too good to him. He even, apparently, got Johnno a screen test for *Survive the Night* which, of course, didn't come to anything. When I asked Will why he sticks with Johnno, he put it down to simple "history." "We don't have much in common, these days," he said. "But we go back a long way."

But Will can be fairly ruthless. To be honest, that was probably one of the things that attracted me to him when we first met, one of the things I immediately recognized we had in common. As much as his golden looks, his winning smile, the thing that drew me was the ambition I could smell coming off him, beneath his charm.

So this is what worries me. Why would Will keep a friend like Johnno around simply because of a shared past? Unless that past has some sort of hold over him.

JOHNNO
The Best Man

WILL CLIMBS OUT OF THE TRAPDOOR CARRYING A PACK OF Guinness. We're up on the Folly's battlements, looking through the gaps in the stonework. The ground's a long way down and some of the stones up here are pretty loose. If you didn't have a good head for heights it would do a number on you. From here you can see all the way to the mainland. I feel like a king up here, with the sun on my face.

Will breaks a can out of the case. "Here you go."

"Ah, the good stuff. Thanks, mate. And sorry I walked in on you back there." I give him a wink. "Thought you were meant to save it for after marriage, though?"

Will raises his eyebrows, all innocence. "I don't know what you're talking about. Jules and I were going through the table plan."

"Oh, yeah? That's what they call it now? Honest, though," I say, "I'm sorry about the suit, mate. I feel like such a tool for forgetting." I want him to know I feel bad—that I'm serious about being a good best man to him. I really am, I want to do him proud.

"Not an issue," Will says. "Not sure my spare's going to fit, but you're welcome to it."

"You're sure Jules is going to be all right about it? She didn't look all that happy."

"Yeah." Will waves a hand. "She'll be fine." Which I guess means she probably isn't fine, but he'll work on it.

"OK. Thanks, mate."

He takes a swig of his Guinness, leans against the stone wall behind us. Then he seems to remember something. "Oh. By the way, you haven't seen Olivia, have you? Jules's half sister? She keeps disappearing. She's a little—" He makes a gesture: *cuckoo,* that's what it means, but "fragile" is what he says.

I met Olivia earlier. She's tall and dark-haired, with a big, sulky mouth and legs that go up to her armpits. "Shame," I say. "'Cause . . . well, don't tell me you haven't noticed?"

"Johnno, she's nineteen, for Christ's sake," Will says. "Don't be disgusting. Besides, she also happens to be my fiancée's sister."

"Nineteen; so she's legal, then," I say, looking to wind him up. "It's tradition, isn't it? The best man has the pick of the brides-maids. And there's only one, so it's not like I have all that much choice . . ."

Will twists his mouth like he's tasted something disgusting. "I don't think that rule applies when they're fifteen years younger than you, you idiot," he says. He's acting all prim now, but he's always had an eye for the ladies. They've always had an eye for him in return, lucky bastard. "She's off-limits, all right? Get that through your thick skull." He knocks my head with his knuckles.

I don't like the "thick skull" bit. I'm not necessarily the bright-est penny in the till. But I don't like being treated like a moron, either. Will knows that. It was one of the things that always got my back up at school. I laugh it off, though. I know he didn't mean it.

"Look," he says. "I can't have you blundering around making passes at my teenage sister-in-law. Jules would *kill* me. She'd kill you, too."

"All right, all right," I say.

"Besides," he says, lowering his voice, "there's also the fact that she's, you know . . ." He makes that *cuckoo* gesture again. "She must get it from Jules's mum. Thank God Jules missed out on any of those genes. Anyway, hands off, all right?"

"Fine, fine . . ." I take a swig of my Guinness and do a big belch.

"You had a chance to do much climbing lately?" Will asks me, obviously trying to change the subject.

"Nah," I say. "Not really. That's why I've got this." I pat my gut. "Hard to find time when you're not being paid for it, like you are."

The funny thing is, it was always me who was more into that stuff. All the Outward-Bound stuff. Until recently, it's what I did for a living too, working at an adventure center in the Lake District.

"Yeah. I guess so," Will says. "It's funny—it's not quite as much fun as it looks, really."

"I doubt that, mate," I say. "You get to do the best thing on earth for a living."

"Well—you know . . . but it's not that authentic; a lot of smoke and mirrors . . ."

I'd bet anything he uses a stuntman to do the harder stuff. Will has never liked getting his hands that dirty. He claims he did a lot of training for the show, but still.

"Then there's all the hair and makeup," he says, "which seems ridiculous when you're shooting a program about survival."

"Bet you love all that," I say with a wink. "Can't fool me."

He's always been a bit vain. I say it with affection, obviously, but I enjoy getting him riled. He's a good-looking bloke and he knows it. You can tell all the clothes he's wearing today, even the jeans, are good stuff, expensive. Maybe it's Jules's influence: she's a stylish lady herself and you can imagine her marching him into a shop. But you can't imagine him minding much either.

"So," I say, clapping him on the shoulder. "You ready to be a married man?"

He grins, nods. "I am. What can I say? I'm head over heels."

I was surprised when Will told me he was getting married, I'm not going to lie. I've always thought of him as a lad about town. No woman can resist that golden boy charm. On the stag, he told me about some of the dates he went on, before Jules. "I mean, in a way it was crazy good. I've never had so much action with so many different women as when I joined those apps, not even at uni. I had to get myself tested every couple of *weeks*. But there were some crazy ones out there, some clingy ones, you know? I don't have time for all that anymore. And then Jules came along. And she was . . . perfect. She's so sure of herself, of what she wants from life. We're the same."

I bet the house in Islington didn't hurt either, I didn't say. *The loaded dad.* I don't dare rib him about it—people get weird talking about money. But if there's one thing Will has always liked, maybe even more than the ladies, it's money. Maybe it's a thing from childhood, never having quite as much as anyone else at our school. I get that. He was there because his dad was headmaster, while I got in on a sports scholarship. My family aren't posh at all. I was spotted playing rugby at a school tournament in Croydon when I was eleven and they approached my dad. That sort of thing actually happened at Trevs: it was that important to them to field a good team.

A voice comes from down below us. "Hey hey hey! What's going on up there?"

"Boys!" Will says. "Come up and join us! More the merrier!"

Bollocks. I was quite enjoying it being just Will and me.

They're climbing up out of the trapdoor—the four ushers. I shift over to make room, giving each a nod as they appear: Femi, then Angus, Duncan, Peter.

"Fuck me, it's high up here," Femi says, peering over the edge.

Duncan grabs hold of Angus's shoulders and pretends to give him a shove. "Whoa, saved you!"

Angus lets out a high-pitched squeal and we all laugh. "Don't!"

he says angrily, recovering himself. "Jesus—that's *fucking* dangerous." He's clinging on to the stone as though for dear life, inching his way along to sit down next to us. Angus was always a bit wet for our group, but got social credit for arriving in his dad's chopper at the start of term.

Will hands out the cans of Guinness I'd been eyeing up for seconds.

"Thanks, mate," Femi says. He looks at the can. "When in Rome, hey?"

Pete nods to the drop beneath us. "Think you might have to have a few of these to forget about that, Angus, mate."

"Yeah but you don't want to drink *too* many," Duncan says. "Or you won't care enough about it."

"Oh shut it," Angus says crossly, coloring. But he's still pretty pale and I get the impression he's doing everything he can not to look over the edge.

"I've got gear with me this weekend," Pete says in an undertone, "that would make you think you could jump off and fucking fly."

"Leopards don't change their spots, eh, Pete?" Femi says. "Raiding your mum's pill cabinet—I remember that kit bag of yours rattling when you came back after exeat."

"Yeah," Angus says. "We all owe her a thank-you."

"*I'd* thank her," Duncan says. "Always remember your mum being a bit of a MILF, Pete."

"You better share the love tomorrow, mate," Femi says.

Pete winks at him. "You know me. Always do well by my boys."

"How about now?" I ask. I suddenly feel I need a hit to blur the edges and the weed I smoked earlier has worn off.

"I like your attitude, J-dog," Pete says. "But you gotta pace yourself."

"You better behave yourselves tomorrow," Will says, mock-sternly. "I don't want my groomsmen showing me up."

"We'll behave, mate," Pete says, throwing an arm around his shoulder. "Just want to make sure our boy's wedding is an occasion to remember."

Will's always been the center of everything, the anchor of the group, all of us revolving round him. Good at sport, good enough grades—with a bit of extra help here and there. Everyone liked him. And I guess it seemed effortless, as though he didn't work for anything. If you didn't know him like I did, that is.

We all sit and drink in silence for a few moments in the sun.

"This is like being back at Trevs," Angus says, ever the historian. "Remember how we used to smuggle beers into the school? Climb up onto the roof of the sports hall to drink them?"

"Yeah," Duncan says. "Seem to remember you shitting yourself then, too."

Angus scowls. "*Fuck* off."

"Johnno smuggled them in really," Femi says, "from that shop in the village."

"Yeah," Duncan says, "because he was a tall, ugly, hairy bastard, even at fifteen, weren't you, mate?" He leans over, punches me on the shoulder.

"And we drank them warm from the can," Angus says, "'cause we didn't have any way to cool them down. Best thing I've ever drunk in my life, probably—even now, when we could all drink, you know, chilled fucking Dom every day of the week if we wanted to."

"You mean like we did a few months ago," Duncan says. "At the RAC."

"When was this?" I ask.

"Ah," Will says. "Sorry, Johnno. I knew it would be too far for you to come, you being in Cumbria and everything."

"Oh," I say. "Yeah, that makes sense." I think of them having a nice old champagne lunch together at the Royal Automobile Club, one of those posh members-only places. Right. I take a big long swig of my Guinness. I could really do with some more weed.

"It was the kick of it," Femi says, "back at school, at Trevs. That's what it was. Knowing we could get caught."

"Jesus," Will says. "Do we really have to talk about Trevs? It's bad enough that I have to hear my dad talking about the place." He says it with a grin, but I can see he's got this slightly pinched look, as if his Guinness has gone down the wrong way. I always felt sorry for Will having a dad like his. No wonder he felt he had to prove himself. I know he'd prefer to forget his whole time at that place. I would too.

"Those years at school seemed so grim at the time," Angus says, "but now, looking back—and Christ knows what this says about me—I think in some ways they feel like the most important of my life. I mean, I definitely wouldn't send my own kids there—no offense to your dad, Will—but it wasn't all bad. Was it?"

"I dunno," Femi says doubtfully. "I got singled out a lot by the teachers. Fucking racists." He says it in an offhand way but I know it wasn't always easy for him, being one of the only black kids there.

"I loved it," Duncan says, and when the rest of us look at him, he adds: "Honest! Now I look back on it I realize how important it was, you know? Wouldn't have had it any other way. It bonded us."

"Anyway," says Will, "back to the present. I'd say things are pretty good now for all of us, wouldn't you?"

They're definitely good for him. The other blokes have done all right for themselves too. Femi's a surgeon, Angus works for his dad's development firm, Duncan's a venture capitalist—whatever that means—and Pete's in advertising, which probably doesn't help his coke habit.

"So what are you up to these days, Johnno?" Pete asks, turning to me. "You were doing that climbing instructor stuff, right?"

I nod. "The adventure center," I say. "Not just climbing. Bush-craft, building camps—"

"Yeah," Duncan says, cutting me off, "you know, I was think-ing of a team-bonding day—was going to talk to you about it. Cut me some mates' rates?"

"I'd love to," I say, thinking someone as minted as Duncan doesn't need to ask for mates' rates. "But I'm not doing it anymore."

"Oh?"

"Nah. I've set up a whiskey business. It'll be coming out pretty soon. Maybe in the next six months or so."

"And you've got outlets?" Angus asks. He sounds rather put out. I suppose it doesn't fit with his image of big, stupid Johnno. I've somehow managed to avoid the boring office job and come out on top.

"I have," I say, nodding. "I have."

"Waitrose?" Duncan asks. "Sainsbury's?"

"And the rest."

"There's a lot of competition out there," Angus says.

"Yeah," I say. "Lots of big old names, celebrity brands—even that UFC fighter, Connor MacGregor. But we wanted to go for a more, I dunno, artisanal feel. Like those new gins."

"We're lucky enough to be serving it tomorrow," Will says. "Johnno brought a case with him. We'll have to give it a try this evening, too. What's the name again? I know it's a good one."

"Hellraiser," I say. I'm quite proud of the name, actually. Dif-ferent from those fusty old brands. And a little annoyed Will's forgotten—it's only on the labels of the bottles I gave him yester-day. But the bloke's getting married tomorrow. He's got other stuff on his mind.

"Who'd have thought it?" Femi says. "All of us, respectable adults. And having come out of that place? Again, no offense to your dad, Will. But it was like somewhere from another century. We're lucky we got out alive—four boys left every term, as I recall."

I couldn't ever have left. My folks were so excited when I got the rugby scholarship, that I got to go to a posh school—a *boarding* school. All the opportunities it would give me, or so they thought.

"Yeah," Pete says. "Remember, there was that boy who drank ethanol from the science department because he was dared to— they had to rush him to hospital? Then there were always the kids who had nervous breakdowns—"

"Oh, shit," Duncan says, excitedly, "and there was that little weedy kid, the one who died. Only the strong survived!" He grins round at us all. "The ones who raised hell, am I right, boys? All back together this weekend!"

"Yeah," Femi says. "But look at this." He leans over and points to the patch where he's going a bit thin on top. "We're getting old and boring now, aren't we?"

"Speak for yourself, mate!" Duncan says. "I reckon we could still fire things up if the occasion demanded it."

"Not at my wedding you won't," Will says, but he's smiling.

"*Especially* at your wedding we will," Duncan says.

"Thought you'd be the first to get married, mate," Femi says to Will. "Being such a hit with the ladies."

"And I thought you never would," Angus says, sucking up like always, "too *much* of a hit with them. Why settle?"

"Do you remember that girl you shagged?" Pete asks. "From the local comp? That topless Polaroid you had of her? Jesus."

"One for the wank bank," Angus says. "Still think about that photo sometimes."

"Yeah, because you never get any action yourself," Duncan says.

Will winks. "Anyway. Seeing as we're all together again—even if we're old and boring, as you so charmingly put it, Femi—I think that deserves a toast."

"I'll drink to that," Duncan says, raising his can.

"Me too," says Pete.

"To the survivors," Will says.

"The survivors!" We echo him. And just for a moment, when I look at the others, they look different, younger. It's like the sun has gilded them. You can't see Femi's bald spot from this angle, or Angus's paunch, and Pete looks less like he only goes out at night. And, if possible, even Will looks better, brighter. I have this sudden sense that we're back there, sitting on that sports hall roof and nothing bad has happened yet. I'd give a fair amount to return to that time.

"Right," Will says, draining the dregs of his Guinness. "I better get downstairs. Charlie and Hannah will be arriving soon. Jules wants a welcoming party on the jetty."

I suppose once everyone's here the weekend will kick off in earnest. I wish for a moment we could go back to just Will and me, shooting the breeze, like we were before the others arrived. I haven't seen all that much of Will recently. Yet he's the person who knows more about me than anyone in the world, really. And I know the most about him.

OLIVIA
The Bridesmaid

MY ROOM USED TO BE A MAID'S QUARTERS, APPARENTLY. I worked out pretty quickly that I'm directly below Jules and Will's room. Last night I could hear *everything*: I did try not to, obviously. But it was like the harder I tried, the more I heard every tiny sound, every groan and gasp. Almost as if they *wanted* to be heard.

They did it this morning too, but at least then I could get out, escape the Folly. We're all under instructions not to go walking around the island after dark. But if it happens again this evening there's no way I'm going to stay here. I'd prefer to take my chances with the peat bog and the cliffs.

I toggle my phone on to Airplane mode and off again, to see if anything happens to the little NO SIGNAL message, but it does fuck all. I doubt I have any new messages. I've sort of lost contact with all my mates. It's not like we've fallen out. It's more that I've left their world since I dropped out of uni. They sent me messages at first:

Hope you're OK babes

Call if you need to chat Livs

See you soon, yeah?

We miss you! 💔

What happened????

Suddenly I feel like I can't breathe. I reach for the bedside table. The razor blade is there: so small, but so sharp. I pull down my jeans and press the razor's edge to my inner thigh, up near my knickers, drag it into my flesh until the blood wells. The color's such a dark red against the blue-white skin there. It's not a very big cut; I've made bigger. But the sting of it focuses everything to a point, to the metal entering my flesh, so that for a moment nothing else exists.

I breathe a little easier. Maybe I'll do one more—

There's a knock on my door. I drop the blade, fumbling to get my jeans closed. "Who is it?" I call.

"Me," Jules says, pushing the door open before I tell her she can come in, which is so Jules. Thank God I reacted quickly. "I need to see you in your bridesmaid dress," she says. "We've got a bit of time before Hannah and Charlie arrive. Johnno's forgotten his *bloody* suit so I want to make sure that at least one member of the wedding party looks good."

"I've already tried it on," I say. "It definitely fits." *Lie.* I have no idea whether it fits or not. I was meant to come to the shop to try it on. But I found an excuse every time Jules tried to get me there: eventually she gave up and bought it, on condition I tried it on and told her it fitted straightaway. I told her it did but I couldn't make myself put it on. It's been in its big stiff cardboard box since Jules had it delivered.

"*You* may have tried it on," Jules says, "but *I* want to see it." She smiles at me, suddenly, like she's just remembered to do so. "You can do it in our bedroom, if you like." She says it as if she's offering some amazing privilege.

"No thanks," I say. "I'd prefer to stay here—"

"Come on," she says. "We've got a nice big mirror." I realize it isn't optional. I go to the wardrobe and lift out the big duck-egg-blue box. Jules's mouth tightens. I know she's pissed off I haven't hung it up yet.

Growing up with Jules sometimes felt like having a second mother, or one who was like other mums—bossy, strict, all that stuff. Mum was never really like that, but Jules was.

I follow her up to their bedroom. Even though Jules is *super* tidy and even though there's a window open to let the fresh air in, it smells of bodies in here, and men's aftershave and, I think (*I don't want to think*), of sex. It feels wrong being in here, in their private space.

Jules closes the door and turns to me with her arms folded. "Go on, then," she says.

I don't feel like I have much choice. Jules is good at making you feel that. I strip down to my underwear, keeping my legs pressed together in case my thigh's still bleeding. If Jules sees I'll have to tell her I've got my period. My skin prickles into goose bumps in the slight breeze coming through the window. I can feel her watching me; I wish she'd give me a bit of privacy. "You've lost weight," she says critically. Her tone is caring, but it doesn't quite ring true. I know she's probably jealous. Once, when she got drunk, she went on about how kids had got at her at school for being "chubby." She's always making comments about my weight, like she doesn't know I've always been skinny, ever since I was a little girl. But it's possible to hate your body when you're thin, too. To feel like it's kept secrets from you. To feel like it's let you down.

Jules is right, though. I have lost weight. I can only wear my smallest jeans at the moment, and even they slip down off my hips. I haven't been trying to lose weight or anything. But that feeling of emptiness I get when I don't eat as much . . . it matches how I feel. It seems right.

Jules is taking the dress out of the box. "Olivia!" she says crossly. "Has this been in here the whole time? Look at these creases! This silk's so delicate . . . I thought you'd look after it a bit better." She sounds as though she's talking to a child. I guess she thinks she is. But I'm not a child anymore.

"Sorry," I say. "I forgot." *Lie.*

"Well. Thank *goodness* I've brought a steamer. It'll take ages to get all of these out, though. You'll have to do that later. But for now just try it on."

She has me put out my arms, like a child, while she shrugs the dress down over my head. As she does I spot an inch-long, bright pink mark on the inside of her wrist. It's a burn, I think. It looks sore and I wonder how she did it: Jules is so careful, she's never normally clumsy enough to burn herself. But before I can get a better look she has taken hold of my upper arms and is steering me toward the mirror so both of us can look at me in the dress. It's a blush pink color, which I would never wear, because it makes me look even paler. The same color, almost, as the swanky manicure Jules made me get in London last week. Jules wasn't happy with the state of my nails: she told the manicurist to "do the best you can with them." When I look at my hands now it makes me want to laugh: the prissy princess-pink shimmer of the polish next to my bitten down, bleeding cuticles.

Jules steps back, her arms folded and eyes narrowed. "It's quite loose. God, I'm sure this was the smallest size they had. For *Christ's sake,* Olivia. I wish you'd told me it didn't fit properly—I would have had it taken in. But . . ." She frowns, moving around me in a slow circle. I feel that breeze through the window again, and shiver. "I don't know, maybe it works a little loose. I suppose it's a *look,* of sorts."

I study myself in the mirror. The shape of the dress itself isn't too offensive: a slip, bias cut, quite nineties. Something I might even have worn if it was another color. Jules isn't wrong; it doesn't look terrible. But you can see my black pants and my nipples through the fabric.

"Don't worry," Jules says, as though she's read my mind. "I've got a stick-on bra for you. And I've bought you a nude thong—I knew you wouldn't have one yourself."

Great. That will make me feel a lot less fucking naked.

It's weird, standing together in front of the mirror, Jules behind me, both of us looking at my reflection. There are obvious differences between us. We're totally different shapes, for one, and I have a slimmer nose—Mum's nose—while Jules has better hair, thick and shiny. But when we're together like this I can see that we're more similar than people might think. The shape of our faces is the same, like Mum's. You can see we're sisters, or nearly.

I wonder if Jules is seeing it too: the similarity between us. Her expression is all odd and pinched-looking.

"Oh, Olivia," she says. And then—I see it happen, in the mirror in front of us, before I actually feel it—she reaches out and takes my hand in hers. I freeze. It's so unlike Jules: she is not big on physical contact, or affection. "Look," she says, "I know we haven't always got along. But I *am* proud to have you as my bridesmaid. You do know that—don't you?"

"Yes," I say. It comes out as a bit of a croak.

Jules gives my hand a squeeze, which for her is like a full-blown hug. "Mum says you broke up with that guy? You know, Olivia, at your age it can feel like the end of the world. But then later you meet someone who you *really* click with and you understand the difference. It's like Will and me—"

"I'm fine," I say. "It's fine." *Lie.* I do *not* want to talk about any of this with anyone. Jules least of all. She's the last person who would understand if I told her I can't remember why I ever bothered to put makeup on, or nice underwear, or buy new clothes, or go and get my hair cut. It seems like someone else did all those things.

Suddenly I feel really weird. Sort of faint and sick. I sway a bit, and Jules catches me, her hands gripping my upper arms hard.

"I'm fine," I say, before she can even ask what's wrong. I bend down and unfasten the over-fancy gray silk shoes Jules has chosen for me, with their jeweled buckles, which takes ages because my hands have become all clumsy and stupid. Then I reach up and drag the dress over my head, so hard that Jules gives a little gasp, like she thinks it might tear. I didn't use her pillow.

"Olivia!" she says. "What on *earth* has gotten into you?"

"Sorry," I say. But I only mouth the word, no actual sound comes out.

"Look," she says. "Just for these few days I'd like you to try and make a bit of an effort. *OK?* This is my wedding, Livvy. I've tried so hard to make it perfect. I bought this dress for you—I'd like you to wear it because I want you there, as my bridesmaid. That *means* something to me. It should mean something to you, too. Doesn't it?"

I nod. "Yeah. Yeah, it does." And then, because she seems to be waiting for me to go on, I add, "I'm OK. I don't know what . . . what that was before. I'm fine now."

Lie.

JULES
The Bride

PUSH OPEN THE DOOR TO MY MOTHER'S ROOM INTO A CLOUD OF Shalimar perfume and, possibly, cigarette smoke. She better not have been smoking in here. Mum is sitting at the mirror in her silk kimono, busy outlining her lips in her signature carmine. "Goodness, that's a murderous expression. What do you want, darling?"

Darling.

The strange cruelty of that word.

I keep my tone calm, reasonable. I am being my best self, today. "Olivia is going to behave herself tomorrow, isn't she?"

My mother gives a weary sigh. Takes a sip of the drink she's got next to her. It looks suspiciously like a martini. Great, so she's already on the strong stuff.

"I made her my bridesmaid," I say. "I could have picked from twenty other people." Not quite true. "But she's acting as though it's this big drag. I've hardly asked her to do anything. She didn't come to the hen do even though there was a room free in the villa for her. It did look odd—"

"I could have come instead, darling."

I stare at her. It would never have occurred to me that she might have wanted to come. Besides, no bloody *way* was I ever going to invite my mother to the hen do. It would, inevitably, have morphed into the Araminta Jones show.

"Look," I say. "None of that really matters. It's in the past now, I suppose. But is she at least going to try and *look* happy for me?"

"She's had a difficult time," Mum says.

"You mean because her boyfriend broke up with her or whatever it was? They were only going out for a few months according to what I've seen on Instagram. Clearly a romance of epic proportions!" A note of petulance has crept in, despite my best intentions.

My mother is now concentrating on the more precise work of outlining her Cupid's bow. "But, darling," she says, once she has finished, "when you think about it, you and the gorgeous Will haven't been together all *that* long, have you?"

"That's rather different," I say, nettled. "Olivia's nineteen. She's still a teenager. Love is what teenagers *think* has happened when actually they're just stuffed full of hormones. *I* thought I was in love when I was about her age."

I think of Charlie at eighteen: the deep biscuit tan, the white line sometimes visible beneath his board shorts. It occurs to me that my mother never knew—or cared to know—about my adolescent affairs of the heart. She was too busy with her own love life. Thank God; I'm not sure any teenager wants that kind of scrutiny. And yet I can't help but feel that this all proves she and Olivia are much closer than we ever were.

"When your father left me," Mum says, "you have to remember that I was about the same age. I had a newborn baby—"

"I know, Mum," I say, as patiently as I can. I've heard more times than I ever needed to about how my birth ended what definitely, probably, *maybe,* would have been a highly successful career for my mother.

"Do you know what it was like for me?" she asks. Ah, here it comes: the same old script. "Trying to have a career and a tiny baby? Trying to make a living, to make something of myself? Just so I could put food on the table?"

You didn't have to continue trying to get acting jobs, I think. *If you'd really wanted to put food on the table that probably wasn't the most sensible way to do it. We didn't have to spend your tiny income on an apartment off Shaftesbury Avenue in Zone One and not be able to afford to eat as a result. It's not my fault you made some bad decisions when you were a teenager and got yourself knocked up.*

As usual, I don't say any of this. "We were talking about Olivia," I say, instead.

"Well," Mum says, "let's just say that there was a little more to Olivia's experience than a bad breakup." She examines the glossy finish of her nails—carmine, too, as though her fingers have been dipped in blood.

Of course, I think. This is Olivia, so it had to be special and different in some way. *Careful, Jules. Don't be bitter. Best behavior.* "What, then?" I ask. "What else was there?"

"It's not my place to say." This is surprisingly discreet, coming from my mother. "And besides," she says, "Olivia's like me in that—an empath. We can't simply . . . smother our feelings and put a brave face on it like some people can."

I know that in a sense this is true. I know that Olivia *does* feel things deeply, too deeply, that she does take them to heart. She's a dreamer. She was always coming home from school with playground scrapes, and bruises from bumping into things. She's a nail-biter, a hairsplitter, an overthinker. She's "fragile." But she's also spoiled.

And I can't help sensing implied criticism in Mum's reference to "some people." Just because the rest of us don't wear our hearts on our sleeves, just because we have found a way of *managing* our feelings—it doesn't mean they're not there.

Breathe, Jules.

I think of how Olivia looked so oddly at me when I told her I was happy to have her as my bridesmaid. I couldn't help feeling a small pang as, trying on the dress, she slipped out of her clothes and revealed her slender, stretch mark–free body. I know she felt me staring. She is definitely too thin and too pale. And yet she looked undeniably gorgeous. Like one of those nineties heroin-chic models: Kate Moss lounging in a bedsit with a string of fairy lights behind her. Looking at her, I was caught between those two emotions I always seem to feel when it comes to Olivia: a deep, almost painful tenderness, and a shameful, secret envy.

I suppose I haven't always been as warm toward her as I might. Now she's older, she's wised up a little—and of late, since the engagement party especially, she has been noticeably cool. But when Olivia was younger she used to trail around after me like an adoring puppy. I got quite used to her displays of unrequited affection. Even as I envied her.

Mum turns around on her chair now. Her face is suddenly very somber, uncharacteristically so. "Look. She's had a difficult time, Jules. You can't possibly begin to know the half of it. That poor kid has been through a lot."

That poor kid. I feel it, at that. I thought I'd be immune to it by now. I'm ashamed to find that I am not: the little dart of envy, under my ribs.

I take a deep breath. Remind myself that here I am, getting married. If Will and I have kids their childhood will be nothing like mine was—Mum with her string of boyfriends, all actors, always "on the verge of a big break." Someone finding me a place to sleep on the coats at all the inevitable Soho afterparties, because I was six years old and all my classmates would have been tucked up hours before.

Mum turns back to the mirror. She squints at herself, pushes her hair one way, then the other, twists it up behind her head. "Got to look good for the new arrivals," she says. "Aren't they *handsome,* all of Will's friends?"

Oh, *Christ.*

Olivia doesn't know how good she had it, how lucky she was. To her it was all normal. When her dad, Rob, was around, Mum became this proper mother figure: cooked meals, insisted on bed by eight, there was a playroom full of toys. Mum eventually got bored of playing happy family. But not before Olivia had had a whole, contented childhood. Not before I had begun half *hating* that little girl for everything she didn't even know she had.

I'm itching with the need to break something. I pick up the Cire Trudon candle on the dressing table, heft it in my hand, imagine how it would feel to watch it splinter to smithereens. I don't do this anymore—I've got it under control. I definitely wouldn't want Will to see this side of me. But around my family I find myself regressing, letting all the old pettiness and envy and hurt come rushing back until I am teenage Jules, plotting to get away. I must be bigger than this. I have forged my own path. I have built it all on my own, something stable and powerful. And this weekend is a statement of that. My victory march.

Through the window I hear the sound of a boat's engine guttering. It must be Charlie arriving. Charlie will make me feel better.

I put the candle back down.

HANNAH

The Plus-One

B Y THE TIME WE FINALLY REACH THE STILLER WATERS OF THE IS-land's inlet I've been sick three times and I'm soaked and cold to the bone, feeling as wrung out as an old dish cloth and clinging to Charlie like he's a human life raft. I'm not sure how I'm going to walk off the boat, as my legs feel like they've got no bones left. I wonder if Charlie's embarrassed to be turning up with me in the state I'm in. He always gets a bit funny around Jules. My mum would call it "putting on airs."

"Oh, look," Charlie says, "see those beaches over there? The sand really is white." I can see the way the sea turns an astonishing aquamarine color in the shallows, the light bouncing off the waves. At one end the land shears away in dramatic cliffs and giant stacks that have become separated from the rest. At the other end is an improbably small castle, right out on a promontory, perched over a few shelves of rocks and the crashing sea below.

"Look at that castle," I say.

"I think that's the Folly," Charlie says. "That's what Jules called it, anyway."

"Trust posh people to have a special name for it."

Charlie ignores me. "We'll be staying in there. It should be fun. And it'll be a nice distraction, won't it? I know this month's always tough."

"Yeah," I nod.

Charlie squeezes my hand. We both fall silent for a moment.

"And, you know," he says, suddenly, "being without the kids for a change. Being adults again."

I shoot him a look. Is there a touch of wistfulness in his tone? It's true that we haven't done very much recently other than keep two small people alive. I even feel, sometimes, that Charlie's a bit jealous of how much love and attention I lavish on the kids.

"Remember those days in the beginning," Charlie said an hour ago, as we drove through the beautiful countryside of Connemara, admiring the red heather and the dark peaks, "when we'd get on a train with a tent and go camping somewhere wild for the weekend? God, that seems a long time ago."

We'd spend whole weekends having sex back then, surfacing only to eat or go for walks. We always seemed to have some spare cash. Yeah, our lives are rich now in another way, but I know what Charlie's getting at. We were the first in our group of friends to have kids—I got pregnant with Ben before we got married. Even though I wouldn't change any of it, I've wondered whether we missed out on a couple more years of carefree fun. There's another self that I sometimes feel I lost along the way. The girl who always stayed for one more drink, who loved a dance. I miss her, sometimes.

Charlie's right. We've needed a weekend away, the two of us. I only wish that our first proper escape in ages didn't have to be at the glamorous wedding of Charlie's slightly terrifying friend.

I don't want to think too hard about when the last time we had sex was, because I know the answer will be too depressing. A while, anyway. In honor of this weekend I've had my first bikini wax in . . . Jesus, quite a long time, anyway, if you don't count those little boxes of DIY strips mainly left unused in the bathroom cupboard. Sometimes, since the kids, it's as though we're more like colleagues, or partners in a small, somewhat shaky start-up that we have to devote all our attention to, rather than lovers. *Lovers.* When was the last time we thought of ourselves as that?

"Crap," I say, to distract myself from this line of thought, "look at that marquee! It's enormous." It's so big it looks like a tented city rather than a single structure. If anyone were going to have a *really* fancy marquee, it would be Jules.

The rest of the island looks, if possible, even more hostile than it did from far away. It seems incredible that this forbidding place is going to accommodate us for the next few days. As we get closer I can see a cluster of small, dark dwellings behind the Folly. And on the crest of a hill rising up beyond the marquee is a bristle of dark shapes. At first I think they're people; an army of figures awaiting our arrival. Only they seem oddly, impossibly still. As we draw closer I realize that the strange, upright forms seem to be grave markers. And what looked like large bulbous heads are crosses, Celtic ones, the round circle enclosing the even-sided cross.

"There they are!" Charlie says. He gives a wave.

I see the cluster of figures on the jetty now, waving. I comb my fingers through my hair, although I know from long experience that I'm probably making it more wild. I wish I had a bottle of water to swig from to help the sour taste in my mouth.

As we draw closer, I can make them all out a little better. I see Jules, and even from this distance, I can see that she looks immaculate: the only person who could wear all white in a place like this and not immediately stain her clothes. Near Jules and Will stand two women who I can only assume must be Jules's family—the glossy dark hair gives them away.

"There's Jules's mum," Charlie says, pointing to the elder woman.

"Wow," I say. She's not what I expected at all. She wears black skinny jeans and little cat's-eye black glasses pushed back onto a glossy dark bob. She doesn't look old enough to have a thirty-something daughter.

"Yeah, she had Jules pretty young," Charlie says, as if reading my mind. "And that must be—Jesus Christ! I suppose that must be Olivia. Jules's little half sister."

"She doesn't look so little now," I say. She's taller than both Jules and her mum; a totally different shape to Jules, who's all curves. She's very striking-looking, beautiful, even, and her skin is pale pale pale in the way that only really looks good with black hair, like hers. Her legs in her jeans look as though they've been drawn with two long thin lines of charcoal. God, I'd kill for legs like that.

"I can't believe how much older she is," Charlie says. He's half whispering now, we're close enough that they might hear us. He sounds a bit freaked out.

"Is she the one who used to have a crush on you?" I ask, dredging this fact up from some half-remembered conversation with Jules.

"Yes," he says, with a rueful grin. "God, Jules used to tease me about it. It was pretty embarrassing. Funny, but embarrassing, too. She used to find excuses to come and talk to me and lounge around in that disturbingly provocative way thirteen-year-olds can."

I look at the gorgeous creature on the jetty and think—*I bet he wouldn't be so embarrassed now.*

Mattie is suddenly busying himself around us, putting out fenders on one side, readying a rope.

Charlie steps forward: "Let me help—"

Mattie waves him away, which I suspect Charlie's a little offended by.

"Chuck it here!" Will strides up the jetty toward us. On TV, he's good-looking. In the flesh, he's . . . well, he's pretty breathtaking. "Let me help you!" he calls to Mattie.

Mattie throws him a rope and Will catches it expertly in mid-air, revealing a slice of muscular stomach beneath his Aran knit sweater. I wonder if I'm imagining Charlie bristling next to me.

Boats are his thing: he was a sailing instructor in his youth. But *everything* outdoorsy, it seems, is Will's thing.

"Welcome, you two!" He grins and reaches out a hand to me. "Need a lift?" I don't really, but I take it anyway. He grabs me under my armpit and lifts me over the side of the boat as though I'm as light as a child. I catch a gust of some subtle, masculine scent—moss and pine—and realize with dismay how I must smell in return, like vomit and seaweed.

He has it in real life, I can tell already, that charm, that magnetism. In one of the articles I read about him, while watching the show—because obviously I had to start googling everything I could find about him—the journalist joked that she basically just watched it because she couldn't tear her eyes away from Will. Lots of people became outraged, claimed it was objectification, that if the same piece had been written by a man the journalist would have been roasted alive. But I bet the show's PR team opened the champagne.

If I'm honest, I can see what she meant. There are lots of shots of Will stripped to the waist, or grunting his way up a rock face, always looking incredibly attractive. But it's more than that. He has a particular way of talking to the camera, an intimacy, so that you feel you might be lying next to him in the temporary shelter he's built out of branches and tree bark, blinking in the light of his headlamp. It's the feeling of a companionable solitude, that it's just you and him in the wilderness. It's a seduction.

Charlie reaches out a hand to Will. "Oh, what the hell?" Will says, ignoring it to envelop Charlie in a big hug. I can see the tension in Charlie's back from here.

"Will," Charlie says, with a curt nod, stepping away immediately. It's borderline rude when Will's being so welcoming.

"Charlie!" Jules is coming forward now, reaching out her arms. "It's been so long. God, I've missed you."

Jules, the other woman in Charlie's life. The most significant woman in his life—until I came along. They hug for a long time.

At last we follow Jules and Will up toward the Folly. Will tells us it was originally built as a coastal defense, then converted by some wealthy Irishman into a holiday home a century ago: a place to retreat to for a few days, entertain friends. But if you didn't know you could almost believe it was medieval. There's a small turret and in among the bigger windows are tiny ones: "false arrow slits," Charlie says—he's quite into castles.

As we make our way there we see a chapel, or what remains of a chapel, hidden behind the Folly. The roof seems to be completely gone, leaving only the walls and five tall pillars—what might once have been the spires—reaching for sky. The windows are gaping empty holes in the stone and the whole front of it must have fallen away. "That's where the ceremony will take place tomorrow," Jules says.

"It's beautiful," I say. "So romantic." All the right things. And I suppose it is beautiful, in a stark way. Charlie and I got married in the local registry office. Definitely not beautiful: a poky municipal room, a bit scuffed and cramped. Jules was there, too, of course, looking rather out of place in her designer outfit. The whole thing was over in what felt like twenty minutes, we met the next couple coming in on our way out.

But I wouldn't have wanted to get married in a place like the chapel. It is beautiful, yes, but there's definitely something tragic about its beauty, even slightly macabre. It stands out against the sky like a twisted, long-fingered hand, reaching up from the ground. There's a haunted look about it.

I watch Will and Jules as we follow them. I would never have had Jules down as a very tactile person but her hands are all over him, it's as if she can't not touch him. You can tell they are having sex. A lot of it. It's hard to watch as her hand slides into the back pocket of his jeans, or up beneath the fabric of his T-shirt. I bet

Charlie's noticed, too. I won't mention it, though. That would only draw attention to the lack of sex we're having. We used to have really good, adventurous sex. But these days we're so knackered all the time. And I find myself wondering whether, since kids, I feel different to Charlie, or whether he fancies me as much now my boobs are not the same boobs they were before breastfeeding, now I have all this strange slack skin on my belly. I know I *shouldn't* ask, because my body has performed a miracle; two, in fact. And yet it is important for a couple to still desire each other, isn't it?

Jules has never really had a lasting relationship in all the time Charlie and I have been together. I always sensed she didn't have time for anything serious, so focused was she on *The Download*. Charlie liked predicting how long they would last: "Three months, tops." Or, "This one's already past its expiry date, if you ask me." And he was always the one she called when she did break up with them. Part of me wonders how he feels now, seeing her settled at last. I'd guess not entirely happy. My suspicions about the two of them threaten to surface. I push them back down.

As we near the building a big cackle of laughter erupts from somewhere above. I glance up and see a group of men on top of the Folly's battlements, looking down at us. There's a mocking note to the laughter and I'm suddenly very aware of the state of my clothes and hair. I'm convinced that we're the butt of their joke.

OLIVIA

The Bridesmaid

SEEING CHARLIE AGAIN REMINDS ME OF HOW I USED TO MOON about after him. It was only a few years ago, really, but I was a kid then. It's embarrassing, thinking of the girl I used to be. But it also makes me kind of sad.

I'm looking for somewhere to hide from them all. I take the track past the ruined houses, left over from when people used to live on this island. Jules told me that the islanders abandoned their homes because they found it easier to live on the mainland, that they wanted electricity and stuff. I get that. Just the fact of being stuck here would drive you mental. Even if you managed to get a boat to the mainland you'd still be a million miles away from anywhere. Your nearest, I don't know, H&M, say, would be hundreds of miles away. I've always felt like Mum and I lived out in the sticks, but now I'm just grateful that we don't live on an island in the middle of the Atlantic. So, yeah, I can see why you'd want to leave. But looking at these deserted houses with their empty windows and tumbledown appearance, it's hard not to feel like bad things happened here.

Yesterday, I saw something on one of the beaches; it was bigger than the rest of the rocks, gray but smoother, softer-looking somehow. I went to get a closer look. It was a dead seal. A baby, I think, because it was so small. I crept a bit closer and then I got a shock.

On the other side, which had been hidden from me before, the seal's body was all open, dark red, spilling out. I can't get the image of it out of my head. Since then this place has made me think of death.

It only takes me a few minutes to get down to the cave, which is marked on a map of the island in the Folly. The Whispering Cave, it's called. It's like a long wound in the ground—open at both ends. You could fall into it without realizing it was there because the opening is hidden by all this long grass. When I came across it yesterday I nearly did fall in. I would have broken my neck. That would ruin Jules's perfect wedding, wouldn't it? The thought almost makes me smile.

I climb down into the cave, down the rocks at the side that resemble a flight of steps. All the noise in my head dials down a notch and I start to breathe easier, even if there is a weird smell in this place—like sulfur, and maybe also of things rotting. It could be coming from the seaweed, lying all around in here in big dark ropes. Or maybe the stink's coming from the walls, which are spotted with yellow lichen.

In front of me is a tiny shingled beach, and the sea beyond. I sit down on a rock. It's damp, but then this whole place is damp. I could feel it on my clothes when I dressed this morning, like they'd been washed and hadn't quite dried. If I lick my lips I can taste salt on my skin.

I think about staying here for a long time, even overnight. I could hide here until after the ceremony is over, until it's all done and dusted. Jules would be livid, of course. Although . . . maybe she'd *pretend* to be angry, but actually she'd be secretly relieved. I don't think she really wants me at her wedding at all. I think she resents me because Mum gets on better with me and because I have a dad who wants to see me at least occasionally. I know I'm being a bitch. Jules does do nice stuff for me, sometimes, like when she let me stay in her flat in London last summer. And when I remember that, I feel bad, like there's a nasty taste in my mouth.

I take out my phone. Because of the rubbish signal here my Instagram is stuck with one photo at the top. Of course it would be Ellie's latest post. It's like they're mocking me. The comments underneath:

> You GUYS! ❤❤❤
> OMG sooooo cute. 😍
> mum + dad
> #mood ❤
> so can we assume its official now, yeh? *winks*

It hurts, still. A pain at the center of my chest. I look at their smug, smiling faces, and part of me wants to lob my phone as hard as I can at the wall of the cave. But that wouldn't sort my problems out. They're all right here with me.

I hear a noise in the cave—footsteps—and almost drop my phone in shock. "Who's there?" I say. My voice sounds small and scared. I really hope it's not the best man, Johnno. I caught him looking at me earlier.

I stand up and start to clamber out of the cave, keeping close to the wall, which is covered with thousands of tiny rough barnacles that graze my fingertips. Finally I put my head around the wall of rock.

"Oh Jesus!" The figure stumbles backward and puts a hand to her chest. It's Charlie's wife. "*Christ!* You gave me a right shock. I didn't think anyone was down here." She's got a nice accent, Northern. "You're Olivia, aren't you? I'm Hannah, I'm married to Charlie."

"Yeah," I say. "I got that. Hi."

"What are you doing down here?" She does a quick glance over her shoulder, like she's checking there's no one listening. "Looking for a place to hide? Me too."

I decide I like her a little bit for that.

"Oh," she says, "that probably sounded bad, didn't it? I just—I guess Charlie and Jules will catch up better if I'm not around. You know, they have all this history and it doesn't include me."

She sounds a bit fed up. History. I'm like 90 percent sure Charlie and Jules have screwed at some point in the past. I wonder if Hannah's ever thought about that.

Hannah sits down on a shelf of rock. I sit, too, because I was here first. I really wish she'd take the hint and leave me alone. I take my pack of cigarettes out of my pocket and tip one out. I wait to see if Hannah's going to say anything. She doesn't. So I go one step further, to test her, I suppose, and offer her one, along with my lighter.

She screws up her face. "I shouldn't," she says. Then she sighs. "But why not? We had such a mental crossing over here—I've got the shakes now." She holds up a hand to show me.

She lights up, takes a deep drag and gives another big sigh. I can see she's gone a bit dizzy. "Wow. That's gone straight to my head. Haven't had one for so long. Gave up when I got pregnant. But I smoked a lot in my clubbing days." She gives me a look. "Yeah, I know—you're thinking that must have been a million years ago. Certainly feels like it."

I feel a bit guilty, because I had thought it. But looking at her more closely I can see that she has four piercings in one ear and there's a tattoo on the inside of her wrist, half-hidden by her sleeve. Maybe there's another side to her.

She takes another big drag. "God, that's good. I thought when I gave them up that I'd eventually go off the taste, or wouldn't miss them anymore." She gives a big, deep laugh. "Yeah. Didn't happen." She blows out four perfect rings of smoke.

I'm kind of impressed, despite myself. Callum used to try that but he never got the hang of it.

"So you're at uni, right?" she asks.

"Yeah," I say.

"Whereabouts?"

"Exeter."

"That's a good one, isn't it?"

"Yeah," I say. "I suppose so."

"I didn't go," Hannah says. "No one in my family went to uni," she coughs, "except for my sister, Alice."

I don't know what to say to that. I don't really know anyone who didn't go to uni. Even Mum went to acting school.

"Alice was always the clever one," Hannah goes on. "I used to be the wild one, if you can believe it. We both went to this crummy school but Alice came out of there with amazing grades." She taps ash from her cigarette. "Sorry, I know I'm banging on. She's on my mind a lot at the moment."

Her face has changed, I notice. But I don't feel like I can ask her about it, seeing as we're total strangers.

"Anyway," Hannah says. "You like Exeter?"

"I'm not there anymore," I say. "I dropped out." I don't know what made me say it. It would have been so much easier to play along, pretend I was still there. But I suddenly felt like I didn't want to lie to her.

Hannah frowns. "Oh, yeah? You weren't enjoying it, then?"

"No," I say. "I guess . . . I had this boyfriend. And he broke up with me." Wow, that sounds pathetic.

"He must have been a real shit," Hannah says, "if you left uni because of him."

When I think about everything that happened in the last year my mind goes hot, and blank, and I can't think about it properly or sort it all out in my head. None of it makes sense, especially now, trying to piece it all together. I can't explain it, I think, without telling her everything. So I shrug and say, "Well, I guess he was my first proper boyfriend."

Proper as in more than someone to hook up with at house parties. But I don't say this to Hannah.

"And you loved him," she says.

She doesn't say it like a question, so I don't feel I have to answer. All the same, I nod my head. "Yeah," I say. My voice comes out very small and cracked. I didn't believe in love at first sight until I saw Callum, across the bar at Fresher's Week, this boy with black curls and beautiful blue eyes. He gave me a sort of slow smile and it was like I knew him. Like we had always meant to come together, to find each other.

Callum said he loved me first. I was too scared of making an arse of myself. But eventually I felt like I *had* to say it too, like it was bursting out of me. When he broke up with me, he told me that he would love me forever. But that's total crap. If you love someone, really, you don't do *anything* to hurt them.

"I didn't leave just because he broke up with me," I say, quickly. "It was . . ." I take a big drag on my cigarette. My hand's trembling. "I guess if Callum hadn't broken up with me, none of the rest would have happened."

"None of the rest?" Hannah asks. She's sitting forward, interested.

I don't answer. I'm trying to think of a way to go on, but I can't find the right words. She doesn't push me. So there's a long silence, both of us sitting there and smoking.

Then: "Shit!" Hannah says. "Is it me or has it got quite a lot darker while we've been sitting here?"

"I think the sun's started to set," I say. We can't see it from here as we're not facing in the right direction, but you can make out the pink glow in the sky.

"Oh dear," Hannah says. "We should probably make our way back to the Folly. Charlie hates being late for anything. He's such a teacher. I reckon I can hide for another ten minutes but—" She's stubbing out her cigarette now.

"You go," I say. "It's fine. It's not important."

She squints at me. "It kind of sounded like it was."

"No," I say. "Honestly."

I can't believe how close I came to telling her about it all. I haven't told anyone the other stuff. Not even any of my mates. It's a relief, really. If I'd told her, there'd be no taking it back. It would be out there in the world: what I've done.

AOIFE
The Wedding Planner

SEVEN O'CLOCK. THE TABLE IS LAID FOR DINNER IN THE DINING room. Freddy's got supper covered, which means it's a free half hour, which means I decide to pay a visit to the graveyard. The flowers need refreshing and tomorrow we'll be run off our feet.

When I step outside the sun is just beginning to go down, spilling fire upon the water. It tinges pink the mist that has begun to gather over the bog, that shields its secrets. This is my favorite hour.

The ushers are sitting up on the battlements: I hear their voices floating down as I leave the Folly—louder and slightly more slurred than earlier, the work of the Guinness, I'll bet.

"Got to send them off with a bang."

"Yeah, we should do *something*. Would only be traditional . . ."

I'm half-tempted to stay and listen, to check they aren't plotting mayhem on my watch. But it sounds harmless. And I've only got this brief window of time to myself.

The island looks at its most starkly beautiful this evening, lit up by the glow of the dying sun. But perhaps it will never seem quite so beautiful to me as I remember from those trips we took here when I was a child. The four of us, my family, here to stay for the summer holidays. Nowhere on earth could possibly live up to those halcyon days. But that's nostalgia for you, the tyranny of those memories of childhood that feel so golden, so perfect.

There is a whispering in the graveyard when I get there, the beginnings of a breeze stirring between the stones. A harbinger of tomorrow's weather, maybe. Sometimes, when the wind is really up, it seems to carry from here the echoes of women from centuries past performing the *caoineadh,* their keening for the dead.

The graves here are unusually close together, because true dry land is in short supply on the island. Even then, at the outer edges the bog has begun to nibble away at it, swallowing several of the graves until only the top few inches remain. Some of the stones have moved closer still, leaning in toward one another as though sharing a secret. The names, the ones that remain visible, are common to Connemara: Joyce, Foley, Kelly, Conneely.

It's a strange thing when you consider that the dead on this island far outnumber the living, even now that some of the guests have arrived. Tomorrow will redress the balance.

There is a great deal of local superstition about the island. When Freddy and I bought the Folly a year or so ago, there was no other bidder. The islanders were always mistrusted, seen as a species apart.

I know the mainlanders view Freddy and me as outsiders. Me the townie "Jackeen" from Dublin and Freddy the Englishman, a couple who don't know better, who have probably bitten off more than we can chew. Who don't know about Inis an Amplóra's dark history, its ghosts. Actually, I know this place better than they think. It is more familiar to me in some ways than any other place I have known in my life. And I'm not worried about it being haunted. I have my own ghosts. I carry them with me wherever I go.

"I miss you," I say, as I crouch down. The stone stares back at me, blank and mute. I touch it with my fingertips. It is rough, cold, unyielding—so far from the warmth of a cheek, or the soft, springy hair that I recall so vividly. "But I hope you'd be proud of me." I feel it as I do every time I crouch here: the familiar, impotent anger, rising up in me to leave its bitter taste in my mouth.

And then I hear a cackling, from somewhere above me, as though in mockery of my words. No matter how many times I hear it, that sound will never cease to make my blood run cold. I look up and see it there: a big cormorant perched on the highest part of the ruined chapel, its crooked black wings hung open to dry like a broken umbrella. A cormorant on a steeple: that's an ill omen. The devil's bird, they call it in these parts. The *cailleach dhubh*, the black hag, the bringer of death. Here's hoping that the bride and groom don't know this . . . or that they aren't the superstitious sort.

I clap my hands, but the creature doesn't budge. Instead it rotates its head slowly so I can see its stark profile, the cruel shape of its beak. And I realize that it is watching me, sidewise, out of its beady gleaming eye, as though it knows something I do not.

BACK AT THE FOLLY, I carry a tray of champagne flutes through to the dining room, ready for this evening's drinks. As I open the door I see a couple sitting there on the sofa. It takes me a moment to realize that it's the bride and another man: one of the couple that Mattie brought across on the boat. The two of them are sitting very close together, their heads touching, talking in low voices. They don't exactly spring apart on noticing my entrance, but they do move a few inches away from one another. And she takes her hand off his knee.

"Aoife," the bride calls out. "This is Charlie."

I remember his name from the list. "Our MC for tomorrow, I believe?" I say.

He coughs. "Yes, that's me."

"Sure, and your wife's Hannah, isn't she?"

"Yes," he says. "Good memory!"

"We were going through Charlie's duties for tomorrow," the bride tells me.

"Of course," I say. "Good." I wonder why she felt the need to explain anything to me. They looked rather cozy together on the sofa but I'm not here to cast any moral judgment upon my clients, or even to have likes and dislikes, to have opinions on things. That isn't how this sort of thing works. Freddy and I, if everything goes well, should simply fade into the background. We will only stand out if things go wrong, and I shall take care to ensure they will not. The bride and groom and their nearest and dearest should feel that this place is theirs, really, that they are the hosts. We are merely here to facilitate everything, to ensure that the whole weekend runs smoothly. But to do that I can't be completely passive. It is the strange tension of my role. I'll have to keep an eye on all of them, watch for any threatening developments. I will have to try and stay one step ahead.

THE WEDDING NIGHT

T HE SOUND OF THE SCREAM RINGS IN THE AIR AFTER IT HAS FIN-
ished, like a struck glass. The guests are frozen in its wake. They
are looking, all of them, out of the marquee and into the roaring
darkness from where it came. The lights flicker, threatening another blackout.

Then a girl stumbles into the marquee. Her white shirt marks
her out as a waitress. But her face is a wild animal's, her eyes huge
and dark, her hair tangled. She stands there in front of them, staring. She does not appear to blink.

Finally a woman approaches her, not one of the guests. It is
the wedding planner. "What is it?" she asks gently. "What's happened?"

The girl doesn't answer. It seems to the guests that all they can
hear is her breathing. There is something animal about that too:
rough and hoarse.

The wedding planner steps toward her, places a tentative hand
on her shoulder. The girl doesn't react. The guests are transfixed,
rooted to the spot. Some of them vaguely remember this girl from
earlier. She was one of many who smilingly handed them their
starters and main courses and desserts. She cleared their plates and
refreshed their wineglasses, pouring expertly, her red ponytail
bobbing smartly with every step, her shirt white and clean and

crisp. Some of them recall her gentle singsong accent: Could she top them up, could she get them anything more? Otherwise she was, for want of a better expression, part of the furniture. Part of the well-oiled machinery of the day. Less worthy of proper notice, really, than the chic arrangements of greenery, the wavering flames atop the silver candlesticks.

"What happened?" the wedding planner asks again. Her tone is still compassionate, but this time there's more firmness in it, a note of authority. The waitress has begun to tremble, so much so that she looks as though she might be having some sort of fit. The wedding planner puts a hand on her shoulder again, as though to quiet her. The girl holds a hand over her mouth, and it seems for a moment that she might vomit. Then, finally, she speaks.

"Outside." It is a rasp of sound, hardly human.

The guests crane in to listen.

She lets out a low moan.

"Come on," the wedding planner says, calmly, quietly. She gives the girl a gentle shake, this time. "Come on. I'm here, I want to help—we all do. And it's OK, you're safe in here. Tell me what has happened."

Finally, in that terrible rasping voice, the girl speaks again. "Outside. *So much blood.*" And then, right before she collapses: "A body."

HANNAH
The Plus-One

BITE DOWN ON A TISSUE TO BLOT MY LIPSTICK. THIS PLACE SEEMS worthy of lipstick. Our room here is huge, twice the size of our bedroom back home. Not a single detail has been forgotten: the ice bucket with a bottle of expensive white wine in it, two glasses; the antique chandelier in the high ceiling; the big window looking out to sea. I can't go too close to the window or I'll get vertigo, because if you look straight down you can see the waves smashing on the rocks below and a tiny wet sliver of beach.

This evening the dying glow of the sunset lights the whole room rose gold. I've had a big glass of the wine, which is delicious, while getting ready. On an empty stomach and after the cigarettes I smoked with Olivia I already feel a bit light-headed.

It was fun smoking in the cave—it felt like a blast from the past. It's inspired me to go for it this weekend. I've felt jittery and sad all month: now here's a chance to cut loose a bit. So I've squeezed myself into a pre-kids black silky dress from & Other Stories; I've always felt good in it. I've blow-dried my hair smooth. It's worth the effort, even if it comes into contact with the moist air from outside and turns into a massive ball of frizz again, like a hairdo version of Cinderella's pumpkin. I thought Charlie would be waiting for me, crossly, but he only returned to the room a couple of minutes ago himself, so I've had time to brush my teeth and remove any scent of cigarettes, feeling like a naughty teenager. I'd half-hoped he would be here, though. We could have had a bath together in the claw-footed tub.

I've barely seen Charlie since we got off the boat, in fact: he and Jules spent the early evening cozied up together, going through his duties as MC. "Sorry, Han," he said, when he got back. "Jules wanted to go through all this stuff for tomorrow. Hope you didn't feel abandoned?"

Now he does an appreciative once-over as I emerge from the bathroom. "You look," he raises his eyebrows, "*hot.*"

"Thank you," I say, doing a little shimmy. I *feel* hot; I suppose it's been a while since I've gone all out. And I know I shouldn't mind that I can't remember the last time he said that.

We join the others in the drawing room, where we're having drinks. It's as well put together as our room: an ancient brick floor, a candelabra bristling with candles, glass boxes on the walls holding vast glistening fish, which I think may be real. How on earth do you taxidermy a fish, I wonder. Small windows show rectangles of blue twilight and everything outside now has a misty, slightly otherworldly quality.

Standing surrounded by a cluster of guests, Jules and Will are lit by candlelight. Will seems to be telling some anecdote: the others all listening to whatever he's saying, hanging off his every word. I notice that he and Jules are holding hands, as though they can't bear not to be touching. They look so good together, impossibly tall and elegant, she in a tailored cream jumpsuit and he in dark trousers and a white shirt that makes his tan appear several shades darker. I'd been feeling good about myself but now my own outfit feels inadequate by comparison: while for me, & Other Stories is a wild extravagance, I'm sure Jules hardly ventures into high-street chains.

• • •

I END UP STANDING QUITE near to Will, which isn't a total accident—I seem to be drawn to him. It's a heady experience, being so close to someone you've seen on your TV screen. This feeling of familiarity and strangeness at the same time. I can feel my skin tingling, being in such close proximity. I was aware when I walked over of his gaze raking my face, quickly up and down my person, before he went back to finishing his anecdote. So I *am* looking good. A guilty thrill goes through me. In the years since I've had kids—probably because I'm always *with* the kids—I've apparently become invisible to men. It only dawned on me, when I stopped feeling them on me, that I had taken men's glances for granted. That I enjoyed them.

"Hannah," Will says, turning to me with that famous, generous smile of his. "You look stunning."

"Thanks." I take a big gulp of my champagne, feeling sexy, a little bit reckless.

"I meant to ask, on the jetty—did we meet at the engagement drinks?"

"No," I say, apologetically. "We couldn't make it up from Brighton, sadly."

"Maybe I've seen you in one of Jules's photos, then. You seem familiar."

"Maybe," I say. I don't think so. I can't imagine Jules displaying a photo that includes me; she's got plenty of just her and Charlie. But I know what Will's doing: helping me feel welcome, one of the gang. I appreciate the kindness. "You know," I say, "I think I'm getting the same feeling about you. Might I have seen *you* somewhere before? You know . . . like on my TV set?"

It was corny but Will laughs anyway, a rich, low sound, and I feel as though I've just won something. "Guilty!" he says, raising his hands. As he does I get a gust of that cologne again: moss and pine, a forest floor via an expensive department store perfume hall.

He asks me about the kids, about Brighton. He seems fascinated by what I'm saying. He's one of those people who makes you feel wittier and more attractive than normal. I realize I'm enjoying myself, enjoying the delicious glass of chilled champagne.

"Now," Will says, palm on my back as a gentle steer, warm through my dress, "let me introduce you to some people. This is Georgina."

Georgina, thin and chic in a column of fuchsia silk, gives me a wintry smile. She can't move her face much and I try hard not to stare—I'm not sure I've ever seen Botox in real life. "Were you on the hen do?" she asks. "I can't remember."

"I had to give it a miss," I say. "The kids . . ." Partly true. But there's also the fact that it was at a yoga retreat in Ibiza and I could never in a million years have afforded it.

"You didn't miss much." A man—slender, dark-red hair—swoops into the conversation. "Just a load of bitches burning their tits off and gossiping over bottles of Whispering Angel. Goodness," he says, giving me a once-over before bending in to kiss my cheek. "Don't *you* scrub up well?"

"Er—thanks." His smile suggests it was meant kindly, but I'm not totally sure it was a compliment.

This man is Duncan, apparently, and he's married to Georgina. He's also one of the ushers, along with the other three guys. Peter—hair slicked back, a party-boy look. Oluwafemi, or Femi—tall, black, seriously handsome. Angus—Boris Johnson blond and similarly potbellied.

But in a funny way they all look quite similar. They're all wearing the same striped tie plus crisp white shirts, polished brogues and tailored jackets that definitely don't come from Next, like Charlie's. Charlie bought his especially for this weekend and I hope he's not feeling too put out by the comparison. But at least he looks fairly dapper next to the best man, Johnno, who despite his size somehow reminds me of a kid wearing clothes from the school lost property cupboard.

On the face of it they're so charming, these men. But I remember the laughter from the tower as we walked up to the Folly. And even now there's definitely an undercurrent beneath the charm. Smirks, raised eyebrows, as though they're having a secret joke at someone's expense—possibly mine.

I move over to chat to Olivia, who looks ethereal in a gray dress. It felt like we bonded a bit earlier in the cave but now she answers me in monosyllables, darting her eyes away.

A couple of times my gaze snags with Will's over her shoulder. I don't think it's my fault: sometimes I'll have the impression that his eyes have been on me for a while. It shouldn't be, but it's exciting. It reminds me—I know it's totally inappropriate to say this—but it reminds me most of that feeling you get when you start to suspect that someone you're attracted to fancies you back.

I catch myself in the thought. Reality check, Hannah. You're a married mother of two and your husband is right there and you're talking to a man who is about to get married to your husband's best friend, who is standing looking like Monica Bellucci, only better dressed. *Probably* ease off the champagne a little. I've been knocking it back. It's partly nerves, surrounded by this lot. But it's also the sense of freedom. No babysitter to embarrass ourselves in front of later, no small people to have to wake up for in the morning. There's something exotic about being all dressed up with only other adults for company, a plentiful supply of booze, no responsibility.

"The food smells incredible," I say. "Who's cooking?"

"Aoife and Freddy," Jules says. "They own the Folly. Aoife's our wedding planner, too. I'll introduce you all at dinner. And Freddy is doing the catering for us tomorrow."

"I can tell it's going to be delicious," I say. "God, I'm hungry."

"Well, your stomach's completely empty," Charlie says. "Got rid of it all on the boat, didn't you?"

"Had a vom?" Duncan asks, delighted. "Fed the fish?"

I shoot Charlie an icy look. I feel like he's just undone some of the effort I made this evening. I feel like he's playing for laughs, trying to get in on the joke at my expense. I swear he's put on a different voice—posher—but I know if I called him out on it he'd pretend he hadn't a clue what I was talking about.

"*Anyway*," I say, "it'll make a nice change from chicken nuggets, which I seem to end up eating every other night with the kids."

"Do you have any good restaurants in Brighton, these days?" Jules asks. Jules always acts like Brighton is the sticks.

"Yes," I say, "there are—"

"Except we never go to them," Charlie says.

"That's not true," I say. "We went to that new Italian place . . ."

"It's not new now," Charlie counters. "That was about a year ago."

He's right. I can't think of the last time we ate out, other than that. Money has been a bit tight and you have to add the cost of a babysitter on top of the meal. But I wish he hadn't said it.

Johnno tries to top up Charlie's champagne and Charlie quickly puts his hand over his glass. "No thanks."

"Oh come on, mate," Johnno says. "Night before the wedding. Got to get a little loose."

"Come on!" Duncan chides. "It's only bubbly, not crack. Or are you going to tell us you're pregnant?"

The other ushers snicker.

"No," Charlie says again, tightly. "I'm taking it easy tonight." I can tell he's embarrassed saying it. But I'm glad he hasn't forgotten himself on this front.

"So Charlie boy," Johnno says, "tell us. How did you two first meet?"

I think at first he means Charlie and I. Then I realize he's looking between Charlie and Jules. Right.

"A million years ago . . ." Jules says. She and Charlie raise their eyebrows at each other in perfect unison.

"I taught her to sail," Charlie says. "I lived in Cornwall. It was my summer job."

"And my dad has a house there," Jules says. "I hoped if I learned he might take me out on his boat with him. But it turns out taking your sixteen-year-old daughter for a sail along the south coast wasn't quite the same as having your latest girlfriend sunbathe on the prow in St. Tropez." It comes out more bitterly than I think she might have intended. "Anyway," she says. "Charlie was my instructor." She looks at him. "I had a *big* crush on him."

Charlie smiles back at her. I laugh along with the others but I'm not really feeling it. It's hardly the first time I've heard this story. It's like a double act they do together. The local boy and the posh girl. Still, my stomach twists as Jules continues.

"*You* were mainly concerned with trying to sleep with as many girls of your own age as possible before you went to uni," Jules says to Charlie. It's suddenly like she's speaking only to him. "It seemed to work for you, though. That permanent tan and the body you had back then probably helped—"

"Yes," Charlie says. "Best body of my life. It was like having a gym membership with the job, working out on the water every day. Sadly you don't get quite as ripped teaching geography to fifteen-year-olds."

"Let's have a look at those abs now," Duncan says, leaning forward and grabbing the bottom of Charlie's shirt. He lifts the hem to show a few inches of pale, soft stomach. Charlie steps back, reddening, tucks himself in.

"And he seemed so grown-up," Jules says, heedless of the interruption. She touches Charlie's arm, proprietary. "When you're sixteen, eighteen seems so much older. I was shy."

"That's hard to believe," Johnno mumbles.

Jules ignores him. "But I know at first you thought I was this stuck-up princess."

"Which was probably true," Charlie says, raising an eyebrow, getting back into his stride.

Jules flicks him with champagne from her glass. "Oi!"

They're *flirting*. There's no other word for it.

"But no, I realized you were actually quite cool in the end," he says. "Discovered that wicked sense of humor."

"And then I suppose we just stayed in touch," Jules says.

"Mobiles had started to become a thing," Charlie says.

"*You* were the shy one the next year," Jules said. "I'd finally got some boobs. I remember seeing you do a double take when I walked down the jetty."

I take a big swig of my champagne. I remind myself that they were teenagers. That I am feeling envious of a seventeen-year-old who no longer exists.

"Yeah and you had that boyfriend and everything," Charlie says. "He wasn't my biggest fan."

"Yes," Jules says, with a secretive smile. "He didn't last very long. He was very jealous."

"So did you ever fuck?" Johnno asks. And just like that: it's the question I've never been able to ask outright.

The ushers are delighted. "He went there!" they cry. "Holy shit!" They crowd in, excited, gleeful, the circle growing tighter. Maybe that's why I'm suddenly finding it harder to breathe.

"Johnno!" Jules says. "Do you mind? This is my *wedding*!" But she hasn't said they didn't.

I can't look at Charlie. I don't want to know.

Then, thank God, there's an interruption: a big bang. Duncan has opened the bottle of champagne he's been holding.

"Christ, Duncan," Femi says. "You nearly took my eye out!"

"How do you guys all know each other?" I ask Johnno, keen to capitalize on the distraction.

"Ah," Johnno says, "we go back years." He puts a hand on Will's shoulder, and somehow this gesture sets him and Will apart from the others. Next to him Will looks even more handsome. They're like chalk and cheese. And there's something a bit weird about Johnno's eyes. I spend a while trying to work out exactly what's off about them. Are they too close together? Too small?

"Yup," Will says. "We were at school together." I'm surprised. The other men have that public schoolboy polish, while Johnno seems rougher—no cut-glass accent.

"Trevellyan's," Femi says. "It was like that book with all the boys on a desert island together, killing each other, oh Christ, what's it called—"

"*Lord of the Flies,*" Charlie says, the faintest trace of superiority in his tone. *I might have gone to state school,* it says, *but I'm better read than you.*

"It wasn't as bad as all that," Will says quickly. "It was more . . . boys running a bit wild."

"Boys will be boys!" Duncan chips in. "Am I right, Johnno?"

"Yeah. Boys will be boys," Johnno echoes.

"And we've been friends ever since," Will says. He slaps Johnno on the back. "Johnno here used to drive up in his ancient banger while I was at Edinburgh for uni, didn't you, Johnno?"

"Yeah," Johnno says. "I'd take him out into the mountains for climbing and camping trips. Make sure he didn't get too soft. Or spend all his time shagging around." He pretends to look contrite. "Sorry, Jules."

Jules tosses her head.

"Who do we know who went to Edinburgh, Han?" Charlie says. I stiffen. How can he possibly have forgotten who it was? Then I see his expression change to one of horror as he realizes his mistake.

"You know someone?" Will says. "Who?"

"She wasn't there for very long," I say quickly. "You know, Will, I've been wondering. That bit in *Survive the Night*, in the Arctic tundra. How cold was it? Did you really nearly get frostbite?"

"Yep," says Will. "Lost all the feeling in the pads of these fingers." He holds up one hand toward me. "The fingerprints have gone from a couple of them." I squint. They don't actually look all that different to me. And yet I find myself saying, "Oh yes, I think I can see that. Wow." I sound like a fangirl.

Charlie turns to me. "I didn't realize you'd seen the show," he says. "When did you watch it? We've never watched it together." *Oops*. I think of those afternoons, setting the kids up with CBeebies, and watching Will's show on my iPad in the kitchen as I heated up their dinner. He looks to Will. "No offense, mate—I do keep meaning to catch it." This isn't true. You can tell from the way he says it that it isn't true. He hasn't made any attempt to sound genuine.

"No offense taken," Will says mildly.

"Oh," I say. "I've never watched the whole thing. I . . . caught the highlights, you know."

"Methinks the lady does protest too much," Peter says. He takes hold of Will's shoulder, grinning. "Will, you've got a fan!"

Will laughs it off. But I can feel the heat prickling up my neck into my cheeks. I'm hoping it's too dark in here for anyone to see that I'm blushing.

Fuck it. I need more champagne. I hold my glass out for a top-up.

"At least your wife knows how to party, mate," Duncan says to Charlie. Femi pours for me, filling the flute close to the top. "Whoa," I say, as it reaches the rim, "that's plenty."

Suddenly there's a loud *plink!* and a little splash up over my wrist. I look in surprise to see that something has been dropped into my drink.

"What was that?" I say, confused.

"Have a look," Duncan says, grinning. "Pennyed you. Have to drink it all now." I stare at him, then at my glass. Sure enough, at the bottom of my very full glass sits the little copper coin, the Queen's stern profile.

"Duncan!" Georgina says, giggling. "You're *too* awful!"

I don't think I've been pennyed since I was about eighteen. Suddenly everyone's looking at me. I look to Charlie, for agreement that I don't have to drink it. But his expression is oddly pleading. It's the sort of look Ben might give me: *Please don't embarrass me in front of my friends, Mum.*

This is crazy, I think. I don't have to drink it. I'm a thirty-four-year-old woman. I don't even know these people, they have no hold over me. I won't be made to do it—

"Down it . . ."

"Down it!"

God, they've started to chant.

"Save the Queen!"

"She's drowning!"

"*Down it down it down it.*"

I can feel my cheeks reddening. To get their eyes off me, to stop their chanting, I knock the glass back and gulp it all down. I'd thought the champagne was delicious before but it's awful like this, sour and sharp, stinging my throat as I cough mid-swallow, rushing up inside my nose. I feel some of it spill out over my bottom lip. I feel my eyes tear up. I'm humiliated. It's like everyone has understood the rules of whatever is happening. Everyone but me.

Afterward, they cheer. But I don't think they're cheering me. They're congratulating themselves. I feel like a child who's been surrounded by a ring of playground bullies. When I glance in Charlie's direction he gives me a kind of apologetic wince. I suddenly feel very alone. I turn away from the others to hide my face.

As I do I catch sight of something that makes my blood run cold.

There is someone at the window, looking in at us out of the blackness, observing silently. The face is pressed against the glass, its features distorted into a hideous gargoyle mask, its teeth bared in a horrible grin. As I continue to stare, unable to look away, it mouths a single word.

BOO.

I'm not even aware of the champagne glass leaving my hand until it explodes at my feet.

THE WEDDING NIGHT

I T IS A FEW MOMENTS BEFORE THE WAITRESS REGAINS CONSCIOUS-
ness. She is, it appears, uninjured, but whatever she has seen out
there has struck her nearly mute. The most they can get from her
are low moans, wordless nonsense.

"I sent her over to the Folly for a couple more bottles of champagne," the head waitress—only twenty or so herself—says help-
lessly.

There is a palpable hush in the tent. The guests are looking
among the throng of people for their loved ones, to check that they
are safe and accounted for. But it is difficult to spot anyone among
the seething crowd, all a little worse for wear after a day of carous-
ing. It is difficult, too, because of the structure of this state-of-the-
art venue: the dance floor in one tent, the bar in another, the main
dining section in the largest.

"She could have had a scare," a man suggests. "She's a teenage
girl. It's pitch-black out there and it's blowing a gale."

"But it sounds like someone needs help," another man says.
"We should go and see—"

"We can't have everyone wandering all over the island." They
listen to the wedding planner. She has an innate authority, though
she looks as shocked as the rest of them, her face drawn and white.
"It *is* blowing a gale," she says. "It's dark. And there's the bog, the

cliffs. I don't want someone else to . . . to injure themselves, if that is what has happened."

"Must be shitting herself about her insurance," a man mutters.

"We should go and look," one of the ushers says. "Some of us blokes. Safety in numbers and all that."

THE DAY BEFORE

JULES
The Bride

DAD!" I SAY. "YOU TERRIFIED POOR HANNAH!" I MEAN IT WAS A *BIT* of an overreaction from her, dropping her glass like that. Did she really have to make such a scene? I stifle my annoyance as Aoife begins sweeping up the shards, moving discreetly around us with a broom.

"Sorry." Dad grins at us all as he enters the room. "Thought I'd give ye all a little fright." His accent is more pronounced than usual, presumably as he's on home turf, or nearly. He grew up in the Gaeltacht, the Irish-speaking part of Galway, not far from here. Dad's not a big man but he manages to take up quite a bit of space and presents an imposing figure: the set of his shoulders, the broken nose. It's difficult for me to see him objectively, because of what he is to me. But I suppose an outsider might assume he was a boxer or something similarly pugilistic, rather than a very successful property developer.

Séverine, Dad's latest wife—French, not far off my age, one part décolletage and three parts liquid eyeliner—slinks in behind him, tossing her long mane of red hair.

"Well," I say to Dad, ignoring Séverine (I can't be bothered to spend much time on her until she passes the five-year mark, Dad's record to date). "You've made it . . . at last." I'd known they were scheduled to arrive about now—I had to ask Aoife to arrange the boat. But even then I'd wondered if there might be some excuse, some delay that meant they couldn't make tonight. It wouldn't be the first time.

I notice Will and Dad sizing each other up surreptitiously. In Dad's company, oddly, Will seems a little diminished, a little less himself. Looking at him, in his pressed shirt and trousers, I'm worried that to Dad he might seem privileged and glib, very much the ex–public schoolboy.

"I can't believe this is the first time you've met," I say. Not for want of bloody trying. Will and I flew to New York specially a few months ago. At the last minute, we learned, Dad had been called away on business in Europe. I imagined our planes crossing somewhere over the Atlantic. Dad is a Very Busy Man. Too busy, even, to meet his daughter's fiancé until the eve of her wedding. Story of my bloody life.

"It's a pleasure to meet you, Ronan," Will says, holding out a hand.

Dad ignores the gesture and cuffs him on the shoulder instead. "The famous Will," he says. "We meet at last."

"Not particularly famous yet," Will says, giving Dad a winning grin. I wince. It's a rare misstep. It sounded like a humblebrag and I'm fairly sure Dad didn't mean "famous" as a reference to the TV stuff. Dad's not a fan of celebrities, of anyone making their fortune by anything other than proper hard work. He's a proudly self-made man.

"And this must be Séverine," Will says, reaching across to give her a kiss on both cheeks. "Jules has told me so much about you— and about the twins."

No, I haven't. The twins, Dad's latest progeny, were not invited.

Séverine simpers, melting beneath Will's charm. This does not seem likely to endear Will further to Dad. I wish it didn't matter to me what my father thinks. And yet I stand, transfixed, watching

as the two of them circle each other in the small space. It is excruciating. It's some relief when Aoife comes through and tells us that
dinner is about to be served.

Aoife is a woman after my own heart: organized, capable, discreet. There's a coolness to her, a detachment, which I suppose
some might not like. I prefer it. I don't want someone pretending to be my best friend when I'm paying her to do something. I
liked Aoife the moment we first spoke on the phone and I'm half-
tempted to ask if she'd consider leaving all of this and coming to
work at *The Download*. She might look quite homely, but she has a
steelier side.

We make our way through to the dining room. Mum and
Dad, as planned, are seated either end of the table, as physically
distant from one another as it is possible to get. I'm genuinely
not sure if my parents have spoken more than a few words to one
another since the nineties and it's probably better for the harmony
of the weekend if that continues. Séverine, meanwhile, is sitting
so close to Dad that she might as well be on his lap. Ugh: she may
not be far off half his age but she's still a thirty-something, not a
teenager.

Tonight, at least, everyone seems to be on pretty good behavior. I think the several bottles of 1999 Bollinger we've drunk are
probably helping. Even Mum is being fairly gracious, acting the
role of mother of the bride with aplomb. Her skills as an actress
have always seemed to come to the fore in real life rather than on
the stage.

Now Aoife and her husband come in bearing our starters: a
creamy chowder flecked with parsley. "This is Aoife and Freddy," I
tell the others. I don't say that they're our hosts because, really, I'm
the host. I'm paying for that privilege. So I settle on: "The Folly
belongs to them."

Aoife gives a neat little nod. "If you need anything, come to
either of us," she says. "I hope you'll all enjoy your stay here. And

the wedding tomorrow is our first on the island, so it will be particularly special."

"It's beautiful," Hannah says graciously. "And this looks delicious."

"Thank you," Freddy says, finding his voice. He's English, I realize—I'd assumed he was Irish like Aoife.

Aoife nods. "We picked the mussels ourselves this morning."

Once we're all served the conversation around the table resumes, with the exception of Olivia, who sits there mutely, staring at her plate.

"Such fond memories of Brighton," Mum is saying to Hannah. "You know, I performed down there a couple of times." Oh God. Not long before she starts telling everyone about that time she had penetrative sex on-screen for an art-house film (never got a release, probably now on PornHub).

"Oh," Hannah replies, "we feel a bit guilty about not getting to the theater more often. Where did you perform? The Theatre Royal?"

"No," Mum says, with that slightly haughty tone that creeps into her voice when she's been shown up. "It's a little more boutique than that." A toss of her head. "It's called the Magic Lantern. In the Lanes. Do you know it?"

"Er—no," Hannah says. And then, quickly, "But as I say, we're so out of the loop we wouldn't know anywhere, even if it's the place to go."

She's kind, Hannah. That is one of the things I know about her. It sort of . . . spills out of her. I remember meeting Hannah for the first time and thinking: oh, that's who Charlie wants. Someone nice. Someone soft, and warm. I'm too much for him. I'm too angry, too driven. He would never have picked me.

I'm not envious of Hannah anymore, I remind myself. Charlie might once have been the sailing club hottie but he's softened now, a paunch where that flat brown stomach used to be. And he's settled in his career, too. If I had anything to do with it he'd be gunning for a deputy head position. There's nothing less sexy than a lack of ambition, is there?

I watch Charlie until his gaze snags on mine—I make sure I'm the first to glance away. And I wonder: *Is he now the jealous one?* I've seen the mistrustful way he acts around Will, as though he's trying to find the flaw. I caught him observing the two of us over drinks. And I felt it again, how good we look together, imagining it through his eyes.

"How *sweet*," Mum's saying to Hannah. "Five's a lovely age." She's certainly doing a very good job of acting interested. "And how are your two, Ronan?" she calls down the table. I wonder if it is an intentional slight, not to have included Séverine in her question. Actually—scrap that, I don't need to wonder. Despite the impression she works hard to convey of bohemian vagueness, very little my mother does is unintentional.

"They're good," he says. "Thank you, Araminta. They're starting at nursery soon, aren't they?" He turns to Séverine.

"*Oui*," she says. "We are looking for a French-speaking nursery for them. So important that they grow up—ah—bileengual, like me."

"Oh, you're bilingual?" I ask. I can't help the slight.

If Séverine notices, she doesn't react. "*Oui*," she says with a shrug. "I went to a girls' boarding school in the UK when I was leetle. And my brudders, they attended a school for boys there too."

"Goodness," Mum says, still speaking only to Dad. "It must all be so *exhausting* at your age, Ronan." Before he has a chance to reply she claps her hands. "While we're between courses," she says, getting to her feet, "I'd like to say a little something."

"You don't have to, Mum," I call. Everyone laughs. But I'm not joking. Is she drunk? It's difficult to gauge, we've all had quite a bit. And I'm not sure it makes much of a difference with Mum anyway. She's never had any inhibitions to lose.

"To my Julia," she says, raising her glass. "Ever since you were a little girl you've known *exactly* what you wanted. And woe betide anyone who got in your way! I've never been like that—what I want always changes from week to week, which is probably why I've always been so bloody unhappy.

"Anyway: you've always known. And what you want, you go after." Oh, God. She's doing this because I've banned her from doing a speech at the wedding itself. I'm sure of it. "I knew it from the moment you told me about Will that he was what you wanted."

Not *quite* so clairvoyant as it sounds, seeing as I told her, in the same conversation, that we were already engaged. But Mum has never let inconvenient facts get in the way of a good story.

"Don't they *look* wonderful together?" she asks. Murmurs of assent from the others. I don't like the way the emphasis seemed to land on the "look."

"I knew Jules would need to find someone as driven as her," Mum says. And was there an edge to the way she said "driven"? It's difficult to be sure. I catch Charlie's eye across the table—he knows of old what Mum is like. He winks at me and I feel a secret fizz of warmth deep in my belly. "And she has such style, my daughter. We all know that about her, don't we? Her magazine, her beautiful house in Islington, and now this stunning man here." She puts a red-nailed hand on Will's shoulder. "You've always had a good eye, Jules." Like I picked him out to go with a pair of shoes. Like I'm marrying him just because he fits perfectly into my life—

"And it might seem like madness to anyone else," Mum goes on. "To haul everyone out to this freezing godforsaken island in the middle of nowhere. But it is important to Jules, and that's what matters."

I don't like the sound of that, either. I'm laughing along with the others. But I'm secretly bracing myself. I want to stand up and say my own piece, as though she's the prosecuting barrister, and

I'm the defense. That's not how you're meant to feel, listening to a speech from a loved one, is it?

Here's the truth my mother won't speak: if I hadn't known what I wanted, and worked out how to get it, I wouldn't have got anywhere. I had to learn how to get my way. Because my mother wasn't going to be any bloody help. I look at her, in her frothy black chiffon—like a negative of a wedding gown—and her glittering earrings, holding her sparkling glass of champagne, and I think: You don't get this. This isn't your moment. You didn't create it. I created it in *spite* of you.

I grip the edge of the table with one hand, hard, anchoring myself. With the other I pick up my glass of champagne and take a long swig. *Say you're proud of me*, I think. And it will just about make everything all right. *Say it, and I'll forgive you.*

"This might sound a little immodest," Mum says, touching her breastbone. "But I have to say that I'm proud of myself, for having brought up such a strong-willed, independent daughter."

And she does a little bow, as though to an adoring audience. Everyone claps dutifully as she sits down.

I'm trembling with anger. I look at the champagne flute in my hand. I imagine, for one delicious, delirious second, smashing it against the table, bringing everything to a halt. I take a deep breath. And instead I rise to make my own toast. I will be gracious, grateful, affectionate.

"Thank you so much for coming," I say. I strive to make my tone warm. I'm so used to giving talks to my employees that I have to work to keep the note of authority out of my voice. I know some women complain about not being able to get people to take them seriously. If anything, I have the opposite problem. At our Christmas party one of my employees, Eliza, got drunk and told me I have permanent resting bitch face. I let it go, because she was drunk and wouldn't remember saying it in the morning. But *I* certainly haven't forgotten it.

"We're so happy to have you all here," I say. I smile. My lipstick feels waxy and unyielding on my lips. "I know it was a long way to come . . . and difficult to get time away from everything. But from the moment this place came to my attention I knew it was perfect. For Will, so Outward Bound. And as a nod to my Irish roots." I look to Dad, who grins. "And to see you all gathered here—our nearest and dearest—it means so much to me. To both of us." I raise my glass to Will, and he raises his in return. He's so much better at this than I am. He exudes charm and warmth without even trying. I can get people to do what I want, sure. But I haven't always been able to get them to like me. Not in the way that my fiancé can. He gives me a grin, a wink, and I find myself imagining carrying on what we started earlier, in the bedroom—

"I didn't believe this day would ever come," I say, remembering myself. "I've been so busy with *The Download* over the last few years that I thought I'd never have the time to meet someone."

"Don't forget," Will calls. "I had to work pretty hard to persuade you to go on a date."

He's right. It seemed somehow too good to be true. He told me later that he'd recently got out of something toxic, that he wasn't looking for anything either. But we really hit it off at that party.

"I'm so glad you did." I smile down at him. It still feels like a kind of miracle, how quickly and easily it all happened. "If I believed in it," I say, "I might think we were brought together by Fate."

Will beams back at me. Our gazes lock, it's like there's no one else here. And then out of nowhere I think of that bloody note. And I feel the smile waver slightly on my lips.

JOHNNO
The Best Man

IT'S PITCH-BLACK OUTSIDE NOW. THE SMOKE FROM THE FIRE FILLS THE room, so that everyone looks different, hazy around the edges. Not quite themselves.

We're on to the next course, some fiddly dark chocolate tart. I try to cut into it and it goes shooting off my plate, crumbs of pastry exploding everywhere.

"Need someone to cut your food for you, big boy?" Duncan jeers, from the far end of the table. I hear the other blokes laugh. It's like nothing has changed. I ignore them.

Hannah turns to me. "So, Johnno," she says, "do you live in London too?" I like Hannah, I've decided. She seems kind. And I like her Northern accent and the studs in the top of her ear which make her look like a party girl, even though she's apparently a mum of two. I bet she can be pretty wild when she wants to be.

"Christ no," I tell her. "I hate the city. Give me the countryside any day. I need space to roam free."

"Are you pretty outdoorsy yourself?" Hannah asks.

"Yeah," I say. "I guess you could say that. I used to work at an adventure center in the Lake District. Teaching climbing, bush-craft, all that."

"Oh wow. I suppose that makes sense, because it was you who organized the stag, right?" She smiles at me. I wonder how much she knows about it.

"Yeah," I say, "I did."

"Charlie hasn't said much about any of it. But I heard there was going to be some kayaking and climbing and stuff."

Ah, so he didn't tell her anything about what went down. I'm not surprised. I probably wouldn't if I were him, come to think of it. The less said about all of that the better. Let's hope he's decided to let bygones be bygones on that front. Poor bloke. It wasn't my idea, all of that.

"Well, yeah," I continue. "I've always been into that sort of thing."

"Yes," Femi interjects. "It was Johnno who worked out how to scale the wall to get up on top of the sports hall. And you climbed that massive tree outside the dining hall, didn't you?"

"Oh God," Will says to Hannah. "Don't get this lot started on our school days. You'll never hear the end of it."

Hannah smiles at me. "It sounds like you could have your own TV series, Johnno."

"Well," I say. "Funny you should say that, but I did actually do a tryout for the show."

"You did?" Hannah asks. "For *Survive the Night*?"

"Yeah." Ah, Christ. Why did I say anything? *Stupid Johnno, always shooting my mouth off.* Jesus, it's humiliating. "Yeah, well, they did a screen test, with the two of us, and—"

"And Johnno decided he wasn't up for any of that crap, didn't you?" Will says. It's good of him to try to save my blushes. But there's no point in lying now, I might as well say it. "He's being a good mate," I say. "Truth is I was shit at it. They basically told me I didn't work on-screen. Not like our boy here—" I lean over and muss up Will's hair, and he ducks away, laughing. "I mean, he's right. It wasn't for me anyway. Couldn't stand any of that makeup they slap on you, the clothes they make you wear. Not that that's any shade on what you do, mate."

"No offense taken," Will says, putting up his hands. He's a natural on-screen. He has this ability to be whoever people want him to be. When he's on the program I notice he drops his "h's," sounds a bit more like "one of the people." But when he's with posh, public school–educated blokes, blokes who came from the better versions of the sort of school we both went to, he's one of them—100 percent.

"Anyway," I say to Hannah. "It makes sense. Who'd ever want this ugly mug on TV, eh?" I pull a face. I see Jules glance away from me as though I've just exposed myself. Stuck-up cow.

"So where did the idea for the show come from, Will?" Hannah asks. I appreciate that she's trying to move the conversation on, spare me any more humiliation.

"Yeah," Femi says. "You know, I was wondering about that. Was it Survival?"

"Survival?" Hannah turns to him.

"This game we used to play at school," Femi explains.

Duncan's wife, Georgina, chips in: "Oh God. Duncan's told me stories about it. Really awful stuff. He told me about boys being taken out of their beds at night, left in the middle of nowhere—"

"Yeah, that's what happened," Femi says. "They'd kidnap a younger boy from his bed and take him as far as they could away from the school, deep into the grounds."

"And we're talking big grounds," Angus says. "And the middle of nowhere. Pitch-black. No light from anything."

"It sounds barbaric," Hannah says, her eyes wide.

"It was a big tradition," Duncan says. "They'd been doing it for hundreds of years, since the start of the school."

"Will never had to do it, did you, mate?" Femi turns to him.

Will holds up his hands. "No one ever came and got me."

"Yeah," Angus says, "because they were all shit-scared of your dad."

"The chap would have a blindfold on at the start," Angus says, turning to Hannah, "so he didn't know where he was. Sometimes he'd even be tied to a tree or a fence, and had to get free. I remember when I did mine—"

"You pissed yourself," Duncan finishes.

"No I didn't," Angus replies.

"Yeah you *did*," Duncan says. "Don't think we've forgotten that. Pisspants."

Angus takes a gulp of wine. "Fine, well, *loads* of people did. It was fucking terrifying."

I remember my Survival. Even though you knew it would happen at some point, nothing prepared you for when they actually came to get you.

"The *craziest* thing is," Georgina says, "Duncan doesn't seem to think it was a bad thing." She turns to him. "Do you, darling?"

"It was the making of me," Duncan says.

I look over at Duncan who's sitting there with his hands in his pockets and his chest thrown out, like he's king of all he surveys, like he owns this place. And I wonder what it made him into, exactly.

I wonder what it made me into.

"I suppose it was harmless," Georgina says, "it's not like anyone died, is it?" She gives a little laugh.

I remember waking up, hearing the whispers in the dark all around me. *Hold his legs . . . you go for the head.* Then how they laughed as they held me down and tied the blindfold round my eyes. Then voices. Whoops and cheers, maybe—but with the blindfold over my ears too they sounded like animals: howls and screeches. Out into the night air, freezing on my bare feet. Rattling fast over the uneven ground—a wheelbarrow I guess it was—for so long I thought we must have left the school grounds. Then they left me, in the woods. All alone. Nothing but the beat of my heart and the secret noises of the woods. Getting the blindfold off and finding it just as dark, no moon to see by. Tree branches scratching at my cheeks, trees so close it felt like there was no way between them, like they were pressing in on me. So cold, a metallic taste like blood at the back of my throat. Crackle of twigs beneath my bare feet. Walking for miles, in circles probably. The whole night, through the woods, until the dawn came.

When I got back to the school building, I felt like I'd been reborn. Fuck the teachers who told me I'd never amount to much. Like they'd ever survived a night like that. I felt like I was invincible. Like I could do anything.

"Johnno," Will says, "I was saying I reckon it's time to get your whiskey out. Give it a sample." He jumps up from the table, and goes and gets one of the bottles.

"Oh," Hannah says, "can I look?" She takes it from Will. "This is such a cool design, Johnno. Did you work with someone on it?"

"Yeah," I say. "I've got a mate in London who's a graphic designer. He's done a good job, hasn't he?"

"He really has," she says, nodding, tracing the type with her finger. "That's what I do," she says. "I'm an illustrator, by trade. But it feels like a million years ago now. I'm on permanent maternity leave."

"Can I have a look?" Charlie says. He takes it from her and reads the label, frowning. "You must have had to partner with a distillery? Because it says here it's been aged twelve years."

"Yeah," I say, feeling like I'm being interviewed, or doing a test. Like he's trying to catch me out. Maybe it's the whole schoolteacher thing. "I did."

"Well," says Will, opening the bottle with a flourish. "The acid test!" He calls into the kitchen, "Aoife . . . Freddy. Could we have some glasses for whiskey please?"

Aoife carries some in on a tray.

"Get one for yourself too," Will says, like he's lord of the manor, "and for Freddy. We'll all try it!" Then, as Aoife tries to shake her head: "I insist!"

Freddy shuffles in to stand next to his wife. He keeps his eyes down and fiddles with the cord of his apron as they both stand there awkwardly. *Fucking weirdo,* Duncan mouths at the rest of us. It's probably a good thing the bloke's looking at the floor.

I check Aoife out. She's not as old as I thought at first: maybe only forty or so. She just dresses older. She's good-looking, too—in a refined kind of way. I wonder what she's doing with such a wet blanket of a husband.

Will pours out the rest of the whiskey. Jules asks for a couple of drops: "I've never been much of a whiskey drinker, I'm afraid." She takes a sip and I see her wince, before she has time to cover it by putting her hand over her mouth. But the hand only draws attention to it. Which maybe, come to think of it, she meant it to do. It's pretty clear she's not my biggest fan.

"It's good, mate," Duncan says. "It *kind* of reminds me of a Laphroaig, you know?"

"Yeah," I say. "I guess so." Trust Duncan to know his whiskies.

Aoife and Freddy down theirs as quickly as possible and high-tail it back to the kitchen. I get that. My mum used to work at the local country club—the sort of place Angus and Duncan's parents probably had memberships to. She said the golfers sometimes tried to buy her a drink, thinking they were being so generous, but it only made her feel awkward.

"I think it's dead tasty," Hannah says. "I'm surprised. I have to tell you, Johnno, I'm not normally a whiskey fan." She takes another sip.

"Well," Jules says. "Our guests are very lucky." She smiles at me. But you know that thing they say about someone's eyes not smiling? Hers aren't.

I grin at them all. But I'm feeling a bit out of sorts. I think it's all that talk about Survival. Hard to remind myself that to them—to pretty much all the other ex-Trevellyan boys—it's all just a game.

I look over at Will. He's got his hand on the back of Jules's head and he's grinning round at everyone. He looks like a man who has everything in life. Which, I suppose, he does. And I think: Does it not affect him too, all the talk about the old days? Not even the tiniest bit?

I've got to shake off this weird mood. I lunge toward the middle of the table and pick up the bottle of whiskey. "I think it's time for a drinking game," I say.

"Ah—" says Jules, probably about to call it off, but she's drowned out by the howls of approval from the blokes.

"Yes!" Angus shouts. "Irish snap?"

"Yeah," Femi says. "Like we played at school! Remember doing shots of Listerine mouthwash? 'Cause we worked out it was fifty percent proof?"

"Or that vodka you smuggled in, Dunc," Angus says.

"Right," I say, jumping up from the table. "I'll go get us a deck." I'm already feeling better now I've got a purpose to distract myself with.

I go to the kitchen and find Aoife standing with her back to me, going through some sort of list on a clipboard. When I cough she gives a little jump.

"Aoife, love," I say, "you got a deck of cards?"

"Yes," she says, taking a step away from me, like she's scared of me. "Of course. I think there's one in the drawing room." She's got a nice accent. I've always liked an Irish girl. "Tink" rather than "think"—that makes me smile.

Her husband's in there too, busying himself with the oven.

"You making stuff for tomorrow?" I ask him, while I wait for Aoife.

"Mm-hmm," he says, without making eye contact. I'm glad when Aoife returns after a minute or so with the cards.

Back at the table I deal the deck out to the others.

"I'm off to get my beauty sleep," Jules's mum says. "I've never been one for the hard stuff." *Not true,* I see Jules mouth. Jules's dad and the hot French step-mum excuse themselves too.

"Nor me," Hannah says. She looks over at Charlie. "We've had a long day, haven't we, love?"

"I don't know—" Charlie says.

"Come on, Charlie boy," I call to Charlie. "It'll be fun! Live a little!"

He doesn't look convinced.

Things got a bit loose on the stag. Charlie, poor bloke, didn't go to a school like ours, so he wasn't really prepared for it. He's just such a . . . geography teacher. I felt like he went to a dark place that night. Anyone would have, I guess. He barely talked to any of us for the rest of the weekend.

It was being back together with that group of blokes again, I suppose. Most of them went to Trevellyan's. We were all bonded by that place. Not in the same way that Will and I are bonded— that's only the two of us. But we are tied by the other stuff. The rituals, the male bonding. When we get together there's this kind of pack mentality.

We get carried away.

HANNAH
The Plus-One

SINCE THE PENNYING INCIDENT I'VE BECOME VERY WARY OF THE ushers. The more they drink the more it emerges: something dark and cruel hiding behind the public schoolboy manners. And I hate that right now my husband's behaving like a teenager who wants to be accepted into their gang.

"Right," Johnno says. "Everyone ready?" He looks around the table. I've worked out what's weird about his eyes. They're so dark you can't tell where the irises end and the pupils begin. It gives him a strange, blank look, so that even while he's laughing, it's like his eyes aren't quite playing along. And the rest of his face is a bit too expressive by comparison, changing every couple of seconds, his mouth very large and mobile. There's this kind of manic energy about him. I hope it's harmless. Like a dog that jumps up at you, big and scary, but all it really wants is to be thrown a ball—not to maul your face.

"Charlie," Johnno says. "You *are* joining us?"

"Charlie," I whisper, trying to catch my husband's eye. He's barely looked my way all evening, too wrapped up in Jules or trying to be one of the lads. But I want to get through to him.

Charlie's such a mild man: hardly ever raises his voice, hardly ever gets cross with the kids. If they get a telling off, it's normally from me. So it isn't like he becomes a more intense version of himself when he drinks, or that alcohol amplifies his bad qualities. In ordinary life he doesn't really have many bad qualities. Yeah, maybe all that anger is there, hidden, somewhere beneath the surface. But I could swear, on the couple of times I have seen him drunk, that it is like my husband has been taken over by someone else. That's what makes it all the more frightening. Over the years I've learned to spot the smallest signs. The slight slackening of his mouth, the drooping of his eyelids. I've had to learn because I know that the next stage isn't pretty. It's like a small firework has suddenly detonated in his brain.

Finally Charlie glances in my direction. I shake my head, slowly, deliberately, so he can make no mistake of my meaning. *Don't do it.*

"What the fuck's going on here?" Duncan crows. Oh God, he's caught me doing it. He swivels to Charlie. "She keep you on a leash, Charlie boy?"

Charlie's ears have gone bright red. "No," he says. "Obviously not. Yeah, fine. I'm in."

Shit. I'm torn between wanting to stay so I can try to stop him doing anything stupid and thinking I should leave him to it and let him take himself out, no matter the consequences. Especially after all that unsubtle flirting with Jules.

"I'm going to deal," Johnno says.

"Wait," Duncan says, getting to his feet, clapping his hands. "We should do the school motto first."

"Yeah," Femi agrees, joining him. Angus stands too. "Come on, Will, Johnno. Old times' sake and all that."

Johnno and Will rise.

I look at them—all, except Johnno, so elegantly dressed in their white shirts and dark trousers, expensive watches at their wrists. I wonder why on earth these men, who have apparently done so well for themselves since, are still obsessing about their school days. I can't imagine banging on about crappy old Dunraven High. I never had any resentment toward it but it's also not somewhere

I think about all that much. Like everyone else, I left in a scribbled-on leaver's shirt and never really looked back. No leaving school at 3:30 P.M. and heading home to watch *Hollyoaks* for these guys—they must have spent a chunk of their childhoods locked in that place.

Duncan begins to drum slowly with a fist on the table. He looks around, encouraging the others to join him. They do. Gradually it gets louder and louder, the drumming faster, more frenzied.

"*Fac fortia et patere,*" Duncan chants, in what I guess must be Latin.

"*Fac fortia et patere,*" the others follow.

And then, in a kind of low, intent murmur:

> *Flectere si nequeo superos,*
> *Acheronta movebo.*
> *Flectere si nequeo superos,*
> *Acheronta movebo!*

I watch the men, how their eyes seem to gleam in the flickering candlelight. Their faces are flushed—they're excited, drunk. There's a prickle up my spine. With the candles and the dark pressing in at the windows and the strange rhythm of the chanting, the drumming, I feel suddenly like I'm watching some satanic ritual being performed. There's a menacing element to it, tribal. I put a hand to my chest and I can feel my heart beating too fast, like a frightened animal's.

The drumming intensifies to a climax, until it's so frenzied that the crockery and cutlery are leaping about all over the place. A glass hops its way off the corner of the table and smashes on the floor. No one apart from me pays it any attention.

> *Fac fortia et patere!*
> *Flectere si nequeo superos,*
> *Acheronta movebo!*

And then, finally, right when I feel I can't bear it any longer, they all give a roar and stop. They stare at each other. Their foreheads glisten with sweat. Their pupils seem bigger, like they've taken a hit of something. Big hyena laughs now, teeth bared, slapping each other on the back, punching each other hard enough to hurt. I notice Johnno's not laughing as hard as all the others. His grin doesn't convince, somehow.

"But what does it mean?" Georgina asks.

"Angus," Femi slurs, "you're the Latin geek."

"The first part," Angus says, "is: 'Do brave deeds and endure,' which was the school motto. The second part was added in by us boys: 'If I can't move heaven, then I shall raise hell.' It used to get chanted before rugby matches."

"And the rest," says Duncan, with a nasty smile.

"It's so menacing," Georgina says. But she's staring up at her red, sweaty, wild-eyed husband as though she's never found him so attractive.

"That was kind of the point."

"Right, *ladies*," Johnno shouts. "Time to stop fannying around and get some drinking done!"

Another roar of approval from the others. Femi and Duncan mix the whiskey with wine, with sauce left over from the meal, with salt and pepper, so it forms a disgusting brown soup. And then the game begins—all of them slamming down their hands on the table and yelling at the top of their voices.

Angus is the first to lose. As he drinks, the mixture slops onto the immaculate white of his shirt, staining it brown. The others jeer him.

"You idiot!" Duncan shouts. "Most of it's going down your neck."

Angus swallows the last gulp, gags. His eyes bulge.

Will's next. He puts it away expertly. I watch the muscles of his throat working. He turns the glass upside down above his head and grins.

Next to end up with all the cards is Charlie. He looks at his glass, takes a deep breath.

"Come on, you pussy!" Duncan shouts.

I can't watch this. I don't have to watch this. Sod Charlie, I think. This was meant to be our weekend away together. If he wants to take himself down it's his bloody lookout. I'm his wife, not his mother. I stand up.

"I'm going to bed," I say. "Night all."

But no one answers, or even glances in my direction.

I PUSH INTO THE DRAWING room next door and as I walk through I stop short in shock. A figure's sitting there on the sofa, in the gloom. After a moment I recognize it to be Olivia. "Oh, hey there," I say.

She looks up. Her long legs stick out in front of her, her feet bare. "Hey."

"Had enough in there?"

"Yeah."

"Me too," I say. "You staying up for a bit?"

She shrugs. "No point in going to bed. My room's right next to *that*."

As if on cue, from the dining room comes a burst of mocking laughter. Someone roars: "Drink it—drink it all down!"

And now a chant: *Down it, down it, down it*—switching suddenly into *raise hell, raise hell, RAISE HELL!* Sounds of the table being smashed with fists. Then of something else shattering—another glass? A slurred voice: "Johnno, you fucking idiot!"

Poor Olivia, unable to escape from all that. I hover in the doorway.

"It's fine," Olivia says. "I don't need anyone to keep me company."

But I feel I should stay. I feel bad for her. And actually, I realize I *want* to stay. I liked sitting with her in the cave earlier, smoking.

There was something exciting about it, a strange thrill. Talking to her, with the taste of the tobacco on my tongue, I could almost imagine I was nineteen again, talking about the boys I'd slept with—not a mum of two and mortgaged up to the eyeballs. And there's also the fact that Olivia reminds me of someone. But I can't think who. It bothers me, like when you're trying to think of a word and you know it's there on the tip of your tongue, just out of reach.

"Actually," I say, "I'm not all that tired. And I don't have to get up early tomorrow morning to deal with two crazy kids. There's some wine in our room—I could go and grab it."

She gives a small smile at this, the first I've seen. And then she reaches behind the sofa cushion and pulls out an expensive-looking bottle of vodka. "I nicked it from the kitchen earlier," she says.

"Oh," I say. "Well, even better." This really *is* like being nineteen again.

She passes me the bottle. I unscrew the cap, take a swig. It burns a freezing streak down my throat and I gasp. "Wow. Can't think of the last time I did that." I pass the bottle to her and wipe my mouth. "We got cut off, earlier, didn't we? You were telling me about that guy—Callum? The breakup."

Olivia shuts her eyes, takes a deep breath. "I guess the breakup was only the beginning," she says.

Another big roar of laughter from the next room. More hands thumping the table. More drunken male voices shouting over each other. A crash against the door, then Angus falls through it, trousers about his ankles, his dick flopping out obscenely.

"Sorry, ladies," he says, with a drunken leer. "Don't mind me."

"Oh for Christ's sake," I explode, "just . . . just fuck off and leave us alone!"

Olivia looks at me, impressed, like she didn't think I had it in me. I didn't, either. I'm not quite sure where it came from. Maybe it's the vodka.

"You know what?" I say. "This probably isn't the best place to chat, is it?"

She shakes her head. "We could go to the cave?"

"Er—" I hadn't planned on a nighttime foray about the island. And I'm sure it's dangerous to wander around at night, with the bog and things.

"Forget it," Olivia says, quickly. "I get it. I just—it's weird—I just felt it was easier talking in there."

And suddenly I have the same feeling I did earlier. An odd thrill, the feeling of breaking the rules. "No," I say. "Let's do it. And bring that bottle."

We sneak out of the Folly via the rear entrance. It's really creepy at night, this place. It's so quiet, apart from the sound of the waves on the rocks in the near distance. Occasionally there comes a strange, guttural cackling that raises all the hairs on my arms. I finally realize that the noise must be made by some sort of bird. A pretty big one from the sound of it.

As we continue, the ruined houses loom up next to us in the beam of my flashlight. The dark, gaping windows are like empty eye sockets and it feels unnervingly as though someone might be in there, looking out, watching us pass. I can hear noises coming from inside, too: rustles and creaks and scratchings. It's probably rats—but then, that's not a particularly reassuring thought either.

I'm aware of things moving around us as we walk—too fast to see properly, caught momentarily by the weak light of the moon. Something flies so near to my face that I feel it brush the sensitive skin of my cheek. I jump back, put a hand up to fend it off. A bat? It was definitely too big to be an insect.

As we climb down into the cave a dark figure appears on the rock wall in front of us, human shaped. I almost drop the bottle in shock until, after a beat, I realize it is my own shadow.

This place is enough to make you believe in ghosts.

THE WEDDING NIGHT

THE FOUR USHERS HAVE FORMED A SEARCH PARTY. THEY TAKE A first-aid kit. They take the big paraffin torches from the brackets at the entrance of the marquee for illumination.

"Right, boys," Femi says. "Everyone ready?"

There has been a strange, fervent energy about their preparations, bordering on an inappropriate excitement. They might be scouts preparing for a mission, the schoolboys they once were on some midnight dare.

The other guests gather around silently watching the preparations, relieved that the thing has been taken out of their hands, that they are permitted to stay here in the light and warmth.

To those inside the marquee who watch them go, they look like medieval villagers on a witch hunt: the lighted torches, the fervor. The wind and the blackout have added to the sense of the surreal. The macabre discovery that supposedly lies in wait out there has taken on a fantastical dimension: not quite real. Besides, it's difficult to know what to believe, whether they can really trust the word of a hysterical teenager. Some of them are still hoping that it has all just been a terrible misunderstanding.

They watch, silently, as the small group marches through the thrashing flaps of the marquee entrance. Out into the loud ragged night, into the storm, holding their torches aloft.

OLIVIA
The Bridesmaid

IN THE CAVE THE SEA HAS COME IN, SO IT'S PRACTICALLY LAPPING AT our feet, the water black as ink. It makes the space feel smaller, more claustrophobic. Hannah and I have to sit nearer to each other than we did before, our knees touching, a candle we nicked from the drawing room perched on the rock in front of us in its glass lantern.

Now I understand why it's called the Whispering Cave. The high water has changed the acoustics in here so that this time everything we say is whispered back to us, as though someone's standing there in the shadows, repeating every word. It's hard to believe there isn't. I find myself turning to check, every so often, to make certain we're alone.

I can't make Hannah out all that well in the soft light of the candle. But I can hear her breathing, smell her perfume.

We pass the bottle of vodka between us. I'm already a bit drunk, I think, from dinner. I couldn't eat much and the booze went straight to my head. But I need to be drunker to tell her, drunk enough that my brain can't stop the words. Which seems silly, as recently I have been needing to tell someone about it so badly that sometimes I feel like it's going to erupt out of me, without any warning. But now it has actually come down to it, I feel tongue-tied.

Hannah speaks first. "Olivia."

The cave replies in a whisper: *Olivia, Olivia, Olivia.*

"God," Hannah says, "that echo. Did your ex . . . did he do anything to you? Someone I know—" She stops, starts again: "My sister, Alice. She had this boyfriend when she was at university. And he reacted really badly to the breakup. I mean, really *really* badly—"

I wait for Hannah to say more, but she doesn't. Instead she takes the bottle from me and has a very long drink, about four shots' worth.

"No, it wasn't anything like that," I say. "Yeah, Callum was a bit of a shit. I mean, he wasn't very subtle about hooking up with Ellie straight after. But he was the one who broke it off, so it wasn't that." I grab the bottle from her, take a big gulp. I can taste her lipstick on the rim. "It was in the summer holidays after term had ended. I was staying at Jules's place in Islington, while she was away for work for a few days."

I speak into the darkness, the cave whispering my own words back to me. I find myself telling Hannah how lonely I felt. How I was in this great big city, which I've always found so exciting, but realized I had no one to share it with. How it was Friday night and I'd gone to the Sainsbury's down the road from Jules's flat and bought myself some crisps, milk and cereal for the morning, and how my walk home took me past all these people standing outside pubs, drinking, having a laugh in the sun. How I felt like such a fucking saddo, with my orange carrier bag and a night of Netflix to look forward to. How it was at times like that I always thought of Callum, and what we might be doing together, which made me feel even more alone.

I still can't quite believe I'm telling her all this, when I hardly know her. But maybe that's the point. Maybe, of all the people here, she's the one person I can tell, *because* she's basically a stranger. The vodka definitely helps, too, and the fact that it's so gloomy in here that I can hardly see her face. Even so, I don't think I can tell her all of it. The thought of doing that makes me feel panicky. But maybe I can start at the beginning and see if, once I've told her most of it, I'm brave enough to tell her the whole thing.

"I was on my phone," I say, "and I could see that Callum was with Ellie. She'd shared all these pics on Snapchat. There was one of her sitting on his lap. And then another one of her kissing him, while she held one middle finger up to the camera like she didn't want anyone to take the picture . . . except then she went and shared it for the whole world to see, for fuck's sake."

Hannah takes a drink from the bottle, breathes out. "That must have made you feel pretty awful," she says. "Seeing that. Jeez, social media has a lot to answer for."

"Yeah." I shrug. "It did make me feel a bit . . . shit." In case I sound like a total stalker I don't tell her how many times I looked at those photos, how I sat there clutching my Sainsbury's bag and crying while I did it. "My mates had been saying I should have some fun," I say. "You know, like show Callum what he was missing. They kept telling me to get myself on some dating apps, but I didn't want to do it at uni, where it was all so incestuous."

"What, apps like Tinder?"

I think she's trying to show she's down with the kids. "Yeah, but no one really uses Tinder anymore."

"Sorry," she says. "I'm ancient, remember. What do I know?" She says it a bit wistfully.

"You're not that old," I tell her.

"Well . . . thanks." Her knee bumps against mine.

I take another swig of vodka. And remember how that night in Jules's flat I drank some of her wine, which made me realize how all the stuff we drank at uni for £3 a glass in the local bars tasted like absolute piss. I remember how I felt quite sophisticated walking around in my pants and bra with one of her big glasses. I imagined it was my flat, that I was going to go out and find some man and bring him back here and screw him. And *that* would show Callum.

Obviously I didn't *actually* plan to do that. I'd only had sex with one person before, with Callum. And even that had been pretty tame.

"I set up a profile," I tell Hannah. "I decided in London it was different. In London I could go on a date and it wouldn't be all over the whole of campus the next morning."

"I'm kind of impressed," Hannah says. "I'd never have been brave enough to do something like that. But weren't you, you know . . . worried about safety?"

"No," I say. "I'm not an idiot. I didn't use my real name. Or my age."

"Ah," Hannah nods. "Right." I get the impression she's not convinced by that and is trying very hard not to say anything else.

I put my age as twenty-six, in fact. The profile photo I put up didn't even look like me. I ransacked Jules's closet, did my makeup perfectly. But it was kind of the *point* not to look like me.

"I called myself Bella," I say. "You know, as in Hadid?"

I tell Hannah how I sat there on the bed and scrolled through photos of all these guys until my eyes burned. "Most of them were rank," I say. "In the gym, like lifting up their shirts, or wearing sunglasses that they thought made them look cool." I almost gave up.

"But I did match with this one guy," I tell Hannah. "He caught my eye. He was . . . different."

I MADE THE FIRST MOVE. So unlike me, but I was a bit pissed from Jules's wine.

Free to meet up? I wrote.

Yes, his reply came. I'd like that, Bella. When suits you?

How about this evening?

There was a long pause. Then: You don't hang about.

This is my only free evening for the next few weeks. I liked how that sounded. Like I had better places to be.

Fine, he messaged back. It's a date.

"WHAT WAS HE LIKE?" HANNAH asks, her chin in her hand. She seems fascinated, watching me closely.

"Hotter than his photo. And a bit older than me."

"How much older?"

"Um . . . maybe fifteen years?"

"OK." Is she trying not to sound shocked? "And what was he like? When you actually met up?"

I think back. It's hard for me to see him as he appeared at the beginning. "I guess I thought he was hot. And . . . he seemed like more of a man. He made Callum look like a boy in comparison." He had broad shoulders, like he worked out a lot, and a tan. In comparison Callum was a scrawny little pretty boy. Proper men were my new thing, I decided. "But," I shrug, even though she can't see me, "I don't know. I suppose however hot he was, at first, a part of me would have preferred him to be Callum."

Hannah nods. "Yeah," she says sympathetically. "I get that. When you've got your heart set on someone Brad Pitt could walk in and he wouldn't be enough—"

"Brad Pitt is really fucking *old*," I say.

"Um—Harry Styles?"

That almost makes me smile. "Yeah. Maybe. Or Timothée Chalamet." I always thought Callum looked a bit like him. "But Callum probably hadn't thought about me for a moment, especially not while Ellie's stupid big tits were in his face." I told myself I had better stop fucking thinking about him.

"And did this guy . . . what was his name?"

"Steven."

"Did he say anything? When you met, about you being so much younger?"

I give her a look. That sounded a bit judge-y.

"Sorry," she says, with a laugh. "But, seriously, did he?"

"Yeah, he did. He asked me if I was really twenty-six. But he didn't say it in a suspicious way, more like it was, I dunno—a joke we were both in on. It didn't really seem to matter to him, not then. And he was nice," I say, though it's hard to remember that now. "I was having a good time. He laughed at all my jokes. He asked me *loads* of questions about myself."

I CAST MY MIND BACK to that night. Being in that bar with the drinks going to my head—I was drinking Negronis because I thought that would make me seem older. "My original plan was to get a photo," I say, "post it to my Instagram." Let Callum see what he was missing.

"I'm guessing . . . ," Hannah looks at me, "a bit more than that happened?"

"Yeah." I take a gulp of vodka.

THERE WAS THIS MOMENT, I remember, when I thought maybe he was going to say goodbye, but he opened the door of the cab and turned to me and said: "Well, are you getting in?" And in the taxi (not even an Uber, a proper black cab), how this little voice kept piping up: *What are you doing? You hardly know him!* But the drunk part of me, the part of me that was up for it, kept telling it to shut up.

We went back to Jules's place, because he'd just moved house and didn't have any proper furniture. I felt a bit bad about it, but I told myself I'd wash the sheets.

"Wow," he said. "*This* is impressive. And it all belongs to you?"

"Yeah," I said, feeling like I'd got a whole lot more sophisticated in his eyes.

"And then we had sex," I tell Hannah. "I guess I wanted to do it before the booze wore off."

"Was it good?" Hannah asks. She sounds excited. And then: "I haven't had sex for ages. Sorry. I know that's TMI."

I try not to think of her and Charlie having sex. "Yeah," I say. "It was a bit—y'know. A bit rough? He pushed me up against the wall, pushed my skirt up around my waist, pulled my knickers down. And he—Can I have a bit more of that?" Hannah passes me the bottle and I take a quick slug. "He went down on me, even though I hadn't had a shower. He said he preferred it like that."

"Right," Hannah says. "OK. Wow."

Callum and I had never done anything very adventurous. I guess the sex I had with Steven was better than anything I'd had with Callum, even if, after he'd made me come with his mouth that first time, I weirdly felt like crying for a moment.

"I saw him, like, quite a few times after that," I tell Hannah.

I feel rather than see Hannah nod, her head so close to mine that I sense the movement of the air. I find myself telling her how I liked seeing myself the way he seemed to: as someone sexy, someone adventurous. Even if sometimes I felt like I was out of my depth, not always totally comfortable with all the stuff he asked me to do in bed.

"I mean," I say, "it wasn't like it was with Callum, when it felt like we were . . ."

"Soul mates?" Hannah asks.

"Yeah," I say. It's a pretty cringe word, but it's also exactly right. "This was different, I guess. With Steven it was like he only showed me a tiny bit of himself, which—"

"Left you wanting to see more?"

"Yeah. I was sort of obsessed by him, I think. And he was so grown-up and so sophisticated, but he wanted *me*. And then—" I shrug. "I fucked up."

Hannah frowns. "What do you mean?"

"I dunno. I suppose I wanted to prove to him I was *mature*. And we never seemed to *do* anything together, other than meet up and, you know, have sex. I had this—this feeling that he might only be interested in me for that."

Hannah nods.

"But at the end of the summer Jules's magazine was throwing this party at the V&A, and I thought it would be a cool thing to bring him to. A proper date. Like, impress him a bit. Make him think I was grown-up and mature."

I tell Hannah about walking up those steps and seeing all these very grown-up, glamorous people milling around inside, all looking like film stars. And how the guy who checked our names looked over me like he didn't think I should be there, whereas Steven seemed to fit in so perfectly.

"I got a bit nervous," I say. "Especially of having to introduce him to Jules. And there were all these free drinks. I had way too many of them, to try and feel more confident. I made a total twat of myself. I had to go and be sick in the loos—I was a state. And then Steven put me in a cab back to Jules's, and I couldn't even ask him to come with me because she would be there later on. I remember him counting out the notes to the cabdriver. And then asking him to make sure I got home safe, like I was a child."

"He should have gone with you," Hannah says. "*He* should have made sure you were all right. Not left it to some taxi driver."

I shrug. "Maybe. But I was such a fucking embarrassment. I'm not surprised he wanted to be rid of me."

I remember watching him out of the window and thinking: *I've blown it*. And thinking, if I were him, maybe I'd just go back inside and hang out with people my own age who could hold their booze.

"After that he started ghosting me." In case she doesn't know what that means I say, "You know, like not replying? Even though I could see the two little blue ticks."

She nods.

"I went back to uni. One night I got a bit drunk and sad after a night out and I sent him *ten* messages. I tried to call him on the walk to Halls at two A.M. He didn't answer. Didn't reply to my texts. I knew I'd never see him again."

"Shit," Hannah says.

"Yeah."

"So was that it?" she asks, when I don't say any more. "*Did* you see him again?" And then, when I don't answer: "Olivia?"

But I can't speak. It's like I was under some sort of spell before, it was so easy to talk. Now it feels as though the words are stuck in my throat.

There's this image in my brain. Red on white. All the blood.

WHEN WE GET BACK TO the Folly, Hannah says she's knackered. "Straight to bed for me," she says. I get it. It was different in the cave. Sitting there in the dark with the vodka and the candlelight, it felt like we could say anything. Now it feels almost like we over-shared. Like we crossed a line.

I know I won't be able to go to sleep, though, especially not while all the blokes are still playing their game outside my room. So I stand against the wall outside for a bit and try to slow down the thoughts racing round my head.

"Hello there."

I nearly jump out of my skin. "What the fuck—"

It's the best man, Johnno. I don't like him. I saw how he looked at me earlier. And he's drunk—I can tell that, and *I'm* pretty drunk. In the light spilling from the dining room I can see him give a big grin, more of a leer. "Fancy a puff?" He holds out a big joint, sickly smell of weed. I can see it's wet on the end where it's been in his mouth.

"No thanks," I say.

"Very well behaved."

I make to go inside, but as I reach for the door he catches my arm, his hand tight about it. "You know, we should have a dance tomorrow, you and I. Best man and the bridesmaid."

I shake my head.

He steps nearer, pulls me closer to him. He's so much bigger than me. But he wouldn't do anything right here, would he? Not with everyone upstairs?

"You should think about it," he says. "Might surprise you. An older man."

"Get the fuck off me," I hiss. I think of my razor blade, upstairs. I wish I had it with me, just so I knew it was there.

I yank my arm out of his grip as I fumble with the door, my fingers not working properly. I feel him watching me the whole time.

JOHNNO
The Best Man

'M BACK UP IN MY ROOM, HAVING FINISHED MY JOINT. I MANAGED to pick up the grass in Dublin when I arrived, hanging around Temple Bar with all the tourists. Not sure it's as strong as the stuff I get from my usual guy but hopefully it will help me sleep. I need a bit of help tonight.

Here on the island it's like we're back there, at Trevellyan's. Maybe it's to do with the land. The cliffs, the sea. All I can hear is the sound of the waves outside the windows, slamming into the rocks below. I remember the dorm room: the rows of beds and the bars outside the windows. To keep us safe or to keep us in—maybe a bit of both. And the sound of the waves there, too, rushing up the beach. *Shush, shush, shush.* Reminding me to keep the secret.

I haven't thought about it, not properly, for years. I can't. Some things you've got to put behind you. But it's like being here is forcing me to look right at it. And when I do I can't fucking breathe properly.

I lie in bed. I've drunk enough to pass out, and then the weed on top. But I feel like something's crawling all over my skin, a million cockroaches in the bed with me. They're here to stop me getting any rest. I want to scratch at myself, tear into my skin if I have to, to make it stop. And I'm afraid that if I do sleep I'll have dreams like I did last night. I haven't had them for as long as I can remember . . . years and years. It's the company. It's this place.

It's so dark in here. It's too dark. I feel like it's pressing down on me. Like I'm drowning in it. I sit up in bed, remind myself that I'm fine. Nothing trying to suffocate me, no cockroaches. It could be the weed—different stuff, making me more paranoid. I'll go take a shower, that's what I'll do. Get the water nice and hot, have a good scrub.

Then I think I see this thing, in the corner of the room. Growing, gathering itself together, out of the darkness.

Nah. I'm imagining it. Must be. Don't believe in ghosts.

It's got to be the weed, the whiskey. My brain playing tricks on me. Fuck, but I'm sure there's something there. I can see it out of the corner of my eye, but when I look directly at it, it seems to disappear. I shut my eyes like a little kid scared of monsters under the bed, press my eyelids with my fingers until I see silver spots. It's no good. I can see it even with my eyes closed. It had a face. And it's not an it, it's a someone. I know who it is.

"Get the fuck away from me," I whisper. Then I try a different way: "I'm sorry. It wasn't my fault. I didn't think—"

My stomach gives a heave. I just make it to the bathroom in time before I'm spewing over the bowl of the toilet, my whole body shaking with fear.

JULES
The Bride

CHARLIE AND I ARE UP ON THE BATTLEMENTS, LOOKING OUT AT the glitter of lights along the mainland. We left the others to their disgusting game. There's something illicit about it, just the two of us up here. Something reckless. Perhaps it's being on top of the world with the steep drop beneath us—invisible but very much there—adding a frisson of excitement, making everything feel slightly freighted with danger. Or that we're cloaked by darkness. That anything could happen up here and no one would know.

"It's so good to have you here," I tell him. "You know you're *my* best man, really?"

"Thanks," he says. "It's good to be here. Why did you choose this place?"

"Oh, you know. My Irish roots. And it's so exclusive, I like the idea of being first. There's the remoteness, too: good for deterring any paps."

"They'd really try and get photos of his wedding?" He sounds incredulous, like he doesn't believe Will's celebrity justifies it.

"They might. And it's so on-brand for Will, having his wedding in such a wild place."

All of what I've told him is true, in a way. But not the whole truth.

I rest my head against his shoulder. I think I feel him go still.

Perhaps it doesn't feel quite so natural as it once did, being physically close like this. Come to think of it, did it ever?

Charlie clears his throat. "Can I ask you a question?"

He sounds serious. I sense a touch of wariness. "Go ahead."

"He does makes you happy, doesn't he?"

I lift my head a fraction off his shoulder. "What do you mean?"

I feel him shrug. "Just that. You know how much I care about you, Jules."

"Yes," I say. "He does. And I could ask you the same about Hannah."

"That's *very* different—"

"Really? How so?" I don't want to hear his reply; I don't need yet another person telling me that it has all been so quick, between Will and me. And then, because I've drunk more than I meant to this evening—and because when else am I going to be able to?—I say it: "Are you saying that *you* would have made me happier?"

"Jules—" He says it as a kind of groan. "Don't do that."

"Do what?" I ask innocently.

"We wouldn't have worked. We're friends, good friends. You know that." At that I feel him pulling away from me, retreating from the cliff edge.

Do I, though? And is he *really* so convinced of that? I know he wanted me once. I still think about that night. The memory I have returned to so many times . . . when I have needed some inspiration in the bath, for example. We have never spoken of it since. And because we haven't, it has retained its power. I'm sure he still thinks about it too.

"We were different people back then," he says, as though he might have read my mind. I wonder if he's as convinced by his words as he's making out. "I wasn't asking because of anything like *that*," he says. "Not out of jealousy . . . or anything."

"*Really?* Because it sounds to me like you're a bit jealous."

"I'm not, I—"

"Did I tell you how good he is in bed? That's the sort of thing friends are meant to tell each other, isn't it?" I know I'm pushing it, but I can't help myself.

"Look," Charlie says. "I just want you to be happy."

How bloody patronizing. I lift my head fully away from his shoulder. I feel the distance between us expanding now, metaphorically as well as physically. "I'm perfectly capable of knowing what does and doesn't make me happy," I say. "In case you haven't noticed I'm thirty-four. Not a sixteen-year-old virgin totally in awe of you."

Charlie grimaces. "God, I know. Sorry, I didn't mean it like that. I care, that's all."

Something has suddenly occurred to me. "Charlie?" I ask. "Did you write me a note?"

"A note?"

I hear the answer to my question in his confusion. It wasn't him.

"It's nothing," I say. "Forget it. You know what? I think I'm going to turn in. If I go now, I can get eight hours' sleep before tomorrow."

"OK," he says. I sense that he is relieved I've called it a night and that pisses me off.

"Give me a hug?" I ask.

"Sure."

I lean into him. His body is softer than Will's, so much less taut than it used to be. But the scent of him is the same. So familiar, somehow, which is strange—considering how long it's been.

It's still there, I think. He must feel it too. But then attraction never really goes away, does it? I'm sure of it: he's jealous.

WHEN I GET BACK TO the room Will's getting undressed. He grins at me, I move toward him.

"Shall we pick up where we left off earlier?" he murmurs.

It's one way, I think, to erase the humiliation of that conversation with Charlie.

I tear open the remaining buttons on his shirt, he rips one of the straps of my jumpsuit trying to get it off me. It's always like the first time with him—that haste—only better, now we know exactly what the other wants. We fuck braced against the bed, him entering me from behind. I come, hard. I'm not quiet about it. In a strange way, it feels as though much of the evening since we got interrupted earlier has been a kind of foreplay. Feeling the gaze of the others upon us: envious, awed. Seeing in their reactions to us how good we look together. And yes, the hurt of having crossed a line with Charlie and being rebuffed. Maybe he'll hear us.

Afterward Will goes for a shower. He takes impeccable care of himself—his routine even makes my own look rather slapdash. I remember being a little surprised when I realized his permanently brown face wasn't actually due to the constant exposure to the elements but to Sisley's self-tan, the same one I use.

IT'S ONLY NOW, SITTING IN the armchair in my robe, that I become aware of a strange odor, more powerful than the evanescently marine scent of sex. It is stronger, undeniably the smell of the sea: a briny, fishy, ammoniac tang at the back of the throat. And as I sit here it seems to gather itself from the shadowy corners of the room, gaining texture and depth.

I go to the window and open it. The air outside is pretty icy, now that it's dark. I can hear the slam of the waves against the rocks down below. Farther out the water is silver in the light of the moon, like molten metal, so bright that I can hardly look at it. You can see the swell in it even from here, great muscular movements beneath the surface, full of intent. I can hear a cackling above me, up on the roof, perhaps. It sounds like a gleeful mocking.

Surely, I think, the smell of the sea should be stronger outside than in? Yet the breeze that wafts in is fresh and odorless by comparison. I can't make sense of it. I reach over to the dressing table and light my scented candle. Then I sit in the chair and try for calm. But I can practically hear the beat of my own heart. Too fast, a flutter in my chest. Is it just the aftermath of our exertions? Or something more than that?

I should talk to Will about the note. Now is the moment, if I'm ever going to do it. But I've already had one confrontation this evening—with Charlie—and I can't quite bring myself to face the thing head-on, to plow ahead and raise it. And it's probably nothing. I'm 99 percent sure, anyway. Maybe 98.

The door to the bathroom opens. Will steps into the room, towel knotted around his waist. Even though I have just had him I'm momentarily distracted by the sight of his body: the planes and ridges of it, the muscles corded in stomach, arms and legs like a statue molded by a Renaissance sculptor.

"What are you doing still up?" he asks. "We should get some rest. Big day tomorrow."

I turn my back to him and drop my robe to the floor, sure I can feel his eyes on me. Enjoying the power of it. Then I lift the cover and slip into the bed and as I do my bare legs make contact with something. Solid and cold, the consistency of dead flesh. That seems to yield as I push my feet unwittingly into it and yet at the same time wraps itself around my legs.

"Jesus Christ! Jesus fucking Christ!"

I leap from the bed, trip, half sprawl on the floor.

Will stares at me. "Jules? What is it?"

I can hardly answer him at first, too scared and repulsed by what I just felt. The panic has risen into my throat in a choke. The shock reverberates through me, deep and visceral and animal. It was the stuff of a nightmare—the sort of thing you dream about finding in your bed, only to wake in a chill sweat and realize it was all in your imagination. But this was real. I can still feel the cold imprint of it against my legs.

"Will," I say, finally finding my voice. "There's something—in the bed. Under the covers."

He strides over in two great bounds, takes the duvet in both hands and rips it away. I can't help screaming. There, in the middle of the mattress, sprawls the huge black body of some marine creature, tentacles stretching in all directions.

Will leaps back. "What the fuck?" He sounds more angry than frightened. He says it again, as though the thing on the bed might somehow answer for itself: "What the fuck . . . ?"

The smell of the sea, of briny, rotting things, is overpowering now, emanating from that black mass on the bed.

And then quickly, recovering much more rapidly than I do, Will moves closer to it again. As he puts out a hand I shout, "Don't touch it!" But he has already grasped the tentacles, given them a yank. They come free, the thing seems to break apart—horribly, sickeningly. It was there while we fucked, waiting for us beneath the covers . . .

Will gives a short, hard laugh, entirely without humor. "Look— it's only seaweed. It's bloody seaweed!"

He holds it aloft. I lean closer. He's right. It's the stuff I've seen strewn along the beaches here, great thick, dark ropes of it washed up by the waves. Will tosses it onto the floor.

Gradually, the whole spectacle loses its macabre, monstrous aspect and is reduced to a horrible mess. I become aware of the indignity of my position, sprawled as I am, naked, upon the floor. I feel my heartbeat slow. I breathe more easily.

Except . . . how did it come to be here in the first place? Why is it here?

Someone has done this to us. Someone has brought this in,

hidden it beneath the duvet, knowing that we would only find it once we got into bed.

I turn to Will. "Who could have done this?"

He shrugs. "Well, I have my suspicions."

"What? About who?"

"It was a prank we used to play on the younger boys at school. We'd go down via the cliff path and collect seaweed on the beaches—as much as we could carry. Then we'd hide it in their beds. So my guess is Johnno or Duncan—possibly all of the guys. They probably thought it was funny."

"You'd call this a *prank*? We're not at school, Will, it's the night before our wedding! What the fuck?" In a way, my anger is a relief.

Will shrugs. "It's not a prank for you, it's for me. You know, for old times' sake. They wouldn't have meant you to get upset—"

"I'm going to go and get them all up now, find out which one of them it was. Show them exactly how funny I think it is."

"Jules." Will takes hold of my shoulders. And then, soothingly: "Look, if you were to do that . . . well, you might say things you'd regret. It would spoil things for tomorrow, wouldn't it? It could change the whole dynamic."

I do, sort of, see what he means. God, he's always so reasonable—sometimes infuriatingly so, always taking the measured approach. I look at the black mass, now on the floor. It's hard to believe that some darker message wasn't intended by it.

"Look," Will says gently. "We're both tired. It's been a long day. Let's not worry about it now. We can get a new sheet from the spare room."

The spare room was intended for Will's parents. They balked at the outlandish idea of actually staying on the island. Will didn't seem surprised: "My father's never been particularly impressed by anything I've done—getting married is undoubtedly no exception." He seemed bitter. He doesn't talk about his father much—

which paradoxically gives me the impression that he's a bigger influence upon my fiancé than he likes to admit.

"Get a new duvet, too," I tell Will now. I'm half-tempted to say I want to swap to the other room. But that would be irrational, and I pride myself on being the opposite.

"Sure." Will gestures to the seaweed. "And I'll sort out this, too—I've dealt with much worse, trust me."

On the program Will has escaped from wolves and been swarmed by vampire bats—though he's never far from the help of the crew—so this must all seem a little pathetic to him. A bit of seaweed on the sheets is hardly a big deal, in the grand scheme of things.

"I'll have a word with the guys tomorrow morning," he says. "Tell them they're fucking idiots."

"OK," I say. He's so good at providing comfort. He's so—well, there's only really one word for it—perfect.

And yet, in this moment, with particularly nasty timing, the words on that horrible little note surface.

Not the man you think he is . . . cheat . . . liar . . .

Don't marry him.

"A good night's sleep," Will says, soothingly. "That's what we need."

I nod.

But I don't think I'm going to sleep a wink.

AOIFE
The Wedding Planner

THERE'S A NOISE OUTSIDE. IT'S A STRANGE NOISE, A KEENING. IT sounds more human than animal—but at the same time it doesn't sound entirely human either. In our bedroom, Freddy and I look at one another. All the guests have gone to bed too, about half an hour ago now. I thought they would never get tired. We had to wait until the bitter end in case they needed anything of us. We listened to the drumming from the dining room, the chanting. Freddy, who has a little schoolboy Latin, could translate the thing they were chanting: "If I cannot move heaven, I shall raise hell." I felt the gooseflesh rise on my skin at that.

They're like overgrown boys, the ushers. I'd say they lack the innocence of boys: but some boys aren't ever really innocent. What I mean is that as grown men they should know better. And there is a pack feeling about them, like dogs that might behave well on their own but, once all together, don't have their own minds. I'll have to keep my eye on them tomorrow, make sure they don't get carried away. It is my experience that some of the smartest affairs, populated by the most well-heeled and upstanding guests, have been those that have got most out of control. I organized a wedding in Dublin that contained half Ireland's political elite—even the Taoiseach was there—only for things to come to blows between the groom and father-in-law before the first dance.

Here there's the added danger of the whole island. The wildness of this place gets under your skin. These guests will feel themselves far from the normal moral codes of society, safe from the prying eyes of others. These men are ex–public schoolboys. They've spent much of their lives being forced to follow a strict set of rules that probably didn't end with their leaving school: choices around what university to attend, what job to do, what sort of house to live in. In my experience those who have the greatest respect for the rules also take the most enjoyment in breaking them.

"I'll go," I say.

"It's not safe," Freddy says. "I'll come with you." I tell Freddy I'll be fine. To reassure him I tell him I'll pick up the poker from beside the fire on my way out. I'm the braver of the two of us, I know. I don't say this with any great pride. It's simply that when the worst has happened, you rather lose your fear of anything else.

I step into the night, appreciating the quality of the darkness, the velvet black as it folds me into itself. Any light from the Folly makes very little impact upon it, though the kitchen is aglow—and also one of the upstairs windows, the room the soon-to-be-married couple are occupying. Well, I know what's keeping them up. We heard the rhythmic shudder of the bed against the floorboards.

I won't use the flashlight yet. It will make me stupid in the darkness. I stand here, listening intently. All I can make out at first is the slam of the water on the rocks and an unfamiliar, susurrating sound which I finally identify as the marquee, the fabric rustling in the gentle breeze some fifty yards away.

And then the other noise begins again. I'm better able to recognize it, now. It's the sound of someone sobbing. Man or woman, though, it's impossible to tell. I turn in its direction and as I do I think I catch a shimmer of movement out of the corner of my eye, in the direction of the outbuildings behind the Folly. I don't know how I saw it, it being so dark. But it is hardwired into us, I think, into our animal selves. Our eyes are alert to any disturbance, any change in the pattern of the darkness.

It might have been a bat. Sometimes in the early evening you can see them flit above in the twilight, so quick you're not sure you've seen them. But I think it was bigger. I'm sure it was a person, the same person who sits weeping cloaked in darkness. Even when I came here all those years ago, even though the island was inhabited then, there were ghost stories. The grieving women mourning their husbands, brutally slain. The voices from the bog, denied their proper burial. At the time we scared ourselves silly with them. And in spite of myself I feel it now, the sensation of my skin shrinking over my bones.

"Hello?" I call. The sound stops, abruptly. When there is no answer I click my torch on. I swing the beam this way and that.

The beam catches on something as I move it in a slow arc. I train it on the same spot, and guide it up the figure that stares back at me. The beam marks out the dark wild hair, the gleaming eyes. Like a being straight from folklore—the Pooka: the phantom goblin, portent of impending doom.

In spite of myself I take a step back, the torch beam wavering. But gradually, recognition dawns. It's only the best man, slumped against the wall of one of the outbuildings.

"Who's there?" His voice sounds slurred and hoarse.

"It's me," I say. "Aoife."

"Oh, Aoife. Come to tell me it's time for lights out? Time to get into bed like a good little boy?" He gives me a crooked grin. But it's a halfhearted affair, and I think those are tear tracks that catch in the beam.

"It's not safe for you to go wandering around the outbuildings," I say, all practicality. There's old farm machinery in there that could cut a person in half. "Especially without a torch," I add. And especially when you're as drunk as you are, I think. Although, oddly enough, I feel as though I am protecting the island from him—rather than the other way round.

He stands up, walks toward me. He's a big man, drunk and more besides—I catch a sickly sweet vegetable waft of weed. I take another step away from him and realize that I'm gripping the poker hard. Then he grins, showing crooked teeth. "Yeah," he says. "Time for Johnny boy to go to bed. Think I had a bit too much of the old, you know." He mimes drinking from a bottle, then smoking. "Always makes me feel a bit off, having too much of both together. Thought I was fucking seeing things."

I nod, even though he can't see me. *So did I.*

I watch as he turns on his heel and lurches his way toward the Folly. The forced good humor didn't convince me for a second. Despite the grin he seemed caught between miserable and terrified. He looked like a man who had seen a ghost.

HANNAH
The Plus-One

WHEN I WAKE, MY HEAD ACHES. I THINK OF ALL THAT champagne—then the vodka. I check the alarm clock: 7 A.M. Charlie's fast asleep, flat on his back. I heard him come in last night, take his clothes off. I waited for the stumbling, the swearing, but he seemed surprisingly in control of his faculties.

"Han," he whispered to me, as he got into bed. "I left the drinking game. I only did the one shot." That made me feel a bit less hostile toward him. Then I wondered where else he'd been, for all that time. With whom. I remembered his flirting with Jules. I remembered how Johnno had asked if they'd slept together—and how they never answered.

So I didn't reply. I pretended to be asleep.

But I've woken up feeling turned on. I had some pretty crazy dreams. I think the vodka was partly responsible. But also the memory of Will's eyes on me at the beginning of the evening. Then talking in the cave with Olivia at the end: sitting so close in the dark with the water lapping at our feet and only the candle for light, passing the bottle between us. Secret, somehow sensual. I found myself hanging on her every word, the images she painted for me vivid in the darkness. As though it were me up against the wall, my skirt pushed up over my hips, someone's mouth upon me. The guy might have been a dickhead but the sex sounded pretty hot. And it made me remember the slightly dangerous thrill of sleeping with someone unknown, where you're not anticipating their every move.

I turn to Charlie. Perhaps now is the time to break our sex drought, regain that lost intimacy. I sneak a hand beneath the covers, grazing the springy hair that covers his chest, moving my hand lower—

Charlie makes a sleepy, surprised noise. And then, his voice claggy with sleep: "Not now, Han. Too tired."

I pull my hand away, stung. "Not now": like I'm an irritation. Tired because he stayed up late last night doing God knows what, when on the boat over here he spoke of this as a weekend for *us*. When he knows how raw I feel at the moment. I have a sudden frightening urge to pick up the hardback on the nightstand and hit him over the head with it. It's alarming, the rush of anger. It feels like I might have been harboring it for a while.

Then a sneaking thought. I allow myself to wonder what it must be like for Jules, to wake up next to Will. I heard them, last night—everyone in the Folly must have. I think again of the strength of Will's arms as he lifted me out of the boat yesterday. I think, too, of how I caught him looking at me last night with that strange questioning look. The sense of power, feeling his eyes on me.

Charlie murmurs in his sleep and I catch a waft of sour morning breath. I can't imagine Will having bad breath. Suddenly, I feel it's important to remove myself from this bedroom, from these thoughts.

THERE'S NO SOUND OF MOVEMENT inside the Folly, so I think I'm the first one up.

There must be quite a breeze today, as I can hear it whistling about the old stones of the place as I creep down the stairs, and every so often the windowpanes rattle in their frames as though someone's just smacked a palm against them. I wonder if we had the best of the weather yesterday. Jules won't like that. I tiptoe into the kitchen.

Aoife's standing there in a crisp white shirt and slacks, a clipboard in her hand, looking as if she's been up for hours. "Morning," she says—and I sense she is scrutinizing my face. "How are you today?" I get the impression Aoife doesn't miss a lot, with those bright, assessing eyes of hers. She's quietly rather beautiful. I sense that she makes an effort to underplay it but it shines through. Beautifully shaped dark eyebrows, gray-green eyes. I'd kill for that sort of natural, Audrey Hepburn–esque elegance, those cheekbones.

"I'm good," I say. "Sorry. Didn't realize anyone else was up."

"We started at the crack of dawn," she says. "With the big day today."

I'd practically forgotten about the actual wedding. I wonder how Jules is feeling this morning. Nervous? I can't imagine her being nervous about anything.

"Of course. I was going to go for a walk. Bit of a sore head."

"Well," she says, with a smile. "Safest to walk to the crest of the island, following the path past the chapel, leaving the marquee on the other side. That should keep you out of the bog. And take some wellies from by the door—you need to be careful to stick to the drier parts, or you'll find yourself in the turf. There's some signal up there too, if you need to make a phone call."

A phone call. Oh God—the kids! With a swoop of guilt, I realize they have totally slipped my mind. *My own children.* I'm shocked by how much this place has already made me forget myself.

I head outside and find the path, or what remains of it. It's not quite as easy as Aoife made out: you can just about see where it must have been trodden into existence, where the grass hasn't grown quite as well as elsewhere. As I walk the clouds scurry overhead, whirling out toward the open sea. It's definitely breezier today, and more overcast, though every so often the sun bursts dazzlingly through the cloud. The huge marquee, on the left of me, rustles in the wind as I pass it. I could sneak inside and have a look. But I am drawn toward the graveyard, instead, to the right of me beyond the chapel. Maybe this is a reflection of my state of mind at this time of year, the morbid mood that descends on me every June.

Wandering among the markers I see several very distinctive Celtic crosses, but I can also make out faint images of anchors, flowers. Most of the stones are so ancient that you can hardly read the writing on them anymore. Even if you could, it's not in English: Gaelic, I suppose. Some are broken or worn down until they have no real shape at all. Without really thinking what I am doing I touch a hand to the one nearest to me and feel where the rough stone has been smoothed by wind and water over the decades. There are a few that look a bit newer, perhaps from shortly before the islanders left for good. But most are pretty overgrown with weeds and mosses, as though they haven't been tended for a while.

Then I come across one that stands out because there's nothing growing over it. In fact it's in good nick: a little jam jar of wildflowers in front of it. From the dates—I do some quick maths—it must have been a child, a young girl: *Darcey Malone*, the stone reads, *Lost to the sea*. I look toward the sea. Many have drowned in making the crossing, Mattie told us. He didn't actually tell us *when* they drowned, I realize. I had assumed that was hundreds of years ago. But maybe it was more recent. To think: this was someone's child.

I bend down and touch the stone. There's an ache at the back of my throat.

"Hannah!" I turn toward the Folly. Aoife stands there, looking at me. "It's not that way," she says, then points to where the path continues at an angle away from the chapel. "Over there!"

"Thanks!" I call to her. "Sorry!" I feel as though I have been caught trespassing.

• • •

AS I GET FARTHER AWAY from the Folly any sign of the path seems to disappear completely. Patches of earth that look safe and grassy give way beneath my feet, collapsing into a black ooze. Cold bogwater has already seeped into my right welly and my foot squelches inside its soaked sock. The thought of the bodies somewhere beneath me makes me shiver. I wonder if anyone will know tonight how close they're dancing to a burial pit.

I hold up my phone. Full signal, as Aoife promised. I ring home. I can make out the tone at the other end over the wind, then my mum's voice saying: "Hello?"

"It's not too early is it?" I ask.

"Goodness no, love. We've been up for . . . well, it *feels* like hours."

When she passes me to Ben I can hardly make out what he's saying, his voice is so high and reedy.

"What was that, darling?" I press the phone to my ear.

"I said hello, Mum." At the sound of his voice I feel it deep down inside, the powerful tug of my bond to him. When I look for something to compare my love for the kids with it's actually not my love for Charlie. It's animal, powerful, blood-thick. The love of kin. The closest thing I can find to it is my love for Alice, my sister.

"Where are you?" Ben asks. "It sounds like the sea. Are there boats?" He's obsessed with boats.

"Yes, we came over on one."

"A big one?"

"Big-ish."

"Lottie was really sick yesterday, Mum."

"What's wrong with her?" I ask, quickly.

The thing that most worries me is the thought of anything happening to my loved ones. When I was little and woke in the night I'd sometimes creep over to my sister Alice's bed to check that she was definitely breathing, because the worst thing I could imagine was her being taken from me. "I'm OK, Han," she'd whisper, a smile in her voice. "But you can get in if you want to." And I'd lie there, pressed against her back, feeling the reassuring movement of her ribs as she breathed.

Mum comes on to the line. "Nothing to worry about, Han. She overdid herself yesterday afternoon. Your dad—the dolt—left her on her own with the Victoria sponge while I was at the shops. She's fine now, love, she's watching CBeebies on the sofa, ready for her breakfast. Now," she says to me, "go have fun at your glamorous weekend."

I don't feel very glamorous right now, I think, with my soggy sock and the breeze stinging tears from my eyes. "All right, Mum," I say, "I'll try and call tomorrow, on our way home. They're not driving you too crazy?"

"No," Mum says. "To be honest—" The little catch in her voice is unmistakable.

"What?"

"Well, it's a nice distraction. Positive. Looking after the next generation." She stops, and I hear her take a deep breath. "You know . . . it's this time of year."

"Yeah," I say. "I get it, Mum. I feel it too."

"Bye, darling. You take care of yourself."

As I ring off it hits me. Is *that* who Olivia reminds me of? Alice? It's all there: the thinness, the fragility, the deer-in-headlights look. I remember when I first saw my sister after she came home from university for the summer holidays. She had lost about a third of her body weight. She looked like someone with a terrible disease— like something was eating her from the inside out. And the worst part was that she didn't think she could talk to anyone about what had happened to her. Not even me.

I START WALKING. AND THEN I stop, look about me. I'm not sure I'm going the right way but it's not obvious which way *is* right.

I can't see the Folly or even the marquee from here, hidden as they are by the rise of the ground. I'd assumed it would be easier going on my return, because I'd know the route. But now I feel disoriented—my thoughts have been somewhere else completely. I must have taken a different way; it seems even boggier here. I'm having to hop between drier tussocks of grass to avoid soft, wet black patches of peat. I plow on. Then I get a bit stuck and chance a big leap. But I've misjudged it: my footing slips and my left welly lands not on the grassy hillock but on the soft surface of the peat.

I sink—and I keep sinking. It happens so fast. The ground opens up and swallows my foot. I lose my balance, staggering backward, and my other foot goes in with a horrible slurp of suction, quick as the black throat of that cormorant swallowing the fish. Within moments, the peat seems to be over the top of my boots and I'm sinking further. For the first few seconds I'm stupid with surprise, frozen. Then I realize I have to act, to rescue myself. I reach out for the dry patch of land in front of me, and grip hold of two hunks of grass.

I heave. Nothing happens. I seem to be stuck fast. How embarrassing this is going to be, I think, when I get back to the Folly absolutely filthy and have to explain what happened. Then I realize that I'm still sinking. The black earth is inching over my knees, up my lower thighs. Little by little it is drinking me in.

Suddenly I don't care about embarrassment any longer. I'm genuinely terrified. "Help!" I shout. But my words are swallowed by the wind. There's no way my voice is going to carry a few yards, let alone all the way to the Folly. Nevertheless, I try again. I scream it: "Help me!"

I think of the bodies in the bog. I imagine skeletal hands reaching up toward me from deep beneath the earth, ready to drag me down. And I begin to scrabble at the bank, using all my strength to haul myself upward, snorting and growling with the effort like an animal. It feels like nothing's happening but I grit my teeth and try even harder.

And then I am aware of the distinct feeling of being watched. A prickle down the spine.

"You want a hand there?"

I start. I can't quite twist myself round to see who has spoken. Slowly they move around to stand in front of me. It's two of the ushers: Duncan and Pete.

"We were having a little explore," Duncan says. "You know, get the lay of the land."

"Didn't think we'd have the pleasure of rescuing a damsel in distress," Pete says.

Their expressions are almost completely neutral. But there's a twitch at the corner of Duncan's mouth and I get the feeling they were laughing at me. That they might have been observing me for a while as I struggled. I don't want to rely on their help. But I'm also not really in any position to be picky.

They each take one of my hands. With them pulling, I finally manage to yank one foot from the bog's hold. I lose the boot as I pull my foot from the last of the muck and the earth closes over it as quickly as it had opened. I pull my other foot out and scrabble on to the bank, safe. For a moment I'm sprawled upon the ground, trembling with exhaustion and adrenaline, unable to find the energy to rise to my feet. I can't quite believe what just happened. Then I remember the two men looking down at me, each holding one of my hands. I scramble to my feet, thanking them, dropping their hands as quickly as seems polite—the clasp of our fingers suddenly feels oddly intimate. Now that the adrenaline is receding I'm becoming aware of how I must have looked to them as they pulled me out: my top gaping to expose my old bra, cheeks flushed and sweaty. I'm also aware of how isolated we are, here. Two of them, one of me.

"Thanks, guys," I say, hating the wobble in my voice. "I think I'm going to head back to the Folly now."

"Yes," Duncan drawls. "Got to wash all that filth off for later." And I can't work out if I'm reading too much into it or whether there really is something suggestive in the way he says it.

I start back in the direction of the Folly. I'm moving as fast as I can go in my socked feet, while being careful to pick only the safest crossings. I suddenly want very much to get back inside, and yes, back to Charlie. To put as much space as possible between myself and the bog. And, to be honest, my rescuers.

AOIFE

The Wedding Planner

SIT AT MY DESK GOING THROUGH THE PLANS FOR TODAY. I LIKE THIS desk. Its drawers are full of memories. Photographs, postcards, letters—paper yellowed with age, handwriting a childish scrawl.

I tune the radio in to the forecast. We get a few Galway stations here.

"It's likely to get a little windy later today," the weatherman's saying. "We have conflicting evidence about the gale-force number, but we can say that most of Connemara and West Galway will be affected, particularly the islands and coastal areas."

"That doesn't sound good," Freddy says, coming in to stand behind me.

We listen as the man on the radio announces that the winds will hit properly after 5 P.M.

"By that time they'll all be safely inside the marquee," I say. "And it should hold fast, even in a bit of wind. So there will be nothing to worry about."

"What about the electrics?" Freddy asks.

"They're pretty good, aren't they? Unless we have a real storm on our hands. And he didn't say anything about that."

We have been up since dawn this morning. Freddy has even made a trip over to the mainland with Mattie to get a few last-minute supplies, while I am checking everything is in order here.

The florist will arrive shortly to arrange the sprays of local wild-flowers in the chapel and marquee: speedwell and wild spotted orchids and blue-eyed grass.

Freddy returns to the kitchen to put the finishing touches to whatever food can be prepared in advance: the canapés and hors d'oeuvres, the cold starters of fish from the Connemara Smoke-house. He's passionate about food, is my husband. He can talk about a dish he's thought up in the way that a great musician might rhapsodize about a composition. It stems from his childhood; he claims that it comes from not having any variety in his diet when he was young.

I walk over to the marquee. It occupies the same higher land as the chapel and graveyard, some fifty yards to the east of the Folly along a tract of drier land, with the marshier stuff of the turf bog on either side. I hear frantic scurryings ahead and then in front of me they appear: hares startled out of their "forms," the hollows they make in the heather to bed down in. They sprint in front of me for a while, their white tails bobbing, their powerful legs kicking out, before veering off into the long grasses on either side and dis-appearing from view. Hares are shape-shifters in Gaelic folklore; sometimes when I see them here I think of all of Inis an Amplóra's departed souls, materializing once more to run amidst the heather.

In the marquee I begin my duties, filling up the space heat-ers and putting certain finishing touches on the tables: the hand-watercolored menus, the linen napkins in their solid silver rings, each engraved with the name of the guest who will take it home. There'll be a striking contrast later between the refinement of these beautifully dressed tables and the wildness outdoors. Later, when we light them, there'll be the scent of the candles from Cloon Keen Atelier, an exclusive Dublin perfumer, shipped over from the bou-tique at no small expense.

The marquee shivers around me as I do my checks. It's quite amazing to think that in a few hours this echoing empty space will be filled with people. The light in here is dull and yellow compared to the bright cold light of outside but tonight this whole structure will glow like one of those paper lanterns you send up into the night sky. People on the mainland will be able to look across and see that something exciting is going on, on Inis an Amplóra—the island they all speak about as the dead place, the haunted isle, as though it only exists as history. If I do my job right, this wedding will make sure they'll be talking about it in the present again.

"Knock knock!"

I turn. It's the groom. He's got one hand up and he's pretending to knock on the side of the canvas flap as though it were a real door.

"I'm looking for two errant ushers," he says. "We should be getting into our morning suits. You haven't seen any sign of them?"

"Oh," I say. "Good morning. No, I don't think I have. Did you sleep well?" I still can't believe it's really him, in the flesh: Will Slater. Freddy and I have watched *Survive the Night* since the start. I haven't mentioned this to the bride and groom, though, in case they worry that we're crazed superfans who are going to embarrass ourselves and them.

"Well!" he says. "Very well." He is very good-looking in real life, more so even than he looks on-screen. I reach down to straighten a fork, in case I'm staring. You can tell he's always had these looks. Some people are awkward and unformed as children but grow into attractive adults. But this man wears his beauty with such ease and grace. I suspect he uses it to great effect, is clearly very aware of its power. Every movement is like watching the working of a finely tuned machine, an animal in the peak of its condition.

"I'm pleased you slept well," I say.

"Ah," he says, "although we discovered a slight issue on going to bed."

"Oh?"

"Some seaweed under the duvet. The ushers' little prank."

"Oh my goodness," I say. "I'm very sorry. You should have

called Freddy or me. We would have sorted it out for you, remade the bed with new sheets."

"You don't have to apologize," he says—that charming grin again. "Boys will be boys." He shrugs. "Even if Johnno is a somewhat overgrown one." He comes to stand beside me, close enough that I can detect the scent of his cologne. I take a small step back. "It's looking great in here, Aoife. Very impressive. You're doing a wonderful job."

"Thank you." My tone does not invite conversation. But I imagine Will Slater isn't used to people not wanting to talk to him. I realize, when he doesn't move, that it's even possible he sees my curtness as a challenge.

"So what's your story, Aoife?" he asks, his head tilted to one side. "Don't you get lonely, living here, only the two of you?"

Is he really interested, I wonder, or simply feigning it? Why does he want to know about me? I shrug. "No, not really. I'm what you might call a loner anyways. In the winter it just feels like survival, to be honest. The summers are what we stay for."

"But how did you end up here?" He seems genuinely intrigued. He really is one of those people that has you convinced they are fascinated by your every word. It's all part of what makes him so charming, I suppose.

"I used to come here on summer holidays," I say, "when I was little. My family, we all used to come here." I don't often talk about that time. There's a lot I could tell him, though. Of cheap strawberry ice lollies on the white sand beaches, the stain of red food coloring on lips and tongues. Of rock-pooling on the other side of the island, filleting through the contents of our nets with eager fingers to find shrimp and tiny, translucent crabs. Splashing about in the turquoise sea in the sheltered bays until we got used to the freezing temperature. I won't tell him any of this, obviously: it would not be appropriate. I need to maintain that essential boundary between myself and the guests.

"Ah," he says. "I didn't think you had the local accent." I wonder what he expects. *Top o' the morning* and *to be sure, to be sure* and shamrocks and leprechauns?

"No," I say, "I have a Dublin accent, which perhaps sounds less pronounced. But I've also lived in different places. When I was younger we moved around a lot, because of my father's job—he was a university professor. England for a bit—even the States for a while."

"You met Freddy abroad? He's English, isn't he?" Still so interested, so charming. It makes me feel a little uneasy. I wonder exactly what he wants to know.

"Freddy and I met a long long time ago," I tell him.

He smiles that charming, interested smile. "Childhood sweethearts?"

"You could say that." It's not quite right, though. Freddy's several years younger than me and we were friends first, for years before anything else. Or perhaps not even friends, more clinging to one another as each other's life rafts. Not long after my mother became a shell of the woman she had once been. Several years before my father's heart attack. But I'm hardly going to tell the groom all of that. Besides everything else, in this profession it is important to never allow yourself to seem too human, too fallible.

"I see," he says.

"Now," I say, before the next question can form on his lips, whatever it may have been. "If you don't mind, I'd better be getting on with everything."

"Of course," he says. "We've got some real party animals coming this evening, Aoife," he says. "I only hope they don't cause too much mayhem." He pushes his hand through his hair and grins at me in what I think is probably intended to be a rueful, winning way. His teeth are very white when he smiles. So bright, in fact, that it makes me wonder if he gets them specially lightened.

Then he moves a little closer and puts a hand on my shoulder.

"You're doing a fantastic job, Aoife. Thank you." He leaves his hand there a beat too long, so that I can feel the heat of his palm seeping through my shirt. I am suddenly very aware that it is just the two of us in this big echoing space.

I smile—my politest, most professional smile—and take a small step away. I suppose a man like him is very sure of his sexual power. It reads as charm at first, but underneath there is something darker, more complicated. I don't think he is actually attracted to me, nothing like that. He put his hand on my shoulder because he can. Perhaps I'm reading too much into it. But it felt like a reminder that he is the one in charge, that I am working for him. That I must dance to his tune.

THE WEDDING NIGHT

THE SEARCH PARTY MARCHES OUT INTO THE DARKNESS. INSTANTLY the wind assaults them, the screaming rush of it. The flames of the paraffin torches billow and hiss and threaten to extinguish. Their eyes water, their ears ring. They find themselves having to push against the wind as though it were a solid mass, their heads bent low.

The adrenaline is coursing through them, it's them versus the elements. A feeling remembered from boyhood—deep, unnameable, feral—stirring memories of nights not altogether unlike this. Them against the dark.

They move forward, slowly. The longish tract of land between the Folly and the marquee, hemmed in by the peat bog on either side: this is where they will begin their search. They call out: "Is anyone out there?" and "Is anyone hurt?" and "Can you hear us?"

There is no reply. The wind seems to swallow their voices.

"Maybe we should spread out!" Femi shouts. "Speed up the search."

"Are you mad?" Angus replies. "When there's a bog in either direction? None of us knows where it starts. And especially not in the dark. I'm not—I'm not frightened. But I don't fancy finding, you know . . . shit on my own."

So they remain close together, within touching distance.

"She must have screamed pretty loud," Duncan shouts. "That waitress. To be heard over this."

"She must have been terrified," Angus shouts.

"You scared, Angus?"

"No. Fuck off, Duncan. But it's—it's really hard to see—"

His words are lost to a particularly vicious gust. In a shower of sparks, two of the big paraffin torches are snuffed out like birthday candles. Their bearers keep the metal supports anyway, holding them out in front like swords.

"Actually," Angus shouts. "Maybe I am a bit. Is that so shameful? Maybe I'm not enjoying being out here in a bloody gale, or . . . or looking forward to what we might find—"

His words are cut off by a panicked cry. They turn, holding their torches aloft to see Pete grasping at the air, the lower half of one leg submerged.

"Stupid fucker," Duncan shouts, "must have wandered away from the drier part." He's relieved though, they all are. For a moment they thought Pete had found something.

They haul him out.

"Jesus," Duncan shouts, as Pete, freed, sprawls on hands and knees at their feet, "second rescue of the day. Pete and I found Charlie's wife squealing like a stuck pig earlier in this bloody bog."

"The bodies . . . ," Pete moans, "in the bog . . ."

"Oh pack it in, Pete," Duncan shouts angrily. "Don't be an idiot." He swings his torch nearer to Pete's face, turns to the others. "Look at his eyes—he's tripping out of his mind. I knew it. Why did we bring him? He's a bloody liability."

They are all relieved when Pete falls silent. No one mentions the bodies again. It is a piece of folklore, they know this. They can dismiss it—albeit less easily than they might in the light of day, when everything felt more familiar. But they can't dismiss the purpose of their own mission, the possibility of what they may find. There are real dangers out here, the landscape unfamiliar and treacherous in the dark. They are only now beginning to realize it fully. To understand just how unprepared they are.

JULES
The Bride

OPEN MY EYES. THE BIG DAY.

I didn't sleep well last night and when I did I had a strange dream: the ruined chapel crumbling to dust around me as I walked into it. I woke up feeling off, uneasy. A touch of hungover paranoia from a glass too many, no doubt. And I'm sure I can still detect the lingering stench of the seaweed, even though it's hours since it was removed.

Will moved to the spare room first thing in a nod to tradition, but I find myself rather wishing he were here. No matter. Adrenaline and willpower will carry me through: they'll have to.

I look over at the dress, hanging from its padded hanger. Its wings of protective tissue dance gently to and fro in some mysterious breeze. I've learned by now that there are currents in this place that somehow find their way inside, despite closed doors and shut windows. They eddy and caper through the air, they kiss the back of your neck, they send a prickle down your spine, soft as the touch of fingertips.

Beneath my silk robe I'm wearing the lingerie I picked out for today from Coco de Mer. The most delicate Leavers lace, fine as cobweb, and an appropriately bridal cream. Very traditional, at first glimpse. But the knickers have a row of tiny mother-of-pearl buttons all the way through, so that they can be completely opened. Nice, then very naughty. I know Will will enjoy discovering them, later.

A shiver of movement through the window catches my attention. Below, on the rocks, I see Olivia. She's wearing the same baggy sweater and ripped jeans as yesterday, picking her way in bare feet toward the edge, where the sea smashes up against the granite in huge explosions of white water. Why on earth isn't she getting ready, as she should be? Her head is bent, her shoulders slumped, her hair blowing in a tangled rope behind her. There's a moment when she's so close to the edge, to the violence of the water, that my breath catches in my throat. She could fall and I wouldn't be able to get down from here in time to save her. She could drown right there while I stand here helpless.

I rap on the window, but I think she's ignoring me or—I admit it's likely—can't hear me above the sound of the waves. Luckily, though, she seems to have stepped a little farther away from the drop.

Fine. I'm not going to worry anymore about her. It's time to start getting ready in earnest. I could easily have had a makeup artist shipped over from the mainland, but there is no way in hell I'd hand over control of my appearance to someone else on such an important day. If doing your own makeup is good enough for Kate Middleton, it's good enough for me.

I reach for my makeup bag but a little unexpected tremor of my hand sends the whole thing crashing to the floor. Fuck. I'm *never* clumsy. Am I . . . nervous?

I look down at the spilled contents, shining gold tubes of mascara and lipsticks rolling in a bid for freedom across the floorboards, an overturned compact leaking a trail of bronzing powder.

There, in the middle of it all, lies a tiny folded piece of paper, slightly soot-blackened. The sight of it turns my blood cold. I stare at it, unable to look away. How is it possible that such a small thing could have occupied such a huge space in my mind over the last couple of weeks?

Why on earth did I keep it?

I unfold it even though I don't need to: the words are imprinted on my memory.

Will Slater is not the man you think he is. He's a cheat and a liar. Don't marry him.

I'm sure it's some random weirdo. Will's always getting mail from strangers who think they know him, know all about his life. Sometimes I get included in their wrath. I remember when a couple of pictures emerged of us online. *"Will Slater out shopping with squeeze, Julia Keegan."* It was a slow day at the *Mail Online*, no doubt.

Even though I knew—*knew*—it was a terrible idea, I ended up scrolling down to the comments section underneath. Christ. I've seen that bile on there before, but when it's directed at you it feels particularly poisonous, especially personal. It was like stumbling into an echo chamber of my own worst thoughts about myself.

—God she thinks shes all that doesn't she?

—Looks like a proper b*tch if you ask me.

—Jeez love haven't you heard your never meant to sleep with a man with thighs thinner than your own?

—Will! ILY! Pick me instead!:):):) She doesn't deserve you. . . . . .

—God, I hate her just from looking at her. Snotty cow.

Nearly all of the comments were like this. It was hard to believe that there were that many total strangers out there who felt such vitriol for me. I found myself scrolling down until I found a couple of naysayers:

—He looks happy. She'll be good for him!

—BTW she's behind The Download—favorite site everrrr. They'll make a good match.

Even these kinder voices were as unsettling in their own way—the sense some of them seemed to have of knowing Will—knowing *me*. That they were in a position to comment on what was good for him. Will's not a household name. But at his level of celebrity you get even more of this sort of thing, because you haven't yet risen above people thinking they have ownership of you.

The note is different to those comments online, though. It's more personal. It was dropped through the letterbox without a stamp, meaning it had to have been hand delivered. Whoever wrote it knows where we live. He or she had come to our place in Islington—which was, until Will moved in recently, *my* place. Less likely, surely, to have been a random weirdo. Or it could have been the very worst kind of weirdo.

But it occurs to me it could conceivably be someone we know. It could even be someone who's coming to this island today.

THE NIGHT THE NOTE ARRIVED I threw it into the log burner. Seconds later I snatched it back, burning my wrist in the process. I've still got the mark—a shiny, risen pink seal on the tender skin there. Every time I've caught sight of it I've thought of the note, in its hiding place. Three little words:

Don't marry him.

I rip the note in half. I rip it again, and again, until it is paper confetti. But it isn't enough. I take it into the bathroom and pull the chain, watching intently until all the pieces have disappeared, swirling out of the bowl. I imagine them traveling down through the plumbing, out into the Atlantic, the same ocean that surrounds us. The thought troubles me more than it probably should.

Anyway, it is out of my life now. It is gone. I am not going to think about it anymore. I pick up my hairbrush, my eyelash curler, my mascara: my arsenal of weapons, my quiver.

Today I am getting married and it is going to be bloody brilliant.

THE WEDDING NIGHT

CHRIST, IT'S HARD GOING IN THIS." DUNCAN PUTS UP A HAND TO shelter his face from the stinging wind, waving his torch with the other, letting off a spray of sparks. "Anyone see anything?"

See what, though? This is the question that occupies their thoughts. Each of them is remembering the waitress's words. *A body.* Every lump or divot in the ground is a potential source of horror. The torches that they hold in front of them don't help as much as they might. They only make the rest of the night seem blacker still.

"It's like being back at school," Duncan shouts to the others. "Creeping around in the dark. Anyone for Survival?"

"Don't be a dick, Duncan," Femi shouts. "Have you forgotten what we're supposed to be looking for?"

"Well, yeah. Guess you can't call it Survival, then."

"That's not funny," Femi shouts.

"All right, Femi! Calm down. I was only trying to lighten the mood."

"Yeah, but I don't think now's the time for that either."

Duncan rounds on him. "I'm out here looking, aren't I? Better than those cowardly fucks in the marquee."

"Survival wasn't funny, anyway," Angus shouts. "Was it? I

can see that now. I'm—I'm done with pretending it was all some big lark. It was totally messed up. Someone could have died . . . someone did die, actually. And the school let it carry on—"

"That was an accident," Duncan cuts in. "When that kid died. That wasn't because of Survival."

"Oh yeah?" Angus shouts back. "How'd you figure that one? Just because you loved all of that shit. I know you got off on it, when it came to your turn, freaking the younger boys out. Can't go around being a sadistic bully now, can you? I bet you haven't had such a big thrill since—"

"Guys," Femi, ever the peacekeeper, calls to them. "Now is *not* the time."

For a while they fall silent, continuing to trudge through the darkness, alone with their own thoughts. None of them has ever been out in weather like this. The wind comes and goes in squally gusts. Sometimes it drops enough for them to hear themselves think. But it is only gathering itself for the next onslaught: a busy murmuring, like the sound of thousands of insects swarming. At its highest it rises to a howl that sounds horribly like a person shriek-ing, an echo of the waitress's scream. Their skin is flayed raw by it, their eyes blinded by tears. It sets their teeth on edge—and they are in its teeth.

"It doesn't feel real, does it?"

"What's that, Angus?"

"Well, you know—one minute we're all in the marquee, pranc-ing around, eating wedding cake. Now we're out here looking for . . ." He summons his courage to say it out loud: "A *body*. What do you think could have happened?"

"We still don't know what we're looking for," Duncan answers. "We're going off the word of one kid."

"Yeah, but she seemed pretty sure . . ."

"Well," Femi calls, "there were a lot of drunk people about. It got seriously loose in there. It's not all that difficult to imagine, is it? Someone wandering out of the marquee into the dark, having an accident—"

"What about that Charlie bloke?" Duncan suggests. "He was in a total state."

"Yeah," Femi shouts, "he was definitely the worse for wear. But after what we did to him on the stag—"

"Less said about that the better, Fem."

"Did you see that bridesmaid, earlier, though?" Duncan shouts. "Anyone else think the same thing I did?"

"What?" Angus answers. "That she was trying to . . . you know . . ."

"Top herself?" Duncan shouts. "Yeah, I do. She's been acting funny since we arrived, hasn't she? Clearly a bit of a basket case. Wouldn't put it past her to have done something stup—"

"Someone's coming," Pete shouts, cutting him off, pointing into the darkness behind them, "someone's coming for us—"

"Oh shut *up*, you twat." Duncan rounds on him. "Christ, he's doing my head in. We should take him back to the marquee. Because I swear—"

"No." There's a wobble in Angus's voice. "He's right. There's something there—"

The others turn to look too, moving in a clumsy circle, bumping into each other, fighting down their unease. All of them fall silent as they stare behind them, into the night.

A light bobs toward them through the darkness. They hold out their own torches, strain to see what it is.

"Oh," Duncan shouts, in some relief. "It's just him—that fat bloke, the wedding planner's husband."

"But wait," Angus says. "What's that . . . in his hand?"

OLIVIA
The Bridesmaid

OUT OF THE WINDOW I CAN SEE THE BOATS CARRYING THE WEDding guests to the island, still distant dark shapes out on the water but moving ever closer. It will all be happening soon. I'm supposed to be getting ready, and God knows I've been up since early. I woke with this ache in my chest and a throbbing head, and took myself outside to get some air. But now I'm sitting here in my room in my bra and pants. I can't bring myself to get changed yet, into that dress. I found a little crimson stain on the pale silk where the small cut I'd made on my thigh must have bled a bit yesterday when I was trying it on. Thank God Jules didn't notice. She really might have lost her shit at that. I've scrubbed it in the sink down the hall with some cold water and soap. It's nearly all come out, thank God. Just a tiny darker pink patch was left, as a reminder.

It made me remember the blood, all those months ago. I hadn't known there would be so much. I shut my eyes. But I can see it there, beneath my eyelids.

I glance out of the window again, think about all those people arriving. I've been feeling claustrophobic in this place since we arrived, feeling like there's no escape, nowhere to run to . . . but it's going to get so much worse today. In less than an hour, Jules will call for me and then I'll have to walk down the aisle in front of her, with everyone looking at us. And then all the people—family, strangers—who I'll have to talk to. I don't think I can do it. Suddenly I feel like I can't breathe.

I think about how the only time I've felt a bit better, since I've been here, was last night in the cave, talking with Hannah. I haven't been able to speak to anyone else the way I did with her: not my mates, not anyone. I don't know what it was about her. I guess it was because she seemed like an odd one out, like she was trying to hide from everything too.

I could go and find Hannah. I could talk to her now, I think. Tell her the rest. Get it all out in the open. The thought of it makes me feel dizzy, sick. But maybe I'd feel better too, in a way—less like I can't get any air into my lungs.

My hands shake as I pull on my jeans and my sweater. If I tell her, there'll be no taking it back. But I think I've made up my mind. I think I have to do it, before I go totally mental.

I creep out of my room. My heart feels like it's moved up into my throat, beating so hard I can hardly swallow. I tiptoe through the dining room, up the stairs. I can't bump into anyone else on the way—if I do I know I'll chicken out.

Hannah's room is at the end of the long corridor, I think. As I get closer, I realize I can hear the murmur of voices coming from inside, growing louder.

"Oh for God's sake, Han," I hear. "You're being completely ridiculous—"

The door's open a crack, too. I creep a little closer. Hannah's out of sight but I can see Charlie in just a pair of boxers, gripping onto the edge of the chest of drawers as though he's trying to contain his anger.

I stop short. I feel like I've seen something I shouldn't, like I'm spying on them. I stupidly hadn't thought about Charlie being in there too—Charlie, who I used to have that cringeworthy teenage crush on. I can't do it. I can't go up and knock on their door, ask Hannah if she'll come for a chat . . . not when they're half-dressed, clearly in the middle of some sort of argument. Then I nearly jump out of my skin as another door opens behind me.

"Oh, hello, Olivia." It's Will. He's wearing suit trousers and a white shirt that hangs open to show his chest, tanned and muscular. I glance quickly away.

"I *thought* I heard someone outside," he says. He frowns at me. "What are you doing up here?"

"N-nothing," I say, or try to say, because hardly any sound comes out of my mouth, just a hoarse whisper. I turn to leave.

Back in my room I sit down on the bed. I've failed. It's too late. I've missed my chance. I should have found a way to tell Hannah last night.

I look out through the window at the boats approaching: closer now. It feels like they are bringing something bad with them to this island. But that's silly. Because it's here already, isn't it? It's me. I'm the bad thing. What I've done.

AOIFE

The Wedding Planner

THE GUESTS ARE ARRIVING. I WATCH THE APPROACH OF THE BOATS from the jetty, ready to welcome them. I smile and nod, try to present a front of decorum. I'm wearing a plain, navy dress now, low wedge heels. Smart, but not too smart. It wouldn't be appropriate to look like one of the guests. Though I needn't have worried about that. It's clear they have all made a *big* effort with their outfits: glittering earrings and painfully high heels, tiny handbags and real fur stoles (it might be June, but this is the cool Irish summer, after all). I even see a smattering of top hats. I suppose when your hosts are the owner of a lifestyle magazine and a TV star, you have to step up your game.

The guests disembark in groups of thirty or so. I can see them all taking in the island, and feel a little surge of personal pride as they do. We'll be a hundred and fifty tonight—that's a lot of people to introduce to Inis an Amplóra.

"Where's the nearest loo?" one man asks me urgently, rather green about the gills, plucking at his shirt collar as though it's strangling him. Several of the guests, in fact, are looking worse for wear beneath their finery. And yet it's not too choppy at the moment, the water somewhere between white and silver—so bright with the cold sunlight on it that you can hardly look at it. I shield my eyes and smile graciously and point them on their way. Perhaps I should offer some strong seasickness pills for the return journey, if it's going to get as windy as the forecast suggests.

I remember the first time we came here as kids, stepping off the old ferry. We didn't feel seasick, not that I remember. We stood out at the front and held on to the rail and squealed as we soared over the waves, as the water came up in big arcs and soaked us. I remember pretending we were riding a huge sea serpent.

It was warm for this part of the world that summer, and the sun would soon dry us. And children are tough. I remember running down the beaches into the water like it was nothing. I guess I hadn't yet learned to be wary of the sea.

A smart couple in their sixties get off the final boat. I somehow know even before they come over and introduce themselves that they are the groom's parents. He must get his looks from his mother and probably his coloring, too, though her hair is gray now. But she doesn't have anything like the groom's easy confidence. She gives the impression of someone trying to hide herself away, even within her own clothes.

The groom's father's features are sharper, harder. You'd never call a man like that good-looking, but I suppose you could imagine seeing a profile like his on the bust of a Roman emperor: the high, arched eyebrows, the hooked nose, the firm, slightly cruel thin-lipped mouth. He has a very strong handshake, I feel the small bones of my hand crushing into one another as he squeezes it. And he has an air of importance about him, like a politician or diplomat. "You must be the wedding planner," he says, with a smile. But his eyes are watchful, assessing.

"I am," I say.

"Good, good," he says. "Got us a seat at the front of the chapel, I hope?" On his son's wedding day it is to be expected. But I think this man would expect a seat at the front of any event.

"Of course," I tell him. "I'll take you up there now."

"You know," he says, as we walk up toward the chapel, "it's a funny thing. I'm a headmaster, at a boys' school. And about a quarter of these guests used to go there, to Trevellyan's. Odd, seeing them all grown up."

I smile, show polite interest: "Do you recognize all of them?"

"Most. But not all, not all. Mainly the larger-than-life characters, as I think you'd call them." He chuckles. "I've seen some of them do a double take already, seeing me. I have a reputation as a bit of a disciplinarian." He seems proud of this. "It's probably put the fear of God in them, catching sight of me here."

I'm sure it has, I think. I feel as though I know this man, though I have never met him before. Instinctively, I do not like him.

Afterward, I go and thank Mattie, who's captained the last boat over.

"Well done," I say. "That all went very smoothly. You've done a great job synchronizing it all."

"And you've done a fine job getting someone to hold their wedding here. He's famous, isn't he?"

"And she has a profile too." I doubt Mattie's up-to-date on women's online magazines, though. "We offered a big discount in the end, but it'll be worth it for the write-up."

He nods. "Put this place on the map, sure it will." He looks out over the water, squinting into the sunlight. "It was easy sailing this morning," he says. "But it will be different later on, to be sure."

"I've been keeping an eye on the forecast," I say. It's hard to imagine the weather turning, with the blustery sunshine we've got now.

"Aye," Mattie says. "The wind's set to get up. This evening is looking quare bad. There's a big one brewing out to sea."

"A storm?" I say, surprised. "I thought it was just a little wind."

He gives me a look that tells me just what he thinks of such Dubliner naïveté—however long we've been here, Freddy and I, we'll forever be the newcomers. "You don't need some forecast fella sitting in a studio in Galway City to tell you," he says. "Use your eyes."

He points and I follow his finger to a stain of darkness, far out, upon the horizon. I'm no seaman like Mattie, but even I can see that it doesn't look good.

"There it is," Mattie says triumphantly. "There's your storm."

JOHNNO

The Best Man

WILL AND I ARE GETTING READY IN THE SPARE ROOM. THE OTHER guys should be joining us in a sec, so I want to say the thing I've been planning first. I'm bad at stuff like this, speaking about how I feel. But I go for it anyway, turning to Will. "I wanted to tell you, mate . . . well, you know, I'm properly honored to be your best man."

"There was never anyone else in my mind for the job," he says. "You know that."

Yeah, see, I'm not *totally* sure that's true. It was a bit desperate, what I did. Because maybe I was wrong, but I got this impression that, for a while, Will's been trying to cut me out of his life. Since all the TV stuff happened, I've hardly seen the bloke. He hadn't even told me about the engagement—I read about it in the papers. And that stung, I'm not going to pretend it didn't. So I called him up and said I wanted to take him for a drink, to celebrate.

And over drinks I said it. "I accept! I'll be your best man."

Did he look a bit awkward, then? Difficult to tell with Will—he's smooth. After a short pause he nodded and said: "You've read my mind."

It wasn't totally out of the blue. He'd promised it, really. When we were kids, at Trevellyan's.

"You're my best mate, Johnno," he said to me once. "Numero

uno. My best man." I didn't forget that. History ties us together, him and me. Really, I think we both knew I was the only person for the job.

I look in the mirror, straighten my tie. Will's spare suit looks like shit on me. Hardly surprising, really, considering it's about three sizes too small. And considering I look like I was up all night, which I was. I'm sweating already in the too-tight wool. Next to Will I look even more shit because his seems to have been sewn onto his body by a host of fucking angels. Which it has, in a way, because he got it made to measure on Savile Row.

"I'm not at my best," I say. Understatement of the century.

"That's your comeuppance," Will says, "for forgetting your suit." He's laughing at me.

"Yeah," I say. "I'm such an idiot." I'm laughing at me, too.

I went to get my suit with Will a few weeks ago. He suggested Paul Smith. Obviously all the shop assistants in there looked at me like I was going to steal something. "It's a good suit," Will told me, "probably the best you can get without going to Savile Row." I did like how I looked in it, no doubt about it. I've never had a good suit before. Haven't worn anything all that smart since school. And I liked how it skimmed my belly. I've let myself go a bit over the last couple of years. "Too much good living!" I'd say, and pat the paunch. But I'm not proud of it. This suit, it hid all that. It made me look like a fucking boss. It made me look like someone I am definitely not.

I turn sideways in the mirror. The buttons on the jacket look like they're about to ping off. Yeah, I miss that belly-skimming Paul Smith wool. Anyway. No point in crying over spilled milk, as my mum would say. And not much use in being vain. I was never much of a looker in the first place.

"Ha—Johnno!" Duncan says, barreling into the room and looking very slick in his own suit, which fits perfectly. "What the fuck is that? Did yours shrink in the wash?"

Pete, Femi and Angus are close behind him. "Morning, morning, chaps," Femi says. "They're all arriving. Just went and accosted a load of old Trevs boys down at the jetty."

Pete lets out a howl. "Johnno—Jesus. Those trousers are so tight I can see what you had for breakfast, mate."

I hold my arms out to the side so my wrists stick out, prance around for them, playing the fool like always.

"Christ and look at you." Femi turns to Will. "Like butter wouldn't fucking melt."

"He was always a bad'un that looked like a good'un though," Duncan says. He leans over to ruffle Will's hair—Will quickly picks up a comb and smooths it flat again. "Wasn't he? That pretty boy face. Never got in trouble with the teachers, did you?"

Will grins at us all, shrugs. "Never did anything wrong."

"Bollocks!" Femi cries. "You got away with murder. You never got caught. Or they turned a blind eye, with your dad being head and all that."

"Nope," Will says. "I was good as gold."

"Well," Angus says, "I'll never understand how you aced those GCSEs when you did no fucking work."

I shoot a look at Will, try to catch his eye—could Angus have guessed? "You're such a jammy bastard," he says now, leaning over to give Will a pinch on the arm. Nah, on second thought he doesn't sound suspicious, just admiring.

"He didn't have any choice," Femi says. "Did you, mate? Your dad would have disowned you." Femi's always been sharp like that, reading people.

"Yeah." Will shrugs. "That's true."

It could have been social leprosy, being the headmaster's kid. But Will survived it. He had tactics. Like that girl he slept with from the local high school, passing those topless Polaroids of her all around our year. After that, he was untouchable. And actually, Will was always the one pushing me to do stuff—because he knew

THE GUEST LIST 163

he could get away with it, probably. Whereas I was scared, at least in the beginning, of losing the scholarship. It would have destroyed my parents.

"Remember that trick we used to play with the seaweed?" Duncan says. "That was all your idea, mate." He points at Will.

"No," Will says. "I'm sure it wasn't." It definitely was.

The younger ones, who it had never been done to before, would lose their shit while the rest of us lay there listening to them, cracking up. But that was how it was if you were one of the younger boys. We'd all been there. You had to take the shit that was thrown at you. You knew that in the end you'd get your turn to throw it at someone else.

There was one kid at Trevellyan's who was a pretty cool customer when we put the seaweed in his bed. A first year. He had a weird, effeminate name. Anyway, we called him Loner, because it fit. He was completely obsessed with Will, who was his head of house, maybe even a bit in love with him. Not in a sexual way, at least I don't think so. More in the way little kids sometimes are with older ones. He started doing his hair in the same way. He'd sort of trail around after us. Sometimes we'd find him lurking behind a bush or something, watching us, and he'd come and watch all our rugby matches. He was the smallest boy in the school, spoke with a funny accent and wore these big glasses, so he was a prime candidate for shitting on. But he tried pretty hard to be liked. And I remember actually being quite impressed by the fact that he survived that first term without having some sort of breakdown, like some boys did. Even when we did the seaweed trick he didn't bitch and moan about it like some of the other kids, like that chubby little friend of his—Fatfuck, I think we called him— who ran off to tell Matron. I remember being pretty impressed by that.

I tune back in to the others. I feel like I'm coming up from underwater.

"It was always the rest of us who got hauled up for it," Duncan says, "who ended up having to do the lines."

"Me most of all," Femi says. "Obviously."

"Speaking of seaweed," Will says, "it wasn't funny, by the way. Last night."

"What wasn't funny?" I look at the others, they seem confused.

Will raises his eyebrows. "I think you know. The seaweed in the bed. Jules *freaked* out. She was pretty pissed off about it."

"Well it wasn't me, mate," I say. "Honest." It's not like I'd do anything that would bring back memories of our time at Trevs.

"Not me," Femi says.

"Or me," Duncan says. "Didn't have an opportunity. Georgina and I were otherwise engaged before dinner, if you get what I'm saying . . . certainly had better things to be doing than wandering around collecting seaweed."

Will frowns. "Well, I know it was one of you," he says. He gives me a long look.

There's a knock on the door.

"Saved by the bell!" Femi says.

It's Charlie. "Apparently the buttonholes are in here?" he says. He doesn't look at any of us properly. Poor bloke.

"They're over there," Will says. "Chuck Charlie one, will you, Johnno?"

I pick one up, little sprig of green stuff and white flowers, and toss it to Charlie, but not *quite* hard enough to reach him. Charlie makes a sort of lunge for it and doesn't manage to catch it, fumbles around on the floor.

When he's finally picked it up he leaves as quickly as possible, without saying anything. I catch the others' eyes and we all stifle a laugh. And for a moment it's like we're kids again, like we can't help ourselves.

"Fellas?" Aoife calls. "Johnno? The guests are all here. They're in the chapel."

"Right," Will says, "how do I look?"

"You're an ugly bastard," I say.

"Thanks." He straightens his jacket in the mirror. Then, as the others go ahead, he turns to me. "One other thing, mate," he says, in an undertone. "Before we go down, as I know I won't get a chance to mention it later. The speech. You're not going to totally embarrass me, are you?" He says it with a grin, but I reckon he's serious. I know there's stuff he doesn't want me to get into. But he doesn't need to worry—I don't want to get into it either. It doesn't reflect well on either of us.

"Nah, mate," I say. "I'll do you proud."

JULES
The Bride

LIFT THE GOLD CROWN ONTO MY HEAD, WITH HANDS THAT—I CAN-not help noticing—betray a telltale tremble. I turn my head, this way and that. It's the one capricious element of my outfit, the one concession to a romantic fantasy. I had it made by a hatmaker's in London. I didn't want to go for a full flower crown, because that would be a bit hippy child, but I felt this would be a stylish solution. A vague nod to a bride from an Irish folktale, say.

The crown gleams nicely against my dark hair, I can see that. I pick my bouquet out of its glass vase, a gathering of local wildflowers: speedwell, spotted orchids and blue-eyed grass.

Then I walk downstairs.

"You look stunning, sweetheart."

Dad stands there in the drawing room, looking very dapper. Yes, my father is going to walk me down the aisle. I considered other possibilities, I really did. Obviously my father is not the best representative of the joys of marriage. But in the end that little girl in me, the one who wants order, who wants things done in the right way, won out. Besides, who else was going to do it? My *mother*?

"The guests are all seated in the chapel," he says. "So everything's just waiting on us now."

In a few minutes we will make the short journey along the

gravel drive that divides the chapel from the Folly. The thought makes my stomach do a somersault, which is ridiculous. I can't think of the last time I felt like this. I did a TEDx Talk last year about digital publishing to a room of eight hundred people and I didn't feel like this.

I look at Dad. "So," I say, more to distract myself from the roiling in my stomach than anything else, "you've finally met Will." My voice sounds strange and slightly strangled. I cough. "Better late than never."

"Yep," Dad says. "Sure have."

I try to keep my tone light. "What is that supposed to mean?"

"Nothing, Juju. Just—yep, sure have met him."

I know, even before it crosses my lips, that I should not ask this next question. But I can't *not* ask it. I need to know his opinion, like it or not. More than anyone else's, I have always sought my dad's approval. When I opened my A-level results in the school car park, his, not Mum's, was the expression of delight I imagined, his the "Nice one, kiddo." So I ask. "*And*?" I say. "And did you *like* him?"

Dad raises his eyebrows. "You really want to have this conversation now, Jules? Half an hour before you get married to the fella?"

He's right, I suppose. It's spectacularly bad timing. But now we've started down this path, there's no going back. And I'm beginning to suspect that his lack of an answer might be an answer in itself.

"Yes," I say. "I want to know. *Do you like him?*"

Dad does a sort of grimace. "He seems like a very charming man, Juju. Very handsome, too. Even I can see that one. A catch, to be sure."

Nothing good can come of this. And yet I can't stop. "But you must have had a stronger first impression," I say. "You've always told me you're good at reading people. That it's such an important skill in business, that you have to be able to do it very quickly . . . yada yada yada."

He makes a noise, a kind of groan, and puts his hands on his knees as though he's bracing himself. And I feel a small, hard kernel of dread, one that's been there ever since I saw the note this morning, beginning to unfurl itself in my belly.

"Tell me," I say. I can hear the blood pounding in my ears. "Tell me what your first impression of him was."

"See, I don't reckon what I think's important," Dad says. "I'm only your old da. What do I know? And you've been with him for what now . . . two years? I should say that's long enough to know."

It's not two years, actually. Nowhere near it. "Yes," I say. "It is long enough to know when it's right." It's what I've said so many times before, to friends, to colleagues. It's what I said last night, effectively, in my toast. And every time before, I meant it. At least . . . I think I did. So why, this time, do my words seem to ring so hollowly? I can't help feeling that I'm saying it not to convince my dad so much as myself. Since finding that note again the old misgivings have reared their heads. I don't want to think about those, so I change tactic. "Anyway," I add. "To be honest, Dad, I probably know him better than I know you—considering we've only spent about six weeks together in my entire life."

It was meant to wound and I see it land: he recoils as though struck by a physical blow. "Well," he says, "there you go. That's all you need to say. You won't be needing my opinion."

"Fine," I say. "Fine, Dad. But you know what? Just this once, you could have come out and told me you thought he was a great guy. Even if you had to lie through your teeth to do it. You know what I needed to hear from you. It's . . . it's selfish."

"Look," Dad says. "I'm sorry. But . . . I can't lie to you, kid. Now I understand if you don't want me to walk you up the aisle." He says it magnanimously, like he's handed me some great gift. And I feel the hurt of it go right through me.

"Of course you're going to walk me up the bloody aisle," I snap. "You've barely been in my life, you were barely free to even attend this wedding. Yes, yes, I know . . . the twins are teething or whatever it is. But I've been your daughter for thirty-four years. You know how important you are to me, even though I wish to God it were otherwise. You are one of the reasons I chose to have my wedding here, in Ireland. Because I know how much you value that heritage, I value it too. I *wish* it didn't matter to me, what you think. But it bloody does. So you're going to walk me up the aisle. That's the very least you can do. You can walk me up that aisle and look bloody delighted for me, every step of the way."

There's a knock on the door. Aoife pops her head round. "All ready to go?"

"No," I say. "I need a moment, actually."

I MARCH UPSTAIRS TO THE bedroom. I'm looking for something, the right shape, the right weight. I'll know it when I see it. There's the scented candle—or, no, the vase that held my bridal bouquet. I pick it up and heft it in my hand, readying myself. Then I hurl it at the wall, watching in satisfaction as the top half of it explodes into shards of glass.

Next I wrap my hand in a T-shirt—I've always been careful to avoid cuts, this is not about self-harm—pick up the unbroken base and slam it into the wall, again and again until I am left with smithereens, panting with the effort, my teeth gritted. I haven't done this for a while, for too long. I haven't wanted Will to see this side of me. I had forgotten how good it feels. The *release* of it. I unclench my teeth. I breathe in, out.

Everything feels a little clearer, calmer, on the other side.

I clean up the mess, as I have always done. I take my time about it. This is my day. They can all bloody well wait.

In the mirror I put my hands up and rearrange the crown on

my head where it has slipped to one side. I see that my exertions have lent a rather flattering color to my complexion. Rather appropriate, for the blushing bride. I bring my hands up to my face and massage it, rearranging, remolding my expression into one of blissful, expectant joy.

If Aoife and Dad heard anything, their faces don't belie it when I reemerge. I nod to them both. "Ready to go." Then I yell for Olivia. She emerges, from that little room next to the dining room. She looks even paler than normal, if that's possible. But miraculously she is ready—in her dress and shoes, holding her garland of flowers. I snatch my own bouquet from Aoife. Then I stride out of the door, leaving Olivia and Dad following in my wake. I feel like a warrior queen, walking into battle.

AS I WALK THE LENGTH of the aisle my mood changes, my certainty ebbs. I see them all turn to look at me and they seem a blur of faces, each oddly featureless. The Irish folksinger's voice eddies around me and for a moment I am struck by how mournful the notes sound, though it is meant to be a love song. The clouds scud overhead above the ruined spires—too fast, as in a nightmare. The wind has picked up and you can hear it whistling among the stones. For a strange moment I have the feeling that our guests are all strangers, that I'm being observed, silently, by a congregation of people I have never met before. I feel dread rise up through me, as though I've stepped into a tank of cold water. All of them are unknown to me, including the man waiting at the end, who turns his head as I approach. That excruciating conversation with Dad pinballs around in my brain—but loudest of all are the words he didn't say. I loosen my grip on his arm, try to put some distance between the two of us, as though his thoughts might further infect me.

Then suddenly it is as though a mist clears and I can see them properly: friends and family, smiling and waving. None of them, thank God, pointing phones at us. We got round that with a stern note on the wedding invite telling them to refrain from pictures during the ceremony. I manage to unfreeze my face, smile back. And then beyond them all, standing there in the center of the aisle, literally haloed in the light that has momentarily broken through the cloud: my husband-to-be. He looks immaculate in his suit. He is incandescent, as handsome as I have ever seen him. He smiles at me and it is like the sun, now warm upon my cheeks. Around him the ruined chapel rises, starkly beautiful, open to the sky.

It is perfect. It is absolutely as I had planned: better than I had planned. And best of all is my groom—beautiful, radiant—awaiting me at the altar. Looking at him, stepping toward him, it is impossible to believe that this man is anything other than the one I know him to be.

I smile.

HANNAH
The Plus-One

DURING THE CEREMONY I'VE BEEN SITTING ON MY OWN, CRAMMED onto a bench with some cousins of Jules's—Charlie had a seat reserved at the front, as part of the wedding party. There was a weird moment, as Jules walked up the aisle. She wore an expression I've never seen on her before. She looked almost afraid: her eyes wide, her mouth set in a grim line. I wondered if anyone else noticed it, or even if I'd imagined it, because by the time she joined Will at the front she was smiling, the radiant bride everyone expects to see, greeting her groom. All around me there were sighs, whispers about how wonderful they both looked together.

The whole thing has gone very smoothly since: no fumbles over the vows, like at some weddings I've been to. The two of them speak the words loudly, clearly, as we all look on silently, the only other sound the whistling of the breeze among the stones. I'm not actually looking at Jules and Will, though. I'm trying to get a glimpse of Charlie, instead, all the way down at the front. I want to try and see what expression he wears as Jules says *I will*. But it's impossible: I can see only the back of his head, the set of his shoulders. I give myself a little mental shake: What did I think I was going to see, anyway? What proof am I looking for?

And suddenly it's all over. People are getting up around me with a sudden explosion of noise, laughing and chattering. The same woman who sang while Jules walked into the chapel sings us out, too, the notes of the accompanying fiddle tripping along behind. The words are all in Gaelic, her voice ethereally high and clear, echoing slightly eerily around the ruined walls.

I follow the trail of guests outside, dodging the huge floral arrangements: big sprays of greenery and colorful wildflowers which I suppose are very chic and right for the dramatic surroundings. I think of our wedding, how my mum's friend Karen gave us mates' rates on our flowers. It was all done in rather retro pastel shades. But I wasn't about to complain; we could never have afforded a florist of our choice. I wonder what it must be like to have the money to do exactly what you want.

The other guests are a very well-dressed, well-heeled bunch. When I looked around at the rest of the congregation in the chapel I realized no one else here is wearing a fascinator. Maybe they're not the thing, in circles like this? Every other woman seems to be in an expensive-looking hat, the sort that probably comes in its own specially made box. I feel like I did on the day at school when we hadn't realized it was home clothes day and both Alice and I wore our uniforms. I remember sitting in assembly and wishing I could spontaneously combust, to avoid spending the day feeling everyone's eyes on me.

We're given crushed dried rose petals to throw as Will and Jules step out of the chapel. But the breeze is stiff enough that they're whipped quickly away. I don't see a single petal land on the newlyweds. Instead they're carried off in a big cloud, up and out toward the sea. Charlie's always telling me I'm too superstitious, but I wouldn't like that, if I were Jules.

The bridal party are taken off for photographs, while everyone else pours away to the outside of the marquee where there's a bar set up. I need some Dutch courage, I decide. I pick my way across the grass toward it, my heels sinking in with every couple of steps. A couple of barmen are taking orders, sloshing cocktail shakers. I ask for a gin and tonic, which comes with a big sprig of rosemary in it.

I chat to the barmen for a bit because they seem like the friendliest faces in this crowd. They're a couple of young local guys, home for the summer from university: Eoin and Seán.

"We normally work in the big hotel on the mainland," Seán tells me. "Used to belong to the Guinness family. Big castle on a lough. That's where people usually want to get married. Never heard of a wedding here, other than in the old days. You know this place is meant to be haunted?"

"Yeah." Eoin leans across, dropping his voice. "My gran tells some pretty dark tales about this place."

"The bodies in the turf," Seán says. "No one knows for sure how they died, but they think they were hacked to pieces by the Vikings. They're not buried in hallowed ground, so there's all this talk about them being unquiet souls."

I know they're probably just pulling my leg but I feel a prickle of disquiet all the same.

"And the rumors are that's why the latest folk all left this place in the end," Eoin says. "Because the voices from the bog got too loud for them." He grins at Seán, then at me. "I'm not looking forward to being here after dark tonight, I tell you. It's the island of ghosts."

"Excuse me," a man in aviators and a tweed jacket behind me says, crossly. "This all sounds very bloody interesting, but would you mind making me an old-fashioned?"

I take that as my cue to leave them to their work.

I decide to sneak a peek inside the marquee, via the entranceway lit by flaming torches. Inside there's a delicious floral scent from lots of expensive-looking candles. And yet (I'm not proud to be pleased by this) there's definitely a whiff of damp canvas underneath. I suppose at the end of the day it's still a big tent. But *what* a tent. "Tents" plural, actually: in a smaller one at one end there's a laminate dance floor with a stage set up for a band and at the other end is a tent containing another bar. Jesus. Why have one bar at your wedding when you can have two? In the main tent white-shirted waiters are moving with the grace of ballet dancers, straightening forks and polishing glasses.

In the middle of everything, on a silver stand, sits a huge cake. It's so beautiful that it makes me sad to think that later Jules and Will will take a knife to it. I can't begin to guess how much a cake like that costs. Probably as much as our entire wedding.

I step outside the marquee again and shiver as a gust catches me. The wind's definitely picking up. Out to sea there are white horses on the caps of the waves now.

I look at the crowd. Everyone I know at this wedding is in the bridal party. If I don't pluck up my courage I'll be standing here on my own until Charlie returns—and as soon as he's finished with the photos I suppose he'll be straight into the MC duties. So I take a big swig of my gin and tonic and launch myself into a nearby group.

They're friendly enough on the surface, but I can tell they're a group of friends catching up—and I don't belong. I stand there and sip my drink, trying not to poke myself in the eye with the rosemary. I wonder how everyone else with a gin and tonic is managing it without injuring themselves. Maybe that's a thing you get taught at private school: how to drink cocktails with unwieldy garnishes. Because everyone here, without a shadow of a doubt, went to private school.

"Do you know what the hashtag is?" one woman asks. "You know, for the wedding? I checked the invitation but I couldn't see it."

"I'm not sure there is one," her friend replies. "Anyway, the signal here's so awful you wouldn't be able to upload anything while you're on the island."

"Maybe that's *why* they chose this place for the wedding," the first says, knowingly. "You know, because of Will's profile."

"It's very mysterious," the other woman says. "I have to admit I'd have expected Italy—the Lakes, perhaps. That seems to be a trend, doesn't it?"

"But then Jules is a trend*setter*," a third woman chips in. "Perhaps this is the new thing"—a great gust of wind nearly sends her hat flying and she clamps it down with a firm hand—"weddings on godforsaken islands in the middle of nowhere."

"It's rather romantic, isn't it? All wilderness and ruined glory. Makes you think of that Irish poet. Keats."

"Yeats, darling."

The women have the deep, real tans of summer holidays on Greek islands. I know this because they start talking about them next, comparing the benefits of Hydra over Crete. "God," one of them says now, "why would anyone fly economy with kids? I mean, talk about starting the holiday on a bad note." I wonder what they'd say if I chipped in and started debating the benefits of one New Forest campsite versus another. *Personally I think it's all about which has the best chemical loos,* I could say, in the same tone in which they're comparing which waterfront restaurant has the best views. I'll have to save that one up to tell Charlie later. Though, as proven last night, Charlie always gets a bit funny around posh people—a little unsure of himself and defensive.

The guy on my right turns to me: an overgrown schoolboy, one of those very round, pink-and-white faces at odds with a receding hairline. "So," he says, "Hannah, is it? Bride or groom?"

I'm so relieved that someone's actually deigned to talk to me I could kiss him.

"Er—bride."

"I'm groom. Went to school with the bastard." He sticks out his hand, I shake it. I feel like I've walked into his office for an interview. "And you know Julia, how . . . ?"

"Oh," I say. "I'm married to Charlie—he's Jules's mate? He's one of the ushers."

"And where's that accent from then?"

"Um, Manchester. Well—the outskirts." Though I always feel like I've lost a lot of it, having lived down south for so long.

"Support United, do you? You know, I went up for a corporate thing a few years ago. OK match. Southampton I think it was. Two-one, one-nil—not a draw, anyway, which would have been fucking boring. Dreadful food, though. Fucking inedible."

"Oh," I say. "Well, my dad supports—"

But he's turned away, bored already, and is in conversation with the guy next to him.

So I introduce myself to an older couple, mainly because they don't seem to be in conversation with anyone else.

"I'm the groom's father," the man says. This strikes me as an odd way to phrase it. Why not just say: "I'm Will's dad"? He indicates the woman next to him with one long-fingered hand: "and this is my wife."

"Hello," she says, and looks at her feet.

"You must be very proud," I say.

"Proud?" He frowns at me, inquiringly. He's tall, with no stoop, so I find myself having to crane my neck slightly to look up at him. And maybe it's the long, hooked shape of it, but I feel that he is looking down his nose at me. I'm aware of a slight tightness in my stomach which most reminds me of being told off by a teacher at school.

"Well, yes," I say, flustered. I didn't think I'd have to explain myself. "Mainly because of the wedding, I suppose, but also because of *Survive the Night*."

"Mm." He seems to be considering this. "But it's not a *profession*, is it?"

"Well, um—I suppose not in the traditional sense—"

"He wasn't always the best student. Got himself into a few scrapes, you know—but he's a bright enough boy, all told. He managed to get into a fairly good university. Could have gone into politics or law. Perhaps not of the first rank in those, but respectable."

Jesus Christ. I've remembered that Will's dad is a headmaster. Right now it sounds as though he could be talking about any random boy, not his own son. I'd never have thought I'd feel pity for Will, who seems to have everything going for him—but right now I think I do.

"Do you have children?" he asks me. "Any sons?"

"Yes, Ben, he's—"

"You could do worse than to think of Trevellyan's. I know our methods may be considered a little . . . severe by some, but they have made great men out of some unpromising raw materials."

The idea of handing Ben into the clutches of this profoundly cold man fills me with horror. I want to tell him that even could I afford it and even if Ben were anywhere near senior school age there'd be no way I'd send my son to a place run by him. But I smile politely and excuse myself. If Will's parents are here, the bridal party must have returned from having their photos taken. And if so, why hasn't Charlie come to find me? I search the crowd, finally spotting him in a big group with the rest of the ushers and several other men. I feel a little dart of anger and move toward him as quickly as my heels will let me.

"Charlie," I say, trying not to sound hectoring. "God, it feels like you've been gone hours. I had the weirdest conversation—"

"Hey, Han," he says, a bit absently. By the slight squint he gives me, and perhaps some other subtle change in his features, I'm certain he's already had a bit to drink. There's a full glass of champagne in one of his hands, but I don't think it's his first. I remind myself that he's always in control, that he knows what his limit is. He's a grown-up. "Oh," he says. "By the way. You can probably take that thing off your head now."

He means the fascinator. I feel my cheeks grow hot as I lift it off. Is he ashamed of me?

One of the men Charlie has been talking to walks over and claps Charlie on the shoulder. "This your old lady, Charlie?"

"Yeah," Charlie says. "Rory, this is my wife, Hannah. Hannah, this is Rory. He was on the stag."

"Lovely to meet you, Hannah," Rory says, with a flash of teeth. So much *charm*, all these public schoolboys. I think of the ushers outside the chapel: *Can I offer you a program? Would you like some dried rose petals?* Butter wouldn't melt. But I saw how they got last night. I wouldn't trust any of them further than I could throw them.

"Hannah," Rory says, "I think I should apologize for the state we sent your boy back in after the stag do. But it was all fun and games, wasn't it, Charlie, mate? Last one in and all that."

I don't know what that means, exactly. I'm watching Charlie. And I see it as it happens, the transformation of my husband's face. The tightening of the features, lips disappearing into a taut line, until he wears the very same expression he did when I collected him from the airport after that weekend.

"What on earth *did* you all get up to?" I ask Rory, keeping my tone playful. "Charlie definitely won't tell me."

Rory seems relieved. "Good man," he says, clapping Charlie on the shoulder again. "What happens on the stag stays on the stag and all that." He winks at me. "All good fun, anyhow. Boys will be boys."

"Charlie?" I ask, as Rory peels away and we have a moment alone together. "Have you been drinking?"

"Only a sip," he says. I don't *think* he's slurring. "You know, to lubricate things."

"Charlie—"

"Han," he says, firmly. "A couple of glasses aren't going to derail me."

"And—" I think of him emerging from Stansted airport, looking hollow-eyed and shell-shocked. "What *happened* on the stag do? What was he talking about?"

"Ah, God." Charlie runs a hand through his hair, screws up his face. "I don't know why it got to me so much. It's—well it's because I'm not one of them, I suppose. But it was pretty horrible at the same time."

"Charlie," I say, feeling disquiet curl through my stomach. "What did they do?"

And then my husband turns to me and hisses, between his teeth, that nasty little trace of something—someone—else creeping into his words. "I don't want to *fucking* talk about it, Hannah."

There it is. Oh God. Charlie *has* been drinking.

JOHNNO

The Best Man

I DOWN MY GLASS OF CHAMPAGNE AND TAKE ANOTHER OFF A PASS-
ing waitress. I'll drink this one quickly, too, then maybe I'll feel
more—I dunno, myself. This morning, seeing all of this, seeing
everything Will has . . . well, it's made me feel a little shitty. I'm
not proud of that. I feel bad about it, of course I do. Will's my best
mate. I'd like to just be happy for him. But it's dredged it all up,
being with the boys again. It's like none of it affected him, none of
it held him back. Whereas I've always felt, I don't know, like I don't
deserve to be happy.

There are so many familiar faces in the crowd outside the
chapel: blokes from the stag and others who didn't go but who
were at school with us. "No plus-one, Johnno?" they ask me.
And, "Gonna be putting the moves on some lucky lady tonight
then?"

"Maybe," I say. "Maybe."

There's a bit of betting about who I'm going to try to crack on
with. Then they're off talking about their jobs, their houses. Share
options and portfolios. Some story about the latest politician who's
made an arse of himself—or herself. Not much I can add to this
conversation as I can't catch the name and even if I could I probably
wouldn't know it. I stand here feeling stupid, feeling like I don't
belong. I never really have.

They all have high-powered jobs now, this lot. Even the ones that I don't remember as being all that bright. And they all look pretty different to how they did at school. Not surprising, considering it's not all that far off twenty years ago. But it doesn't feel that way. Not to me. Not right now, standing here, in this place. Looking at each face, it doesn't matter how much time has passed, or that there are bald spots where there was once hair, or dark where there was once blond, or contacts now, instead of glasses. I can place them all.

See, even now, even though I've been such a fucking disappointment, my folks have still got the school photo in pride of place on the mantelpiece in our living room. I've never seen it with a speck of dust on it. They're so proud of that photo. *Look at our boy, at his big posh school. One of them.* The whole school out on the pitches in front of the main building, with the cliffs on the other side. All of us perched on one of those metal stands, looking good as gold, with our hair brushed into side-partings by Matron and big, stupid grins: *Smile for the cameras, boys!*

I'm grinning at them all now, like I did in that photo. I wonder if they're secretly all looking at me and thinking the same old thoughts. Johnno: the waster. The fuckup. Always good for a laugh—not much more. Turned out exactly how they thought. Well, that's where I'll prove them wrong. Because I've got the whiskey business to talk about, haven't I?

"Johnno, mate. Can't believe how long it's been." Greg Hastings—third row, second from the left. Had a hot mum, whose looks he definitely didn't inherit.

"Ha, trust you, Johnno, to forget your bloody suit!" Miles Locke—fifth row, somewhere in the middle. Bit of a genius, but not too much of a geek about it, so he got by.

"Didn't forget the rings at least! Wish you had done, that would have been the *ultimate*." Jeremy Swift—up in the far-right-hand corner. Swallowed a fifty-pence piece in a dare and had to go to hospital.

"Johnno, big fella—you know, I have to tell you, I'm still recovering from the stag. You did a number on me. Christ and that poor bloke! We *really* did a number on him. He's here, isn't he?" Curtis Lowe—fourth row, fifth from the right. Nearly played tennis professionally but ended up an accountant.

See? They call me thick. But I've got a pretty good memory, when it comes down to it.

There's one face in that photo I can't ever bring myself to look at. Bottom row, with the smallest kids, out to the right. *Loner,* the little kid who worshipped Will, would do anything to please him. Anything we asked. He'd steal extra rolls and butter from the kitchens for us, brush the mud off our rugby boots, clean our dorm. All stuff we didn't actually *need* or could've done ourselves. But it was fun, in a way, to think up things for him to do.

We'd find ourselves asking for more and more stupid things. One time we told him to climb up onto the school roof and hoot like an owl, and he did it. Another time we got him to set off all the fire alarms. It was hard not to keep pushing, to see how far he would go. Sometimes we'd go through his stuff, eat the sweets his mum had sent him or pretend to get off from the photo of his hot older sister on the beach. Or we'd find the letters he'd written to send home and read them aloud in a whiny voice: *I miss you all so much.* And sometimes we'd even knock him about a bit. If he hadn't cleaned our rugby boots well enough, say—or what we *said* wasn't clean enough, because he always did a pretty good job. I'd get him to stand there while I hit him on his arse with the studded side of the boot as an "incentive." Seeing what we could get away with. And he'd have let us get away with anything.

I grab another glass of champagne, down it. This one hits home, finally; I feel myself float a little higher. I move into the big group

of Old Trevellyans. I want to tell them all about the whiskey business. Just for the next half an hour or so. Just so they might finally
realize I'm as good as any of them. But the conversation has moved
on and I can't think of a way to get it back.

Someone taps me on the shoulder, hard. I turn round and I'm
face-to-face with him: Mr. Slater. Will's dad—but first and foremost, always, headmaster of Trevellyan's.

"Jonathan Briggs," he says. "You haven't changed one bit." He
doesn't mean this as a compliment.

Shit, I'd been hoping to give him a wide berth. The sight of
him has the same effect on me it always did. Would have thought
now, my being an adult, it might be different. But I'm as shit-
scared of him as ever. Funny, considering he was the one that once
saved my bacon, really.

"Hello, sir," I say. My tongue feels like it's stuck in my throat.
"I mean, Mr. Slater." I think he'd prefer it if I called him "sir." I
glance over my shoulder. The group I was in before has closed up,
so we're stuck on the outside of it now: just him and I. No escape.

He's looking me up and down. "I see you're dressed in the same
unusual way. That blazer you had at Trevellyan's: too large at the
beginning and far too small at the end."

Yeah, because my folks could only afford the one.

"And I see you're still hanging around my son," he says. He
never liked me. But then I can't imagine him liking anyone much,
not even his own child.

"Yeah," I say. "We're best mates."

"Oh is that what you are? I was always rather under the impression you simply did his dirty work for him. Like when you broke
into my office to steal those GCSE papers."

For a moment everything around me goes still and quiet. I'm so
surprised I can't even get a word out.

"Oh yes," Mr. Slater continues, unfazed by my silence. "I know.
You think that simply because it wasn't reported you'd got away

with it? It would have been a disgrace on the school, on my name, if it had got out."

"No," I say, "I dunno what you're talking about." But what I think is: You don't know the half of it. Or maybe you do and you've got an even better poker face than I realized.

I manage to get away after this. I go and search for more drink. Something stronger. There's a bar they've set up, near the marquee. They can't pour the stuff fast enough. People are asking for two, three drinks, pretending they're for friends and plus-ones when really I can see them necking them as they walk away. It's going to get loose, this evening, especially with the gear Peter Ramsay's brought. When I pick up my whiskey—the stuff I brought—I notice that my hand is trembling.

Then I see this bloke I recognize, across the crowd of people. He looks at me, frowning. But he's *not* from Trevellyan's. He's about fifty, anyway, way too old to be in that photo. And it annoys me at first, because I can't work out where I know him from.

He has a too-fashionable hipster haircut, even though he's gray and going a bit bald and wears a suit with sneakers. He looks like he's stepped out of some wanky Soho office and isn't quite sure how he ended up here in the middle of nowhere on some random island.

For a few minutes, genuinely, I haven't got a single clue where I could have met someone like him. Then I think we both work it out at the same time. Shit. It's the producer of *Survive the Night*. Something French and fancy-sounding. *Piers*. That's it.

He walks toward me. "Johnno," he says. "It's good to see you."

I'm kind of flattered that he remembers my name, that he recognizes my face. Then I remember that he hadn't liked my face enough to put me on his TV show, so I dial down my enthusiasm. "Piers," I say, sticking out a hand. I have no fucking idea why he wants to come and speak to me. We only met the once, when I came to do the screen test with Will. Surely it would be less embarrassing if we just raised a glass to each other over everyone's heads and left it at that?

"Long time no see, Johnno," he says, rocking back and forth on his heels. "I hardly recognized you . . . with all that hair." He's being polite. My hair's not that much longer. But I probably look about fifteen years older than the last time we met. It's all the drinking, I guess. "And what have you been up to?" he asks. "I know there must have been something very worthwhile keeping you busy."

I feel like there's something strange about how he put that, but I gloss over it. "Well." I puff myself up. "I've been making whiskey, Piers." I try hard to do the big spiel, but to be honest I can't stop thinking about the way this bloke rejected me with a few lines in an email.

Not quite the right fit for the show.

People don't realize this about me, you see. They see old Johnno, the wild one, the crazy one . . . without much going on backstage. And of course I like them thinking that, I play up to it. But I do feel stuff too, and I am embarrassed by this conversation, just like I was when the production company dropped me. At least I got paid a couple of grand for the concept, I guess.

See, the idea for the show was mine. I'm not saying I thought up the whole thing. But I know it was me who planted the seed. A while ago Will and I were sitting in a pub, having a drink. It had always been me who suggested we meet up. Will was always too busy, even though he didn't have much of a TV career to speak of in those days, just an agent. But even if he puts me off a couple of times he never cancels. There's too much of a bond between us for this friendship to die. He knows that too.

I must have got pretty drunk, because I even brought up the game we used to play at school: Survival. I remember Will giving me this look. I think he was afraid of what I might say next. But I wasn't going to go into any of that. We never do. I'd been watching this show the night before with some adventurer guy and it seemed so soft. So I said, "That would have made a much better idea for a TV program than most of the so-called survival stuff you see, wouldn't it?"

He had looked at me differently, then.

"What?" I asked.

"Johnno," he said. "That might be the best idea you've ever come up with."

"Yeah, but you couldn't actually do it. You know . . . because of what happened."

"That was a million years ago," he said. "And it was an accident, remember?" And then, when I didn't respond: "Remember?"

I looked at him. Did he really believe that? He was waiting for an answer.

"Yeah," I said. "Yeah it was."

Next thing I knew, he'd got us both the screen test. And the rest, you could say, was history. For him, anyway. Obviously they didn't want my ugly mug in the end.

I realize that Piers is looking at me a bit funny. I think he's just asked me something. "Sorry," I say. "What was that?"

"I was saying that it sounds like you've got your work cut out for you. I suppose at least our loss is whiskey's gain."

Our *loss*? But it wasn't their loss: they didn't want me, full stop.

I take a big swig of my drink. "Piers," I say. "You didn't *want* me on the show. So, with the greatest possible respect, what the fuck are you talking about?"

AOIFE
The Wedding Planner

ON THE HORIZON THE STAIN OF BAD WEATHER IS ALREADY spreading, darkening. The breeze has stiffened. Silk dresses flap in the wind, a couple of hats cartwheel away, cocktail garnishes are whisked into the air.

But over the growing sound of the wind the voice of the singer rises:

> *is tusa ceol mo chroí,*
> *Mo mhuirnín*
> *is tusa ceol mo chroí.*
> *You're the music of my heart,*
> *My darling,*
> *You're the music of my heart.*

For a moment it is as though I have forgotten how to breathe. That song. My mother sang it to us when we were little. I force myself to inhale, exhale. Focus, Aoife. You have too much to be getting on with.

The guests are already crowding about me with demands:

"Are there any gluten-free canapés?"

"Where's the best signal here?"

"Will you ask the photographer to take some photos of us?"

"Can you change my seat on the table plan?"

I move among them, reassuring, answering their questions, pointing them in the right direction for the lavatories, the cloakroom, the bar. There seem to be so many more than a hundred and fifty of them: they are everywhere, streaming in and out of the fluttering doors of the marquee, thronging in front of the bar, swarming across the grass, posing for smartphone pictures, kissing and laughing and eating canapés from the army of waiters. I've already corralled several guests away from the bog before they can begin to get in trouble.

"Please," I say, heading off another group who are trying to enter the graveyard, clutching their drinks, as though they're looking around some fairground attraction. "Some of these stones are very old and very fragile."

"It doesn't look as though anyone's visited them in a while," says one of the men in a calm-down-dear sort of voice as they leave, a little begrudgingly. "It's a deserted island, isn't it? So I don't *think* anyone's going to mind." Evidently he hasn't spotted my own family's little patch yet and I am glad of that. I don't want them milling about among the stones, spilling their drinks and treading upon the hallowed ground in their spike heels and shiny brogues, reading the inscriptions aloud. My own tragedy written there for them all to pore over.

I had prepared myself for how strange it would feel, having all these people, here. It is a necessary evil: This is what I have wanted, after all. To bring people to the island again. And yet I hadn't realized quite how much of a trespass it would seem.

OLIVIA
The Bridesmaid

THE CEREMONY WENT ON FOR HOURS—OR THAT'S HOW IT FELT. IN my thin dress I couldn't stop shivering. I held my bouquet so tightly that the thorns of the rose stems bit through the white silk ribbon into my hands. I had to suck the little drops of blood from my palms while no one was watching.

Eventually, though, it was over.

But after the ceremony there were photos. My face hurts from trying to smile. My cheeks *ache*. The photographer kept singling me out, telling me I need to "turn that frown upside down, darling!" I tried. I know it can't have seemed like a smile on the other side—I know it must have looked like I was baring my teeth, because that's how it felt. I could tell Jules was getting annoyed with me, but I didn't know how to do anything about it. I couldn't remember how to smile properly. Mum put a hand on my shoulder. "Are you all right, Livvy?" She could see something was up, I guess. That I'm not all right, not at all.

People crowd around: aunts and uncles and cousins I haven't seen for ages.

"Livvy," my cousin Beth asks, "you still with that boyfriend? What was his name?" She's a few years younger than me: fifteen. And I've always felt like she's kind of looked up to me. I remember telling her all about Callum last year, at my aunt's fiftieth, and feeling proud as she hung on my words.

"Callum," I say. "No . . . not anymore."

"And you've finished your first year at Exeter now?" my aunt Meg asks. Mum hasn't told her about me leaving, then. When I try to nod my head it feels too heavy for my neck. "Yeah," I say, because it's easier to pretend, "yeah, it's good."

I try to answer all their questions but it's even more exhausting than the smiling. I want to scream . . . inside I *am* screaming. I can see some of them looking at me in confusion—I even see them glancing at each other, like: "What's up with her?" *Concerned looks.* I suppose I don't seem like the Olivia they remember. That girl was chatty and outgoing and she laughed a lot. But then I'm not the Olivia *I* remember. I'm not sure if or how I'll ever get back to her. And I can't act out a role for them. I'm not like Mum.

Suddenly I feel like I can't breathe again, like I can't get the air into my lungs properly. I want to get away from their questions and their kind, concerned faces. I tell them I'm going off to find the loo. They don't seem bothered. Maybe they're relieved. I peel away from the group. I think I hear Mum call my name but I keep on walking and she doesn't call again, probably because she's got distracted talking to someone. Mum loves an audience. I go a little faster. I take off my stupid heels, which have already got covered in dirt. I'm not sure where I'm going exactly, other than in the opposite direction to everyone else.

On my left are cliffs of black stone, shining wet from the water spray. The land drops away in places, like a big chunk of it has suddenly disappeared into the sea, leaving a jagged line behind. I wonder what it would feel like to have the ground suddenly fall away under me, suddenly disappear, so I'd have no choice but to go down with it. For a moment I realize I'm standing here almost hoping for it to happen.

Below the track I'm following I see little pockets in between the cliffs with beaches of white sand. The waves are big, whitecapped far out. I let the wind blow over me, till my hair feels like it's being ripped from my head, till my eyelids feel like they're trying to turn inside out, the wind pushing at me like it's trying its best to shove me over. There's a sting of salt on my face.

The water out there is a bright blue, like the color of the sea in a photo of a Caribbean island, like the one where my mate Jess went last year with her family and from which she posted about fifty thousand photos on Instagram of herself in a bikini (all totally Facetuned, of course, so her legs looked longer and her waist looked smaller and her boobs looked bigger). I suppose that it's all quite beautiful, what I am looking at, but I can't *feel* it being beautiful. I can't properly feel any good things anymore: like the taste of food, or the sun on my face or a song I like on the radio. Looking out at the sea all I feel is a dull pain, somewhere under my ribs, like an old injury.

I find a way down where it's not so steep, where the ground meets the beach in a slope, not a cliff. I have to fight my way through bushes that are growing on the slope, small and tough and thorny. They snag at my dress as I go past and then I trip on a root, and I'm falling down the bank, tripping, tumbling forward. I can feel the silk tear—Jules will flip—and then I'm down on my knees—bam! And my knees are stinging and all I can think is that the last time I fell like this I was a kid, at school, maybe nine years ago. I want to cry like a kid as I stumble down to the beach, because it should hurt, my whole body should hurt, but no tears will come—I haven't been able to make them come for a long time. If I could cry it might all be better, but I can't. It's like an ability I've lost, like a language I've forgotten.

I sit on the wet sand, and I can feel it soaking through my dress. My knees are covered with proper playground grazes, pink and raw and gravelly. I open my little beaded bag and carefully take out the razor blade. I lift up the fabric of my dress and press the razor to my skin. Watch the tiny bright red beads of blood come up—slow at first, then faster. Even though I can feel the pain it doesn't feel like my blood, my leg. So I squeeze the cut, bringing more blood to the surface, waiting to feel like it belongs to me.

The blood is bright red, so bright, kind of beautiful. I put a finger to it and then taste my finger, taste the metal of it. I remember the blood after the "procedure," which is what they called it. They said that "a little light spotting" would be totally normal. But it went on for weeks, it felt like; the dark brown stain appearing in my knickers, like something inside me was rusting away.

I REMEMBER EXACTLY WHERE I was when I realized I hadn't had my period. I was with my friend Jess, at a house party some second years were holding at their place, and she'd been telling me she'd had to raid the cupboards in the bathroom for tampons, as hers had come early. I remember how when she told me I felt this odd feeling, like indigestion in my chest, like I couldn't draw a breath—a little like now. I realized I couldn't think of the last time I had to use a tampon, to use anything. And I'd felt strange, kind of bloated and gross and tired, but I thought that was the crap food I ate and feeling shitty over things with Steven. It had been a while. Some months, my periods are really light, so they hardly bother me at all. But they're always there. They're still regular.

It was halfway through the new term. I went to the uni doctor and took a pregnancy test with her, because I didn't trust myself to do it properly. She told me it was positive. I sat there, staring at her, like I wasn't going to fall for it, like I was waiting for her to tell me she was joking. I didn't really believe it could be true. And then she started talking about what my options were, and did I have anyone I could talk to about it? I couldn't say anything. I remember how I opened my mouth a couple of times and nothing came out, not even air, because again I could hardly breathe. I felt like I was suffocating. She sat there, looking sympathetic, but of course she couldn't come and give me a hug because of all that legal stuff. And right then I really, really needed a hug.

I got out of there and I was all shaky and weird, I couldn't walk properly—I felt like a car had slammed into me. My body didn't feel like mine. All this time it had been doing this secret, strange thing . . . without me knowing about it.

I couldn't even make my fingers work on my phone. But eventually I unlocked it. I WhatsApped him. I saw that he'd read it straightaway. I saw the three little dots appear—it told me that he was "typing," at the top. Then they disappeared. Then they appeared again, and he was "typing" for about a minute. Then nothing again.

I called him, because clearly he had his phone right there, in his hand. He didn't answer. I called him again, it rang out. The third time, it went straight to the voice mail message. He'd declined it. So I left him a voice mail—though I'm not sure he would have been able to work out what I was actually saying, my voice was wobbling so much.

Mum took me to the clinic to have it done. She drove all the way from London to Exeter, nearly four hours door to door, and waited for me while I had it done and then drove me home afterward.

"It's the best thing," she told me. "It's the best thing, Livvy darling. I had a baby when I was your age. I didn't think I had any other choice. I was at the beginning of my life, of my career. It ruined everything."

I knew Jules would like hearing that one. I heard an argument with them once, when Jules had screamed at Mum: "You never wanted me! I know I was your biggest mistake . . ."

It was the only thing I could have done. But it would have been so much easier if he'd answered, if he'd let me know he understood, felt it too. Just a line—that's all it would have taken.

"He's a little bastard," Mum told me. "For leaving you to go through all of this on your own."

"Mum," I told her—in case through some freak chance she happened to bump into Callum and go off on a tirade against him, "he doesn't know. I don't want him to know."

I don't know why I didn't tell her it wasn't Callum. It's not like Mum's a prude, like she would judge me for the whole thing with Steven. But I suppose I knew how much worse it would make me feel, reliving it all, feeling that rejection all over again.

I remember everything about that drive back from the clinic. I remember how Mum seemed so different to usual, how I'd never really seen her like that before. I saw how her hands gripped the steering wheel, hard enough that the skin went white. She kept swearing, under her breath. Her driving was even worse than normal.

She told me, when we got home, to go and lie on the sofa, and she brought me biscuits and made me tea and arranged a rug over me, even though it was pretty warm. Then she sat down next to me, with her own cup of tea, even though I'm not sure I'd ever seen her drink tea before. She didn't drink it, actually, she just sat there with her hands clenched around her mug as tight as they had been on the steering wheel.

"I could kill him," she said again. Her voice didn't even sound like her own; it was low and rough. "He should have been there with you, today," she said, in that same strange voice. "It's probably a good thing I don't know his full name. The things I would do to him if I did."

I STARE OUT INTO THE waves. I think being in the sea will make me feel better. I think it's the only thing that will work, all of a sudden. It looks so clean and beautiful and flawless, like being inside it would be like being inside a precious stone. I stand up, brush the sand off my dress. Shit . . . it's cold in the wind. But actually it's kind of a good cold—not like the cold in the chapel. Like it's blowing every other thought out of my head.

I leave my shoes in the wet sand. I don't bother stepping out of my dress. I walk into the water and it's ten degrees cooler than the air, absolutely freezing freezing cold, it makes my breath come all fast and I can only take in little gulps of air. I feel the sting of the cut on my leg as the salt gets in it. And I push farther into it, so that the water comes up to my chest, then my shoulders and now I really can't breathe properly, like I'm wearing a corset. I feel tiny fireworks explode in my head and on the surface of my skin and all the bad thoughts loosen, so I can look at them more easily.

I put my head under, shaking it to encourage the bad thoughts to float away. A wave comes, and the water fills my mouth. It's so salty it makes me gag and when I gag I swallow more water and don't manage to breathe and more water goes in, and it's in my nose too and each time I open my mouth for air more water comes in instead, great big salty gulps of it. I can feel the movement of the water under my feet and it feels like it's tugging me somewhere, trying to take me with it. It's like my body knows something I don't because it's fighting for me, my arms and legs thrashing out. I wonder if this is a bit what drowning is like. Then I wonder if I *am* drowning.

JULES
The Bride

W ILL AND I HAVE BEEN AWAY FROM THE MELEE, HAVING OUR photos taken beside the cliffs. The wind has definitely picked up. It did so as soon as we stepped outside the protection of the chapel and the handfuls of thrown rose petals were whipped away and out to sea before they could even touch us. Thank goodness I decided to wear my hair down, so the elements can only do so much damage. I feel it rippling out behind me, and the train of my skirt lifts in a stream of silk. The photographer loves this. "You look like an ancient Gaelic queen, with that crown—and your coloring!" he calls. Will grins. "*My* Gaelic queen," he mouths. I smile back at him. My husband.

When the photographer asks us to kiss I slip my tongue into his mouth and he responds in kind, until the photographer—somewhat flustered—suggests that these photos might be a little "racy" for the official records.

Now we return to our guests. The faces that turn toward us as we walk among them are already flushed with warmth and booze. In front of them I feel oddly stripped bare, as though the stress of earlier might be visible on my face. I try to remind myself of the pleasure of friends and loved ones being here together in one place, clearly enjoying themselves. And that it's worked: I have created an event that people will remember, will talk about, will try—and probably fail—to replicate.

On the horizon, darker clouds mass ominously. Women clasp their hats to their heads, their skirts to their thighs, with small shrieks of hilarity. I can feel the wind tugging at my outfit, too, flinging up the heavy silk skirt of my dress as though it were light as tissue, whistling through the metal spokes of my crown as if it would quite like to rip it from my head and hurl it out to sea.

I glance across at Will, to see if he's noticed. He's surrounded by a gaggle of well-wishers and is being his usual, charming self. But I sense that he's not fully engaged. He keeps glancing distractedly over the shoulders of the various relatives and friends who come up to greet us as though he's searching for someone, or looking at something.

"What is it?" I ask. I take his hand. It looks different to me now, foreign, with its plain band of gold.

"Is that—Piers—over there?" he says. "Talking to Johnno?"

I follow his gaze. There, indeed, is Piers Whiteley, producer of *Survive the Night,* balding head bent earnestly as he listens to whatever Johnno has to say.

"Yes," I say, "that's him. What's the matter?" Because *something* is the matter, I'm sure of it—I can see it from Will's frown. It's an expression I rarely see him wear, this look of slightly anxious distraction.

"Nothing—in particular," he says. "I—well, it's just a little awkward, you know. Because Johnno was turned down for the TV stuff. Not sure who it's more awkward for, to be honest. Perhaps I should go over and rescue one of them."

"They're grown men," I say. "I'm sure they can handle themselves."

Will hardly seems to have heard me. In fact, he's dropped my hand and is making his way across the grass toward them, pushing politely but decisively past the guests who turn to greet him as he goes.

It's very out of character. I look after him, wondering. I'd thought the sense of unease would leave me, after the ceremony, after we'd said those all-important vows. But it's still with me, sitting like sickness in the pit of my stomach. I have the sense that there's something malign stalking me, as though at the very edge of my vision, of which I can never get a proper glimpse. But that's crazy. I just need a moment to myself, I decide, away from the fray.

I move quickly past the guests on the outskirts of the crowd, head down, stride purposeful, in case one of them tries to stop me. I enter the Folly via the kitchen. It's blissfully quiet inside. I close my eyes for a long moment, in relief. On the butcher's block in the center of the kitchen, something—part of the meal for later, no doubt—is covered with a large cloth. I find a glass, run myself a cold drink of water, listen to the soothing tick of the clock on the wall. I stand there facing the sink and as I sip my water I count to ten and back down again. *You're being ridiculous, Jules. It's all in your head.*

I'm not sure what it is that makes me aware I am not alone. Some animal sense, maybe. I turn and in the doorway I see—

Oh God. I gasp, stumble backward, my heart hammering. It's a man holding a huge knife, his front smeared with blood.

"Jesus Christ," I whisper. I shrink away from him, just managing not to drop my glass. A beat of pure fear, of racing adrenaline . . . then logic reasserts itself. It's Freddy, Aoife's husband. He's holding a carving knife, and the blood smears are on the butcher's apron he wears tied about his waist.

"Sorry," he says, in that awkward way of his. "Didn't mean to give you a fright. I'm carving the lamb in here—there's a better surface than in the catering tent."

As if to demonstrate, he lifts the cloth from the butcher's block and beneath I see all the clustered racks of lamb: the crimson, glistening meat, the upthrust white bones.

As my heartbeat returns to normal, I'm humiliated to think how naked the fear must have been on my face. "Well," I say, trying to inject a note of authority. "I'm sure it will be delicious. Thank you." And I walk quickly—but careful not to hurry—out of the kitchen.

AS I REJOIN MY MILLING guests I become aware of a change in the energy of the crowd. There's a new hum of interest. It seems that something's going on out to sea. Everyone is beginning to turn and look, caught by whatever's happening.

"What is it?" I ask, craning to see over heads, unable to make out anything at all. The crowd is thinning around me, people drifting away wordlessly, toward the sea, trying to get a better view of whatever is going on.

Maybe some sea creature. They see dolphins from here regularly, Aoife told me. More rarely, a whale. That would be quite a spectacle, even a nice bit of atmospheric detail. But the noises coming from those at the front of the crowd of guests don't seem the right pitch for that. I'd expect shrieks and exclamations, excited gesturing. They're watching whatever it is, intently, but they're not making very much noise. That makes me uneasy. It suggests it's something bad.

I press forward. People have become pushy, clustering for position as though they're vying for the best view at a gig. Before, as the bride, I was like a queen among them, cutting a swath through the crowd wherever I walked. Now they have forgotten themselves, too intent on whatever it is that is going on.

"Let me through!" I shout. "I want to see."

Finally, they part for me and I move forward, up to the front.

There is something out there. Squinting, eyes shielded against the light, I can make out the dark shape of a head. It could be a seal or some other sea creature, save for the occasional appearance of a white hand.

There is *someone* in the water. It's difficult to get a proper glimpse of him or her from here. It must be one of the guests; it's not like anyone could swim here from the mainland. I wouldn't be surprised if it were Johnno—although it can't be, he was chatting to Piers moments ago. So if it's not him, perhaps it's one of the other exhibitionists in our number, one of the ushers, showing off. But as I look more closely I realize the swimmer isn't facing the shore, but out to sea. And they aren't swimming, I see now. In fact—

"They're drowning!" a woman is shouting—Hannah, I think. "They're caught in the current—look!"

I'm moving forward, trying to get a better look, pushing through the watching crowd of guests. And then finally I'm at the front and I can see more clearly. Or perhaps it's simply that strange deep knowledge, the way we know those closest to us from a long distance, even if we only see the back of a head.

"Olivia!" I shout. "It's Olivia! Oh my God, it's Olivia." I'm trying to run, my skirt catching under my heels and hampering me. I hear the sound of tearing silk and ignore it, kick off my shoes, keep running, losing my footing as my feet sink into wet, marshy patches of ground. I've never been a runner, and it's a whole other issue in a wedding dress. I seem to be moving unbelievably slowly. Will, thank God, doesn't seem to have the same problem—he tears past me, followed by Charlie and several others.

When I finally get to the beach it takes a few moments for me to work out what's going on, to understand the scene in front of me. Hannah, who must have started running too, arrives next to me, breathing hard. Charlie and Johnno stand thigh-deep in the water, with several other men behind them, on the water's edge—Femi, Duncan and others. And beyond them, emerging from the depths, is Will, with Olivia in his arms. She seems to be struggling, fighting him, her arms windmilling, her legs kicking out desperately. He holds on tight. Her hair is a black slick. Her dress is absolutely translucent. She looks so pale, her skin tinged with blue.

"She could have drowned," Johnno says, as he returns to the beach. He looks distraught. For the first time I feel more warmly toward him. "Lucky we spotted her. Crazy kid, anyone could see it's not sheltered here. Could have got swept straight out to the open sea."

Will gets to shore and lets Olivia go. She launches herself away from him and stands staring at us all. Her eyes are black and impenetrable. You can see her near-naked body through the soaked dress: the dark points of her nipples, the small pit of her navel. She looks primeval. Like a wild animal.

I see that Will's face and throat are scratched, red marks springing up livid on his skin. And at the sight of these a switch is flicked. Where a second ago I had been full of fear for her, now I feel a violent, red-hot solar flare of rage.

"The crazy little *bitch*," I say.

"Jules," Hannah says gently—but not so gently that I can't hear the note of opprobrium in her voice. "You know, I don't think Olivia's OK. I—I think she might need help—"

"Oh for God's sake, Hannah." I spin toward her. "Look, I get how kind and maternal you are, and whatever. But Olivia doesn't need a fucking mother. She's already got one—who gives her a lot more attention, let me tell you, than I ever got. Olivia doesn't need help. She needs to get her fucking act together. I'm not going to have her ruining my wedding. So . . . back off, OK?"

I see her step, almost stumble, backward. I'm dimly aware of her expression of hurt, of shock. I've gone beyond the pale: there, it's done. But, right now, I don't care. I turn back to Olivia. "What the *hell* were you doing?" I scream at her.

Olivia merely gazes back at me, dully, mute. She looks like she's drunk. I grab hold of her shoulders. Her skin is freezing to the touch. I want to shake her, slap her, pull her hair, demand answers. And then her mouth opens and closes, open and closes. I stare at her, trying to work it out. It is as though she is attempting to form words but her voice won't come. The expression in her eyes is intent, pleading. It sends a chill through me. For a moment I feel as though she is trying hard to semaphore a message I don't have the means to decipher. Is it an apology? An explanation?

Before I have a chance to ask her to try again, my mother is upon us. "Oh my girls, my girls." She clasps us both in her bony embrace. Beneath the billowing cloud of Shalimar I smell the sharp, acrid tang of her sweat, her fear. It is Olivia she's really reaching for, of course. But for a moment I allow myself to yield to her embrace.

Then I glance behind me. The other guests are catching up with us. I can hear the murmur of their voices, sense the excitement coming off them. I need to defuse this whole situation.

"Anyone else fancy a swim?" I call. No one laughs. The silence seems to stretch out. They all seem to be waiting, now the show is over, for some cue as to where to go now. How to behave. I don't know what to do. This is not in my playbook. So I stand, staring back at them, feeling the dampness of the beach soaking into the skirt of my dress.

Thank God for Aoife, who appears among them, neat in her sensible navy dress and wedge shoes, absolutely unflustered. I see them turn to her, as though recognizing her authority.

"Everyone," she calls. "Listen up." For a small, quiet woman, her voice is impressively resonant. "If you'll follow me back this way. The wedding breakfast will be served soon. The marquee awaits!"

JOHNNO
The Best Man

LOOK AT HIM. PLAYING THE HERO, CARRYING JULES'S SISTER OUT OF the water. Just fucking look at him. He's always been so good at getting people to see exactly what he wants them to see.

I know Will better than other people, maybe better than anyone in the world. I'll bet I know him a lot better than Jules does, or probably ever will. With her he's put on the mask, put up the screen. But I have kept his secrets for him, because they are both of ours to keep.

I always knew he was a ruthless fucker. I've known it since school, when he stole those exam papers. But I thought I was safe from that side of his character. I'm his best friend.

That's what I thought until about half an hour ago, anyway.

"It was such a shame," Piers said, "when we heard you didn't want to do it. I mean, Will goes down an absolute storm with the ladies, of course. He's made for TV. But he can be a bit too . . . smooth. And between you and me, I don't think male viewers like him all that much. The consumer research we've done has suggested they find him a bit—well, I think the expression one participant used was 'a bit of an arse.' Some viewers, the men, especially, are turned off by a host who they see as a bit too good-looking. You'd have balanced all that."

"Hang on, mate," I said. "Why did you think I *didn't* want to do it?"

Piers looked a bit put out at first—I don't think he's the sort of bloke who likes to be cut off in full flow when he's talking about demographics. Then he frowned, registering what I'd said.

"Why did we think—" He stopped, shook his head. "Well, you never turned up at the meeting, that's why."

I didn't have a clue what he was talking about. "What meeting?"

"The meeting we had to discuss how everything would progress. Will turned up with his agent and said unfortunately you and he had had a long discussion, and you'd decided it wasn't for you after all. That you weren't 'a TV sort of bloke.'"

All the stuff I've been saying to everyone these past four years. Except I never said it to Will. Not then, anyway. Not before some sort of important meeting. "I never heard of any meeting," I said. "I got an email saying you didn't want me."

It seemed to take a while for the penny to drop. Then Piers's mouth opened and closed gormlessly, silently, like a fish: bloop bloop bloop. Finally he said, "That's impossible."

"Nope," I told him. "No, it isn't. And I can tell you that for certain—because I never heard about a meeting."

"But we emailed—"

"Yeah. You never had *my* email, though, did you? It all went through Will, and his agent. They sorted everything like that."

"Well," Piers said. I think he'd just worked out that he'd opened up a massive can of worms. "Well," he went on, like he might as well say it all now. "He definitely told us that you weren't interested. That you'd had this whole period of soul searching and told him you'd decided against it. And it was such a shame, because you and Will, as we'd always planned . . . the rough and the smooth. Now, that could be TV dynamite."

There was no point in saying any more to Piers about it. He already looked like he wished he could teleport to anywhere else. *We're on a small island, mate,* I nearly told him. *Nowhere to go.* I wasn't surprised he felt like that, though. I could see him glancing over my shoulder, searching for someone to save him.

But my beef wasn't with him. It was with the bloke I thought was my best friend.

Speak of the devil. Will had started striding toward us, grinning at us both, looking so fucking handsome with not a hair out of place, despite the wind. "What are you two over here gossiping about?" he asked. He was close enough that I could see the beads of sweat on his forehead. See, Will is the sort of bloke who hardly ever sweats. Even on the rugby pitch, I barely saw him break much of one. But he was sweating now.

Too late, *mate*, I thought. *Too fucking late.*

I think I get it. He was too clever to cut me off at the beginning. The idea for *Survive the Night* was mine and we both knew it. If he'd done that, I could have spilled the beans, told everyone about what had happened when we were kids. I didn't have nearly so much to lose as him. So he brought me in, made me feel a part of it, and then he made it look like it was down to someone else that I was chucked out. Not his fault at all. *Sorry about that, mate. Such a shame. Would have loved working with you.*

I REMEMBER HOW MUCH I liked doing the screen test. I felt natural, talking about all that stuff, stuff I knew. I felt like I had something to say—something people would listen to. If they'd asked me to recite my times tables, or talk about politics, I would have been fucked. But climbing and abseiling and all that: I taught those skills at the adventure center. I didn't even think about the camera, after the first bit.

The most fucking offensive thing about it is how simple it all must have felt to Will. Stupid Johnno . . . so easy to pull the wool over his eyes. Now I understand why he's been so hard to get hold of recently. Why I've felt like he's pushed me away. Why I practically had to beg to be his best man. When he agreed he must have thought of it as a consolation prize, a Band-Aid. But being best man doesn't pay the bills. It's not a big enough Band-Aid. He's used me, the whole time, ever since school. I've been there to do his dirty work for him. But he didn't want to share the spotlight with me, oh no. When it came to it he threw me under the bus.

I swallow my whiskey in one long gulp. That double-crossing motherfucker. I'll have to find a way to get my own back.

HANNAH

The Plus-One

OLIVIA IS SOMEONE ELSE'S SISTER, SOMEONE ELSE'S DAUGHTER. Perhaps I should back off, as Jules told me to. And yet I can't. As the others are streaming into the marquee I find myself walking in the other direction, toward the Folly.

"Olivia?" I call, once I've stepped inside. There's no answer. My voice is echoed back to me by the stone walls. The Folly seems so silent and dark and empty now. It's hard to believe that there's anyone else in here. I know where Olivia's room is, the door that leads off the dining room—I'll try that first, I decide. I knock on the door.

"Olivia?"

"Yeah?" I think I hear a small voice from inside. I take it as my cue to push open the door. Olivia's sitting there on the bed, a towel wrapped around her shoulders.

"I'm fine," she says, without looking up at me. "I'm coming back to the marquee in a minute. I've just got to change first. I'm fine." The second time doesn't make it sound any more convincing.

"You don't really *seem* fine," I say.

She shrugs but doesn't say anything.

"Look," I say. "I know it's not my business. I know we hardly know each other. But when we talked yesterday, I got the sense that you've been going through some pretty major stuff . . . I imagine it must be hard to put on a happy face over all that."

Olivia remains silent, not looking at me.

"So," I say, "I guess I wanted to ask—what were you doing in the water?"

Olivia shrugs again. "I dunno," she says. A pause. "I—it all got a bit much. The wedding, all the people. Saying I must be so happy for Jules. Asking me how I was doing. About uni . . ." She trails off, looks at her hands. I see how the nails are bitten down as a child's, the cuticles red and raw-looking against the pale skin. "I just wanted to get away from all of it."

Jules had made out that it was all a stunt, that Olivia was being a drama queen. I suspect it was the opposite. I think she was trying to disappear.

"Can I tell you something?" I ask her.

She doesn't say no, so I go on.

"You know how I mentioned my sister, Alice, last night?"

"Yeah."

"Well, I . . . I suppose you remind me of her a little bit. I hope you don't mind me saying that. I *promise* it's a compliment. She was the first one in our family to go to university. She got the best GCSEs, straight A's for her A-levels."

"I'm not all that clever," Olivia mumbles.

"Yeah? I think you're cleverer than you like to let on. You did English lit at Exeter. That's a good course, isn't it?"

She shrugs.

"Alice wanted to work in politics," I say. "She knew that she had to have an impeccable record and to get the right grades for it. She got them, of course, she was accepted into one of the UK's top universities. And then in her first year, after she'd realized that she was easily knocking off Firsts for every essay she turned in, she relaxed a bit and got her first boyfriend. We all found it quite funny, me and Mum and Dad, because she was suddenly *so* into him."

Alice told me all about this new guy when she came home for the Christmas holidays. She'd met him at the Reeling Society, which was some posh club she'd joined because they had a fancy ball at the end of term. I remember thinking she brought the same intensity to this new relationship as she brought to her studies. "He's dead fit, Han," she told me. "And everyone fancies him. I can't believe he'd even *look* at me." She told me, swearing me to secrecy, that they'd slept together. He was the first boy she'd ever slept with. She told me that she felt so close to him, that she hadn't realized it could be like that. But I remember she qualified this, said it was probably the hormones and all the sociocultural idealization of young love. My beautiful, brainy sister, trying to rationalize away her feelings . . . classic Alice.

"But then she started going off him," I tell Olivia.

Olivia raises her eyebrows. "She got the ick?" She seems a bit more engaged now.

"I think so. By the Easter holiday she'd stopped talking about him so much. When I asked her she told me that she realized he wasn't quite the guy she thought he was. And that she'd spent too much time wrapped up in him, that she really needed to get her head down and focus on her studies. She'd got a low 2.1 in an essay she'd handed in and that had been her wake-up call."

"Jeez," Olivia says, rolling her eyes. "She sounds like a massive geek." And then she catches herself. "Sorry."

I smile. "I told her exactly the same thing. But that was Alice, all over. Anyway, she wanted to make sure that she did the decent thing by him, told him in person." That was Alice all over too.

"How did he take it?" Olivia asks.

"It didn't go that well," I say. "He was pretty horrible about it all, said he wouldn't let her humiliate him. That she would pay for it." I remember that because I remember wondering what he could possibly do. How do you make someone "pay" for a breakup?

"She didn't tell me what he did, to get her back," I tell Olivia. "She didn't tell me or Mum or Dad. She was too ashamed."

"But you found out?"

"Later," I say. "I found out later. He'd taken this video of her."

A video of Alice had been uploaded to the university's intranet. It was a video she had let him take, after the fancy Reeling Society ball. It was taken down from the server the second the university found out about it. But by then the news had spread, the damage was done. Other versions of it had been saved on computers around campus. It was posted to Facebook. It was taken down. It was posted again.

"So, like . . . revenge porn?" Olivia asks.

I nod. "That's what we'd call it now. But then it was this, you know, more innocent time. Now you're warned to be careful, aren't you? Everyone knows that if you let someone take photos or a video of you it could end up on the internet."

"I guess," Olivia says. "But people forget. In the moment. Or you know, if you really like someone and they ask you. So I suppose everyone at uni saw it, right?"

"Yes," I say. "But the worst part is we didn't know at the time, she didn't tell us. She was too ashamed. I think maybe she thought it would spoil our image of her. She'd always been so perfect, though of course that wasn't why we loved her."

The fact that she didn't even tell *me*. That's the part that still hurts so much.

"Sometimes," I say, "I think it's too difficult to tell the people closest to you. The ones you love. Does that sound familiar?"

Olivia nods.

"So. I want you to know: you can tell me. Yeah? Because here's the thing. It's always better to get it out in the open—even if it seems shameful, even if you feel like people won't understand. I wish Alice had been able to talk to me about it. I think she might have got some perspective she couldn't see herself."

Olivia looks up at me, then away. It comes out as little more than a whisper. "Yeah."

And then the tinny sound of an announcement comes from the

direction of the marquee. "Ladies and gents"—it's Charlie's voice, I realize, he must be doing his MC bit—"Please take your seats for the wedding breakfast."

I DON'T HAVE TIME TO tell Olivia the rest—and perhaps that's for the best. So I don't tell her how the whole thing was like a huge stain upon Alice's life, on her person—like it was tattooed there. None of us had realized quite how fragile Alice was. She had always seemed so capable, so in control: getting all those amazing grades, playing on the sports teams, getting her place at university, never missing a trick. But underneath that, fueling all this success, was a tangled mass of anxiety that none of us saw until it was too late. She couldn't cope with the shame of it all. She realized she would never—*could* never—work in politics as she had dreamt. It wasn't just that she didn't have her B.A., because she'd dropped out. There was a video of her giving some guy a blow job—and more—on the internet, now. It was indelible.

So I didn't tell Olivia how one June, two months after she came home from uni, Alice took a cocktail of painkillers and pretty much anything else she could find from the medicine cabinet in the bathroom while my mum was collecting me from netball practice. How, seventeen years ago this month, my beautiful, clever sister killed herself.

AOIFE
The Wedding Planner

T'S MY FAULT, WHAT JUST HAPPENED, WITH THE BRIDESMAID. I SHOULD
have seen it coming. I *did* see it coming: I knew there was trouble
brewing with that girl. I knew it when I gave her her breakfast this
morning. She held it together during the ceremony, even though
she looked like she wanted to turn and bolt out of there. Afterward, of course, I tried to keep my eye on her. But there have been
so many other demands on me: the guests were so insistent, so ra-
bid, that the waiting staff—all mostly older schoolkids and students
on their summer holidays—could hardly cope.

The next thing I knew, there was the commotion, and she was
in the water. Seeing her I was suddenly transported back to a different day. Powerless to help. Having seen the signs, but ignoring
them until it was too late. Those insistent images in my dreams:
the water rising, my hands reaching out as though I might be able
to do something . . .

This time rescue was possible. I think of the groom walking out
of the water with her, savior of the day. But maybe I could have
prevented it from happening at all, if I had paid more attention at
the right time. I am angry with myself for having been so lax. I
managed to keep a veneer of cool professionalism in front of the
guests, for the time it took to marshal them all into the marquee
for the wedding breakfast. Even if I hadn't kept such a firm hold

of myself, I doubt anyone would have noticed anything was amiss. After all, it is my job to be invisible.

I need Freddy. Freddy always makes me feel better.

I find him out of sight of the guests, in the catering area of the back of the marquee: plating up with a small army of helpers. I get him to step outside with me, away from the curious gaze of his kitchen aides.

"The girl could have drowned, out there," I say. When I think about it, I can hardly breathe. I'm seeing it all, how it could have happened, playing out before my eyes. It is as though I've been transported back to a different day, when there was no happy ending. "Oh God—Freddy, she could have drowned. I wasn't paying enough attention." It is the past, all over again. All my fault.

"Aoife," he says. He takes a firm hold of my shoulders. "She didn't drown. It's all OK."

"No," I say. "He saved her. But what if—"

"No what-ifs. The guests are in the marquee, now. Everything is going to go perfectly, trust me. Go back out there and do what you do best." Freddy has always been good at soothing me. "It's a minor blip. Otherwise everything is going beautifully."

"But it's all different to how I imagined," I say. "Harder, having them all here, wandering about all over the place. Those men, with their horrible games last night. And now this—bringing it all back . . ."

"It's nearly done," Freddy says, firmly. "All you have to do is get through the next few hours."

I nod. He's right. And I know I need to get a grip on myself. I can't afford to fall apart, not today.

THE WEDDING NIGHT

NOW THEY CAN MAKE HIM OUT, THE MAN, FREDDY, HURRYING toward them as quickly as he is able. He holds a torch in his hand: nothing more sinister than that. The light of their own torches picks out the sheen of sweat on his pale forehead as he draws near. "You should come back to the marquee," he shouts, between gasps of breath. "We've called the Gardaí."

"What? Why?"

"The waitress has come round a little. She says she thinks she saw someone else out there, in the dark."

"WE SHOULD LISTEN TO HIM," Angus shouts to the others, once Freddy has left them. "Wait for the police. It's not safe."

"Nah," Femi shouts. "We've come too far."

"You really think they're going to be here *soon* do you, Angus?" Duncan asks. "The police? In this weather? No fucking way, mate. We're all alone out here."

"Well, all the more reason. It's not safe—"

"Aren't we jumping to conclusions?" Femi shouts.

"What do you mean?"

"He only said she *might* have seen someone."

"But if she did," Angus calls, "that means—"

"What?"

"Well, if someone else was involved. It means it might not—it might not have been an accident."

He doesn't go so far as to spell it out but they hear it, all the same, behind his words. *Murder.*

They grip their torches a little tighter. "These would make good weapons," Duncan shouts. "If it comes down to it."

"Yeah," Femi shouts, straightening his shoulders a little. "It's us against them. Four of us, one of them."

"Wait, has anyone seen Pete?" Angus says, suddenly.

"What? Shit—no."

"Maybe he went with that Freddy bloke?"

"He didn't, Fem," Angus replies. "And he was really out of it. Shit—"

They call for him: "Pete!"

"Pete, mate—you out there?" There is no answer.

"Christ . . . well, I'm not going to wander around looking for him, too," Duncan shouts, a faint but telling tremor in his voice. "It's not the first time he's been in that state, is it? He can look after himself. He'll be fine." The others suspect he's made an effort to sound more certain than he really is. But they aren't going to question it. They want to believe it too.

JULES
The Bride

NSIDE THE MARQUEE, AOIFE HAS CONJURED SOMETHING MAGICAL. It's warm in here, a respite from the increasingly cool wind outside. Through the entrance I can see the lighted torches flicker and dip and every so often the roof of the marquee billows and deflates gently, flexing against the wind outside. But in a way it only adds to the sense of coziness inside. The whole place is scented by the candles, and the faces clustered about the candlelight appear rosy, flushed with health and youth—even if the true cause is an afternoon of drinking in the penetrating Irish wind. It's everything I could have wanted. I look around at the guests and see it in their faces: the awe at their surroundings. And yet . . . why am I left feeling so hollow?

Everyone already seems to have forgotten about Olivia's crazy stunt; it could have happened on another day entirely. They are throwing back the wine, guzzling it down . . . growing increasingly loud and animated. The atmosphere of the day has been recaptured and is following its prescribed track. But I can't forget. When I think about Olivia's expression, about that pleading look in her eyes when she tried to speak, all the little hairs on the back of my neck prickle to attention.

The plates are cleared away, every one practically licked clean. Alcohol has given the guests a real hunger and Freddy is a great talent. I've been to so many weddings where I've had to force down mouthfuls of rubbery chicken breast, school canteen–style vegetables. This was the most tender rack of lamb, velvet on the tongue, crushed potatoes scented with rosemary. It was perfect.

IT'S TIME FOR THE SPEECHES. The waiters fan out about the room, carrying trays of Bollinger, ready for toasts. There's a sourness in the pit of my stomach and the thought of yet more champagne makes me feel slightly queasy. I've drunk too much already, in an effort to match the bonhomie of my guests, and feel strange, untethered. The image of that dark cloud on the horizon during the reception drinks keeps playing upon my mind.

There's the sound of a spoon on a glass: *ding ding ding*!

The chatter in the marquee subsides, replaced by an obedient hush. I feel the attention of the room shift. Faces swivel toward us, to the top table. The show is about to begin. I rearrange my expression into one of joyful anticipation.

Then the lights in the marquee shiver, going out. We are plunged into a twilit gloom that matches the fading light outside.

"Apologies," calls Aoife, from the back of the marquee. "It's the wind, outside. The electricity's a bit temperamental here."

Someone, one of the ushers, I think, lets out a long, lupine howl. And then others join in, until it sounds as though there is a whole pack of wolves in here. They're all drunk by now, all getting looser and more wild. I want to scream at them all to shut up.

"Will," I hiss, "can we ask them to stop?"

"It'll only encourage them," he says soothingly. His hand closes over mine. "I'm sure the lights will come on again in a second."

Just when I think I can't bear it any longer, that I really will scream, the lights flicker on again. The guests cheer.

Dad stands, first, to give his speech. Perhaps I should have banished him at the last minute as a punishment for his earlier behavior. But that would look odd, wouldn't it? And so much of this whole wedding business, I have realized, is about how things *appear*. As long as we can make it through with all seeming joyful, jubilant . . . well, perhaps then we can suppress any darker forces stirring beneath the surface of the day. I bet most people would guess that this wedding is all down to my dad's generosity. Not quite.

Everyone's been asking me what made me decide to hold the wedding here. I put a shout-out on social media: "Pitch me your wedding venue." All part of a feature for *The Download*. Aoife answered the call. I admired the level of planning in her pitch, the consideration of practicalities. She seemed so much hungrier than all the rest. It knocked spots off the competition, really. But that's not why this place won our business. The whole unvarnished truth of why I decided to hold my wedding here was because it was nice and cheap.

Because Daddy dearest, standing up there looking all proud, turned off the tap. Or Séverine did it for him.

No one's going to guess that one, are they? Not when I've got a cake that cost three grand, or solid silver engraved napkin rings, or Cloon Keen Atelier's entire year's output of candles. But those were exactly the sort of things my guests expected from me. And I could only afford them—and a wedding in the style to which I am accustomed—because Aoife also offered a 50 percent discount if I held it here. She might look dowdy but she's savvy. That's how she clinched it. She knows I'll feature it in the magazine now, knows it'll get press because of Will. It'll pay dividends in the end.

"I'M HONORED TO BE HERE," Dad says, now. "At the wedding of my little girl."

His little girl. *Really*. I feel my smile harden.

Dad raises aloft his glass. He's drinking Guinness, I see—he's always made a point of not drinking champagne, keeping true to his roots. I know that I should be gazing back adoringly but I'm still so cross about what he said earlier that I can barely bring myself to look at him.

"But then Julia has never really been my little girl," Dad says. His accent is the strongest I've heard it in years. It always gets more pronounced at times of heightened emotion . . . or when he's had a fair amount to drink. "She's always known her own mind. Even at the age of nine, always knew exactly what she wanted. Even if I . . ." He gives a meaningful cough, "tried to persuade her otherwise." There's a ripple of amusement from the guests. "She went after whatever she wanted with a single-minded ambition." He smiles, ruefully. "If I were to flatter myself I might try to say that she takes after me in that respect. But I'm not the same. I'm not nearly so strong. I pretend to know what I want but really it's whatever has taken my fancy. Jules is absolutely her own person, and woe betide anyone who gets in her way. I'm sure any employees of hers will agree." There's some slightly nervous laughter from the table of *The Download* crowd. I smile at them beatifically: None of you are going to get in trouble. Not today.

"Look," Dad says, "sure, I'm not the best role model for this wedding stuff, I'll be totally honest. I believe I have wife number one and number five here this evening. So I suppose you could say I'm a card-carrying member of the club . . . though not a very good one." Not very funny—though there are some dutiful titters from the spectators. "Jules was—ahem—quick to point that out to me earlier today when I attempted to offer some words of fatherly advice."

Fatherly advice. Ha.

"But I would say that I've learned a thing or two over the years, about how to get it right. Marriage is about finding that person you know best in the world. Not how they take their coffee or what their favorite film is or the name of their first cat. It's knowing on a deeper level. It's knowing their soul." He grins at Séverine, who positively preens.

"Besides, I hardly felt qualified to give that advice. I know I haven't always been around. Scratch that. I have hardly ever been around. Neither of us have been. I think Araminta will probably agree with me on that."

Wow. I look toward Mum. She wears a rictus smile that I think might well be as taut as my own. She won't have enjoyed the first wife bit because it'll make her feel old and she'll be livid at the suggestion of parental neglectfulness, considering how much she's been enjoying playing the gracious mother of the bride today.

"So in our absence, Julia has always had to forge her own path. And what a path she has forged. I know I haven't always been very good at showing it, but I am so proud of you, Juju, of all that you have achieved." I think of the school prize-giving ceremony. My graduation. The launch for *The Download*—none of which my father attended. I think about how often I have wanted to hear those words, and now, here they are—right when I'm most furious at him. I feel my eyes fill with tears. Shit. That really caught me unawares. I never cry.

Dad turns to me. "I love you so much . . . clever, complicated, fierce daughter of mine." Oh God. They aren't pretty tears, either, a subtle glistening of the eyes. They spill over onto my cheeks and I have to put up the heel of a hand, then my napkin, to try and staunch them. What is *happening* to me?

"And here's the thing," Dad says, to the crowd. "Even though Jules is this incredible, independent person, I like to flatter myself that she is my little girl. Because there are certain emotions, as a parent, that you can't escape . . . no matter what a shite one you've been, no matter how little right you have to them. And one of those is the instinct to protect." He turns to me again. I have to look at him now. He wears an expression of genuine tenderness. My chest hurts.

And then he turns to Will. "William, you seem like . . . a great guy." Was it just me, or was there a dangerous emphasis on the "seem"? "But," Dad grins—I know that grin. It isn't a smile at all. It's a baring of teeth. "You better look after my daughter. You better not feck this up. And if you do anything to hurt my girl—well, it's simple." He raises his glass, in a silent toast. "I'll come for you."

There's a strained silence. I force out a laugh, though it seems to come out more like a sob. There's a ripple in its wake, other guests following suit—relieved, perhaps, to know how to take it. *Ah, it's a joke.* Only it wasn't a joke. I know it, Dad knows it—and I suspect, from the look on Will's face, he knows it too.

OLIVIA

The Bridesmaid

JULES'S DAD SITS DOWN. JULES LOOKS A WRECK: HER FACE BLOTCHY and red. I saw her dabbing her eyes with her napkin. She does feel stuff, my half sister, even if she does a good impression of being so tough all the time. I feel bad about earlier, honestly. I know Jules wouldn't believe it if I told her, but I *am* sorry. I still feel cold, like the chill from the sea got deep under my skin. I've changed into the dress I wore last night, because I thought that would piss Jules off the least, but I wish I could have got into my normal clothes. I'm keeping my arms wrapped around myself to try and stay warm but it doesn't stop my teeth chattering together.

Will gets to his feet to hollers and whistles, a few catcalls. Then the room falls silent. He has their total attention. He has that sort of effect on people. I guess it's how he looks and how he is; his confidence. How he's always totally in control.

"On behalf of my new wife and I," he says—and is almost drowned out by the whoops and cheers, the drumming on the tables, the stamping of feet. He smiles around until everyone settles down. "On behalf of my new wife and I, thank you so much for coming today," he says. "I know Jules will agree with me when I say that it is a wonderful thing to celebrate with all of our most cherished loved ones, our nearest and dearest." He turns to Jules. "I feel like the luckiest man in the world."

Jules has dried her eyes now. And when she looks up at Will her expression is totally different, transformed. She seems suddenly happy enough that it is hard to look at her, like staring at a lightbulb. Will beams back at her.

"Oh my God," I hear a woman whisper, at the next table. "They're just *too* perfect."

WILL'S GRINNING AROUND AT EVERYONE. "And it really *was* luck," he says. "Our first meeting. If I hadn't been in the right place at the right time. As Jules likes to say, it was our sliding doors moment." He raises his glass: "So: to luck. And to making your own luck . . . or giving it a little helping hand, when it needs it."

He winks. The guests laugh.

"First of all," he says, "it's customary to tell the bridesmaids how beautiful they're looking, isn't it? We only have one, but I think you'll agree she's beautiful enough for seven. So a toast to Olivia! My new sister."

The whole room turns toward me, raising their glasses. I can't bear it. I look at the floor until the cheers die down and Will begins to speak again.

"And next, to my new wife. My beautiful, clever Jules . . ."— the guests go wild again—"Without you, life would be very dull indeed. Without you, there would be no joy, no love. You are my equal, my counterpart. So, please be upstanding to raise a toast to Jules!"

The guests all rise to their feet around me. "To Jules!" they echo, grinning. They're all smiling at Will, the women especially, their eyes not leaving his face. I know what they're seeing. Will Slater: TV star. Husband, now, to my half sister. Hero: look how he rescued me earlier, from the water. All-round good guy.

"Do you know how Jules and I met?" Will asks, when they've all sat down. "It was the work of Fate. She threw a party at the

V&A museum, for *The Download*. I was just a plus-one: I had come along with a friend. Anyway, my friend had to leave the party and I was left behind. I was just deciding whether to leave myself. So it was a total spur-of-the-moment decision, to go back inside. So who knows what would have happened, if I hadn't? Would we ever have met? So—even though Jules works so hard that I sometimes feel it's the third person in our relationship, I'd also like to thank it for bringing us together. To *The Download*!"

The guests get to their feet. "To *The Download*!" they parrot.

I DIDN'T MEET JULES'S NEW fiancé until after they were engaged. She had been very hush-hush about him. It was like she hadn't wanted to bring him home before she got the ring on her finger, in case we put him off. Maybe I sound like a bitch for saying that, but Jules has always been pretty ruthless about some things. I suppose I don't blame her, exactly. Mum *can* be a bit much.

Jules being Jules, she'd stage-managed the whole thing. They were going to arrive at Mum's for coffee, stay for half an hour, then we'd all head off to the River Café for lunch (their favorite place, Jules told us; she had booked). Her instructions to Mum and me were pretty clear: do not fuck this up for me.

I honestly didn't mean to fuck it up, that first meeting with Jules's fiancé. But when the two of them arrived, and they first walked in through the door, I had to run to the bathroom and throw up. Then I found I couldn't move. I sank down next to the loo and sat on the floor for what felt like a very long time. I felt winded, like someone had punched me in the stomach.

I saw exactly how it had happened. He'd gone back into the V&A, after he put me in that taxi. There he'd met my sister, belle of the ball—so much better suited to him. Fate. And I remember what he'd said when we first met: "If you were ten years older, you'd be my ideal woman." I saw it all.

After a little while—because she had her important schedule, I suppose—Jules came upstairs. "Olivia," she said, "we need to go off for lunch now. Of course, I'd love you to join us, but if you're not feeling well enough then, well, I suppose that's fine." I could hear that it wasn't fine, not at all, but that was the least of my worries.

Somehow I managed to find my voice. "I—I can't come," I said, through the door. "I'm . . . ill." It seemed the easiest thing to do, right then, to go along with what she'd said. And anyway, I wasn't feeling well—I was sick to my stomach, like I'd swallowed something poisonous.

I've thought about it since, though. What if right then I'd had the balls to open that door and tell her the truth, right then and there to her face? Rather than waiting and hiding, until it was way too late?

"OK," she said. "Fine, then. I'm very sorry you can't come." She didn't sound in the least bit sorry. "I'm not going to make a big deal out of this now, Olivia. Maybe you really are ill. I'll give you the benefit of the doubt. But I'd really like your support in this. Mum told me you've had a tough time lately, and I'm sorry for that. But for once, I'd like you to try and be happy for me."

I slumped down against the bathroom door and tried to keep breathing.

HE COVERED IT SO QUICKLY, his own reaction. When he walked in through Mum's door, that first time we "met," there was maybe a split second of shock. One that maybe only I would have noticed. The flicker of an eyelid, a slight tightening of the jaw. Nothing more than that. He covered it up so well, he was so smooth.

So you see, I can't think of him as Will. To me he'll always be Steven. I hadn't thought of that, when I renamed myself for the dating app. I hadn't thought that he might have lied too.

• • •

THE GUEST LIST 227

AT THEIR ENGAGEMENT DRINKS, I decided I wouldn't run away and hide like before. I'd spent the couple of months in between thinking of all the ways I could have reacted that would have been so much better, so much less pathetic, than scarpering and throwing up. I hadn't done anything wrong, after all. This time I'd confront him. He was the one that had all the explaining to do, to me, to Jules. He was the one who should be feeling pretty fucking sick. I had let him win that first one. This time, I was going to show him.

He threw me off at the beginning. When I arrived he gave me a big grin. "Olivia!" he said. "I hope you're feeling better. It was such a shame we didn't get to meet properly, last time."

I was so shocked I couldn't say anything. He was pretending we'd never met, right to my face. It made me even start to doubt myself. Was it really him? But I *knew* it was. There was no doubt about it. Closer up I could see how the skin around his eyes creased the same, how he had these two moles on his neck, below the jaw. And I remembered, so clearly, that split second's reaction, when he'd first seen me.

He knew exactly what he was doing: making it harder for me to get my own version of the truth out. And he'd also banked on me being too pathetic to say anything to Jules, too scared that she wouldn't believe anything I said.

He was right.

HANNAH
The Plus-One

THERE WAS SOMETHING WEIRD ABOUT WILL'S SPEECH JUST NOW. Something that felt strangely familiar, a sense of déjà vu. I can't quite put my finger on it but while everyone around me cheered and clapped I was left with an uneasy feeling in the pit of my stomach.

"Here we go," I hear someone at the table whisper, "is everyone ready for the main event?"

Charlie's not on my table. He's on the top table, right there at Jules's left elbow. It makes sense, I suppose: I'm not one of the wedding party after all, while Charlie is. But everywhere else husbands and wives seem to be seated next to one another. It occurs to me that I have barely seen Charlie since this morning, and then only outside at the drinks—which somehow made me feel more disconnected from him than if we hadn't seen one another at all. In the space of a mere twenty-four hours, it feels as though a gulf has opened up between us.

The guests sitting near me have done a poll on how long the best man's speech is going to last. Fifty quid for a bet, so I declined. They've also designated our table "the naughty table." There's a manic, intense feeling around it. They're like children who have been cooped up for too long. Over the last hour or so they've knocked back at least a bottle and a half each. Peter Ramsay—who's

THE GUEST LIST 229

sitting on the other side of me—has been speaking so quickly that it's starting to make me feel dizzy. This might have something to do with the crusting of white powder around one of his nostrils; it's everything I can do not to lean over and dash it off with the corner of my napkin.

Charlie rises to his feet, resuming his MC role, taking the mic from Will. I find myself watching him carefully for any sign that he might have had too much to drink. Is his face drooping slightly in that telltale way? Is he a little unsteady on his feet?

"And now," he says, but there's a scream of feedback as people—especially the ushers, I notice—groan and jeer and cover their ears. Charlie flushes. I cringe inwardly for him. He tries again: "And now . . . it's time for the best man. Everyone give a big hand for Jonathan Briggs."

"Be kind, Johnno!" Will shouts, hands cupped around his mouth. He gives a wry smile, a pantomime wince. Everyone laughs.

I always find the best man's speech hard to watch. There's so much expectation. There's that tiny, hair-thin line between being too vanilla and causing offense. Better, surely, to stay on the PC side of it than to try and nail it completely. I get the impression Johnno's not the sort to worry about offending anyone.

Maybe I'm imagining it, but he seems to be swaying slightly as he takes the mic from Charlie. Beside him, my husband looks sober as a judge. Then, as Johnno makes his way round to the front of the table, he trips and nearly falls. There's lots of heckling and catcalling from my table companions. Next to me Peter Ramsay puts his fingers in his mouth and lets out a whistle that leaves my eardrums ringing.

By the time Johnno gets out in front of us all it's pretty clear he's drunk. He stands there silently for several seconds before he seems to remember where he is and what he's meant to be doing. He taps the mic a few times and the sound booms around the tent.

"Come on, Johnners!" someone shouts. "We're growing old waiting here!" The guests around my table start drumming with their fists, stamping with their feet. "Speech, speech, speech! Speech, speech, speech!" The hairs on my arms prickle. It's a reminder of last night: that tribal rhythm, that sense of menace.

Johnno does a "calm down, calm down" motion with his hand. He grins at us all. Then he turns and looks toward Will. He clears his throat, takes a deep breath.

"We go a long way back, this fella and I. Shout-out to all my Old Trevellyans!" A cheer goes up, particularly from the ushers.

"Anyway," Johnno says as the sound dies down, sweeping a hand to indicate Will. "Look at this guy. It would be easy to hate him, wouldn't it?" There's a pause, a beat too long, maybe, before he picks up again. "He's got everything: the looks, the charm, the career, the money"—was that pointed?—"and . . ."—He gestures to Jules—"The girl. So, actually, now I think about it . . . I suppose I *do* hate him. Anyone else with me?"

A ripple of laughter goes around the room; someone shouts: "Hear, hear!"

Johnno grins. There's this wild, dangerous glitter in his eyes. "For those of you who don't know, Will and I were at school together. But it wasn't any normal school. It was more like . . . oh, I don't know . . . a prison camp crossed with *Lord of the Flies*—thanks for giving us that one last night, Charlie boy! See, it wasn't about getting the best grades you could. It was all about survival."

I wonder if I imagined the emphasis on the last word, spoken as though it were a proper noun. I remember the game they told us about, at dinner last night. That was called Survival, wasn't it?

"And let me tell you," Johnno goes on. "We have got into our fair share of shit over the years. I'm talking about the Trevellyan's days in particular. There were some dark times. There were some mental times. Sometimes it felt like it was us versus the rest of the world." He looks over at Will. "Didn't it?"

Will nods, smiles.

There's something a bit strange about Johnno's tone. There's a dangerous edge, a sense that he could do or say anything and take it all completely off the rails. I look around the other tables, I wonder if the other guests are sensing it too. The room has certainly gone a little quiet, as though everyone is holding their breath.

"That's the thing about a best mate, isn't it?" Johnno says. "They've always got your back."

I feel like I'm watching a glass teeter on the edge of a table, unable to do anything about it, waiting for it to shatter. I glance over at Jules and wince. Her mouth is set in a grim line. She looks as though she's waiting for this to all be over.

"And look at this." Johnno gestures to himself. "I'm a fat fucking slob in a too-tight suit. Oh," he turns to Will, "you know how I said I'd *forgotten* my suit? Yeah, there's a little story behind that one." He swivels round to face us, the audience.

"So. Here's the truth—the honest truth. There was never any suit. Or . . . there was a suit, then there wasn't. See, at the beginning, I thought Will might get it for me. I don't know much about these things, but I'm pretty sure that happens with bridesmaids' dresses, doesn't it?"

He looks inquiringly at us all. No one answers. There's a hush in the marquee now—even Peter Ramsay next to me has stopped jiggling his leg up and down.

"Doesn't the bride buy them?" Johnno asks us. "It's the rule, isn't it? You're making someone wear the fucking thing. It's not like it's their choice. And old Will here especially wanted me to have a suit from Paul Smith, nothing less would do."

He's getting into the swing of things now. He's striding back and forth in front of us like a comedian at an open mic night.

"Anyway . . . so we're standing in the shop and I see the label and I think to myself—bloody hell, he's being generous. *Eight hundred quid.* It's the sort of suit that gets you laid, right? But for eight hundred quid? Better to pay to get laid. Like, what use do I have in my life for an eight hundred quid suit? It's not exactly like I've got some fancy do to attend every couple of weeks. Still, I thought. If that's what he wants me to wear, who am I to argue?"

I glance toward Will. He's smiling, but there's a strained look to it.

"But then," Johnno says, "there's this awkward moment by the till, when he sort of stands aside and lets me get on with it. I spend the whole time praying it goes through on my credit card. Total fucking miracle it did, to be perfectly honest. And he stands there, smiling the whole time. Like he'd really bought it for me. Like I should turn round and thank him."

"Shit's just got real," Peter Ramsay whispers.

"So, the next day, I returned the suit. Obviously I wasn't going to tell Will all this. So you see I concocted this whole plan, way before I got here, that I'd pretend I'd left it at home. They couldn't make me go all the way back to Blighty to get it, could they? And thank Christ I live in the middle of nowhere so that none of you lot could 'kindly offer' to go and get it for me—as that would have landed me in hot water, ha ha!"

"Is this meant to be funny?" a woman across from me asks.

"Eight hundred quid for a suit," Johnno says. "Eight hundred. Because it's got some random bloke's name stitched inside the jacket? I'd have had to sell a fucking *kidney*. I'd have had to sell this shit," he runs his hands down his body, lasciviously, to a few half-hearted catcalls, "on the street. And you know there's only limited interest in fat hairy slobs in their midthirties." He gives a big, wild roar of a laugh.

Following suit—like they've been given their cue—some of the audience laugh with him. They're laughs of relief, like the laughs of people who have been holding their breath.

"I mean," Johnno says, not done. "He *could* have bought me the suit, couldn't he? It's not like he's not *loaded*, is it? Mainly thanks to you, Jules love. But he's a stingy bastard. I say that, of course, with *all my love*." He pretends to flutter his eyelashes at Will in a weird, camp parody.

Will's not smiling anymore. I can't even bring myself to look at Jules's expression. I feel like I shouldn't watch; this is not all that different to that horrible, dark compulsion you have to look at the scene of a car crash.

"Anyway," Johnno says. "Whatever. He lent me his spare, no questions asked. That's stand-up-bloke behavior, isn't it? Though I have to warn you, mate"—he stretches, and the jacket strains against the button holding it closed—"it may never be the same again." He turns to face all of us again. "But that's the thing about a best mate, isn't it? They've always got your back. He might be a tightwad. But I know he's always been there for me."

He puts a big hand on Will's shoulder. Will looks as though he's slightly buckling under the weight, as though Johnno might be putting some downward pressure on it. "And I know, I truly know, that he would never screw me over." He turns to Will, dips in close, as though he's searching Will's face. "*Would you, mate?*"

Will puts up a hand and wipes his face where it seems Johnno's saliva has landed.

There's a pause—an awkward, lengthening pause, during which it becomes clear that Johnno's actually waiting for an answer. Finally, Will says: "No. I wouldn't. Of course I wouldn't."

"Well that's good," Johnno says. "That's great! Because ha ha . . . the *things* we've been through together. The things I know about you, man. It wouldn't be wise, would it? All that history we share together? You remember it, don't you? All those years ago."

He turns back to Will again. Will's face has gone white.

"What the *fuck*," someone on the table whispers, "is Johnno going on about? Is he *on* something?"

"I know," I hear in reply. "This is *mental*."

"And you know what?" Johnno says. "I had a little chat with

the ushers, earlier. We thought it might be nice to bring a bit of tradition to the proceedings. For old times' sake." He gestures to the room. "Chaps?"

As if on cue the ushers rise. They all move to surround Will, where he's sitting.

Will shrugs, good-humoredly: "What can you do?" Everyone laughs. But I see that Will's not smiling.

"Seems only fair," Johnno says. "Tradition, and all that. Come on, mate, it'll be fun!"

And between them they grab hold of Will. They're all laughing and cheering—if they weren't it would appear a whole lot more sinister. Johnno has taken his tie off and he wraps it around Will's eyes, tying it, like a blindfold. Then they hoist him up on their shoulders and march off with him. Out of the marquee, into the growing darkness.

JOHNNO
The Best Man

WE DROP WILL ON THE FLOOR OF THE WHISPERING CAVE. I guess he won't be delighted about his precious suit touching the wet sand or the fact that the smell in here hits you like a punch in the face: rotting seaweed and sulfur. It's starting to get darker and you have to squint a bit to see properly. The sea's rougher than it was earlier, too: you can hear it crashing against the rocks on either side. The whole way here, as we carried him, Will was laughing and joking with us. "You boys better not be taking me anywhere messy. If I get anything on this suit Jules will kill me," and "Can't I bribe any of you with an extra crate of Bolly to take me back?"

The guys are all laughing. For them, this is all great fun, a bit of a blast from the past. They've been sitting in the marquee for a couple of hours getting drunker and more restless, especially those like Peter Ramsay who have powdered their noses. Before I did my speech I too had a bump in the toilets, with some of the blokes, which was maybe a bad idea. It's only made me more jittery. It's also made everything weirdly clear.

The others are all just excited to be outside. It's a bit like the stag. All the boys together, like it was back in the day. The wind, blowing a gale now, makes it all the more dramatic. We had to bend our heads low against it. It made carrying Will all that much harder.

It's a good spot, here, the Whispering Cave. Pretty out of the way. You can imagine, if there had been a cave like this at Trevellyan's, it would have been used in Survival.

Will is lying on the shingle: not *too* close to the water. Don't know what the tides are like around here. We've bound his wrists and ankles with our ties, as per old school tradition.

"All right, boys," I say. "Let's leave him here for a bit. See if he can make his own way back."

"We're not going to actually leave him there, are we?" Duncan whispers to me, as we climb out of the cave. "Until he works out how to untie himself?"

"Nah," I tell him. "Well, if he hasn't returned in half an hour we'll come get him."

"You better!" Will calls. He's still acting like this is all a big joke. "I've got a wedding to get to!"

I head toward the marquee with the rest of the ushers. "Know what," I say, as we pass the Folly. "I'm gonna peel off here. Gotta take a leak."

I watch them all return to the marquee, laughing and jostling each other. I wish I could be like one of them. I wish for me it was only harmless school memories, a bit of fun. That it could still be a game.

When they're all out of sight, I turn around and start walking back to the cave.

"Who's that?" Will calls, as I approach him. His words echo in the space, so it sounds as though there are five of him saying it.

"It's me," I say. "*Mate.*"

"Johnno?" Will hisses. He's managed to sit up, is leaning against the cave wall. Now the boys have gone he's dropped the act. Even with his eyes covered I can see he's fairly pissed off, his jaw tight. "Untie me, get this blindfold off! I should be at the wedding—Jules will be livid. You've had your joke now. But this isn't funny."

"No," I say. "No, I know it's not. See, I'm not laughing either.

It's not that much fun when you're on the other end of it, is it? But you wouldn't know, not up until now. You never did a Survival, did you, at Trevs? Somehow got out of that one too."

I see him frown behind the blindfold. "You know, Johnno," he says, his tone light, friendly. "That speech . . . and now this—I think you might have had a bit too much of the good stuff. Seriously, mate—"

"I'm not your mate," I say. "I think you might be able to guess why."

I played drunker than I am, during the speech. I'm not actually all that drunk. Plus the coke has sharpened me. My mind feels very clear now, like someone's turned on a big bright spotlight in my brain. Lots of stuff is suddenly lit up, making sense.

This is the last time anyone plays me for the fool.

"Up until about two this afternoon I was your mate," I tell him. "But not now, not any longer."

"What are you talking about?" Will asks. He's starting to sound a bit unsure of himself. Yeah, I think. You're right to be scared.

I could see him looking at me the whole way through that speech, wondering what the fuck I was doing. Wondering what I was going to say next, tell all his guests about him. I hope he was shitting himself. I wish I'd gone the whole hog in my speech, told them everything. But I chickened out. Like I chickened out all those years ago—when *I* should have gone to the teachers, too, backed up whichever kid it was that snitched on us. Told them exactly what we had done. They wouldn't have been able to ignore two of us, would they?

But I couldn't do it then, and I couldn't do it in the speech. Because I'm a fucking coward.

This is the next best thing.

"I had an interesting chat with Piers earlier," I say. "Very *educational*."

I see Will swallow. "Look," he says, carefully, his tone very reasonable, man-to-man. It only makes me more angry. "I don't know what Piers said to you, but—"

"You fucked me over," I say. "Piers didn't actually need to say all that much. I worked it out for myself. Yeah, me. Stupid Johnno, must try harder. You couldn't have me there, could you? Too much of a liability. Reminding you of what you once were. What you did."

Will grimaces. "Johnno, mate, I—"

"You and me," I say. "See, it was meant to be you and me, sticking up for each other, always. Us against the world, that's what you said. Especially after what we'd done, what we knew about each other. I had your back, you had mine. That's how I thought it was."

"It is, Johnno. You're my best man—"

"Can I tell you something?" I say. "The whole whiskey business?"

"Oh yeah," Will says quickly, eagerly. "Hellraiser!" He's remembered it this time. "See, there you go! You're doing so well for yourself. No need for all this bitterness—"

"Nah." I cut him off again. "See, it doesn't exist."

"What are you talking about? Those bottles you've given us . . ."

"Are fakes." I shrug, even though he can't see me. "It's some single malt from the supermarket, decanted into plain bottles. Got my mate Alan to make up labels for me."

"Johnno, what—"

"I mean, I did actually think I could do it at the beginning. That's what makes it so tragic. It's why I got Alan to mock the design up at first, to see how it might look. But do you know how hard it is to launch a whiskey brand these days? Unless you're David Beckham. Or you have rich parents to bankroll you, or connections with important people? I have none of that. I never did. All the other boys at Trevs knew it. I know some of them called me a pikey behind my back. But what *we* had, I thought that was solid."

Will's shifting on the ground, trying to get to his feet. I'm not going to help him. "Johnno, mate, Jesus—"

"Yeah, oh, and I didn't leave the wilderness retreat to set up the whiskey brand. How pathetic is this? Wait for it . . . I got fired for being stoned on the job. Like a teenager. This fat bloke on a team-bonding course—I let him go down too fast on the rope and he broke an ankle. And do you know why I was stoned?"

"Why?" he asks, wary.

"Because I have to smoke it, to get by. Because it's the only thing that helps me forget. See, it feels like my whole life stopped at that point, all those years ago. It's like—it's like . . . nothing good has happened since. The one good thing that's happened to me in the years after Trevs was that shot at the TV show—and you took it away from me." I pause, take a deep breath, prepare to say what I've finally come to realize, after nearly twenty years. "But it's not like that for you, is it? It's like the past doesn't affect you. It didn't matter to you at all. You carry on taking what you need. And you always get away with it."

HANNAH
The Plus-One

THE FOUR USHERS EXPLODE BACK INTO THE MARQUEE. PETER RAM-
say does a knee-slide across the laminate, nearly crashing into the
table bearing the magnificent wedding cake. I see Duncan leap on
to Angus's back, his arm making a tight headlock around his neck
so his face begins to turn purple. Angus staggers, half-laughing,
half-gasping for breath. Then Femi jumps on top of both of them
and they collapse in a tangled heap of limbs. They're pumped up,
excited by their stunt I suppose, carrying Will out of the marquee
like that.

"To the bar, boys!" Duncan roars, leaping to his feet. "Time to
raise hell!"

The rest of the guests follow them, taking this as their cue,
laughing and chattering. I stay sitting in my seat. Most seem
thrilled, titillated, by the speech and the spectacle that came after
it. But I can't say I feel the same—though Will was smiling there
was a disturbing undertone about it all: the blindfold, tying his
hands and feet like that. I look across to the top table and see that it
is almost completely deserted apart from Jules, who is sitting very
still, apparently lost in thought.

Suddenly there's a commotion from the bar tent. Raised voices.

"Whoa—steady on!"

"What the fuck is your problem, mate?"

"Jesus, calm down—"

And then, unmistakably, my husband's voice. Oh God. I get to my feet and hurry toward the bar. There's a press of people, all avidly watching, like children on a playground. I shove my way through to the front as quickly as I can.

Charlie is crouched on the floor. Then I realize that his fist is raised and he's half-straddling another man: Duncan.

"Say that again," Charlie says.

For a moment I can only stare at him: my husband—geography teacher, father of two, usually such a mild man. I haven't seen this side of him for a very long time. Then I realize I have to act. "Charlie!" I say, rushing forward. He turns and for a moment he just blinks at me, like he hardly recognizes me. He's flushed, trembling with adrenaline. I can smell the booze on his breath. "Charlie—what the hell are you doing?"

He seems to come to his senses a little at this. And, thank God, he gets up without too much fuss. Duncan straightens his shirt, muttering under his breath. As Charlie follows me, the crowd parting to let us pass, I can feel all the guests watching silently. Now that my immediate horror has receded I simply feel mortified.

"What on earth was that?" I ask him as we return to the main tent, sit down at the nearest table. "Charlie—what's got into you?"

"I had enough," he says. There's definitely a slur to his speech and I can see how much he's drunk by the bitter set of his mouth. "He was mouthing off about the stag, and I've had enough."

"Charlie," I say. "What *happened* on the stag?"

He gives a long groan, covers his face with his hands.

"Tell me," I say. "How bad can it be? Really?"

Charlie's shoulders slump. He seems resigned to telling me, suddenly. He takes a deep breath. There's a long pause. And then, at last, he begins to talk.

"We got a ferry to this place a couple of hours' ride from Stockholm, made a camp there on an island in the archipelago. It was very . . . you know, boy's own, putting up tents, lighting a fire. Someone had bought some steaks and we cooked them over the embers. I didn't know any of the blokes other than Will, but they seemed all right, I suppose."

Suddenly it's all tumbling out of him, the booze he's drunk loosening his tongue. They'd all been to Trevellyan's together, he tells me, so there was a lot of boring reminiscing about that; Charlie just sat there and smiled and tried to look interested. He didn't want to drink much, obviously, and they mocked him about that. Then one of them—Pete, Charlie thinks—produced some mushrooms.

"You ate mushrooms, Charlie? *Magic* mushrooms?" I nearly laugh. This doesn't sound at all like my sensible, safety-conscious husband. I'm the one who's up for trying stuff out, who dipped her foot into it a couple of times in my teenage years on the Manchester club scene.

Charlie screws up his face. "Yeah, well, we were all doing it. When you're in a group of blokes like that . . . you don't say no, do you? And I didn't go to their posh school, so I was already the odd one out."

But you're thirty-four, I want to say to him. What would you say to Ben, if his friends were telling him to do something he didn't want to? Then I think of last night, as I downed that drink while they all chanted at me. Even though I didn't want to, knew I didn't actually have to. "So. You took magic mushrooms?" This is my husband, Deputy Head, who has a strict zero-tolerance policy of drugs at his school. "Oh my God," I say, and I do laugh now—I can't help it. "Imagine what the PTA would say about that!"

Next, Charlie tells me, they all got into the canoes and went to another island. They were jumping in the water, naked. They dared Charlie to swim out to a third tiny island—there were lots of dares like that—and then when he got back, they'd all gone. They had left him there, without his canoe.

"I had no clothes. It might have been spring, but it's the fucking Arctic Circle, Han. It's freezing at night. I was there for hours before they finally came for me. I was coming down from the mushrooms. I was so cold. I thought I was going to get hypothermia . . . I thought I was going to die. And when they found me I was—"

"What?"

"I was crying. I was lying on the ground, sobbing like a child."

He looks mortified enough to cry now and my heart goes out to him. I want to give him a hug, like I would Ben—but I'm not sure how it would go down. I know men do stupid stuff on stags, but this sounds targeted, like they were singling Charlie out. That's not right, is it?

"That's—horrible," I say. "That's like bullying, Charlie. I mean, it is bullying."

Charlie has a fixed, faraway expression. I can't read it. The arrogance of having always assumed I know my husband inside out. We've been together for years. But it has taken less than twenty-four hours in this strange place to show that assumption up for the illusion it is. I've felt it ever since we made that crossing over here. Charlie has seemed increasingly like a stranger to me. The stag do is one more confirmation of this: the discovery of a horrific experience that he has kept from me, that I now suspect might have changed him in some complex, invisible way. The truth is, I don't think Charlie is quite himself at the moment: or not the self I know. This place has done something to him—to us.

"It was all *his* idea," Charlie says. "I'm sure of it."

"Whose idea? Duncan's?"

"No. He's an idiot. A follower. Will. He was the ringleader. You could tell. And Johnno too. The others were all acting on instructions."

I can't quite imagine Will making the others do that. Anyway, the stags are normally the ones to call the shots, not the groom. Yeah, I can see *Johnno* being behind it, no problem, especially after that stunt just now. He has that slightly wild air about him. Not malicious, but like he might push things too far without really meaning to. Definitely Duncan. But not Will. I think Charlie prefers to hang the blame on Will simply because he doesn't like him.

"You don't believe me, do you?" Charlie says, his expression darkening. "You don't think it was Will."

"Well," I say. "If I'm honest, not really. Because—"

"Because you want to screw him?" he snarls. "Yeah, did you think I hadn't noticed? I saw the way you looked at him last night, Hannah. Even the way you say his name." He does a horrible little falsetto. "Oh Will, tell me about that time you got frostbite, oh, you're so masculine . . ."

The ferocity of his tone is so unexpected that I recoil from him. It's been so long since Charlie's been drunk that I'd forgotten the extent of the transformation. But I'm also reacting to the tiny element of truth in it. A flicker of guilt at the memory of how I found myself responding to Will. But it quickly transforms itself to anger.

"Charlie," I hiss, "how . . . how *dare* you speak to me like that? Do you realize how offensive you're being? All because he made some effort to make me feel welcome—which is a hell of a lot more than *you* did."

And then I remember last night, that flirting with Jules. That slinking into our bedroom in the small hours when he definitely hadn't been drinking with the men.

"Actually," I say, my voice rising, "you haven't got a leg to stand on. That whole horrible charade with you and Jules last night. She's always acting like she has you wrapped around her little finger—and you play along. Do you know how it makes me feel?" My voice cracks. "Do you?" I'm caught between anger and tears, the pressure and loneliness of the day catching up with me.

Charlie looks slightly chastened. He opens his mouth to speak but I shake my head.

"You've had sex with her, haven't you?" I've never wanted to know before. But now, I'm feeling brave enough to ask it.

There's a long pause. Charlie puts his head in his hands. "Once," he says, voice muffled through his fingers. "But . . . ages and ages ago, honestly . . ."

"When? When was it? When you were teenagers?"

He lifts his head. Opens his mouth, as though to speak, then closes it again. His expression. Oh my God. *Not* when they were teenagers. I feel as though I have been punched in the stomach. But I have to know now. "Later?" I ask.

He sighs, then nods.

My throat seems to close up so that it's a struggle to get the words out. "Was it . . . was it when we were together?"

Charlie folds over into himself, puts his face in his hands again. He lets out a long, low groan. "Han . . . I'm so sorry. It didn't mean anything, honest. It was so stupid. You were . . . it was, well, it was when we hadn't had sex for ages. It was—"

"After I had Ben." I feel sick to my stomach. I'm suddenly certain. He doesn't say anything and that's all the confirmation I need.

Finally, he speaks. "You know . . . we were going through a rough patch. You were, well . . . you were so down all the time, and I didn't know what to do, how to help—"

"You mean, when I had borderline postnatal depression? When I was waiting for the stitches to heal? Jesus Christ, Charlie—"

"I'm so sorry." All the bluster has gone out of him now. I could almost believe he's completely sober. "I'm so sorry, Han. Jules had just broken up with that boyfriend she had at the time—we went out for drinks after work . . . I had too much. We both agreed it was a terrible idea, afterwards, that it would never happen again. *It didn't mean anything.* I mean, I barely remember it. Han—look at me."

I can't look at him. I won't look at him.

It's so horrible I can barely begin to think about it clearly. I feel like I'm in shock, like the full hurt of it hasn't sunk in yet. But it throws all that flirting, all that physical closeness, into a new, terrible light. I think of all the times I have felt Jules has purposefully excluded me—cordoning off Charlie for herself.

That bitch.

"So all this time," I say, "all this time that you've been telling me you've only ever been friends, that a bit of flirting means nothing, that she's like a sister to you . . . that's not fucking true, is it? I have no idea what the two of you were doing last night. I don't want to know. But how *dare* you?"

"Han—" He reaches out a hand, touches my wrist, tentatively.

"No—don't touch me." I snatch my arm away, stand up. "And you're a state," I say. "An embarrassment. Whatever they did to you on the stag, there's no excuse for your behavior just now. Yeah, maybe it was awful, what they did. But it didn't do you any lasting harm, did it? For Christ's sake, you're a grown man—a father . . ." I almost add "a husband" but can't bring myself to. "You've got responsibilities," I say. "And you know what? I'm sick of looking after you. I don't care. You can sort out your own bloody mess." I turn and stride away.

JOHNNO
The Best Man

JOHNNO," WILL SAYS, WITH A LITTLE LAUGH. THE CAVE WALLS ECHO the laugh back at us. "I really don't know what you're talking about. All this talk of the past. It isn't good for you. You have to move on."

Yeah, I think, but I can't. It's like some part of me got stuck there. As much as I've tried to forget it, it has been there at the center of me, this toxic thing. I feel like nothing has happened in my life since, nothing that matters anyway. And I wonder how Will has been able to carry on living his life, without even a backward glance.

"They said it was a tragic accident," I say. "But it wasn't. It was us, Will. It was all our fault."

"I'VE BEEN TIDYING THE DORM," Loner said, when we came in from rugby practice. I'd told him to do it, as I'd run out of other stuff for him to do. "But I found these." He held them in his hand as though they might burn him: a stack of GCSE exam papers.

He looked at Will. You'd think from Loner's expression that someone had died. I suppose for him someone had died: his hero.

"Put them back," Will said, very quiet.

"You shouldn't have taken them," Loner said, which I thought showed courage, considering we were both about twice his height. He was a pretty brave kid, and decent, too, when I think about it. Which I try not to. He shook his head. "It's—it's cheating."

Will turned to me, after he'd left the room. "You're a fucking idiot," he said. "Why'd you get him to tidy it when you knew they were there?" He was the one that had stolen them, not me. Though I'm sure now that he'd have let me take the blame if it got out.

I remember how he gave a grin then that wasn't really a grin at all. "You know what?" he said. "I think tonight we'll play Survival."

"YOU COULDN'T BEAR IT," I say to Will. "Because you knew you'd get expelled if it got out. And your fucking reputation has always been so important to you. It's always been like that. You take what you want. And fuck everyone else, if they might get in your way. Even me."

"Johnno," Will says, his tone calm, rational. "You've had too much to drink. You don't know what you're saying. If it had been our fault, we wouldn't have got away with it. Would we?"

IT ONLY TOOK THE TWO of us. There were four boys in Loner's dorm that night—a couple of them had got sick and were in the infirmary. That helped. I felt like maybe one of them stirred when we came in, but we were quick. I felt like an assassin—and it was fucking brilliant. It was fun. I wasn't really thinking. Just adrenaline, pumping through me. I shoved a rugby sock into his mouth while Will tied the blindfold, so that any noises he made were pretty muffled and quiet. It wasn't hard to carry him: he weighed nothing at all.

He struggled a bit. He didn't wet himself, though, like some of the boys did. As I say, he was a pretty brave kid.

I thought we'd go into the woods. But Will motioned to the cliffs. I looked at him, not understanding. For one horrible moment it felt like he might suggest we throw the kid off them. "The cliff path," he mouthed at me. "Yeah, OK." I was relieved. It took us ages, climbing down the cliff path, with the chalk disintegrating with every step, our feet skidding, and we couldn't even use the handrail, hammered into the rock, because our hands were full. The kid had stopped struggling. He'd gone very still. I remember I was worried he couldn't breathe, so I went to take the gag out, but Will shook his head. "He can breathe through his nose," he said. Maybe it was around then that I started feeling bad. I told myself that was stupid: We had all been through it, hadn't we? We kept on going.

Finally we were on the beach, down on the wet sand. I couldn't work out how we were going to make this hard. It would be obvious where he was, once he'd got the blindfold off, even without his glasses. It wasn't that far from the school and anyone could climb up that cliff path—a little kid, especially. Boys went down to the beach all the time. But I thought: maybe Will wanted to make it easy for him, after all, because of all the stuff he'd done for us—cleaning our boots and tidying our dorm and all of the rest. That seemed fair.

"YOU KNOW IT, WILL," I say. A noise comes up from somewhere deep inside my chest, a sound of pain. I think I might be crying. "We *should* have paid for it, what we did."

I REMEMBER HOW WILL POINTED to the bottom of the cliff path. That was when he produced some laces. Nothing fancy, the laces from a pair of rugby boots.

"We're going to tie him up," he said.

It was easy in the end. Will got me to tie him to the handrail at the bottom of the cliff path—I was pretty good with knots, that sort of thing. *Now* I got it. That would make it a bit more difficult. He'd have to do a Houdini to get out of there, that was the part that would take the time.

Then we left him.

"FOR *GOD'S SAKE*, JOHNNO," WILL says. "You heard what they said, at the time. It was a terrible accident."

"You know that isn't true—"

"No. That is the truth. There isn't anything else."

I REMEMBER WAKING UP THE next day and looking out of the window in our dorm and seeing the sea. And that was when I realized. I couldn't believe how stupid we'd been. The tide had come in.

"Will," I said, "Will—I don't think he could have untied himself. The tide . . . I didn't think. Oh God, I think he might be—" I thought I might throw up.

"Shut up, Johnno," Will said. "Nothing happened, OK? First of all, we need to work that out between us, Johnno. Otherwise, we're in big trouble, you get that, right?"

I couldn't believe it was happening. I wanted to go to sleep and wake up and none of it be real. It didn't seem real, something so fucking terrible. All for the sake of a few bits of stolen paper.

"OK," Will said. "Do you agree? We were in bed. We don't know anything."

He'd jumped so quickly ahead. I hadn't even thought about that stuff, telling someone. But I guess I would have assumed that was what we had to do. That was the right thing, wasn't it? You couldn't keep something like this secret.

But I wasn't going to disagree with him. His face kind of scared me. His eyes had changed—like there was no light behind them.

I nodded, slowly. I guess I didn't think then about what it would mean, later, how it would destroy me.

"Say it out loud," Will told me.

"Yeah," I said, and my voice came out as a croak.

HE WAS DEAD. HE HADN'T been able to get himself free. It was a Tragic Accident. That was what we all got told a week later in assembly after he had been found, washed up farther along the beach, by the school caretaker. I suppose the ties must have come undone after all, just not in time to save him. You'd have thought there would have been marks, anyway. The local police chief was a mate of Will's dad. The two of them would drink together in Will's dad's study. I guess that helped.

"I REMEMBER HIS PARENTS," I say to Will now. "Coming to the school, after. His mum looked like she wanted to die, too." I saw her, from the dorm upstairs, getting out of her car. She looked up and I had to step out of sight, trembling.

I crouch down so I'm level with Will. I grip his shoulders, hard, make him look me in the eye. "We killed him, Will. We killed that boy."

He fights me off, throwing his arms out blindly. His fingernails catch my neck, scratching under my collar. It stings. I shove him against the rock with one hand.

"Johnno," Will says, breathing hard. "You need to get a grip of yourself. You need to shut the *fuck* up." And that's when I know I've gotten to him. He hardly ever swears. It doesn't fit with his golden boy image, I guess.

"Did you know?" I ask him. "You did know, didn't you?"

"Did I know what? I don't know what you're talking about. For Christ's sake, Johnno—untie me. This has gone on long enough."

"Did you know that the tide would come in?"

"I don't know what you're talking about. Johnno—you're not making sense. I knew it last night, mate, and in the speech. You've been drinking too much. Do you have a problem? Look. I'm your friend. There are ways to get help. I can help you. But stop with this fantasizing."

I push my hair out of my eyes. Even though it's cold I feel the sweat come away on my fingers. "*I* was a fucking idiot. I've always been the slow one, I know that. I'm not saying it's an excuse. I was the one who tied him up, yeah, when you told me to. But I didn't think about the tide. I didn't think about it until the next morning, when it was too late."

"Johnno," Will hisses, like he's scared someone might come.

It only makes me want to be louder. "All this time," I say. "All this time, I've wondered that. And I gave you the benefit of the doubt. I thought: yeah, Will could be a dick at school at times, but we all were. You had to be, to survive in that place."

It made us into animals.

I think of the kid, how he was an example of what happened if you weren't—if you were too good, too honest, if you didn't understand the rules.

"But," I say, "I thought: 'Will's not *evil*. He wouldn't kill a kid. Not over some stolen exam papers. Even if it meant he might get expelled.'"

"I didn't kill him," Will says. "No one killed him. The water killed him. The game killed him, maybe. But not *us*. It's not our fault he didn't get away."

"Yeah," I say. "Yeah, that's what I've told myself, all these years. I've repeated the story you created. It was the game. But we *were* the game, Will. He thought we were his mates. He trusted us."

"Johnno." Now he's angry. He leans forward. "Get a *fucking* grip. I'm not going to let you ruin all of this for me. Because you've got some regrets about the past, because your life is a mess and you don't have anything to lose. A little kid like him—he wouldn't ever have survived in the real world. He was a runt. If it wasn't us, it would have been something else."

THE TERM ENDED EARLY, BECAUSE of the death. Everyone turned their attention to the upcoming summer holidays and it seemed like the kid had never existed. I suppose he barely had for the rest of the school: he was a first year, a nonentity.

Except there was a snitch. One pupil who sneaked on us. I was always sure it was Loner's fat little friend. He said he'd seen us come into the dorm room, tie Loner up. It didn't get very far. Will's dad was headmaster, of course. He was a dick, most of the time—more to Will than anyone else. But for this, he had Will's back and mine too.

And we had each other's.

ALL THESE YEARS WE'VE STUCK together—bound by memories, by the dark shit we went through together, the thing we did. I thought he felt the same way about it too, that we needed each other. But what the TV stuff shows is that all that time he wanted out of our friendship. I'm too much of a liability. He wanted to distance himself from me. No wonder he looked so fucking uncomfortable when I told him I would be his best man.

"Johnno," Will says. "Think about my dad. You know what he's like. That's why I was desperate to try and get those grades. I *had* to do it. And if he'd found out the truth, how I hid those papers—he would have killed me. So I wanted to scare the kid—"

"Don't you dare," I say. "Don't you start feeling sorry for yourself. Do you know how many free passes you've been given? Because of how you look, how you manage to convince people that you're this great bloke?" It's only made me angrier, his self-pity.

"I'm going to tell them," I say. "I can't deal with it any longer. I'm going to tell them all—"

"You wouldn't dare," Will says, his voice changed now—low and hard. "You'd ruin our lives. Your life too."

"Ha!" I say. "It already ruined my life. It's been destroying me ever since that morning, when you told me to keep my mouth shut. I never would have stayed silent in the first place if it weren't for you. Since that boy died there hasn't been a day when I haven't thought about it, felt like I should have told someone. But you? Oh, no, it hasn't affected you in any way, has it? You've just gone on, like you always have. No consequences. Well you know what? I think it's about time that there are some. It'd be a relief, as far as I'm concerned. I'd only be doing what we should have done years ago."

There's a sound in the cave then, a woman's voice: "Hello?"

Both of us freeze.

"Will?" It's the wedding planner. "Are you in here?" She appears around the bend of the rock wall. "Oh, hello, Johnno. Will, I've been sent to find you—the other ushers told me that they'd left you in here." She sounds totally calm and professional, even though we're all standing in a bloody great cave, and one of us is slumped on the ground tied up and blindfolded. "It's been nearly half an hour, so Julia wanted me to come and . . . well, rescue you. I should warn you that she's not—" She looks like she's trying to find a way to put it delicately. "She's not as delighted as she might be by this . . . and the band are about to start."

She waits, as I untie Will and help him up, watching over us like a schoolteacher. Then we follow her out of the cave. I can't help wondering if she heard or saw anything. Or what I would have done if she hadn't interrupted us.

AOIFE

The Wedding Planner

IN THE MARQUEE THE CELEBRATIONS HAVE MOVED INTO ANOTHER gear. The guests have drunk the champagne dry. Now they are moving on to the stronger stuff: cocktails and shots at the temporary bar. They are high on the freedom of the night.

In the toilets in the Folly, refreshing the hand towels, I find telltale spills of fine white powder on the floor, scattered across the slate sink surround. I'm not surprised, I've seen guests wiping their noses furtively as they return to the marquee. They have behaved themselves for the rest of the day, this lot. They have traveled long distances to be here. They have come bearing gifts. They have dressed themselves appropriately and sat through a ceremony and listened to the speeches and worn the proper expressions and said the right things. But they're adults who have briefly left their responsibilities behind; they're like children without their parents present. Now this part of the day is theirs for the taking. Even as the bride and groom wait to begin their first dance they press forward, ready to make the dance floor their own.

An hour or so earlier, on a trip back to the Folly, I heard a strange noise, upstairs. The rest of the building was barricaded off, of course, but there are only so many measures you can take to stop drunk people going where they want. I went up to inspect, pushed open the door of the bride and groom's bedroom and found, not the happily married couple, but another man and woman, bent low over the bed. At my intrusion they scrambled to cover themselves, she yanking down her skirts red-faced, he covering his bobbing erection with his own top hat. Only a little while later, I saw them both returning innocently to different corners of the marquee. What particularly interested me about this was that they both appeared to be wearing wedding bands. And yet—and I've probably memorized the table plan as well as Julia herself now—I happen to know that all husbands and wives are seated opposite each other.

They weren't worried about me, though: not really. Their initial panic at my entrance gave way to a kind of giggly relief. They know I won't expose their secret. Besides, I wasn't particularly surprised. I've seen much of the same before. This extremity of behavior is very much par for the course. There are always secrets around the fringes of a wedding. I hear the things said in confidence, the bitchy remarks, the gossip. I heard some of the best man's words in the cave.

This is the thing about organizing a wedding. I can put together a perfect day, as long as the guests play along, remember to stay within certain bounds. But if they don't, the repercussions can last far longer than twenty-four hours. No one is capable of controlling that sort of fallout.

JULES
The Bride

THE BAND HAVE BEGUN TO PLAY. WILL—WHO RETURNED TO THE marquee looking slightly unkempt—takes my hand as we step onto the laminate floor. I realize I'm holding his hand hard enough to hurt, probably—and I tell myself to loosen my grip. But I'm incensed by the interruption to the evening caused by the ushers and their stupid prank. The guests surround us, whooping, hollering. Their faces are flushed and sweaty, their teeth bared, their eyes wide. They're drunk—and more. They press forward, leaning in, and the space suddenly feels too small. They're so close that I can smell them: perfume and cologne, the sour, yeasty smell of Guinness and champagne, body odor, booze-soured breath. I smile at them all because that is what I am meant to do. I smile so much that there is a dull ache somewhere beneath my ears and my whole jaw feels like an overstretched piece of elastic.

I hope I'm giving an impression of having a good time. I've drunk a lot, but it hasn't had any discernible effect other than making me more wary, more jittery. Since that speech I've been feeling a mounting unease. I look around me. Everyone else is having a great time: their inhibitions truly thrown off now. To them the train wreck of a speech is probably a mere footnote to the day—an amusing anecdote.

Will and I turn one way, then the other. He spins me away from him and back again. The guests shout their appreciation of these modest moves. We didn't go to dance lessons, because that would be unspeakably naff, but Will is a naturally good dancer. Except that a couple of times he treads on the train of my dress; I have to yank it away from under his feet before I trip. It's unlike him, to be so graceless. He seems distracted.

"What on earth was all of that?" I ask, when I'm drawn to his chest. I whisper it as though I am whispering a sweet nothing into his ear.

"Oh, it was stupid," Will says. "Boys being boys. Messing around, you know. A little leftover from the stag, maybe." He smiles, but he doesn't look quite himself. He downed two large glasses of wine when he returned to the marquee: one after the other. He shrugs. "Johnno's idea of a joke."

"The seaweed was supposedly a little joke last night," I say. "And that wasn't very bloody funny. And now this? And that speech—what did he mean by all of that? What was all that about the past? About keeping secrets from each other . . . what secrets did he mean?"

"Oh," Will says, "I don't know, Jules. It's only Johnno messing around. It's nothing."

We turn a slow circle about the floor. I have an impression of beaming faces, hands clapping.

"But it didn't *sound* like nothing," I say. "It sounded very *much* like something. Will, what sort of hold does he have over you?"

"Oh for God's sake, Jules," he says sharply. "I said: it's nothing. *Drop* it. *Please*."

I stare at him. It's not the words themselves so much as the way he said them—that and the way he has tightened his hold on my arm. It feels like as strong a corroboration as one could ask for that whatever it is, it's very much *not* nothing.

"You're hurting me," I say, pulling my arm out of his grip.

He is immediately contrite. "Jules—look, I'm sorry." His voice is totally different now—any hint of hostility immediately gone. "I didn't mean to snap at you. Look, it's been a long day. A wonderful day, of course, but a long one. Forgive me?" And he gives me a smile, the same smile I haven't been able to resist since I saw it that night at the V&A museum. And yet it doesn't have the same effect it normally does. If anything, it makes me feel more uneasy, because of the speed of the change. It's as though he's pulled on a mask.

"We're a married couple, now," I say. "We are meant to be able to share things with one another. To confide in each other."

Will spins me away under his arm, and toward him again. The crowd cheer this flourish.

Then, when we're facing one another once more, he takes a deep breath. "Look," he says. "Johnno has got this bee in his bonnet about this thing that he says happened in the past, when we were young. He's obsessed by it. But he's a fantasist. I've felt sorry for him, all these years. That's where I went wrong. Feeling I should pander to him, because my life has worked out, and his hasn't. Now he's envious: of everything I have, we have. He thinks that I owe him."

"Oh for God's sake," I say. "What could *you* possibly owe him? He's the one that's clearly been hanging on your coattails for too long."

He doesn't answer this. Instead he pulls me close, as the song comes to its crescendo. A cheer goes up from the crowd. But they sound suddenly far away. "After tonight, that's it," Will says firmly, into my hair. "I'll cut him from my life—our life. I promise. I'm done with him. Trust me. I'll sort it out."

HANNAH
The Plus-One

'VE WANDERED INTO THE DANCE TENT. THE FIRST DANCE IS OVER, thank God, and all the guests who were watching have swarmed in to fill the space. I'm not sure what I want to find in here, exactly. Some distraction, I suppose, from the churn of thoughts in my head. Charlie and Jules. It's too painful to think about.

It feels as though every single guest is crammed in here, a hot press of bodies. The band's vocalist takes to the mic: "Are you ready to dance, girls and boys?"

They begin to play a frenzied rhythm—four fiddles, a wild, foot-tapping tune. Bodies are crashing around as everyone attempts, unsuccessfully, drunkenly, to do his or her version of an Irish jig. I see Will grab Olivia out of the crowd: "Time for the groom to claim his dance with the bridesmaid!" But they seem oddly out of step as they career onto the dance floor, as though one of them is resisting the other. Olivia's expression gives me pause. She looks trapped. There was this bit in the speech. I thought that before. What was it? It had struck me as oddly familiar. I grope about in my memory for it, trying to focus.

The V&A museum, that was it. I remember her telling me last night about how she brought Steven there, to a party, held by Jules. And everything goes still as it occurs to me—

But that's completely crazy. It *can't* be. It wouldn't make any sense. It must be a weird coincidence.

"Hey," a guy says, as I push past him. "What's the hurry?"

"Oh," I say, glancing vaguely in his direction. "Sorry. I was . . . a bit distracted."

"Well, maybe a dance will help with that." He grins. I look at him more closely. He's pretty attractive—tall, black-haired, a dimple forming in one cheek when he smiles. And before I can say anything he takes hold of my hand and gives me a gentle tug toward him, onto the laminate of the dance floor. I don't resist.

"I saw you earlier," he shouts, over the music. "In the church, sitting on your own. And I thought: *She* looks worth getting to know." That grin again. Oh. He thinks I'm single, here by myself. He can't have caught that scene with Charlie in the bar.

"Luis!" he shouts now, pointing to his chest.

"Hannah."

Maybe I should explain that I'm here with my husband. But I don't want to think about Charlie right now. And holding this flattering new image of myself through his eyes—not the badly dressed imposter I thought I was, but someone attractive, mysterious—I decide not to say anything. I allow myself to begin to move in time with him, to the music. I allow him to move a little nearer, his eyes on mine. Perhaps I move closer, too. Close enough that I can smell his sweat—but clean sweat, a good smell. There's a stirring in the pit of my stomach. A little sting of want.

THE WEDDING NIGHT

SOMEONE ELSE OUT THERE. THE THOUGHT HAS THEM SPOOKING AT shadows, cringing away from shapes in the blackness, which seem to loom up at them and then reveal themselves to be nothing more than tricks of the eye. They move in a tight, close pack, afraid of losing another of their number. Pete is still missing.

They seem to feel the prickle of unknown eyes upon them. They feel clumsier now, more exposed. They trip and stumble over the uneven ground, over hidden tussocks of heather. They try not to think about Pete. They can't afford to: they have to look out for themselves. Every so often they shout to one another for reassurance more than anything else, their voices like another light held against the night, uncharacteristically caring: "All right there, Angus?" "Yeah—you OK, Femi?" It helps them to keep going. It helps them forget about their mounting fear.

"Jesus—what's that?" Femi sweeps his flashlight in a wide arc. It illuminates an upright form, rising palely out of the shadows, nearly as tall as a man. And then several similar shapes, some smaller, too.

"It's the graveyard," Angus calls, softly. They gaze at the Celtic crosses, the crumbling stone forms: an eerie, silent army.

"Christ," Duncan shouts. "I thought it was a person." For a moment they all thought it: the round shape and thin upright base conspired briefly to seem human. Even now, as they retreat some-what gingerly, it is hard to shake the feeling of being watched, reproachfully, by the many sentinel forms.

They continue for a time in a new direction.

"Do you hear that?" Angus shouts. "I think we've got too close to the sea now."

They stop. Somewhere near at hand they are vaguely aware of the crash of water against rock. They can feel the ground shudder-ing beneath their feet at the impact of it.

"OK. Right." Femi thinks. "The graveyard's behind us, the sea's here. So I think we need to go—that way."

They begin to creep away from the sound of the crashing surf.

"Hey—there's something there—"

Instantly, they all stop where they are.

"What did you say, Angus?"

"I said there's something there. Look."

They hold out their flashlights. The beams they cast tremble on the ground. They are bracing themselves to find a grisly sight. They are surprised, and rather relieved, when it reflects brightly off the hard gleam of metal.

"It's a—what is it?"

Femi, bravest among them, steps forward and picks it up. Turn-ing to them, shielding his eyes from the glare, he lifts it so they can all see. They recognize the object immediately; although it is man-gled out of shape, the metal twisted and broken. It is a gold crown.

WANDER ROUND THE CORNERS OF THE MARQUEE. I MOVE BETWEEN the tables. I pick up half-full glasses, the remains of people's drinks, and down them. I want to get as drunk as possible.

I pulled away from Will as quickly as I could, after he grabbed me for that dance. It made me feel sick, being so close to him, feeling his body pressed up against me, thinking of the things I've done with him . . . the things he got me to do . . . the horrible secret between us. It was like he was getting off on it. Right at the end he whispered in my ear: "That crazy stunt you pulled earlier . . . that's the end of it, OK? No more. Do you hear me? No more."

No one seems to notice me as I go about minesweeping their discarded drinks. They're all pretty wasted by now and, besides, they've abandoned the tables for the dance floor. It's absolutely crammed in there. There are all these thirty-somethings slut-dropping and grinding on each other as though they're in some shit strip club dancing to 50 Cent, not a marquee on a deserted island with some guys playing fiddles.

The old me might have found it funny. I could imagine texting my mates, giving them a live running commentary on the absolute cringe fest going on in front of me.

A few of the waiters are watching everyone from the corners of the marquee, sort of hovering on the edges of things. Some of them are about my age, younger. They all hate us, it's so obvious. And I'm not surprised. I feel like I hate them too. Especially the men. I've been touched on the shoulder, on the hip and on the bum tonight by some of the blokes here, Will and Jules's so-called friends. Hands grabbing, stroking, squeezing, cupping—out of sight of wives and girlfriends, as though I'm a piece of meat. I'm sick of it.

The last time it happened, I turned around and gave the guy such a poisonous stare that he actually backed away from me, making a stupid wide-eyed face and holding his hands up in the air—all mock-innocent. If it happens again I feel like I might really lose it.

I drink some more. The taste in my mouth is foul: sour and stale. I need to drink until I don't care about that sort of thing. Until I can't taste or feel anymore.

And then I'm seized by my cousin Beth and dragged toward the dance tent. Other than earlier, outside the church, I haven't seen Beth since last year at my aunt's birthday. She's wearing a ton of makeup but underneath you can see she's still a child, her face round and soft, her eyes wide. I want to tell her to wipe off the lipstick and eyeliner, to stay in that safe childhood space for a while longer.

On the dance floor, surrounded by all these bodies, moving and shoving, the room begins to spin. It's like all the stuff I've drunk has caught up with me in one big rush. And then I trip—maybe over someone's foot or maybe it's my own stupid, too-high shoes. I go down, hard, with a crack that I hear a long time before I feel it. I think I've hit my head.

Through the fug, I hear Beth speaking to someone nearby. "She's really drunk, I think. Oh my God."

"Get Jules," someone says. "Or her mum."

"Can't see Jules anywhere."

"Oh, look, here's Will."

"Will, she's pretty drunk. Can you help? I don't know what to do—"

He comes toward me, smiling. "Oh Olivia. What happened?" He reaches out a hand to me. "Come on, let's get you up."

"No," I say. I bat his hand away. "Fuck off."

"Come on," Will says, his voice so kind, so gentle. I feel him lifting me up, and it doesn't seem like there's much point in struggling. "Let's get you some air." He puts his hands on my shoulders.

"Get your hands off me!" I try to fight my way out of his grip.

I hear a murmur from the people watching us. I'm the difficult one, I bet that's what they're saying to each other. I'm the crazy one. An embarrassment.

OUTSIDE THE MARQUEE, THE WIND hits us full force, so hard it nearly knocks me over. "This way," Will says. "It's more sheltered round here." I feel too tired and drunk to resist, all of a sudden. I let him march me round the other side of the marquee, toward where the land gives way to the sea. I can see the lights of the mainland in the distance like a trail of spilled glitter in the blackness. They go in and out of focus: pin-sharp, then fuzzy, like I'm seeing them through water.

Now, for the first time in a long time, it's just the two of us.

Me and him.

JULES
The Bride

MY NEW HUSBAND SEEMS TO HAVE DISAPPEARED. "HAS ANYONE seen Will?" I ask my guests. They shrug, shake their heads. I feel like I've lost any control I might have had over them. They've apparently forgotten that they're here for my big day. Earlier they were circling around me until it almost got unbearable, coming forward with their compliments and well-wishes, like courtiers before their queen. Now they seem indifferent to me. I suppose this is their opportunity for a little hedonism, a return to the freedom they enjoyed at university or in their early twenties, before they were weighed down with kids or demanding jobs. Tonight is about them—catching up with their mates, flirting with the ones who got away. I could get angry, but there's no point, I decide. I've got more important things to be concerning myself with: Will.

The longer I look for him the more my sense of unease grows.

"I saw him," someone pipes up. I see it's my little cousin Beth. "He was with Olivia—she was a bit drunk."

"Oh, yeah. Olivia!" another cousin chimes in. "They went toward the entrance. He thought she should get some air."

Olivia, making a spectacle of herself yet again. But when I go outside there's no sign of them. The only people hanging around in the entrance of the marquee are a group of smokers—friends from university. They turn toward me and say all the things you're

meant to say about how wonderful I look, what a magical ceremony it was—I cut them off.

"Have you seen Olivia, or Will?"

They gesture vaguely around the side of the marquee, toward
the sea. But why on earth would Will and Olivia go out there? The
weather has started to turn now and it's dark, the moonlight too
dim to see by.

The wind screams about the marquee and around me when I
step into the brunt of it. Remembering the near-drowning scene
earlier, I feel my stomach pitch with dread. Olivia couldn't have
done something stupid, could she?

I FINALLY CATCH SIGHT OF their faint outlines beyond the main spill
of light from the marquee, toward the sea. But some intuition beyond naming stops me from calling out to them. I've realized that
they're very close to one another. In the near-dark the two shapes
seem to blur together. For a horrible moment I think . . . but no,
they must be talking. And yet it doesn't make sense. I'm not sure
I've ever seen my sister and Will speak to one another, beyond
polite conversation at least. I mean, they barely *know* each other.
They've met precisely once before. And yet they seem to have a
great deal to say to one another. What on earth can they be talking
about? Why come all the way round here, away from the sight of
the other guests?

I begin to move, silent as a cat burglar, edging forward into the
growing darkness.

OLIVIA
The Bridesmaid

'M GOING TO TELL HER," I SAY. IT'S AN EFFORT TO GET THE WORDS out, but I'm determined to do it. "I'm going to . . . I'm going to tell her about us." I'm thinking of what Hannah said, earlier. *It's always better to get it out in the open—even if it seems shameful, even if you feel like people will judge you for it.*

He clamps a hand over my mouth. It's a shock—so sudden. I can smell his cologne. I remember smelling that cologne on my skin, afterward. Thinking how delicious it was, how grown-up. Now it makes me want to vomit.

"Oh no, Olivia," Will says. His voice is still *almost* kind, gentle, which only makes it worse. "I don't think you will, actually. And you know why? You won't do it because you would be destroying your sister's happiness. This is her wedding day, you silly little girl. Jules is too special to you for you to do that to her. And for what purpose? It's not like anything is going to happen between us now."

There's a burst of chatter from the other side of the marquee, and perhaps he's worried someone is going to see us like this because he takes his hand away from my mouth.

"I know that!" I say. "That's not what I mean . . . that's not what I want."

He raises his eyebrows, like he isn't sure whether he believes me. "Well, what do you want, Olivia?"

Not to feel so awful any longer, I think. To get rid of this horrible secret I've been carrying around. But I don't answer. So he goes on: "I get it. You want to lash out at me. I will be the first to admit, I haven't behaved impeccably in all of this. I should have broken it off with you properly. I should perhaps have been more transparent. I never meant to hurt anyone. And can I tell you what I honestly think, Olivia?"

He seems to be waiting for a reply so I nod my head.

"I think that if you were going to do it, you would have done it by now."

I shake my head. But he's right. I have had so much time to do it, really, to tell Jules the truth. So many times I have lain in bed in the early hours of the morning and thought about how I'd get Jules on her own—suggest lunch, or coffee. But I never did it. I was too chicken. I avoided her instead, like I avoided going to the shop to try on my bridesmaid dress. It was easier to hide, to pretend it wasn't happening.

I've thought about what I would do in this situation if I were Jules, or Mum. How I would have made a big display, probably the first time I saw him—embarrassed him in front of everyone at the engagement drinks. But I'm not strong like them, not confident.

So I tried with the note. I printed it out and dropped it through Jules's letterbox:

Will Slater is not the man you think he is. He's a cheat and a liar. Don't marry him.

I thought it might at least make her question him. Make her think. I wanted to sow a tiny bit of doubt in her mind. It was pathetic, I can see that now. Maybe Jules didn't even get it. Maybe Will saw it first, or it got swept up with a load of flyers and trashed. And even if she did see it, I should have realized Jules isn't the sort of person to be bothered about a note. Jules isn't a worrier.

"You don't want to destroy your sister's life, do you?" Will says, now. "You couldn't do it to her."

It's true. Even though at times I feel like I hate her, I love her more. She'll always be my big sister, and this would ruin things between us forever.

He has such confidence in his own story. My own version of it all is falling apart. And I suppose he's right in saying that he didn't lie, not really. He just didn't tell the truth. I don't seem to be able to hold on to my anger anymore, the bright burning energy of it. I can feel it slipping away from me, leaving in its place something worse. A kind of nothingness.

And then, suddenly, I think of Jules, the smile on her face as she stood next to him in the chapel, not having a clue about who he really is. Jules never lets anyone make a fool of her . . . but he has. I feel angry for her in a way I haven't been able to for myself.

"I've kept your texts," I tell him. "I can show them to her." It's the last thing I have over him, the last bit of power I hold. I hold my phone out in front of him, to emphasize it. I should see it coming. But he's been speaking so softly, so gently, that somehow I don't. His arm darts out. He grabs my wrist in midair. He grabs my other wrist, too. And in one quick motion he's got my phone off me. Before I can even work out what he's doing he's hurled it, far away from us, into the dark water. It makes a tiny *plop!* as it enters.

"There'll be backups—" I say, even though I'm not sure how I'd find them.

"Oh yes?" He sneers. "You want to mess people's lives up, Olivia? Because you should know that I have some photos on my phone—"

"Stop!" I say. The thought of Jules—of anyone—seeing me like that . . .

I felt so uncomfortable when he was taking them. But he was so good at asking for them, telling me how sexy I looked while I was performing for him, how much it would turn me on. And I was worried that not doing them would make me look like a prude, a child. And he wasn't in them at all—not his face, not his voice. He could claim I sent them to him, I realize, that I had shot them myself. He could deny it all.

His face is very near to mine, now. For a crazy moment I think he might be about to kiss me. And even though I hate myself for it, a tiny part of me wants him to. Part of me wants *him*. And that makes me sick.

He's still got ahold of my other wrist. It hurts. I make a sound and try to pull away but he only grips me harder, his fingers digging into my flesh. He's strong, so much stronger than me. I realized that earlier, when he carried me out of the water, looking like the big hero, playing to the crowd. I think of my little razor blade, but it's in my beaded bag, somewhere in the marquee.

Will gives me a yank forward and I trip over my feet. My shoe comes off. It is only now that I realize it's not all that far to the cliff edge. And he's pulling me toward it. I can see all the water out there, glossy black in the moonlight. But . . . he wouldn't, would he?

THE WEDDING NIGHT

THE USHERS STARE AT THE MANGLED GOLD CROWN IN FEMI'S HAND. It seemed so out of place where they found it—sitting on the black earth, in the midst of the storm—that it takes all of them a few moments to work out where they have seen it before.

"It's Jules's crown," Angus says.

"Shit," Femi says. "Of course it is."

Each wonders silently what violence it might have taken to so brutally deform the metal.

"Did you see her face?" Angus asks. "Jules? Before she cut the cake? She looked really angry, I thought. Or . . . or maybe really frightened."

"Did anyone see her in the marquee?" Femi asks. "After the lights came on?"

Angus quails. "But surely you can't think . . . you don't mean you think something really bad could have happened to her?"

"Fuck." Duncan lets out a hiss of breath.

"I'm not saying that exactly," Femi answers. "I'm only saying—does anyone remember seeing her?"

There's a long silence.

"I can't—"

"No, Dunc. Neither can I."

They look about them in the darkness, eyes straining for any movement, ears pricked for any sound, breath catching in their throats.

"Oh God. Look, there's something else over there." Angus bends to retrieve the object. They all see how his hand trembles as he lifts it to the light, but none of them mocks him for his fear this time. They are all afraid now.

It's a shoe. A single court pump in a pale gray silk, a jeweled buckle on the toe.

HANNAH
The Plus-One

THIS GUY, LUIS, IS A GREAT DANCER. THE BAND IS WHIPPING THE guests into a frenzy, forcing us closer together as bodies career around us. And I find myself thinking about how bloody stressful and lonely my whole day has been. Charlie's largely responsible for that. I don't want to think about him right now, though. I'm too angry with him, too sad. Besides, when was the last time I abandoned myself to some music . . . when was the last time I had a really good dance? When was the last time I felt this desired, this bloody sexy? It feels like I lost that part of myself somewhere along the way. For these few hours I'm going to enjoy having it back. I put my hands above my head. I swing my hair, feel it brush the bare skin of my shoulders. I feel Luis watching me. I find the rhythm of the music with my hips. I was always a good dancer— those years of practice in Manchester clubs in my teens, raving to all the latest anthems from Ibiza. I'd forgotten how much in tune it makes me feel with my own body, how much it turns me on. And I can see how good I look reflected in Luis's approving expression, his gaze only leaving mine to travel down the length of my body as I move.

The music slows. Luis pulls me closer. His hands are on my waist and I can feel his heartbeat through his shirt, the heat of his chest beneath the fabric. I can smell his skin. His lips are inches away from mine. And I'm becoming aware, now our bodies are touching, that he's hard, pressing against me.

I pull away a little, try to put a few centimeters of space between us. I need to clear my head. "You know what," I say. My voice has a tremor in it. "I think I'm going to go and get a drink."

"Sure," he says. "Great idea!"

I hadn't meant him to come with me. I feel all of a sudden as though I need a bit of space, but at the same time I don't have the energy to explain. So we head to the bar tent together.

"How do you know Will?" I shout, over the music.

"What?" He moves closer to hear, his ear brushing my lips.

I repeat the question. "Are you from Trevellyan's too?" I ask.

"Oh," he says. "You mean the school? Nah, we went to the same uni in Edinburgh. We were on the rugby team together."

"Hey, Luis." A guy standing at the bar raises a hand and envelops him in a hug as we draw near. "Come join a lonely bloke in a drink, won't you? I've lost Iona to the dance floor. Won't be seeing her till the bitter end now." He catches sight of me. "Oh, *hello*. Pleased to meet you. Been keeping my boy company, have you? He spotted you in the chapel, you know—"

"Shut up," Luis says, flushing. "But yeah, we've had a dance, haven't we?"

"I'm Hannah," I say. My voice comes out a little strangled. I'm wondering what I'm doing here.

"Jethro," Luis's friend says. "So, Hannah, what you fancy drinking?"

"Er—" I waver, thinking I should be sensible. I've already had so much to drink today. Then I think of Charlie, and what he told me about him and Jules. I want to regain that sense of freedom I felt, briefly, on the dance floor. I want to be a lot less sober. "A shot," I say, turning to the barman: it's Eoin, from earlier. "Of . . . er—tequila." I don't want to mess around.

Jethro raises his eyebrows. "Okaaay. I'm in. Luis?"

Eoin pours us three tequilas. We down our shots. "Christ," Luis says, slamming his down, his eyes tearing up. But I feel like mine hasn't done anything. It might as well have been water.

"Another," I say.

"I like her," Jethro says to Luis. "But I'm not sure my liver does."

"I think it's fucking sexy," Luis says, beaming at me.

We do another shot.

"You weren't at Edinburgh," Jethro says, squinting at me. "Were you? Know I'd remember you if you had been. Party girl like you."

"No," I say. That place again. The mere mention of it makes me feel a whole lot more sober. "I—"

"We were," Jethro says, slinging an arm around Luis's neck. "Time of our lives, right, Lu? Still miss it. Miss playing rugby too. Though it's probably good for my own safety that I don't." He points at the bridge of his nose, which is flattened, clearly an old break.

"I lost a tooth," Luis says.

"I remember!" Jethro laughs. He turns to me. " 'Course, Will never got a scratch on him. Played winger, the bastard. Pretty boy position. That's why he's so disgustingly handsome."

"He was the worst blocker," Luis says, "when we went out after a match. You'd be there trying to chat up some girl and then Will would trundle over to ask if you wanted a round and they'd only have eyes for him."

"His hit rate was insane," Jethro says, nodding. "Only reason he joined the Reeling Society, because of the totty. Let's not forget he wasn't always such a player, though. Remember the one who got away?"

"Oh, yeah," Luis says. "I'd forgotten about that. The Northern girl, you mean? The clever one?"

Oh God. It feels as though horrible is coming into focus. And I can only stand here and watch it.

"Yeah," Jethro says. "Like you." He winks at me. "He got his own back, though, when she dumped him. Remember, Luis?"

Luis squints. "Not really. I mean . . . I remember she left uni. Didn't she? I remember him being pretty cut up when she broke it off. Always thought she was a bit too smart for him."

The sick feeling in the pit of my stomach grows.

"That video that did the rounds, remember?" Jethro says.

"Shiiiiit," Luis says, eyes widening. "Yeah, of course. That was . . . savage."

"It's probably found its way onto PornHub now," Jethro says. "Vintage section, obviously. Wonder what she's doing now. Knowing it's out there somewhere."

"Hey," Luis says suddenly, looking at me. "You all right? Jesus—" He puts a hand on my arm. "You've actually gone white." He grimaces, sympathetically. "That last shot go down the wrong way?"

I shove him away and stumble away from them. I need to get outside. I barely make it out in time before I fall onto my hands and knees and vomit onto the ground. My whole body is trembling as though I am running a fever. I'm dimly aware of a couple of guests, standing inside the entrance, murmuring their shock and disgust, the tinkle of a laugh. I vaguely register that the weather out here has become so much wilder, whipping my hair away from my head, stinging the tears from my eyes.

I vomit again. But unlike with my seasickness on the boat I don't feel any better. This sickness cannot be alleviated. It has gone down deep inside me, the poison of this new knowledge. It has found its way to my very core.

THE WEDDING NIGHT

WHO WAS WEARING THIS?" ANGUS HOLDS THE SHOE UP. HIS hand shakes.

"I know I've seen it before," Femi replies. "But I can't think where—it all seems so long ago." It is the day that feels surreal now. This: the night, the storm, their fear, has become all that exists for them.

"Should we take it with us?" Angus asks. "It might—it might be some sort of clue as to what happened."

"No. We should leave it where it is," Femi says. "We shouldn't have even touched it. Or the crown, to be honest."

"Why?" Angus asks.

"Because, you idiot," Duncan snaps, "it could be evidence."

"Hey," Angus says, as they leave the shoe and carry on. "The wind—it's stopped."

He's right. Somehow, without their noticing it, the storm has worn itself out. In its wake it leaves an eerie stillness that makes them long for its return. This quiet feels like a held breath, a false calm. And they can hear their own frightened breathing now, hoarse and shallow.

It has been difficult to make much progress when they're checking in all directions—anxiously scanning the velvet darkness for any threat, any sign of movement. But now, finally, the

Folly looms into view in the distance, its windows reflecting a black glitter.

"There." Femi stops short. The others behind him freeze.

"I think—" he says, "I think there's something there."

"Not another fucking shoe," Duncan shouts. "What is this? Cinderella? Hansel and bloody Gretel?" None of them is convinced by this attempt at a joke. All of them hear the rattle of fear in his voice.

"No," Femi says. "It's not a shoe."

All of them have heard the edge to his voice. It makes them want very much *not* to look, to cringe away from whatever it is. Instead they force themselves to stand and watch as he moves his flashlight in a slow arc, the beam traveling weakly across the ground.

There is something there. Though it's not a something, this time. It's someone. They look on in growing horror as a long shape appears in the light upon the earth. Prone, terrible, definitely human. It lies fairly close to the Folly, on the edge of where the peat bog takes over from the more solid ground. In the wind the edges of the body's clothing fidget and snicker, and this, along with the wavering light from the phone's flashlight, gives an unnerving impression of movement. A macabre trick, a sleight of hand.

To the ushers it doesn't seem likely that there can really be a human being inside those clothes. A human who was, until recently, talking and laughing. Who was among them all, celebrating a wedding.

AOIFE

The Wedding Planner

WITH THE HELP OF SEVERAL OF THE WAITING STAFF, AND IN-finite care, we have lifted the great cake into the center of the marquee. Shortly the guests will be called in here to gather around it, to witness the cutting of the first slice. It feels as much of a sacrament as the ceremony in the chapel earlier.

Freddy emerges from the catering area, carrying the knife. He frowns at me. "Are you all right?" he asks, looking closely at me.

"I'm fine," I tell him. I suppose I must be wearing the tension of the day on my face. "Just feeling a little overwhelmed, I suppose."

Freddy nods, he understands. "Well," he says. "It'll all be over soon." He passes me the knife, to place beside the cake. It's a beautiful thing, finely wrought: a long blade and an elegant mother-of-pearl handle. "Tell them to be really careful with this. It could give you a nick from the slightest touch. The bride asked for it to be sharpened specially—madness really, as a knife like this is really meant for cutting through meat. It'll go through that sponge like it's butter."

JULES
The Bride

OLIVIA AND WILL, BY THE CLIFF EDGE: I HEARD IT ALL. OR, AT LEAST, enough to understand. Some of it was snatched away by the wind and I had to move so close to them that I was certain that they would glance in my direction and see me. But apparently each was too intent on the other—their confrontation—to notice. I couldn't make sense of it at first.

"I'll tell her about us," Olivia shouted. At first I resisted understanding. It couldn't be, it was too horrific to contemplate—

I thought then about Olivia, when she came out of the water. How it seemed, for a moment, like there was something she was trying to tell me.

Then I heard the way his voice changed. How he put his hand over her mouth. How he grabbed her arm. That shocked me even more than the actual substance of what he was saying. Here was my husband. Here was also a man I barely knew.

As I watched them from the shadows I noticed a kind of physical familiarity between them that spoke more eloquently than any words.

When I saw them by the cliff edge the whole hideous shape of it began to coalesce before me.

There wasn't time for anger at first. Only for the huge, existential shock of it: the bottom dropping out of everything. Now I am beginning to feel differently.

He has humiliated me. He has played me for a fool. I feel the rage, almost comforting in its familiarity, blossoming up inside of me and obliterating everything else in its wake.

I rip off my gold crown, cast it to the ground. I stamp down until it is reduced to a mangled piece of metal. It's not enough.

OLIVIA
The Bridesmaid

WILL!" IT'S JULES'S VOICE. AND THEN A BRIGHT BLUISH LIGHT—
the flashlight on her phone. It feels like we've been caught in a spotlight. Both of us freeze. Will drops my arm, straightaway, like my skin has burned him, and steps quickly away from me.

I couldn't tell anything from the way she said his name. It was completely neutral—maybe a bit of impatience. I wonder how much she has seen, or, more important, how much she has heard. But she can't have heard all that much, can she? As otherwise— well, I know Jules. We'd probably both be lying at the bottom of that cliff by now.

"What on earth are you two doing out here?" Jules asks. "Will, everyone's wondering where you are. And Olivia—someone said you fell?" She comes closer. Something's different about her, I think. She's missing her gold crown: that's it. But maybe there's another change, too, something that I can't quite put my finger on.

"Yes," Will says, all charm again. "I thought it best if I took her out for a bit of air."

"Well," Jules says. "That was kind of you. But you should come inside now. We're going to cut the cake."

THE WEDDING NIGHT

T HE USHERS MOVE TOWARD THE BODY CAREFULLY.

It lies a little off the tract of drier land, where the peat takes over. Already the bog has begun to gather itself around the edges of the corpse, hemming it in diligently, lovingly—so that even if the dead one were suddenly to miraculously come to life, to stir itself and try to stand, they might find it a little more difficult than expected. Might struggle to free a hand, a foot. Might find themselves held close and tight to the wet black breast of the earth.

The bog has swallowed other bodies before, swallowed them whole, yawned them deep down into itself. This was a long time ago, though. It has been hungry for some time.

As they creep closer, disparate parts are revealed in the sweeps of light: the legs, splayed clumsily outward, the head thrown back against the ground. The vacant, sightless eyes, gleaming in the beam. They glimpse a half-open mouth, the tongue protruding slightly, somehow obscene. And at the sternum a stain of dark red blood.

"Oh fuck," Femi says. "Oh fuck . . . it's Will."

For the first time, the groom does not look beautiful. His features are contorted into a mask of agony: the staring clouded eyes, that lolling tongue.

"Oh Jesus," someone says. Angus retches. Duncan lets out a

sob: Duncan, who none of them have seen moved by anything. Then he crouches and shakes the body—"Come on, mate. Get up! Get up!" The movement creates a horrible pantomime of animation as the head rolls from side to side. "Stop it!" Angus shouts, grabbing at Duncan. "Stop it!"

They stare and stare. Femi's right. It is. But it *can't* be. Not Will, the anchor of their group, the untouchable one, loved by all.

They are all so focused upon him—their fallen friend—so caught up in their shock and grief, that they have let their guard down. None of them notice the movement a few feet away: a second figure, very much alive, stepping toward them out of the darkness.

WILL
The Groom

JULES AND I WALK BACK TO THE MARQUEE TOGETHER. I LEAVE OLIVIA to make her own way. For one crazy moment there, realizing how near we were to the cliff edge, I was tempted. It wouldn't have come as that much of a surprise. She tried to drown herself earlier, after all—or that's certainly how it looked, before I saved her. And with this wind—it's really blowing a gale now—there would have been so much confusion.

But that's not me. I'm not a killer. I'm a good guy.

It's all somewhat out of control, though, everything getting out of hand. I'll have to sort things out.

Obviously I could never have told Jules about Olivia. Not by the time I made the connection between them that day at her mum's house, not when it had gone so far. What would have been the point in hurting Jules unnecessarily? The thing with Olivia— that was never going to be real, was it? It was a temporary attraction. With her it was all based on lies, hers as much as mine. In fact it was the pretense that got me going when we met on that date, her trying to be someone she wasn't. Pretending to be older, pretending to be sophisticated. That insecurity. It made me want to corrupt her, rather like a girlfriend I had at uni once, who was one of the good girls—smart, a hard worker, who came from some crummy school and didn't think she was good enough to be there.

When I met Jules at that party, however, that was different. It was like Fate. I saw how good we would be together straight-away. How good we'd *look* together—physically, yes, but also in how well-matched we were. Me, on the brink of a promising new career, her, such a high flyer. I needed an equal, someone with self-confidence, ambition—someone like me. Together we'd be invincible. And we are.

Olivia will keep quiet, I think. I've known that since the be-ginning. Knew she wouldn't feel anyone would believe her. She doubts herself too much. Except—and perhaps I'm simply being paranoid—it does feel like she's changed since we've been here. Everything seems changed on this island. It's as though the place is doing it, that we've been brought here for a reason. I know that's ridiculous. It's the fact of having so many people in one spot at once: past and present. I'm usually so careful, but I admit I hadn't thought it all through, how it might play out having them all here together. The consequences of it.

So. Olivia: I think I'm fine there. But I'll have to do something about Johnno, soon as I get back to the marquee. I can't have him running his mouth off to anyone and everyone. I underestimated him, perhaps. I thought it was safer to have him here than not, to keep him close. But Jules invited Piers without my knowing. Yes, actually, *that's* where it all went wrong. If she hadn't, Johnno would never have known about the TV thing and we could have carried on as normal. It would never have worked, him on the show, he must know that. He does, in fact: he put it so well himself. He's an absolute liability. With his pot smoking and his drinking and his long fucking memory. He'd have had some sort of freak-out in front of a journalist and it would all have come out. If he can see that—what a disaster he would have been—then I don't really understand why is he so cut up about it. Anyway, he's dangerous. What he knows, what he could tell. I'm fairly sure no one would believe him—some absurd story from twenty years ago. But I won't run that risk. He's dangerous in other ways too. I have no idea what he was about to do in the cave, because I had the blindfold on, but I'm bloody glad Aoife found us when she did, otherwise who knows what might have happened.

Well. This time, he's not going to catch me unawares.

HANNAH

The Plus-One

'M TRYING TO LOOK AT IT RATIONALLY, WHAT I LEARNED FROM JETHRO and Luis. Is there the smallest chance it's a coincidence? I am trying to listen to my sensible voice. Imagining what I would tell Charlie in a similar situation: You're drunk. You're not thinking coherently. Sleep on it, think again in the morning.

But really—even without having to reflect properly—I know. I can feel it. It fits, too neatly to be any coincidence.

The video of Alice was posted anonymously, of course. And we were too lost in grief at the time to think about seeking out her friends, who might have been able to help us find the culprit. But later, I vowed that if I ever had a chance to get my revenge on the man who ruined my sister's life—who *ended* her life—I would make him suffer. Oh God . . . and to think I fancied him. I dreamt about him last night—the thought makes more bile rise into my mouth. It is yet another insult, that I fell for the same charm that destroyed Alice.

I think of Will at the rehearsal dinner. *Did we meet at the engagement drinks? You seem familiar. I must have seen you in one of Jules's photos.* When he said he recognized me, he didn't recognize *me*. He recognized Alice.

• • •

BENEATH MY CALM EXTERIOR, AS I step back into the marquee, is a rage so powerful it frightens me. The man responsible for my sister's death has flourished, has carved a career out of false charm, out of essentially being good-looking and privileged. While Alice, a million times brighter and better than him—my clever, brilliant sister—never got her chance.

I'm surrounded by a sea of people. They're drunk and stupid, bumbling about. I can't see through them, past them. I push my way through, at times so forcefully that I hear little exclamations, sense heads turning to look at me.

The lights seem to be failing again. It must be the wind. As I walk through the crowd they flicker and go out, then come on again. Then out. Earlier, when it was twilight, you could still see pretty well. But now without the electric lights it's nearly pitch-black. The little tea lights on the tables are no use. If anything it's more confusing, being able to see vague shapes of people, shadows moving this way and that. People shriek and giggle, bump into me. I feel like I'm in a haunted house. I want to scream.

I clench and unclench my fists so hard I feel my nails puncture the flesh of my palms.

This is not me. This is a feeling like being possessed.

The lights come on. Everyone cheers.

Charlie's voice, amplified by the mic, echoes from the corner of the room. "Everyone: it's time to cut the cake." Over the guests crowding in front of me I stare at my husband, holding his microphone. I have never felt so far away from him.

There is the cake, white and glistening and perfect with its sugar flowers and leaves. Jules and Will stand, poised, next to it. And in fact, they look like the perfect figurines atop a wedding cake: him lean and fair in his elegant suit, her dark and hourglass-shaped in her white dress. I would never say I have hated anyone before. Not properly. Not even when I heard about Alice's boyfriend, what he had done to her, because I didn't have a real figure to focus it on. Oh, but I *hate* him, now. Standing there, grinning into the flashes of a hundred mobiles. I move closer.

THE WEDDING PARTY IS CLUSTERED around them. The four ushers, grinning away, patting Will on the back . . . and I wonder: Have any of them glimpsed his true nature? Do they not care? Then there's Charlie, doing a pretty good impression—and I'm certain it's just that—of looking sober and in control of his faculties. Nearby stand Jules's parents and Will's, smiling on proudly. Then Olivia, looking as miserable as she has all day.

I move a little closer. I don't know what to do with this feeling, this energy that is crackling through me, as though my veins have been fed with an electric current. When I put out a hand I see my fingers tremble with it. It frightens me and excites me at the same time. I feel that if I were to test it out, right now, I'd find that I have a new, unnatural strength.

Aoife steps forward. She passes a knife to Jules and Will. It's a big knife, with a long, sharp blade. There is a mother-of-pearl handle to it, as though to make the whole thing look softer, to conceal its sharpness, as though to say: this is a knife for cutting a wedding cake, nothing more sinister than that.

Will puts his hand over Jules's. Jules smiles at us all. Her teeth gleam.

I move closer still. I'm nearly at the front.

They cut down, together, her knuckles white around the handle, his hand resting upon hers. The cake cleaves away, exposing its dark red center. Jules and Will smile, smile, smile, into the phone cameras around them. The knife is placed back on the table. The blade gleams. It is right there. It is within reach.

And then Jules leans down and picks up a huge handful of cake. While smiling for the cameras, quick as a flash, she smashes it into

Will's face. It looks as violent as a slap, a punch. Will staggers away from her, gaping through the mess at her as chunks of sponge and icing fall, landing on his immaculate suit. Jules's expression is unreadable.

There is a moment of appalled silence as everyone waits to see what will happen. Then Will puts a hand to his chest, does an "I've been hit" pantomime, and grins. "I better go and wash this off," he says.

Everyone whoops and cheers and shrieks and forgets the strangeness of what they just saw. It is all a part of the ceremony.

But Jules, I notice, is not smiling.

Will walks from the marquee, in the direction of the Folly. The guests have resumed their chatter, their laughter. Perhaps I am the only one who turns to watch him go.

The band begins to play again. Everyone spills toward the dance floor. I stand here rooted to the spot.

And then the lights go out.

OLIVIA
The Bridesmaid

HE WAS RIGHT. I'M NEVER GOING TO TELL JULES NOW.

I think about how he twisted it all around. How he made me feel it was my fault, somehow, everything that happened. He played on the shame he made me feel: the same shame I have felt ever since I saw him walk through the door with Jules. He has made me feel small, unloved, ugly, stupid, worthless. He has made me hate myself and he has driven a wedge between me and everyone else, even my own family—especially my own family— because of this horrible secret.

I think about how he grabbed my arm just now, by the cliff. I think of what might have happened if Jules hadn't come along. If she had seen, everything would be different. But she didn't and I've missed my moment. No one would believe me, if I told them now. Or they'd blame me. I can't do it. I'm not brave enough for that.

But I could do *something*.

And then the lights go out.

JULES
The Bride

THE CAKE WASN'T ENOUGH. IT FELT PETTY, PATHETIC. HE HAS LET ME down, irrevocably. Like every other bloody person in my family. I overrode all of my carefully constructed security measures for him. I made myself vulnerable to him.

The thought of him smiling at me as we cut down, our hands joined on the cake. His hands that have been all over my own sister's body, that have—God, it's all too disgusting to contemplate. Did he think about her, when we slept together? Did he think I was too stupid to ever guess? He must have done, I suppose. And he was right. That's one more small part of what makes it so insulting.

Well. He has underestimated me.

The rage is growing inside me, overtaking the shock and grief. I can feel it blossoming up behind my ribs. It's almost a relief, how it obliterates every other feeling in its path.

And then the lights go out.

JOHNNO
The Best Man

'M OUTSIDE IN THE DARKNESS. IT'S BLOWING A BLOODY GALE OUT here. It feels like things keep appearing out of the night. I put up my hands to fight them off. Most of all I'm seeing that face again, the same one I saw last night in my room. The big glasses, that look he wore in the dorm that last time, a few hours before we took him. The boy we killed. We *both* killed him. But only one of our lives has been destroyed by it.

I'm feeling pretty out of it. Peter Ramsay was passing stuff out like after-dinner mints—the effects are finally taking hold of me.

Will, that fucker. Going into the marquee like nothing had happened, like none of it had touched him: big fat grin on his face. I should have finished him off in that cave, I think, while I still had the chance.

I'm trying to get back to the marquee. I can see the light of it, but it's like it keeps appearing in different places . . . nearer then farther away. I can hear the noise of it, the canvas in the wind, the music—

And then the lights go out.

AOIFE
The Wedding Planner

THE LIGHTS GO OUT. THE GUESTS SHRIEK.

"Don't worry, everyone," I shout. "It's the generator, failing again, because of the wind. The lights should come on again in a few minutes, if you all stay here."

WILL
The Groom

I'M WASHING THE CAKE OFF MY FACE IN THE BATHROOM AT THE Folly. Getting here was no picnic, even having the lights of the building to follow, because the wind kept trying to blow me off course. But perhaps it's good to have some space, to clear my thoughts. Jesus, there's icing in my hair, even up my nose. Jules really went for it. It was humiliating. I looked up afterward and saw my father, watching me. Same expression he's always worn—like when the first team was announced for the big match and I wasn't on it. Or when I didn't get into Oxbridge, or when I got those GCSE results and they were a whisker too perfect. More like a sort of grim satisfaction, like he'd been proven right about me all along. I have never *once* seen him look proud of me. That in spite of the fact that I've only ever tried to better myself, to achieve, as he always told me to. In spite of everything I *have* achieved.

Jules's expression when she picked up that slice of cake. *Fuck.* Has she worked something out? But what? Perhaps she was still just annoyed about the ushers carrying me off like that: the interruption to our evening. I'm sure it was that and nothing more. Or, if needs be, I'm sure I can convince her otherwise.

It wasn't meant to be like this. It all suddenly feels so fragile. Like the whole thing could come crashing down at any moment.

I need to go back there and get a handle on everything. But what to sort out first?

I look up, catch sight of my reflection in the mirror. Thank God for this face. It doesn't show one bit of any of it, the stress of the last couple of hours. It's my passport. It earns me trust, love. And this is why I know I'll always win, in the end, over a bloke like Johnno. I wipe one last tiny crumb from the corner of my mouth, smooth my hair. I smile.

And then the lights go out.

THE WEDDING NIGHT

THEY CROUCH OVER THE BODY. FEMI—A SURGEON IN ORDINARY life, which feels very far away right now—bends down over the prone form, puts his face close to the mouth and listens for any sounds of breathing. It's futile, really. Even if it were possible to hear anything over the sound of the wind, it is quite clear from the open, cloudy eyes, the gaping mouth, the dark stain of crimson at the chest, that he is very dead.

They are all so focused on the motionless form in front of them that none of them has noticed that they are not alone, none of them glimpsing the figure that has remained shrouded in darkness on the edge of their circle. Now he steps into the light of their torches, looming out of the blackness like some terrible, ancient figure—Old Testament, the personification of vengeance. They don't even recognize him at first. The first thing they see is all the blood.

He appears to have bathed in it. It covers his shirt front: the garment now more crimson than white. His hands are steeped to the wrists in it. There is blood up his neck, blood crusted along his jaw, as though he has been drinking it.

They stare at him in silent horror.

He is sobbing quietly. He raises his hands toward them and now they catch the glint of metal. So the second thing they see is the knife. If they had time to think about it they might recognize it, the blade. It's a long, elegant blade with a mother-of-pearl handle, most recently seen slicing through a wedding cake.

Femi is the first to find his voice. "Johnno," he says, very slowly and carefully. "Johnno—it's all over, mate. Put the knife down."

WILL

The Victim

FUCK. ANOTHER POWER CUT. I FUMBLE IN MY TOP POCKET FOR MY phone, flick on the torch as I step out into the night. It's really blowing a gale out here. I have to put my head down and lean into it to make any headway. Christ, I hate it when my hair gets messed up by the wind. Not the sort of thing I'd ever admit out loud—it wouldn't be very on-brand for *Survive the Night*.

When I look up to check the direction I am walking in, I realize that there's someone coming toward me, visible only by the light of their phone. I must be lit up to them while they remain invisible to me.

"Who's there?" I ask. And then, finally, I can make the shape of them out.

Make her out.

"Oh," I say, in some relief. "It's you."

"HELLO, WILL," AOIFE SAYS. "GOT all that cake off?"

"Yes, just about. What's going on?"

"Another power cut," she says. "Sorry about this. It's this weather. The forecast didn't say it would be nearly as bad as this. Our generator can't keep up with it. It should really have kicked in by now . . . I was going to see what had happened. Actually—you wouldn't be able to help me, would you?"

I'd really rather not. I need to get back, there are things to sort out—a wife to placate, a bridesmaid and a best man to . . . deal with. But I suppose I can't do any of those things in the dark. So I might as well be of help. "Of course," I say gallantly. "As I said this morning, I'm only too eager to be of assistance."

"Thank you. That's very kind."

"It's a wee way over here." She leads me off the path, round toward the back of the Folly. We're sheltered from the wind here. And then—odd—she turns to face me, even though we haven't reached anything that looks like a generator. She's shining the light in my eyes. I put up a hand. "That's a bit bright," I say. I laugh. "It feels like I'm at an interrogation."

"Oh," she says. "Does it?"

But she doesn't lower the light.

"Please," I say, getting annoyed now but trying to remain civil. "Aoife—the light is in my eyes. I can't see anything, you know."

"We don't have very much time," she says. "So this will have to be quick."

"What?" For a very strange moment I feel as though I am being propositioned. She is certainly attractive. I noticed that this morning, in the marquee. All the more so for trying to cover it up—I've always liked that, as I've said, that unawareness in a woman, that insecurity. What she's doing with a fat fuck of a husband like Freddy is anyone's guess. Even so, my hands are rather full right now.

"I suppose I just wanted to tell you something," she says. "Perhaps I should have told you when you mentioned it this morning. I didn't think it would be prudent, then. The seaweed in the bed last night. That was me."

"The seaweed?" I stare into the light, trying to work out what on earth she's talking about. "No, no," I say. "It must have been one of the ushers, because that was—"

"What you used to do at Trevellyan's—to the younger boys. Yes. I know. I know all about Trevellyan's. Quite a bit more than I would like to, really."

"About . . . but I don't understand—" My heart is beginning to beat a little faster in my chest, though I'm not quite sure why.

"I looked for you for so long online," she says. "But William Slater—it's a pretty common name. And then *Survive the Night* came out. And there you were. Freddy recognized you instantly. And you hadn't even changed the format, had you? We've watched every episode."

"What—?"

"So. It's why I tried so very hard to get you here," she says. "Why I offered that ridiculous discount to be featured in your wife's magazine. I *would* have expected her to question it a little more than she did. But I suppose that's why she's so well suited to you. Entitled enough to believe that the world simply owes her something. She must have realized that there would be no way we could make a profit from it. But I am getting something out of it, so it happens."

"And what's that?" I am beginning to back away from her. This is suddenly feeling a little fishy. But my right foot lands upon a piece of ground that gives way beneath it. It begins to sink. We're right on the edge of the bog. It's almost like she's planned it that way.

"I wanted to talk to you," she says. "That's all. And I couldn't think of a better way to do it."

"What—than like this, in the middle of a gale, in the pitch-black?"

"Actually I think it's the perfect way to do it. Do you remember a little boy called Darcey, Will? At Trevellyan's?"

"Darcey?" The light in my face is so bright I can't fucking think straight. "No," I say. "I can't say I do. *Darcey*. Is that even a boy's name?"

"Surname Malone? I believe you used surnames only there."

Actually, come to think of it, it does ring a bell. But it can't be. Surely not—

"But of course you'll remember him as Loner," she says. "Malone . . . Loner. That was the name you called him by, wasn't it? I still have all the letters from him, you see. I have them here with me on this island. I looked at them only this morning. He wrote to me about you, you know. You and Jonathan Briggs. His 'friends.' I knew something wasn't right about the friendship—and I didn't do anything. That is my cross to bear.

"His grave's right here. Where we were all happiest."

"I—I don't understand."

And then I remember a photo, of a teenage girl on a white sand beach. The one Johnno and I used to tease him about. The hot sister. But it *can't* be—

"I don't have time to explain everything," she says. "I wish I did. I wish we had time to talk. All I *wanted* was to talk, really, to find out why you did what you did. That's why I was so keen for you to come here, to hold your wedding on the island. There were so many things I wanted to ask you. Was he frightened, at the end? Did you try to save him? Freddy says when you came into the dorm you seemed excited, the two of you. Like it was all some big lark."

"Freddy?"

"Yes, Freddy. Or, as I think you used to call him: Fatfuck. He was the only boy awake in the dorm that night. He thought you might be coming for him, to take him for his Survival. So he hid, and pretended to be asleep, and didn't say a word when you carried off Darcey. He's never forgiven himself. I've tried to explain to him that he carries no guilt for it. It was the two of you who took him. But you most of all. At least your friend Johnno feels sorry for what he's done."

"Aoife," I say, careful as I can, "I don't understand. I don't know . . . what are you talking about?"

"Only—maybe I don't need to ask all those questions now. I know the answer. When I came to find you earlier, in the cave, I got all my answers then. Of course, now I have other questions. Why you did it, for example. Stolen exam papers? Does that really seem like enough of a motive to take a boy's life? Just because you'd been found out?"

"I'm sorry, Aoife, but I really must be getting back to the marquee now."

"No," she says.

I laugh. "What do you mean, no?" I use my most winning voice. "Look. You don't have any proof of what you're saying. Because there isn't any. I'm terribly sorry for your loss. I don't know what you're thinking about doing. But whatever it is it wouldn't do any good. It would be simply your word against mine. I think we know who would be believed. According to all records it was just a tragic accident."

"I thought you'd say that," she says. "I know you won't admit it. I know that you don't regret it. I overheard you in the cave, after all. You took everything from me that night. My mother as good as died that night too. We lost my father to a heart attack a few years later, certainly due to the stress of his grief."

I'm not afraid of her, I remind myself. She has no hold over me. I have *slightly* bigger fish to fry here, things with real consequences. She's just a bitter, confused woman—

And then I catch a glimpse of something. A gleam of metal, that is. In her other hand, the one not holding the light.

JOHNNO
The Best Man

COULDN'T SAVE HIM.

I shouldn't have pulled the knife out, I know that now. It would only have increased the bleeding, probably.

I wanted to make them understand, when they found me out in the dark. Femi, Angus, Duncan. But they wouldn't listen. They had these burning torches that they held out like weapons, like I was a wild animal. They were shouting at me, screaming at me, to drop the knife, to just PUT IT DOWN and there was so much noise in my head. I couldn't get the words out. So I couldn't make them see that it wasn't me. I couldn't explain.

How I'd been coming down off whatever Peter Ramsay had given me, out there in the storm.

How the lights went out.

How I found Will, out there in the dark. How I bent over him and saw the knife, sticking from his chest like something growing out of him, buried so deep you couldn't see any of the blade. How I realized, then, that in spite of all of it, I still loved him. How I hugged him to me and cried.

They surrounded me, the other ushers. They held me like an animal until the Gardaí arrived on their boat. I could see it in their eyes, how they feared me. How they knew I had never really been one of them.

· · ·

THE GARDAÍ ARE HERE NOW. They've put me in cuffs. They've arrested me. They'll take me back to the mainland. I'll be tried back home, for the murder of my best friend.

Yeah, I did think about it, in the cave. Killing Will, I mean. Picking up a rock close to hand. And there was definitely a moment when I *really* thought about it. When it felt like it would have been the easiest thing. The best thing.

But I didn't kill him. I know that—even though things did go a bit hazy after I'd had that pill from Pete Ramsay, a couple of slightly blank spots. I mean, I wasn't even in the tent. How could I have grabbed the knife? But the police don't seem to think that's a problem.

I don't *think* of myself as a killer, anyway.

Except I am, aren't I? That kid, all those years ago. I was the one who tied him up, in the end. Will made sure of that, but I still did it. And it's not really an excuse that will stand up to anything, is it, saying that you were too thick to properly think out the consequences?

Sometimes I think of what I saw the night before the wedding. That thing, that figure, crouched in my room. Obviously there's no point in telling anyone about that. Imagine it: "Oh, it wasn't me, I think Will might actually have been stabbed with a great fucking cake knife by the ghost of a boy we killed—yeah, I think I saw him in my bedroom the night before the wedding." Doesn't sound all that convincing, does it? Anyway, it's more than likely that it came from inside my head, what I saw. That would make a kind of sense, because in a way the boy's been living there for years.

I consider that jail cell waiting for me. But when I think about it, I've been in a prison since that morning when the tide came in. And maybe it's like justice catching up with me, for that terrible thing we did. But I didn't kill my best friend. Which means someone else did.

AOIFE
The Wedding Planner

I LIFT UP THE KNIFE. I TOLD FREDDY I ONLY WANTED TO GET WILL HERE to speak to him. Which was true, at least in the beginning. Perhaps it was what I overheard in the cave that changed my mind: the lack of remorse.

Four lives destroyed by that one night. One guilty life in recompense for an innocent: it seems a more than fair trade.

I hope he sees the blade, catching in the flashlight beam. For a moment I want him—so golden, so untouchable—to feel a tiny fragment of what my little brother might have experienced that night as he lay on the beach, waiting for the sea to come in. The terror of it. I want this man to be more terrified than he has ever been in his life. I keep the light trained on him, on his widening eyes.

And then, for my little brother, I stab him. In his heart.

I have raised hell.

EPILOGUE

OLIVIA
The Bridesmaid

THE WIND HAS STOPPED, FINALLY. THE IRISH POLICE HAVE ARRIVED. We're all gathered in the marquee, because they want us in one place. They've explained to us what has happened, what they found. Who they found. We know that someone's been arrested, but not who, yet.

It's amazing how little noise a hundred and fifty people can make. People sit around at the tables, talking in whispers. Some of them are wearing foil blankets, for the cold and shock, and these are louder than the sound of voices, rustling as people move.

I haven't said anything at all, not to anyone, not since he and I stood by the clifftop. I feel like all the words have been stolen from me.

All I've thought about for months is him. And now he's dead, they say. I'm not pleased. At least, I don't think I am. Mainly I'm still just shocked.

It wasn't me. But it *could* have been. I remember how I felt the last time I saw him, cutting the cake with Jules. Seeing that knife . . . The thought was in my head. It was only for a couple of seconds. But I did think it, feel it, strong enough that a part of me wonders whether maybe I *did* do it, and somehow blanked it out. I can't catch anyone's eye, in case they see it in my face.

I jump in shock as I feel someone's hand on my bare shoulder. I look up. It's Jules, a foil blanket over her wedding dress. On her it looks like it's a part of the outfit, like a warrior queen's cape. Her mouth is set in such a thin line that her lips have disappeared and her eyes glitter. Her hand is on my shoulder, her fingers are gripping tight.

"I know," she whispers. "About him—you."

Oh God. So after all that soul-searching about whether to tell her, she somehow worked it out on her own, anyway. And she hates me. She must do. I can see it. I know there's nothing I can do to change Jules's mind once she's made it up, nothing I can say.

Then there's a shift and I think I glimpse something new in her expression.

"If I'd known . . ." I see her mouth the words more than hear them. "If I'd—" She stops, swallows. She closes her eyes for a long moment and when she opens them again I see that they have filled with tears. And then she's reaching for me and I'm standing up and she's hugging me. And then I tense as I feel her body begin to shake. She's crying, I realize, great loud, angry sobs. I can't remember the last time Jules cried. I can't remember the last time we hugged like this. Maybe never. There's always been that distance between us. But for a moment it's gone. And in the middle of everything else, all the shock and trauma of this whole night, it's just the two of us. My sister and me.

THE NEXT DAY

HANNAH
The Plus-One

CHARLIE AND I ARE ON THE BOAT BACK TO THE MAINLAND. MOST of the guests left earlier than us, the family are staying behind. I look back toward the island. The weather has cleared now and there's sunlight on the water but the island is cast in the shadow of an overhanging cloud. It seems to crouch there like a great black beast, awaiting its next meal. I turn away from it.

I've barely been bothered by the movement of the boat this time. A little nausea is nothing compared to the deep sickness of the soul I felt when I made my discovery last night, that it was Will who as good as killed my sister.

I think of how I clung to Charlie on the ferry crossing to the island less than forty-eight hours ago, how we laughed together, despite my feeling so awful. The memory of it stings.

Charlie and I have hardly talked to one another. We have barely glanced at one another. Both of us, I think, have been lost in our own thoughts, remembering the last time we spoke before everything happened. And I don't think I'd have the energy to speak right now, even if I wanted to. I feel physically and emotionally shattered . . . too weary to even begin to organize my thoughts, to work out how I feel. No one slept at all last night, obviously, but it's more than that.

We'll have to face everything once we're home, of course. We'll have to see, when we return to reality, whether we can mend what has been ruptured by this weekend. So much has been broken.

And yet one thing has emerged, complete, from that wreckage. A missing part of the puzzle has been found. I wouldn't call it clo-sure, because that wound will never fully heal. I am angry that I never got my chance to confront him. But I got my answer to the question I have been asking ever since Alice died. And in killing him, you could say that Will's murderer avenged my sister too. I am only rather sorry I didn't get the chance to plunge the knife in myself.

ACKNOWLEDGMENTS

To my editors, Kate Nintzel, Kim Young and Charlotte Brabbin: This book has been such a collaborative effort that I definitely feel your names should be on the front of it too. Kate, thank you for your brilliant editorial eye and for being such a fantastic cheerleader for my writing from the outset.

To my U.S. publishing team—Liate Stehlik, Jennifer Hart, Kate Nintzel, Brittani Hilles, Kaitlin Harri, Imani Gary, Stephanie Vallejo, Elina Cohen, Jeanne Reina, Owen Corrigan and Molly Gendell— thank you for bringing my books to the U.S. audience!

To my agents, Alexandra Machinist and Cath Summerhayes: Thank you for championing me and my books at every opportunity. Thank you, too, for being such fun to work with!

To Luke Speed: Fantastic film agent and the loveliest man. Thank you for your vision and wisdom.

To all the booksellers who have hand-sold my book and who have such love of the written word and who create such exciting, welcoming spaces in which to discover it.

To all the readers who have read the book and told me they've enjoyed it: I love hearing from you—I can't tell you how much joy your messages bring.

To my parents, for your pride and love. For always encouraging me to do what I love best, right from the beginning.

To Kate and Max, Robbie and Charlotte: Thank you for making life such fun and for all your encouragement.

Last, but definitely not least . . . to Al: Always my first reader. Thank you for everything you do—your constant support and encouragement, your willingness to spend an entire six-hour car journey thrashing out a new book idea, for rescuing me from the despairing depths of a plot hole, for spending your whole weekend reading through my first draft. This book would not have been finished without you.

Insights,
Interviews
& More...

Meet Lucy Foley

Philippa Gedge

Lucy Foley studied English literature at Durham University and University College London and worked for several years as a fiction editor in the publishing industry. She is the author of *The Book of Lost and Found*, *The Invitation*, and *The Hunting Party*. She lives in London.

Wild and Perfect: Playing with Contrasts in *The Guest List*

I love weddings. Don't get me wrong—they're wonderful occasions. But as someone in her early thirties, I've attended a LOT of them in the past few years . . . and as an author there's a sneaky little part of me that's always on the lookout for inspiration. And it occurred to me that a wedding might be the *ideal* setting for a murder mystery.

You've got old friends, newer friends, and family members all gathered together in one place—and perhaps some hidden histories, buried secrets, and resentments bubbling away under the surface. You've got nerves and emotions running high, that expectation that everything has to turn out *perfectly*. You've got free-flowing alcohol, people leaving their inhibitions behind as they get into the swing of things.

And then there's all the stuff about how much it costs to get to the venue, the price of gifts on the registry, the angst over whether you're at the good table or whether you've been relegated to the one with all the weird uncles and oddballs, the anticipation of the drama that comes with the speeches; will they cross a line, go too far? I knew I could have a lot of (evil!) fun with all of it.

Then I decided I'd dial up the tension a notch by setting this fictional wedding on an island so that I could trap all my characters together in one place and make sure all those tensions are dialed up a ▶

3

Wild and Perfect: Playing with Contrasts in *The Guest List*
(*continued*)

notch further. As a result, they're forced to look rather too closely at one another and at themselves. Of course, there's also the practical fact that when someone is murdered no one can escape, not even the killer . . .

I chose the west coast of Ireland for the setting. It's a beautiful part of the world, with white sands and turquoise waters and wildflower-strewn moors, totally the sort of place in which you might choose to get married. But it's also very remote—and the islands just off the coast are even more so. When I traveled to them on my research trip, I genuinely thought I might drown on the terrifyingly rough boat crossing over. Obviously, that had to go straight into the book itself!

Some of the islands off the west coast of Ireland used to be inhabited but are now deserted—as is the case with the fictional Cormorant Island in the book—and when you listen to the wind howling through the ruined houses it's hard not to think of ghosts. Standing looking out at the Atlantic Ocean you realize there's nothing between you and the North American continent except thousands of miles of water: a very isolating thought. There's a real feeling of being cut off from the rest of the world, and a sense that it wouldn't be all that easy to get back . . .

I wanted the wildness of the island to form a contrast with the glamour and perfection of the wedding in the book: the big white tent, the no-expenses-spared catering, the magnificent spectacle of the wedding cake. Jules, the bride, is something of a perfectionist—and she expects everything to *be* perfect. But you can't control nature, and unbeknownst to any of them, a storm is approaching from far out in the Atlantic. A storm that will mirror the one taking place within the wedding party itself, with devastating—and deadly!—consequences.

As a civilization it feels as though we float somewhere between a kind of savage wilderness and our self-curation—that perfect veneer we try to present to the outside world. I wanted to really play with that contrast in the book. On the one hand we have the wedding, which is really the ultimate facade of perfection. On the other we have the wilderness of the island, which gradually brings out a wildness within the characters themselves, revealing something violent and animal within as their masks fall away. ∽

Lucy Foley on Writing Characters You Love to Hate

When I think about my favorite characters in thrillers, I realize they're often the "baddies." If I made a list it would have to include Tom Ripley in *The Talented Mr. Ripley*, Villanelle in the books of the same name (*Killing Eve* in the TV version), and the unrepentant boyfriend-murdering Ayoola in *My Sister, the Serial Killer*. None of these are cardboard-cutout bad guys: they're witty, or sympathetic, or just downright charismatic. They even have elements we might recognize in ourselves. These are the kinds of characters I'm drawn to create as a writer.

Don't get me wrong, I do enjoy writing "good" characters: the ones the reader empathizes with and roots for and could even imagine themselves being friends with. But I also love writing the ones you love to hate. Those with guilty secrets, dark pasts, evil intentions—characters that you resolutely dislike as a reader, but also find yourself more than a little fascinated by. Or you could flip it and say that some of these characters are those you hate to love: the ones you know you *shouldn't* like because they're deeply flawed in some way—and yet find yourself drawn to in spite of those flaws.

As a writer I enjoy the challenge of creating characters that are perhaps objectively bad, but also compellingly so. I don't want the reader to be so appalled with them that they don't want to read on or fail to find anything to empathize with. It's an important balancing act. My test for myself when I'm writing is: Do I want to spend a little more time in this person's company? Am I having fun creating this character? If the answers are yes, then I'm hopefully on the right track. Conversely, if I find myself increasingly turned off by them, then it's unlikely the reader's going to want to hang around long enough to find out what they have to say for themselves!

Of course, you're likely to find more examples of this sort of love-to-hate figure in a murder mystery, in which everyone may have a motive to kill. A cast of badly behaved characters is pretty much a hallmark of the traditional murder mystery novel. In *The Guest List*, even those characters that I want the reader to actively like—that are on balance "good"—aren't without their own secrets. I hope it makes them feel more rounded as characters to have that complexity. ▶

About the book

Likewise, my characters that are on balance "bad" aren't without their redeeming features, or without personal struggles and disappointments that we can empathize with. This, I think, humanizes them. I want the reader to have some level of understanding of their motivations, perhaps even to feel some degree of compassion for them. I never want to write mustache-twirling "evil" villains: they're boring and not particularly believable. After all, no one thinks of themselves as the bad guy in their own narrative. Everyone can justify their own actions to themselves. That's why I enjoy using the first-person point of view in my murder mysteries, so that my characters can tell their story to you, the reader, directly. It's confessional, intimate. This way you can really get inside their heads. Perhaps you might even begin—uncomfortably—to understand their motivations.

None of us is perfect and without our own flaws, petty jealousies, uncharitable thoughts, so why should a character in a book be? That just wouldn't feel believable. Because, after all, aren't we all a little bit bad? ∽

Reading Group Guide

1. Did you guess who the killer was? What (if any) clues did you pick up on throughout the book that helped contribute to your theory?

2. Throughout the story, we're introduced to pairs of biological siblings—Jules and Olivia, Hannah and Alice, Aoife and her brother—as well as characters who consider themselves like brothers, namely Will and his friends. How are each of these relationships different? What do you think the author is saying about the strength of biological family bonds versus the bonds of found families?

3. How did the setting add to your experience of the story? In what ways does the isolation affect each of the characters? Do you think things might have gone differently if they weren't brought together in such a remote location?

4. *The Guest List* is a modern take on the murder mystery. In what ways does Foley modernize and update the classic murder mystery?

5. Both Will's and Jules's best friends are friends from their youth. Why is this significant, and how does it affect the atmosphere of the wedding?

6. How reliable did you find the different narrators? As you were reading, did you trust what each narrator was saying? Did your opinion change as you read further?

7. There are several twists throughout the book. Which of these surprised you the most? Were there any you saw coming?

8. Many of the characters experience feeling like outsiders, whether at the wedding or at some point in their pasts. How does this affect their actions throughout the book and their relationships with others?

9. Who was your favorite character? Who was your least favorite? Was there one you related to the most? ▸

10. "This place is enough to make you believe in ghosts," Hannah thinks while exploring the island. In what way do ghosts—metaphorical and maybe even literal—come back to haunt each of the characters?

11. Many of the characters commit crimes or do things that could be considered villainous, for very different reasons. Which characters did you empathize with, and which did you not feel sympathy for?

12. What did you think of the ending? Was justice served? Were you satisfied with where each of the characters ended up? ◠

An Excerpt from
The Hunting Party

·1

H E A T H E R

Now
January 2, 2019

I SEE A MAN COMING THROUGH THE
falling snow. From a distance, through
the curtain of white, he looks hardly
human, like a shadow figure.

As he nears me I see that it is Doug,
the gamekeeper.

He is hurrying toward the Lodge,
I realize, trying to run. But the fallen,
falling snow hampers him. He stumbles
with each step. Something bad. I know
this without being able to see his face.

As he comes closer I see that his
features are frozen with shock. I know
this look. I have seen it before. This
is the expression of someone who has
witnessed something horrific, beyond the
bounds of normal human experience.

I open the door of the Lodge, let him
in. He brings with him a rush of freezing
air, a spill of snow.

"What's happened?" I ask him.

There is a moment—a long pause—
in which he tries to catch his breath.
But his eyes tell the story before he can,
a mute communication of horror. ▶

An Excerpt from *The Hunting Party* (continued)

Finally, he speaks. "I've found the missing guest."
"Well, that's great," I say. "Where—"
He shakes his head, and I feel the question expire on my lips.
"I found a body."

2

E M M A

Three days earlier
December 30, 2018

NEW YEAR. ALL OF US TOGETHER FOR THE FIRST TIME IN AGES. ME and Mark, Miranda and Julien, Nick and Bo, Samira and Giles, their six-month-old baby, Priya. And Katie.

Four days in a winter Highland wilderness. Loch Corrin, it's called. Very exclusive: they only let four parties stay there each year—the rest of the time it's kept as a private residence. This time of year, as you might guess, is the most popular. I had to reserve it pretty much the day after New Year last year, as soon as the bookings opened up. The woman I spoke with assured me that with our group taking over most of the accommodations we should have the whole place to ourselves.

I take the brochure out of my bag again. A thick card, expensive affair. It shows a fir-lined loch, heather-red peaks rising behind, though they may well be snow-covered now. According to the photographs, the Lodge itself—the "New Lodge," as the brochure describes it—is a big glass construction, über-modern, designed by a top architect who recently constructed the summer pavilion at the Serpentine Gallery. I think the idea is that it's meant to blend seamlessly with the still waters of the loch, reflecting the landscape and the uncompromising lines of the big peak, the Munro, rising behind.

Near the Lodge, dwarfed by it, you can make out a small cluster of dwellings that look as though they are huddling together to keep warm. These are the cabins; there's one for each couple, but we'll come together to have meals in the shooting lodge, the bigger building in the middle. Apart from the Highland Dinner on the first night—"a showcase of local, seasonal produce"—we'll be cooking for ourselves. They've ordered food in for me. I sent a long list in advance—fresh truffles, foie gras, oysters. I'm planning a real feast for New Year's Eve, which I'm very excited about. I love to cook. Food brings people together, doesn't it?

T HIS PART OF THE JOURNEY IS PARTICULARLY DRAMATIC. WE HAVE the sea on one side of us, and every so often the land sheers away so that it feels as if one wrong move might send us careering over the edge. The water is slate gray, violent-looking. In one cliff-top field the sheep huddle together in a group as though trying to keep warm. You can hear the wind; every so often it throws itself against the windows, and the train shudders.

All of the others seem to have fallen asleep, even baby Priya. Giles is actually snoring.

Look, I want to say, *look how beautiful it is!*

I've planned this trip, so I feel a certain ownership of it—the anxiety that people won't enjoy themselves, that things might go wrong. And also a sense of pride, already, in its small successes . . . like this, the wild beauty outside the window.

It's hardly a surprise that they're all asleep. We got up so early this morning to catch the train—Miranda looked particularly cross at the hour. And then everyone got on the booze, of course. Mark, Giles, and Julien hit the drinks trolley early, somewhere around Doncaster, even though it was only eleven. They got happily tipsy, affectionate, and loud (the next few seats along did not look impressed). They seem to be able to fall back into the easy camaraderie of years gone by no matter how much time has passed since they last saw each other, especially with the help of a couple of beers.

Nick and Bo, Nick's American boyfriend, aren't so much a feature of this boys' club, because Nick wasn't part of their group at Oxford . . . although Katie has claimed in the past that there's more to it than that, some tacit homophobia on the part of the ▶

other boys. Nick is Katie's friend, first and foremost. Sometimes I have the distinct impression that he doesn't particularly like the rest of us, that he tolerates us only because of Katie. I've always suspected a bit of coolness between Nick and Miranda, probably because they're both such strong characters. And yet this morning the two of them seemed thick as thieves, hurrying off across the station concourse, arm in arm, to buy "sustenance" for the trip. This turned out to be a perfectly chilled bottle of Sancerre, which Nick pulled from the cool-bag to slightly envious looks from the beer drinkers. "He was trying to get those G-and-Ts in cans," Miranda told us, "but I wouldn't let him. We have to start as we mean to go on."

Miranda, Nick, Bo, and I each had some wine. Even Samira decided to have a small one, too, at the last minute: "There's all this new evidence that says you can drink when you're breastfeeding."

Katie shook her head at first; she had a bottle of fizzy water. "Oh, come on, Kay-tee," Miranda pleaded, with a winning smile, proffering a glass. "We're on holiday!" It's difficult to refuse Miranda anything when she's trying to persuade you to do something, so Katie took it, of course, and had a tentative sip.

THE BOOZE HELPED LIGHTEN THE ATMOSPHERE A BIT; WE'D HAD a bit of a mix-up with the seating when we first got on. Everyone was tired and cross, halfheartedly trying to work it out. It turned out that one of the nine seats on the booking had somehow ended up in the next carriage, completely on its own. The train was packed, for the holidays, so there was no possibility of shuffling things around.

"Obviously that's my one," Katie said. Katie, you see, is the odd one out, not being in a couple. In a way, I suppose you could say that she is more of an interloper than I am these days.

"Oh, Katie," I said. "I'm so sorry—I feel like an idiot. I don't know how that happened. I was sure I'd reserved them all in the middle, to try to make sure we'd all be together. The system must have changed it. Look, you come and sit here . . . I'll go there."

"No," Katie said, hefting her suitcase awkwardly over the heads of the passengers already in their seats. "That doesn't make any sense. I don't mind."

Her tone suggested otherwise. For goodness' sake, I found myself thinking. It's only a train journey. Does it really matter?

The other eight seats were facing each other around two tables in the middle of the carriage. Just beyond, there was an elderly woman sitting next to a pierced teenager—two solitary travelers. It didn't look likely that we'd be able to do anything about the mess-up. But then Miranda bent across to speak to the elderly woman, her curtain of hair shining like gold, and worked her magic. I could see how charmed the woman was by her: the looks, the cut-glass—almost antique—accent. Miranda, when she wants to, can exert *serious* charm. Anyone who knows her has been on the receiving end of it.

Oh yes, the woman said, of course she would move. It would probably be more peaceful in the next carriage anyway: "You young people, aha!"—though none of us are all that young anymore—"And I prefer sitting forward, as it is."

"Thanks, Manda," Katie said, with a brief smile. (She sounded grateful, but she didn't look it, exactly.) Katie and Miranda are best friends from way back. I know they haven't seen as much of each other lately, those two; Miranda says Katie has been busy with work. And because Samira and Giles have been tied up in baby land, Miranda and I have spent more time together than ever before. We've been shopping, we've gone for drinks. We've gossiped together. I have begun to feel that she's accepted me as her *friend*, rather than merely Mark's girlfriend, last to the group by almost a decade.

Katie has always been there to usurp me, in the past. She and Miranda have always been so tight-knit. So much so that they're almost more like sisters than friends. In the past I've felt excluded by this, all that closeness and history. It doesn't leave any new friendship with room to breathe. So a secret part of me is—well, rather pleased.

I REALLY WANT EVERYONE TO HAVE A GOOD TIME ON THIS TRIP, for it all to be a success. The New Year's Eve getaway is a big deal. They've done it every year, this group. They've been doing it for long before I came onto the scene. And I suppose, in a way, planning this trip is a rather pitiful attempt at proving that I am ▶

really one of them. At saying I should be
properly accepted into the "inner circle"
at last. You'd think that three years—
which is the time it has been since
Mark and I got together—would be
long enough. But it's not. They all go
back a very long way, you see: to Oxford,
where they first became friends.

It's tricky—as anyone who has been
in this situation will know—to be the
latest addition to a group of old friends.
It seems that I will always be the new
girl, however many years pass. I will
always be the last in, the trespasser.

I look again at the brochure in my
lap. Perhaps this trip—so carefully
planned—will change things. Prove that
I am one of them. I'm so excited. ❧